THE DARK DEFILES

Also by Richard Morgan from Gollancz:

Takeshi Kovacs novels:
Altered Carbon
Broken Angels
Woken Furies

Market Forces
Black Man

The Steel Remains
The Cold Commands

RICHARD MORGAN

THE DARK DEFILES

GOLLANCZ
LONDON

The right of Richard Morgan to be identified as the author
of this work has been asserted by him in accordance with the
Copyright, Designs and Patents Act 1988.

First published in Great Britain in 2014 by Gollancz
An imprint of the Orion Publishing Group
Orion House, 5 Upper St Martin's Lane, London WC2H 9EA
An Hachette UK Company

A CIP catalogue record for this book is available
from the British Library.

ISBN 978 0 575 07794 2 (Cased)
ISBN 978 0 575 08859 7 (Export Trade Paperback)

1 3 5 7 9 10 8 6 4 2

Typeset by Input Data Services Ltd, Bridgwater, Somerset

Printed and bound by CPI Group (UK) Ltd, Croydon, CRO 4YY

The Orion Publishing Group's policy is to use papers that
are natural, renewable and recyclable products and made from
wood grown in sustainable forests. The logging and manufacturing
processes are expected to conform to the environmental
regulations of the country of origin.

www.richardkmorgan.com
www.orionbooks.co.uk
www.gollancz.co.uk

This book is for Daniel

I'll be there for the seaweed, mate

Dinnae ask me how majic wurks . . . but wun way or the uthir it canny be oll its craked up tae be or ah suppose the wurld woold be toatally fukin wunderffil an happy an aw that an folk woold live in peece an harminy an so on; thatill be the day, if ye ask me. Enyway its no like that ataw, so it isnay, an just as well to say I, coz utherwyse thay wooldnae need peepil like me (an itid be ded fukin boarin to).

Naw, ahm doin no to bad these days; servises mutch in dimand . . .

Iain Banks
The Bridge

Call for justice or explanation, and the sea will thunder back with its mute clamour. Men's accounts with the gods do not balance.

George Steiner
The Death of Tragedy

BOOK I
ARSE END OF THE WORLD

*'Once there was a High Quest to Northern Lands, a Bright Fellowship
led out in Sunlit Glory by three Heroes from the Great War, companied
with the Finest Warriors and Wise Men of Empire, and guided by an
Angel fallen from On High . . .'*

The Grand Chronicle of Yhelteth
Court Bard Edition

ONE

'Well, that's that, I suppose.'

Ringil Eskiath weighed the desiccated human jawbone glumly in the palm of his hand. He crouched on the edge of the opened grave, fighting off a vague urge to jump down into it.

Looks cosy down there. Out of the wind, dark and warm . . .

He rubbed at his unshaven chin instead. Three days of stubble, rasping on calloused fingers, itching on hollow cheeks. His cloak, puddled about him where he crouched, was soiled at the border and soaking up water from the rain-drenched grass. The shoulder of his sword arm nagged from the unrelenting damp.

He shut out the ache and brooded on what lay below him in the grave.

They'd come a long way for this.

There wasn't much – shards of wood that might once have formed a casket, a few long strips of leather, cured stiff and crumbling. A mess of small bone fragments, like the leavings of some overenthusiastic sooth-sayer on the scry . . .

Gil sighed and levered himself back to his feet. Tossed the jawbone back in with the rest.

'Fucking waste of five months.'

'My lord?'

Shahn, the marine sergeant, who'd climbed back out of the grave, and now waited close by the mounds of earth his men had dug out. Behind him, the work party stood around, soil- and sweat-streaked, entrenching tools in hand, scowling against the weather. Whoever dug this plot all those centuries ago, they'd chosen a spot close to the cliffs, and right now there was a blustery wind coming in off the ocean, laced with fistfuls of sleet and the promise of another storm. The three Hironish guides they'd hired back in Ornley already had their hoods up – they stood further from the grave, were watching the sky and conversing in low tones.

Ringil brushed the traces of dirt off his hands.

'We're all done here,' he announced loudly. 'If this is the Illwrack Changeling, the worms sorted him out for us a while back. Stow tools, let's get back to the boats.'

A tremor of hesitation – hands working at tool handles, feet shifting. The sergeant cleared his throat. Gestured half-heartedly at the soft-mounded earth beside the grave.

'Sire, should we not . . .?'

'Fill that in?' Ringil grinned harshly. 'Listen, if those bones stand up and follow us down to the beach, I'll be very surprised. But you know what? – if they do, I'll deal with it.'

His words carved out their own patch of quiet in the rising wind. Among the men, a touching of talismans. Some muttering.

Ringil cut them a surreptitious glance, counting faces without seeming to. A couple of those he saw had been around when he took down the kraken, but most were on the other ships at the time; or they were aboard *Dragon's Demise* but in their bunks. It had been a filthy night anyway – rain and howling wind, band-light muffled up in thick, scudding cloud, and the encounter was over almost as soon as it began. All but a handful missed the action.

They had report from their comrades, of course, but Ringil couldn't blame them for doubting it. Killing a kraken, at the height and heart of an ocean storm by night – yeah, *right*. It was a stock scene out of myth, a lantern-light story to frighten the cabin boy with. It was a fucking *tale*.

It was five weeks now, and no one was calling him Krakenbane that he'd noticed.

He supposed it was for the best. He'd held enough commands in the past to know how it went. Best not to disabuse your men of their tight-held notions, whatever those might be. That went in equal measure for those who doubted him and those who told tales of his prowess. The actual truth would probably scare both parties out of their wits, and that, right here and now, was going to be counterproductive.

They were twitchy enough as it was.

He faced them. Put one booted foot on the forlorn, shin-high chunk of mossed over granite that served the grave as marker. He pitched his voice for them all to hear – pearls of dark wisdom from the swordsman sorcerer in your midst.

'All right, people, listen up. Anyone wants to sprinkle salt, go right ahead, get it done. But if we stay here to fill this hole in, we're going to get drenched.'

He nodded westward, out to sea. It was not long past noon, but the sour afternoon light was already closing down. Cloud raced in from the north, boiling up like ink poured in a glass of water. Overhead, the sky was turning the black of a hanged man's face.

Yeah – be calling that *an omen before you know it.*

His mood didn't improve much on the way back to the boats. He took point on the meandering sheep track that brought them down off the cliffs. Set a punishing pace over the yielding, peaty ground. No one made the mistake of trying to stay abreast or talk to him.

By way of contrast, there was raucous good cheer at his back. The marines had loosened up with the permission to lay wards. Now they tramped

4

boisterously along behind him, good-natured bickering and jeering in the ranks. It was as if they'd poured out their misgivings with the salt from their tooled leather bags, left it all behind them in the tiny white traceries they'd made.

Which, Ringil supposed, they had, and wasn't that the whole point of religion anyway?

But he was honest enough to recognise his own released tension as well. Because, despite all the other pointless, empty graves, despite his own increasingly solid conviction that they were wasting their time, he too had gone up to those cliffs expecting a fight.

Wanting a fight.

Little vestiges of the feeling still quivered at the nape of his neck and in his hands. Enough to know it had been there, even if he hadn't spotted it at the time.

Last resting place of the Illwrack Changeling.

Again.

This being the ninth last resting place to date. The ninth grave of the legendary Dark King they'd dug up, only to find the detritus of common mortality beneath.

Has to be an easier way to do this shit.

Really, though, there wasn't, and he knew it. They were all strangers here, himself included. Oh, he'd read about the Hironish Isles in his father's library as a boy, learnt the arid almanac facts from his tutors. And growing up in Trelayne he'd known a handful of people who'd spent time there in exile. But this was not knowledge with practical application, and anyway it was decades out of date. Fluent Naomic aside, he had no useful advantage over his fellow expedition members.

Meanwhile, Anasharal the Helmsman, full of ancient unhuman knowing when they planned the expedition back in Yhelteth last year, was now proving remarkably cagey about specifics. The Kiriath demon was either unwilling or unable to point them with any clarity to the Changeling's grave, and instead suggested – somewhat haughtily – that they do the legwork themselves and inquire of the locals. *I fell from on high for your benefit*, went the habitual gist of the lecture. *Is it my fault that I no longer have the vision I gave up in order to bring my message to you? I have steered you to journey's end. Let human tongues do the rest.*

But the Hironish islanders were a notoriously closed-mouth bunch – even Gil's dull-as-dishwater tutors had mentioned that. Historically, they'd been known to harbour popular pirates and tax evaders despite anything the League's heavy-handed customs officers could do about it. To lie with impassive calm in the face of threats, to spit with contempt at drawn steel, and to die under torture rather than give up a fellow islander.

So they certainly weren't about to spill the secrets of settled generations to some bunch of poncy imperials who showed up from the alien south and started asking, *Oh, hey, we hear there's this dark lord out of legend buried around here somewhere; any chance you could take us to him?*

Not just like that, anyway.

It took a week of careful diplomacy in and out of the taverns in Ornley and then out to the hamlets and crofts beyond, just to find a handful of locals who would talk to them. It took soft words and coin and endless rounds of drinks. And, even then, what these men had to say was sparse and contradictory:

– *the Illwrack Changeling, hmm, yes, that'd be the one from the dwenda legend. But he was never buried up here, the dwenda took him away in a shining longship, to where the band meets the ocean . . .*

– *crucified him on Sirk beach for a betrayer, was what I heard, facing the setting sun as he died. His followers took him down three days later and buried him. It's that grave up behind the old whaler's temple.*

– *the Illwrack Betrayer was brought to the Last Isle, to the Chain's Last Link, just as the legends say. But the isle only manifests to mortal eyes at Spring solstice, and even then, only with much purifying prayer. To land there would require an act of great piety. You should ask at the monastery on Glin cliffs, perhaps they can make offerings for you when you return next year.*

Yeah, that's right – jeers from further down the tavern bar – *you should ask his brother out at Glin. Never known him turn down a request for intercession if it came weighted with enough coin . . .*

You know, I've had about enough out of you whelps. My brother's a righteous man, not like some worthless bastard sons I could—

They'd had to break that one up with fists. Start all over again.

– *the grave you seek is on a promontory of the Grey Gull peninsula, no more than a day's march north of here. On approach, Grey Gull may seem a separate island, but do not be deceived. Certain currents cause the inlets to fill enough at certain times to make it so – but you can always cross, at worst you might have to wade waist deep. And most of the time, you won't even get your boots wet.*

Hagh! – a greybeard fishing skipper hawks and spits something unpleasantly yellow onto the tavern's sawdust floor, rather close to Ringil's boot – *not going to find that grave this side of Hell! That's where the Aldrain demons took that one – screaming to Hell!*

No, no, my lords, forgive him, this is just fisherfolk superstition. The last human son of Illwrack is buried at the compass crossroads, on a rise just south of here. Some say the hill itself is the Changeling's barrow.

– *the truth, my lords, is that the dwenda hero was laid to rest in the stone circle at Selkin, where his retainers . . .*

So forth.

It was a lot of digging.

But in the absence of the imperial expedition's other main prize – the legendary floating city of An-Kirilnar, which they also couldn't seem to find right now – there really wasn't much else to do but tramp out to site after site and dig until disappointed.

Disappointment is a slow poison.

Initially, and for some of the closer sites, practically every figure of note on the expedition tagged along. There was still a palpable air of journey's end hanging over them all at that point – a sense that, after all that planning, all those sea miles covered, *this* was *it*. And whatever *it* was, no one wanted to miss it.

True above all for Mahmal Shanta – he went out of sheer academic curiosity and at the cost of some substantial personal discomfort. Really too old for a voyage into such cold climes anyway, Shanta was still getting over flu and had to be carried on a covered litter by six servants, which was awkward over rough ground and slowed everybody else down. Gil rolled his eyes at Archeth, but in the end what were you going to do? The elderly naval engineer was a primary sponsor of the expedition: his family's shipyards had built two of the three vessels they sailed in and reconditioned the third, and even in illness he held onto stubborn and canny command of the flagship *Pride of Yhelteth*.

If anyone had earned the right, it was Shanta.

Archeth's reasons for riding along were twofold, and a little more pragmatic. She went because she was overall expedition leader and it was expected of her. But more than that, she badly needed something to take her mind off the lack of any Kiriath architecture standing above the waves off-shore. Not finding An-Kirilnar had hit her hard.

Marine commander Senger Hald went ostensibly to supervise those of his men detailed to the search, but really to put an unquestionable marine boot on the proceedings. And Noyal Rakan went beside him, to show the Throne Eternal flag and remind everyone who was supposed to be in charge. The two men were coolly amicable, but the inter-service rivalry was never far beneath the surface, in them or the men they commanded.

Lal Nyanar, captain of *Dragon's Demise* mostly on account of Shab Nyanar's substantial investment in the expedition, went along even when the prospecting was done overland, apparently out of some belief that he was representing his absent father's interests in the quest. Gil didn't really begrudge him; Nyanar wasn't much of a sea captain – the sinecure commands his family had secured for him back in Yhelteth were largely ceremonial or involved river vessels – but he did at least know how to follow orders. Out of sight of his ship, he deferred to the expedition leaders and kept his head down.

The same could not be said of the others.

Of the expedition's other investors who'd actually made the trip north, Klarn Shendanak stuck close to the action because he didn't trust Empire men any further than you could throw one, and that included Archeth Indamaninarmal, jet-skinned half-human imperial cipher that she was. Menith Tand followed suit and stuck close to Shendanak because he harboured a standard Empire nobleman's distaste for the Majak's rough-and-ready immigrant manners and would not be one-upped. And Yilmar Kaptal went along because he mistrusted both Shendanak and Tand in about equal measure. The three of them didn't quite spit at each other outright, but having them at your back was like leading a procession of alley cats. Shendanak never went anywhere without an eight-strong honour guard of thuggish-looking second cousins fresh down from the steppes, which in turn meant that Tand brought along a handful of his own mercenary crew to balance the equation and Kaptal flat-out de-manded that Rakan muster a squad of Throne Eternal just in case . . .

Egar usually tagged along at Gil's shoulder just to see if there'd be any kind of fight.

One grey morning, on the way to a talisman-warded grave that would prove to contain nothing but the skeleton of a badly deformed sheep, Ringil stopped and looked back from the top of a low rise, squinting against the rain. The whole bedraggled entourage spilled up the trail behind him like the survivors of a shipwreck. He reckoned sourly that he hadn't seen such a mess since he led the expeditionary retreat back to Gallows Gap eleven years ago.

Bit harsh, was Egar's considered opinion. *On the expeditionary, I mean. That was an army we had. You imagine trying to lead this lot into a battle and out the other side? We'll be lucky if they're not all at each other's throats before noon.*

Don't, Ringil told him wearily. *Just – don't.*

They went. They dug. Found nothing and came back, mostly in the rain.

But – to the Dragonbane's evident disappointment – there never was a fight.

Instead, Gil's train of gawkers and minders slowly began to whittle away in the face of repeated let-down and the god-awful weather. Each found other, more compelling matters to occupy them. Archeth withdrew into brooding isolation aboard *Sea Eagle's Daughter*, and could occasionally be heard right across the harbour, yelling abuse at Anasharal in the High Kir tongue. Nyanar went back to residence aboard *Dragon's Demise*, where he instructed and supervised an endless series of small deck repairs and wrote self-importantly about it in the captain's log. On the shore side of things, Yilmar Kaptal took to his rooms at the inn on Gull's Flight Wynd and asked Rakan for a brace of Throne Eternal to guard his door. Shen-danak and Tand stomped about the streets of Ornley, shadowed by their men, glaring at the locals and each other whenever they crossed paths. Desperate to bring the temperature down, Hald and Rakan both habitu-ally stayed in town with the bulk of their respective commands, put their men through punishing work schedules, held exhaustive training sessions, did anything they could to head off the simmering sense of boredom and frustration.

Egar found himself some local whores.

And Mahmal Shanta sat with a racking cough in his stateroom aboard the flagship *Pride of Yhelteth*, spitting up phlegm, drinking hot herbal infusions and poring over charts, all the while trying to pretend he was not planning their empty-handed return home.

The search went on, pared back to Ringil and a marine detachment under Hald's occasional command to do the digging. The unspoken understanding – Gil was the sharp end. He had the spells and the alien iron blade; if the Illwrack Changeling popped up out of the next grave in fighting temper, Ringil Eskiath was the man to put him down. As they exhausted the more promising fragments of legend and hearsay closer to town, Nyanar and *Dragon's Demise* were detailed to carry them whenever a site was – or was reputed to be – sailing distance away. Which was all the time these days.

It was starting to feel like clutching at straws. Like going through the motions. Gil's patience, never his strong suit, was frayed down to shreds. The itch to kill something stalked him day and night. What he wouldn't give for the Illwrack Changeling to erupt from the damp earth and grass right in front of him right now, sword in hand, undead eyes aflame.

He'd cut the fucker down like barley.

The sheep track wound its unhurried way across the shoulder of the hill, dropping by hairpin increments into the valley below. A couple of ruined crofts showed hearth ends and tumbled dry stone walls rising out of the heather like longboats drowned in shallow water. Bedraggled-looking sheep dotted the slope, stood at a distance, chewing patiently, watching them pass. One or two of the nearer ones beat ungainly, lumbering retreat from the path, as if warned in advance of Gil's state of mind.

I'm going to put that fucking Helmsman over the rail when we get back. I'm going to sink it in Ornley Sound without a cable and leave it there to rot.

If Archeth doesn't beat me to it.

I'm going to—

He jerked to a halt, awareness of the thing that blocked his path coming late through his seething mood. He teetered back a couple of inches.

Behind him, he heard the marines' banter dry up.

The ram stood its ground on the path. It was big, bulking nearly twice the size of the sheep they'd seen, and it was old, fist-thick horns coiling twice around and then out to wicked downward-jabbing spikes. Its fleece was a filthy yellowish white, matted across a back as broad as a mule's. It stood well over waist height on Ringil, and it stared him down out of pupils that were slotted black openings into emptiness. Its chin was raised towards him, and it seemed to be smiling at some private joke.

Ringil took a sharp step forward. Jerked arms upward and wide – not unlike, it suddenly dawned on him, one of the charlatan witches you saw pissing about at magic in Strov Square.

The ram stayed where it was.

'I'm in no mood for you,' Gil barked. 'Go on, fuck off.'

Silence. A couple of nervous guffaws from the marines.

The moment stretched and broke. The ram took a step sideways, tossed its head in a gesture as if to say *look up there*, and ambled off towards one of the ruined crofts.

Ringil looked, a flinching glance, back up the rain-soaked hillside and—

Black flap of cloak, glimmer of faint blue fire in motion.

A dark figure, moving on the ridgeline, head down as if watching him.

He blinked. Stood there, locked still, trying to be sure. The flicker of movement, out of the corner of his eye.

There and gone.

Oh, come off it.

He came back round, spotted the ram standing at the wall of the ruin. It still seemed to be watching him.

'Sir?'

Shahn was at his side, face carefully expressionless. Ringil looked past him at the men, who were mostly squaring away twitchy grins, squinting up at the sky and trying to seem serious. He couldn't really blame them; he was about to shrug off the whole thing himself, when he noticed the Hironish guides. They stood apart, off the path, and hastily averted their eyes as soon as he looked their way. He stared at them for a couple of moments, and they steadfastly refused to meet his gaze. But he caught the glance one of them could not help casting towards the ruin and the ram.

Ringil followed the man's gaze. He felt his pulse pick up.

The *ikinri 'ska*, pricking awake in him like some dozy hound by the fireside at the sound of the latch.

'Sergeant,' he said with distant calm. 'Get everybody down to the boats, would you?'

'Sir.'

'Wait for me there. Tell Commander Hald and the captain I won't be long.'

'Yes sir.'

Ringil was already moving towards the ruin. He barely heard the man's response, was barely aware of the marines as they mustered behind Shahn's snapped order and tramped off at a brisk march. He was off the path now, knee-deep in the rain-soaked heather, and he had to force his legs through it to make headway. Ahead of him, the ram, apparently satisfied, tossed its head again and trotted through a gap in the tumbled wall of the croft that might once have been a doorway.

The sky had darkened overhead with the gathering cloud. The wind seemed to be picking up.

He reached the ruin and looked in over a wall that barely came up to his waist. The ram was nowhere to be seen. Ringil prowled the wall, swept a speculative glance up and down the interior, making sure. Knee-high growth of grass across the floor space, shaped stones from the tumbled walls scattered here and there, the splintered, rotted-wood remnants of what might have been furniture a long time ago. At one end wall, the stonework was blackened where hearth and chimney had once stood.

Something was gathered there, crouched by the hearth-space, waiting for him.

He couldn't quite see what it was.

At the ruined doorway, gusts from the rising wind agitated the long grass, bowed it back as if offering him passage inside.

Ringil nodded to himself. 'All right, then.'

He stepped in over the threshold.

TWO

He'd paid the whores for the whole afternoon, but in the end couldn't summon much enthusiasm for a third go round. Usually, two women at once solved that kind of problem for him, but not today. Maybe it was the smell of damp wool that still clung to their bodies even after they'd peeled naked for him, maybe the fact he caught the mask of fake arousal falling off the face of the younger one a couple too many times in the act. That kind of thing stabbed at him, took him out of the moment. He knew he was paying, but he didn't like to be reminded of the fact, and back in Yhelteth he wouldn't have been.

What's the matter, Dragonbane? You never fucking happy? Up on the steppe, you craved all that southern sophistication you'd left behind. Put you back in the imperial city and you wish you could have the simple life again. Now here you are with simple whores in a simple little town, and that's not right for you either.

Ye Gods, he missed Imrana.

Wasn't talking to the bitch currently, but missed her still.

So when the young one knelt before him on the floor and slipped his flaccid cock into her mouth, while her older companion sat on a stool in the corner, legs apart, lifting one pendulous tit at a time and tonguing the nipple with leering glances in his direction, he just grunted and shook his head. Hoisted the girl bodily from her knees – his cock slipped back out of her mouth, still pretty much flaccid – and set her aside. The older whore eyed him warily as he got up off the dishevelled bed. He read her thoughts as if they were tattooed across her face. No telling what any paying customer might do when they couldn't get it up, and this one here was big and battle-scarred, and a foreigner to boot. Harsh alien accent and hair all tangled up with talismans in iron. Lurid tales of the Majak had percolated right across the continent in the last couple of centuries – they'd doubtless got as far as the Hironish Isles long ago. *Bloody steppe savages, disembowel a girl and cook her on a spit soon as look at her most likely if they got out of bed the wrong side one morning . . .*

He forced a reassuring grimace and went to stare out of the window. Heard them move behind him with alacrity, start gathering up their clothes and the coin he'd left on the table. Light-footed, they left in what seemed like seconds and the door of his room clunked shut. He felt the relief it brought go through his whole frame. He slumped against the window, rested his head on cool glass. Outside, a light rain was falling into the street, clogging up daylight that was already past its best. A couple of children went past, splashing deliberately in the puddles and yattering some rhyme he could barely make out. He'd learnt the League tongue, more or less, while on campaign in the north during the war, but the Hironish accent was hard work.

Yeah, like their fucking awful food and their fucking awful weather and their fucking awful whores. Five weeks in this shit-hole already, and still no—

Commotion downstairs. A woman shrieked. Furniture went over.

He frowned. Cocked his head at the sound.

Another shriek. Coarse laughter, and men calling to each other. The words were indistinct, but the rhythms were Majak.

Uh-oh.

He grabbed his breeches off the bed, trod hurriedly into them on his way to the door. Shirt off the table as he passed, out into the corridor still bare-chested. Shouldered into the garment as he went down the stairs. No time for boots or other refinement, because—

He arrived on the ground floor of the inn, barefoot and undone. Surveyed the scene before him. Thin crop of locals at tables and bar, gazes fixed steadfastly down on their drinks, eyes averted from the quick chaos erupting in their midst, the new arrivals . . .

There were three of them. Shendanak's men, just in from the street by the look of it, felt coats still buttoned up and damp across the shoulders from the rain. One had the younger of Egar's whores grasped firmly by the crotch and one tit, was nuzzling and licking at her neck. The other two seemed engaged in facing down the innkeeper.

'Oi!' Egar barked, in Majak. 'Fuck do you think you're doing?'

The one holding the whore looked up. 'Dragonbane!' he bawled. 'Brother! We were just looking for you! Get your drinking boots on! 's time to light this shit-hole town *right* the fuck up – Majak style!'

Egar nodded slowly. 'I see. Whose idea was that, then?'

'Old Klarn, mate! The man himself.' The whore bucked and twisted in the speaker's grip. She sank teeth into his forearm. He winced and grinned, let go of her crotch, used the free hand to squeeze her jaws open and force her head back, clear of his flesh. Looked like she'd left a pretty distinct bite there in the thick muscle behind the wrist, welling blood and everything, but the Majak's voice barely wavered from its previous slurring good cheer. Egar estimated he'd been drinking a while. 'Fucking bitch. Yeah, Klarn says we've been soft-soaping around these fish-fuckers for long enough. Time to get steppe-handed on their arses. In't that right, boys?'

Growls of approval from the other two. By now they had the innkeeper bent back over his own bar with the flat of a knife blade tapping under his chin and his feet dangling a couple of inches off the sawdusted floor. They flashed cheery, inclusive grins at the Dragonbane.

Egar jerked his chin at the girl. 'That's my whore you've got there. Let her go.'

'*Your* whore?' The other Majak's face was suddenly a lot less friendly. 'Who says she's yours? She's down here waggling her tits and arse in grown men's faces, she—'

'She's paid until sunset.' Egar shifted his stance a little, squaring up. He nodded at the older whore. 'They both are. They're down here getting me a drink and a platter. So let her go. And you two – let him up as well. How's the poor cunt supposed to pull me a pint if you have him pinned?'

The two Majak at the bar were happy enough to obey. Maybe they'd been drinking less, maybe they were just more intelligent men. They nodded amiably, backed off the innkeeper and let him scramble loose. The one with the knife put his weapon away with a sheepish grin. But the guy with his arm round the whore was going to be a harder push. As Egar watched, he tightened his grip.

'My coin's as good as anybody's,' he growled.

Egar took a casual step forward. Measured the room without seeming to. 'Then get in the queue with it. Or find yourself another whore. You're not having mine.'

The other Majak's hand strayed down towards his belt and the big-hilted killing knife sheathed there. He barely seemed aware of the motion.

'You've got 'til sunset,' he said gruffly, almost reasonably, as if trying to put the case to some court in his own head. 'I'll not need long.'

'I'm not going to tell you again. *Let her go.*'

Egar saw the other man make his decision, saw it in his eyes even before he went for the knife. His hand clamped down on the hilt, but the Dragonbane was already in motion. Across the scant space between them, bottle snatched up off the table to his right, sweeping in, and a braining stroke across the Majak's head. He gave it all he had, was actually a bit surprised when the bottle didn't break first time. The other man reeled from the blow, Egar stepped in after him, swung again, back-handed, and this time – *yes!* – the glass came apart in a bright burst of shards and cheap wine. The Majak went down, bleeding from multiple gouges in his forehead. The whore got loose and scurried behind her colleague; the injured man crawled dizzily about on the floor, blood running into his eyes. Egar curled one foot back, mindful of his naked toes, and kicked the Majak hard in the face before he could get up. He brandished the business end of the shattered bottle admonishingly at the other two.

'You boys plan to paint the town, you aren't going to start in here. Got it?'

Quiet. Wine dripped wetly off the jagged angles of the bottle stump.

The two remaining Majak looked at their companion, curled up on the floor and twitching, then back to the wet gleam of Egar's makeshift weapon. Rage and confusion struggled on their faces, but that was as far as it went. He saw they were both pretty young, reckoned he might be able to brazen this one out. He waited. Watched one of them rake a hand perplexedly back through his hair and make an angry gesture.

'Look, Dragonbane, we thought—'

'Then you thought wrong.' He had his reputation and his age – things that would have counted for something among Majak back on the steppe, and might play here, if these two hadn't been away from home too long.

If not, well . . .

If not, he had bare feet and a broken bottle. And glass shards on the floor.

Nice going, Dragonbane.

Better make this good.

He put on his best clanmaster voice. 'I am *guesting here*, you herd-end fuckwits. My bond with these people *compels* me, under the eyes of the Dwellers, to defend them. Or don't the shamans teach you that shit any-more when you're coming up?'

The two young men looked at each other. It was a dodgy interpretation of Majak practice at best – outside of some small ritual gifts, you didn't *pay* for guesting out on the steppe. And lodging at a tavern or a rooming house, say, in Ishlin-ichan, wasn't considered the same thing at all. But Egar was Skaranak and these two were border Ishlinak, and they might not know enough about their northerly cousins to be sure, and in the end, hey, this old guy killed a fucking *dragon* back in the day, so . . .

The one on the floor groaned and tried groggily to prop himself up.

Time running out.

Egar pointed downward with the bottle. Played out his high cards. 'And what do your clan elders have to say about *this* shit? Stealing another man's whore out from under his nose? That okay, is it?'

'He didn't kn—'

'Pulling a *knife* on a brother? That okay with you, is it?'

'But you—'

'*I'm done fucking talking about this!*' Egar let the bottle hang at his side, like he had no need for it at all. He stabbed a finger at them instead, played the irascible clan elder to the hilt. 'Now you get him up, and you get him the fuck out of my sight. Get him out of here while I'm still in a good mood.'

They dithered. He barked. 'Go on! Take your fucking party some-where else!'

Something gave in their faces. Their companion stirred on the floor again and they hurried to him. Egar gave them the space, relieved. Bottle still ready at his side. They propped the injured man up between them, got his arms over their shoulders, and turned for the door. One of them found some small piece of face-saving bravado on the way out. He twisted awkwardly about with his half of the burden. The anger still hadn't won out on his face, but it was hardening that way.

'You know, Klarn isn't going to wear this.'

Egar jutted his chin again. 'Try him. Klarn Shendanak is steppe to the

15

bone. He's going to see this exactly the way it is – a lack of fucking respect where it's due. Now *get out.*'

They went out, into the rain, left the door swinging wide in their wake. The Dragonbane found himself alone in a room full of staring locals.

Presently, someone got up from a table and shut the door. Still, no one spoke, still they went on staring at him. He realised the whole exchange had been in Majak, would have been incomprehensible to everybody there.

He was still holding the jag-ended bottle stump.

He laid it down – on the table he'd swiped the bottle from in the first place. Its owner flinched back in his chair. Egar sighed. Looked over at the innkeeper.

'You'd better keep that door barred for the time being,' he said in Naomic. To the room more generally, he added: 'Anyone has family home alone right now, you might want to drink up and get on back to them.'

There was some shuffling among the men, some muttering back and forth, but no one actually got up or moved for the door. They were all still intent on him, the barefoot old thug with iron in his hair and his shirt hanging open on a pelt going grey.

They were all still trying to understand what had just happened.

He sympathised. He'd sort of hoped—

Fucking Shendanak.

He picked his way carefully through the shards of broken glass on the floor, past the stares, and went upstairs to get properly dressed.

He wanted his boots on for the next round.

He found Shendanak holding court outside the big inn on League Street where he'd taken rooms. The Majak-turned-imperial-merchant had ordered a rough wooden table brought out into the middle of the street, and he was sat there in the filtering rain, a flagon of something at his elbow, watching three of his men beat up a Hironish islander. He saw Egar approaching and raised the flagon in his direction.

'Dragonbane.'

'Klarn.' Egar stepped around the roughing up, fended his way past an overthrown punch that skidded inexpertly off the islander's skull. He shoved the tangle of men impatiently aside. 'You want to tell me what the fuck's going on?'

Shendanak surfaced from the flagon and wiped his whiskers. 'Not my idea, brother. Tand's getting his tackle in a knot, shouting about how these fish-fuckers know something they're not telling us. Starts in on how I'm too soft to do what it takes to find out what we need to know. Come on, what am I supposed to do? Can't take that lying down, can I? Not from Tand.'

'So instead, you're going to take orders from him?'

'Nah, it's not like that. It's a competition, isn't it, boys?' The Majak warriors stopped what they were doing to the islander for a moment. Looked up like dogs called off. Shendanak waved them back to the task. 'Tand sets his mercenaries to interrogating. I do the same with the brothers. See who finds out where that grave and that treasure is first. Thousand elemental pay-off and a public obeisance for the winner.'

'Right.' Egar sat on the edge of the table and watched as two of the Majak held the islander up while a third planted heavy punches into his stomach and ribs. 'Menith Tand's a piece-of-shit slave trader with a hard-on for hurting people, and he's bored. What's your excuse?'

Shendanak squinted at him thoughtfully.

'Heard about your little run in with Nabak. You really bottled him over some fishwife whore you wouldn't share? Doesn't sound like you.'

'I bottled him because he pulled a knife on me. You need to keep a tighter grip on your cousins, Klarn.'

'Oh, indeed.'

It was hard to read what was in Shendanak's voice. Abruptly, his eyes widened and he grabbed the flagon again, lifted it off the table top as the islander staggered back into the table and clung there, panting. The man was bleeding from the mouth and nose, his lips were split and torn where they'd been smashed repeatedly into his teeth. Both his eyes were blackening closed and his right hand looked to have been badly stomped. Still, he pushed himself up off the table with a snarl. The Majak bracketed him, dragged him—

'You know what,' said Shendanak brightly. He gestured with the flagon 'I really don't think this one knows anything. Why don't you let him go? Just leave him there. Go on and have a drink before we start on the next one. It's thirsty work, this.'

The Majak looked surprised, but they shrugged and did as they were told. One of them gave the beaten man a savage kick behind the knee and then spat on him as he collapsed in the street. Laughter, barked and bitten off. The three of them went back into the inn, shaking out their scraped knuckles and talking up the blows they'd dealt. Shendanak watched them through the door, waited for it to close before he looked back at Egar.

'My cousins are getting restless, Dragonbane. They were promised an adventure in a floating alien city and a battle to the death against a black shaman warrior king. So far, both those things have been conspicuous by their absence.'

'And you think beating the shit out of the local populace is going to help?'

'No, of course not.' Shendanak leaned up and peered over the table at where the islander lay collapsed on the greasy cobbles. He settled back in his seat. 'But it will let the men work out some of their frustration. It will exercise them. And anyway, like I said, I really can't lose face to a sack of shit like Menith Tand.'

'I'm going to talk to Tand,' growled Egar. 'Right now.'

Shendanak shrugged. 'Do that. But I think you'll find he doesn't believe these interrogations are going to help any more than I do. That's not what this is about. Tand's men are better trained than mine, but in the end they're soldiers just the same. And you and I both know what soldiers are like. They need the violence. They crave it, and if you starve them of it for long enough, you're going to have trouble.'

'Trouble.' Egar spoke the word as if he was weighing it up. 'So let me get this straight – you and Tand are doing this because you want to *avoid* trouble?'

'In essence, yes.'

'In *essence*, is it?' *Fucking court-crawling wannabe excuse for a . . .* He held it down. Measured his tone. 'Let me tell you a little war story, Klarn. You know, the war you managed to sit out, back in the capital with your horse farms and your investments?'

'Oh, here we fucking go.'

'Yeah, well. You talk about soldiers like you ever were one, so I thought I'd better set you straight. Back in the war, when we came down out of the mountains at Gallows Gap, I had this little half-pint guy marching at my side. League volunteer, never knew his name. But we talked some, the way you do. He told me he came from the Hironish Isles, cursed the day he ever left. You want to know why?'

Shendanak sighed. 'I guess you're going to tell me.'

'He left the islands, married a League woman and made a home in Rajal. When the Scaled Folk came, he saw his wife and kids roasted and eaten. Only made it out himself because the roasting pit collapsed in on itself that night and he got buried in the ash. You want to try and imagine that for a moment? Lying there choking in hot ash, in silence, surrounded by the picked bones of your family, until the lizards fuck off to dig another pit. He burnt his bonds off in the embers – I saw the scarring on his arms – then he crawled a quarter of a mile along Rajal beach through the battle dead to get away. Are you listening to me, you brigand fuckwit?'

Shendanak's gaze kindled, but he never moved from the chair. Horse thief, bandit and cut-throat in his youth, he'd likely still be handy in a scrap, despite his advancing years and the prodigious belly he'd grown. But they both knew how it'd come out if he and the Dragonbane clashed. He made a pained face, sat back and folded his arms.

'Yes, Dragonbane, I'm listening to you.'

'At Gallows Gap, that same little guy saved my life. He took down a pair of reptile peons that got the jump on me. Lost his axe to the first one, he split its skull and while it was thrashing about dying, it tore the haft right out of his grip. So he took the other one down *with his bare hands*. He died with his arm stuffed down its throat to block the bite. Tore out its tongue before he bled out. Am I getting through to you at all?'

'He was from here. Tough little motherfucker. Yeah, I get it.'

'Yeah. If you or Tand stir these people up, you're going to have a local peasant uprising on your hands. We won't cope with that, we're not an army of occupation. In fact,' Egar's lip curled, 'we're not an army of any kind. And we are a long way from home.'

'We have the marines, and the Throne Eternal.'

'Oh, don't be a fucking idiot. Even with Tand's mercenaries and your thug cousins, we have a fighting muster under two hundred men. That's not even garrison strength for a town this size. These people know the countryside, they know the in-shore waters. They'll melt out of Ornley and the hamlets, they'll disappear, and then start picking us off at their leisure. We'll be forced back to the ships – if some fisher crew doesn't manage to sneak in and burn those to the waterline as well – and we haven't even provisioned for the trip back yet. It's better than three weeks south to Gergis, and I don't know about you, but I don't want to do it on skewered rat and rainwater.'

'Well, now.' Shendanak made a show of examining his nails – it was pure court performance, something he must have picked up on the long climb to wealth and power back in Yhelteth. It made Egar want to crush his skull. 'Getting a bit precious about our campaigning in our old age, aren't we? Tell me, did you *really* kill that dragon back in the war? I mean, it's just – you don't *talk* much like a spit-blood-and-die dragon-slayer.'

Egar bared his teeth in a rictus grin. 'You want a spanking, Klarn, right in front of your men? I'll be happy to oblige. Just keep riding me.'

Again, the glint of suppressed rage in Shendanak's eye. His jaw set, his voice came out soft and silky.

'Don't get carried away here, Dragonbane. You're not your faggot friend, you know. And he's not here to back you up, either.'

Egar swore later, if it hadn't been for that last comment, he would have let it slide.

THREE

'You are not being *reasonable*, daughter of Flaradnam.'

Archeth grunted, gritted teeth and hauled on the rope again. Below her, the Helmsman Anasharal spindled about and bumped up a couple more of the companionway steps. Its weighty iron carapace clanked dully on the wood, its under-folded limbs twitched feebly about. As ever, it looked and moved like a crippled giant crab.

And talked like an exasperated schoolmaster.

'Krinzanz has clouded your judgement.'

'Uh-huh.'

She took a turn of rope about her forearm, set her boot against the hatch frame and leaned her weight steadily backwards. She'd run the rope over the top strut of the companionway rail and then under the rail itself to create a makeshift pulley. Now the cabled hemp came slithering round the polished wood rail at really quite promising speed. She staggered backwards, semi-controlled. Anasharal came up again, a solid yard this time. Whatever krinzanz was or was not doing to her judgement, it ran in her muscles like liquid rage.

'You are going to regret this.'

'Doubt it.' Words bitten off, she was panting hard from the exertion. 'This is the *best* fucking idea. I've had in *months*.'

Another savage tug backwards on the last word and she made three more steps across the deck, away from the hatch at a tight angle that kept the rope pulleyed around that strut. Damp grey daylight and the cold wrap of drizzle across her face. Summer in the Hironish. If the sun was up there somewhere, you'd never have known it. The rail was beginning to warp visibly with Anasharal's weight, but there was a krinzanz certainty in her head that said it would hold, it *would* hold, if she could just . . .

Knees bent almost to sitting, Archeth dropped her weight near the deck to stop her feet slipping on the rain-greased timbers. She heaved backward, felt the throb of a krin-elevated pulse in her neck as she strained. The companionway was built amidships and equidistant from either bulwark. *Sea Eagle's Daughter* was a decent-sized ship, starboard was a good fifteen feet away, but once Anasharal was up on deck, dragging it across the wet planking would be child's play. She wasn't quite sure how she'd get the Helmsman up and over the bulwark – work something out once she got that far – truth was, she hadn't been much in the mood for careful planning when she went below with the rope.

'Daughter of Flaradnam. You cannot believe any of this is my *fault*.'

'No?' *Haul-l-l* – and suddenly the Helmsman's carapace cleared the top of the companionway. Anasharal hung and swung there like some big, misshapen ship's bell. A couple of its legs reached half-heartedly for purchase on the rail, but as always, the effort of motion alone seemed to defeat them. Archeth felt a vicious surge of satisfaction jolt through her at the sight. 'So who dragged us the fuck up here in the first place? Whose idea was this fucking quest? Who told us we'd find a Kiriath city in the ocean up here?'

'I had no reason not to believe—'

'Or wait – what about a phantom island that comes and goes like the weather? Ring any motherfucking bells, does it?'

'I understand that you may be disappointed, Archeth.'

'Oh, you do?' Leaning back into the tension on the rope, getting some breath back. 'That's good, then.'

She began to track an arc sideways across the deck, opening the angle on the taut rope and hauling herself back in closer, leant steeply backward the whole way. Another couple of steps and the rope should snap free of the rail end, yanking the Helmsman over the edge of the companionway hatch and out onto the deck.

'But what exactly do you think this will achieve?'

She thought there might be the faintest trace of panic in the Helmsman's voice now.

'Do you expect me to confess some secret I've been keeping from you?'

'Nope.' Shortening rope, hand over hand. 'I expect you to sink.'

'Daughter of Flaradnam, you *cannot*—'

'Just watch me.'

Footfalls on wood. Off to her left, where the ship's gangplank lay lowered, a figure came hurriedly aboard. She spared a glance, saw one of Rakan's Throne Eternal approaching. Nodded breathless acknowledgement at him and went back to hauling on the rope.

'My lady, I am sent to—'

'Not!' Through gritted teeth. 'Now!'

The rope twanged free of its wrap on the rail. Anasharal tumbled to the decking, tipped over on its back with the momentum, legs flailing. Slack leapt through the rope, Archeth went over on her arse. The Throne Eternal sprang forward.

'My lady—'

'*I'm fine*,' she snarled, and the sheer force of it drove him back a step. She scrambled to her feet, gathered the rope in burning palms. Anasharal looked pretty helpless upended like that, but she wouldn't have put it past the Helmsman to somehow right itself, drag itself back to the edge of the hatch and fall to the relative safety at the bottom of the companionway; safe because – and she suspected that Anasharal would somehow know this – she was pretty sure she wouldn't have the focal strength to do all this a second time today, krinzanz or no krinzanz. She was, in fact, already starting to feel that maybe—

'Help me,' she snapped at the confused soldier. 'Don't just stand there with your prick in your hand! Grab the rope!'

'My lady?'

But he was Throne Eternal, and she, here in this godforsaken miserable place, *was* the throne, or its closest representative at least. He was charged with obeying her to the death if need be. He did as he was told. He took up station behind her, and she felt the easing on her own scorched-palm grip as he added his strength to hers. They hauled in unison, and the upended Helmsman skated a couple of feet across the greasy timbers, rocking gently. The Throne Eternal tried again, panting somewhat now. 'My lady, what is . . . your intention?'

'Intention?' She twisted her head to look back at him, treated him to a gritted krinzanz grin. 'Dump this fucker in the harbour, why?'

She caught the look of dismay on his face. Turned herself back to face front.

'Just pull,' she told him.

'That would be ill-advised, Selak Chan, as I'm sure you already realise,' said the Helmsman. 'The lady Archeth has ingested—'

'*You shut up!*' she screamed jaggedly. '*You shut the fuck up!*'

And abruptly, as if the scream had punctured some inner chamber in the workings of her anger, she was done. She felt the precious load of her fury leaking away, turning into tears. Suddenly, her muscles were no longer on fire, they only ached. Her palms stung, her mouth tasted sour and dry. Every one of her two hundred and nine years fell on her like stones.

She dropped the rope and stood there in the rain, head down.

'Shut the fuck up,' she murmured to herself.

'My lady? Are you hale, my lady?'

Archeth shook herself like a wet dog. She turned to face the man properly for the first time since he'd come aboard.

'What do you want?'

'It's the Dragonbane, my lady. And Shendanak's men. Well, and my lord Tand as well. There's been fighting. At the inn on League Street. Commander Rakan requests your presence.'

'Wait, *fighting?* Who's fighting, who—?' She drew a breath deep enough to shake her whole body. 'All right, never mind. Go back, tell them I'm on my way.'

'Yes, my lady.' Relief flooding the young face. He saluted, fist to heart, turned and hurried away. She watched him cross the gangplank and head off into the drizzle. She wiped some of the rain off her face.

Fighting.

Just what we needed.

Better get strapped, then.

'Not one fucking word,' she told the Helmsman, as she passed its up-ended carapace on her way to her cabin and her knives.

For once, Anasharal was silent.

They had Shendanak laid out on the bed in his rooms. Grim-faced Majak cousins lined the narrow corridor outside and took up space on the stairs, bulky and damp-smelling in their felt coats and boots. Shouldering her way up past them, Archeth caught impassive stares and muttered snatches of conversation in the steppe tongue. Covert warding gestures forked in her direction, hands touched to talisman purses. Here and there, she saw the glint of a knife being used – for now – to pick at nails or teeth.

There was an ugly, purposeful quiet to it all, and it kicked her straight back to the war. Armed men, waiting for violence to ensue.

At the top of the stairs, one of the cousins rocked to his feet and got in her face, berating her loudly until two of his companions forced him to sit back down. She couldn't decipher any of what he said, her understanding of the various Majak dialects was limited to a handful of Skaranak phrases Egar had taught her over the years. But she didn't really need a translator.

She masked her misgivings, kept her hands well away from the hilts of her own knives, and rapped sharply at the door. Rakan opened for her.

'Got your message,' she said.

'I would not have disturbed you, my lady, but—'

'Skip it.' She slid through the meagre gap he'd opened, let him close up again after her. Saw two brace of Throne Eternal at his back with hands on sword hilts. 'That really necessary?'

Rakan's young face was grim. 'We had to break a couple of heads just to calm things down. I think if Tand's crew hadn't shown up when they did, it might actually have been worse. It might have come down to steel.'

'Wait a minute.' Archeth frowned. 'If this wasn't Tand and Shendanak going at it, who the fuck started the fight?'

'I did.' Egar, in from the next room, pressing a wet cloth to the right side of his head. His face was a mess, one eye bruising up, fresh gouge on the cheek. He grinned at her. 'Afternoon, Archidi.'

'Yeah.' She was in no mood. 'What happened to you?'

The Dragonbane lowered the cloth and peered into its bloodstained folds. 'Bit my ear,' he said apologetically. 'Still bleeding a bit, look. I kind of lost it when he did that. Wouldn't have hurt him nearly as bad otherwise.'

'*You* were fighting with Shendanak? What the fuck for?'

'Basically?' Egar shrugged. 'Because he's a fat imperial fuck who's forgotten where he's from, and he needed a good spanking to help him remember.'

The Throne Eternal bristled. Archeth closed her eyes. 'Great. Where is he?'

'In here.'

Shendanak lay on the big four poster bed, belly up, unconscious. He'd

23

been stripped down to a loincloth and Archeth thought the impression was rather like a butchered whale she'd once seen landed at the docks in Trelayne. One arm was splinted, the head was bandaged with windings through which blood had already soaked. The face was a torn up mess – broken nose, both eyes blackened, the jaw looked lopsided with bruising, might be dislocated . . .

She gave up trying to assess him. Salbak Barla, ship's doctor from *The Pride of Yhelteth*, was bent over Shendanak with a poultice. He nodded absently at her.

'My lady.'

'How is he, doctor?'

Barla sucked in air through his teeth. 'Well, he'll live. Your barbarian friend here was restrained enough for that. But it may be a while before he walks anywhere unaided. He's taken a lot of heavy blows to the skull. One knee is badly bruised, the joint may be cracked. Severe bruising to the groin as well. Ribs broken in numerous places. The arm' – a gesture – 'as you see.'

'Yeah, that was when he did the ear.' Egar, behind her, voice still apologetic. 'Like I said, I just lost it.'

'You certainly did,' agreed Barla.

Archeth held down the edges of a krinzanz rage. She turned to face the Dragonbane, who'd gone to stand at the window.

'So what was the plan, Eg?' she asked mildly. 'I mean, I assume you had one.'

He would not look at her. Stared out at the rain instead. 'I already told you, I lost my temper. But that fat fuck and Tand have both got their men out there beating up the locals for information they don't have. Something you'd know about, if you got off the boat occasionally.'

'Don't you fucking try to make this my fault.'

He spun from the window. 'Archeth, they are *betting* on who gouges some information out of these poor bastards first. Someone had to put a stop to it.'

'Yeah – that's what Rakan and Hald are here for.'

'Hald went with Gil. And anyway, I didn't need any help.'

Breathe, Archidi. Keep it together.

'And what's going to happen now, Eg? Who's going to keep Shendanak's steppe cousins in line now he's not awake to do it?'

'I will.'

'*You* will?' Disbelieving. 'Eg, the mood they're in on the stairs, I'm surprised they haven't broken in here and lynched you already.'

He gave her a grim smile. 'Not the way it works, Archidi. Those kids are pure steppe. I can handle them just fine.'

'The two down in the stable were handled well enough,' said Barla, without turning from his work with the poultice.

'The two in the stable?' Archeth asked with dangerous calm.

Egar nodded. 'Yeah, couple of Shendanak's guys came out in the street while I was stomping him. That was before Tand showed up. I had to take them down as well. No big deal.'

'No big deal, I see. Doctor?'

'Superficial injuries,' Barla confirmed. 'I've given both men a grain of flandrijn to keep them happy. They should sleep it off and be fine by the morning.'

'I see. Egar – let's get this straight. Exactly how many men have you . . . damaged today?'

'Just the three. The others backed right off.' The Dragonbane paused. 'Well, and there was the one in the tavern earlier, the other tavern, where I'm billeted. I bottled him because he was groping my whore, wouldn't give it up.'

Archeth shook her head. 'I'm sorry? You bottled him because *what?*'

'Yeah, it's how I knew this shit was going down in the first place. The way they came in, throwing their weight around. Two he was with probably would have let it go, but—'

'Wait, *wait.*' She held up her hands, palm out. 'Stop. Eg, suppose you act like I don't know what the fuck is going on for a moment, and *tell* me what the fuck is going on. From the start. What happened? How did we end up like this?'

How did we end up like this?

It would have been a reasonable question for anyone on the expedition to ask.

Five months back, it was all bright spring sunlight and cheering, as the freshly minted flotilla sailed downriver through Yhelteth and out to sea. Fair winds and a high quest, the Emperor's blessing and the city turned out in force to see them off. Jhiral, in a shrewdly calculated crowd-pleasing gesture, had made the day of their departure a public holiday, and the banks of the river were thronged on both sides. Every ship in the harbour flew sky-blue and silver pennants for luck. Even the Citadel – or at least the more collaboration-minded among its mastery – had been prevailed upon to offer up prayers for the expedition's success and safe homecoming. Incense billowed from blessing braziers along the river, smoked out over the water, mingled with the criss-crossed traceries of a thousand fireworks set off.

Pretty noisy for a secret mission, Ringil reckoned as they left the estuary, shadowed on all sides by a mob of smaller craft filled with waving, bellowing well-wishers. But you could see even he was enjoying himself.

That's 'voyage of scientific discovery' to you, son, Mahmal Shanta told him, grinning.

And the wind stropped at the unfurled canvas overhead, the sun glistened on the foaming churn of their bow-wave, and Archeth, who was already starting to miss Ishgrim, found a quiet smile despite herself.

Now two out of three vessels sat storm-battered and damp, huddled into Ornley harbour like whipped dogs in a kitchen corner. *Dragon's Demise* was off up the coast, chasing another pointless lead, and it seemed the rain would never stop.

And for lack of other enemies, we're tearing each other apart.

She heard Egar out with weary patience – the brawl over whores, Tand and Shendanak's bet, the fight with Shendanak in the street, the stand-off with his angry cousins over his beaten body, the arrival of Tand and his men . . .

'Didn't really need them,' sniffed the Dragonbane. 'But it got things wrapped up a lot faster, you know.'

No surprise there – Tand's mercenaries were a cold-eyed, scary bunch, a couple of hundred years' brutal enforcement experience between them and all the scars to show for it. You'd have to be either pretty sure of yourself or pretty far gone to get into it with them. Shendanak's cousins were tough enough in their unseasoned steppe-grown fashion, they were mostly younger men, and there were more of them. But in the end, methodical battle-trained competence was always going to tell. It was the axiomatic truth they'd all learnt in the war.

'Where is Tand?' she asked.

Egar shrugged. 'He got them to call Rakan, then he fucked off. Went back to his rooms, I reckon. You know how much he hates the rain.'

'Right. I'm going to talk to him.'

'I'll come with you.'

'No. You won't.' Archeth jerked a thumb in the direction of the door and the men gathered on the stairs beyond it. 'You say you can handle Shendanak's crew? Then you stay here with Rakan in case we need you to do exactly that. You let me worry about Tand.'

It was bravado she didn't much feel. The krin had peaked on her back aboard *Sea Eagle's Daughter*, and now it was starting to wane. All she really felt was tired. But she lacquered on a thin shell of pretence as she went up through the streets to Tand's inn, forced the ghost of strength down into her legs with each step and reminded herself that she was the Emperor's Named Envoy for the expedition, the Authority of the Burnished Throne made Flesh.

And an immortal black-skinned witch with dark magic from the veins of the Earth at her command.

Let's not forget that one, Archidi.

She found Menith Tand sat at a table in one corner of the otherwise empty tavern bar, flanked by two of his mercenary crew and playing out a deck of cards in some version of solitaire she didn't know. If he was concerned about the path of recent events, it didn't show. Lamps had been lit for him against the late afternoon gloom, and in the light they cast, his narrow features were composed to the point of boredom. She saw he'd recently had a shave, and his ostentatiously undyed grey hair was gathered back on either side of his head with twinned clips the colour of ivory, carved, so the rumour went, from the bones of an escaped slave. He met Archeth's eye as she came through the tavern door and nodded, then leaned back in his chair to speak with one of his men. As she approached the table, the man stepped forward and for a moment her pulse ratcheted up. But the mercenary just made a clumsy bow and set out the chair opposite Tand for her to sit down.

'Greetings, my lady.' The slave magnate placed a new card, frowning at the pattern for a moment before he looked up. 'Won't you be seated?'

Archeth ignored the snub. She rested her hands on the back of the chair. 'I hear you've taken some kind of bet with Klarn Shendanak.'

'Yes.' Tand went back to brooding on his cards. 'What of it?'

'Are you entirely fucking stupid, Tand?'

The slaver turned over a card, did not look up. 'Not entirely, my lady, no. Why, what seems to be the problem?'

'You really think going to war with the locals for a bet is a smart thing to do? You think we can afford that right now?' Quick, dark pulse of krinzanz rage. 'I'm *talking* to you, Tand! *Did your krin-whore mother drop you on your fucking head when you were a baby?*'

The mercenary who'd put out the chair stiffened, laid hand to sword-hilt. Archeth peeled him her best lethal-black-witch look and watched with satisfaction as the hand slid away again. Tand, meanwhile—

The slaver had paused, theatrically, mid-way through playing out a card. Momentary stillness, and it was hard to tell if she'd got to him or if it was for show, but – yes, *there*. A vein pulsed in one temple. Archeth cheered inwardly at the sight. Then Tand completed his play, laid aside the slim sheaf of cards in his hand and sat back in his chair.

'My mother was a noblewoman of Baldaran stock, my lady.' The pale, cold eyes swivelled up to meet her own, and for just a moment she saw the fury chained there, she saw how dangerous he was. But the slave magnate's voice, when it came, was cool and even. 'And as for krinzanz, I think it's likely she saw less of it in the course of her whole life than is currently coursing through your half-blood veins. So. Perhaps we can dispense with the cheap insults now and behave a little more as befits our station, yes?'

She leaned on the back of the chair. 'I'm all in favour of that, Tand. Let's start by knocking off the occupation tactics. You were there at Lanatray, you signed the accord like everybody else. We are diplomatic guests of the Trelayne League, permitted access to the Hironish Isles on that basis. Let's act as such.'

'They made us their guests because they had no choice. The peace is fragile, my lady. They'd hardly deny us passage and risk the Emperor's displeasure.'

'I think you overestimate imperial influence. By the best route home, we're nearly three thousand miles from Yhelteth.'

Tand made a dismissive gesture. 'We're the best part of a thousand miles from Trelayne as well. By the time word of what we do here reaches anyone who matters, we'll be long gone. That's if anyone cares in the first place, which – if my knowledge of Trelayne Chancellery affairs is anything to go by – they won't.'

He probably had a point. Ringil had told her exactly how remote from League affairs the Hironish Isles were. Some of the dignitaries they met with in Lanatray had even been a little vague on where exactly the islands were to be found, how far north or west they would have to sail to reach them. And Tand, in his capacity as major player in the slave markets, had spent enough time back and forth between League and Empire in the last few years to be accurately informed. Still . . .

'The peace is fragile on both sides, Tand. What you're doing here could be just the tinder it needs. You throw your weight around like this under the auspices of an imperial expedition and you're creating a perfect pretext for war.'

'Frankly, I doubt that. But in any case, what we've done so far is considerably more controlled and less destructive than what will probably happen if the men are left much longer without some outlet for their frustrations. You have dragged us to the ends of the Earth, my lady, and now we're here, you give us nothing to do. That's not an ideal situation for fighting men.'

'So you don't believe there's anything to learn from these interrogations? The whole thing's a sham, just to keep the men exercised?'

The slave magnate nodded sagely. 'No call to let Klarn Shendanak know that, of course, but – yes, more or less.'

'I doubt I'll be telling Shendanak anything in the near future. The Dragonbane put him in a coma.'

'Did he now?' There might have been admiration in Tand's voice.

'You didn't know that? You were there, weren't you?'

'Yes, I thought the old tub of guts looked rather mauled when we arrived. But you know what these Majak are like – up on the steppe, they're beating the shit out of each other the minute they drop out of the womb. They breed for thick skulls.'

'Well, Shendanak not so much, it seems.'

'No.' Tand looked genuinely thoughtful for the first time since she'd walked in. 'That does put a different complexion on things. We'd better—'

The door of the tavern banged back. Twitchy with the crashing krin, Archeth jumped at the noise it made.

'Sire!' It was one of Tand's men, grinning triumphantly in the doorway. 'Sire, we've got it!'

He advanced into the room, campaign cap off for respect, shaven head gleaming with sweat in the low light. He seemed to have been running, he was panting hard. Took a moment to get his breath under control.

'We've got it,' he said again.

'I'm sure you have, Nalmur,' said Tand patiently. 'But perhaps you could tell the lady Archeth and myself *what* exactly it is that you've got?'

Nalmur glanced at Archeth, apparently noticing her for the first time in the gloom. His expression grew a little more wary, but his face was still suffused with delight.

'The thousand elementals, my lord. The bet. We know what happened to the Illwrack Changeling!'

FOUR

He felt the change as soon as he stepped over the threshold of the croft. It came on like icy water, sprinkling across the nape of his neck.

He tilted his head a little to send the feeling away, traced a warding glyph in the air, like taking down a volume from a library shelf. Around him, the croft walls grew back to an enclosing height they likely hadn't seen in decades. The boiling grey sky blacked out, replaced with damp smelling thatch overhead. A dull, reddish glow reached out to him from the hearth. Peat smoke stung his throat. He heard the slow creak of wood.

A worn oak rocking chair, angled at the fireside, tilting gently back and forth. From where he stood, Ringil could not tell what was seated there, only that it was wrapped in a dark cloak and cowl.

The ward he'd chosen was burning down around him like some torched peasant's hut. He felt the fresh exposure shiver through him. Reached for something stronger, cracked finger-bones etching it into the air.

'Yes – becoming quite adept at that, aren't we?' It was a voice that creaked like the chair. Wheeze and rustle of seeming age, or maybe just the breathlessness at the end of laughing too hard at something. 'Quite the master of the *ikinri 'ska* these days.'

His fresh ward shattered apart, no better than the first – the chill of the Presence rushed in on him. The rocking chair jerked violently around, from no agency he could see. The thing it held was a corpse.

The shrunken mounds it made within the wrap of the cloak were unmistakable, the way it skewed awkwardly in the seat, as if blown there by the wind. The cowl was tipped forward like the muzzle of some huge dark worm, shrouding the face. One ivory-pallid hand gripped an armrest, flesh shrunk back from long, curving nails. The other hand was lost in the folds of the cloak, and seemed to be holding something.

His own hand leapt up, across, closed on the hilt of the Ravensfriend where it jutted over his left shoulder.

'Oh, please,' creaked the voice. 'Put that away, why don't you? If I can break your wards like sticks for kindling, how hard do you think it's going to be for me to break that dinky little sword of yours as well? You know, for an up-and-coming sorcerer, you show remarkably little breadth of response.'

Ringil let go the Ravensfriend, felt the pommel slip through his hands as the Kiriath-engineered scabbard sucked the hand's breadth of exposed blade back into itself. He eyed the slumped form before him and held down the repeated urge to shiver.

'And you are?'

'And still he does not know me.'

Abruptly, the corpse loomed to its feet, out of the chair as if tugged there by puppet's strings. Ringil found himself face to face with the worm's-head cowl and the blank darkness it framed. He made himself stare back, but if there was a face in there, dead or alive, he could not make it out. The whispering voice seemed to come from everywhere at once – down from the eaves of the thatch – up amidst the crackle of the hearth – out of the air just behind his ear.

'You did not know me at Trelayne's Eastern Gate, when your destiny was first laid out in terms you could understand. You did not know me at the river, when the first of the Cold gathered to you, and your passage to the Dark Gate began. And I sent a whole *shipload* of corpses for you when you were finally ready to come back. So tell me, Ringil Eskiath – how many times must I look out at you through the eyes of the dead, before I am given my due?'

It fell in on him like the thatched roof coming down. The cloak and cowl, the stylised placement of hands, one raised to the arm of the chair, the other gathered in the lap, holding—

'*Firfirdar?*'

'Oh, well done.' The corpse turned and shuffled away from him, back towards the hearth. 'Took you long enough, didn't it? Wouldn't have thought it'd be so hard to recognise the Queen of the Dark Court when she comes calling. We are your ancestral gods, are we not?'

'Not by my choice,' he said starkly.

But through his head it went, all the same – the call-and-response prayer to the Mistress of Dice and Death:

Firfirdar sits
Upon her molten iron throne
And is not touched
By fire

Is kernel heart of darkness to the blaze

It was ingrained – a decade of foot-dragging attendance at the Eskiath family temple, every week like clockwork until, finally, at fifteen years of age, he found the words to face his father down and refuse the charade.

By then, though, the cant was worked into his brain like tanner's dung.

Firfirdar smiles
In shadows lit by liquid fire
And holds the dice
Of days

Holds dice for all, and all that is to come

Firfirdar lifts
The dice of days in one cold hand
And rolls them free
In fire

Calls luck like sparks from out the forge of fate

'Yes, well.' The corpse bent stiffly into the shadows beside the fire-glow, and the pallid, long-nailed hand reached a poker from its resting place against the stonework. Firfirdar prodded at the fire, and a log fell loose, cascading embers. 'Fortunately, we're not all dependent on *your* choices in such matters.'

'Then why am I here?'

'Oh.' The poker stabbed into the hearth a couple more times. Sparks billowed up the chimney. The voice rustled about in the flicker-lit, haunted spaces of the croft. 'You were passing. It seemed as good a time as any.'

'You know, for a goddess of death and destiny, you show remarkably little sense of divine grandeur.'

The corpse leaned over the hearth, cowl pressed to the low stone mantelpiece as if tired by its exertions. The echo of Ringil's words seemed to hang in the silence. For a long, cold-sweat moment, he wondered if the Dark Queen would take offence.

His fingers flexed and formed a brief fist—

Look, I won't lie to you, Gil. No ikinri 'ska ward is going to actually back down a member of the Dark Court. Hjel the Dispossessed, almost apologetic when Ringil asks him. *It's his magic, after all, his heritage he's teaching here. But if you throw enough of them around, well* – a faint shrug – *you might buy yourself some time, I suppose.*

Time to do what?

But to that, he gets no answer beyond the dispossessed prince's customary slipshod grin. Hjel is not what you'd call a consistent guide.

What he is, exactly, Ringil has yet to work out.

—and so . . .

He loosened the fist, forced his fingers to hang slack. Waited for the Dark Queen's response.

'Funny.' The corpse had not moved, was still bent there over the hearth. It was as if Firfirdar was talking to the flames. 'Yes. They did say that. That you think you're *funny*.'

A thick silence poured into the croft behind the snap in that final word. All the hairs on Ringil's forearms and the back of his neck leapt erect. He mastered the shudder, thrust it down and stared at the hunched black form. The *ikinri 'ska*, swirling like water just below his fingertips . . .

32

The corpse straightened up. Set the poker aside in the shadows by the wall.

'We're wasting time,' said Firfirdar sibilantly. 'I am not your enemy. You would not still be standing there if I were.'

'Perhaps not.' Behind the mask he kept, a cool relief went pummelling through his veins. He let the *ikinri 'ska* subside. 'But please don't claim the Dark Court has my best interests at heart either. I've read a few too many hero legends to believe that.'

'Legends are written down by mortals, floundering in the details of their world, seeking significance for their acts where usually there is none.' The corpse hobbled back to its seat by the fire. 'You would do well not to set too much store by such tales.'

'Is it inaccurate, then, my lady, to say that heroes in the service of the gods rarely end well?'

'Men who carry steel upon their backs and live by it rarely end well. It would be a little unjust to blame the gods for that, don't you think?'

Ringil grimaced. 'The Mistress of Dice and Death complains to me of injustice? Have you not been paying attention, my lady? Injustice is the fashion – for the last several thousand years, as near as I can determine, more than likely before that too. I think it unlikely the Dark Court has not had a hand in any of it.'

'Well, our attention has been known to wander.' It was hard to be sure with that whispering, rustling voice, but the Dark Queen seemed amused. 'But we are focused on you now, which is what counts. Rejoice, Ringil Eskiath – we are here to help.'

'Really? The lady Kwelgrish gave me to understand that mortal affairs are a game you play at. It's hard to rejoice in being treated as a piece on the board.'

Quiet. The corpse lolled back in the rocking chair's embrace. The nails of its left hand tapped at the wooden armrest, like the click of dice in a cupped palm.

'Kwelgrish is . . . forthright, by the standards of the Court.'

'You mean she shouldn't have told me?'

The soft crackle of the fire in the hearth. Gil thought, uneasily, that the leaping shadows painted on the wall behind Firfirdar were a little too high and animated to fit the modest flames in the hearth that supposedly threw them. A little too *shaped*, as well, a little too suggestive of upward tilted jaws and teeth, as if some invisible, inaudible dog-pack surged and clamoured there in the gloom behind the Dark Queen's chair, only waiting to be unleashed . . .

Very slowly, the corpse lifted both hands to the edges of the cowl it wore. Lifted the dark cloth back and up, away from the visage it covered.

The breath stopped in Ringil's throat.

With an effort of will, he looked back into Firfirdar's eyes.

It was not that the corpse she had chosen was hideous with decay – far from it. Apart from a tell-tale pallor and a sunken look around the eyes, it was a face that might still have belonged with the living.

But it was beautiful.

It was the face of some fine-featured, consumptive youth you'd readily kiss and risk infection for. A face you might lose yourself in one haunted back-alley night, then wake without in the morning and spend fruitless months searching the stew of streets for again. It was a face that gathered you in, that beckoned you away, that rendered all thought of safety and common sense futile. A face you'd go to gladly, when the time came; no regrets and nothing left behind but a faint and fading smile, printed on your cooling lips.

'*Do you see me, Ringil Eskiath?*' asked the hissing, whispering voice.

It was like flandrijn fumes through his head, like stumbling on a step that suddenly wasn't there. He reeled and swayed from the force of it, and the corpse's mouth did not move at all and the voice seemed to come from everywhere at once.

'*Do you see me now?*'

Out of the seething, chilling confusion of his own consciousness, Ringil mustered the will to stay on his feet. He drew in breath, hard.

'Yes,' he said. 'I see you.'

'*Then let us understand each other. It isn't easy being a god, but some of us are better at it than others. Kwelgrish has her intricate games and her irony, Dakovash his constant rage and disappointment with mortals, and Hoiran just likes to watch. But I am none of these. You would be ill-advised to judge me as if I were. Is that clear?*'

Ringil swallowed, dry-throated. Nodded.

'*That's good.*' The corpse raised pallid hands once more and lifted the cowl back in place. Something went out of the space around them, as if someone had opened a window somewhere to let in fresh air. 'Now – to the business at hand. Walk with me, Ringil Eskiath. Convince me that my fellow gods have not been overly optimistic in their assessment of your worth.'

'Walk with you whe—?'

The fire billowed upward in the hearth, blinded him where he stood. Soundless detonation that deafens his gaze. The croft walls and thatch ripped back, no more substantial than a Majak yurt torn away by cyclone winds. He thought he caught a glimpse of them borne away at some angle it hurts his eyes to look at. Gone, all gone. He blinked – shakes his head – is standing suddenly before a roaring bonfire, on a deserted beach, under an eerily luminescent sky.

Walk with me here, says Firfirdar quietly.

She's unhooded again, it's the same achingly beautiful dying youth's face, but here it seems not to have the power it had back in the croft. Or maybe it's him – maybe he has a power here the real world will not permit him. Either way there's no punch-to-the-guts menace, no fracturing of his will and sense of self. Instead, he thinks, the Mistress of Dice and Death looks overwhelmingly saddened by something, and maybe a little lost.

There is not much time, she murmurs. *The dwenda have found a way back – though* back *is a relative term, as they'll discover soon enough – and with them comes every dark thing men have ever feared.*

Ringil shivers. There's a hard wind coming off the sea, stoking the bonfire, whipping up the flames and leaching the heat away.

Then stop them, why don't you?

A gossamer smile touches Firfirdar's mouth at the corners, but it's etched with that same sadness. Her eyes tilt to the sky.

That was tried, she says quietly. *Once. And your sky still bears the scars.*

He follows her gaze upward. The source of the eerie radiance slips from behind the clouds – the dying, pockmarked little sun he's heard the dwenda call *muhn.* He shrugs.

So try again.

It will not be permitted again. Even if we could find some way to press upon the sky as hard and deeply as before, such powers must remain leashed. That was the pact, the gift of mending the Book-Keepers gave. We are bound by the codes they wrote.

Ringil stares into the orange-red heart of the bonfire, as if he could pull some of its heat out and cup it to himself. *So much for the gods. Maybe I should just talk to one of these Book-Keepers instead.*

You already have. How else would you have returned through the Dark Gate except with its blessing? How else would you have come back from the crossroads?

Memory stabs at him on that last word. The creature at the crossroads, the book it held in its multiple arms. The razor talons it touched him with.

I should hate to tear you asunder. You show a lot of promise.

The branches buried in the heart of the fire suddenly look a lot like bones in a pyre. He turns away. He stares away along the shoreline, where the wind is piling up waves and dumping them out incessantly on the sand. Over the sound it makes, he grows aware that Firfirdar is watching him.

That was the Book-Keeper? he asks reluctantly.

One of them, yes.

He locks down another shiver. Sets his jaw. *I was under the impression that I owed my passage through this Dark Gate of yours to Kwelgrish and Dakovash.*

In a manner of speaking, yes, you do. But – come. Firfirdar gestures, away along the ghost-lit beach and into the gloom. *Walk with me. Let us talk it through. All will become clear.*

Yeah? Ringil grimaces. *That'd be a first.*

But he walks with her anyway, away from the useless glare of the bonfire, the heat it apparently cannot give him. He lets her link her arm through his – he can feel the chill it gives off through his clothing and hers – and she leads him away, under the dwenda *muhn*.

In the ghost light it casts, he notices, looking back, that her feet leave no trace on the sand at all.

After a while, nor do his.

FIVE

When the doctor was done with Shendanak, Egar went out onto the stairs and called in a couple of the cousins for witness. He picked two faces he knew, men he'd shared grog and grumbling with on the long voyage north. Both had been down off the steppe for a good few years, both had survived in Yhelteth in a number of more or less thuggish capacities before they went to work for Shendanak. They had a flexible city manner about them as a result, and ought to understand the situation beyond any initial dumb-as-fuck tribal loyalties they still might own.

He hoped.

He led them to Shendanak's bedside and let them look.

'See,' he told them breezily. 'Cleaned up and sleeping like a baby.'

'Yeah?' Durhan, the younger of the two, glowered across to where Salbak Barla was packing up his doctor's satchel. 'So when's he going to wake up?'

Egar shot Barla a warning look.

'Sleep is a great healer,' the doctor said smoothly. 'It unmounts the rider of consciousness so that the horse – the body – may rest from its exertions and recover from any wounds it has sustained. The wise rider does not attempt to mount an ill-used horse too soon.'

Durhan was not appeased. 'Don't fucking talk to me about horses, you city-dwelling twat. I asked you when he's going to wake up.'

'Couple of days,' Egar improvised rapidly. 'Right, doc?'

Barla nodded. 'Yes, I was going to say. Given the nature of his wounds, a few days should suffice.'

Durhan's companion, a blunt, taciturn Ishlinak name of Gart, nodded slowly and fixed Egar with a speculative look.

'You sure about that, Dragonbane?' he rumbled. 'Couple of days? That's the word you want put out?'

Egar feigned lack of concern. 'You heard the bone man.'

'Yeah. But I wouldn't want to be you or your pet bone man here, three days hence, if Klarn still hasn't made it back. That happens, the brothers are going to take it hard.'

'That happens,' Durhan echoed. 'The brothers are going to want blood.'

Egar grinned fiercely, no need to fake it this time. 'Anyone wants blood – that can be arranged. You just tell them to come see the Dragonbane.'

Alarm on Salbak Barla's face, but the two Majak just grunted acknowledgement. It was steppe custom, close enough. It would wash.

'Couple of days it is,' said Gart.

'Yeah.' Durhan nodded at the doctor. 'You keep him well, bone man, you hear? If you know what's good for you.'

'Right, good.' Egar, shepherding them out of the bedchamber. 'Now get everybody off the stairs and about their business. I want a sickbed honour vigil out there at most – five men or less, cool heads. You pick them. And no more shaking down the locals in the meantime. We need that shit like a pony needs skates.'

Durhan balked. 'Tand's men—'

'The lady Archeth has gone to deal with Tand. That's her end, this is ours. You get the brothers straightened out for me, we'll talk about the rest later.'

He got them to the door, ejected them into the hall and nodded to the Throne Eternal to close up again. Through the wooden panels of the door, he heard Gart's voice raised against a growing storm of questions in Majak. He closed his eyes, allowed himself the brief moment.

Here we go again.

Back in Yhelteth, he'd sworn he was done giving other men orders. He wanted no rank, he wanted no responsibility. He'd tagged along on the expedition for a whole tangle of reasons that he now had trouble teasing apart, but longing for command was not one of them. There was gratitude to Ringil, some vague sense of obligation to Archeth – he was, after all, supposed to be her bodyguard these days – and the common-sense discretion attached to getting out of town after his clash with clan Ashant. And underlying, he knew, was a generous helping of nostalgia for the camaraderie of the war years. The quest had *felt* like the war again, at least the preparatory part. But he'd reasoned that while there might indeed be some fighting along the way – pirates, unruly locals, maybe finally the minions of this long undead warlord they couldn't seem to find – still, he'd thought he could take his place in the line without having to worry about what other men thought or feared or needed.

Yeah, some fucking chance.

He went back through to the bedchamber, found Barla fastening up his satchel and looking distinctly queasy. He manufactured an easy grin.

'Don't worry, doc. I'll walk you out.'

'Is that, uh,' the doctor swallowed, 'really necessary?'

'No, probably not,' Egar lied. 'But it's best not to take any chances, tempers the way they are right now.'

Also best not to mention that for most of Shendanak's crew, the ones who hadn't been off the steppe longer than a couple of years, a doctor was just a shaman without the Sky Dwellers to call upon. And fail to deliver the magical goods without the gods at your back, you could end up in a ditch with a slit throat – he'd seen it happen more than once to itinerant doctors from the south in Ishlin-ichan.

'Yes, well, uhm.' Barla put both hands on the closed satchel and looked down at it, as if considering a rapid change of profession. 'Thank you. But could not Captain Rakan and his men, uh . . .?'

'Better if it's me.' Egar's smile was starting to feel like smeared jam on his face. 'Come on, let's get you back aboard the *Pride*. Shanta could probably use another one of those stinking herbal infusions you make, and he won't drink it if you're not there to force it down.'

In the other chamber, Rakan heard the plan and nodded agreement with barely a word. He was a pretty shrewd lad for his age, he saw the sense in this. But as his men got the door, he beckoned Egar aside for a moment and the Dragonbane saw how his youth leaked through the facade of soldierly calm.

'When do you think my lord Ringil will return?' he asked quietly.

Egar shook his head. 'Your guess is as good as mine, Captain. A day there by boat, they said. A day back. That's two, plus a day to do the digging and rest . . .'

'It's been four days already. What if something's wrong?'

'Well, they might have a hard time finding the grave marker, sure. Or, if the weather's against them—'

'No.' Rakan's voice grew tighter, lower. 'Not that. What if this time he *found* the Illwrack Changeling?'

Near the opened door, Salbak Barla cleared his throat. Egar shot a glance that way, saw Rakan's men hanging off their captain's every word. He pitched his own voice loud and brisk.

'If that has happened, Captain, then pity the Changeling. Because Gil's going to be bringing us his head on a spike and his balls wrapped around the haft.'

It raised weak grins among the men, which he counted a victory of sorts. He wagged a finger in salute at Rakan, led Barla out the door.

To his relief, both corridor and stairs outside were cleared of men. Durhan and Gart appeared to have followed their instructions to the letter. Downstairs in the tavern's main bar, four Majak sat at a table, burning a blessing taper and playing half-heartedly at dice. Serving staff and a couple of local patrons aside, they were the bar's only occupants. They grew quieter as the doctor and the Dragonbane came down the stairs, but they all lowered their eyes with appropriate respect. Egar paused at the table and sketched obeisance at the taper, nodded acknowledgement at the man he judged the eldest. Then he ushered Salbak Barla past, one proprietary hand on the doctor's shoulder for all to see.

He felt their stares at his back, all the way to the tavern's front door.

Out in the street, it was still raining and the daylight had all but given up. A damp grey gloom hung over everything. Ornley had no formal street lighting, even here on League Street, one of the town's main thoroughfares. There was a local ordinance commanding residents to burn candles in their windows during the hours of darkness, but around here this kind of murk apparently didn't count as dark, so no candles yet. Egar and the doctor picked their way with care over rain-slick cobbles they could barely make out, and presently the street began to slope downward towards the harbour.

'What will you do if Shendanak does not waken in three days?' Barla asked him when they'd negotiated a hairpin curve that took them out of sight of the tavern.

'I'll think of something.'

'That's very reassuring.'

Egar shrugged. 'Look on the bright side. Maybe he'll be up and about day after tomorrow. I didn't hit him that hard in the head.'

'No, but you did it repeatedly. Which makes it far more like . . .'

Volume soaking out of Barla's voice like piss into sand. Then silence. Egar glanced over at him curiously.

Saw where the doctor was staring and followed his gaze, down League Street to the next bend, over the low roofs of houses to the harbour waters beyond.

And the big, lean League man o' war anchored there.

He sprinted the rest of the slope downward, left Barla puffing in his wake. Skidded on greasy cobbles, stayed upright with the long habit of battle-field charges in his past. Round the final curve on League Street, where it splayed wide to meet the wharf, down the broad cobbled mound it made, and so out onto the waterfront proper. He let his pace bleed down to a slow jog and came to a halt at the edge of the wharf, staring out at the new arrival.

Trying to calculate exactly how much bad news this might be.

The League ship was a little smaller than *Pride of Yhelteth*, but with that sole exception, she dominated the harbour. Her bulk dwarfed the few local fishing boats tied up along the southern quay, her lines rebuked the sturdy merchantman build of *Pride* and *Sea Eagle's Daughter*, and she somehow gave the impression of having shunted the moored imperial vessels aside to make room for herself in the centre of the little bay. Shielded archers' platforms armoured her railings fore and aft. The cumbersome snout of a war-fire tube poked over her bows like some huge sleeping serpent's head.

She was anchored squarely across the harbour exit.

Her colours flapped wetly at stern and mainmast – he'd recognised them from that first glimpse up on the hill, had seen plenty like them on the ships in Lanatray harbour a few weeks back, while the expedition re-stocked provisions and waited on the diplomatic niceties. The eleven-star-and-band combination of the League topped the mainmast, above a bigger flag denoting city of origin – in this case some piece of nonsense involving a gate, a river, sacks of silver and a couple of large buzzards; Trelayne itself, he recalled. The League flag was repeated at the stern, and dark reddish pennants flew off both secondary masts. He'd seen those before too, couldn't remember where. Couldn't remember what they meant.

Footfalls behind him – he glanced round, saw Barla crossing the deserted wharf at a limping trot, lugging his bag from one hand to the other as he came.

'Sacred Mother of Revelation,' he panted. 'What's that doing here?'

Egar shook his head. 'I'd love to believe it's a standard patrol. But from what we heard in Lanatray, I don't think they bother with that sort of thing up here. Fits with what Gil told me too – no one in the League gives a shit about these islands.'

'Apparently they do now.'

'Yeah.'

Movement on *Pride of Yhelteth's* main deck. Egar squinted in the failing light, made it for Mahmal Shanta, up out of his cabin for the first time in days, huddled in a heavy blanket and trailed by solicitous slaves. He stood at the starboard rail with a spyglass at his eye, scoping the League vessel. Egar saw him turn to one of his retinue and issue commands. The man bowed and went below again.

'All right, come on.' Egar jogged along the wharf to *Pride*'s gangplank, waited for Barla to catch him up and then went aboard. The watchmen waved them through, clearly distracted. Which, Egar reflected grimly, wasn't good to see in men supposedly trained to marine standard.

We're all getting way too slack. This place is sapping us. We're in no shape to . . .

To what?

He joined Mahmal Shanta at the starboard rail.

'Dragonbane.' The old naval engineer did not take the spyglass from his eye. His voice was hoarse with long bouts of coughing. 'You've seen our new friends, I take it?'

Egar grunted. 'Hard to miss.'

'Indeed. Hard to take as coincidence too. One doubts such savage beauty graces Ornley harbour on a regular basis.'

'Beauty?'

'Beauty.' Reedy emphasis on the word. Shanta lowered the spyglass and looked at the Dragonbane. He'd grown gaunt with his illness, but his eyes still gleamed. 'I don't expect anyone from a horse tribe to appreciate it, but that's a poem in timber floating out there, a veritable ode to maritime speed and manoeuvrability. There's a reason the Empire always comes off worse in naval engagements with the League, and you're looking at it. Superior design, born of constant competition between city states warring for an edge.'

'Right.' Egar gestured. 'You know what those red pennants mean?'

'Indeed I do—'

Shanta stopped abruptly, caught and then creased over with a spasm of coughing. One of his retinue came forward to hold him up, but the engineer waved him violently away. He braced himself on the rail with one age-knobbed hand, got himself upright again by wheezing stages. Slaves fussed about, re-arranging the blanket on Shanta's trembling shoulders. The man Egar had seen Shanta order below returned with a steaming mug of something that reeked of mint and other less palatable herbs. The engineer tucked the spyglass under his arm and cupped the mug with both hands. He drank gingerly. Grimaced but forced the liquid down.

'My lord, this is madness.' Salbak Barla knew his patient well and was not crowding him, but his tone was urgent. 'You should not be out in this weather. We must get you below, we must get you warm.'

'Yes, yes, all in good time. Here.' Shanta handed the mug to the doctor and took hold of his spyglass again. 'It is unfortunate, but I am the expert here, and I am not done perusing. I must fix the details in my head, doctor, and thus save myself the necessity of further sojourns on deck.'

'The pennants,' Egar persisted.

'Yes, the pennants.' Shanta pointed with the spyglass, schoolmasterish. 'Heart's blood red, snake's tongue trim, at foremast and aft. Northern League naval convention. It signifies that the vessel is flagship to a flotilla.'

'A fucking *flotilla?*'

Shanta stifled another, weaker cough with his fist. 'Three to five vessels, if my memory serves me correctly. More and the pennants would not be split tongued. Or they would have gold trim. Or is it both?'

The rain seemed abruptly to be falling that little bit harder. The gloom beyond the harbour exit grew that much more menacing. Egar scowled.

'So where are the rest of them?'

'There'd hardly be room for more vessels in the harbour anyway,' Barla offered. 'Perhaps they anchored further out.'

Egar tried to stave off a creeping sense of doom.

'How long have they been there?' he asked Shanta.

'Oh, not long. The watchmen called me as soon as they sighted the colours. It's taken me some time to get up and dressed, and then I waited below to see if they'd come to us. When they didn't, I came up on deck and I've been here a while. Say half an hour since they anchored? A little longer?'

'And no landing party.' Egar squinted against the rain. 'They've not even started lowering a boat.'

'No.'

'But . . . what would they be waiting for?' wondered Barla.

Shanta and the Dragonbane traded glances. Shanta nodded. Egar felt a sickly weight settling in his guts.

'Should I tell him?' wheezed the naval engineer. 'Or will you?'

The doctor blinked in the rain. 'What?'

'Encirclement,' said Egar grimly. 'They're not here to send anyone ashore, they're here to plug up the harbour. Stop us getting out. While the rest of the flotilla lands an assault force somewhere up the coast, and they come overland to fence us in.'

'Then – but, then . . .' Salbak Barla gaped back and forth at the two of them. 'Well, we have to warn Captain Rakan. And the marines. We have to . . . to . . .'

'Forget it.' Egar gripped the rail in front of him, tightened his hands on it with crushing force as the anger swept through him. 'Way too late now.'

Can't believe we've been this fucking stupid.

But who would have looked for it, Eg? Here, at the damp arsehole end of the world? Why would they fucking bother?

'What do you mean too late?' The doctor's voice, plaintive now, like a child tugging at his sleeve. It seemed to be coming from a long way off.

'He means,' explained Mahmal Shanta patiently, 'that if they've chosen to show themselves in the harbour now, it's because the land forces are already in place.'

Egar made an effort, reeled himself back in. He scanned the rise of the town where it backed up the hill above the bay, the briefly seen winding of streets and alleys between the dark stone houses, the crappy little watch-tower on the ridge to the north. All harsh and alien now, and just to really crown it, a thick fog had settled in on the upper reaches of the hill. Half the fucking town was gone into it already.

Steep ground, bad weather, hostile forces closing from all sides. And a local population we've just succeeded in pissing off.

'Gentlemen,' he said flatly. 'We are royally fucked.'

SIX

The house Tand's men took her to was on the upper fringes of the town, just before Ornley thinned out into a scattering of isolated crofts. It was high ground, and there would have been a great view back down the slope of the bay to the harbour, if the air below hadn't been quite so clogged with drifts of murky, low-lying cloud.

At least we're out of the rain.

It was something Tand appeared to take comfort from as well. As they walked the last couple of turns in the street, he put back the hood on his cloak and nodded approvingly up at the sky. He was doing his best not to look smug.

'Seems to be clearing,' he said.

She tried not to sound too bad-tempered. 'You really think we can trust this confession, Tand?'

'Oh, most certainly. Nalmur's a good man, one of my best. He knows his work.'

Nalmur was leading the group. He glanced back at the mention of his name.

'I'd stake my life on it, my lady. We got at least three other squealers leading us to this bloke by name, and when he talked, well – you know it when a man cracks, you can almost hear it happen. Like a rotten tree branch going, it is.'

She masked a desire to bury one of her knives in his throat. 'Right. And have you left this cracked man in any fit state to talk to us?'

'Oh, yes, my lady. Didn't need to rough him up much past the usual.' An opened palm, explanatory. 'He's a family man, see. Good lady wife, a pair of strapping young sons. Plenty to work with.'

Smirks edged the expressions of the other men in the group.

'Yes, thank you, Nalmur.' Perhaps Tand saw something in her face. 'You can spare us the details, I think.'

'Just as you like, my lord. My lady. But that confession is rock solid. You could build a castle on it, sir.'

Tand tipped her a told-you-so look. She worked at not grinding her teeth.

They took the final turn in the street, found themselves facing a short row of cottages, dwellings more hunched and huddled than the buildings lower down the hill. A brace of Tand's men were loitering outside an opened door about halfway along the row. They were guffawing about something, but when they saw the approaching party, they stiffened into quiet and an approximation of drilled military attention.

A curtain twitched in Archeth's peripheral vision. She didn't bother to look round. You could feel the eyes on you all the way along the street. Gathered at the edges of the darkened windows and in the gap of doors cracked a bare inch open, waiting to slam. Watching, hating as the booted feet tramped by.

It was the post-war occupations all over again.

Greetings from the Emperor of All Lands – we come to you in peace and the universal brotherhood of the Holy Revelation.

But if you don't want those things, then we're going to fuck you up.

Tand had taken the lead. He nodded at his saluting men and stepped between them, ducking in under the low lintel. Archeth followed, into the soft glow of a banked fire in the grate, and candles lit against the day's end gloom. There was a pervasive smell of damp from the earthen floor and the whiff of voided bowels to go with it. A sustained, hopeless keening leaked in from the next room. Three more of Tand's mercenaries stood guard over a man stripped to the waist and strapped to an upright chair.

Nalmur and the rest of the squad crowded in after her.

'Well then,' said Tand. 'Nalmur, will you do the honours?'

Nalmur took a theatrical turn around the chair and its occupant. As Archeth's eyes adjusted to the light, she made out bruising on the man's face, crusted blood from the broken nose, a series of livid burn marks across chest and upper arms. His breeches were soaked through at the crotch. Nalmur dropped a friendly arm around his shoulders, and the man flinched violently against his bonds.

'My lord, my lady – meet Critlin Tilgeth, first warden of the Aldrain flame, Hironish chapter. Master Critlin here likes to get together with his pals a couple of times a year in stone circles and invoke the spirits of the Vanishing Folk. Which they do, apparently, by dancing around naked and fucking each other's wives senseless. I guess you got to find something to fill your evenings with up here.'

Belly laughs from the men around her.

'Get on with it,' she said harshly.

'Yes, my lady.' Nalmur slapped the tied man amiably on one cheek. Straightened up. He switched to accented but serviceable Naomic. 'Tell us about the grave again, Critlin. Tell us what you did.'

'Yes. Yes, we dug—' Critlin swallowed hard. His voice sounded as broken as his face. Low and shaky, a pleading in it, like raindrops trembling on the underside of a roof's edge. His eyes kept darting to the doorway into the other room, the source of the endless weeping. 'We dug it up. We – we went at night. The day before Quickening Eve, when the waters are low.'

Archeth frowned. 'What waters?'

'He means the gap at Grey Gull peninsula, my lady.' Nalmur, for all the world like a tutor helping out a feeble student under examination.

'Says the currents bring more water in at certain times, make it harder to cross.'

'But—' She shook her head irritably. 'There was a dead sheep in that grave, that's all we found, we didn't . . .'

They'd been using Tethanne, while Critlin gaped uncomprehendingly back and forth, between this evil-eyed black woman and his tormentor-in-chief. Archeth made an effort, shunted the constant keening to the back of her mind, summoned her own creaky Naomic.

'You uh – you took the Illwrack Changeling out – and put a, uhm – deformed? Yeah – a deformed sheep in his place? What – position? – no, wait, what *condition* – what condition was the body in?'

Critlin hesitated. He seemed puzzled by the question, maybe confused by her fumbling, error-strewn speech. Nalmur fetched him a massive clout across the side of the head.

'The lady Archeth asks you a question! Answer, and be quick about it! Or perhaps you think little Eril's jealous of the caresses his big brother's had from my men. Perhaps he'd like some of the same?'

The wailing from the next room re-doubled. Critlin moaned deep in his chest and strained against his bonds. Nalmur grinned and raised his hand again.

'That's enough!' Archeth snapped.

The hand came down. A small, angry smile played around the corners of Nalmur's mouth for a moment, but he bowed his head. Archeth leaned in closer to Critlin. He shrank from her, as far as the chair-back would allow. The stench of shit wafted as he moved. She raised her hands, palms outward, backed away again.

'Just tell me,' she said quietly. 'Was the body intact? Had it decayed at all?'

'Intact,' blurted Critlin. 'It was intact! The sheep was but recently slaughtered. We took it from Gelher's flock and—'

'All right, that's it you little goat-fucker!' Nalmur, stepping in with fist clenched and swinging. Archeth swung up and round, put a knife-fighter's block in the way.

'I *said* that's enough.'

Nalmur recoiled from touching her, whether out of respect for rank or superstitious dread, it was hard to tell. But there was a tight anger in his face.

'My lady, he is taking the piss. He's—'

'He is *broken!*' Her yell froze the room. One of Nalmur's men, already on his zealous way to the other chamber, stopped dead his tracks. Archeth swung on him, pointed. 'You! You step through that door, I will fucking kill you.'

Tand stirred. 'My lady, the man shows a distinct lack of respect, given his station. Joking at our expense should hardly go unpunished.'

'I *will* kill you.' Still eye-balling Nalmur's man. 'Don't test me, human.'

And abruptly it was there in her head, like some unfolding map of a battle campaign she'd only heard rumour of until now. How it could be done, how it would go. The rest of Tand's men, their positions in the room, the gnarled hilt of each knife she carried, how to reach them, in what sequence, how many bloody seconds it would take to *fucking kill them all . . .*

These fucking humans, Archidi. Grashgal's voice, almost toneless, empty of anything but the distant trickle of despair, as the Kiriath laid their plans to leave. *They're going turn us into something we never used to be.*

Hadn't he called it right?

Didn't she feel it herself, day-in day-out, the corrosive rub of human brutality, human cruelty, human *stupidity* against the weave of her soul. The slow erosion of her own moral certainties, the ground she gave up with every political compromise, every carefully balanced step in the Great Kiriath Mission, every lie she told herself about necessary sacrifice in the name of building something better . . .

Through the doorway, the constant keening. Her hands itched for the hilts of her knives.

Maybe it was just fucking *time*.

Menith Tand was watching her, fascinated. She felt his gaze like shadow in the corner of one eye, and something about it pulled her back from the brink.

'You want to live, you stand down,' she told the mercenary by the door. Voice flat now, as flat and emptied out as Grashgal's had ever been. 'Nalmur, get your men out of here.'

Nalmur looked at Tand, outraged. The slave magnate nodded soberly.

'But my lord, this man is—'

'Broken. Remember?' Archeth fixed her eyes on Critlin as she spoke, didn't look round, didn't look at Nalmur at all. She didn't trust herself to. 'You heard him break, you said, "Like a rotten tree branch. Couldn't miss it." Your work here is done, sellsword. Now get out, and take your thugs with you.'

It took less than a minute to clear the house. Give Nalmur his due, he ran a tight enough crew. A sharp whistle brought a couple of younger mercenaries out of the room the keening was coming from. A gruff command and everybody trooped out, leaving Archeth and Tand alone with Critlin. Nalmur was last man out, slamming the door ungraciously shut.

The room seemed suddenly larger, less oppressive. Even the weeping next door seemed to ebb a little.

Archeth crouched in front of Critlin's chair, made herself as unthreatening as she knew how. The Naomic came a little easier this time around. Just getting Tand's men out of the house felt like a headache lifting.

'Listen to me, Critlin. Just listen. No one's going to hurt you anymore. You have my word. No one's going to hurt your family, no one's going to hurt you. Just tell me again about the body.'

'The . . . the sheep?'

She breathed deep. 'No, not the sheep. The body in the grave. What state was the body in?'

'But . . .' Critlin stared. His voice quavered. 'There *was* no body in the grave.'

Archeth shot a glance at Tand.

'Look,' the slave magnate began angrily. 'You told my men—'

Critlin cringed as if Nalmur had just come back through the door.

'There was bone,' he gabbled. 'Just bone, just fragments of it, tiny, nothing left but that. The rest was just . . . rotted . . .'

His voice petered out. He was staring at them both as if they were insane. Archeth groped for some context.

'Well – were you surprised by that?'

He looked back at her numbly.

'Surprised?'

'That the Illwrack Changeling's body had rotted? Did that surprise you?'

'N-no, my lady. He has been dead these four thousand years.'

'Yeah, but—'

She shut her mouth with a snap. Recognising suddenly which side of reasonable they'd all somehow ended up.

Because if these last weeks have been anything at all, Archidi, it's a lesson in how badly myth and legend butt up against the real world. And yet here she still was, wanting to know why a body put in the ground four millennia ago wouldn't be in decent condition when you dug it up.

This place is driving us all insane.

'All right, so there was no body.' Tand seemed to have moved past his previous anger – there was a deadly metronome patience in his voice now. 'Or at least nothing much left of one. And you expected that. So why bother digging up the grave in the first place?'

'The lodge elder ordered it, my lord.' Critlin's head sagged forward. He seemed to be giving up some final thing. 'To take the sword.'

Archeth gave Tand another significant look. 'There's a sword now?'

The slave magnate shrugged. 'He was a warrior, was he not, this Illwrack Changeling? Makes sense that they'd bury him with his weapons.'

'All right, so you took the sword.' Archeth rubbed at her closed eyes with finger and thumb. 'But, look – why bury a fucking sheep in its place? Why would you do that?'

'The lodge elder ordered that too, my lady.' The words were falling out of Critlin's mouth now, stumbling to get out. He was done, he was over some kind of hill, and his eyes flickered more and more to the door into the other room. 'Gelher's flock have the run of Grey Gull – several were born last season with deformities – the lodge-master said it was a sign, that the soul of the Changeling had awakened – most died at birth, but two or three survived until this year. So the elder said – we must sacrifice one such in thanks – lay it in place of the sword. We did only as he ordered us, as our oath demanded.'

Archeth drew Quarterless from the sheath in the small of her back. The knife blade glimmered in the low light.

'Where is the sword now?'

'Taken back, my lady.' His eyes were fixed dully on the blade. For one chilly moment, Archeth thought she saw a longing in that gaze that made no distinction between Quarterless cutting his bonds or his throat. 'Back to Trelayne. There will be a ceremony. The lodge elder says rejoice, the Aldrain are returning.'

She shivered, not sure if it was his words or the look in his eyes that caused it. Shook it off, either way. Knelt at his side and sliced through the cords binding his legs to the chair. He began to weep then, like a small child. The stench from where he'd pissed and shat himself was stronger this close in. She cut the cords off his chest and arms, ripped them loose with unneeded violence. She swallowed hard.

'Go to your family,' she said. 'You will not be harmed further. You have my word.'

Critlin staggered upright, clutching at one arm. He limped away into the other room. Archeth stared after him, locked up in a paroxysm of something she could not name.

Menith Tand cleared his throat. 'Perhaps, my lady—'

'Give me your purse,' she said distantly.

'I *beg* your pardon?'

She stirred as if awakening. Turned on him, Quarterless still in her hand. Words like hammered nails into wood. '*Give me your motherfucking purse!*'

Tand's lips tightened almost imperceptibly. The same chained rage she'd seen in his eyes at the inn was there again. But he reached carefully beneath his cloak and fished out an amply swollen soft black leather purse. Weighed it gently in the palm of his hand.

'I do not care for your tone, my lady.'

'Yeah?' She reached back and put Quarterless away in its sheath. Safer there, the way she felt right now. 'Then take it up with the Emperor when we get back. I'm sure you'll be able to buy yourself an audience.'

'Yes, no doubt. Using the same funds that have made me a significant sponsor of this expedition—'

She chopped him down. 'Of which I am nominated imperial commander. Are you going to give me that purse, or am I going to take it from you?'

Brief stillness between them. The faint reek of shit from the stained torture chair she stood beside. Horseplay commotion from Tand's men out in the street. Raised voices – they seemed to be squabbling about something. In the next room, the keening went on as if Critlin had never been released.

Tand tossed the purse at her, hard. Two centuries of drilled reflex took it out of the air with knife-fighter aplomb.

'Thank you.'

The slave magnate turned away and headed for the door. He paused, hand on the latch, and looked back at her. The fire was out in his eyes now, and he looked merely – thoughtful.

'You know, my lady – you would be ill-advised to make an enemy of me.'

She should have left it alone, but the krin still sputtered and smoked in her like a pissed out campfire. The words were out of her mouth before she knew it.

'I think you have that backwards, Tand. I've seen better than you strapped to an execution board in the Chamber of Confidences.'

He held her gaze for a sober moment, then shrugged.

'Understood,' he said tonelessly. 'Thank you for your candour.'

He turned the latch and went outside to his men. Archeth watched the door close on him, then cast about in the dampish, shit-smelling room as if she'd dropped something of value somewhere on the earthen floor. She closed her eyes briefly, too briefly, then forced herself to the door into the next room and the source of the keening. She leaned there in the doorway, curiously unwilling to actually step over the threshold.

On the big sagging bed that constituted the room's only real furniture, like huddled shipwreck survivors on some fortuitous raft, a young woman sat and hugged two young boys to her. All three had had their clothing torn or sliced apart and now only the woman's tight embrace held the remnants against their pallid flesh. The eldest boy looked to be about ten or eleven, the younger more like six or seven. Both their faces and bodies were marked, beginning to bruise. The woman's eyes were closed tight, one swollen cheek was gouged where someone had struck her, most likely with a belt-end or maybe just the back of a heavily ringed hand. Her lips were moving in some voiceless litany, but it was her throat the keening came from, the only sound she made, and she rocked in time with it, back and forth, back and forth, a rigid couple of inches either way.

Critlin was slumped on the ground near the doorway in a way that suggested he'd simply leaned there and slid down the stonework until the floor stopped him. He was less than four feet from his family and staring at them as if they'd just sailed from some harbour quay without him. His left hand reached helplessly out for them, rested on one of his own up-jutting knees, hung there limp and lifeless.

Archeth swallowed and stepped into the room. Crouched at Critlin's side, tried to fold his nerveless fingers around the purse. 'Here. Take this.'

He barely looked at her.

'Take – look, here – just fucking *take it*, will you.'

The purse hung in his hand a scant second. Then it tugged loose with its own weight, fell from his slackened grip and into the dirt he sat on.

Muffled clink of imperial silver within.

Greetings from the Emperor of All Lands.

She got up and backed out.

Went back through the room they'd tortured Critlin in, as if pushed by a gathering wind. Yanked open the door and stepped out into the murky evening street.

Found a sword tip at her throat.

SEVEN

He woke to the crash of waves and the cold, coarse press of damp sand against his cheek. Harsh grey light insisted at his eyelids until he opened them. He blinked, lifted his head and saw eyes on stalks, watching him from less than a foot away.

Shudder and shiver with the chill.

He pushed himself more or less upright and the crab scuttled away. Seen clearly, it wasn't much bigger than the palm of his hand. It found a burrow in the sand some distance off and stood half in, half out, still watching him. Ringil sat and stared back for a while, trying to put his head back together.

Along the curve of the beach, away from bonfire glow, she told him the Truth behind Everything, and then he forgot it.

Or more precisely, he drops it, cannot hold onto it with sufficient strength – the Truth, it turns out, is a delicate, ineffable thing. It will not fit in his head any more than the wind will fit in a helmet. It tumbles and falls away instead. Bruises on impact, like fruit lost off some heavily overladen market barrow, while Ringil Eskiath, sorcerer warlord apparent, runs around grabbing and groping for the scattered, rolling pieces.

He rubbed ferociously at his face and forehead with both hands, but it was gone, scrubbed away, leaving only a truth-shaped stain on his memory and a loose, sandy feeling in his head.

The rest came back presently, in tawdry chunks – sparse fragments of recall, like soiled pieces of crockery from some lavish feast he'd attended and then been ejected from for lack of sufficiently noble blood.

They steered you as best they could, she tells him. Dakovash and Kwelgrish, juggling the myriad factors between them, with a little side help now and then from Hoiran and myself. They made the introductions, so to speak. Borrowed scrapings of steppe nomad myth, crafted them into an exchange and a U-turn, just beyond the shadow of death. Your tithe for the Dark Gate, paid. But in the end, we of the Dark Court can only request such passage. Permission is for the Book-Keepers to give or withhold. And even that permission may be qualified, truncated, subject to change.

Ringil's lip curls. *You'll forgive me if I say this all sounds rather clerkish. The gods of the Dark Court stooping to abject negotiation.*

Well, now – most human prayer is exactly that, is it not? He thinks he can hear pique in the Dark Queen's voice, and the waves seem to crash a little harder on the sand. *Abject negotiation with higher powers for aid, for intercession, for benefits not otherwise obtainable?*

Yes, but that's humans. We're a conniving, carping bunch.

As above, so below, she says tartly. *And since the results have saved your life on more than one occasion, perhaps you should be a little less snide.*

He got to his feet, swaying.

The Ravensfriend lay in the sand beside him – evidently at some point he'd taken it off, but he didn't remember that either.

He bent, clumsy-limbed with the cold. Gathered the sword to him like the body of some dead and broken lover.

They stand together on a promontory overlooking the ocean. They must have climbed there from the beach below, though his memory on this is vague. The sky has darkened, but there's a loose, buttery glow from the *muhn*, seeping through the torn up cloud like a weaker version of bandlight, dusting the sea with soft gold. Around them, the wind cuts through the long coarse grass, bending it in circles so it seems to be making obeisance to the Dark Queen.

You are seeking the Ghost Isle, the Chain's Last Link. There's no question in her voice.

Among other things, yes.

You found it a week ago. You have been deceived.

Ringil makes a restless gesture. *An island that comes and goes from existence with the wind and weather? With respect, my lady, I'm fairly certain we would have noticed such a thing if we'd stumbled on it.*

Would you now? Firfirdar's eyes glitter in the sparse light. *And how exactly would you do that? How would you recognise such an island, unless you had seen it materialise? How, in its manifest form, would it be any different than any other island? Would you expect it to glow with witch fire as the chronicles claim?*

No, I'd expect the locals to know about it and be able to point it out to me.

They do. And they did.

You are mistaken, my lady. Outside of myth and old wives' tales, the locals made no mention of any island at all. The closest they came was—

And realisation dawns. He hears the rough Hironish-accented voice again, one among the many *many* they'd listened to in and out of Ornley's taverns until they all began to blur into a single, incoherent stream. *On approach, Grey Gull may seem a separate island, but do not be deceived. Certain currents cause the inlets to fill enough at certain times to make it so – but you can always cross, at worst you might have to wade waist deep. And most of the time, you won't even get your boots wet.*

He closes his eyes. *Oh, for Hoiran's fucking sake.*

Just so. As I said, you have been deceived. More specifically, you have been tricked into thinking that a legend distorted over millennia of telling and re-telling can still be taken literally.

It comes and goes with the weather, Ringil says heavily, laying it out like some theological proof. *There's an island there, then it's gone – because there's a peninsula in its place. I'm going to fucking drown that Helmsman.*

The Helmsmen have agendas of their own. It would be a mistake to believe they are your friends.

He snorts. *Yeah, they told me the same thing about you.*

He slung the Ravensfriend across his back by its harness and felt immediately somewhat better. The ache the truth had left in him receded, became more or less manageable. He'd had worse hangovers.

He cast about, trying to get his bearings. The beach wasn't one he recognised, either from his time in the Grey Places or anywhere he'd been in more prosaic realms. But the landscape behind was a close match for what he'd seen of the Hironish Isles so far – windswept and low-lying, not much in the way of trees, some low rock outcroppings and what looked like cliffs out at one distant headland. He wondered for a brief moment if Firfirdar had sent him back to Grey Gull peninsula with his newly minted understanding, to finally face the Illwrack Changeling. He dismissed the idea after a moment's groggy thought.

We dug that grave up. It had a dead sheep in it.

For a moment, it seemed he recalled the Dark Queen advising him that looking for the Illwrack Changeling's corpse was in itself a mistake, a waste of time. But he couldn't be sure. There was too much missing around the ragged wound in his memory where the gift tore loose.

Yeah, yeah. You had the truth, and then you dropped it, and it broke. Poets weep, the sky falls down. Get a fucking grip, Gil.

He shook his head to clear it. Found a high point on the spine of the land behind him and started walking towards it.

The churned up memories scampered after him.

Yes, you may ask.

What? She's fallen behind so he turns to look back at her. *Ask what?*

She grins, not fooled. *The question that echoes through your thoughts so clearly. All those adolescent evenings at temple back in Glades House, Eskiath. You remember the cant. Now you're wondering how much truth lies in it. You're wondering – does the Dark Queen really grant favours to those bold enough to face her and ask?*

They face each other across a half dozen steps in the sand. The wind buffets noisily between them. It's a tense little moment.

Well? Ringil gestures impatiently. *Does she?*

It has been known. What would you ask for, supplicant?

He grimaces at the epithet. Hesitates, then plunges in. *Grashgal the*

Wanderer told me once that the Ravensfriend will hang behind museum glass in a city where there is no war.

That is one possible end for it, yes. I ask again – what do you want?

He swaps the grimace for a weary smile, and turns away. His words trail back over his shoulder like a scarf caught up in the wind. *Well, if you can really catch the echo of my thoughts, Mistress of Dice and Death, then you already know that.*

Ah, grim and gritty little Ringil Eskiath. Yes, walk away, why don't you? And then, abruptly, she's close at his side again, voice intimate, a caressing whisper at his ear. *The fractured heavens forbid that Gil Eskiath should ever beg a favour of anybody, even of the gods themselves. That he should ever show weakness or need. How unbecoming that would be in the scarred bearer of the dread blade Ravensfriend. Oh yes, I can see why they both like you so much.*

He kept his eyes straight ahead, kept walking. Voice just about steady. *Like I said, if you can catch the echo of my thoughts—*

You want to go there. It's out in a rush, and then Firfirdar is abruptly silent. She seems, in some indefinable way, to have surprised herself. For just a moment, her tone grows almost wondering. *They're right, you do it every fucking time. All right, Ringil Eskiath, you want to play the game that way, let's lay down those pathetic cards you're holding. What do you want? What is your heart's desire? You want to go there, to that city without war. You want to live out the rest of your days in the peace it offers. Standard twilight-of-a-warrior happy ending shit. Your basic profession-of-violence retirement dream. There. Satisfied? Did the goddess read your mind? Or did she read your mind?*

It's his turn to be silent, oddly embarrassed to hear his own barely conscious longing laid out so brutally naked in words. He clears his throat to chase the quiet away.

Grashgal told me there was no way to reach it. He said the quick paths are too twisted for a mortal to take, and the straight path is too long.

True as far as it goes, yes.

He glances sideways at her. *But?*

But it misses the larger point. Grashgal's vision was incomplete. Like so many of his Kiriath kin, he never fully recovered from the passage through the veins of the Earth and the gifts it inflicted. He had the sight, but not the critical instinct to interpret it well. In the case of the Ravensfriend, he saw the resting place, but not how it came to be. He did not appreciate the irony of that sword in that museum.

For what it's worth, nor do I. You want to explain in words a mere mortal can understand?

Well, irony really does better unelaborated, but if you insist. The Dark Queen's voice drifts, as if reciting some empty cant. *The city you speak of will be built – will stand in all its undeserved serenity – on the bones of a billion unjust, unremembered deaths. Its foundation stones are mortared with the blood of ten thousand suffering generations that no one there recalls or cares about. Its citizens live out their safe, butterfly lives in covered gardens and brilliant halls without the slightest idea or interest in how they came to have it all.* She comes abruptly back to the here and now. Turns and flashes him a hard little smile. *Do you really think that you could stand to live among such people?*

Ringil shrugs. *I lived among my own people nine years after the war. Most couldn't forget the past fast enough. The fortunate among them spend their lives now ignoring the misery their good fortune squats upon. If I have to live amidst ignorance, I'll take a people who've forgotten what suffering is any day over a society that eats, sleeps and breathes it daily and still turns a blind eye to the pain.*

Very well. She walks ahead of him now, raising her voice a little. *Then ask yourself another question, hero. Do you think they could stand to have you in their midst – a bloody-handed monster, a living, breathing reminder of all they do not appreciate or understand?*

I'm used to that too, he says curtly.

They've reached the end of the beach's sweep. A darkened tumble of rock looms ahead of them, fringed along its edges with the luminous shatter of waves. Wind-blown spray from the breakers dampens the air, puts a faint sheen on everything. The Dark Queen picks her way up onto the outcrop without apparent effort, turns and beckons him after her.

Disappears.

He follows awkwardly, places each booted step with care on the wet, unyielding tilt of the rocks. A couple of times, he slips and curses, nearly goes over – the long habit of battlefield poise keeps him up. Further along, with some relief, he finds small, pale expanses of barnacles he can gain some crunching purchase on. His steps firm up.

He catches up with Firfirdar at the edge of a minor drop, six or eight feet down to where the waves hurl themselves into the jagged line of the rocks. She's watching them burst high and spatter, suck back and slide away off wet-gleaming granite surfaces, then surge in again, tireless.

She waits until he's at her side. Pitches her voice to carry over the sound it makes.

Supposing I could take you to that city – how would you live there? Your blade would be behind glass in a museum, and no use for it even if it were not. The languages you speak would be millennia dead. What would you do for money, for food? Do you see yourself cleaning tables, perhaps, in some eatery whose owner does not mind your halting attempts at the local tongue? A brief career as a tavern whore, maybe, while your looks last? Do you see yourself washing dishes or mucking out horses, as you grow old and grey? Does that appeal?

He grimaces. *Well, now you come to mention it . . .*

Quite. And here is our difficulty. Your daydreamed retirement is no more honest than the daydreamed heroics of young boys who've never picked up a blade. It is a fantasy staple – stale, learnt longing, incurious of any human detail, a mediocre hand dealt out from the grubby, endlessly reshuffled myths and legends and comforting lies you people like to tell each other. There is less weight to it in the end than in all your boyhood fantasies of a life with the gypsies, out on the marsh at Trelayne. *That at least was something you might once have attempted, a path you might have taken. But this – this is a lie to yourself that you carry around in your heart because you'd rather not face the truth.*

And what truth would that be?

Firfirdar gestures at the waves breaking below them. *That there is rest and there is motion. And that once set in motion, none of us are ever truly at rest again as long as we live. That the only truly important thing is to move well while you can, to go to rest only when rest is all that remains.*

Yeah? So where does that leave me?

The Dark Queen looks almost embarrassed for him. *Well,* she says. *What else, aside from slaughter with sharp steel, are you really good for?*

There's a long, quiet pause, broken only by the roar and suck of the sea. Ringil feels the sound stuffing itself into his ears, emptying him out. They stand, goddess and man, a foot and a half apart, like two statues carved from the granite underfoot.

I suppose a blow-job's out of the question, he says at last.

She turns to look at him, glitter-eyed. *You said* what *to me, mortal?*

You're not going to take me to Grashgal's city. I get it.

I cannot.

Cannot or will not?

Cannot. The codes the Book-Keepers wrote are very specific. Though I may grant wishes, they must be genuine, they must come from the heart and soul of the supplicant. There's a soft, persuasive urgency to her words now. *I read your mind for you – now I will read you your heart. Look inside yourself, Hero of Gallows Gap, Dragonbane unacknowledged – look deep, find the flame inside, and tell me what you* really *want.*

He stares into the crash and foam of the waves below, for what seems like quite a while. Long, vertiginous moments of letting go. Grashgal's vision of a city at peace receding, sucking back and sliding away, leaving hard, wet rock gleaming beneath.

Finally, he sees what she's talking about.

I want them dead, he says quietly. *I want them all fucking dead.*

Ah. The Mistress of Dice and Death puts a companionable arm around his shoulders. Her touch bites through his clothes like freezing iron. *Now that's* more *like it.*

From the top of the long slope he'd climbed, the landscape sprang into some comprehensible focus. Familiar folds in the rolling terrain. Off to the west, the long, slumped spine that led up to the cliffs where they'd dug out the grave. He pivoted about, gauging the angles in the wind and the pallid light. He squinted – could just make out the spike and tracery of mast-tips beyond a fold in the land to the east.

Dragon's Demise, moored where they'd left her.

It seemed he hadn't been away for long.

*

57

Let me show you something, she tells him, as they emerge from a grotto of tumbled granite blocks onto another beach. *Perhaps it will help.*

They leave the shadow of the rocks behind, pass over low white sand dunes and down towards a broad waterline that curves away to the horizon. The waves run in to meet them, soft and muted, lapping up the beach with creamy tongues. But further out they're breaking twice the height of a man, and the sound of it echoes off the cliffs behind them like distant thunder.

Something flickers past Ringil's shoulder.

He tears loose of the Dark Queen's arm. Flinches around, fingers twitching.

Sees only a leaf of pale light, something like a candle flame detached from its wick and grown to the size of a man. It skitters around them for a moment, then darts away along the beach.

Fuck was that? he asks, watching it go.

One of the locals. Firfirdar presses on down the slope of the beach towards the waves. She calls back to him. *Don't worry, they're not interested in us.*

True enough – as he follows the Dark Queen down, he sees a dozen or more of the same living flames flickering about on the sand, gathering briefly then scattering apart again, sprinting short straight lines, then dodging playfully aside, skidding out over the creamy broken surface of the water in broad curves, then skimming back again. Some of them make wobbling circuits around him or Firfirdar or both, but it's fleeting, as if there's simply not enough in either visitor to hold their attention, and soon they're gone again, out across the water, away . . .

It's like watching energetic moths at play on some lamplit balcony.

He joins the Dark Queen at the waterline.

So what are they interested in? he asks her.

She gestures out over the ocean. *See for yourself.*

Out where the waves are breaking big, the same flickering lights dance up and down, back and across the smoothly rising, advancing face of each breaker. It looks weirdly as if some naval vessel has left small patches of float-fire burning fiercely on the surface of the waves – but patches that slide giddily around on some unfeasible clash of currents beneath.

Nalumin, says Firfirdar, as if this is explanation enough.

Ringil watches a pair of the glimmering things race in on a wave. They seem to grow paler as they reach the shallows.

Are they alive?

That depends on your working definition. Once, long ago even in the memory of the gods, the Nalumin were men and women like you. But a flame possessed them at the core, and they spent their lives stripping away all layers that did not feed that flame. Something changes in the Dark Queen's voice and when Ringil looks round, he sees that distant sadness smoking off her again. *When the Book-Keepers came, the Nalumin made a choice. Like so many of us, they perhaps did not fully understand what that choice would mean.*

And what did it mean?

Firfirdar shrugs. *That all layers were stripped away. That they gave them-selves over wholly to the flame. Just as you see.*

They burn brighter on the water than on the land. He's speaking more to himself than to the goddess at his side. But Firfirdar nods.

Yes. Brighter on water than on land, guttering to nothing if they leave the sea behind for very long. And brightest of all when they ride the waves. A crooked smile. *It was, by all accounts, what they wanted.*

They're trapped here, then?

To the extent that all mortals are, I suppose. The Dark Queen appears not to have given it much thought. *A flickering limen of existence between the salt waters you all come from and a darkened hinterland beyond. Yes, trapped – you could say so. Though they seem not to mind. Eternity is what you make of it, I'd say.*

They're eternal, then? Immortal?

So far, yes.

It conjures out the ghost of his own smile. He rolls her a sardonic look. *Right. And this is supposed to make me feel better about my own situation, is it?*

Firfirdar shrugs again.

There are worse fates, are there not, than being forced into a place where your choice of acts is limited to those that cause your soul to burn the brightest?

He draws a breath that hurts his throat, because he can see where this is going. *Right. And now we get down to where my soul burns brightest, do we?*

The goddess looks at him – no, not at him, past him – past his face and left shoulder to where the hilt of the Ravensfriend spikes in silhouette. Her eyes glitter, like the Nalumin dancing on the waves.

Oh, I think you already know that, she whispers.

He cut across the land, staying out of dips as much as he could – climate in the Hironish made for boggy ground wherever water could easily col-lect. He picked up sheep tracks along his path, used them where they helped, ignored them when they meandered too far wide of the direction he wanted. Less than half an hour in, sweat had collected on his brow and under his clothing. He'd set a marching pace without realising it.

As if battle lay ahead, or something behind was gaining on him.

About an hour later, he came over a rise, panting the steady rhythm of the march, took in the ruined croft and the short column of men on the sheep track below, not really grasping the detail for what it was.

He stopped anyway, half-wary, an alarm bell tolling somewhere in the back of his head.

A large sheep – no, he narrowed his gaze, saw horns, make that a ram – broke from the path, ambled away through the long grass towards the croft. Guffawing laughter drifted up to him on the damp air. The man in the vanguard of the column looked up.

Long hair, gaunt face, all round evil-seeming motherfucker, looked like a scar on one ch—

Understanding knifed through Gil's hangover blur, hit him like a mace blow from some unsuspected attacker off his flank. He staggered backward, cloak flapping around him in the wind. Sat down hard on the wet grass at the top of the rise. Rolled frantically for cover.

You didn't see me. You did not *see me.*

It came through gritted teeth, part wishful thinking, part statement of fact, part *ikinri 'ska* incantation.

If magicking against that thing down there was even possible.

We can swim to the shallows, yes. Seethlaw, on the possibilities of existing within the Grey Places. *With practice, we can step into places where time slows to a crawl, slows almost to stopping point, even dances around itself in spirals . . .*

And so could the Dark Court, it seemed.

Not for the first time, he wondered what real difference lay between the dwenda and the gods. What powers and interests they might share.

He lay with his cheek pressed into the soaking grass, and a fresh chunk of memory dropped into his head.

Risgillen of Illwrack told me she negotiated with the Dark Court to bring about my downfall. In essence, that you gave me up to her.

Is that how it seemed to you? Yet you did not fall down, as near as I recall. Or, let us say, you did not fall very far.

He shivers. It's the best part of a year since the assault on the Citadel in Yhelteth, the horror he was plunged into as a result. He will not revisit those memories if he can avoid it.

The dwenda do not lie, he says, in a voice not quite even.

Do they not?

That was my understanding, from my time spent with Seethlaw. He saw deceit as a human trait he must learn. He was quite bitter about it. Risgillen was his sister, and junior to him in their schemes. It seems unlikely she would have learnt the trick any faster.

Well, then, she perhaps told you the truth as she understood it.

Gil sets his jaw. *You lied to her.*

Does that upset you? A wry smile. *We are human gods, after all.*

You set us both up. He can hear the bitterness surge in his voice. *And then you fuckers sat back and watched us fight it out.*

The Dark Queen shrugs. *Risgillen was coming for you anyway. It might be more accurate to say we provided you with the tools to withstand her revenge.*

Yeah – tools I learnt how to use only at the eleventh hour, and no thanks to the Dark Court along the way.

But you are the apple of our eye, Ringil. The Court has always had faith in your ability to find your own way. It is what draws us to you.

Oh, fuck off.

No, really. Ask yourself – what use does any god have for worshippers who tug *constantly at her sleeve like so many over-mothered children?* The Dark Queen's lip curls and contempt etches her tone. *Wanting, praying, needing, begging, asking for comfort, guidance, confirmation, a great big blanket of righteousness to wrap themselves up in from cradle to grave. We grow weary of it, and faster than you'd think. Give me some arrogant unbeliever over that any day of the week, and twice on holy days.* That's *how heroes are made.*

Yeah? Well, this hero's done.

She looks at him like a doting mother. *No, you aren't. You are not made that way.*

All blades have a breaking point. It's a line from his treatise on modern warfare, the one no one in Trelayne would touch with a publishing barge pole. *All men too.*

Firfirdar inclines her head. *You are all made to run yourselves against the grindstone, true enough. But some take longer to wear down than others, and some give out brighter sparks. You shower incandescence at every unyielding turn, Ringil.*

I won't do it, he says quickly.

You won't do what?

Whatever it is you want. I won't take up your fucking tools and be your cat's paw. Not anymore.

She breaks out into soft, throaty laughter. It's as if he told a very sophisticated joke, and the punchline has only just dawned on her.

Oh Ringil, she says fondly. *That's not how it works. You should know that by now. I do not send you back to the world with* instructions. *I offer only guidance, I tell you only what you might anyway wish to know.*

Which is what?

Another regal shrug. *That Ornley is fallen in your absence, that your friends are now captive and your enemies lie in wait. That war is declared and battle soon to be joined. That the Aldrain are bringing the Talons of the Sun to light the skies once more with the glare from a myriad undeserved deaths – unless you can stop the machine in time.* She gestures cheerfully. *Things like that.*

You think you'll hook me again? He manages a shaky laugh. He clears his throat, clears out the hoarseness in his voice. *You've had your fun, you and the court both. I broke Risgillen for you. But that's the end of it. Show's over, time to go home. I am done playing this game.*

But the Dark Queen only shakes her head.

No, she tells him gently. *You're only just beginning.*

Propped up to peer cautiously over the ridge once more, he watched himself poke about in the long grass along the ruined wall of the croft. Watched himself step over the threshold of a doorway that barely existed. Watched the uncertain storm-light gather there nonetheless, and wrap itself in some indefinable way around his black-cloaked form.

Watched it fold him somehow *away*.

When he was sure the scar-faced sorcerer assassin had really gone, he got himself upright and scuttled down the grassy bank to the path. He stood there, eyes fixed on the croft doorway, until his vision blotched with the imagined lines and angles of its shape, and his head was wiped clean of everything but the white, rinsed-out whisper of the wind.

He wondered dizzily – the thought went fleeting half-unformed, through his head like a cold-sweat twinge of pain – what if he followed himself through that doorway? What would he find on the other side, what would he have to face?

He turned hastily away.

Blinked to clear his vision, and hurried down the path after the marines.

EIGHT

Archeth had one brief, blind moment in which to curse Menith Tand for a traitorous piece of shit. Then she saw him on the other side of the narrow street, pinioned by armed men in unfamiliar garb, and she woke up to what was really happening.

The sword at her throat belonged to a grim-faced stranger.

'Easy there,' she said, lifting hands wide and well away from her knives. 'Let's not get off on the wrong foot.'

The flat of the blade chucked her roughly under the chin. She had to rise on tip-toe to avoid getting cut.

'Shut your fucking face, sorceress.'

He spoke Naomic, and she realised she had done too – some reflexive carry-over from her words with Critlin before she walked out into the street. But even without the exchange, she'd have made this one for a northerner right off. Pale-faced and craggy-featured, none too clean-smelling. The blade at her throat was a League navy cutlass, shorter and chunkier than anything you'd get out of an Empire smithy, and the man's clothing was cut from drab shades of grey and green no self-respecting imperial would have been seen dead in. There was a woollen seaman's cap crammed on his head, a cheap metal badge in the shape of a cross pinned into the cloth.

Up on tip-toe, Archeth was unable to focus on the design of the badge, but she didn't need to. She already knew what it depicted – a rolled and sealed scroll crossed with a cutlass not unlike the one now nestling under her chin. Letter of marque and a blade.

Privateers.

'I think you're making a mistake,' she said conversationally. 'We are a licensed and authorised—'

'Sogren, get over here.' Her captor didn't turn to speak to his comrade. The eyes behind the cutlass blade stayed narrow on her the whole time. 'Come and take this fucking witch's knives off her before she starts getting any ideas. Check her over good.'

Sogren was bigger than his companion, a capless, long-haired giant with a face that looked oddly cheery despite the various scars it bore. He carried no blades, had only a long sealing club slung at his belt, but he didn't look like he'd need much else in a fight. He collected her weapons with the brusque efficiency of long custom – unbuckled the harness that held the knives sheathed about her waist and at her breast, lifted it away in one hand entire, then bent and took Falling Angel out of her boot. He handed everything off to someone else she couldn't see clearly, then went over her body with blunt-fingered care, pressing and prodding for hidden blades, inevitably taking the opportunity to grope her between the legs and squeeze approvingly at her breasts. Swell of chuckling as his companions saw it. She bit her tongue, stared straight ahead. Submitted, because, realistically, what else was she going to do right now. Sogren finished up his fun, checked through her stiffly braided hair with his fingertips, stepped back and nodded.

'We're good. Nothing on her.'

The cutlass under her chin dropped a grudging couple of inches. She was able to look around and take in the full extent of the shit they were in.

The street was thronged with the drab privateer uniforms. She counted two dozen in her first sweep, possibly there were more. She saw crossbows, cocked and levelled, a variety of unsheathed steel. Tand's men must have been overwhelmed on the instant, no chance to stand and fight or even run. Then the privateers had simply waited on Tand to come out, and then her. It showed an admirable level of patience and tactical smarts she didn't generally associate with the League's licensed pirates, whose depredations up and down Yhelteth's coasts in earlier years had been legendary for senseless blood-letting and terror.

She heard the clop of horse's hooves, coming steadily up the darkened street. Saw how the men stiffened around her at the sound. She turned gingerly to face the new arrival, mindful of the blade still hovering at her chest.

An explanation of sorts offered itself.

The rider wore the martial colours of Trelayne – rich cream cloak bordered in sunset red, the tunic in blue slashed across with the same tones of red and cream. There was a lightweight open helm on his head and the spike of a broadsword pommel over his left shoulder. A second, shorter sword was sheathed at his hip. And he was flanked by six men in skirmish ranger attire – Trelayne's nearest equivalent to the Throne Eternal.

Privateers or not, the newcomers looked to be under formal military command.

She met Menith Tand's gaze across the street. The slaver raised one eyebrow, nodded down to where his captors' hands still had him firmly pinned. He shrugged apologetically.

And you, in any case, are expedition leader, Archidi . . .

She made eye-contact with the man behind the cutlass, pitched her voice for calm and command. 'I'll speak with your commander now. You may stand down.'

The man bared his teeth at her, made a noise in his throat like a wary hound. But he voiced no actual objection, and when she lifted – slowly, slowly – one loosely curled hand and gently pushed his blade aside, he let it happen. She stepped out into the centre of the street, just as the Trelayne knight reined in. She made a brief dip of obeisance, just enough to meet etiquette, then drew herself up.

'My lord, I am kir-Archeth Indamaninarmal, imperial envoy of his majesty Jhiral Khimran the Second of Yhelteth, and leader of an accredited expedition in good faith to the Hironish Isles, as licensed by the city council of Lanatray in certain letters of—'

'Yeah, good.' The rider waved it away with one gauntleted hand. He leaned forward on the pommel of his saddle, seemingly fascinated by what he saw. 'Been looking for you, my lady. Glad we found you so easily, in fact. I'd not want an officer of the southern court to come to any unwarranted harm, even in these times.'

These times?

'You have not given us *your* name, sire.' Menith Tand, apparently also let free by his captors and now standing haughtily at Archeth's side. 'Which is, at a minimum, our diplomatic due. Perhaps you would care to remedy your lack of manners.'

The mounted man scratched under his helm at the back. Grinned. 'You'd be Tand, right? The slaver? Yeah, they said you was a scrawny, arrogant fuck.'

Tand grew very still.

'Klithren of Hinerion,' The helm came off, doffed as if it were some peasant's cloth cap. The head beneath was recently shaven, showing less growth than the man's stubbly beard. One ear was chopped and notched from some past near miss. 'Knight supplemental in the united land armies of the Trelayne League. I'm not much for protocol, I'm afraid. But I have a feeling that's why they sent me.'

'This is an outrage,' said Tand coldly. 'I have good friends in the Trelayne Chancellery, Captain Klithren. I'm not entirely sure how you managed to attain your present commission, but I assure you, your lack of respect will not be allowed to stand. I will see you whipped for this.'

Klithren sighed.

'Sogren.' He raised an arm, snapped his fingers and beckoned. 'Explain the situation to my lord Tand, would you? Without breaking anything.'

Archeth turned just in time to see the giant who'd searched her earlier come up behind Tand with a grin. He grabbed the slaver by the hair yanked him about and punched him solidly in the belly. Tand grunted with shock, sagged and would have fallen to the floor if Sogren hadn't still been holding him up by his immaculately groomed grey locks. The giant landed another punch and Tand threw up, hung there by Sogren's grip on his hair with vomit spilling down over his chin and onto his clothes. Sogren clubbed him solidly back and forth across the face three times, let him drop to the cobbles, and then put the boot in with judicious, repeated force until Tand stopped trying to get up.

Klithren of Hinerion fitted his helm carefully back on his head.

'We are at war, my lady. My lord. Empire forces took my home city by storm nine weeks ago yesterday. The League has responded with a formal declaration of unity in the face of imperial aggression. Armed levy to be raised in every city, an army of liberation to march on Hinerion before season's end. All imperial citizens found within the borders of the League to be detained pending exchange or ransom.' A wintry smile. 'Or trial and execution for spying.'

Archeth gaped up at him. 'You *what?*'

'You heard, my lady. You are now my prisoners under terms of war.' Klithren nodded to Sogren, and the giant hauled Menith Tand upright with no more effort than you'd use picking up a saddlebag. Klithren looked the slave magnate over. 'As my prisoners, you can expect to be treated with the courtesy that befits your station. Provided, of course, that you observe that same courtesy yourselves. Got that, my lord Tand?'

Tand's lips moved but nothing audible came out. He made a jerked coughing sound and tried to collapse again. Sogren grinned and held him up.

'I'll take that as a yes.' Klithren glanced at Archeth. 'Yes, my lady, you have a question?'

'I, yes, I – for what cause?' Her head still whirling, krinzanz-fogged. 'The assault on Hinerion – what cause was given?'

Klithren sniffed and rubbed at his stubbled chin. 'Well, not that it much matters – we all know you lot been spoiling for another fight ever since Vanbyr – but the charge given was murder of an imperial legate and impeding the actions of imperial authority in bringing the culprits to justice. Which I think your ladyship would agree is pretty fucking thin as an excuse to tear up a whole city.'

She stopped herself nodding, just. Her thoughts skittered about like panicked rats, seeking logical boltholes from the madness.

What the fuck are you playing at down there, Jhiral?

Who's been pouring poison into your ears while I'm gone? Which buggered excuse for an imperial counsellor thought this shit *was a good idea?*

Citadel pressure?

Impossible. Following the death of Pashla Menkarak and the collapse of the Afa'marag Temple cabal, the Citadel Mastery had been meek as a gaggle of fresh-bought harem initiates. Jhiral had them eating out of his hand when she left.

Shield-beating at the Empire's edge, then?

But garrison command on the marches was chosen with exactly that kind of risk in mind. The commanders were shrewd and sanguine to a man, the cream of Yhelteth's officer class even in these pinched times. None of them would be so stupid.

Did something else force your hand?

Is there something new in play, something I missed?

Not for the first time since they arrived in the Hironish Isles, Archeth had the dizzying-urgent sense that she was in the wrong place. That somewhere, a serious miscalculation had been made, and now they were all going to pay.

'And so.' Klithren leaned forward on his saddle once more, eyes fixed directly on Archeth's face, holding her gaze. 'To our next point of business. I'd be grateful if you'd confirm for me the continued presence on this expedition of the Trelayne renegade and declared outlaw Ringil Eskiath.'

'You did not know of this, my lady?'

In the low yellow light from the tavern lamps, Klithren watched her shrewdly for reaction. She made her face stone. Shrugged.

'I knew he wasn't getting on well with his family.'

'That's putting it mildly.' He leaned forward on the table, poured wine for them both. Around them, his men bustled about the business of setting up billets with the landlord and getting drinks of their own. 'His family have disowned him before the Chancellery. Gingren Eskiath has declared him outlaw and forsworn blood vengeance on anyone who brings in his son's head. Cheers. Your very good health.'

Archeth left her brimming goblet where it was, though she too was forced to huddle into the table somewhat. It was a small tavern, basically someone's converted kitchen in a farmhouse on the outer corner of the drover's road where it came into town. There wasn't a lot of space with Klithren's men milling around.

'Curious,' she said. 'At Lanatray his mother was quite civil. Helpful even. We were guests at her residence for a week and she said nothing of this. In fact, I'm told it was her word in council that expedited our licence to come here.'

'Well – mothers with their sons.' Klithren made her a tight little smile as he sipped his wine alone. 'Never had a mother myself, but I've known a few. Women often lack the mettle to do what is needful. They don't deal well with the harsher realities of life.'

'Is that a fact?'

'And, frankly, Lanatray's pretty much a one-horse town. Been the lady Ishil's summer residence for a couple of decades now, I hear she dominates the place like Firfirdar on the throne. Of course, the outlaw proclamation is Trelayne's alone, so Lanatray is no more obliged to recognise it than any other League city. But still, it was smart of Ringil, putting in there. Took a couple of weeks before the news leaked back to Trelayne.'

'Lanatray was five hundred miles closer along the coast.' She tried to keep the annoyance out of her voice, because, whore's breath and *fuck* it, Gil should have told her this shit ahead of time – not left her to find it out second hand from some hacked-about over-the-hill League captain with a bounty gleam in his eye. 'Since we were told any incorporated city may issue licence of passage for the whole League territory, there was no need for us to cover the extra distance.'

A sober nod. 'Yeah. And, but for the war, that licence would have been a fine pair of bollocks to wave in Gingren's face. Nice trick, really. Show up on your dad's doorstep an accredited imperial officer and dare him to do something about it.'

'Do you see everything in such childish personal terms?'

'In my experience, my lady, the whole stinking dung cart of history is hauled along on such childish personal terms.' Klithren grimaced, as if surprised by his own sudden reach into gravitas. He shrugged. 'In any case, I think it's safe to say your comrade is some significant distance past *getting on badly* with his family. House Eskiath has cast him out utterly. They have named him outlaw. Seen the declaration of amnesty from blood vengeance myself, and Gingren Eskiath's seal is on it. Ringil's own father wants him dead.'

'And so do you.' Challenging him with her eyes.

Klithren made a throwaway gesture. 'I am charged with bringing him to Trelayne in chains. If he sees fit to surrender, that's what I'll do.' His voice hardened. 'But if he wants a fight, he can have that instead, and I'll settle for his head in a bounty bag. Now, where is he?'

She touched the goblet's base with a finger. Grinned down at the scarred wooden table it stood on. Prodded circular ripples awake in the wine.

'Something amuses you, my lady?'

'Yes, my lord Klithren. You amuse me, if you think you're going to take Ringil back to Trelayne in a bounty bag.'

'Are you refusing to tell me where he is?'

'Not at all. I'm warning you what to expect when you find him.'

Klithren rubbed at his mutilated ear. 'I do this for a living, my lady. I fought at Hinerion and Baldaran during the war, and since then I've been gainfully employed hunting outlaws for both the League and you imperials at Tlanmar. In '59 I brought in five of the Silverleaf Brotherhood single-handed.'

'I'm afraid I have no idea what that implies,' Archeth said politely. 'Were they dangerous men?'

'The Tlanmar garrison commander thought so. Dangerous enough to pay three hundred elementals a head. And one of them claimed to be a black mage, just like your friend.' Another shrug. 'Didn't help him much, when the steel came out.'

'I've never heard Ringil Eskiath claim to be a black mage.' Still she toyed with the goblet, still she did not pick it up. 'But I have seen him stand and kill things that would turn most men's bowels to jelly.'

'Yeah – the Hero of Gallows Gap, the Scourge of the Scaled Folk, Last Man Standing on the Walls of Trelayne. Heard it all before, my lady, out of a thousand flapping mouths, most of whom were never actually there. But you know what? When I last encountered this war hero he was skulking behind an assumed name and denial of his origins, and the only way he could best me was to strike me down from behind, under cover of false camaraderie.'

A jagged pause. Klithren had not quite been shouting when he stopped, but the quiet that followed was tight with the rise in his voice. At the other tables in the tavern, his men paused in their drinking and chatter and glanced towards their leader.

Archeth nodded. 'I see. So it would be fair to say, my lord, that your interest here is personal.'

'I am here on assignment from the Trelayne Chancellery,' said Klithren stiffly. 'To secure the Hironish Isles against invading forces, to dispatch or detain all enemies of the League discovered therein. Speaking of which, I think it's time we cut the courtier pleasantries and I get on with my job. So I'll ask you once more, politely, and hope you'll give me a straight answer this time, because I'd not want to put a noble captive to the question quite this early in the game – *where is Ringil Eskiath?*'

She picked up the wine, examined it intently. 'Along the coast somewhere. Searching for a grave that probably isn't there. Your good health, sir.'

Klithren watched her drink, nodding. Waited until she set the goblet down.

'Do you think you could be a little more fucking vague, my lady?' Leaning in with a sudden, fierce grin. 'Only – I have a few hundred men at my disposal and I worry that *along the coast somewhere* may not quite soak up all their efforts.'

She tucked away the little nugget of information he'd let slip. Shrugged. 'I believe *Dragon's Demise* sailed north from here.'

Klithren hung there, still leaned in over the table towards her. Something old and unkind glittered in his eyes.

'You are not taking me seriously, my lady.'

'My lord Klithren, I assure you I am. I was otherwise occupied the day Ringil Eskiath departed, I did not see him sail.' *True enough – otherwise occupied shivering and hugging yourself in your bunk, waiting out a krinzanz crash that made it feel like your eyeballs might fall out of your skull if you moved your head too suddenly.* 'Others did, however, and I shall instruct them to answer your questions openly. I believe they'll tell you that *Dragon's Demise* took sail northward along the coast, but I cannot personally vouch for that fact.'

'You show so little interest, then, in your officers' comings and goings?'

She built him a weary smile. 'We are not a military expedition, my lord. Lanatray would hardly have permitted us passage if we were. We are explorers and scientists.'

'Yes. And latterly torturers, it seems.'

She left that where it was. 'If Ringil Eskiath has deceived the imperial court as to his status in the League, then he has done my command a grave disservice, and I have no interest in protecting him from his enemies. As I said, I believe you will find him to the north.'

Klithren held her gaze pinned for a moment. Not many men could look her in the eye so long and hard. Then he sat back in his chair.

'All right. How many men are with him?'

She gestured apologetically. 'Again, my lord. I cannot be precise. But let's see; full crew for *Dragon's Demise*; a substantial detachment of imperial marines. Say about eighty in all? Maybe a hundred?'

She saw how he worked to hide his disquiet. 'A lot of men to dig up a grave, my lady. What were you expecting to find – a barrow full of guardian undead?'

She shrugged again. 'These are unfamiliar climes for us. We try not to take unnecessary chances.'

'Hmm. And these imperial marines of yours – are they amenable to reason? Will they stand down if challenged under League authority?'

Archeth drank again, deeply – harsh metallic taste to the cheap wine as it went down. But she'd had time now to fumble through the new hand they'd all been dealt, and she saw only one useful way it could be played. She emptied the goblet and put it down.

'They will if I tell them to,' she said.

NINE

'You fucking *what?*'

Egar, bristling, still had eyes to see Archeth flinch at the hissed fury in his voice. But she rallied pretty quick.

'You need to calm down,' she told him. 'If we're going to turn this thing around, we have to be smart. We need to think things through.'

Well, maybe. But right now, he was in no fucking mood for strategy. He'd just spent an unpalatable half hour talking the Majak down from a suicidal last stand around the sleeping body of Klarn Shendanak. Now, he stood downstairs in the inn on League Street, face knotted up with mingled shame and rage, watching his countrymen hand over their killing iron to Klithren's skirmish ranger elite without a fight.

Like you had some other choice.

The privateer incursion had been meticulously planned, and now it yielded near enough a perfect victory. Aside from a couple of messy skirmishes with some die-hard Throne Eternal – whose bodies now lay heaped together, pin-cushioned through with arrows and crossbow bolts, on the cobbled street outside – this Klithren fuck had rolled up the imperial forces almost without incident.

'I am thinking things through,' he snapped at Archeth. 'We're fucked in the arse, and you've just sold Gil out like a barrel of gone-over ale.'

'Keep your voice down.'

She took his arm. He shook her off angrily.

'We should have seen this coming, we should have *fucking* seen it coming!'

'How?' She came round to face him, voice low and urgent. 'War declared out of nowhere, and a flotilla sent chasing up here after us before the declaration ink is even dry. Tell me how we could have seen that coming, Eg.'

Egar drew a deep breath and held it in. Let go his anger with a growl. It got a couple of wary looks from among the League men, but they soon looked away again, when they saw he presented no threat. They went back to their drinking or their card games, or simply watched with fascinated gaze this bloodless humbling of the dread barbarians from the Majak steppe.

'You don't want to worry too much about being overheard,' he muttered. 'Pirate scum like this, they won't speak Tethanne worth a shaman's fuck.'

'Yeah? Klithren, for your information, almost certainly has fluent Tethanne. He's been careful enough not to show it to me, but he let slip that he grew up in Hinerion, and apparently he's worked both sides of the border as a bounty hunter. There's no way you get by in that world without Naomic and Tethanne both. And chances are he's brought a few other schooled borderlanders up here with him too. So keep your fucking voice *down*.'

'All right.' Muttering tightly now. 'But I still don't see how selling Gil out is supposed to help.'

Dull crumping clunk – like emphasis, as the next Majak in the line dumped his axe and knives onto the table in front of Klithren's armourer. The skirmish ranger ran a rapid professional hand over the tangle of sheaths and belts and steel, calling it to the man seated at his side with pen and parchment. *Axe – machete – couple of knives, and – what's this – oh, right, blade-edged bolas. Nice.* He indicated where the Majak should ink his thumb and make mark on the parchment, then nodded him aside. *Next.*

The Majak turned away, fixed Egar with a baleful, blaming stare and spat in the sawdust on the floor. But he went quietly enough, out the door under guard to whatever makeshift lock-up Klithren's men had cobbled together for the defeated rank and file.

Great. Just fucking great.

'I haven't sold Gil out,' Archeth said patiently. 'All I've done is give Klithren information he could have had from the locals in about five minutes anyway. The whole town saw *Dragon's Demise* set sail north. The whole town knows what we're doing here. But you want to know the interesting thing?'

He puffed out a disinterested breath. 'Sure. Tell me the interesting thing.'

'Klithren already knew.'

'Knew what?'

'Knew we were busy digging up graves. I told him Gil was up the coast looking for a grave that might not be there. He never blinked. He already knew.'

Egar shrugged. 'So he had advance scouts, and they already talked to the locals.'

'No, I don't think so. It doesn't fit. Look, Eg, I can see a man like Klithren working a grudge, hearing about the expedition from someone in Lanatray and coming up here after Gil on his own hook. I can even see someone – Gil's father, some slave merchant or other with an axe to grind – paying him to do it. Outfitting him for the trip. But a fucking *flotilla?* Hundreds of men? Diverted a thousand miles north of Trelayne, when the fight's shaping up nearly five hundred miles south? That takes major resources. Connections. Yeah, maybe Klithren blagged himself the command, but someone in Trelayne made this happen, someone with a lot of rank and influence. And you know what that means, right?'

Egar nodded. 'There was something here to find all along.'

'Yeah. And they were afraid we'd find it.'

'Oi, dragonfucker!'

It was one of the privateers by the table, a youngish-looking thug, built in the chest and arms, possessed of a raucous Naomic drawl that carried. Conversation elsewhere in the tavern petered out at the sound. Egar gave him a measured look.

'You talking to me?'

'Yeah – what you so busy boiling up with that midnight bitch? Cooking up your fucking escape, are you? Pack that in if you are, you're both of you fucking done.'

Egar grimaced at Archeth, left her in the corner and advanced deliberately towards the table. He heard a couple of low whoops from the spectators, anticipatory glee for the fight that looked to be brewing. And every Majak eye in the room was on him – the queue of those still to be disarmed rustled and muttered, the armed men around them tensed. Egar nailed the privateer who'd spoken with a hard stare, tapped fingers on the broad red-silk ribbon tied around his upper right arm.

'See this?' he asked the man coldly. 'Me and that midnight bitch, we're both prisoners-in-honour to your commanding officer. So you want to watch your step, son. Else I reckon he'll kick your ignorant bilge-rat arse all the way down to the harbour and in.'

The privateer leered. 'Oh yeah?'

'Yeah.' Aping the leer, mocking it. 'And something else. That midnight bitch? Been my comrade-in-arms since you were a pissing, shitting bundle at your mother's tit. You got the balls to take off your steel, I'll give you a spanking for lack of respect, right here and now.'

It played well – approving laughter sounded loud across the room, much of it from the same men who'd whooped low before. The privateer's face mottled and he clamped a hand on his sword hilt. But one of Klithren's skirmish rangers stepped in. He locked the other man's hand down and shoved him back, eye to eye, voice a corrosive low-toned hiss. Egar didn't hear exactly what was said, but the wind went out of the younger man like wine from a slashed skin. The ranger twisted the privateer's hand off the sword hilt, let him go with another contemptuous shove. Looked back to Egar and made an apologetic gesture.

'He's young, Dragonbane, what are you going to do? Let's just try to keep things civilised, shall we?'

'Suits me,' Egar lied.

He rejoined Archeth in the shadowy corner of the room. Kept his voice to a murmur that didn't suit the words he uttered or the low pounding in his blood.

'All right, so what was there to find that has them scurrying up here after us? Tell me that much, please, because it sure as shit isn't anything we've managed to dig up so far. The graves have all been empty of anything worth having. Your Kiriath city in the ocean isn't here. And this

73

dwenda Vanishing Isle is living up to its fucking name. So what else is there?'

'There's a sword,' she began.

'A sword?' Voice tight with disbelief. 'You're telling me we came all this way for a fucking *sword?*'

'Just listen, Eg.'

He listened.

They got a table, off in an alcove, ordered drinks for show and watched the tail end of the Majak queue get stripped of their weapons. Egar slumped moodily in his chair, not entirely for show. The wine tasted bitter and iron on his tongue. He barely sipped at it, felt nonetheless as if he'd downed the whole bottle. He was dizzy with the implications of the last four hours, and nothing Archeth was saying made much useful sense.

'Look.' Hands down on the tabletop in an attempt to stop the spinning. 'If they've already got this sword – already got away with it – then why send this lot up here afterwards?'

'I don't know,' Archeth admitted. 'Maybe it's bad communication. Ringil told me there's a cabal at the heart of things in Trelayne, and he thinks they're the ones who had dealings with the dwenda. Said he thinks the Trelayne Chancellery didn't necessarily know about it. So maybe this cabal sent for the sword, but they haven't let the Chancellery know it's in the bag.'

Egar scowled. 'That's pretty fucking thin. Why would they do something like that?'

'All right, then maybe the ship with the sword never made it back. Maybe they got wrecked on the way home and the sword's at the bottom of the ocean. Or washed up somewhere on the Wastes coast. It doesn't much matter, does it? The point is they're here and they want Gil—'

'Yeah, and you've told them where to find him.'

'What I've done is buy us a little time, and a fighting chance. We've got prisoner-in-honour status, flexibility to come and go within reason. And tomorrow at first light, Klithren is going to rig up and sail north after Gil. He's going to split his forces to do it, and he's going to take me with him.'

He shot her a sceptical look. 'He told you that?'

'He didn't have to. He's got a hard-on for Gil like a fucking tent pole.'

'Ought to make the man happy,' Egar said sourly. 'But if Klithren's spoiling for that much of a fight, I don't see him taking you along to talk the marines down.'

'You didn't see his face when I gave him the numbers.' Archeth cut him a grim little smile. 'Eg, this isn't some meat-head bounty hunter we're dealing with. This guy's built himself a knight's commission and a naval command on a war only nine weeks old. That makes him pretty fucking smart.'

'Yeah. Smart enough to take us all up the arse before we saw it coming.'

She lost her smile. 'Agreed. And we were slack, and we were stupid, and we deserved to get fucked over the way we did. Now can we stop wailing and beating our breasts about it, and *for fuck's sake* concentrate on getting out of this mess instead?'

A flicker of old admiration woke in him. Archeth Indamaninarmal, sat there across from him in all her battered glory. The woman who'd pulled him out of a jail cell, out from under certain death, back in Yhelteth last year. The woman who'd rallied the engineers at Demlarashan when the dragon came. The krinzanz crash was there in all the jerky gestures she made, in the dark smears under her eyes and the hollow stare – but something else coiled there too, at the core of it all, and he would have trusted that something at his back in a fight on foot with steppe ghouls.

He cleared his throat. Nodded.

'I'm still listening.'

'Good to know.' Maybe she'd seen the change in him. She leaned in a little closer. 'Klithren grew up in the borders, so he knows a little something about imperial marines. And he probably saw them in action during the war as well. End result, he won't want to get in a fight with them if he can avoid it. So he'll take me with him, but he'll take a fair few of his pirate pals as well, just in case. He'll leave a rump force here because he figures this battle is won. At which point – it's up to you and Rakan to prove him wrong.'

She sat back. He went on looking at her.

'You put all this together off one conversation with this Klithren? On the fly, while you were still talking to him?'

'More or less, yeah.' She rubbed at one eye with a knuckle. Sniffed. 'Why?'

'Nothing, it's, uh . . .'

'Oh, right. You think that's fancy footwork?' She gave him a weary smile. 'Try a hundred and fifty years at the imperial court.'

He scooted a surreptitious glance around the room. Now the disarmament of the Majak was done, they were getting more attention from the victorious privateers in the tavern lounge. But none of it amounted to more than muttering and speculative looks, and both died away as soon as he glanced in their direction. No one was listening in, nor realistically could have been, as near as he could judge.

'All right, so young Noyal and I turn the tables here. What then?'

'You get the fuck out of Ornley. Take back *Pride* and *Sea Eagle's Daughter*, burn anything else in the harbour to the waterline. Tell Shanta he's to run south under full sail. Skip Lanatray, skip anything bigger than a village you can scare. Re-provision fast, and then swing out wide around the Gergis cape. If there's a League cordon, it'll be sticking close to the coast, you should slip by them easily enough.'

'And you?'

'Don't worry about me.'

'I'm supposed to be your fucking bodyguard, Archidi.'

It drew a smile from her, and for a moment she bowed her head in homage to something he couldn't quite work out. Then she looked up, and her face was set.

'Look, Eg,' she said quietly. 'Maybe this business about the sword is so much superstitious horseshit, just like the Illwrack Changeling, just like the Vanishing Isle. But if it isn't – if the sword really is some talisman for bringing back the dwenda, then the Empire needs to know what's coming. And that means you have to get home, with or without me.'

Egar shook his head. 'The Empire's on a war footing already. And if Jhiral's not expecting dwenda to the feast, then he's even more of a useless wanker than I thought. Not like he hasn't had enough warning the last couple of years.'

'That isn't—'

He chopped across it. 'We all need to go home, Archidi. That includes you. The Empire, I could give a stiff shit about, it's a decade since I took their coin. But I took an oath to keep you in one piece, and that's still in force. You don't really get a say in it.'

'I saved your life last year,' she reminded him.

'Yeah – which is really going to encourage me to leave you up here on the wrong side of a war while the rest of us run south. Forget it, I'm not—'

The tavern door unlatched, slammed back on a gust of wind. Cold air scooped the room. Klithren of Hinerion loomed in the doorway, bodyguards at his back. No helm or mail, but he bore a longsword over one shoulder and another sheathed in leather at his belt.

'Here we go,' murmured Archeth.

The League commander pretty clearly spotted them, but there was no sense of acknowledgement in the way his gaze swept the room. He headed over to speak to his skirmish rangers instead. For a while, the men prodded at the piled Majak weaponry and swapped comments that were, apparently, funny.

'Easy, Eg.'

'Yeah, yeah.' He made an effort, wiped his face of all expression. Took a measured sip from his wine and settled lower in his chair. 'All under control.'

Presently, Klithren found time for them.

He came to their table alone, bodyguards dismissed to their own devices over by the bar. Arms spread wide with avuncular good humour, a cheerful grin on his face. Ease of victory had evidently put him in an expansive mood.

'So you'd be the Dragonbane,' he said loudly. 'Sitting right there in the fucking flesh! Couldn't believe it when they told me. Can't be too many like you left above ground, eh?'

Egar grunted into his goblet.

Klithren seemed to take it for an invitation. He hooked out a stool from under the unoccupied portion of the table. Sat down with the satisfied sigh of a craftsman at the end of a long day's work. He looked amiably from Egar to Archeth and back again.

'Fought the reptiles myself, of course, back in the day. Hinerion, Baldaran, like that. We had some Majak lads billeted in Hinerion back in '51.'

'Not me.'

'Right, no, I guess not.' Klithren helped himself to the wine bottle, swigged deep, set it down. Wiped his mouth with evident relish. 'Anyway – an honour to meet you, Dragonbane. Only sorry about the circumstances. And I want to thank you for talking down your brethren earlier. That was a smart move, saved a lot of bloodshed all round.'

Egar stared into the middle distance. 'Think nothing of it.'

'Yeah, 'cause otherwise we would have rolled over you like a twenty stone whore. No one wants that, eh?'

'Don't know,' the Dragonbane said, teeth still not quite clenched. 'Never had a twenty stone whore, I guess it'd be an interesting challenge.'

'We're all keen to avoid bloodshed,' said Archeth hurriedly. 'We are not, as I've already said, a military expedition. Can I ask what provision you've made for the internment of our men?'

Klithren switched his attention to the woman across the table from him. There was a small smile playing about his mouth that Egar didn't like at all.

'Those who have surrendered will be treated well, my lady. But it seems a handful of your Throne Eternal have taken weapons and a small boat with their captain, and escaped along the shoreline. They will, of course, be executed if captured alive. I can allow no mercy there.'

'Of course.' She made it come out it pretty smoothly, Egar thought.

Count young Noyal out of any schemes we have for now, then. Crafty fucker, wish I'd had the same idea first.

'Of Menith Tand's mercenaries,' Klithren went on, 'quite a few have offered to change sides if the purse is right. But that's a matter for my masters back in Trelayne to decide. For now, imprisonment will be according to rank and station.'

Archeth nodded. 'Yes, that's fair. Thank you.'

'For yourselves, I would like you both to report to the harbour at dawn tomorrow. *Lord of the Salt Wind* is now at dock and re-provisioning, so she'll be ready to sail at first light.'

'Both of us?' Caution edging her tone now.

'Yes, it's my intention to have you conveyed back to Trelayne with all due speed along with the other prisoners. Matters of ransom and interrogation can be decided by the proper authorities once you arrive. I'm afraid I shall not be accompanying you myself.'

'*Trelayne?* But . . .'

Egar saw how she clamped down hard on her dismay. How she came back smooth-voiced and court-mannered once more.

'My lord Klithren, I understood you required my help in negotiating a surrender from the marine force accompanying Ringil Eskiath up the coast.'

'Did you now?' Klithren grinned. *He knows, he fucking knows.* 'My apologies, my lady, for that little misunderstanding. I have no intention of sailing out in search of the outlaw Eskiath – that would, after all, entail splitting my forces with an enemy still at large. Tactically unwise, given that I am now weighed down with captives, most of whom are canny professional soldiers. Wouldn't you say, Dragonbane?'

Egar took the bottle and concentrated minutely on pouring his goblet full. 'I'd say you worry overly about men whose weapons you have already taken away.'

'Well, we differ, then.' The League commander sniffed, but showed no sign of losing his good humour. 'In any case, I have it on pretty good authority from some of the locals that Ringil Eskiath will be back very shortly. The grave he went to rob, it seems, is not all that far from here. A little something you neglected to mention there, my lady.'

'Specifics, my lord.' Archeth, working at elaborate unconcern. 'As I told you—'

'Yes, yes, I recall. You are not a military expedition, you do not concern yourself with details, Ringil Eskiath went, uhm, let's see . . . north.' Klithren's grin sharpened a little. 'But it seems he didn't go very *far* north, so I think an ambush here in Ornley will serve me better than hunting him along the coast. And clearly it's better that such honoured prisoners as yourselves should not be caught up in the action.'

'My lord, without my presence,' Archeth cleared her throat, 'well, I'm not sure the marines can be relied upon to surrender, even under ambush.'

'Well, then they'll die.' Sudden, gravelled drop in Klithren's tone, and the grin was gone. 'My men will hold the high ground and the cover, and I'll close up the harbour from the outside once Eskiath's ship is in. Surrender will be offered – once. If a detachment of imperial marines can't see the writing on that particular wall, then I've no sympathy for them. We are, after all, at war.'

They all sat there while that sank in.

And across the silence, Klithren's long arm reaching, as he helped himself to the wine bottle once again.

TEN

They waited a full day and night for Ringil Eskiath to show.

Everyone was briefed, everyone knew their place. The League war-ship *Mayne's Moor Blooded* sat quietly at quay as decoy, while *Star of Gergis* and *Hoiran's Grin* took picket station at points north and south along the nearby coast. The privateers held ambush positions down at the harbour and all along the edges of the bay. Lookouts took the high ground at either end, and the watchtower at Dako's Point. Certain among the im-perial marine prisoners were held in cellars not far from the docks, ready to be hauled out and used for bargaining or simply as shields. Klithren sat at a table in the inn on League Street, played dice against himself and waited for word.

The locals hid in their homes. Ornley held its breath.

The privateers were sanguine – they knew how to sit tight. It was part of their trade to wait, sifting the haze at the horizon for signs of enemy ship-ping or a change in the weather. You waited sometimes for days on end, and nothing to break the monotony but the soft rocking of your vessel on the swell. You learnt patience out there, you had to. No percentage in get-ting all riled up ahead of time. The fight, the storm – these things would be upon you soon enough. Take the quiet empty hours and breathe them in like pipe-house smoke – they'd be yours for a meagre enough span in the end.

The townspeople were less sanguine. Maybe if you were a soldier boy you could sit scratching your arse like this all day long, but gouging a living out of the Hironish took work. You were up with the dawn or before, out to sea and casting your nets, or into the surrounding hills to tend your livestock. There were dry-stone walls to be maintained, crops to be checked for blight, crows and gulls to be kept at bay, eventually the harvest; thatches to be renewed or repaired after storms, peat to be dug and cut and stacked for drying. Nets to be mended, hulls to be ripped of barnacles, scrubbed and pitched; there was gutting and cleaning, salting, packing, the smokehouse to tend. Did these bloody blade artists ever stop to think how food ended up on their plates and fire in the grate to keep out the chill? Thank the Dark Queen we never got that garrison they promised us after the war, if this is all they're good for . . .

The hours limped by like ageing mules, overladen with expectation, one slow step at a time. Late into the afternoon, some representation was made to Klithren, that they could not sit like this indefinitely and when did he expect to be done? Because the goats out on Whaler's Rise wouldn't milk themselves, you know, and there were—

At which point, Klithren looked up at the little knot of spokesmen, and gave them a thin smile that dried the words in their throats. He waited a couple of beats and then, when no more complaints looked to be forthcoming, he nodded. Two privateers stepped in from the corners of the room, and the spokesmen were ushered away, to recriminate bitterly with each other out in the street.

Klithren, for his part, stared after them until the tavern door slammed, then he went back to his dice. Cup and roll, out onto the scarred wooden table top with a bony rattle. Scrutinise the faces the worn cubes offered up.

Scoop and cup, and roll again.

'He'll come, Venj,' some later claimed they heard him murmur. 'You've not long to wait now, mate.'

But whoever he was talking to seemed destined to disappointment. Afternoon turned into evening, and what miserable grey light there'd been all day went down into dark without any sign of the outlaw or his ship. The customary lamps were lit along the harbour wall and the wharf-front, the waiting privateers stretched cramped limbs, and cursed, and settled in to wait some more.

'Going to be a long fucking night,' someone grumbled out on the harbour wall and the men down the line all laughed.

'Figure it'll be worth your while,' someone else called back. 'I was at Rajal beach in the war, I saw Ringil Eskiath fight. Never seen anything like that, before or since. He was a fucking maniac. We take him down tonight, you're going to have a tale to get you laid the rest of your natural life.'

More laughter, punctuated this time with lewd commentary.

'Yeah, or you'll be dog meat,' sneered a grizzled and corpulent privateer sprawled spread-legged with his back to the wall a couple of yards down from the original speaker. 'And your soul sent screaming to hell.'

And he prodded morosely with the tip of his killing knife at the crack between two of the harbour wall flagstones he sat on. Around him, the laughter damped down a bit. Stares fell on him. A few of the men shifted out from the wall so they could see him more clearly.

'Say what?'

The grizzled privateer glanced up, saw he had an audience.

'Yeah, that's right,' he said. 'I don't know nothing about Rajal beach, but before I got this gig, I worked muscle for Slab Findrich back in Trelayne—'

'That slaver piece of shit?' A younger privateer hawked and spat.

'Too fucking right, that slaver piece of shit. Findrich pays double the going rate for good men in Etterkal.'

'What'd he pay you, then?'

Jeers. Further down the line, a sergeant bellowed for quiet.

'Yeah, laugh it up.' The corpulent privateer glowered and dug harder with his dagger. The blade tip made a tiny scraping that put your teeth on edge. 'I was in Etterkal when Ringil Eskiath came calling last year, when Findrich put the bounty out on him. I saw what was left of the Sileta brothers when they finally found them.'

The jeers dried up with the mention of the name. Everyone knew that story, some version or other. Tavern tale spinners in Trelayne had been drinking off it ever since the news broke. Mothers down in Harbour End used it these days to quieten their unruly infant sons – *behave, or Ringil Eskiath'll come for you in the night* – *do you up like the Sileta brothers.*

The privateer looked round with a bleak smile, nodding.

'Slab Findrich threw up when he saw what was left,' he said. 'I was there at his side. And I'll tell you this much for free. Nothing human could have done that.'

'Ah, come off it,' somebody scoffed. 'What is this Eskiath, a fucking demon now? You think there aren't half a hundred whores and losers in Harbour End who'd have cut the Siletas up the exact same way if they got the chance.'

'But they weren't cut up.' *Scrape, scrape* went the knife point, along the crack and the listeners' nerves. 'It wasn't a blade that did it; it wasn't that kind of damage.'

Silence. Lamplight dappled out in thin lines across the black harbour waters. Out to sea, a barely heard sound that might have been gathering thunder.

Someone cleared their throat. 'Look—'

'He's just a man,' snapped the privateer who claimed to have been at Rajal beach. 'Fast with a blade and not afraid to die is all. Seen it before plenty of times.'

The corpulent storyteller scowled. 'That's what you think. Maybe he was still a man back at Rajal, but no man could have—'

'You!' The sergeant, grown tired of the raised voices, had stirred himself and come stalking down the line. 'Yeah, you – fatty. Shut the fuck up, before I kick your larded arse down in the cellar with the prisoners.'

The rest of the privateers broke up – ripples of snorting laughter along the harbour wall. The sergeant rounded on them.

'That goes for anyone else around here who thinks this is all one big fucking joke. You stow that shit, right now. Call yourselves men of war? You're on watch, all of you – not down the tavern with your pox-ridden sisters on your arm.'

The laughter died abruptly. The sergeant glared up and down the line, spaced his words for impact.

'When this outlaw faggot piece of shit comes creeping into harbour tonight, I want men on this wall, not a gaggle of fucking fishwives. Do I make myself clear?'

It seemed, from the ensuing quiet, that he did.

Still, he stood a while longer, daring anyone to catch his eye. When no one looked like taking up the challenge, he evidently judged his point made and headed back to his post. Muttering snaked in his wake, but it was muted, and there was no more conversation along the harbour wall for quite a while.

The privateers settled once more to waiting.

But the only thing that came creeping into harbour as the night wore on was a thick, low-lying sea fog that blanketed vision, muffled sound and chilled them all to the bone.

'I know you can't see to steer in it,' Ringil said patiently. 'You don't *need* to steer in it. The ship will steer itself.'

Not really accurate, but about as close to the truth as he wanted to get. If he'd told captain and crew what was really going to steer *Dragon's Demise* through the fog, Gil suspected he'd have an all-out mutiny on his hands.

This swordsman-sorcerer gig was turning out harder to balance than you'd expect.

Lal Nyanar, for instance. There he stood on the helm deck now, fine aristo features pinched up in a frown, shaking his head. Torches bracketed at the rail gave a flickering yellow light, enough to make out the salients. Below them on the main deck, the mist roiled and crept like something alive. Above and ahead of them it wrapped tendril fingers through the rigging and around the masts.

'But this . . .' Nyanar gestured weakly. 'This is no natural fog.'

Ringil held onto his temper. 'Of course it's not natural – you saw me summon it, didn't you? Now can we please get underway while it lasts.'

'You put all our souls in danger with this northern witchery, Eskiath.'

'Oh, *please*.'

'I think,' said Senger Hald dryly, 'that my lord Ringil is most concerned at the moment with our temporal well-being. To which I must concur. There will be time enough to worry about the salvation of our immortal souls once we've saved our mortal skins.'

Ringil masked his surprise. 'Thank you, Commander. I do believe you've stated the case admirably there. Captain?'

Nyanar looked betrayed. Hald was probably the closest thing to a soul-mate he had on the expedition. Both men had washed up in the company through sheer chance. Both had been witness to the arrival of the Helms-man Anasharal whilst they were about entirely routine duties, and so in the interests of keeping the secrets of the quest between as few as possible, both had been promptly seconded to the command.

But more than that, they were both of a *kind*. Both were Yhelteth born-and-bred, both came of noble stock – Hald might lack the stagger-ing wealth of the Nyanar clan in his own family backdrop, but like most home-grown military commanders in the Empire, his lineage would be impeccable – and both had contented themselves with moderate careers in soldiering that kept them close to home. Neither man had seen more than superficial deployment during the war. Neither man had previously been outside the Empire's borders.

Now here they were, up on the mist-ridden outer rim of the world, the sun-baked certainties of Yhelteth three thousand miles astern, and suddenly Hald was breaking ranks. Buying into this infidel sorcery and the dark northern powers it called on. Casting off the sober tenets of the Revelation and trusting to an unholy alien faith. Worse still, they had no Citadel-assigned invigilator along to weigh in – Jhiral moved swiftly enough to crush *that* custom as soon as events at Afa'marag gave him the upper hand. The palace, he declared, *could not possibly* trouble the Mastery for valued officers of the faith when they must *surely* be needed here at home to help with the purges; the northern expedition must perforce rely on the individual piety and moral strength of its members without recourse to clerical support; as, in fact, must all naval and military commands, for the time being at least, until this deeply shocking crisis has passed. No, really, such an outpouring of pastoral concern is touching, but his Imperial Radiance *insists*.

No invigilators, no clear moral compass, no working chain of command. And the only viable father figure around wears a scar on his face, fucks men from preference and has unnamed demons at his back.

You had to feel sorry for Nyanar, caught up in it all through no fault of his own and no easy way home.

No, you have to kick his arse and get him moving.

'Captain? Are we agreed?'

Nyanar looked from Ringil to Hald and back, mouth pursed tight as if he'd just been served a platter of peasant gruel. He turned his back and stared out into the fog.

'Very well,' he snapped. 'Sanat, raise anchor, make sail. Inshore rig.'

'Aye sir.' Sanat sent a practised first mate's call rolling down the length of the ship. 'Raise anchor! Make sail!'

The call picked up, was echoed across the decks. Men moved in the rigging, vaguely seen, and canvas came tumbling down. Inshore rig, taken as read. Grunted cadences from the prow and the repeated graunch of wet rope on wood as the anchor came up.

Dragon's Demise shifted and slid on the swell. Began to move with purpose.

Ringil felt himself relax a little with the motion. He thought it had been touch and go for a while back there. Not for the first time, he wondered if the powers he was acquiring under Hjel's tutelage were really worth the trouble spent getting them.

What point, after all, in racking yourself to produce a handy sorcerous mist, if the men you led wouldn't follow you into it?

*

They'd all watched him raise hands to the sky and contort his face, like some barking mad market square prophet of doom. A knot of sailors not otherwise occupied gathered on the main deck below to stare. They'd heard the muttering sounds he made deep in his throat, seen the splay-fingered traceries he cast across the air. He supposed they must have done some muttering themselves, some more clutching at their precious talismans, but he'd been too lost in it by then to notice. Too busy pouring his entire focus into the glyphs he made, because in the end that was the only way it would work.

You must write upon the air like a scribe, Hjel tells him on a cold stony beach somewhere at the margins of the Grey Places. *The air itself is parchment, read continually by powers waiting for command. But such powers can only read what is written clearly, can only answer commands clearly expressed. Cast poorly and you are no better than a clumsy scribe, blotching or scrawling your script. Cast poorly or in error, and there will be no answer.*

Now try again.

It takes days.

It takes morning after bleak early morning, going down to the shore again and again from the cold, coarse-grassed dunes where Hjel's gypsy band are camped; it takes day after day of standing there facing the ocean like an enemy, clawing at the air, grating the learnt strings of poly-syllables until his throat is raw. It takes days, and not even Hjel's caresses under canvas at night can take away the impatient frustration it stirs in him.

But finally, one morning, he goes down to the shore in an odd, emptied-out mood. He goes alone – Hjel turns over under the blankets when he rises, mumbles something, does not open his eyes – and he stands there on the beach, and he casts, and this time he does it right.

The mist rolls in from the sea, blots out everything around him, wraps him in its damp grey embrace.

Now, aboard *Dragon's Demise*, it came as second nature. His throat had long since accustomed itself to the harsh sounds he needed to make, his fingers had grown supple with practice. And whatever elemental powers lurked in the coves and straits of the Hironish, now they leapt to do his bidding. He sensed them – rising off the darkened ocean's surface like cold steam, pouring down out of gullies and caves in the ancient cliffs along this coast, circling the anchored vessel in fitful band-light like curious wolves, darting in now and then to stalk the decks unseen by human eyes, to ruffle the flames of a torch, or brush past crew members with wild, unhuman hilarity, leaving the brief touch of chilly tendril fingers and shivers on the spine.

He felt them gather on the helm deck at his back.

He felt them breathing down his neck.

He gathered their cold breath to him like a cloak, he breathed it in. He smiled as the *ikinri 'ska* came on like some icy battlefield drug.

84

He heard, as if in a dream, the lookout overhead, calling out the fog as it rolled in and wrapped them.

The *ikinri 'ska* syllables died away in his throat, scuttling back down under cover, their work done. The muscles in his cheeks and jaw eased, his arms sagged to his sides. His aching fingers hung loose, his eyes – he wasn't aware he'd closed them – snapped suddenly open, and he found himself staring into Senger Hald's face.

The marine commander shuddered visibly in the torchlight.

Turned away.

Dragon's Demise made curiously good time down the coast, as if the same elemental forces that had brought the fog now clung to the masts and filled the cautiously rigged canvas with their breath. As if they were anxious to see the ship arrive. Once or twice, the steersman remarked that it felt as if something was dragging on the hull. But they were a prudent distance out from the shore in five fathoms or more of water, and when Nyanar glanced askance at Ringil, Gil just shrugged.

Now and then, off the port bow, they heard the rumbling prowl of a storm. But it was faint and distant to the east, and showed no signs of coming after them.

These are not trivial sorceries, Hjel warns him, when he finally has the magic down. *The elementals are capricious, and their range is wide. Unleash them, and their mischief will be general. Try not to worry about it too much, it's a price you have no choice but to pay. That they do your will in your immediate vicinity is the trick. What havoc they wreak elsewhere need not be your concern.*

Ringil shrugs. *Sounds no worse than most men I've had under command.*

He stood alert though, throughout the night, listening intently to the storm and ready to pull down the *ikinri 'ska* on the elementals' heads if they showed signs of getting cute.

The fog held. The storm stayed away. He heard it fading, chasing away southeast, some other vessel's problem now.

They made Ornley harbour with the cold pale seep of dawn.

ELEVEN

'Archeth? Archeth?'

There was a numb, pulsing heaviness in her head that she took to be krinzanz crash. She groaned and twitched, thankful it still seemed to be dark outside. Or at least – some hints of light filtered in and prodded at her eyelids, but not enough to force them open. Ishgrim's arm was heavy across her chest, did not shift as Archeth moved. No surprises there – the northern girl habitually dosed herself with wine or flandrijn as night came on, or simply with Archeth's repeated attentions – *again, mistress, do me again* hissed frantically up from the pillows she lay crushed back into, mouth smeared slack and smiling with spent passion, driving a sleepy Archeth back into fresh arousal she hadn't known she owned – until sleep came and took Ishgrim down like prey. Thereafter, she either thrashed with nightmares or slept like the dead, a coin-toss guess as to which it would be any given night. But by morning . . .

'Archeth!'

Sounded like the Dragonbane's voice – be banging through the door and into her bed-chamber any moment, by the tone of it. Yeah, any excuse to leer and peer at Ishgrim's curves. Archeth felt the twitch of a smug, possessive smile at her lips. Reached up to grasp the girl's fingers in her own. Trying now to remember what the hell they'd been playing at last night because she had aches in places that—

Memory crashed in on her, like shutters blown back in a—

Storm.

She found the fingers at the end of the heavy arm. Yelped in shocked revulsion and let them go in a hurry. They were corpse-cold, thick and blunt—

The storm.

Waking to its sudden violence, hurled casually from her bunk aboard Lord of the Salt Wind *as the deck tilted up and the cabin door slammed open, tearing out its feeble lock.*

Stumbling out, thankful she'd slumped on the bunk without the will to undress or even pull off her boots. Slapped in the face with driving rain and spray, heels skidding on a deck awash with water – men stampeding back and forth yelling – and then a sound overhead like the sky tearing open. The savage pitch and roll of the ship, the heaving ocean lit by fitful lightning flash, like some vast angry beast hunching and flexing awake . . .

She opened her eyes.

She was flat on her back on unyielding rock, arms trailing up past her head and curiously weighted down. Pallid light filtered up from somewhere between her feet.

Screams from the lookouts – Lord of the Salt Wind *wallowing like a pig in mud, the veil of rain and spray torn suddenly aside as they washed sideways – the shore coming at them like a cavalry charge – some kind of bay, a jagged lower jaw of rocks like fangs, the sky-high burst of surf like geysers, the roar of it all in her ears . . .*

Wrenching, groaning impact.

Her grip on a companionway rail torn loose, her whole body flung into the rain-filled, thunderous air.

And flight – like magic from a tale.

She was upside down.

Dreams of Ishgrim, memory of the storm – it all flew apart in fragments as she woke up for real. The heaviness in her head was not from krinzanz or its lack, it was gathered blood, clogging there as she hung upside down in some damp and narrow, salt-smelling space. Cold flat rock under her back, the echoing drip-drip of water around her, and a dead man on her chest. The light between her feet wasn't shining upward, it was spilling down from above.

'Archeth?'

'*Here!*' But it came out a strangled squawk, barely louder than the drip of the water and the thud of blood in her ears. She arched up as far as the dead man would let her, coughed and spat sideways, cleared her throat out for a decent attempt at a yell. 'Eg! Down *here!*'

The corpse on her chest pressed her back down. Her head and shoulders hung in empty space, but it seemed the rest of her body lay on solid stone, albeit at an atrocious backward angle. She heaved an arm up and out to the side, touched slick, wet rock – forget it, no chance of purchase on that, even without the dead man's insistent weight to contend with. And back up at the other end of her body, her feet were caught up, tightly wrapped by something and numb inside her boots. She and the corpse seemed to have tumbled headfirst down a steep incline in some kind of cleft and in each other's arms, and whatever had caught them by the feet had apparently stopped them going over the lip of the incline and into the lightless space beneath.

'Archeth?'

'Eg!' Voice stronger now. 'Yeah, I'm down here! I'm caught up! Must be wreckage or someth—'

Something moved, stealthily, in the space below her hanging head.

Fuck!

She flinched violently, tried to lift herself bodily up, and this time the strength of her fear let her shift the corpse off her chest and aside. She twisted about, flailed in vain for handholds anywhere, *anywhere* in the

87

smooth stone she lay on. She craned up at the faint light beyond her boots and yelled again.

'Eg! *Egar!*'

Movement, definitely, and noises like a beggar sucking on midden-heap bones.

She hinged up, hard, elbowed the dangling dead man aside. His slack, lugubrious features wobbled away from her in the gloom, as if offended by the blow.

'*Eg!*'

'Archeth!' The light blotted out, his voice boomed down into the cleft. 'Right here. You're caught up in the bowsprit lines. We're going to have to clear—'

'Never mind that shit, Eg!' Some real panic in her tone now. Briefly, an image flared in her mind – Jhiral's Hanliagh octopods, tearing the condemned apart in the pool in the Chamber of Confidences. She heaved violently up again, felt muscles in her stomach tearing with the force of it. '*Pull me the fuck up! There's something down here!*'

The sucking sound built, rose closer to her ears.

Yelling from overhead, more than one voice. A repeated cracking and suddenly she was whisked a foot up the incline. The corpse came up with her, she could hear grunting effort from above.

'He's dead,' she shouted frantically. 'The other guy, he's dead. Cut him loose!'

Egar gritted something she couldn't hear. They hauled her another couple of feet upward, the corpse came spindling and cuddling at her. A door opened somewhere in her head and abruptly she remembered him in life – some young sailor, not one of the privateer force, *running at her yelling, gesturing, some communication she had no hope of making out in the chaos of the storm, mouth distorted wide around his shouted words and—*

Gone.

Washed away as they hit and her grip was ripped from the railing and she flew—

The thing that was making the sucking noises came up over the lip of the incline.

Vision upside down, dizzied by the tugging and swaying as she was dragged upward, Archeth fixed on it and could make no sense. There were tendrils, she saw that much, a thick, muddy fringe of them like the made-up eyelashes on some gargantuan whore's eye, and they seethed about in search of prey, tasting the surface of the rock as they came, but the body, there was no body, there was only . . .

Icy clutch around her heart as she understood.

The creature filled the cleft like water. It flowed and swelled, was a single amorphous thing rising in the confines of the space it owned. Patterning like giant eyes or plague rings swilled around on the surface of its flesh like oil in a hot pan.

'*Get me the fuck out of here!*' she screamed.

Another yard. She felt hands on her boot, heaved desperately from the waist again and stuck up an arm, somewhere close to her own feet. A calloused hand grabbed her around the wrist, she felt one of the creature's tendrils brush stickily into her hair at the same instant. Pure revulsion wrung the shriek out of her – it dinned in her ears, involuntary, her right hand curled for the grip of a knife that *wasn't fucking there*—

Then she was in the air.

Burst of light and space, the thin roar of the ocean.

She had time for one backward glimpse of the creature rising behind her, cramming up into the cleft like vomit in a throat. Then the Dragonbane swung her up bodily by one hand and boot, tilted and dumped her way off to the side on cold flat rock. Her breath exploded out of her with the impact. Shocked yells rose around her, she twisted about on the rock and saw men staggering back. The creature burst into the open among them like a pan of milk boiling over. Her corpse companion from the cleft was gone, swallowed down somewhere in that heaving mass. Tendrils lashed back and forth, one of the men toppled and was caught by the leg, another seemed to stumble face-first into the creature's fronds.

The Dragonbane whirled about. He had something like a huge broken lance or harpoon held aloft in both hands – later she would realise it was *Lord of the Salt Wind*'s snapped and splintered bowsprit, still trailing lines and fragments of netting. His eyes were wide with berserk fury, there was a rising, grinding roar from his mouth. Like some statue of a warrior god, he lurched forward and over on the yell, buried the length of splintered wood deep into the heart of the seething, tendrilled mass.

Twisted and leaned in. Roared again, dug deeper still.

The tendrils spasmed, some pale fluid leapt across the air, spattered down on the rocks. The rising mass of the creature seemed to deflate. It was, she noted numbly, quite beautiful in the light – all patterned purples and pale violets flowing in and out of each other in the vaguely circular patterns she'd taken for eyes . . .

'*Get on this,*' bellowed Egar. '*Gouge this fucker with me!*'

Two men threw themselves on the leaning bowsprit, hung off it, swinging with all their weight. More splattering leakage, a low gurgling, hissing sound, and it was done. The two men dropped off the end of Egar's improvised harpoon, someone dragged the ones who'd been grabbed by the creature's tendrils out of harm's way. The thing sank back down into the cleft as swiftly as it had risen, taking the bowsprit with it. Egar let go of the shaft with a kiss-off gesture. Spat into the hole after his retreating adversary.

He turned about to check on her – by then she was back on her feet, a little shaky, but otherwise holding up. He grinned at her, still panting.

'Hey, Archidi.' Pause for a mustered breath. A sweeping gesture with one arm 'Welcome to the Kiriath Wastes.'

*

In two hundred years, she'd been there just once, and then only to the southern fringes, on what amounted to a glorified child's dare.

When she was younger, Grashgal and her father continually talked up the possibility of expeditions north to see what had become of the land. It had been thousands of years, they argued, nature would have absorbed and repaired most of the damage done, it *had* to be safe by now. And who knew what they might find that had been lost to memory and record all those centuries? She remembered those conversations, the earliest of them barely comprehensible to her infant ears as she sat in Flaradnam's lap or played on the rug while the adults talked. On later occasions, she perched on the arm of her father's chair and joined in the speculating as best she could. She'd always assumed she'd be going with them.

Her mother put paid to that notion pretty sharply one summer evening. *The Cursed Lands? Are you insane, girl? Do you know what's waiting up there?*

No, Mum. She would have been about eleven at the time, the answer was meant innocently enough. *Do you?*

Don't you smart-mouth me, young lady.

Mum, I'm not. Dad says no one *knows what's up there.*

Yes, and that's precisely why you're not going.

In the end, it didn't matter. Like so many of the Kiriath's latter-day schemes, nothing came of it. The years of talk guttered and went out, focus wavered and was gone. Grashgal and Flaradnam went back to their hobby of tinkering with the Empire's political framework instead.

Forty odd years slipped by.

Archeth was never sure if it was just the nature of her father's people and their subtly damaged mental state that killed the expedition, or if, as her mother feared, there really were things up in the Waste better left undisturbed. Or if those two factors were linked, and Grashgal and her father abandoned their plans because they came to fear that an expedition would somehow – *guilt? ghosts? strange infectious airs?* – further corrode their ability to live in this adopted world as if it were their home.

Then her mother died, as humans were wont to do, and Archeth got the chance to see the Wastes for herself first hand.

Taken north one autumn by Grashgal as part of an extensive diplomatic mission to the recently formed League, she found herself wintering in Trelayne. Nantara's death was barely a couple of years past, and Archeth was still raw, ripe for mischief. Part of Grashgal's intent had in fact been to get her away from An-Monal and her perennially grief-stricken father for a while, in the hope that it would maybe calm her down, get her back on an even keel – all of which pretty much showed how poorly he under-stood the half-blood girl he'd helped raise. Fuck her mother's ghost, fuck her father in his endless self-absorbed gloom; now she was going to *get even* with both of them. While Grashgal and the imperial legate busied themselves with sounding out their new northern neighbours, putting out cautious feelers, getting useful ink on documents of trade and peaceful co-existence, Archeth and a couple of Kiriath lads near to her own age talked each other into mounting an expedition across the northern sound and into the Wastes.

It took them almost the whole winter to put the scheme together. To find a suitable vessel along the ramshackle riverside moorings that passed for Trelayne's harbour in those days, to identify a captain and crew willing not only to make the trip but to have any truck with these jet-skinned demon folk from the south in the first place. And then, with a price agreed for passage and provisions, they had to slowly siphon off the necessary cash from embassy funds without anyone in the mission noticing. It was all painfully gradual, with frequent disappointments and setbacks. But if an immortal life-span was good for anything, it was the learning of methodical patience and planning. Two days into Spring, and a month before the mission was due to go home, they cast off from a quay in Trelayne harbour aboard a grubby-looking longship, and they headed upriver to the estuary and the sea.

By the time Grashgal realised they were gone – and set about tearing the city apart to find them – Archeth and her pals had raised the Wastes coast, made landfall, established an initial camp and pretty soon had a major fight on their hands trying to stop the longship captain sailing straight back home again. The sky above the Wastes shoreline burned as often as not with luminescent greenish fire. Strange cracking and whistling sounds could be heard from further off into the interior. The strand they'd anchored off was replete with all sorts of exciting stuff – outlandish mobile vegetation that seemed as happy in the water as it did on the sand and was given to tangling affectionately around your limbs if you walked or swam near it; clumps of shredded alloy wreckage that looked and mostly was inert, but would occasionally shudder and talk to them beseechingly in High Kir; creatures that might once have been crabs, but were now, well, quite a lot *bigger* for one thing, more lopsided, uglier all round, and made an unpleasant hissing sound if approached . . .

The captain lasted three days at anchor, nailed in place initially by some apparent sense of contractual integrity, then, as tensions built, by improvised threats of Black Folk sorcery if he broke his signatory oath. But when Archeth insisted they proceed into the interior and would need porters, the crew delivered a quiet ultimatum of their own, and the three young Kiriath woke the next morning to find the longship gone.

They had their provisions – the captain had been decent enough at least to off-load these – and a decision to make. Stay on the beach and wait for rescue, or head south-east along the coast with what they could carry and try to walk out. Archeth was all for walking out, but got voted down by her two rather more chastened male companions. Lucky as it happened – a Trelayne navy picket boat carrying an incandescently angry Grashgal showed up off-shore two days later. He came ashore tight-lipped and icily controlled, unwilling to loose his rage on them in front of the humans, but you could see in his face that they were going to catch it as soon as he got them alone. He wouldn't even let them take specimens home, despite Archeth's muted protests. She managed to sneak a cutting of the friendly mobile vegetation aboard in a bottle nonetheless, but she had no idea how to care for it and it died not long after they got back to Trelayne.

They went home to An-Monal in deep disgrace, not least on account of the diplomatic strain caused by Grashgal's rampage through the city in search of them. He thought they'd been taken by slavers, or some weird religious sect or other, and had got pretty heavy-handed with representatives of both constituencies before the Trelayne Chancellery stepped in, posted a reward and turned up the shamefaced longship captain a day or so later. But by then quite a lot of damage had been done. It didn't quite set relations back between League and Empire the hundred years Grashgal ranted at them that it had – the League had in any case only been around in its current form for a couple of decades, as Archeth tried to point out before she was bellowed into silence – but it certainly hadn't been any kind of diplomatic triumph either.

For Archeth, the disgrace lasted a year or so after she got back, though her father, still deep in mourning for Nantara, was half-hearted in his disapproval. He didn't much care how many fucking humans she'd offended in the north – protests that *she* wasn't the one who'd done the offending washed right over his head – he was just glad to see her home in one piece. There were some harsh words between Flaradnam and Grashgal on the subject, though nothing that Grashgal couldn't later forgive as the grief talking, and the millennia-old friendship was never at any real risk. But for well over a century after, they all avoided anything but casual mention of the Kiriath Wastes.

Then the Scaled Folk came, and avoidance was no longer an option.

Year of '52. The great floating purplish-black migration weed rafts, spotted drifting northward on strong coastal currents, up past the Gergis peninsula and onward. Some premature celebrating at the realisation that this fresh wave would not wash ashore in either Empire or League.

And then the Helmsmen, doing the math, talking with iron certainty of what would happen if the rafts hatched out on the shores of the Wastes, of what would come sweeping south in the autumn after.

Archeth was with the Kiriath delegation that went to Trelayne behind Akal the Great and laid it out for the League. She still remembered her father, pacing back and forth in the Chancellery hall, giving a flesh and blood face to the Helmsmen's unhuman wisdom. Seamed ebony features intent as he walked the northerners through the need for yet more sacrifice, yet more blood, yet more men drawn from the war-weary ranks for an expeditionary force into the Wastes.

The lizards can endure some cold, slower though it makes them. But they are drawn to warmth. We estimate there may be enough residual heat among the ruins of the Wastes to keep them happy through the summer months. But with autumn and the chill, they will inevitably turn south. At best, they will be a force as powerful as anything we have yet seen or fought against; at worst, the sorcer-ies at work in the Wastes may have twisted them into new and more dangerous forms.

In either case, the war will begin anew on your northern flank before it is even ended in the south. All we have achieved here in brotherhood will be for nothing.

This time, Archeth was certain she'd get to go.

But Flaradnam would not hear of it. *Your mother was right,* he told her. *And I was foolish beside her wisdom. Enough that we devastated the land back then and poisoned it for centuries to come. Enough that we must now drag more human lives back into that hell. I will not risk my own flesh and blood there too.*

But you're going she said bitterly.

I am going because somebody has to. The humans cannot operate our engineer-ing without help, they will need Kiriath leadership to see it through. Naranash is no longer with us, Grashgal is needed in the south. That leaves me.

I'll be more use at your side than I will in the south. The fighting's all but done, it's just politics down there now. Grashgal doesn't need me for that.

No – but I need you to go. And as fresh protests rose to her lips. *Please, Archeth, don't make this harder for me than it already is. I made your mother a promise on her death-bed. Don't ask me to break it.*

It was a rarely used appeal, but it was one that in all the years since her mother died, Archeth had never learnt to resist.

So she went back to Yhelteth with Grashgal and the others.

And she never saw her father again.

TWELVE

'You hear that?'

'Hear what?' The second privateer stifled a yawn. 'Only thing I can hear is Kentrin snoring. Kick him for me, will ya?'

'Let the kid sleep. I mean, did you hear water dripping just n—'

'Let him *sleep?* He's on fucking watch.'

'We're all on watch – all three of us. Doesn't take six eyes to peer through this murk and see nothing all night. Leave him alone.'

'Leave him a . . .? What's the matter with you, Lhesh? You after a portion of pert buttock pie or something? *We're on fucking watch.*'

'Yeah, like you never dozed off when you were his age?'

'Yeah, I did. And the first mate put stripes on my back for it. You give him a kick in that pretty arse of his and bawl him out, he's getting off lightl—'

Ringil came over the watchtower rampart like a grinning black shadow.

He was chilled and drenched through from his brief swim to the tower's base, his teeth were locked tight to stop them chattering, his fingers and unshod toes ached from the thirty foot climb. He landed right at the feet of the grumbling privateer. Hit the stone flags on haunches and one braced palm, exploded up out of the crouch, dragon-fang dagger already reversed in his right hand, while the man just gaped down at him in disbelief. He struck upward for the soft underside of the jaw, up through tongue, mouth, soft palate and on into the brain.

He lifted the privateer backwards on the force of the blow.

Yanked the knife free.

The man crumpled, eyes rolled up to the whites. Ringil was already turning away.

The other privateer, Lhesh, was a scant five yards off across the flagstone roof of the tower. He turned as his comrade stopped speaking, curious more than alert, and the difference killed him. He had time to glimpse motion, the collapse of a body to the stones, dull red splatter across the fogged palette of the dawn, and a twisted black shape, spinning about . . .

The dragon tooth blade was useless for throwing, it didn't have the balance or the elegance of form. Ringil dropped it. Raked a glyph into the chilly morning air instead, uttered harsh whispered syllables, and Lhesh choked on the cry in his throat. He gaped, staggered, made hoarse sounds and pawing gestures. Ringil crossed the five yard gap in what seemed like a single leap. He reached in, left hand swept across the man's eyes like the gesture of a servant wiping a window, right palm slapped in against the upper ribs. He hissed out the two syllable command.

Stopped the man's heart in his chest.

Lhesh's eyes bulged for a brief moment – shock, terror and the struggle to understand. Then he sagged and went bonelessly to the flagstone floor. Ringil held on to the dead man's chest like a lover, softened the drop, lowered the body down.

Soft snores from one gloomy corner of the tower wall.

Ringil looked round, slightly incredulous. Kentrin, it seemed, had managed to sleep through the whole thing. He was still there, legs pulled up for warmth, leaned slightly into the corner, face slack with sleep. Gil approached, cat-footed, momentarily unsure what to do. He glanced back at the dragon fang blade, sticky with blood where he'd left it, too far to easily fetch. And now, almost as if Kentrin sensed the danger looming over him, he stirred. Muttered something, eyes sliding halfway open, still glazed with sleep . . .

Drop to one knee, press the killing palm into the boy's chest. Ringil made the window-wiping gesture again, again the two grating irrevocable words from the *ikinri 'ska*. Kentrin's eyes jerked wider open at the sound, his mouth fluttered, the beginnings of panic surfacing on his face. Gil put fingers to the boy's lips and pressed. Made his voice soft as warm wool.

'Shsss. Sleep, go back to sleep, it's fine.'

'Nnno, but—' Body twitching sideways, legs shoving for support – in a moment he'd struggle to his feet against the hollow wrongness in his chest. 'You're—'

'A bad dream. That's all I am. Shsssh.' Sing-song soothing, wiping the fear away. Watching the boy's features soften again as death took him back down. 'You're having a bad dream, go back to sleep. Rest now, rest . . .'

The boy's head lolled sideways in the angle of the wall. His legs slid down under their own weight, straightening slowly out. He looked almost as peaceful in death as he had done asleep.

His comrades lay less cosily, but still like sleeping men, flat out on the grey stone flooring, curled just fractionally into themselves as if against the cold. Blood pooling around the first man's head told a different tale, but in this uncertain light even that was easy to miss.

And Ringil was gone.

He met Senger Hald at the base of the tower.

He'd stopped to kill two more men on the way down, but in the twisting spiral confines of the tower's only staircase, it was easier work than he'd had on the roof. Each sleepy privateer heard unhurried motion on the stone steps overhead, glanced up in expectation of a comrade coming down with something to report, saw instead a looming, unfamiliar figure, jagged knife in hand. Ringil stepped down, stepped in close, and it was done.

He used the dragon fang dagger both times – stopping the hearts of the two on the roof had tired him for magic, and anyway, trying to cast glyphs under the low stone roofing of the staircase was asking for trouble and barked knuckles besides.

The ikinri 'ska *works better in open areas,* Hjel tells him apologetically. *Best of all under open skies. The powers are not always attentive in tight or hidden places.*

Great. Some fucking sorcery you're teaching me here.

The dispossessed prince smiles. *Did you think it would be easy?*

Not to learn, no – but I thought it might be a bit handier than this once I had it down.

Your mistake, then.

Yeah.

He edged out of the watchtower doorway, squinted round the curve of the wall to his right. From the raised promontory of Dako's Point, a broad, stepped causeway descended southward over a chaotic tumble of boulders and chunks of collapsed cliff facade each the size of a modest galleon. Beyond, dimly through the fog and the strengthening glimmer of dawn, the lights of Ornley harbour beckoned.

Footfalls to his left. He whipped round and saw Hald emerge from the gloom, sword in hand. Black marine combat rig and cloak, soot-smeared features – Ringil was expecting him, but it was still a little like meeting an unquiet ghost.

'All right?'

The marine commander gestured over his shoulder. 'They're coming up now. Had to brace our way up a chimney from that inlet. Higher than we thought.'

'Yeah, well, the good news is it looks like we guessed right about these guys. I don't see anyone on the causeway.'

Hald grunted and took his own peek round the curve of the tower.

'It is sense,' he allowed. 'If I held the town, and could assume a good watch in the tower, I would not waste men either by stringing them out this far from the harbour.'

More black-clad figures, out of the gloom at his back as he spoke – the marines gathering, two and three at a time, blades out, sooted faces grim. Hald snapped his fingers, gestured for positions. They formed up in a small phalanx. Someone brought up helm and shield for Ringil, the Ravensfriend in its scabbard, a marine issue cloak and his boots, a cuirass – he put it all on, hefted the shield a couple of times to settle it on his arm, then he faced the men and drew the Ravensfriend from his back. Most of them hadn't seen that trick before, how fast the Kiriath sheath would deliver up the blade. It sent a brief murmur through the ranks. Gil showed them the slice of a smile.

'I'm afraid I don't know how many of these motherfuckers we're dealing with down in the harbour,' he began. 'But I can tell you this much for nothing – the ones in the tower died pretty easily. These are League privateers we're dealing with, not soldiers. They're pirate freebooters, out for easy coin. No match for imperial marines, *and they do not know we're coming.*'

Carnivorous grins on some of the faces now, and the murmuring in the ranks grew. Hald tried to look aloof from it, but he couldn't keep the gleam of anticipation off his face either. Ringil kept his smile, wore it like a mask. He was underselling the privateers, he knew; they were generally a pretty hard-bitten lot, the League's hard-nosed mercantile version, in fact, of the Empire's marine soldiery. Back before the war, privateer crews under men like Critlin Blacksail and Sharkmaster Wyr had shown themselves pretty effective in routing imperial forces both aboard ship and on land. They were maybe not as intensively trained nor regimentally committed as the marines, but most among them would be similarly seasoned in the acts of piracy and coastal assault that passed for naval warfare on the western seaboard. They'd be as savage, as hungry for the slaughter.

Truth was, barring terminology and the ink on a few contractual documents signed by men who could barely read what they'd put their names to, there really wasn't a lot to choose between the two sides here.

But now was not the time for that truth. Some of these men would be dead before the hour was out, and collectively they knew it.

So let's keep it upbeat, Gil. Let's give them that at least.

'You have the element of surprise,' he said. 'And you have your training. Follow my lead, keep my pace. We start slow, but we'll be taking the harbour wall at a charge. They're never going to know what hit them. We clean them out, we kill anything that gets in our way. And – this is important – any of them go into the water in the fight, forget them, they're done. They won't be getting back out again, that's a promise.'

'Yeah, and what if *we* fall in?' called someone at the back, a grin in the voice.

'Don't,' he told them, and the grins all evaporated at the chill in his tone. 'I won't be able to help you, there won't be time. Now enough of this advisory shit – *who wants to open some pirate throats?*'

Growling assent. It wasn't dissimilar to the elemental thunder he'd set prowling the sky the night before.

He let it in, he let it carry him forward. Raised an arm. Let it fall.

Down the broad, stepped flow of the causeway, skulking at first, some caution in the pace. Shields carried low, eyes and ears sharp for any straggling re-supply coming up for the watchtower guard. Soft, hurried trample of booted feet behind him, no sign of anyone in their path. And now, sketched in fog below, the blunt outlines of the harbour wall looming closer. Nothing to indicate they'd yet been seen. Caution crumbling, flaking away before the heated fact of what they were about to do. Pace already picked up way past any chance of braking – they were sprinting now, they were *falling* forward, pouring down the steps unstoppable, the heads of men becoming vaguely visible here and there above the line of the harbour wall, there'd be bowmen among them, keep it tight and silent, keep that shrill, hooting cry fenced back behind your teeth. Lips peeling back, grinning hard from the sprint, breath beginning to cost something now each time it's drawn—

'*ware raiders!*'

It rang out, high and panicky, from somewhere on the wall.

Way too late.

Gil leapt the last two steps to the wall, landed among men nodding at the edges of sleep. They had perhaps a glimpse of him – a darkened form unfolding, the terrible strop and glide of the Ravensfriend in the gloom, then it was all blood and screaming as the Kiriath steel found flesh and laid it open. He barely saw the men he killed – pale, blurred faces in the whirl of first contact, shocked, gaping mouths – he knew only that he took the throat out of one – chopped open the neck on a second – took down a third with a slice to the thigh, batted him into the harbour waters with a blow from his shield, the man screamed once, was pulled down, was gone – gutted a fourth on his way past. None among them had managed to even clear their weapons. None among them got out any kind of articulate word before they died.

Ringil hooked back his head as the howl inside him came loose. The fog eddied, seemed to tear apart around him with the sound.

And back came cries from along the wall, as if in answer.

'ware raiders! *This is it, lads!*'

A sneer painted itself on his lips like a lover's smeared kiss. He piled forward, full tilt, into the eddies of fog and vaguely seen forms ahead.

If the harbour wall was for defence against seaborne enemies and the elements, the causeway behind was made with blunt haulage and commerce in mind. It was wide enough to take an ox cart – or a dozen armed and armoured men abreast. Ringil led the imperials in an iron wedge, short swords out to hack and stab. They tore into the disarrayed ranks of the privateers, rolled up a dozen yards of the wall before anyone could grasp what was going on.

Then, somewhere down the line – a voice of gruff command.

'They're coming off the fucking stair!'

Something dark snapped and snarled inside Gil, something reached out smokily for *whoever that fucking loudmouth was*. But he lacked the tools to equip it, to send it on its way, and anyway whatever the dark thing was, it could not find the speaker in the fog, nor break his tongue in time.

'They've taken the tower! *Brace up the north end!*'

The cry was taken up. It was the sound of order in the chaos, the sound of their advantage burning down. Ringil reached inside himself. Dredged up a warped, grating roar. Threw back his head again.

'Whore sons of Trelayne!' He barely understood it as his own voice, it was like something from the Grey Places speaking through him. 'Whore sons of Trelayne – *come meet your unmaker!*'

And on down the red-running causeway path, bringing the killing steel as he came.

It was less than a hundred yards to the end of the wall, but by halfway, he was running into harder pellets of resistance and losing men. That rallying, command voice had done something, built something here that wouldn't give.

At his left shoulder, the first casualty – some privateer with a cutlass proving more than equal to imperial marine training. The marine went down with a groan. But the wedge held – his replacement stepped right over his body and avenged his death in five savage cut-and-thrust blows. Further on, another imperial grappled with a privateer on Gil's right, lost the white-knuckled struggle for grip and took a knife blade in the guts, staggered backward with a howl. But he clung on and took his killer with him, over the edge of the causeway into the harbour below. Boiling thrash of water, vaguely seen through the fog, and then both men were gone.

The next imperial slotted right into the gap. The wedge rolled on.

Salt on the marsh. Mother says . . .

It was the boy, Gerin, the cold voice in his ear. Always the same rote words, the icy urchin touch at the nape of his neck that he'd learnt better than to ignore in moments like these. Tugging him downward to a crouch . . .

Arrow fire came slicing out of the fog.

'Shields!' he bellowed. His own was already up – the shafts split and feathered it like magic, took down three less wary imperials in an eye-blink. They cursed and groaned and tumbled, twisted and fell atop the bodies of men they'd just killed.

'That's it, lads! Hold the line!'

That fucking voice again.

Yelling from across the harbour at the docks, lanterns coming on. Any element of surprise they'd once had was fast transmuting into the dross of a messy pitched battle. If he didn't get this nailed down pretty fast . . .

He summoned force, summoned voice.

'Men of Trelayne!' Grateful for once that his own men would mostly not be able to follow the Naomic well enough for it to affect them. 'Men of Trelayne, *look to the water! The kraken wakes!*'

And leapt forward behind his shield, into the fog and the figures that bulked there.

He heard the oaths and yelps of shock. A shrill, terrified cry went up from somewhere, a volley of arrows scattered wide and harmless. Briefly, he glimpsed the terror that he'd set loose in their minds, the towering, tentacled bulk, rearing over the harbour wall like some vast, uprooted, upended oak tree, studded with unblinking obsidian eyes. Grey flicker glimpse, there and gone. It didn't look a lot like the real article he'd faced a few weeks back – way too big, for one thing – but these men were seafarers and they'd come up on a dripping, woven mass of tales about this beast, each more outlandish and distended than the last. Some few might be smart or awake enough to shake off the glamour for what it was, but not many. For the others, their deepest nightmares and fears would do the rest.

A young privateer ran screaming along the causeway at him, eyes blind with fear. Ringil blocked a wild cutlass slash, stepped aside, tripped the man and shoved him into the water on the harbour side. Something sinuous and muscular coiled up and around him as he flailed, Gil caught a glimpse of the man's screaming face being engulfed and really wished he hadn't . . .

'*Rally!*' The command voice, higher pitched now with desperation. 'Rally, you fools! It's a *trick!* There's nothing there!'

'No, no – *there's something in the water, there is!*'

'The *kraken!*'

'It took Perit!'

'*Stand, you fools!*'

Right.

Time to finish this.

He cut down two more privateers on his way to the commander. It wasn't hard to do, the state they were in. Block and slice, hack out the leg from under one, pommel into the face of the other, then the short chop to the throat as he staggered back. He shouldered them out of the way, cleared space for himself with the Ravensfriend and now – the fog was finally clearing, burning off as the day got underway – he spotted the rallying point. The commander stood there on a crate, bellowing at the panicking muddle of men around him.

'You!' Gil stalked forward, sword point raised at the man. 'Yeah, you! Want to come down off there and give me a fight?'

The moment seemed to lock up. Men froze in mid-motion, weapons half-raised, staring. Tendrils of fog, curling back, blown away on a new breeze.

'It's him,' someone yelled. 'It's Eskiath, I told you he's not fucking hu—'

The commander – by his jacket badges a mere sergeant – came leaping off the crate, blade in his right hand, short axe in his left.

'With me, lads! Throw this filth back into the sea!'

Ringil met him in a whirl, shield up to block the axe, Ravensfriend swooping low. Forced the other man to parry clumsily downward with his sword. The axe hit and bounced off the shield – evil, twanging pain up through Gil's elbow and shoulder with the impact. He rode it, jerked the shield edge in, looking for a chop into face or head. But the privateer sergeant was too canny a fighter – he'd already backed up, two looping rearward steps, weaving a figure-of-eight blur with his two weapons to cover.

'Get in behind this fuck,' he yelled. 'Chop him down.'

But the imperial wedge was already rolling up behind Gil, the other privateers had opponents of their own to worry about now. Battle was joined, tangled up and snarling across the corpse-littered causeway flag-stones. They stared at each other through waxing morning light and an odd moment of calm. Ringil lifted shield and sword, querying.

'Need a rest?'

The sergeant brandished his weapons and roared. 'Outlaw faggot *scum!*'

'Oh, *please.*'

He judged the man's rush, broke it on the instant with his own leaping attack. Led with the Ravensfriend, let the sergeant beat it back with a wild, looping parry and swung in hard with his shield. Got the other man in the chest. Got ground. The axe whistled down and he flung the shield higher, whipped the pommel of the Ravensfriend into the sergeant's face. Hooked the axe head on the shield edge, ripped the privateer forward off balance and chopped in under his ribs. The man screamed, swung wildly with his sword arm, but the axe was still snagged and Ringil just leapt back, hauling the clinch. The sergeant tripped or slipped on blood, fell headlong forward at Gil's feet, still dragged on axe and shield. Ringil flipped the Ravensfriend over from horizontal guard to downward jag, stabbed down hard between the man's back ribs, shoulder turn and full weight behind the blow. There was mail over the man's jerkin, but light-weight and cheap, links most likely rusted with time at sea – the Kiriath steel went through it like an arrow at full draw. The sergeant spasmed and groaned, let go his axe haft and Gil's shield came free.

He withdrew the Ravensfriend, judged the man done, looked about for fresh targets.

But the fight was all but finished. The imperials were still rolling for-ward, and any discipline the privateers had once had was broken. Strictly mopping up from here on in. Gil stalked about anyway, hamstrung a man here, belted another in the head with his shield, just to speed things up. The imperials fell on his victims and finished them.

Unexpected glint off the Ravensfriend's edge – he peered upward through the clearing fog.

Looked like the sun was going to come out after all.

THIRTEEN

They came down off the flat rock in single file behind the Dragonbane, giving clefts and blowholes a suitably wide berth. There was more debris from the wreck along the way – crates here and there, like lost dice from some abandoned game among giants; spars and tangled rigging, some of it up-jutting out of gaps in the rock where wind and waves had driven it or perhaps – she shivered slightly at the thought – where it had later been dragged. Here, the smashed ribs and soggy white spill of a shattered flour barrel. There, a scattering of galley pans. And just once, like so much knotted up wet laundry flung down, a privateer corpse, sprawled bonelessly on the rock.

A couple of the men made sketched gestures of blessing over the dead man as they went past, some business with open palm and a couple of fingers kissed. Hand to chest, briefly bowed head. It dawned on a groggy Archeth, as she watched the ritual, that at least half her rescue party were also privateers.

The others she made for Tand's men, with the exception of a single young Majak and a pair of marines. But they all followed the Dragonbane as one.

She went up the line, caught him up.

'Got these guys eating out of your hand, don't you?' she said in Tethanne. 'How'd you swing that one?'

Egar shrugged. 'Someone's got to be in charge.'

'Okay. But . . . a prisoner of war?'

'Look around you, Archidi. Things have changed.'

She let that go, looked out in silence to the rinsed grey horizon and the unquiet sea. The curve of a shingle beach just ahead of them, the rise of jagged uplands beyond. It was a pretty bleak shore they'd wrecked on.

'You recognise anything?' she asked, more quietly.

'Not here, no. We've got to be a long way further north than the expeditionary ever made it to.' He pointed ahead. 'Follow this coast far enough south, there's a big river delta with Kiriath ruins on the northern shore. It's where we burnt the lizard rafts with your father's machines. We need to find that river. Then I'll know where we are. Then I can get us home.'

They reached the limits of the flat rock, jumped down into the crunch of the shingle. More flotsam strewn along the strand ahead of them, some of it still washing around in the shallows. She stopped, shaded her eyes and looked further out, saw a bobbing carpet of the stuff there as well. No sign of any intact portion of the ship itself.

Further along the beach, someone had built a driftwood fire. Pale flames, barely visible in the harsh grey daylight. Men huddled around, jostling for warmth.

Archeth nodded at them. 'How many we got?'

'Thirty-four, all told. I sent another party to scout the rocks southward, see if we find anybody else.'

She glanced back at her rescue party. 'What's the split?'

Another shrug. 'What you see there – some League, some of Tand's freebooters, a few marines mixed in. There's a few Eternals too, but I left them in charge of the other party and the fire.'

'Any more Majak?'

'A couple.' Egar grimaced. 'Not a lot of use for swimming up on the steppe, most of them never learn.'

'Did you find . . . Kaptal?' She'd been going to ask after Shendanak, or his sodden corpse anyway, then thought better of it. 'Or Tand?'

The Dragonbane shook his head. 'Kaptal, no. No sign. And Tand went on the other ship – *Flight of the . . . going west* or whatever it was. With Shendanak and Shanta, remember?'

She did now. 'Gull – *Flight of the Westward Gull*. Yeah, but . . .'

'But what?'

'Well.' She gestured helplessly. 'There's a lot of wreckage.'

'All from the one ship.' The Dragonbane jerked a thumb back at one of the accompanying privateers. 'According to that guy, anyway, and he was second watch steersman on *Lord of the Salt Wind*. Figure he ought to know what he's talking about. Seems pretty certain the other ship didn't wreck, nor the *Pride*. Or at least – they didn't wreck around here.'

They reached the fire. One of the Throne Eternal, she didn't know him by name, came to meet her and bowed his head. He was bedraggled and damp, but there was still a drilled poise in the way he stood that made her abruptly long for Yhelteth and home.

'Alwar Nash, my lady. At your service. It brings me joy to find you hale. Will you come closer to the fire?'

The solicitude melted some tiny chunk of something inside her, and for the first time she realised that her clothes were damp, that her head and body both ached from bruises she'd collected in the wreck, that she was in fact *pretty fucking cold*—

She locked down a shiver, nodded weary thanks. Nash turned and brusquely ushered the crouched or kneeling men aside to make a path nearer the fire. There were some resentful glances, but between Archeth's alien looks and Nash's take-no-shit Throne Eternal demeanour, no one seemed to want to make an issue of it. She stood at the wall of heat like a supplicant, holding out her hands to it, trying not to shudder with pleasure as the warmth seeped into her chilled and battered body.

There was some muttering among the privateers by the fire, the usual thing, and she would have paid it little attention, except that she saw the second steersman stride in among them, point back at her and murmur something urgent. At which point the muttering dried up faster than a desert martyr's blood. She wasn't sure, but she thought she saw a couple of the men make some gesture of . . . *what's that? Obeisance?*

'What's going on?' she asked Egar as he joined her in the warmth. 'I get that they don't like the burnt-black witch. But this is new.'

The Dragonbane glanced over at the privateer huddle. 'Yeah, forgot to mention. Reason we found you so fast? You were caught up on the bowsprit lines and the snapped top half of the figurehead too. The whole lot was jammed in there, sticking back up into the sky like a big fucking arrow pointing us to where you were.'

'Yeah, so?'

Egar hesitated. 'Thing is, when we got there, it looked like the figurehead had hold of you by one ankle. Ship's called *Lord of the Salt Wind*, remember? That's Takavach – Dakovash of the Dark Court for these guys – and the figurehead was his likeness. Looks like the Salt Lord grabbed you by the leg in the storm, hung on and saved your life.'

She shot him a sidelong look. 'You're not serious?'

'Hey, you're looking at the man Takavach showed up *in person* to save from a brotherslaying back on the steppe. What do I know? And another thing? Privateers and marines both are all muttering that was no natural storm hit us last night. Certainly came on pretty fucking fast.'

'But—'

'Look, it doesn't matter, Archidi. Believe what you want. But if these men think you're some kind of favourite with their Dark Court, going to be handy for keeping order. So don't knock it down.'

'No problem.' She rubbed her hands together thankfully in the warmth from the flames. 'Been the bad smell in the room round here for quite long enough. Adulation's going to make a nice change.'

A little later, she felt well enough to realise she was hungry, and asked Egar quietly about supplies. He shook his head.

'We're pretty low. Couple of oil jars with the seals still on, found them floating in the breakers. And there's a salted ham we might be able to salvage some of. Got an intact crate over there with some ship's biscuit in. Sea water got to some of it, but to be honest you need to soak that shit in brine before you can eat it anyway.' He looked at the backs of his battle-scarred hands. 'It'll do for now. Water's the bigger problem.'

She brooded on the chains of jagged rising rock that formed the hinterland view. 'There's got to be some up there somewhere though, right?'

'Somewhere, yeah. But it could be a long way, and when we find it, it may not be safe to drink. Couple of times on the expeditionary, your father told us not to drink the water we found. Said it was likely poisoned.'

'Great. So do we scout or—'

A cry from someone on the other side of the fire. Egar and Archeth stepped wide of the billowing heat haze the flames gave off. Saw returning figures dotted along the shingle to the south. Moving slowly by the look of it – for some reason Archeth thought of men walking into the teeth of a roaring gale.

'My eyes aren't what they used to be,' the Dragonbane muttered. 'Is that . . . are they carrying someone back there? The last ones in the file?'

'Or some*thing*.' Archeth squinted. 'Hard to tell. I count eleven men walking, anyway. That right?'

Egar grunted. 'Four more than I sent out.'

They watched and waited as the party straggled in. Archeth recognised the Throne Eternal who led them – Selak Chan, the man who'd come aboard *Pride of Yhelteth* and found her trying to sink Anasharal in the harbour. His young face seemed to have aged ten years since she saw it last, but as with Alwar Nash, there was a trained spine of determination to his stance that gave her a little hope. He bowed deeply as he reached her.

'My lady. Such fortune we could not have hoped for. My life at your command. And with the news I bring—'

'You found survivors?' Egar broke in pragmatically.

Chan nodded, gestured back. 'Two League, a Majak kid and one of Tand's. All in pretty good shape – one of the League guys has a couple of broken fingers, but we splinted them up. Tand's dog is limping, says he did something to his knee. But he can walk.'

'So who are you . . . carrying . . .' Voice fading out as she saw.

The last two men in the party were both marines. They'd slung a couple of lengths of three inch rope across their shoulders to form a nifty make-shift carry cable between. Hanging from the rope, like some giant crab caught up on netting, was a Kiriath machine.

Anasharal . . .?

It took her measurable moments to realise it was not the Helmsman.

First of all, no mention of Anasharal had been made by her captors at any point, and she had to assume that it was still skulking aboard *Sea Eagle's Daughter* somewhere, silently imitating some inanimate object.

Yeah, or dazzling Klithren and his men with some sorcerous shit or other, and securing passage south.

In any case, the thing the men carried was no Helmsman. It was smaller than Anasharal, for one thing, and more skeletal in frame. The central mass was dwarfed by powerful limbs, whose articulations would have risen well above the body itself when the thing walked, and by two of which it now hung suspended from the rope sling. It was like some night-mare version of a Helmsman, some predatory fantasy Anasharal might once have dreamed of itself.

'What the fuck is that?' Egar, asking it for all of them.

'Dunno,' grunted one of the men carrying the sling. 'But it's very fuck-ing heavy.'

He nodded to his companion and the two of them shucked the rope sling in a single neat motion. The crab-like thing clanked and rattled loudly on the shingle as it landed. It lay there on its back, legs splayed and draped outward, while the men from the fire crowded round to stare.

'Is it dead?' someone asked wonderingly.

'Looks that way,' said the marine who'd complained about the weight. 'Looks like they burnt it up or something.'

It was true – now she looked at it carefully, Archeth saw that the thing was blackened and charred all over. Parts of it even seemed to have melted, something she found hard to credit despite the evidence of her own eyes. Her people built habitually out of materials that would withstand great heat. Outside of dragon venom, which ate pretty much anything it touched, the only time she'd seen substantial damage to Kiriath alloys was—

Khangset.

She still remembered her first view from the rise above the town – Khangset's seaward ramparts torn and melted through when the dwenda came calling, the damage done as if by gigantic white-hot claws.

The Talons of the Sun, Ringil told her they called it. He wasn't sure what exactly it was, had himself never seen it in action. From what he did know, it seemed the dwenda used it like volleys of flaming arrows to open pas-sage, to sow chaos and terror ahead of an assault, or simply to obliterate everything in their path.

Later, she'd found fleeting reference to it in the war chronicles her people left behind. But the language was ornate and unhelpful – usually a sure sign of the writer covering for their own lack of knowledge or reliable memory. She'd talked to the Helmsmen, and not got much further. They'd been around for the war, four thousand years back, but they couldn't tell her much more than she'd already gleaned elsewhere. They'd seen what the Talons did, had perfect recall of smouldering ruins and whole armies charred to ash, but the strike had always come from a place they could not see. They had some largely incomprehensible explanation of how this might work, one that lost Archeth at the first bend.

'Where did you find this?' she asked Chan.

The Throne Eternal nodded back over his shoulder. 'At the bottom of a gully, my lady, on the other side of the headland. There were quite a few like it, all piled up there. I believe they must have come from the fortress.'

'Fortress?' Hunger, cold, the bruising she'd taken. For the first time, she felt genuinely dizzy. 'You found a . . . fortress? A *Kiriath* fortress?'

'Yes, my lady. I was about to tell you.' Chan shot a reproachful glance at the Dragonbane. 'We saw it from the headland, out to sea at least a mile. It stands in the ocean exactly as the Helmsman described it.'

FOURTEEN

There were three fishing skiffs tied up along the causeway quay. The imperials found a couple of younger privateers cowering among the nets aboard the first, smacked them about a bit and threw them overboard. Splash and roil of waters as they were snatched down screaming – one or two of the marines looked a little queasy as they caught glimpses, but the rest seemed to be getting used to it.

Ringil cobbled together a rough-and-ready kindling spell Hjel had taught him early on and conjured fire from the damp timbers in the prow of the boat. It took a couple of attempts, the first one more smoke and smoulder than flame. But second time around, the spell took. The damp wood snapped and crackled alight like desert scrub kindling. Ringil stepped back, splayed hands towards the flames, as if at once restraining them and warming his hands.

'Get out of the boat,' he suggested to the curious imperials rubbernecking at his back. 'And somebody get that mooring cut.'

He clambered out after them. Watched sombrely as the little improvised fireship drifted away from the causeway, spun about like a floated needle seeking north, and then settled into an eerily rapid and accurate course across the harbour. The imperials clustered about him on the quay's edge, but none got too close.

'There's no current pulling that way,' somebody muttered at his back.

'Yeah, no shit,' came a low response. 'What, did you just get here or something? You didn't see those guys go into the water?'

Ringil turned about as if he hadn't heard. Made for the second skiff. The rhythms for the kindling spell were thrumming in his head now, he had it down. Pretty sure he'd only need the one shot at it this time. More than enough spare attention to track the murmured conversation among the men who followed him.

'This is evil work,' he heard. 'The Revelation is clear. It's forbidden to have dealings with powers like these. Scarface there is going to—'

'*Keep your fucking voice down!* Man's a sorcerer, isn't he?'

Twitch of a grin at the corners of Ringil's mouth. A fresh voice joined in.

'Yeah, Krag, we're all real upset about how it's turning out. We just kicked these pirates' arses into the harbour thanks to *Scarface there*. I'll take that over a barrel of invigilator's indulgences any day of the week.'

'Yeah, you ever see an *invigilator* fight like that?'

Guffaws.

'Ever see an invigilator fight at all?'

'That's blasphemy, Shahn! The Revelation's our guide to salvation of the soul. The invigilators cannot mire themselves in worldly matters.'

'Yeah? Seen a couple of them mire themselves pretty deep in the girls at Salyana's Yard last year.'

'What I hear, most of them prefer boys.'

'Man, now *that's* just fucking obscene—'

'Oh, what – you really going to pull that face, Mahmal? After the way you snuggled up to little rosy cheeks from the galley aboard *Lizardlash* last year?'

'That's different, man. That's at sea. But when you've got the fucking *choice* . . .'

They reached the second skiff. Showing off a little, Gil made the cast from the causeway this time, into the piled up nets in the bottom of the boat. Smoke and smoulder, and for a moment he thought he'd fucked it up again. Then the flames broke out, pale and crackling in the bright morning air. He rested one boot on the side of the skiff, gave the fire a moment to really take, then nodded at the marine nearest the mooring iron. The man hacked a knife blade up through the rope and Ringil gave the boat a heavy, booted shove away from the causeway's edge.

'My lord!' A marine, hurrying along the quay from the stairway end. 'My lord Ringil!'

Gil turned to face him. The imperial bore the marks of the engagement just gone – he was limping somewhat, he'd been bandaged crudely about the head. Blood had trickled down from the binding and was starting to dry on his face. Still, he seemed pretty cheerful.

'My lord, Commander Hald sends word – he is ready to move on the town. Fresh men are coming up at the tower to support the push.'

'Excellent.' Ringil nodded at the last remaining skiff. 'Everybody in the boat, then. Tell Commander Hald we'll see him on the other side.'

He watched with some amusement as the men around him looked at each other in alarm. Then he strode to the third skiff, threw in his borrowed shield and jumped down after it. Looked back expectantly at the marines.

'Gentlemen, if you please.'

They came without much enthusiasm, nine men in all, lowered themselves in with wary care. They sat gingerly away from the sides, while he took station at the prow and waited for the bandaged marine to cut them loose. Out ahead in the harbour waters, the other two skiffs were well ablaze and heading steadily for the League man of war tied up at the main dock. In the brightening light of the morning, the fireships looked harmless and toylike, but he could already hear voices raised in alarm along the dock.

Good enough.

They made good time across the harbour – stood at the prow, Ringil glanced down and saw the lead akyia just below the surface of the water, swimming effortlessly on its side, long, fronded limbs rippling. One claw-tipped hand trailed back to caress the keel, as if guiding the vessel by touch alone. The creature's head was tilted up, one fist-sized eye seeming to watch him through the water, huge lamprey-like mouth irising open and shut in the boneless lower face.

They're talking about you.

Seethlaw's words, the first time they saw the akyia, watching them both from shallow waters, just offshore in the Grey Places. At the time, he'd dismissed the dwenda's words as a joke. But he was pretty sure there'd been an akyia in the river when he came out of the crumbling temple at Afa'marag. He was pretty sure it had left him his dragon tooth dagger, pegged in the mud on the riverbank. And somewhere in the twisted morass of nightmare and memory he carried from that time, was a flicker-lit recollection of taking the Ravensfriend out of a webbed and clawed hand that offered it like a gift from the water.

I see what the akyia saw, Gil. I see what you could become if you'd only let yourself.

He wasn't sure what he was becoming, but he knew they'd shadowed him north. He'd seen them cavorting in the surf one night at Lanatray when he went out to prowl the battlements of his mother's summer re-treat. He'd seen them at play in the band-light-dappled wake of *Dragon's Demise* on more than one occasion, though no one else up on deck those nights seemed to share his vision. And when the kraken came calling, hauling itself meatily up on deck one questing tentacle at a time in search of prey, it was the akyia who swarmed it, tearing at its bulk with claws and mouths, dragging it finally back down into the ocean before Ringil had the chance to do more than hack at it a half dozen times.

They featured in Naomic myth, more often called the Merroigai, though the focus in those tales was usually on their sleek, womanlike bodies and seductive ways with mariners. Not so much mention of the nightmarish bone structure and feeding apparatus of the face, or the rather intimidating claws. But for all that, they were seen as creatures of power. There were legends that made them minor gods, close relatives of the Dark Court nobility. In other myth, they were linked specifically with the Salt Lord Dakovash. In some versions they were his eyes and ears across the ocean, in others his handmaidens.

Seethlaw had been reticent, told him nothing meaningful or useful, but one thing had come across very clearly. The dwenda lord and his sister Risgillen were both obviously wary of offending the akyia, if not actually scared of them. And anything that worried the dwenda, well, that had to be worth something.

We'll take what allies we can get, Akal the Great told his court bluntly, when news of the alliance with Trelayne against the lizards was proclaimed. *And we'll not question our good fortune in finding them.*

Ringil had never much liked the man, but he couldn't fault the thinking.

They were coming up on the shingle beach now, at the end of the quay. No sign of a reception committee. In the wake of the fireships and Hald's encroachment along the far side of the harbour, no one had had time to notice them arrive. The lead akyia let go the boat's keel, executed a slick dive-and-turn that would have broken the back on any human swimmer, and was gone, back into deeper waters. Through the soles of his boots and his own grip on the prow, Gil thought he felt the release of multiple claws from the underside of the skiff and a faint slackening of the boat's momentum.

'Ready it, lads.' Shahn, the ranking imperial present, gruff voice raised. 'I want a nice tight deployment behind my lord Ringil, soon as we hit. Blades out *after* you jump.'

They ran in to the shelving shingle with a sustained, grinding crunch. The boat jammed to a halt and tilted to one side along the keel. Gil leapt out, shield slung, splashing heavily through ankle shallows and up onto dry land. He stood and drew the Ravensfriend, sheer leadership bravado, there was nothing here to kill with it. But he heard the multiple scrape as the men at his back followed suit.

'Shields!'

They stalked up the beach as one. The soft breeze plucked aside his cloak, put a moment's chill back in his damp clothing. He shivered, but it felt exultant.

Dad, if you could only see me now. Leading a pack of imperials in assault on a chartered League town.

Outlaw faggot scum, is it?

Fair enough.

They made the street to the quay unnoticed, traded shingle for cobbles with some relief. A couple of hundred yards off to the right, one of the makeshift fireships had lodged at the waterline of the League warship, flames licking upward at the rail and rigging there. Men swarmed the ship with buckets, trying to get the fire out.

Yeah, good luck with that. Hjel had taught him well; nothing would quench invoked fire until the thing you'd set aflame was ash.

Meantime . . .

The plan was pretty straightforward, a lopsided pincer to clear out the wharf of any hostile forces, then advance up into the town with general slaughter. But as they reached the quay, he heard yelling and the clatter of boots on cobbles, carried down from the street above in the still morning air.

Reinforcements, coming down.

He whipped around to face the imperials, whirl of decision and hurried speech.

'Four men, with me, now. We're going up there and block the next wave. Shahn, you take the others and hack your way through to Hald.'

Six of the eight imperials stepped forward on the instant. Assume the remaining two had to be the pious Krag and a like-minded pal. Ringil grinned and pointed at random with his shield.

'You, you, you and you. Thank you, gentlemen.' Briefly, turning to Shahn. 'Tell Hald we'll hold the slope as long as we can, but some back-up would be nice. Okay, go. Get it done. The rest of you, with me. Let's fucking chase them back up that hill, shall we?'

Grim laughter. They knew what they were being asked to do, they knew the odds. Five blades to stop up the street against who knew how many privateers, and the gradient against them too.

He raised the Ravensfriend like a steel standard.

'For your comrades, gentlemen – for the Empire! Make it count!'

For the Empire, *Gil? Where'd that one come from?*

Hey, whatever works.

They rushed the corner, got there at about the same time as the privateer force hurrying down the street – to that extent, it was an ambush and quite effective as such. The descending soldiers literally stumbled over Ringil's squad. Gil battered the lead privateer with his shield, knocked him down, kicked him in the head and left him for someone else to finish. He cut low on the next man, chopped the legs out from under him almost before the privateer realised he was there. Then slip aside as the maimed and screaming soldier tumbled past, plant your feet, meet the third man with *hew* and *block* and *slice*, all the time looking for that opening. Watch those cobbles underfoot – the night's fog and the morning dew had left them slick and treacherous.

The privateer he faced found out the same thing on too much downward momentum – he staggered on a parry, came round too far – the Ravensfriend scythed down, took off his arm just below the elbow. Gout of blood across the air, and the man bellowed like a slaughterhouse ox as he saw it happen. Ringil grabbed him roughly by the jerkin, shoved him aside. Caught some of the blood, warm and wet, across the side of his face as the man fell screaming to the floor.

The imperials had opened out around him like the petals on some malign black rose. Slam of shields and hack and stab – they scooped the surprised privateers in, set them stumbling about on the incline, had slaughtered a half dozen before anyone managed to back up and mount a decent defence. For long moments, panic and confusion swept the League ranks – they couldn't see exactly what kind of force had got in their way, how strong it was, or how well armed. And this outlaw they'd come to take down, wasn't he a black mage or something, was this some kind of sorcery . . .?

Of course, it couldn't last.

'For Hoiran's fucking sake, there's only *five* of them! Form up!'

Like a dog shaking itself, the privateer troop rallied. Shields came down off shoulders, a ragged line formed, backed away for breathing space. The imperials grabbed the chance, drew breath of their own, stood panting. The privateer who'd shouted pushed his way through to the front, grinning savagely beneath an ornate helm that hid his upper face. There was a sergeant's badge emblem painted crudely across his cuirass, an axe held low in his right hand and – Gil's heart sank – a skirmish ranger's coat beneath the armour.

'Right,' he snapped, and pointed with his axe. 'Now cut these perfumed southern ponces *down*, will you.'

Here we go, Gil. Now or never.

Sword arm thrown up, as if blocking a punch, fist reversed, Ravensfriend held vertical, blade pointing down. He took three fingers off the grip, held on to the sword with circled index finger and thumb. He made the glyph. Hoped Hjel's much vaunted Powers were paying close attention, out here in this, come on now, pretty fucking open space.

The skirmish ranger snorted. 'Fuck's that supposed to mean? You want to surrender now, outcast? That all you got?'

'Your helmet is red hot,' Ringil told him.

And watched as the man screamed, dropped his axe and grabbed his helm with both hands, screamed again as his fingers touched the metal and melted from the heat, went to his knees still screaming. The skirmish ranger spasmed to the cobbles, thrashed and rolled and arched in agony, scream on scream on *scream*, until it was done, and finally lay there twitching, eyes poached white in their sockets.

Faint steam curled out of the wrenched gape of his mouth, like a soul departing.

The cost of it all came and took Gil like a kick in the guts. It was a major effort not to flinch, not to sag in the wake of the forces that had passed through him, not to sit down right there on the cobbled street. He lifted the Ravensfriend instead, trembling fingers clenched once more around the grip. He pointed with the blade at the staring privateers. The voice that grated up out of him seemed to belong to another creature entirely.

'*Who's next?*' it asked them.

They broke and ran.

Luckily.

He led the imperials up the street after the rout. Hald could play catch up when he finally broke through along the wharf. He was a smart lad, he'd work it out.

We certainly left enough bodies for him.

They made no real attempt to catch the fleeing privateers – better to let them sow panic in all they met along the way, then deal with any die-hard hero types who didn't buy the tale and decided to make a stand. They took the slope at no more than a brisk walk. Slow enough to let Gil get some breath back and try to master the trembling in his guts. He'd pushed it too far, he knew – just as Hjel had warned him not to – and here came the price. One thing to put imagined terrors and doubts into the minds of ignorant, ill-educated opponents. That came at a light enough toll, was almost, according to Hjel, not sorcery at all. But *this* trick – pulling furnace heat out of the air's very pores, pulling it down on an elite-trained opponent's head in the midst of combat and the blink of an eye . . .

That, you paid for in heavy coin.

The *ikinri 'ska* snaked about within him, like something wanting to be fed. It coiled and snapped in his chest and guts, watered his eyes, shoved jagged spikes down the nerves in his arms and legs. He had no way to get a grip on it.

'Upper window!' Crisp, controlled alert from one of the imperials. 'Left side.'

He swung to look. Saw only a boy of about ten or twelve gaping down at them, pointing finger raised, turning back into the room behind, lips moving.

And grabbed away by a burly, parental form.

'Nothing—' He cleared his throat, gathered some command back into his voice 'Nothing to worry about. Keep the pace.'

Further up, where the sloping thoroughfare took a hairpin turn, they found blood trickling down between the cobbles and tracked it to a stricken privateer. The man was trying to crawl out of the street and into the sanctuary of a narrow gap between neighbouring houses. He'd either staggered this far and then collapsed, or he'd been carried by comrades who'd thought better of the gesture and shed their burden in favour of a speedier retreat. He heard their boots coming and scrabbled over onto his back, propped himself up on one elbow and groped desperately at his belt for a knife that wasn't there. There were smeared puddles of blood on the cobbles where he'd crawled, and a ragged axe gash in his jerkin just above the hip, marking the wound beneath. He looked up at them as they approached, defiant eyes in a sweat-beaded face contorted with pain.

Grim chuckles among the imperials. Their blood was up with the unexpected victory they'd just enjoyed. One of them crouched at the man's side.

'That looks like your handiwork there, Mahmal.' He prodded at the wound and the privateer convulsed with a weak scream. 'Half-arsed butcher's chop like that.'

'Fuck off. He's down, isn't he?'

The crouched imperial cleared a mercy blade from his belt left-handed. 'Yeah, but you gotta learn to—'

'Hold up.' Ringil, stepping between them. 'Let me talk to him.'

The imperial shrugged and moved aside. Ringil took his place and squatted by the injured man's side. He looked down into the sweating countenance. Saw under the blood and grime a face not much out of boyhood. He switched to Naomic.

'You know who I am, son?'

A shaky nod. The man shrank from him as best he could.

'Not the demon blade . . .' he husked.

It took Ringil a moment to understand that what he was hearing was a plea. He reversed his grip on the Ravensfriend, hefted it by the pommel, up where the man could see it.

'This?'

'No! Don't kill me with that. Please, I – I beg. Not – that blade. Don't take my soul.'

'Hm.' *Don't waste this, Gil. Run with it.* 'You want to save your soul, son, you'd better talk to me. I want some answers. And, ehm, have a care – the demon that sleeps in this blade will know if you lie.'

'Yes.' Voice faint and tight with the pain. 'All right, yes. Ask me.'

'Right, first off – what the fuck are you people doing up here? There's nothing worth having in the Hironish – it's the arse end of the League. Any coast-hugger captain knows that much. What's this about?'

'Came for you – Eskiath, outcast.' It was barely a whisper. 'Capture for judgement – or kill.'

'This many men? Come off it.' Gil hefted the Ravensfriend again. 'I said tell the truth.'

'No – wait, *wait*. It *is truth*.' The injured man, panting with panic as well as pain now, gulped a breath. 'Word came – from Lanatray. The outlaw Eskiath, in company of Empire nobles, of men at arms. A voyage north. And now, with the war—'

Ringil blinked. 'War?'

'—you are all proscribed . . . in League territory. We are ordered – detain all – all imperials . . .'

'*What fucking war?*'

The man flinched. 'The imperials – they began it. They took Hinerion . . . with fire and force. They claimed offence . . . justification. The . . . old story.'

Ringil closed his eyes. *Jhiral – you twisted, arrogant little fuckwit, what have you done? What murderous, pimp-strutting piece of idiocy have you loosed on us all now?*

Aware that he was probably looking less than wholly dark and sorcerous, more just sick and tired, he opened his eyes again.

'How long ago was this?'

'Don't know – couple . . . months . . . Maybe more – by the time word came.'

War is declared and battle soon to be joined. The Dark Queen's words floated back through his head. It had never occurred to him that she might be speaking literally.

'How many men?' And then, on a sudden, grim suspicion. 'How many ships?'

'Five – five vessels – but two are now gone – took the prisoners. I . . . crew for *Star of Gergis*. Her muster is . . . eighty-six—'

And the man o' war in the harbour looked good to carry twice that. Plus three more hulls at anybody's guess of tonnage and crew. It beggared belief.

Five fucking ships. Father, you have really outdone yourself this time.

Come off it, Gil. Let's not let our family rancour run away with us. Gingren doesn't swing the weight to accomplish this.

The cabal, then?

An open question. He still had little real sense of the cabal's reach, the extent to which they might or might not govern behind the scenes in Trelayne or even the League in general. He'd met their agents on occasion, but had scant opportunity to interrogate them – the scuffles were always too brutal, the blades too unforgiving, his own unleashed rage too raw. Seethlaw had been using the cabal to consolidate power and influence in the northern cities, this much he did know. But he had no idea whether the cabal itself was a created tool of the dwenda's hand, or simply an existing power structure Seethlaw had seen fit to subvert. He didn't know if it had shrivelled when Seethlaw went away and Ringil returned to the city to wreak vengeful havoc among those who'd abducted his cousin, or if Findrich and the others had merely hunkered down and waited out Gil's poorly planned and clumsily executed revenge. Gil had warned off Risgillen's incursion in Yhelteth last year in no uncertain terms –

I stand watch here! There is no way to this city except through me! – his own screams, shredding at his ears as the temple hall at Afa'marag came collapsing about him, and Risgillen looked on appalled – *The next time I see a dwenda, I cut its heart out and eat it still beating!*

– but he'd never had much doubt Seethlaw's sister would continue to work whatever levers of power she could find in the north.

The Aldrain are bringing the Talons of the Sun, Firfirdar's whispering voice in his head like feathers falling, *To light the skies once more with the glare from a myriad undeserved deaths . . .*

Never mind the cabal, what would the League itself do for a weapon like that? He'd heard Risgillen's boasts, he'd listened to Archeth's account of what she found at Khangset. He didn't understand what exactly the Talons of the Sun was, but what it could do did not seem much in question. A weapon to set the city of Yhelteth aflame like felled and rotted timber. A weapon to bring the whole Empire to its knees.

What would they *not* offer up to Risgillen for that?

Five ships and a few hundred men to capture or kill your brother's murderer, my otherworldly lady, bringer of victory fire? It'd barely count as a good-faith down payment.

He forced his attention back to the wounded privateer.

'Who commands you in this?'

The man quailed. 'Klithren . . . Klithren of Hinerion. Lately knight . . . knight commander under the war muster.'

Ringil's lip curled. 'Oh, really?'

He knew the sort. Scrambling for cheap title and advancement in the frantic, ill-discerning chaos of mobilisation. The war against the Scaled Folk had seen a flood of noble younger sons into posts they were not remotely equipped to fill – *not least one hot-eyed young Ringil Eskiath, come to think of it* – and he supposed this time around would be no different.

The injured man gulped air again. 'They . . . they say Klithren . . . bears you ill-will. Personal, they say. He . . . speaks your name with hate . . . to his pillow at night.'

'How very romantic.' Ringil got to his feet. Saw how the privateer's eyes darted desperately left and right among the towering figures of the enemies that surrounded him. Terror and quailing hope fighting for the upper hand on his tormented face. 'All right, son. Rest easy, we're done. Your soul is safe.'

He made a show of putting aside the Ravensfriend. Saw the flood of relief in the young man's eyes. He nodded at the imperial with the mercy blade.

'Make it quick.'

The imperial knelt, humming a distracted little tune to himself, and slit the man's throat ear to ear. The privateer's lips moved, gusting prayer. Blood welled up and filled the gash, spilled down onto the man's chest, soaked down his jerkin to join the spreading stain from the wound at his hip. Hard to tell if the relief stayed on his face as he died – the imperial was good at his job and the young features went sullen and slack with blood loss, almost the moment the cut was made. The privateer's eyes fluttered closed, like doves settling to a perch, and then he was gone.

Klithren.

Gil brooded. The name meant nothing to him, but then these blood feud names rarely did. Kill enough men, you built a whole clan's-worth of bereaved brothers, fathers, sons and comrades, and they'd all rip out your entrails if they ever got the chance. The upside was that, contrary to popular tales and legend, that chance almost never came. Few outside the nobility had the luxury of the spare time to track you down, let alone the fighting skills to do the deed, or the purse to hire it done. Oh, you might get called out to the odd inconvenient duel, or hear vague word of sneak assassins set on you, who anyway as often as not pocketed the purse and disappeared rather than take the trouble to fulfil their contract . . .

But mostly, you got to sleep at night untroubled. And your murderous deeds were washed away downstream, leached more or less clean of the blood, lost in the slaughterhouse flow of it all. The world forgot and so, in time, did you.

'Anything useful, sir?' Shahn asked him.

Ringil nodded. 'Seems His Imperial Radiance has, in His infinite wisdom, taken us to war in our absence. Hinerion has already fallen.'

'All hail,' said Shahn reflexively, either missing the irony in Gil's words or perhaps just choosing to. He looked significantly at his comrades, and a muted smattering of *All hails* trickled out among them.

'That puts us a thousand miles the wrong side of the line,' someone muttered.

'Then we fight through it,' snapped Shahn. 'And join our comrades at the front in glory, with blood already on our blades.'

'Indeed,' said Ringil, deadpan. 'But first things first, eh? According to our friend here, there's some arsehole with a personal grudge against me leading this lot. If I can find him, we might be able to wrap this up faster than I thought.'

Shahn frowned. 'Single combat, my lord?'

'If he'll take it, yes.'

'Do we know their strength?' asked one of the others.

'Five vessels. But two are already gone south with prisoners.'

'*Five!* Five fucking—'

'*Silence!* My lord Ringil is speaking.'

'I reckon about two fifty, maybe three hundred men,' he went on evenly. 'Most of them ashore. Skeleton crews for the picket ship we passed in the fog, and its sister to the south.'

'And us with less than eighty men.' The same imperial who'd worried over the thousand miles to the front. 'Come on – who'd take single combat over those odds?'

'*Eskiath!*'

It was a raw bellow from up the slope and beyond the turn in the street ahead. A voice bright with rage in the crisp morning air, thick with unreleased longing. Ringil spun towards it with a look on his face the imperials would later describe to their comrades as close to joy.

'Answer your question for you?' he asked absently, scanning the rise.

'*Coward! Outcast!*' The roared challenges rolled down on top of each other, echoing between the houses like the fall of heavy stones. '*Come meet your rightful doom!!*'

'Be right there,' Ringil murmured.

And stalked up the street, as if to something calling him home.

FIFTEEN

Even for Kiriath architecture, An-Kirilnar was pretty fucking impressive.

Sure, anyone who'd ever lived in Yhelteth knew what the Kiriath could build when the mood took them. Sooner or later, you went out and rubbernecked at the Black Folk Span where it leapt across the river, or the Bracing Twins on the imperial palace's distressed northern flank. At one time or another, you'd have seen the estuary defence walls and the eternally dancing prism of green and violet light atop the lighthouse tower where they ended. You'd maybe have passed the cordoned end of the imperial shipyards, where the last remaining fireship in the city rested on its dry-dock props like some huge pupating iron grub. Or you'd have gone one day to peer into the gaping pit at Kaldan Cross and the eldritch scaffolding there that seemed to lead the eye on downward forever . . .

But still.

Pretty fucking impressive.

Egar muttered the words under his breath, as the party walked the ocean-drenched causeway into the shadow of the city, tilting their heads back to take in the silent, overhead loom of the place. An-Kirilnar stood about a hundred feet above the waves, on five thick, supporting columns that would each have dwarfed the estuary lighthouse back in Yhelteth, in girth if not in height. From the shore, it had looked distant and unreal – blank walls the dirty white of old river ice, wrapped tight around a central cluster of spires that glistened now and then as some wandering shaft of sunlight made it down through the cloud. It was like seeing a frost-giant fortress out of some Voronak hunter's tale – something glimpsed through veils of blizzard snow up north along the edges of the Big Ice. Like some tiny chunk of another world dropped into this one. Like something out of myth.

But up close like this, myth melted into something else. The underside of the city, now they were beneath it, looked derelict and used – a vast, dark expanse of stained and variegated alloy surfacing, scarred here and there with patchwork riveting and ugly metal seams that looked to Eg like repairs carried out in haste. He'd seen similar during the war, when the dragons came and the Kiriath engineering corps had to make good the damage to their defences before the next battle. And still, at intervals across this surface, there were broad gaps, some regular enough to be intended aspects of the structure, others looking ragged and wound-like. The wind swept in and hooted eerily among them, brought with it occasional gusts scented with some indefinable chemical reek. Here and there, cabling drooled down out of a gap, like spittle from the mouth of some drunk collapsed asleep over the edge of a table.

They walked beneath as if afraid of waking something up.

'Think this place is haunted?' he heard at his back in Naomic.

Another privateer hawked and spat. 'Nah. Those burnt-blacks are fucking immortal, in't they? How you going to get ghosts if no one ever dies?'

'Yeah, but they could still die in, like, battles and shit. Like at Rajal beach.'

'Fucking *looks* like someone died around here.'

Egar rolled a look back over one shoulder. 'Shut up.'

The men fell silent.

Just as well, really. Not exactly the time or place for knocking heads together, this. A causeway of interlocking five-sided alloy plates each the size of a small shield, but making a path barely a yard and a half across in total, washed a couple of inches deep each time the ocean swell swept across it, and slippery as fuck if you didn't watch your step. Any punch-ups here and all parties would likely end up in the drink. And having seen what could come crawling up out of cracks in the rock on dry land in these parts, Egar wasn't all that keen to try his luck in deep water a couple of miles from shore.

You worry like a boy at a brothel door, Dragonbane. These men aren't going to break ranks on you now, and you know it.

It was herdsman's wisdom first and foremost, gleaned up on the steppe from boyhood on. The buffalo herds followed the big bulls – get the bulls to behave, you had the herd too. But head south and enlist, and you found that what held for steppe buffalo wasn't far out for men either. The pack followed its leaders pretty much the same way.

Yeah, and you broke the big bull back on the beach this morning. Picked him out of the huddled early survivors at a glance, recognised him from among his and Archeth's captors when they were brought aboard *Lord of the Salt Wind* the day before –

Only yesterday? Urann's balls, time flies when you're having fun.

– beckoned him forward.

You with the hair. What do they call you?

What's it to you, Majak? Stirring, rising to a disconcerting two yards plus of muscled height. Fighting scars on the face, and—

And never mind.

Put on a brief grin, Dragonbane, take it off as fast. *What's it to me? Take a look around, why don't you.* Voice abruptly raised. *Go on – the rest of you too. You realise where we've washed up?*

It's the Wastes coast, someone said.

Yeah, it is. Anyone been here before?

Silence.

Well, I have. I was here with the joint expeditionary under Flaradnam Indamaninarmal back in '52. And I was at Gallows Gap on the way back.

A stir of murmurs at the name. If a single battle had caught the imagination of the League populace, it was the stand at Gallows Gap. For the first time, the giant in front of him looked uncertain. Egar locked gazes. Dropped his voice to a more personal level again.

You want to get out of here? A tight nod towards the huddle around the fire. *You want to get these people home in one piece? I'm your man.*

Yeah? Last time I checked, you were a fucking prisoner of war.

Egar let his hands hang loose at his sides, put everything into his eyes. *Check again.*

Long pause.

The giant shifted. *Sogren,* he said. *They call me Cablehand.*

Egar. They call me the Dragonbane.

The causeway ended. More precisely, it opened into what appeared to be an encircling ring, shadowing the curve on the central supporting column, a dozen yards out from the structure itself. Ahead of Egar, Archeth had been setting the pace, as hurriedly as the treacherous surface they walked on would allow. Now she came to an abrupt halt and Egar was so busy casting glances upward that he walked into her back. She teetered forward, he grabbed her by the shoulders, just avoided sending them both into the water.

They stood very still.

'Sorry,' he muttered.

'That's just fucking great.' There was a dull, bitten-off anger in her tone, but it wasn't for him. She gestured outward. 'How the fuck are we supposed to . . .'

Let her arm fall.

They stood staring across at the support column. The surface of the sea heaved and slopped in the gap between – in the shadow of the city's loom, the water was a murky, impenetrable grey. The face of the column rose featureless from it, dirty white alloy, bloomed here and there with patches of green or purplish brown, as if the metal had somehow bruised. If there was a way in anywhere, it didn't show.

The men were piling up behind them. The muttering started again. *Better give them something to do, Eg.*

He snapped his fingers for attention – his old imperial training, woken to the occasion and rising ready for use. He stayed in Tethanne, looked to one of Tand's men to translate quietly into Naomic for the privateers.

'Right, listen up, all of you. I want fifteen men to make a circuit that way, another fifteen this way. Sogren, you take the first party, pick 'em out now. Alwar Nash you pick fifteen more and go the other way. Go *carefully*. You're looking for a doorway, a bridge, a crack – anything that lets us in. Meet at the mid-point, pass each other and keep on going – what one man's eyes miss, another's may find. The rest of you, back up and check overhead. I don't see how, but maybe we missed something important up there.'

Hesitation, glances exchanged. They were cold, tired, hungry and bruised from surviving the storm and the wreck. Caught up in a place they knew only from nightmare tales and legend, armed with nothing beyond a sparse selection of knives, a few salvaged lengths of chain and one or two shattered ship's timbers with enough heft to make a halfway decent club. They were kitted out for a tavern brawl at best, and they were facing monsters out of myth.

Egar spread his arms. 'Come on, people. Let's get to it.'

He let his own two foot piece of chain dangle from the loop he'd made of it around his right hand. He had no intention of using it – could not afford to start maiming or killing men out of a party not fifty strong over some minor issue of discipline. But the chain was a reminder. It still carried the bolts at either end that had anchored it to the chunk of driftwood he'd found it in. And they'd all watched him tear out those bolts one at a time by sheer brute force.

'Yeah, come on.' Sogren gestured impatiently. 'You heard the man. You. You. You . . .'

The tension drained away. Alwar Nash mustered some limited Naomic to make his own selection – though he chose mainly from among the various imperial contingents anyway – and the two search parties formed up. Egar watched them head off, then waved the remaining men back along the main causeway. He turned back to Archeth, who'd sunk into a crouch on the inner rim edge of the ring.

'Any ideas?' he asked her quietly.

'You got any grip on what your ancestors were doing four thousand years ago? No, I don't have any fucking ideas.'

'I thought Grashgal . . . your father . . .'

'Yeah, they were around back then. They didn't talk about it. I don't think they even remembered it all that well.'

He crouched at her side. 'Well, what about that place you found at Shaktur – that was a city standing in the lake, wasn't it?'

'An-Naranash, yeah.' She shook her head. 'Not like this. It was smaller, and they left the doors open when they abandoned it. Anyway, we had a boat back then.'

Egar studied the blank, colour-bruised surface of the support column. Green and reddish-brown blooms like fungus, but no sign of any crack or opening. Not even a purchase point for climbing out of the ocean.

'I'd swim across there,' he offered. 'But—'

'No, you fucking won't.' She looked sideways at him and he saw the apology in her face. 'You think I'm going to let you put yourself in that water? Let that fuck Sogren do it, see what happens to him.'

Egar blinked. 'Sogren's kind of handy to have around at the moment. He do something to upset you?'

She shook her head wearily. 'Forget it. Anyway, what's the fucking point? There's no way in, even if he did survive the swim.'

'Okay, Archidi, but we got to come up with something. It's cold, and it's going to get colder with the dark. Either we get inside this thing pretty sharpish, or we have to head back to the beach and get a fresh fire built.'

'You think I don't know that?'

He fixed his gaze on the support column and its bruises. Greenish blue and crimson, purplish black. He sighed.

'I think,' he said carefully, 'that you're cold and tired and pissed off that this isn't turning out the way you hoped. And you'd probably sit here until you freeze rather than—'

Wait a minute . . .

'Archidi . . .' Long hesitation because he wanted to be sure. 'Look.'

'Skip it, Eg. I don't want to talk about it.'

'No, *look.*' He leapt upright, pointed. 'Look at it, look at the colours. They're changing, they're . . . shifting or something . . .'

They both stared over the water at the blooms on the dirty white alloy column. The greenish-blue patch lost its last few tinges of green as they watched. The crimson began to darken, tipping towards the colour of old meat. The purplish-black mark paled, crept into violet.

'No,' Archeth, climbing slowly to her feet. 'Fucking. Way.'

'You want to bet?' For some reason there was a grin on his face. 'They're moving around too. Look.'

It was like watching the passage of slow clouds across the sky. Some force inched the patches of colour along, squeezing them thinner, puffing them out, sculpting fresh lines and curves along their edges, all so gradually that if you looked away too soon – or, say, if you stood around with a bunch of tired and worn shipwrecked men looking for a doorway that wasn't there – you'd miss it.

'You know what that is?' Archeth asked him with sudden energy.

'I was hoping you'd tell me.'

'It's a . . .' she stopped, lips moving silently as she mustered, he guessed, a translation from High Kir. 'A species portcullis. Built for the dwenda wars. It locks out anyone who isn't Kiriath. Can't believe I didn't recognise it – the Indirath M'Nal talks about them all the time. All I have to do is name the colours out loud.'

'Well . . .' Egar frowned. 'So anyone who speaks High Kir could get in, really.'

'No. Human eyes don't work the same way as Kiriath – it's a subtle difference, but it's there.' A wan smile. 'Why my mother and I could never agree on clothes. Even if you knew the words in High Kir, you wouldn't have the vision to identify them. I guess that must have been true for the dwenda too.'

She stepped back and narrowed her eyes at the crawling blotches of colour. Cleared her throat, raised her chin and uttered a paced string of syllables.

Waited. A good few seconds.

They exchanged a glance.

'Are you sure you and your mother didn't just—'

The ocean rose up before them, roaring.

SIXTEEN

Klithren of Hinerion, newly minted League knight commander, was not quite the fop Gil had been hoping for.

He stood at the top of the rise, backed by a knot of men in skirmish ranger gear, and in his stance alone, Ringil read trouble. There was nothing affected about it, no trace of show for the men at his back or bravado for his approaching enemy. In fact, for a man bearing a blood grudge, Klithren looked uncommonly relaxed. He stood with a sword held low in each hand, no more tense than a craftsman with his tools contemplating the start of the day's work. He was no youngster, probably had a good few years on Gil himself, but he wore it well – taut midriff showing left and right of his cuirass's lower curves; muscular dancer's legs and probably a nice tight arse at the top of them. Big in the shoulders, long in the arms, the wrap of the cabled muscles easy to read under the mail that covered them.

'How now, Eskiath?' he called, as Ringil got within easy hailing distance. 'Remember me?'

'Not really, no.'

In fact, there was something familiar about the face, but that could just have been the combination of weathered features and warrior calm. He'd rubbed shoulders with men of this temper countless times in the war, faced down a few when his command was called into question, fought and killed a few more in the snapping, snarling mess that followed, when the Scaled Folk were defeated and League and Empire went back to their habitual dogfight scrabbling over territory and the souls of men . . .

This could have been any one of them.

'You *lie*, faggot!' Gil's answer seemed to have shaken Klithren's poise a little. The calm on his face broke up in a scowl. His top lip lifted off his teeth.

Ringil raised sword and shield in a fractional shrug. 'I hear you're upset about something I did, but I'm afraid you're going to have to refresh my memory.'

Klithren twitched forward, and now his voice shook. 'Perhaps, *fucker*, you don't remember my face because when you struck me down in Hinerion, it was from behind, just like the faggot *coward* you are. Perhaps instead you'll remember *Venj*, whose guts you spilled across the street like night soil, like *I'm going to fucking do to yours!*'

Ah.

Through veils of dimly remembered fever and frailty, now he placed the face. The voice.

Some fucking retirement, eh pal? Hunting bandits in a foreign land for fifty florins a pop.

The candled gloom of the bounty office in Hinerion. Grim shared hilarity, and men of violence waiting on the call. His incipient fever-ish trembling, banished by an effort of will as he clung to his assumed disguise and a thin semblance of good health, and joined in the brutal camaraderie as best he could.

I pride myself on being a judge of men with steel. And you're like me, you've held a command. Got the rank, the experience. Man like that, be glad to have you ride with us.

The tavern after, Klithren's bizarre enthusiasm for alliance, and that bullying little turd Venj in his train – the instinctive clash, the looks the axeman shot Gil as he left. And later, on the sloping cobbled street, that same crowing, bullying sneer.

Well, well, well. Thought that was a dodgy fucking Yhelteth accent if ever I heard one. Thought I knew the face from somewhere.

And then the dance of shadows out of nowhere and the fine patter of blood like rain on his face as he watched the slaughter like something that had nothing to do with him at all.

He stood on the sloping cobbled street – this *other* sloping cobbled street – and was dizzied for a moment by the swinging hinge of past over present time. The way his existence seemed to convulse about him like some crumpled parchment tossed onto the fire.

Are we all like this? he had an instant to wonder. *Parchment lives written out in lines and held rigid in time until, one by one, we all crumple and twist and flare away to nothing in Firfirdar's flames?*

'So *now* you know me, Eskiath.' The march of memory must have shown on his face. There was no real question in the other man's voice, only a certitude of hate. Gil remembered the final moment – Klithren bent over Venj's slaughtered form, back turned to Ringil in the confidence of com-radeship or maybe just the emotion of the moment.

He was an arrogant little fuck sometimes. But you couldn't ask for a better man at your back in a scrap. Saved my life a couple of times for sure.

And the nape of Klithren's neck, offered . . .

'Now you remember, coward!'

Ringil took hold, pulled himself back through the storm of time and into the now. Like hauling in canvas on a trimmed sail. He looked into Klithren's newly familiar face.

'Yeah, I remember I spared your life last time around. Want me to remedy that?'

Klithren's hands clenched around each sword hilt. He bared his teeth.

'Let's see you try, faggot.'

But he didn't quite hurl himself forward on the challenge. The imperials had come up on Ringil's flanks and stood there like so many watchful shadows. Only four men, but somehow the balance in the street shifted with their arrival, and a new moment unfolded.

Grab it, Gil.

'All right, darling – you can have me.' he smooched a brief kiss at Klithren. 'But if this is personal, it stays that way. Got it?'

Pause. The mercenary sneered.

'Single combat? Are you fucking dreaming?'

'Ah – not quite so personal after all, then.'

A quiet arose between the faced-off parties, so intense that Ringil caught the soft moan of sea breezes down the rising hairpin streets and alleys of the town around them.

Shifting among the skirmish rangers at Klithren's back. Murmuring.

Klithren gestured. 'Why would I, outcast? The bulk of your force is already defeated and sent south to Trelayne, your nobles included. I hold this town in the palm of my hand. My men outnumber yours three to one.'

One of the imperials, who apparently had some Naomic, coughed out laughter. 'Yeah? Funny how we just chase them up street a minute gone.'

The skirmish rangers bristled. At Ringil's shoulder, another Empire man spat on the cobbled street and mustered his own rough take on the northern tongue.

'Go down to harbour, look for self, pirate scum,' he snapped. 'You're against imperial marine this time. You're fucking done.'

'And that isn't even the point,' said Ringil softly. He held Klithren's eye. 'Is it?'

The moment leaned over them all, like the shade of a passing summer cloud. Klithren twitched. Nodded. He turned his head aside, toward the nearest of the skirmish rangers.

'Captain. If I fall here, you will grant safe passage to the imperials out of Ornley and south. You will not—'

'My lord! We—'

'Shut up and recall your fucking oath, Captain!'

The skirmish ranger subsided, just barely. Klithren waited a couple of beats. Laid out his words like measured paces.

'You will not pursue them, you will let them walk. You will let them sail away. Is that understood? On your soul before the Dark Court, I want your word you'll see it done.'

Brief, stiff silence, while they all waited.

'On my soul before the Dark Court,' gritted the ranger captain. 'I will see it done as you command. But they—'

'Yes, quite.' The mercenary jerked his chin at Ringil. 'Your turn. You lose, your men lay down their arms and submit. I want to hear your marine pals say it. And I warn you, my Tethanne's pretty good – you try and fuck me here, I'm going to hear it.'

Gil nodded. He switched to Tethanne, raised his voice for the imperials so they could all hear. 'Have you understood the terms?' he asked.

'It isn't complicated,' said one of the men who'd spoken in Naomic before.

'Yeah,' agreed another. 'You kick this piece of shit's arse, they surrender. You lose, we do the same. Not going to lose, are you, my lord?'

Ringil held back a smile. 'No, I'm not going to lose. But this is my word, and yours, that we stand on. Under the lady kir-Archeth, I command this expedition, and she is now a prisoner. That leaves me. If I fall, you see to it that Commander Hald honours my terms.'

'It will be done,' said the man who'd slit the injured privateer's throat, and with about as much emotion. 'If this pirate rabble can keep faith, will an imperial marine not?'

'Good enough?' Gil asked Klithren, in Naomic again. He gestured with his shield at the ground between them. 'Shall we?'

The duel space opened around them like some quiet clockwork trick, like the iris of an eye in thickening light. The men at their backs gave instinctive ground, the duellists moved crabwise and cautious, reading each other's movements for error or slack. Gil circled up slope to the right, Klithren let him come, gave ground down and left. Soft scuff of boot leather on the cobbles underfoot. The early morning sun threw slant shadows off the roofs of houses and down on the street. Broad bars of warmth and chill for the two men to move in. A gull carped shrilly at them from its overlooking roof-top perch. A hollow brightness held the air.

Best weather we've had since I got here.

Klithren rushed in.

Conventional enough – the longer of the two swords chopping down, the shorter stabbing in from the side – but very fast. Gil got his shield up in the way of the bigger blade, took the impact of a blow only partly committed, heard the muted clank it made in the morning air. He fended off the short sword with the Ravensfriend reversed downward – harsh scrape of steel on steel as the weapons crossed. He stabbed slantwise down on the same move, and Klithren had to leap backward to avoid getting skewered through the foot. Gil made a hard feint after him with the shield, watched over the rim to see what the mercenary's instinctive guard looked like – answer: it looked pretty good – then let him go.

Testing, testing . . .

Ringil reached inside himself where the magic was, found the *ikinri 'ska* still too slippery and restless to get a hold on. Even the brief effort he made kicked a pit of nausea open in his throat, put tiny sparks across his vision. No chance, no chance at all.

Guess we'll just have to do this the hard way.

He drifted unhurriedly towards Klithren, waited for the other man's reaction. Klithren let him come. He had the slope, a shallow slanting angle on it anyway, and Gil's attack would have to be made uphill, with all the cost that implied. The mercenary's lips were parted as he watched, his sword blades held open as if in invitation, as if to embrace. Ringil grinned and nodded amiably as if something had just been agreed – put an abrupt spurt of speed on his approach, drove hard with one foot, raised his shield in a repeat of the feint he'd made before. Klithren read it, wasn't buying that or Ringil's distracting smile, kept his eyes full on the sweep of the Ravensfriend – and Gil, driving hard from the same foot, rammed the shield all the way home.

Klithren staggered, swung to block, both blades at once. The Ravensfriend leapt into the gap it left, faster than human steel could have moved. Sliced one mailed arm at the shoulder, bit through the metal links with no more effort than if they'd been leather weave. Klithren roared and struck back with his broadsword, in at thigh height. Gil chopped his shield down, killed the blow, snapped his own blade up across the other man's face. Klithren recoiled – but the Ravensfriend kissed a pair of sparks off the cheek-guard of his helm before he got clear.

Something subtly wrong with the pattern of it all . . .

Ringil pressed the attack, gave himself no time to think. *Get this done.* The Ravensfriend went for Klithren's throat like an enraged wolfhound, seemed to drag Gil along more for company than because he was striking the blow. The mercenary blocked with the short blade, swung his other sword in from the side. Gil took it on the shield, was moving aside anyway, dropped his wrist and stabbed low. The Ravensfriend snagged Klithren's mail above the hip, below the curve of his cuirass. Chewed through again – bright spill of blood and wisp of smoke in the shining air. Gil pivoted and withdrew, gouging back hard with the blade's edge, along the wound he'd made. Klithren screamed and—

Smoke?

—the short blade, out of nowhere, glinting down. It screeched on Gil's cuirass, bounced off, punched him back. Fleetingly, he saw Klithren had reversed his grip on the weapon, must have let go, rolled the hilt off his thumb on the blade's own weight in mid-air, grabbed it up inverted and stabbed down, all in the same split second and riding the pain of the wound in his side. There was just time for Gil to appreciate the grit and speed it would take to do all that, the momentary unsettling in his guts at the realisation he was fighting an equal here after all. Then his shield was back in the way, yanked in on instinct to take another blow from Klithren's broadsword that he never actually saw coming.

Fucking smoke?!

He backed up. Klithren snarled a grin across the space it opened between them.

'Ready to die now, faggot?' Klithren, who should have been leaking blood copiously down his left leg from the torn up mess of the wound above his hip. Gil could almost see the way it ought to look, as if it were somehow *there*, in alternate moments, laid over the wound the mercenary actually bore, which looked barely knife-nick deep and didn't seem to trouble him at all. *And let's not forget the shoulder, Gil* – another solid chop that ought to have sliced and levered open the knit of the muscle there, *ought* to have made any major motion of that arm a screaming agony thereafter.

Instead, as Ringil watched, Klithren flipped the reversed short sword in the air with that hand, caught it upright again, barely grimaced as he did it.

Made it look easy.

'Well?' he jeered. 'That all you fucking got?'

'Why don't you ask your friend Venj?' Gil shut out his misgivings, gathered himself. 'You'll be seeing him soon enough.'

He hurled himself forward on the last word. Ravensfriend upflung, inviting the block, then snatched down in the instant that Klithren took the bait. He drove for the other man's leg. Somehow, the mercenary got there first, slammed a block on the Ravensfriend with his broadsword that drove the Kiriath weapon down into the cobbles and locked it there.

The short sword came leaping, in at head height.

Gil felt it more than saw it. Could only drop his chin and hope.

The blade caught him a savage blow across the top of the helm, jarred it almost off his head, then skidded off the metal curve and sent him stumbling, head ringing with the impact, shield wrong-sided and useless, sword hand barely clinging to the Ravensfriend's hilt.

It was all he could do to keep his feet.

Whoop of triumph from Klithren, and abruptly he felt a chilly urchin hand on his arm, tugging him to one side. He went with it, heard the other man's broadsword slice the air apart where he'd been. Reeling, he thought he'd found his feet for a moment, but then there was another urchin tug and this time it took him to the ground. He hit the cobbles hard, full length, banged his head. Felt his helm come loose with the impact, heard it roll clinking away, and realised at the same moment that Gerin's ghostly grip was on the Ravensfriend, dragging it out of his grasp . . .

He rolled soggily onto his back, shield an impossible weight pinning down his left arm at his side, sword hand empty. Saw Klithren walk up to him and block out the sky like some towering, triumphant god he'd managed to upset. He felt the point of the mercenary's broadsword jab in under his chin, press down for a long moment, then snick loose again. Blood welled and trickled where it had been.

He guessed his throat had been slit, and marvelled at how little it hurt.

Klithren crouched down, tucked the fingers of his left hand in where the sword point had gone, then brought them back up into view, smeared wet and red with Ringil's blood. He looked at the blood quizzically for a moment, then got to his feet again.

Spat in Ringil's face.

'Some fucking hero,' he said flatly. 'The Silverleaf crew were a harder take than you.'

Ringil, still belatedly working out that his throat had probably not been cut after all, could make no sense of the words. All he knew was that Gerin's ghost hand was cold on his brow and other hands, bigger but equally chilling, tugged at his arm as if to hurry him away at some impossible angle to the rest of the world

Klithren turned away, then seemed to think better of it. He stepped wide, came back and swung one colossal god-sized boot, hard into the side of Ringil's head.

The sky went out, like candles snuffed.

SEVENTEEN

At times, he feels no more than a tapestry stitching of a man.

He moves, he acts, as ever, but it's as if every action has an echo in his own head, as if he can stand there and watch himself perform it without really being involved. He did this consciously a few times on the voyage north – let his hands go on with a task without him. Stared down at them as if they belonged to another man entirely, as if he could get up and wander away from his own body, and trust it to complete whatever duty had been assigned.

It sits ill with him, this detachment hovering constantly in the corner of his eye. He's a soldier after all, and what's a soldier if not a man of forthright action. Leave maundering down the well of deep thoughts to the inkspurt clerks and greybeards they pay so handsomely to do that stuff. Last time he held a quill was when they asked him to make his mark on the articles of enlistment. His right hand has had other employment since, and ink is not a stain it's familiar with. He is no clerk. His chosen tools are sword and axe and shield, mute iron witnesses to the life he's carved out for himself, and the lives of others he's spilled out in bloody ruin along the way. He has memories of slaughter in a half dozen different places across the Empire, though he doesn't revisit them much. What would be the point? He has the decorations and scars to prove he was there. He has the body, the heart and the brain of a soldier, and all he wants is the simple peace of mind that should go with it.

Is that so much to ask?

Not like he'd done badly for himself until recently either – assignment in honour to the Emperor's own personal advisor, the last remaining Kiriath in the world. He recalls how he swelled inside with rich satisfaction when he woke the morning after that news, and remembered the posting was his. Service aboard a river frigate – not generally something a marine would shout about, Yhelteth doesn't do much of its fighting on rivers; they're strategically important to be sure, and sometimes need policing like any other aspect of Empire, but no one ever launched a real threat to the Burnished Throne from a river. This river frigate, though, appointed specifically to carry the lady Archeth Indamaninarmal to and from her ancestral home at An-Monal, this was something special. He's not sure why, exactly, but from the beginning it felt right. *Destined. The lady Archeth felt* important, *still does in some indefinable way that nothing in his blunt soldier's pragmatism can pin down.*

All he knows is that he needs to be by her side.

He was not in the least surprised when the news broke that she would be leading a quest into the north. But he remembers the crushing anxiety he felt that he might not be among those finally selected to escort her, then the relief and joy when the orders came down that he would. He traded vessel assignment with another comrade, even though it meant a lesser post, so that he could serve aboard Sea Eagle's Daughter *and stay closer to the lady Archeth. He kept an eye on her cabin whenever he took night watches, and whenever she went ashore during the voyage around the cape, he did his utmost to get assignment in her guard. He did these things instinctively, rarely, if ever, questioning the impulses that drove him. Thinking that way, questioning his basic assumptions, didn't feel good. It distanced him from the comfort that soldiering brought, and at times it seemed to bring on that same cursed sense of detachment once more.*

The Kiriath built the Empire, their magic and their learning sustained it even now. There. Service to the last of their kind could only be service of the highest sort to the Empire itself and all its peoples.

Something like that, anyway.

And now it's all up in flames, it's a fucking mess, and not one cursed thing he can do about it. Ornley fallen to League privateer scum, the lady Archeth taken as prisoner and spirited away by ship, most likely south to Trelayne. Lord Ringil defeated, despite his dark arts and lethal steel prowess. Brought low by a common freebooter just when victory seemed within his grasp. And the imperial forces scattered, some already taken in chains with the lady Archeth, the rest awaiting a similar fate. Locked in the town jail or, like him, thrust in small groups into the dark, damp, stinking confines of individual cellars all across Ornley.

He snarls and thumps his fist impotently into the rough stone wall at his side, rakes it sideways so the skin over his knuckles breaks and oozes thick, slow droplets of blood. The others startle for a moment in the gloom, stare at him, see what he's done. The pain burns briefly, but it's distant, no contender anyway for the other scrapes and bumps and minor gashes he collected in the day's fight. He grits his teeth, hisses through them like something cornered. His companions look away, staring wordless into the glow from the candle stubs guttering on the cellar's earthen floor. He can hardly blame them. They have their own demons to contend with – ignominious defeat, forced surrender, most likely torture to look forward to once the League forces get organised, digest their victory and decide it's time to do some questioning.

He turns his clenched fist in the flicker of the candles, looks incuriously at the torn knuckles. In the scant, uncertain light, his blood is black.

Should never have done it.

Should never have accepted assignment to the search parties and Dragon's Demise.

Should never have trusted that the lady Archeth would be safe out of his sight, even in this dull-as-dishwater fish-reeking northern shit-hole.

Should never have bought into the logic that said the real threat now was the undead sorcerer lord whose grave they sought, that being there to take that fucker down quick and hard was the best service he could render both Empire and the lady Archeth too.

Would not have trusted either, not any of it, were it not for the softly murmured persuasion of that fucking Helmsman.

EIGHTEEN

He wakes on a bedroll beside a softly crackling fire. Red sparks escaping skyward over his head, to mingle with the cold white scatter of stars. He props himself up and stares through the waver of flames to where Hjel the Dispossessed sits with mandolin in lap and broad-brimmed hat slanted forward over his eyes.

How'd you find me? he asks.

Hjel nods across the fire. *They brought you.*

Three figures sit cross-legged around the fire to his right, heads bowed as if in prayer. They don't speak or look at him, they give no sign they know Ringil and Hjel are there with them at all. They don't even breathe. Aside from the occasional pluck of the night breeze at their ragged garments, they might be statues, carved there in obsidian to mark some auspicious campfire meeting from whatever chronicled histories this place might own.

But they aren't statues.

They are his dead. His own personal cold command – though actually commanding them in anything is something he still has no inkling how to do. He knows only that they've been with him in one way or another since Hinerion and the slave caravan. That every so often, when his own death looms inescapably close, they will step out of whatever shadows they normally keep to and add a chilly thumb to the scales of chance, to steer him safe and clear.

He supposes he should be grateful for the mechanism, whatever it is. But all he feels when he looks at them is an awful, plummeting grief.

The rangy one with the mutilated head and face, gazing down at a gore-streaked sword he holds balanced on his thighs, cupped lightly in both hands at pommel and point.

The big, blunt one with the scarred hands and the blacksmith's hammer in his lap.

The boy Gerin . . .

Half-starved urchin face intent, thin hands empty – the only one he actually saw die, the only one whose name he knows, but somehow the link that pins the three of them together and cements them all to Gil.

He's not even sure if they know they're dead.

Come to that . . .

He looks at one hand, turns it in the firelight. *Am I . . . ?*

No. Hjel smiles into the flames. *Very far from it. In fact, from what I can see, you are barely here at all. Whatever your shade guard brought here is the thinnest of essences. More's the pity. That hard warrior's body of yours is still back in whichever real world owns it.*

Some fucking warrior. Memory crashes in on him. *I lost. I got my arse handed to me by some low rent border thug with a grudge.*

Hjel's smile melts into a frown. *That seems unlikely.*

Hey, you weren't fucking there.

Did you want to lose?

Oh, yeah. Just tired of life, me.

The dispossessed sorcerer prince lifts his head and nails him with a glitter-eyed stare. *You shouldn't joke about that. I see a weariness and a self-hatred in you that might burn down half the world if you unleashed it, if you finally gave up caring and let go. Now answer me –* did you want to lose?

Ringil sits fully up. Stares down the cold blade of his memories for a while.

No, he says finally. *It was single combat. The lives and freedom of my men if I won.*

The impotent fury of it sits in his belly like the ache of an old wound.

Hjel shrugs. *Then you misjudged your opponent. He is clearly not . . . some low rent border thug after all.*

He fucking is.

Then he had help. Hjel lifts his hands from the strings of his mandolin, gestures open-palmed. *How else would he best you? Think about it. See it again. What went wrong?*

Gil peers back into the last solid moments of the duel. He sees again the damage he dealt, the way Klithren weathered it, shrugged it off as if it didn't matter. He sees again the wisps of blue smoke that join the other man's blood as it spills, the way the wounds didn't—

No, not smoke.

Suddenly, he's certain. He sees it again in his mind's eye, the wisp *and flicker of fragmented blue fire like lightning . . .*

He missed it for what it was in the bright morning air, missed the connection, and in absence of that link, his eyes had made what sense of it they could on their own. He saw smoke. Now, he looks up at Hjel in dawning shock.

Oh, shit.

The dispossessed prince nods. *Tell me.*

I think the dwenda just chose a human champion.

I thought they chose you.

Yeah, well, look how that worked out. Something approaching pique creeping into his tone now. *Looks like they're trying the low end of the market this time.*

That the great Elder race out of legend could be satisfied with someone as, well, as *basic* as Klithren.

You work with the tools at hand, Dakovash told him once of the Dark Court's policies. No reason, he supposed, that the dwenda should be any less pragmatic.

But still, somehow . . .

I've got to go back.

You've got to go back, agrees Hjel, and strums a gently chiming chord out of his mandolin. *In fact—*

He woke with a start, on a low wooden cot in the soft light of a lantern set on the floor at his side. Splutter and splash of water somewhere faint, blank boards and beams of a cabin roof overhead. Way less clearance than the imperial shipwrights habitually built for, and the woodwork was worn and split with age – he was aboard one of Klithren's League vessels, then. Sickly heavy reek like temple incense in his parched throat, a deep ache in his jaws and a banging head. Sluggishness through his veins, and the pain was distant – it felt as though they'd drugged him with something. He tried to sit up and failed – found his hands crossed over his chest like the wings of a bird, roped together at wrists and thumbs, multiple coils of thinner cord wound tightly round his palms and fingers.

Thicker ropes were secured tightly right round the frame of the cot, pinning him in place. He tried to shift his legs, found similar bindings there.

Someone wasn't taking any chances.

And the ache in his jaw – the same someone had jammed his mouth open on a rough wooden wedge, then gagged him with silk strips soaked in some anointing oil and knotted savagely tight at the nape of his neck. Pain from the pressure flowed steadily up and around to join the throb in his head, where a broad contusion gripped hotly at one temple and the side of his brow.

No fucking guesses as to how that got there.

A grunt that wasn't his. He twisted his head awkwardly and glared across the glow of the lantern to where Klithren of Hinerion sat on a low stool, watching him from the other side of the cabin.

'Comfortable?' the mercenary asked him.

Ringil let his gaze turn back up to the wooden ceiling. Judging by the gentle tilt in the cabin space around him, they were at sea. Bound for Trelayne, he assumed.

'If Venj could see you now, eh?'

He flickered Klithren a sideways glance. Rolled his eyes.

Flurry of motion and the other man leant over him, close enough to smell coffee and lemon on his breath. A mercy blade glinted in one raised hand. Gil felt it snick in behind his ear and lift the cartilage a hairs' breadth away from his skull.

'If I were you, *faggot,*' said Klithren, soft and very intent, 'I'd keep what manners you can about you on this voyage. I am charged with delivering you to Trelayne as intact as possible, but there's none to say what harm I might need to inflict on you to staunch your black mage sorceries.'

Gil held the other man's stare with his own. Poured every ounce of contempt he could muster into his look. He wondered briefly if Risgillen was fucking this one to keep him in thrall.

What, the way Seethlaw was fucking you, you mean? To keep you in thrall.

The thought must have kindled some extra measure of hate in his eyes. Klithren broke gaze. Snorted and put his knife away.

'Don't know why I bother. I'm pretty sure what they'll do to you in Trelayne is going to make anything I can put you through here look like tickling.'

He got up and turned away, stood with his back to Ringil a moment or two. Turned back, face still dark with anger. He gestured at the way Gil was trussed.

'You know, my men wanted a more permanent solution than this. They wanted your fingers and thumbs hacked off. Your tongue sliced out at the root. Took some convincing out of it too. You're alone on this vessel, Eskiath. I left your men under guard back in Ornley, pending pick up from my other ships.'

Yeah, you'll be lucky. He'd sent the akyia after the League picket vessels.

'So it's just you, me and a boatload of privateers who hate your black mage guts. These men are plain sailor stock; they're way past superstitious at the best of times, and let me tell you, right now is not the best of times.'

The mercenary prowled the cabin in the low light from the lantern. He seemed distracted, and a lot less happy than you'd expect under the circumstances. If he was pleased with his victory over Ringil, there was precious little sign of it.

'They're nervous, you see. They're full of fears about kraken and mer-roigai and unholy consuming fire, and they've got a fully declared war for an excuse. I don't honestly think it'd take much for them to roll right over me. Break in here to get you and then sacrifice you to the Salt Lord in the old way. And while I have a contract with some very important men in Trelayne, I'm just as well served seeing you strung up from the rigging and torn apart with boathooks, and then telling my employers that dead was the best I could do.'

No Risgillen, then. Or at least not bluntly front and centre the way Seethlaw had been. Maybe Klithren was into the cabal and not the Chancellery for his commission and his new command, but he didn't seem to be aware of the other gifts he'd been given.

Not yet, anyway.

Well, nor were you at the time, Gil. Nor were you.

'Think it over,' the mercenary told him. 'Think about behaving. When I come back, maybe I'll bring you some water.'

He got up, took the lantern and went to the cabin door, passed out of

Ringil's field of vision as he did so. Banged the door on his way out with what sounded like unnecessary force.

Without the lantern, the cabin was sunk in a darkness relieved only by the faint gleam of band-light through a single porthole in the far wall. Ringil waited in the gloom a while to make sure Klithren really had gone, then set about exploring his bonds at greater length, carefully testing each coil and knot for some measure of play. He found none. Sailor stock, sure enough.

He couldn't get loose, and he certainly couldn't use the *ikinri 'ska*.

If it would even work in here.

He spent a while reflecting on the irony of getting sacrificed to the Salt Lord, when Dakovash and his fellow dark courtiers had apparently spent the last couple of years moving heaven and earth and a few other places besides to shape him into their champion.

Dakovash – yeah, where's that slippery fucker when you need him? Or Firfirdar, Hoiran and the rest, for that matter.

The Court has always had faith in your ability to find your own way. It is what draws us to you.

Ask yourself – what use does any god have for worshippers who tug constantly at her sleeve like so many over-mothered children?

Yes, well.

He drifted for a while after that, trying not to focus on the raw pain in his mouth, his dust-dry throat and his stiffened muscles. He wondered if there was some way to get through to the Grey Places that didn't involve actual sorcerous effort. He'd woken there on occasion in the midst of fevers or while drunk, with no clear recollection of how it had happened. He didn't know, looking back, if he owed some dark courtier or other for the passage, or if he'd somehow done it himself and then forgotten. Or if, on those occasions, he'd just been dreaming and never really gone in the first place

Come to that, even if he could push through right now, wouldn't he wake there still bound and roped to this fucking cot?

As you step through from your own world, so exactly you will arrive in the Margins.

Hjel, explaining to Gil as his father once explained it to him. Wisdom handed down the line of dispossessed princes from the Creature at the Crossroads. It was, Hjel tells him, something to do with *conservation*, though what was conserved and in what kind of vessels, he admits he doesn't know. Those mysterious black glass long-jars they sometimes stumble on in rusting waist-high racks or discarded in piles at certain points on their travels, perhaps . . .

The first time Hjel shows him the jars, he tries to pick one up from the top of its rack and is mildly shocked at the weight. They're slim and gently tapered, about the length of a modest broadsword and the girth of a fortification fence pole at the thick end, but they're heavier than the biggest campaign pack he's ever had to lift. The closed ones are faintly warm to the touch and capped off at the tapered end with bluntly rounded stoppers that remind him, frankly, of nothing so much as the end of a gigantic straining cock. There's no sign of handles or even wrapping bolts to knot a carry cord, so he manhandles the thing with open hands, gathers it back in his arms like a big bonfire log, into the crook of his elbows and up against his chest with a rolling impact that makes him grunt. There's space for another one stacked against the first, but he doubts he could hold them both up. He doubts he could carry this one more than fifty feet without setting it down to rest.

What's in *here?* he pants at Hjel.

The sorcerer prince shrugs. *You're asking the wrong man. You can't get them open, and they will not break. Many have tried.*

Ringil lets go with a gasp, leaps back to save his toes and proves Hjel's point as the released canister crashes down against one rusted corner of the rack, then tumbles to the floor apparently none the worse for the impact. He crouches and rolls it carefully over on the ground a couple of times but can find no damage, not even a scratch.

He does, however, in the course of his search come up with a single imperfection in the jar's surface – about a third of the way down from the cap, minute lines of script are etched lengthways into the smooth black glass curve, in an alphabet he cannot read. Next to them is set an equally tiny etched image – a human skull apparently fracturing apart under the influence of what might have been the sun's rays, except that they fall not from a sun but from a curious symbol like a double looped knot or maybe a pair of empty oval eyes just touching in the middle and staring outward.

He can't read it, can't decipher it at all. But if that's not a warding, a binding spell of some sort, then he doesn't know what is.

Hjel shifts impatiently behind him. *If we spend so long poring over every lost thing the Margins offer up, we'll never reach the glyph cliffs at all.*

Are they all marked like this?

The sorcerer prince sighs. *Yes. Every one I've ever looked at is marked like that. And no, I have no clue what it says. Hang around in the Margins long enough, you get used to that sort of thing. Now come on, let's get out of here.*

Ringil brushes his fingertips across the minutely carved glyphs, feels their tiny tracks through the calluses a lifetime of swordsmanship has left on his skin. Then he looks away across the marsh plain around them, the empty grey sky these things have lain abandoned under for who knows how many thousands of years, and a shiver comes to walk up his spine.

Can't read it, can't decipher the spell. And suddenly he doesn't want to.

Later on in the journey – what feels like days later, but in the Grey Places who can tell? – Hjel relents a little and takes them off the paved track they're following. He shows Ringil a place between standing stones where the ground is scattered with more of the same jars, all of them opened. Gil goes to pick one up and finds it almost weightless. It's a comical moment, he staggers upright with the surplus force he's unleashed to lift the thing, nearly goes over on his arse as a result. He recovers, catches Hjel smirking.

Very fucking funny.

Yeah, thought you'd like it.

Gil tips the canister cautiously back and forth on his open palms, mindful of nesting marsh spiders or worse, but nothing falls out. At the narrower end, the glans-shaped stopper is gone entirely, nowhere to be seen on the surrounding ground. The jar's surface is cool to the touch, almost cold, and the black glass has turned a pale, smudged grey, marked out, now he looks closer, with tightly whorled patterns continuous along its length. When he upends the jar to peer inside, there's nothing to see but a slim empty space and the same whorl pattern, filtering the light that gets through the glass so it dapples the interior in the weirdly restful shades of a charcoal sketch.

You'd think something would nest in these, he says, hefting the vessel in both hands.

Hjel nods. *Yes, but nothing ever does. Smell.*

Suspecting another joke at his expense, Gil lifts the open jar end closer to his face and sniffs. Catches a scent like thunder recently departed – must sniff again to be sure he hasn't imagined it – catches it again, clearer and closer this time – the same thick odour the air carries after lightning strikes close by, but pared down to a wavering remnant of itself, as if you could somehow pick up the trailing reek of some storm that passed this way a thousand years ago . . .

He looks up, disbelieving.

Right. Hjel has lost any trace of a grin he might have had. *Now listen to it.*

Past any fear of pranks, Gil lowers one ear to the open end of the jar, and this time his senses are sharpened enough to be sure first time.

Right down at the limits of hearing, he picks it up – a constant seething, chittering, like specks of oil on a heated pan in another room. Or the hisses and clicks of the million invisibly tiny snakes and beetles Grashgal had once told him – *thanks, pal, really needed the extra nightmares* – existed on every patch of his and every other human being's skin no matter how often they washed. Or – his mind groping about ever more feebly for comparison to cling to – like a constant succession of newly tempered swords plunged into a cooling trough down at the end of some unlikely palace hallway a thousand echoing yards in length.

He lifts his head again, cannot prevent the impulse to peer down into the dappled grey light at the bottom of the canister as if, despite Hjel's words and his own previous check, there's something insectile living down there after all.

Hear that?

Ringil nods numbly. Something about the noise has unnerved him out of all proportion to its volume or provenance. The hairs on the nape of his neck are erect in the cool air. He wonders if this is what dogs feel when there's a storm closing in.

Makes you a young man, then. The sorcerer prince's expression is sombre, his smile doesn't quite make it through. *My father told me there's an age you get to, you just can't hear it anymore. Not too old either, he was only in his thirties.*

Gil shakes his head. *Wouldn't bother me, if I never heard that again.* He looks warily around at the scattered canisters. *Are they—?*

Yeah. All like that. Try another one if you like.

Thanks, I'll pass.

And later, as they put the stone circle behind them and head back to the paved path, he asks Hjel quietly what he thinks the long-jars were for, whether he's ever heard anything that might explain them.

Hjel walks in silence at his side for a while before he speaks.

There's nothing in what I've mastered of the ikinri 'ska *about them*, he says finally. *Nothing in the tales my people tell either. I think they're too old for that.*

More quiet, the soft squelch of their boots across the boggy ground. They regain the paved path and pick up their pace.

That looked like some kind of spell written on them, Gil ventures. *Some kind of ward.*

Maybe. Hjel stops and looks back to where the standing stones still puncture a skyline growing dark with some faded simulacrum of evening. He sighs. *Look, I'm just a cheap trick mage, a scavenger along the cliffs of the* ikinri 'ska. *I've got nothing but some vague, eroded hints and my own feelings to go on. I'm just guessing here. But I think something bad happened in the Margins, a very long time ago, so long ago maybe even the gods don't remember it very well. I think men – or beings like men anyway, you saw that death's head – were in it somehow, and I think they brought those vessels here as tools to play whatever part they had. Tools, or maybe weapons.*

He faces Ringil in the gathering gloom on the road.

Whatever it was those men came to do, I think they failed. I think they were, I don't know – a helpless gesture *– swept away somehow, and their tools were the only thing left behind. But whatever it was they did, I think it caused harm that's still not fully healed today, maybe harm that can't ever completely heal.*

He draws a deep breath and looks up and down the faintly luminous dirty white paving of the path they're on.

And I think that's what you can hear. The echo in time of the harm those canisters did when they were opened.

The rasp of the cabin door latch woke him from reverie that had somewhere slipped into a fitful doze. No real sense of how much time had passed. He looked down the length of his roped up, immobilised body in the gloom and saw no useful change – dreams, it seemed, would not get you into the Grey Places unaided after all.

The door creaked open, somewhat less violently than Klithren had banged it on his way out. Maybe he'd calmed down a bit, taken a few turns around the decks and let the fact of his victory sink in. Maybe there'd be some water after all. Ringil's throat clutched and worked with craving at the thought. He fought the urge, the eagerness to twist his head and look. *Give him nothing, Gil. No weakness to work with, no satisfaction, no submission that isn't torn out of you by the fucking roots . . .*

Low, swaying glimmer of the lantern carried into the cabin, the shadows it set dancing on the ceiling and walls. He heard it set down.

A calloused swordsman's hand fell on his cheek. He had a moment to wonder if, under all of Klithren's rough sellsword camaraderie in Hinerion, there had lurked something less rough and manly after all. Some twinge of attraction, maybe, that . . .

The swordsman's fingers stroked up against his stubble. Touched the jut of his cheekbone below the eye. He recognised a sly, torturer's mockery in the caress, prelude to some brutal abuse or other.

So it's going to be like that.

He shut down hope of water, hope of anything at all.

The caressing hand fell away.

NINETEEN

It took Archeth a numb couple of seconds to understand.

The sudden, violent upwelling of the ocean in front of her gave rapid way to structure beneath. A broad array of nestled five-sided platforms, rumbling up out of the water, filling the gap inside the ring and rising higher still, in stepped succession, towards the support column at the centre. Churned gallons of seawater, roaring and streaming down off the jagged alloy terraces like some vast, mounded waterfall, as the platforms built themselves into an even conical ziggurat reaching up in easy steps to touch the support column at about half its full height.

Where, abruptly, there was an opening.

'Have you been tortured, child?'

Water was still pouring down off the sudden structure. Archeth, entranced by the risen spectacle before her, barely registered the voice at all, let alone the language it used or the words it spoke. She glanced at Egar, who stood equally spellbound at her side.

'What?'

'Hm?' The Dragonbane, evidently unable to tear his eyes away from the newly formed ziggurat either. 'What'd you say?'

'I didn't say anything, I asked you what you said.'

'Didn't say anything,' Egar murmured. 'You realise—'

'*I* spoke to you, child!' There was a note of sharp reproach in the voice this time, enough to sting her out of her trance. 'I *asked* if you had been *tortured.*'

High Kir – only now did she register the stark, marching syllables for what they were, only now did she understand, seeing Egar's utter lack of reaction, that the voice spoke only for her. And a scant moment after that, realisation crashed in on her; that tight, wavering edge on the avuncular tones, like a scream held back – she was listening to a Helmsman.

'I, uhm . . .' She mustered command of her people's tongue. Looked upward at the ravaged underside of the city for want of any other direction to address herself. 'Why would you think I'd been tortured?'

Out of the corner of her eye, she caught Egar gaping at her. Raised one rigid flat palm – *give me a minute here.*

'Others have been,' said the voice matter-of-factly. 'Many prisoners were brutalised to gain entry past the species portcullis. And your state corresponds with theirs to some extent – you have not fed well or drunk sufficiently for several days, your body carries substantial bruising and

your mind shows signs of torment. But you need have no more fear, child –
I can withdraw the structure you stand upon to the level of the seabed just
as easily as I have raised this entry. You will be rescued with precision and
your tormenters will be drowned the same way. You have my promise.'

'*No!*' She made an effort at calm. 'No, that won't be necessary. These
men are my . . . uhm . . . friends.'

'Are you sure, child? You seem to be lying to me. There really is no
need to lie on these creatures' behalf. There is not the least risk that they
can harm you further, and to accomplish their deaths is a small matter
for me.'

She thought she detected a hint of leashed eagerness in the voice, a
touch more of the withheld shriek behind the avuncular. Over her head,
An-Kirilnar seemed abruptly to squat lower on its supports, to loom that
much more menacingly. The roar of the water pouring off the ziggurat in
front of them had muted to the tick and trickle of some mountain brook,
and an ominous quiet was building in the space it left. Egar mouthed at
her.

Who the fuck are you talking to?

Unsure of the answer herself, she shook her head.

'Look, there's no *further* about it,' she said rapidly. 'These men haven't
harmed me *at all*. In fact, some of them saved my life earlier today. My
privations are not the fault of anyone here. Well, that is, some of them did,
uhm . . . Look, I bear them no ill will *now*, that's the thing.'

'You lie again, child. A small lie, but—'

'Yes, yes, all right. I know.'

She fought off a panic-stricken vision of Egar and the others, yelling
knee-deep in the ocean as the causeway pentagons sank away under their
feet. Knee-deep, waist-deep, and then just floundering to stay afloat,
thrust back into the nightmare of shipwreck once again, and this time a
couple of miles off-shore.

She was beginning to guess at what the An-Kirilnar Helmsman was.
She formulated her words with care.

'There is one, yes. He put his hands on me when I was his captive, the
one with—'

'I am aware of him, child.'

'But that's done, it's over. The uhm, the circumstances have changed,
the uh . . . Look, it's complicated, all right? Just take my word for it, we're
all friends now.'

'I am not ill-equipped for complexity.' The hint of reproach was back.
'But little can be taken on trust in these troubled lands. The Aldrain have
grown cunning of late.'

'Maybe so, but . . . *What did you say?*'

'I said I am not ill-equipped for—'

'No – about the dwenda. The Aldrain. You said they're getting more
cunning of late?'

'That is correct.'

'Of late?' Her nerves prickled. 'You're saying that there've been dwenda around here recently? And – and my people too, the Kiriath? *Recently?*'

'Most certainly. The last local clashes were considerably less than five thousand years ago. And inconclusive, despite some opinion to the contrary.'

Her shoulders sagged. All the privations the Helmsman had so neatly listed seemed to fall on her again, harder. She was cold, she was hungry and thirsty, she ached from head to foot. The krinzanz need was beginning to bite.

'Five . . . thousand years?' she asked drably.

'Less, my child, far less.'

But that's not fucking recent! she felt like wailing. *Not even my father on one of his bad days would have called that recent.*

Get a grip, Archidi . . .

'I am kir-Archeth,' she said evenly. 'Daughter of kir-Flaradnam of the clan Indamaninarmal. Current overall mission commander of the Kiriath Project, based out of An-Monal. To whom am I speaking?'

There was a long pause. Through the quiet, she heard the wind hoot in the gaps and crannies of the massive structure overhead.

'I am the Warhelm Tharalanangharst, chief among the Seven Summoned from the Void. Please excuse my lack of manners. I have not had visitors for a while.'

'That's, uhm . . . fine.' She nodded, suspicions confirmed. 'I take it we are permitted to enter here, then?'

'But of course.' She couldn't be sure if surprise etched the Warhelm's tones or she just read it there herself. 'The species lock is open, you are of the People. And these others are your allies, however *variegated* their allegiance may be. I have opened portals at three points around the entry tower now. Some of your men are already mounting the steps.'

She shot an alarmed glance at Egar, remembered he could not hear half of the conversation, and the half he heard was gibberish to him anyway. He looked back at her expectantly.

'Explain later,' she told him. 'We'd better get in there.'

Led by outside appearances, and by her sour memories of An-Naranash, she expected dilapidation and decay within.

Instead, the space inside An-Kirilnar's central support column was neatly kept and spotlessly clean. Illumination sprang up as they entered, struck a sheen from burnished dark alloy surfaces in a dozen different colours that all flowed into each other. It was subtly done, it took her a while to work out where exactly the lights were ensconced and, even then, her eye was led back to where their radiance fell instead – on walls and pentagon-patterned floor, the first turn of steps and then the climbing underside of a huge spiral staircase where it swept upward around the curve of the column, and the gold and steel thicket of concertina metal fencing on a massive cage set in the centre.

The men stood and gaped about them. The Dragonbane, who'd seen the inside of An-Monal a couple of times, worked visibly at not being impressed. Archeth went to the cage and cranked the mechanism that opened it. There was a smooth clicking, snipping, the sound of a hundred brisk tailor's scissors at work, and the concertina fencing folded up on itself to the side.

The men looked dubiously at the opening.

'It's an elevator,' she told them. 'It'll carry us to the top.'

'Yes, just a moment.' From the way they all looked fearfully upward and around, it seemed Tharalananghargarst had given up speaking in her ear alone. 'There are one or two matters to be gone through before we proceed. First of all, allow me to welcome you formally to the Overwatch Platform An-Kirilnar. I am the Warhelm Tharalananghargarst, I govern here. Please forgive the somewhat archaic use of your various native tongues, this will improve as I converse with you further. In the meantime, here are some basic ground rules.'

On three sides, the doors they'd come through dropped shut with a rapid triple clang. Out of nowhere, something spiderlike and gleaming leapt down onto one man's shoulders – she realised who it was, felt the pit of her stomach fall out – and bore him to the floor. There was a moment of thrashing, a scream and the crimson glint of blood, then the man lay still. His panicked panting came to her across the air.

'This man,' the Warhelm told them in the same genial tones. 'Laid unwanted hands on the lady kir-Archeth Indamaninarmal when she was powerless to repel such attention.'

She stared fascinated at the thing that had Sogren pinned. It was a machine like the charred crab remnant the men had carried back from the south side of the bay, but poised and menacing and alive. It glimmered and gleamed in the lighting, crouched atop Sogren's head and shoulders for all the world like some arcane helm and shoulder piece he'd somehow fallen over wearing. Or, she thought queasily, some beautifully crafted instrument of torture from the imperial dungeons. Sogren had tried to rise, to cast the thing off, but a narrow, bladed appendage was out near the creature's head – it had drilled the privateer neatly through the right hand, sprouted multiple holding pincers and twisted his arm out and over, locked the elbow joint out. It held him flat to the floor like a wrestler's trick.

One of the other privateers darted forward to help. Soft scuttling sounds came from the walls as he moved.

'I really wouldn't if I were you,' the Warhelm advised.

The man froze where he was.

'Needless to say,' Tharalananghargarst went on, into the horror-struck stillness. 'Such violation of the body of one of the People is also a violation of the alliance terms between the Kiriath and those noble humans who wish to throw off the yoke of dwenda oppression. It is therefore punishable by death. Sogren Cablehand, do you have anything to say?'

Appendages like long, extending jaws clamped on Sogren's head at either side, dragged his face up from the floor. He snarled and thrashed, spat out his rage.

'Nothing of consequence, then,' the Warhelm decided, and the clamping appendages hauled sharply up and to the right. Sogren's eyes bulged with the sudden pain, he made a desperate choking sound, like some giant startled hen, and then his neck snapped with an audible crunch. His contorted features slackened on the instant, but his neck went on making tiny crunching noises as the crab twisted his head around until it faced neatly backwards on his shoulders.

Among the men, she heard shocked oaths, Naomic and Tethanne alike.

The executioner unseated itself from Sogren's neck, prodded once or twice at the newly made corpse, as if to make absolutely sure the job was done. Then it stalked spider-legged away into the shadow beneath the first turn of the staircase, found a small hole in the wall there that Archeth hadn't noticed before, and was gone.

'The body of kir-Archeth Indamaninarmal is sacred,' said the Warhelm Tharalanangharst mildly. 'Other acts of violence here, though lesser in degree, will not be looked well upon either. You would do well to remember this while you are guests in An-Kirilnar. With that proviso, you are, as I have already said, most welcome.

'The elevator will take you to more adequate accommodation.'

'It's a Warhelm, Eg. What can I tell you? They're not like other Helmsmen.'

'Yeah, no shit!' The Dragonbane stalked back to her across the sumptuous black carpet in her rooms, voice savage. 'Think I noticed that about the time it was snapping the head off one of my men!'

'*Your* men? And anyway – don't exaggerate. It broke his neck.'

'And then turned his face around to look backwards on his shoulders! Let's not forget that little detail, shall we? Because it's fixed pretty fucking clearly in my head, and I doubt any of Sogren's privateer pals are going to have trouble remembering it either. I have to *lead* this rabble, Archeth. Sogren Cablehand was a key part of that.'

'Well, he isn't anymore.' She hadn't enjoyed watching Sogren die any more than anyone else, but she was fucked if she was going to tax herself with summoning sympathy or any species of regret. 'So you'd better start getting used to the idea.'

'Yeah, easy for you to—' Egar made a noise in his throat and turned away, whatever else he had to say bitten off and swallowed.

'Easy how?' she demanded.

'Forget it.'

'No! How is this any fucking easier for me than it is for you?'

The Dragonbane gestured around them. 'You're home, aren't you? Apartments fit for a Kiriath queen. The Empress of all you survey.'

She followed the motion. Tharalananghasrst's hospitality was lavish, true enough. She had rooms of palatial expanse, windowed for a view out over the ocean and the coastal headland to the south. The bedchamber was furnished with a bed big enough to sleep a whole family in comfort, there was a bathing annexe with a bath seemingly built with the same family in mind, and the lounge she sat in provided ample scope for the Dragonbane's pacing. The roof space was high, the alloy flooring was polished to a gloss that made it look like well-cared-for wood and strewn with multiple carpets in jagged Kiriath designs. Beyond a discreet archway to one side, there was a dining chamber containing a table set for ten and near enough space to ride a horse round the outside.

If the decor was sombre, metallic and rather thin on adornment of any sort, well, she was used to that from An-Monal.

'That's a bitchy crack, Eg. I'm as far from home as you are, and you know it.'

The Dragonbane sighed. Came to the couch she was seated on, dropped onto it beside her. Pinched finger and thumb to his eyes.

'I know. I'm sorry.' He dropped his hand from his face. 'But Sogren was herd bull for the privateers. Now he's gone, I'm likely going to have to do the whole dominance thing all over again, just to keep them in step.'

'You think they'll try to leave?'

'Not right away, no.' Egar nodded at the stupendous bowl of fruit that stood on an ornamental table beside the couch. A brace of Tharalananghast's smaller creatures spidered about in it, re-stocking and removing the sucked-clean stones and pips Archeth had left when she fell on the fruit earlier. 'I mean, look at that little lot. They're not stupid, they'll fill their bellies while they have the chance. They'll want to get warm and dry, get some rest. But after that . . .'

He scowled.

'You really think they'd mutiny?'

'I think they'll be fed and rested, they'll have had time to think and talk, and they won't be any less pissed off about Sogren. I don't know about outright mutiny, but it'll make them slippery to handle once we set out south. And it's certainly going to put a dent in their liking for you.'

'I thought I was Chosen of the Dark Court since Dakovash grabbed my ankle.'

'Yeah, and now you're friend to a demonic power that's butchered one of their own right before their eyes.'

'And is feeding and sheltering the rest of them in the lap of luxury,' she snapped. 'If I were a privateer, I'd be counting my fucking blessings.'

'Maybe they are, right now. But that kind of gratitude fades pretty fast. What they're going to remember when we head south is that Sogren was killed while we all watched, and none of them did a fucking thing about it. That's going to rankle and rot inside them, and sooner or later, they're going to want to cleanse the wound.' He shook his head. 'It's not a showdown I'm looking forward to.'

'They're not a majority.' She'd been too tired and beaten down and krin-deprived to do the count properly at any point – made her eyes ache just to try. 'Are they?'

'Not outright, no. But they outnumber each of the other factions well enough, and there's no telling where Tand's freebooters are going to stand if it comes to a fight.' Egar sighed again, leaned back on the couch and stared at the iron-beamed ceiling four yards over their heads. 'All right, look, forget it – for now anyway. I guess we're cosy enough here for the moment. Give me another one of those plums.'

She scooped it off the pile, black and ripe, handed it to him. He bit into the flesh, spilled juice down his chin, chewed with his eyes still on the ceiling.

'Ate a ton of these in my room earlier,' he said, a bit indistinctly. 'Still can't believe how good they taste. How long you reckon this place has been here?'

She shrugged. 'My people chased the dwenda out anything between four and five thousand years ago, depending on which sources you want to believe. Tharalananghargarst seems to have had a hand in that, so you're looking at that long at least. Why?'

'Just wondering where all the food came from.' He looked at the remainder of his plum. 'This is fresh off the tree.'

'It's out of store, apparently. They say this part of the world was a garden paradise before the Kiriath came. The Wastes are what was left here after we went to war with the dwenda. They must have harvested for a siege, laid down the stores and then never used them.'

'Stores that last five thousand years?' There wasn't any real incredulity in the Dragonbane's voice, he was mildly surprised at most. He bit into the plum again. 'Neat trick if you can pull it off. So you think any of this stuff can exist outside of the fortress? Or will it turn to dust if we try to take it away.'

'No, why would it?'

'Well, you know.' He gestured. 'Spells and such. They say up on the steppe you can find the finest silver where a falling star hits the Earth, but you have to get to it before the sun comes up or it turns to dross.'

'That's just superstition, Eg. Just tales. My people were engineers, not magicians.'

'There's a difference?'

Since she sometimes had a hard time seeing the difference herself, she let it go. 'So how are your rooms?'

'Good.' Egar spat the plum stone into his palm. Looked around in vain for somewhere to dump it. 'Not as big as these. Got a view out to sea. You think there's any chance of meat in this place? I'd kill for some decent meat.'

'I'd be surprised if there isn't. An-Monal was always pretty well stocked.'

He nodded at the ceiling. 'Think it's listening to us?'

'I have no idea. Like I said, it's a Warhelm. I never met one before, I've only read about them.' She heard how her voice took on the cadences of her father's lectures, the same words and phrases borrowed wholesale, some of them still only partially understood. 'But they reckon the exigencies made for some pretty weird behaviour. Thing is, when you summon something as powerful as a Helmsman from the void, you usually want it leashed pretty tight, kept pretty attentive to your needs. Otherwise, who knows what it'll go off and do that's more interesting than looking after you. So you lay down protocols, you cement a complex dependency. You make what you've summoned need you as much as you need it. But the Warhelms aren't like that, they couldn't be. There wasn't time. They are raw power and purpose, and they were called to the world in a hurry, purely to defeat the dwenda. There were no other considerations, and no other purpose for them once the war was done.'

The Dragonbane frowned. 'You think they'd be any use in a war against someone else? Someone not the dwenda, I mean?'

She shrugged again. 'You saw what happened to Sogren.'

'Yeah. You know Archidi, I got to wonder if this is what your father was really doing up here on the expeditionary. I mean, I know we went to burn the Scaled Folk's rafts before they could hatch out, but what if after that, Flaradnam was planning to come looking for this place, looking to enlist its help.'

'That,' said the voice of the Warhelm suddenly from the air, 'is not likely.'

It spoke Tethanne this time, perhaps intending to be inclusive. She exchanged a look with Egar. 'You've been listening to us?'

'No, but I am listening to you now.'

'Seems a bit convenient,' said the Dragonbane, studiously casual. He dumped his plum stone surreptitiously down by the side of the couch. 'Why now particularly?'

'You mentioned kir-Archeth's father by name. I knew kir-Flaradnam Indamaninarmal well. He was instrumental in my summoning from the void, and we fought side by side to end the Aldrain presence.'

'Well, then.' Archeth spread her hands. 'He probably *was* on his way to see you back in '52. It would make sense, wouldn't it?'

'It would not. Your father and I were not on good terms by the time the Aldrain were driven out, and we certainly never reconciled.' Hard to tell if something shifted now in the tight-strung amiability of Tharalananghargst's tone, but she thought she heard a chill there. 'It was, after all, kir-Flaradnam who crippled and blinded me at the end.'

TWENTY

Ringil tensed for the inevitable blow.

Saw a cloth-muffled face lean over him, familiar eyes above the mask, creased in boyish concern . . .

No fucking way!

He jerked in his bonds. Grunted against the gag.

Noyal Rakan pulled the masking cloth down off his firm young mouth and chin, put fingers slantwise across his lips for quiet.

'Have you loose in just a moment, my lord,' he whispered. 'Don't move.'

Yeah, like I got a fucking choice about that, you stupid gorgeous idiot beautiful wait 'til I get loose of these . . .

Rakan already had fingers at the back of Ringil's neck, exploring the gag. He conjured a knife in his left hand, pressed Gil's head gently over to one side and sliced deftly through the knotted silk. Ringil shoved at the wedge in his mouth with a tongue that felt like a chopped off piece of two inch rope. He coughed the chunk of wood loose as the Throne Eternal captain lifted away the severed silk bonds of the gag. He spat it out onto his chest with a relief that watered his eyes.

'What are you doing here?' he croaked.

'Skulked aboard last night while they were loading.' Rakan worked rapidly on Gil's bonds with the knife as he talked. 'Been hiding in the grain store since we made sail. Took me a while to work out where they were keeping you. Can you walk?'

'I doubt it.' Ringil flexed his hands as Rakan sliced the cords away, grimacing at the numbness. 'Anyway, we're not leaving. I want to be right here when Klithren comes back.'

The Throne Eternal looked baffled. 'You want to stay *put*? My lord, I – this lantern is from the bracket outside the cabin, someone's going to notice it's gone. We need to get you out of here fast.'

'And go where? We're at sea, Noy. What are we going to do, jump over the side? *Swim* back to Ornley?'

'No, but—'

Ringil flexed his mouth in an ugly, down-curved smile. His parched lips split, thin splinters of pain somehow driving the grin.

'We're going to fucking take this ship, Noy. You and me, with a little help from our friend Klithren. Now get my feet and help me up. I'm going to cramp like fuck, but that's fine. Need to work it off.'

Rakan sliced the ropes binding Gil's legs in place, got an arm round his shoulders, helped him into a sitting position on the edge of the cot. Sure enough, cramp sank its fangs into his calf the moment he tried to put pressure on that foot. He grunted, stiffened – felt Rakan's arm tighten around his shoulder. He turned sideways to look at the Throne Eternal in the low light.

'How the . . . I thought you were gone, Noy. Captured, sent south for ransom, or dead or worse, I—' He swallowed painfully, reached down to massage his calf as best he could with numb fingers and palm. 'I mean, what the fuck happened while I was gone?'

The Throne Eternal looked away, something like shame in his face.

'We were unprepared,' he said quietly. 'They landed men down the coast and stormed the town from the top, while one of their vessels stopped up the harbour below. When I saw the ship, I took five men and went looking for the lady Archeth. She was supposed to be at Menith Tand's lodgings, but when I got there both were gone, no way to know where. We cut back to the harbour, but by then this pirate scum were in the streets, along the wharf, everywhere. We fought, but . . .'

He looked back at Ringil.

'I knew you'd be coming back. I took my men, only three left by then and one of them wounded. We cut loose a small boat at the beach, got it past the League ship, out of the harbour and along the shoreline. I hoped to find you, warn you before you sailed back into the trap.'

He stared miserably at the cabin floor.

'I abandoned the lady Archeth. The Emperor's anointed agent in the flesh. I failed my sworn charge. I told myself it was for the best, that saving you would save the others in the end. But that's not – that's not why I, I . . .'

Ringil took the hand he was using to work at his cramped leg, pressed it hard against Rakan's averted face. Hints of pain beginning to spike through the numb flesh now as circulation returned, he couldn't feel much else. But he pulled the young Throne Eternal round fully to face him. Placed the other hand on his other cheek and pulled him close. Kissed him hard on the mouth, for all that it cracked his dried-up lips again and hurt the scorched rag of his tongue. He pushed back and held the other man's face only inches from his own.

'I'm very glad you did,' he said distinctly. 'I'm in your debt, Noy. Really. I'm . . . honoured by this.'

Rakan licked his lips. 'But—'

'And we will get Archeth and the others back, no matter what it takes. Count on it. Your oath is not broken, you have done nothing wrong.'

'We tried to find you.' The Throne Eternal's voice was urgent, pleading. He pulled away from Ringil's grip, stared at the floor again. 'We tried, but night came on. None of us are accomplished seamen, we're not marines. Akal was sinking into a fever, losing blood. In the end we had to beach and build a fire for him. We sat with him, we . . .'

Rakan swallowed. Tears bright in his eyes. Not for the first time, Gil was forcibly reminded how young this tight-muscled lover he'd taken still was.

'When the morning came, he was stiff and cold,' Rakan whispered. 'We buried him as best we could without tools. Offered prayer, scattered salt. There was a peak behind the beach, we climbed it and scanned the horizon northward for your sail. We stayed there all day. But then, with evening, the fog came, the storm blew up out to sea. We couldn't manage the boat in weather like that.'

'No.' *Probably would have got eaten by the akyia into the bargain.*

'We walked inland. We thought to raid some croft, feed ourselves at least and keep our strength up. But we'd walked almost back to Ornley before we saw any signs of life. We made out lights in the mist, but when we got closer, when we realised where we were . . .'

Ringil grunted. 'Yeah, fog'll get you all turned around like that. Lose your sense of distance, direction, everything. Done it myself a few times.'

He forced himself to his feet and hobbled across the cabin to its single porthole. His other leg cramped up in the thigh on the way, but it wasn't as bad as the calf had been. His fingers were starting to really hurt now as blood forced its way back into them. He braced on the cabin wall with both hands, bowed his head to look through the porthole. Saw a narrow slice of band-lit ocean, the dark crumpled rise of a shoreline beyond. Standard night voyage precautions – they were shadowing the Hironish coast, but far enough out to stay safe. Looked like the privateers had put to sea pretty much as soon as they could tidy up the aftermath in Ornley and get Ringil loaded aboard. Klithren must be in a real hurry to get his bounty home.

'We heard the fighting on the breeze as we approached,' Rakan evidently still felt the need to explain. 'But by the time the mist cleared and we could make any sense, it was over. All we could do was skulk and wait for nightfall. Learn what we could, plan from that. Nalak and Jan took the upper town, I went to the harbour, we were supposed to meet back up on the cliff road. But when I saw them carrying you aboard . . .'

'Yeah.' *Enough talk, Gil. And enough bloody brooding – what is this, one of Skimil Shend's poetry soirees?* He turned away from the porthole. 'Listen, Noy, you'd better get that lantern back outside on its bracket.'

He limped back towards the cot, gauging the strength in his legs. Still not great, but getting better by the minute. Across from him, Rakan was already on his feet, like it was parade call. He swept up the lantern and slipped out the door, plunged the cabin back into gloom.

Ringil lowered himself to the cot, swung his legs back up and lay flat. The pain of returning circulation was spiking right through his hands now, but along with the pain there was functional feeling as well.

Yeah, might even be able to hold a sword some time later this month.

'All right, listen,' he told Rakan, as soon as the Throne Eternal was back in the darkened room with the door closed. 'Get back by the hinges. You're going to jump Klithren soon as he comes in here. Hurt him, put him on the floor, but whatever you do, don't stab him. We need him alive.'

Rakan nodded, barely seen in the gloom, and sank into a comfortable crouch in the space where the door would hinge back. As if on cue, the hurrying multitude stomp of feet on wood came from somewhere overhead.

But it faded again and no one came.

'Think it's another ship,' murmured Rakan. 'Heard the crow's nest call out something just before I came down here. I mean, I don't speak Naomic or anything, but if there's one word I have picked up in the last couple of months, it's *ship*. Gave me my best chance to move, too. Must have had every man on deck over at the rail to look.'

'You couldn't work out anything else they said?'

Rakan's dimly seen form shook its head. 'Nothing. They sounded pretty pissed off, though.'

An Empire warship this far north was a flat out impossibility. And Ringil couldn't see any reason why sighting random League traffic of any sort would upset the privateers.

Which left only one explanation, really.

'Get ready,' he told the Throne Eternal cheerfully. 'If this is what I think it is, we're about to have some very angry company.'

A solid, jolting impact that nearly tipped Noyal Rakan out of his crouch. Then another, less violent, and then a couple more gentle bumps. Shouts of satisfaction from above. Gil recognised the pattern from the time they'd been boarded by a customs frigate on the run-in to Lanatray. Whatever ship Klithren's lookout had sighted, they'd come up on it now and were engaged. Grappling irons and boathooks would lock the two vessels together until they could be properly lashed. Meantime, the privateers were amply competent to swing or leap aboard, take stock and then . . .

They waited.

It didn't take long. A shocked cry came in through the porthole, then others, high pitched with fear and disgust. A wider chaos of yelling above as men still on board this ship tried to get sense out of those who had boarded the other.

Now, he wondered if they shouldn't have tried to sneak out of the cabin after all. There'd be enough confusion on deck to maybe let them find some other place to hide. Leave an empty cot and the loose coils of rope, a vanishing trick from the terrifying black mage they'd so foolishly taken captive . . .

Yeah, and then what, Gil?

Over the side and swim? We'd drown before we got halfway to the coast.

Stow away on a boat full of privateers out for blood, who know her stem to stern? How long's that going to last?

And even if we could, even if you could somehow buy time to use the ikinri *'ska and kill them all off – who's going to sail us back to Ornley? Elementals again? The akyia? It was hard enough last time, with a fully competent crew to keep* Dragon's Demise *trimmed. We're two men, and neither of us knows any sea-craft worth a back-alley fuck.*

You need to own this ship, Gil. Ship and crew, stem to stern. There is no other way.

There is nothing wrong with a defensive strategy, he'd written in his treatise on warfare, back when he still thought it might see the published light of day, *save that it hands over the initiative to the enemy. So you'd better hope you're strong enough, fortified enough in defence, to withstand whatever that enemy decides, in the luxury of time and choice you've given them, to start throwing at you.*

And if you are not that strong – then offence and a colossal bluff may be the better option.

He heard boots stamping down on companionway steps close by.

'Showtime,' he hissed at Rakan.

The latch. The door flung back. Klithren stormed into the cabin amidst a spill of light from outside. He hadn't bothered to take the lantern down from its bracket.

'What the fuck have you done, Eskiath? What the fu—'

Rakan hit him from the side like something demonic. Chopping blows into neck and temple, a savage stomp into the back of one knee to fold and take him down, and a vicious kidney punch as the Throne Eternal rode his victim to the floor. Klithren convulsed and groaned, tried to get up and found an arm across his throat, a dagger point at his eye.

'I'd lie still if I were you.' Ringil told him, up off the cot at a speed he felt quite pleased with, all things considered. 'That's a Throne Eternal blade in your face.'

He limped rapidly to the cabin door, hooked the lantern on his arm and brought it in, shut the door solidly and turned back to his new captive. He set the lantern down, well away from Klithren and Rakan's clinch on the floor. He grinned down at the floored mercenary.

'Change of dealer,' he said. 'But the game remains much the same.'

'They're going to fucking kill you now, Eskiath.' The words choked out of Klithren. 'Nothing I can do, nothing anyone can do. You think one imperial sneak assassin at your back is going to change that?'

Ringil nodded up at the cabin ceiling. 'That one of your flotilla up there, is it? Drifting with the wind?'

'What did you do to that ship? What filthy piece of sorcery did you work on those men?'

'Me? Nothing. We sneaked past your picket in the fog, close enough to hear their hour call on the breeze.'

Klithren glared up at him. 'You lie. There are . . . fucking *pieces* of dead men all over her deck. Blood everywhere. They've been . . . *chewed* on, you piece of shit.'

Ringil knew. He'd seen the Sileta brothers after the merroigai got through with them.

'Let's just say I've got some friends you'd prefer not to meet,' he said. 'And if you don't want your crew meeting them either, I suggest you do exactly what I tell you.'

He crouched over Klithren.

'Now where's my fucking sword?'

A rapid search of Klithren for weapons yielded a couple of nasty little knuckle blades tucked up in interesting places, as well as the big killing knife on his hip and a slimmer, nicely balanced piece of cutlery in his right boot.

It wasn't the Ravensfriend, but it was a start. They shared out the blades and took Klithren up on deck.

The companionway was the trickiest part. Gil had Rakan lead, he at least knew the ship's layout a little, would have some sense of what they were climbing up into. The Throne Eternal went up, lifted the companionway hatch by inches to check for close bystanders, then flagged an all-clear to them and clambered up and out. Klithren went next, far enough behind not to grab at the Throne Eternal's ankles, and Gil brought up the rear, the slim, balanced blade pressed close against the artery in the mercenary's inner thigh as he climbed. The moment the mercenary's head cleared the top of the companionway, Rakan's dagger snicked in under his chin, and the Throne Eternal drew him painstakingly up and out like some big, vicious fish he'd just hooked. Gil came swiftly up behind and settled the slim blade in Klithren's back.

'Easy there,' he murmured.

They crouched in a corner of the raised foredeck, shadowed by the rail and the foremast rigging in band-lit bars and squares.

By now, the hubbub down on the main deck was total. The other vessel was roped in tight to the port rail and a mob of men crowded there, yelling and brandishing weapons. Others clung to the mainmast rigging for a ladder and stared down onto the other ship's deck. Even the steersman and his boy had left the wheel and were crowding the poop deck rail in an attempt to see what was going on.

You're not going to get a better chance than this, Gil.

He took the slim balanced knife out of Klithren's back and weighed it loosely on his palm. Knew, with a sudden conviction, that the weapon was worth less to him now than his two empty, unbound hands.

'Don't you fucking move,' he warned the mercenary. 'Noy, you take this blade, keep it right-handed, ready for a throw. Dagger in your left and hard up against our pal here's kidneys. Soon as I give you the nod, get him up against the rail to my left. And get your mask back up. Try to look, uhm, shadowy. Hunched.'

He ignored the look the Throne Eternal shot him, flexed his fingers, wishing they weren't still quite so stiff, and drew in one deep, hard breath. Then he nodded at Rakan and went to stand upright at the rail.

'*Men of Trelayne!*' Voice pitched to roll sonorously out across the main deck below. '*Look upon my work, and repent! I hold your souls in the balance!*'

The men in the rigging heard him first, swung from their points of purchase to stare. So far so good – no one climbs rigging with a primed crossbow, and the range was too great for accurate throwing of knives or clubs.

Down on the deck, though – that was going to be a different matter . . .

'Noy, this is going to be your moment.' He figured the muttered Tethanne was safe enough, was likely going to sound to the rattled northerners below like some kind of spell or incantation, if they heard it at all. 'They'll all have their eyes on me. Reckon you can throw down there accurately, take out the first man that gets too close?'

The Throne Eternal hefted the slim knife below the level of the rail without change of expression or stance.

'What, and *still* look hunched and shadowy?' he muttered back, deadpan.

'Good lad.' Gil raised his hands, switched back to sonorous Naomic. '*Look upon what I have done! Know the power you face!*'

Curses now, panicked and raging in about equal measure. The crammed pack of men at the ship's rail loosened, unknotting itself, spreading back out across the ship's waist as the privateers turned and saw the dark figure up on the foredeck.

A new chaos of voices boiled up among them.

'*He's loose!*' one of them yelled. '*He's out!*'

'How the f—'

'Look, *Klithren* – he's sold us out!' A panicking bellow. '*He's traded our fucking souls!*'

'No, no, use your *eyes* – the mage's familiar has him!'

'Black mage, black mage! Hoiran ward us!'

'Shit, it's true, like that fat git Hort said, he's—'

'*Black mage!* In Hoiran and Firfirdar's name, *ward us!*'

So forth.

Out of the mess, Ringil tracked the dangerous men – snaking their way through the press, largely silent, eyes fixed balefully on the foredeck rail and the dark lord stood there who'd apparently butchered their comrades. Perhaps predictably, at least half of them wore skirmish ranger rig. He let them come on, tried to stave off the rising itch of unarmed exposure it set loose in his guts. Trusting to Rakan's eye and arm *rather a lot here, actually.* If the *ikinri 'ska* had spells for taking thrown weapons safely out of the air or deflecting them away – and he supposed it probably did – Hjel hadn't got around to teaching them to him just yet. And the men down on deck were going to cut loose as soon as they thought they were in safe range, which might or might not be inside a distance Throne Eternal training allowed for, so if even one of them looked like . . .

157

That one for example – ranger rig, out now ahead of the pack, spiked killing club in hand, still moving fleet-footed forward but settling into this sliding crouch that presaged—

Fuck this shit.

He threw up his arm and pointed. Shouted in Tethanne, words spaced in his best attempt at sounding like a spell. *'That one there, Noy!'*

The privateer got his throwing arm up, almost back – went choking, stumbling backward instead with Rakan's knife in his throat. The tipped weight in his stance took him over in a tumble, no time to see if he landed with the knife clearly visible or not, if anyone was interested in checking such details with the black mage calling from the rail . . .

'Will you harm me with your petty blades and clubs?' he roared at them. *'Will you stand against me? Will I bring the kraken's doom upon you all? Don't touch him!'*

This last to a privateer pacing up to the newly made corpse. There was nothing of magic in the shout, just the years of desperate command from the war, but the man froze as if turned to stone. Gil, balanced on the hard edge of the seconds it bought him, saw what had to be done next to keep control—

Did it.

Leapt without thinking.

Up and over the rail, gut-swoop moment of the fall and his cloak flapping out behind him like tattered black wings – with luck they'd see that and believe he flew. He hit the main deck in a solid crouch, dared not roll to absorb the impact – it was only going to wreck the hard-bought dark lord poise of it all – took it in the knees and spine instead, jagged tug and flare through the bone, then straighten up out of the crouch, as if the pain were not there.

You jumped out of raided warehouse windows twice that high, back in the day, back in Trelayne.

Yeah, you were half the age as well.

Flickering stab of nostalgia for the youth and long-withered innocence of those years – it hurt almost as much as the fall. He shook off both, stalked into the scattered ranks of the privateers with hands rising in finger-splayed claws at his sides.

'Who wants to die next then?'

Now it was time for the *ikinri 'ska*, and he welcomed it in – the liquid stir it made through him, the trembling potential in his fingertips. *Yeah and half a hundred more subjects than you can put away with it here, Gil. Let's not get cocky.* He still had the positions of the men he'd marked from the rail, the dangerous ones. He saw a raised hand-axe out of the corner of his eye, swung on the man who wielded it. Carved a glyph from the air and pointed.

'You. You're on your knees.'

And the privateer dropped there, like a puppet with strings abruptly cut.

'That's not an axe, it's a snake.'

The man let go his weapon with a yell of revulsion. Exultation surged through Ringil. He saw reaction run through the other privateers, steps stumbling backward in most, away from the black cloaked thing walking into their midst. He picked another man who'd still not given ground. A glyph like tearing open, another pointing finger—

'You, you're choking.'

And watched him go down, clutching at his throat. Another skirmish ranger off to his left—

'Corpsemite! It's on your back!'

The victim, screaming and staggering, thrashing fit to snap his own spine backwards . . .

'You – where are your weapons? What's that on your *thumbs?*'

And the privateer rearing back, hands held up in horror. The exhilaration of the *ikinri 'ska* washed through Ringil now like flandrijn, washed *around* him like the summery blue and white slop of waves on the beach at Lanatray in his youth. Something had changed, something had shifted inside him. Somehow, the overreach he'd forced through on the sloping street in Ornley had pulled something along with it. Like a knot threaded back through itself and then hauled on so hard it pops out of existence and leaves the cable running clean. Like a muscle, torn up with too much strain, knitting harder and tougher again . . .

A man in ranger rig came at him howling, cutlass raised for the chop. He locked gazes, spoke the simple word *No*, not even very loud. Saw the waver of the upflung blade, the sudden stammer in the skirmish ranger's step. He stepped in, blocked the cutlass blow with an imperial empty-hand technique, hooked and hauled the arm down, smashed an open palm into the man's chest, put him on the deck on his back—

'Lie *still* – you are in your grave!'

The skirmish ranger convulsed on the planking, as if pinned there by an iron spike. He flailed with hands in front of his face, weeping. Ringil turned away, on to the next . . .

He should be weakening, this should be tiring him by now.

'Marsh spider – there in your shirt!'

But all he feels is the appetite for more. He strides unarmed into the midst of his enemies, and it's as if he's wearing tailored plate; as if the Ravensfriend is there in his hand. The privateers are backing away now, scrambling to get clear of him, clear of the clawing, raking, stabbing gestures from raised hands he barely seems to own anymore . . .

'Oh, you think you're going to shoot me with that? It's not *strung*, you twat. And your *eyes* are bleeding!'

The arbalest, tumbling to the deck, landing – reach in there and *flip* – upside down, muffled *twank* and the bolt discharged, spent into the deck planking. The man who'd held it clapped hands to his face and bawled something incomprehensible . . .

Enough.

He bent and gathered up the crossbow, held it briefly aloft in one hand. 'You think *this* is going to save you?'

And threw it to the deck at his feet. Raised his voice for them all.

'*There are two kinds of men aboard this ship! Those who oppose me – and those who will live to see the dawn!*' He snapped out the blade of one hand, gestured at a trembling privateer on his left. Stared into the man's face. 'Which are you?'

Frozen pause.

Then the man's head bowed and he dropped on one knee to the deck. He threw his club away.

Ringil turned his head, and it was like a wave sweeping through the privateers wherever his gaze fell. They began to kneel. By ones and twos at first – then more – then most – and finally the very few stiff-backed resilient ones, broken by his stare as it swept over the bowed heads of their comrades and found them, put the same silent question to them that the others had already faced and answered for themselves.

Soft clatter and thump of discarded weaponry across the deck.

And the slow leak inside of a feeling Ringil couldn't place at first. He thought it might only be the sinking away of the *ikinri 'ska* as it faded into the background again, and he looked around at the men he would not now need to fight and kill . . .

Then he had it. Saw the sensation for what it really was.

Disappointment.

TWENTY-ONE

It seemed like a very long time the silence held, while the Warhelm's accusation soaked away into the quiet. Archeth might have been a statue, rooted to the polished alloy floor where she'd leapt to her feet.

'You said what?' Staring balefully up at the iron-beamed ceiling. 'You'd better back that shit up, Warhelm. You'd better fucking explain to me why my father would *cripple* and *blind* one of his most powerful allies in the fight against the dwenda. Are you accusing him of treachery? Why would he commit such an act of violence against you?'

'It was not treachery, no. But we differed over how to end the Aldrain threat.' Near as Egar could tell, the screech-edged amiability in the demon's voice hadn't changed. If it had ever been pissed off about what 'Nam had supposedly done to it, the passing of a few thousand years certainly seemed to have taken the edge off. 'More precisely, kir-Flaradnam believed that the threat *was* ended, and I did not. He did not like my plans for further action, and he knew I would not obey him when he told me to stand down.'

'But it *was* ended,' Archeth blurted. 'You drove out the dwenda. The Aldrain. It was over, the Indirath M'nal says so. You ended the threat.'

Egar sniffed. ''til now, anyway.'

'Ah, so it begins.'

'Begins?' The Dragonbane looked suspiciously around. 'What begins?'

'The Aldrain reconquest, I imagine. I did wonder about the seismics. I have wondered every time, in fact. They fit so well into the model, each time it was hard to believe that the Aldrain would not see their opportunity and seize it. Though apparently not until now.' Tharalananghars had seemed for a moment to be drifting away. Now, its voice came back tighter. 'A pity your father is not here to see this, kir-Archeth – he was adamant that it would not occur. *Could* not occur, in fact. He was a tower of rhetorical passion on the subject. It was the kind of conviction one only sees in a man when he knows beyond any doubt, beneath all speech and emotion, that he is utterly wrong.'

'What seismics?' Archeth asked the ceiling rigidly.

'Yeah, what is a *size-mix* anyway?' Egar liked to think his Tethanne was pretty good, but it wasn't a word he'd heard before.

'I have detected vibrations from the south, consistent with a significant earthquake event. My *these days somewhat limited* senses tell me its origin is in the Hanliagh fault.'

'Fucking *earthquake?*' Egar blinked. 'What, wait a minute – you talking about the Drowned Daughters?'

One tavern night in Yhelteth, not long arrived in the city, he'd felt the floor lift and sway beneath his feet and thought it was just the drink – until a serving maid shrieked at his elbow, and things started toppling off shelves and tables around him. He rode the shaking with a – drunken – horse breaker's calm, watching faintly bemused as his hardened mercenary colleagues grabbed at the talismans they wore or made forking wards in the air. It was a solid few minutes before everything calmed down and he could grab someone, with bruising, inebriated force, and ask *what the fuck just happened here, brother?*

The Drowned Daughters twist and yearn in their sleep. They dream of waking and rising from their ocean bed in memory of their great father.

There'd been other tremors on and off in the years that followed, mostly of lesser force, nothing you didn't get used to with time. They were far from the weirdest thing a Majak lad might experience, living in the imperial city. But some of the local tales on the subject were pretty dark. They told of a cataclysmic ruin visited upon Yhelteth in earlier times, and the tellers could point you easily enough to cracked and slumped buildings amidst the older architecture to vouch for the truth of the account. It was said that, out to sea, the ocean had boiled, and the Drowned Daughters of Hanliagh had risen from it vomiting fire to scorch the sky.

'Well?' Archeth, looking slightly sick now. 'Is he right? Have the Daughters risen?'

'The nature and intensity of the tremors suggests not, at least not yet. But if these vibrations are only a precursor, then it is not impossible that the submarine caldera at the heart of the Hanliagh scatter could vent again.'

Archeth twitched about, then, just as abruptly, seemed not to know what to do with her sudden will to motion. She stood irresolute on the stark black carpet, glaring through the Dragonbane at something he had no way to see.

'If there are earthquakes in Yhelteth,' she said tightly, 'Then those arseholes up at the Citadel are going to be touting it for evidence that God's angry with the Empire, and that means angry with the Emperor too. This is going to be their wet-dream comeback moment, Eg. They can march right up to the palace gates at the head of a mob ten thousand strong, demand audience and ask for pretty much anything they like. Prophet's prick! No wonder Jhiral's taken us to war.'

Egar nodded. 'Looks like he's taking a leaf out of daddy's campaign manual.'

'Yeah – a new holy war, against the infidel north. Except when Akal did it, he was expanding the Empire for real. Jhiral's going to do it just so he can hang onto the throne.'

'Still – not going too shabbily, if he's taken Hinerion like Klithren said.'

Archeth pulled a sour face. 'He can lose it again just as fast. That border's been back and forth like a wanker's hand as long as I've been alive.'

'Yeah, seen some action there myself, back when I was starting out.' The Dragonbane brooded for a while. 'You reckon Anasharal saw this coming, Archidi?'

'What?'

'Well, look at it this way – Helmsman gets us all fired up for a three thousand mile quest north after things that aren't there—'

'An-Kirilnar's there. Here, I mean.'

'Archidi, come *on*. You're reaching. There's no Illwrack Changeling, there's no fucking Ghost Isle. And this place is nowhere near where we were told it was going to be.'

Archeth looked thoughtful. 'Anasharal said south and east of the Ghost Isle. You know, that's not technically a lie. This coast is east of the Hironish, and the storm did blow us a long way south before we wrecked.'

'Yeah, whatever. Point is, we were sold a nag and told it was a unicorn. So I'm thinking maybe Anasharal just wanted you out of the city before all this earthquake and war shit broke loose. Maybe this whole thing was just one big fucking excuse to protect you.'

He watched her digest the idea. Stare at the carpet underfoot, then shake her head. 'No. Can't be, Eg. It's too elaborate. Helmsmen falling out of the sky? Portents and legends come to life? A quarter million elemental venture, complete with imperial charter, drawing in half the uncrowned heads of Yhelteth commerce? All that to coddle one washed up krinsoaked half-breed?'

He heard the old, tangled damage, the pain and self-hate in her voice.

'Well,' he said, very gently. 'Got to depend on how much the washed up krin-soaked half-breed in question matters to you, I guess. Didn't you tell me Angfal's sworn to the single purpose of your protection? Manathan too, right?'

'Manathan is sworn to the Kiriath mission, not me. Anyway, that's not the fucking point. If this is all about protecting me, why didn't Angfal just tell me to head out to Dhashara for the duration? Or sit things out in the imperial embassy at Shaktur?'

'Dunno, because you wouldn't have gone, maybe?' Egar grinned. 'I've been your bodyguard less than two years, Archidi, and I already know you're a pain in the arse to keep out of harm's way. I don't envy Angfal. You do what's good for you about as often as a shaman gets a shag.'

He thought she smiled, just barely. 'Thanks.'

'Just pointing out some obvious truths here. Anasharal sold you the one pony that would get you a thousand miles out of Yhelteth without blinking. And he sold Jhiral a matching saddle to get you there in style.'

'No.' She shook her head again, emphatically. 'I'm not buying this, Eg. You set out a good stall, but there's too much else that doesn't fit. There's the dwenda. Anasharal didn't make them up. There's Klithren, and the fact that somebody in Trelayne thought it was worth sending him and a whole fucking flotilla of privateers up to the Hironish Isles to detain us. There's the fact somebody in Ornley was told to dig up that sword and take it back to Trelayne before we arrived. That can't all be—'

'*What sword?*'

A hard edge on the Warhelm's voice, unmistakable even to Egar. And he saw how Archeth shot a surprised look at the ceiling.

'What do you care?' she asked curtly.

Into the air evolved a twist of light that rapidly became a writhing calligraphic stroke, then some kind of long tool, then – recognition sidling quickly in – a broadsword.

'If,' said the Warhelm distinctly, 'it is this sword, then I care a great deal, and you had better tell me all about it.'

Egar stared at the image floating in the air before him. He'd been a lot of different places in his time under the imperial standard, slaughtered a lot of different peoples and seen the – usually inferior – weapons they defended themselves with.

He'd never seen anything like this.

The blade glinted blue along its edges and did not taper, was the same slim width from guard to jagged tip – he'd seen similar in the hands of the dwenda when they came to Ennishmin two years ago, right enough, and again in the musty stone depths of the temple at Afa'marag last year. But at the guard end of the weapon, any further familiarity died. This sword was equipped there with a heavy slope-sided cross-piece, studded on the underside with hooked little teeth that gave it the appearance of iron jaws wrenched open to vomit out grip and pommel. And grip and pommel, well . . . Egar caught himself shaking his head as he tried to make sense of what was there. No defined place for hands to grip, no pommel counter-weight, just a long snake-like coil of metal that also gleamed blue in the low light and terminated in a sharp, inward-angled spike.

The whole lower section of the weapon looked more like an instrument of torture than the handling end of a broadsword.

'Is this the sword?' A hint of impatience in the demon's voice now.

'We haven't seen the fucking sword,' Archeth snapped. 'It was taken from a grave in the Hironish Isles before we arrived there. How are we supposed to know what it looks like? You want to tell us what this . . . thing is?'

'This is *Betrayal Becomes You*,' said the Warhelm crisply. 'It is the Illwrack Changeling's Doom. A synthesis – a Kiriath reverse-engineered simulacrum of the Aldrain weapon *Out of Twilight Leaping*, which was gifted by the Illwrack clan to their human champion Cormorion Ilusilin Mayne, called Cormorion the Radiant, on his appointment as battle marshal supreme in the *until right now, it seems* final dwenda war.'

Archeth prowled around the floating image of the sword, fascinated. '*Betrayal Becomes You?* Reverse-engineered why? What for?'

'As its name *I would have imagined* tends to suggest, the Illwrack Changeling's Doom was designed to murder Cormorion when he drew it in battle.'

'Murder him how?' Archeth was still peering at the sword, either oblivious to the Warhelm's sour point-scoring, or just ignoring it.

'The Illwrack Changeling's Doom was reverse-engineered to cut the Changeling's connection with undefined existence and the opportunities for sorcerous strength that it provides, instead of feeding and channelling them as the original weapon was forged to do. It was to then mirror and store Cormorion's selfhood, oppose that copy to his existing self in his own mind and let them obliterate each other.'

Egar frowned. 'You what?'

'To steal his soul,' said the demon more slowly. 'All right?'

'No, it's not all right,' Archeth interjected. 'I've read the Indirath M'nal. That's not science the Kiriath have ever had. There are speculations about the possibility of stealing or mirroring a, whatever you want to call it, a soul. But that's all they ever were. Speculations.'

'I did not say, kir-Archeth, that the forces at the heart of the sword's design were Kiriath. I said only that the Kiriath did the engineering work.'

'On whose instigation?'

Another pause. 'We knew them as the *Ahn Foi* – or the Immortal Watch. Humans on both sides of the conflict called them by a variety of names. Judging by the curses and prayers that I have overheard some of your followers utter in the last several hours, it seems they are currently known as the Dark Court.'

'The fucking Sky Dwellers?' A disbelieving grin on the Dragonbane's face.

'That too.'

'They've been in this fight for that long?' He looked at Archeth, still grinning. 'On your side, against the dwenda from the start? Man, they must be pretty fucking pissed off 'Nam and Grashgal opted for the Revelation.'

She shrugged, a bit defensively. 'We had our reasons. Monotheism's handy if you want a rational development of . . . oh, never mind.' Her voice pitched up again. 'So. This assassination plot. Presumably, it worked?'

'To an incomplete extent, yes. The Changeling's . . . soul was obliterated, and he fell in battle. The Aldrain forces were routed, and not long thereafter, the Aldrain themselves were driven entirely back into the undefined planes.'

'Sounds pretty complete to me.'

'But?' Archeth prompted.

'But the mirrored copy of his self remains, stored in the substance of the sword.' More hesitation, hanging in the empty air. To the Dragonbane at least, it sounded like embarrassment. 'There were those among both

Kiriath and humans who believed this meant the Changeling could one day be brought back to life.'

Egar traded a glance with Archeth. 'Oops.'

'Yes, oops,' said the Warhelm unexpectedly. 'There were solutions to this, but as I explained earlier, kir-Archeth, your father did not want them applied.'

'My father,' Bitten emphasis on Archeth's words. 'Would not have left the job of liberating this world half-done. What solutions are you talking about?'

'For Cormorion to return would require a fresh human host – a new body for his soul. For that matter, for the Aldrain themselves to return would require human collaboration of some sort. It seems from the detail we were able to glean out of myth and legend belonging to both races, that it was human sorcery of some kind that summoned the Aldrain into the world in the first place. And whatever form that initial relationship took, by the time the Kiriath arrived here, Aldrain supremacy was wholly dependent on vassal support from human rulers. There were simply not that many of them, compared to humanity's numbers. They might easily have been overwhelmed, had humans been able to perceive them as an enemy and to act in concert against them. But humans did not. In fact, it was notable how much of humanity seemed to actively crave their presence, their disruption of the natural order, their *magic*, if you will. Many actively preferred it to the science the Kiriath brought, and even those who did not, could often not tell the difference.'

Egar grunted. 'Tell me about it.'

'Are you . . . are you saying humanity didn't *want* to be liberated?'

'You have fallen deep into their ways, daughter of kir-Flaradnam.' Hard to be sure, but the Warhelm seemed amused. 'You think as they do, you abandon all rational grasp. Do you think your father would be proud? Here you stand, attributing will and intent to abstractions. Humanity, even then, was a race many tens of millions strong. Do you really believe that such numbers could have a single, unified wish or purpose?'

'But the Indirath M'nal—'

'The Indirath M'nal was written seven centuries after the events it relates. It was a document designed to rationalise what had gone before, and to vindicate the new Kiriath mission. You should not expect too much accuracy.'

'But if humans were happy with Aldrain rule—'

'Some were, some were not. Most lived with it as they lived with the weather and the shape of local terrain – as an unalterable fact of life. But there were enough malcontents and dreamers, fortunately, for our purposes.'

'Our *purposes*? Our *purpose* was to rid the world of a demonic foe. To liberate humanity from their yoke.' She was almost shouting now, shouting at the impassive roofing over her head. *'My father told me that!'*

'Then perhaps by then he believed it.' No irony in the demon's voice as far as Egar could tell. 'Certainly, he worked hard to destroy or make obscure the original records of those times and what was done in them. But the hard truth is, daughter of kir-Flaradnam, that in the early years of the Arrival, the Kiriath purpose was to survive. No more, no less. They were few in number, stranded in a world they were struggling to understand, a world that appeared not to fully obey the laws of physics they had believed to be universal, and they were faced with a dominant civilisation that wanted them gone. What else could they do but go to war?'

The Dragonbane watched as Archeth floundered for a hold, for something to fling back at the dispassionate voice from the ceiling. She was drowning, as surely as if she'd just been pitched off *Lord of the Salt Wind*'s rail once again.

He cleared his throat ostentatiously.

'Can't help remembering,' he rumbled. 'That we were talking about your solution to the Aldrain's return.'

'Yes. We spoke of this.'

'So what was it? Your solution?'

'I thought I had made that obvious, Dragonbane. The relationship between Aldrain and human was tightly woven and symbiotic. Without—'

'Simi-what?'

'He means they depended on each other,' said Archeth sickly. 'And I see now what my father would not let you do.'

'Yes, you do appear to have grasped it now.' The Warhelm fell silent, then, as if struck by an afterthought. 'Would you like me to explain it to your friend?'

'That'd be nice,' growled Egar.

'Very well. Without *humans*, Dragonbane, the Aldrain would have no hope of a foothold against us, would perhaps not even be interested in a return. Extermination of the human race was the obvious safety measure.'

'Extermination?' Not that he hadn't heard the word before – work the imperial borders long enough and you didn't just hear it, you saw the tactic in action. But that was villages, hill tribes, the odd major town that wouldn't see sense. This, *this* was . . . 'You talking about *everybody?*'

'There were only forty-seven million of them left at the time,' the Warhelm said modestly. 'It would have been a simple matter.'

TWENTY-TWO

'You know, I didn't actually kill your friend Venj.'

'Fuck you – lying faggot piece of shit.'

Ringil made a pained face. 'Says the man who told me I was the only prisoner on this ship.'

He twisted left and right in his chair, gestured with elaborate irony at the grim-featured imperial marines who flanked him. They'd not been out of their irons long, and their faces still bore the marks of the rough handling they'd had from Klithren's men. They stood like statues at attention in the torchlight, but they stared across the table at Klithren like he was food.

Along with Klithren himself, they probably thought they had a pretty good idea of what was coming next.

Ringil was feeling tired and pissed off enough that he'd be sorry to disappoint them.

Finding out about the marines was sheer luck. It seemed they'd been brought aboard in chains and confined below decks early in the day, long before Ringil was stretchered down to the wharf that evening under Klithren's watchful eye. Noyal Rakan wasn't there to see it, he was still hiding somewhere out on the upper fringes of Ornley, waiting for nightfall. And he spoke no Naomic in any case, could not have understood anything he overheard the privateers saying even when he'd stowed away to rescue Gil. He'd never had any reason to suspect there might be any other imperials aboard.

And you, Gil, let an overweening sense of your own importance beat out any suspicion Klithren might not be telling the truth.

Nice going.

In fact, if one trembling young privateer hadn't cracked and started babbling when Ringil quizzed him about the whereabouts of the Ravensfriend, neither he nor Rakan might have been any the wiser.

Senger Hald had been confined, with the rough courtesy due a noble and a commander, to a lower deck bosun's cabin – Gil supposed they might have stumbled on him sooner rather than later. But the dozen or so other marines Klithren had chosen to bring along as secondary trophies were not as lucky. They'd all been crammed into a damp holding space down in the stern, built for exactly this purpose, but with about half that number in mind. They'd had no food or water, and they'd had to share the space with rats who hadn't reacted well to the encroachment. They were in a fine mood by the time Rakan went to let them out – ready to take on the entire privateer crew empty handed if they had to, and a little disappointed to discover that particular piece of heavy lifting had already been done.

Suddenly having a dozen loyal men at his disposal made Ringil's immediate situation a lot easier, but it didn't change the basic problem he faced.

'Check the armoury,' he told Hald, when the more immediate business of lowering an anchor and locking down the privateers in the forward hold was complete. 'Chances are there's a portable torture table packed away down there somewhere. When you find it, bring it to me here.'

'With pleasure.'

'We'll need some torches for those brackets there, too. Oh, and have someone get me a soft chair from the captain's cabin. I have a feeling this is going to be a long session.'

The marines found the table without too much trouble – it couldn't have looked much different from similar imperial equipment they'd be used to working with. They brought it up to the main deck in pieces and set it up for him. Square and sturdy-legged once locked together, it was built of well-seasoned marsh oak and was broad enough to play chess across, or would have been but for the black iron manacle rail in the centre.

It had seen a lot of use. The surface around the rail was scarred and stained with accumulated wear and tear. Hammers and nails, carpenter's drill-bits and chopping blades, poorly scrubbed away blood – all had left their mark.

He ordered the mercenary brought up on deck. Sat in his chair on the inquisitor's side of the table and watched as three imperial marines forced Klithren down onto a stool opposite, cut his bonds, then yanked his arms forward and cuffed his wrists into the appropriate manacles on the rack. Aside from a livid bruise across the forehead and a broken lip, the mercenary looked in reasonable shape. He'd flinched when they first got him up the companionway onto the deck and he saw where he was headed, but it was momentary and then he had it together. The only resistance he offered was a gritted snarl.

Gil supposed he knew they'd just break his arms if he gave them any real trouble.

'Neck too?' asked one of the marines hopefully, gesturing at the chain-link loop and ratchet that would lock Klithren's head flat to the board.

'No, that's fine. Leave him the way he is for now.'

They finished checking the manacles and stood back. Waited expectantly in the flicker from the bracketed torches set about the deck. A couple of them, the ones who'd put the table together, had tooled up from the ship's store for the occasion. Pincers, hammers, galley knives.

He turned his attention back to Klithren.

'Comfortable?' he couldn't resist asking.

'Fuck you, faggot.'

'Don't go giving me ideas.'

Klithren bared his teeth like a street dog at bay.

Which was about as good as it got.

Even cuffed to the torture board, Klithren was hard as nails and tight with hate. A professional lifetime spent rubbing shoulders with death and screaming agony gave him the reserves. He awaited the pain of torture with fatalistic calm, the way any rank-and-file captured soldier would; he lived and breathed the moment by moment luxury of its absence and meantime built what strength he could for when it must finally come. Any fear he had was stashed away deep, to make way for more usefully savage emotions. Any ghost of the uncertainty he'd seemed afflicted with when he held Ringil prisoner was good and buried.

Gil hadn't seen such a depth of will glaring back at him since he murdered Poppy Snarl in the scrub outside Hinerion.

And Klithren was no use to him dead.

Try again.

'Look, I'm not saying I wouldn't have killed the prick if I'd got the chance. But I didn't get the chance. Venj came looking for me, looking to cash me in for the price on my head. Something else cashed him in first.'

Klithren sneered. 'Yeah, I remember – marauding Majak tribesmen.'

'Okay, that was some lizardshit I fed you to get your back turned. Fact remains, it wasn't me.' Gil bent the truth a useful fraction. 'I didn't even see it go down.'

'No?' The rage leaking back into the mercenary's tone again. 'You were standing over his fucking corpse when I got there.'

'I was surrounded by corpses when you got there. Remember? Some of them were torn in pieces. You really think I did all that myself?'

Klithren leaned closer across the table, maybe the better to sneer, maybe just to ease the strain on his stretched arms. 'Why do you give a flying fuck what I think, Eskiath?

'Because I need your help.'

'Then I guess you're fucked.'

Gil lost his temper.

'You know, I could just as well have these boys here applying heated irons up your arse right now,' he snapped. 'Or let them burn your prick and balls off to make way for a new cunt. Both very popular punishments down south for recalcitrant slaves.'

'I ain't your fucking slave.'

Got to be smarter than this, Gil. Got to find another angle.

Actually, he knew what he was probably going to have to do.

He just didn't want to do it.

'Look,' he said evenly. 'You're a mercenary. Down in Hinerion, you were a bounty hunter for whoever paid. It's not such a reach for you to take Empire silver. All I—'

'Go fuck yourself, faggot. I'm a knight commander in the United Land Armies of the Trelayne League. Commissioned in League *gold* to bring in your backstabbing coward skull.'

'Well you're doing a bang-up job of that so far.'

'Fuck you—'

'—faggot, yeah. I think we've covered this ground already.' Ringil gestured impatiently. The torchlight made jumpy shadows off the motion. 'You know, Klithren, you're coming across a lot more stupid than I took you for. You really think that shiny new rank they gave you counts for anything? It's just a licence to stand between richer men than you and their enemies, and bleed on their account. I don't know who hired you exactly – actually, scratch that, I do have a pretty good idea – but do you *really think* that fuckwit cabal plan to do any of the dying in this new war they've got cooking?'

He was watching the mercenary's face – saw the faintest flicker of reaction on the word *cabal*, barely there, but enough. He stowed the confirmation, pressed the point, some genuine anger creeping in and warming his tone.

'Findrich, Kaad, the rest of them – they're using you the exact same way they used us all last time around. What benefits did *you* see for fighting the Scaled Folk after it was done? Five years we bled, and when it was safely over, those fuckers crawled back out of their holes and built a whole new slave trade on the back of what we'd saved from the lizards. Proud of your new employers, are you?'

Klithren shrugged as best he could with the manacles tugging at his arms. 'Proud of yours? Last time I checked, it was your imperial friends started this ball rolling. The Empire walked into a chartered League city unprovoked, a city which also happens to be my home town by the way, and they set loose the troops. You got any fucking idea what that looks like from the inside, sir Glades noble war hero?'

Actually, yes.

Ringil sat silent, wrapped in bloodshot recollection. When the war against the Scaled Folk wound down, he'd spent altogether too long witnessing the depredations of imperial soldiery in disputed border towns. Had, in fact, got himself badly hurt trying to stop it on one occasion, before he wised up and went home.

That the League's forces were engaged in entirely similar behaviour elsewhere in the borders, that the chaos was general and the men committing it as often as not just as bewildered as their victims, that the whole thing was in the end resolved with a flurry of save-face negotiation and the forced relocation of thousands – none of these facts had ever done anything to wash out the bloodied tinge of those memories.

Klithren had him.

Ringil looked across the table into his face and saw that the other man knew it too.

'What's the matter, war hero?' Klithren sat back as far as the iron cuffs would let him. 'Nothing smart to say about that? One scumbag mercenary to another?'

One of the marines stooped to speak beside his ear. 'Want me to slice off a couple of his fingers for you, my lord?' he asked helpfully. 'Just the little ones to start, give him something to think about?'

Ringil grimaced. 'No, that won't be necessary. Thank you.'

'As you like, sir. Happy to do it, though – just give the word. I trained with a torture detachment at Dhashara, sir. Very tough bandits up there, I know what I'm doing.'

You're going to have to do it, Gil. You know you are.

A tiny, trickling calm now he'd accepted it.

'Tell me something, sellsword,' he said quietly. 'How do you think you beat me, back in Ornley?'

Klithren snorted. 'You looking for tuition?'

'I tagged you twice before you took me down. What happened to those wounds?'

'Wounds?' But this time, the snort rang forced. 'I've had worse scratches off the kingsthorn around Tlanmar.'

'Yes, probably.' And now he leaned in towards the other man, certain that this was the weak point, the source of the restless uncertainty he'd spotted in Klithren down in the cabin before their roles were reversed. 'But your mail was sliced right through, wasn't it?'

The mercenary said nothing. His gaze skittered away over Ringil's shoulder. Gil waited a couple of beats, kept his voice soft.

'The Ravensfriend is a Kiriath blade. Kiriath tempered steel, an eternal edge. You've been in this game long enough, you know what that means. Deliver that edge right, it'll go through chain-link like it was cotton. And I delivered it right, you know I did. Right through your mail – twice. Big fucking holes, both times. But, somehow, all you scored under that damage was a couple of scratches.' Ringil was watching the mercenary intently. 'That's not possible, is it?'

Klithren sniffed. Met Gil's eyes. 'All I know about yesterday is you lost, Eskiath. Make up whatever lizardshit you need to, if it makes you feel better. Do whatever you're going to do here. But Kiriath steel or no Kiriath steel, I took you down, motherfucker.'

Ringil shook his head.

'There's a lot more to it than that. You think you've stepped inside the charmed circle back in Trelayne? Seen the real power behind the Chancellery? It goes way deeper than you think. Findrich and his pals are fucking with powers they can't control, powers that are going to roll right over them when the time comes, like a cartwheel over dung.'

'Yeah, *right*. The Dark is abroad, it prowls the marsh. The Aldrain winter is coming.' Klithren spat on the table between them, jerked his chin at Ringil. 'Black mage lizardshit, you think I haven't heard it all before. Go fuck yourself with your Kiriath steel.'

A taut silence. The marines twitched, yearning etched into their young faces.

You're going to have to do it, Gil. Let's just get on with it, shall we?

He sighed. 'You know the real problem here, bounty hunter?'

Klithren showed him the street dog snarl again, but Gil thought he saw a tremor at the edge of it this time. Hard as nails or not, and contrary to Ringil's earlier insult, the mercenary wasn't stupid. He would have picked up on the new calm in his captor, would understand how it presaged the endgame.

He offered Klithren a thin smile.

'The real problem is that you took my friends. And I want them back.'

'Yeah?' The mercenary spread his fingers, studied his hands in their cuffs with affected boredom. His voice missed steady by an inch. 'Well, I want to fuck a Yhelteth virgin princess. Let's see who gets lucky first, shall we?'

Ringil laughed politely. 'No, you haven't understood,' he said.

And launched himself forward.

Grabbed Klithren's fingers between his own and snapped his fists closed. The mercenary reared back in shock, then tried to mend his failed nerve by leaping straight back in with a full force head-butt. Ringil jerked his own head clear by fractions and Klithren's forehead went all the way down. Hit the table and the iron manacle rail with a solid clank.

The marines leapt forward on either side, curses and drawn blades—

'No!' Gil kept his hold on Klithren's fingers, shut the imperials down on voice alone. 'It's okay, we're fine here. We're fine.'

The marines eased back, one muscle at a time. Gil saw them shoot each other glances about equal parts bemusement and anger. A fair bet they'd never attended an interrogation session quite like this one before.

You know you're going to have to—

He lowered his head carefully beside Klithren's. 'Just fighting men, shooting the breeze. Right, Hinerion?'

The mercenary groaned. Lashed sideways with his head, but Ringil was too close for him to make it into a blow of any consequence. Gil pressed back, skull to skull, feeling Klithren's stubble rasp against his own cheek. Both their faces dipped to within inches of the torture table's ravaged wooden surface. He let go Klithren's right hand with his left, slammed his palm up hard against the other side of the mercenary's skull to keep the clinch.

'I *said* you haven't understood,' he hissed low. 'I am going to have my friends back. If I have to burn the whole—'

Klithren bucked against his grip. Ringil clinched harder with head and hand, dug his nails into the mercenary's face.

173

'—the whole fucking city of Trelayne into the marsh to bring them home, *then I will do exactly that.* Those fucks in the cabal, the Chancellery, my own fucking father – if they think I caused trouble last time I was in town, they have seen and understood *nothing.* Are you beginning to get which way the wind blows here, Klithren of Hinerion?'

Grunt of muffled rage, another attempt to butt sideways. He felt Klithren's feet thrashing about for purchase beneath the table.

You know you're going to—

He reached down, reached inward. Spoke in rasping tones, hauled hard, as if pulling some massive root crop fruit up through the dry-baked earth of a pitiless summer. Felt in the pit of his stomach how the power built with each glyph, how it washed about seeking an exit, any exit other than the one he now demanded. Let the rumbling, answering snarl come up his throat and out through his gritted teeth, the sequenced cant, the savage warning to whatever it was he was struggling against here, living thing or insensate matter or something somewhere in between, to *get the fuck out of his way.* He kept his grip on Klithren, kept his weight locked in, *kept on pulling* at the stubborn edges of the rip he'd made, the damage he'd done to whatever fabric this was . . .

And *through.*

Like a fist punched into mud, and out an unexpected other side.

Into weeping quiet.

Ringil shudders and lets go. They're here.

He hears it for sure now – the low keening, like the wind in tall grass, but he knows that's not what it is. He grips Klithren's head for a moment like a drowning man clinging to some smoothly rounded rock. He turns his face and drags a hard, smearing kiss up over the other man's cheek to his ear. Lets go and stands shakily back. Jerks his chin at Klithren's huddled form where it's slumped over the torture table.

He gets his breathing mostly back under control.

Now let's stop fucking about, he says unsteadily.

The Grey Places spread out around them, marsh flats to the horizon in every direction and a vast pale sky above.

Some things shift in substance or form when they come through to the Margins, some things melt completely away. Hjel tells him he suspects it depends on how likely or unlikely the item in question is to exist across a whole range of different times and places.

The torture table hasn't changed very much at all.

The wood is a little more worn and cracked, perhaps, and whitened in the cracks with some lichen or mildew he doesn't recognise. He thinks the scarring on the table top looks different too – suddenly unfamiliar patterns among the scatter of dents and gouges, changed outlines to the blotched and faded stains, a whole new map of atrocity to get used to. The manacle rail is rusted, the manacles themselves are no longer iron, they look to be made of some cured bluish-grey hide.

The keening around him is growing louder now, or maybe just imprinting itself more clearly on his scrambled senses. Ringil casts a glance around him, knowing already what he'll see, still hoping somehow that he won't.

Klithren twitches on the table and mumbles something. Gil turns back and leans over him, glad of the focus. He's not sure how conscious the other man is. Coming through has left him feeling like a morning after too much cheap rum and krin, and he's more or less used to the transition. No telling how the passage must have felt to the mercenary.

Nonetheless . . .

He digs out his dragon tooth dagger, cuts the blue-grey hide bindings. It's harder work than you'd expect from the frayed and faded look of them. He hooks Klithren under the shoulder with one arm, heaves and drags him up off the table, dumps him on the marshy ground. Stares down at him for a moment.

Black mage lizardshit, is it? He kicks the mercenary solidly in the ribs. Stands over him, breathing harder than his exertions merit. *Why don't you take a look around, Klithren of Hinerion? See what you think.*

Another kick. Klithren rouses with a groan. He rolls over on the water-logged, spongy turf, comes up with a bump against what looks at a glance like some ancient, rotted mooring post, driven here untold centuries ago to mark the edge of a river long since dried up or diverted. The mercenary blinks, rubs the back of his hand across his eyes, and then reaches up to steady himself on the protrusion. He props himself blurrily to his knees, glances at the post—

Screams – recoils – falls back over on his arse again.

No, but, no, no, that's, no, no . . . dribbles from his lips as he stares at the thing he's just rested his hand on.

It's a human head. And it's alive.

They took them, Miri, they shone like stars, I tried, I tried, but they took them, please believe me, I couldn't stop them, please forgive me, they shone like stars, they took them . . .

It's the head of an old man, sparsely bearded with white whiskers and mostly bald, mumbling and weeping, endless tears that ribbon down through the grime on his cheeks and into the deep-cut lines that mark his sunken face. His neck has been severed a hand's breadth below his chin and then somehow cemented to a tree stump that matches its circumference perfectly. If his faded blue staring eyes see them at all, he shows no sign.

—took them, please, I couldn't, they shone, shone like stars—

Klithren has seen enough – he's scrabbling backwards on the heels of his hands, still staring, as far away as he can get. Until he bumps solidly into something behind him, jerks his head around to look at what he's hit, and screams again.

It's a young woman this time, dishevelled long hair half-obscuring her face, trailing down to brush at the humped and twisted roots of the stump she's mounted on. Her voice whispers out, as if jolted into speech by Klithren's clumsy shoulder.

—left me, he said he'd come, trust him he said, he'd come for me, it aches, it hurts, please don't, I'm tired, he'd come he said, he swore, I trusted, I'm tired, where is he, oh, it hurts, it hurts, *he left me, he—*

Klithren staggers to his feet. Backs away, tearing his gaze from the babbling woman's face, looking for escape.

He's wasting his time.

The severed heads stretch away in all directions, studding the marsh in endless random succession as far as the eye can distinguish them from the tufted marsh grass. They number in the thousands, maybe the tens of thousands, and all of them are weeping, some low, some high, some screaming their pain, some mumbling, but not a single one at any kind of lasting rest . . .

Ringil can almost see the moment that Klithren makes the connection, understands the low susurrus of moaning on the wind for what it really is.

No, that can't be, that, no . . . he's shaking his head, muttering to himself with a kind of hollow confidence. *No, that, no, no . . .*

Oh, yes, yes, fucking yes. Ringil stands at his shoulder, feeling an unwelcome stab of empathy for the other man. Grinding it back down into anger. *And no, in case you wondered, you are not fucking dreaming. Each one of these is a living soul, kept alive so long as the tree roots draw water from the soil. Look out there and try to count. Some of them will be children.*

The mercenary hangs there for a moment, and then a deep shudder runs through him. He swings on Ringil, sharp enough that Gil's reflexes put up a blocking arm between them, a hand pressed to the other man's shoulder ready to trip him back into the marsh. They're close enough that he can smell Klithren's soured breath. Their eyes lock.

What . . .? The mercenary shakes his head numbly. *What is this?*

This? Ringil presses firmly back a couple of inches to make the point, then drops his arm. He looks around at the harvest of human misery they stand amidst. *This is what's coming – if I can't stop it in time.*

Klithren makes a noise, not even a word. Ringil steps away from him and gestures with the dragon tooth dagger.

You wanted to see some black mage lizardshit? You're looking at it. This is what happens when the original black mages cut loose. This is what the dwenda leave in their wake.

Fucking dwenda? Klithren's still numb by the sound of it, still dislocated and stumbling. *You . . . talking about the Aldrain?*

More steps away – then Gil turns to face the other man. *Call them what you like. They're the power behind Findrich and the rest, just like the cabal is the power behind the Chancellery. You do a deal with Findrich and the cabal, you're* doing a deal with the creatures that did this – that do this habitually *when they're pissed off.*

So like I asked you once before, Klithren of Hinerion – proud of your employers, are you?

Klithren shakes himself like a wet dog. Breathes in hard. Gil watches. Knows what the other man's doing because – *there's that fucking empathy again, Gil, going to get you killed one of these days* – he's done it himself enough times. Close down focus, shut out what you can't stand or can't do anything about, just stare down the blade of what needs to be done.

And then do it.

How do you know all this? Klithren asks him.

Ringil smiles bleakly. *The dwenda and I are old friends.*

That's not an answer.

It's the only one you're getting on that subject. Ask me something else.

Why did you bring me here? Klithren talking deliberately louder now, to drown out the keening around them. But there's a wavering crack in his voice. *Why are you showing me this?*

I told you – because I need your help. Ringil looks away to the horizon. One part of him registers with a tiny shock how used he's grown to this horror, how little it touches him anymore. *See, I think I can probably take back Ornley without you. I've got your crew terrified into submission, I've got the ship, and for a little bonus I've got a handful of my own men to season the mix. I could torture some details out of you—*

You could fucking try!

I could fucking succeed. He says it matter-of-factly, doesn't even look round. *You're from the borders, you know about imperial marines. Well, there are marines back on that ship trained specifically in inquisition, and they're leaping at the leash for a shot at you. I let them loose, you'd spill, you know you would. You'd give up everything I need to know before you died. And the noises you'd make doing it are just going to hammer home my grip on your crew.*

Silence at his back that he takes for assent. Ringil waits regardless. The lost-soul moaning rises to fill the gap. He lets it chew at Klithren for a while before he goes on.

So like I said, I could get the detail. Find out where the prisoners are being held, what defensive set-up you've left in place. Now he turns back to the other man. Sees that Klithren has started, faintly but perceptibly, to tremble. *But here's the thing – it's still going to cost too much. It's another fucking sneak attack, another battle uphill, and I'm going to lose men I can't afford. Some bright spark on shore is likely going to run off to wherever they've stashed the prisoners and start cutting throats – it's what I'd do, anyway. And there'll be reprisals when we're done. We'll probably end up burning the town.*

He sees it in his mind's eye.

In other words, it'll be a bloody fucking mess for all concerned. And when that's done, I've still got to sail to Trelayne, get my friends back somehow, slaughter Findrich and his pals, find some way to stop the dwenda.

That's a lot of work with no intelligence to go on.

Whereas – you give me your allegiance here and now, I can go back to Ornley without drawing a blade. I collect my men in good order, imprison yours. Get my ships back, provision them, set sail. Nobody gets hurt. Then you tell me what I need to know about the cabal. You come back to Trelayne with me, and help me gain entry.

Then, when we're done, I'll give you what you want.

Klithren makes an effort to master his trembling. *Which is what?*

Your much-vaunted revenge. The chance to kill me blade to blade, and no need to hand me over to anyone else. Gil considers for a moment. *And no lizardshit black mage protection for either one of us. You can find out for real what the gods want done about this.*

The mercenary stares at him. *You'll do that?*

Gil sighs. *Yeah, I'll do that. Like I already told you, I didn't kill your friend. But the truth is, I would have cut him apart given half a chance, it would have made my day. And the thing that did cut him apart – well, that was a power sent to protect me, so . . .* A careless shrug. *You want payback? You want a piece of me? I'll give you your shot.*

What p-power? There's no masking the tremors now – Klithren is breaking down. The desolate unhuman chill of the Grey Places is eating into him like fever. But he clings to the last vestiges of his hate. *The thing that . . . what, what are you* talking *about? What* thing?

Do you really want to know? Ringil crushes out another inconvenient flicker of sympathy for the mercenary. Opens a palm to the marsh plain around them and what it contains. *Have you really not seen enough?*

It feels almost cheap this time, the little it takes to break down the other man's gaze and have him look away. Klithren shudders.

And – what, what if I – refuse this? Turn you down?

Oh, that's easy, Ringil tells him. *I'll just leave you here.*

TWENTY-THREE

You didn't see the Dragonbane at a loss very often.

Archeth was one of the few who had, and she couldn't remember the last time she'd seen that expression on his face. She'd forgotten how suddenly young it could make him look. For just those few moments, she was watching the features of a Majak buffalo herdsman not yet out of his teens.

'But – forty-seven . . . *million?*' he murmured. 'You could really have killed forty-seven *million* people?'

'Oh, yes. Sadly no longer, though. Her father saw to that.'

'But.' Egar shook his head. 'Why did you let him? You said you wouldn't obey his orders, why'd you sit still for him to . . . to mutilate you?'

'I was summoned from the void to protect the People, at any and all cost to anything else including myself. That was the pact, those were the terms of my containment. I could not act directly against kir-Flaradnam Indamaninarmal, or against any Kiriath, even in self-defence. It was not in my intrinsic nature, I could no more do it than you, Dragonbane, could breathe beneath the waves. And since I could not act against kir-Flaradnam, he was free to commit such surgery on me as he chose.' A longish pause, an unmistakable note of sour satisfaction creeping into Tharalanangharst's voice. 'I only hope his daughter does not live to regret the fact too much, now that our concerns about humanity have proven accurate.'

'The Kiriath mission,' snapped Archeth. 'Is to *nurture* humanity, to bring the human race eventually to the same levels of civilisation as the Kiriath themselves enjoy.'

'Yes, it is *now*. Didn't use to be. Good luck with that, by the way, when the Aldrain finally wake up to the benefits of volcanic eruption at Hanliagh and give it a little helping hand with their weapon of last resort.'

'You're talking about the Talons of the Sun?'

'Well, well, you are better read than I expected. Yes, kir-Archeth, I am referring to the Aldrain's chief engine of destruction. Which can in all likelihood pour enough destructive force into the volcanic vents at Hanliagh to burst the caldera like a rotten egg.'

'In all likelihood?' She let scorn edge her tone. 'You don't *know?*'

'No.' If the Warhelm noticed or cared about her affected lack of esteem, it didn't show. It lectured methodically on, as if to a none-too-bright student. 'The *rather melodramatically named* Talons of the Sun remains, I'm afraid, a largely unknown quantity. The Aldrain used it several times against us during the war, to obliterate cities and armies or to create obstacles in the landscape. Once, they evaporated the ocean at Inatharam harbour and so created an incoming wave of colossal force. But for all this, the weapon itself never manifested in the real world. It was deployed from, and seems resident in, an undefined plane to which we did not have access.'

'And now? Do you have access now?'

'I have access to very little these days, daughter of kir-Flaradnam. I thought I'd made that clear.' The Warhelm paused again, presumably to let the poetic justice sink in. 'So, no, in answer to your rather obtuse question, I am no more able to locate and quantify the Talons of the Sun now than I ever was.'

Archeth went, as if called by something, to stare out of the run of broad windows in the chamber's south facing wall. There was an ornamental rail below the glass expanse and she placed her hands on it with a conscious effort at calm. The krinzanz craving itched through her grip, made her fingers twitch. She watched evening crowd the thin sunlight westward and out to sea.

'If the dwenda use the Talons of the Sun to force an eruption at Hanliagh,' she said evenly, 'then it's going to affect the whole fault system. Will An-Monal erupt as well?'

'It did not happen the last time the caldera blew. The pressure walls at An-Monal are among the most powerful defensive engineering ever conceived by Kiriath science. The heat exchangers and diversion channelling were all built with exactly such a contingency in mind. And the Helmsman Manathan was called from the void primarily to hold the volcanic forces there in safe equilibrium.'

'But last time was not a dwenda incursion.'

'No.'

Her hands tightened on the rail. 'Then it could happen. Manathan could be overwhelmed.'

'Possibly, yes. But I think you have missed the rather more important consequence of an eruption at Hanliagh, both for Manathan and for everybody else.'

'Which is what?'

'Which is that the ash cloud thrown up when the caldera detonates will darken the skies over Yhelteth for days, veil the sun's force for even longer and so render the region positively hospitable for any invading Aldrain force. After that, whether Manathan is overwhelmed by lava at An-Monal or by Aldrain sorcery is really academic. The Kiriath mission, such as it is, will have failed.'

Archeth leaned in hard against her own grip. Stared out at the darkening ocean and coast, as if she could somehow will herself southward and back to Yhelteth along the line of her own gaze. She was in the wrong place, she was in the wrong *fucking* place. She felt the bitter flood of vindication – could briefly appreciate how Tharalanangharst must feel – and the impotent rage that it brought. She'd known. From the moment their disappointments began at Ornley, she'd fucking *known*.

Hold it down, Archidi. Someone's got to deal with this, and it looks like it's you. Again.

My father would not have left the job of liberating this world half-done. She would have laughed if she hadn't felt so near to weeping. They'd left *everything* half-done or worse, Grashgal and her father, it was practically their defining characteristic. The Empire – the brutal and bloodthirsty men they'd somehow let hold sway over it, let warp its envisaged purposes into the same dreary mash of conquest and slaughter, tribute and oppression, as ever was. The plan to reclaim the Wastes, the plan to cross the western ocean – both abandoned on the drawing board. The search for the Estranged Clans – wherever they'd wandered off to over the slow millennia – abandoned. Re-decorating An-Monal. Her own fucking education. All left half-done or badly handled. About the only thing her father had followed through on in the end was getting himself killed. And then Grashgal and the rest had left *her*, one badly trained half-breed caretaker novice, fumbling to hold up the towering, badly stacked, awkward-to-balance weight of their ridiculous fucking mission to civilise—

All right, Archidi. Old wounds, leave them alone.

'You are powerless to prevent any of this?' she asked tonelessly.

'In direct terms, yes.'

'Are there other Warhelms still in existence?'

'Oh, yes. The Aldrain were only able to bring down three of us in the end. Valdanakrakharn in the east—'

'I don't need the names of the dead. Who's left?'

'In the far south, Anakhanaladras. Up in endless circuit between the world and the band, Ingharnanasharal. And on the shores across the western ocean Gohlahaidranagawr. But I'm afraid they are each as crippled and reduced as I am. They had all reached the same conclusions as I, you see. And your father was most thorough in his determination not to allow the house cleaning we wished to embark on.'

'House cleaning,' she said grimly. 'Right. Did you at least – any of you – manage to gather any useful intelligence about the Talons of the Sun?'

'Useful? No.'

'Well, I don't see how that can be,' she worked at keeping the tinge of desperation out of her voice. 'Even ordinary fucking Helmsmen can make assumptions, projections based on evidence. And you were summoned specifically to fight the dwenda. It was your whole purpose.'

Tharalanangharst's tone turned acidic. 'Be that as it may, daughter of kir-Flaradnam, we were only ever able to determine two basic truths about the Talons of the Sun, *busy as we were* fulfilling our purpose and ensuring that the Aldrain did not obliterate the People. First, despite the name, the weapon does not appear to have anything to do with the sun, or at least not the sun that this world orbits around. And second, the uses to which the dwenda put their device appeared neither to tax it very much nor suit its capacities particularly well. It was a weapon immeasurably more powerful than anything the People had access to, but equally, it seemed hopelessly out of place in the Aldrain armoury. It was, if you like, a broadsword used by school children to cut twine.' Another of the Warhelm's characteristic blank pauses. 'So, then. Do you wish me to make an assumption based on this evidence, kir-Archeth?'

'Yeah, why don't you do that.'

'Then assume this: we are talking about a weapon held over from the cataclysm visited upon this world tens of thousands of years before the Kiriath arrived here through the veins of the earth. A battle relic of what some of your more well-read human protégés five thousand years ago liked to hark back to as *the Time of Dark and Angry Ancient Gods.*'

Archeth watched the sky through the window. Early stars glimmered in the gaps between soft mounded cloud, the band leaned in from the horizon at a drunken angle. She glanced upward at the roof, expectant. Got nothing in return. It took her a couple of moments to understand that Tharalanangharst had stopped talking for good. Had chosen to absent itself in the wake of its last, charged words, and leave her swimming in the implications.

An odd quiet made itself felt, dropping into place like shutters across her view, forcing her back to the room, a half-turn to look at the Dragon-bane still sitting there on the couch. He met her gaze and shrugged.

'Dark and Angry Ancient Gods, eh? Doesn't sound too clever.'

She felt the chilly, dead breath in the phrase, tickling the short hairs at the back of her neck. She shook it off, impatient.

'We have to get out of here,' she said. 'We have to get home. Jhiral isn't going to be able to handle any of this alone.'

'Jhiral isn't going to be able to handle any of this *at all*. But that doesn't put us one foot further south than we already are. And I don't see how we can get back to Yhelteth in time to make a difference.'

'You said you could walk us out of the Wastes.'

'Yeah.' Egar nodded at the fruit bowl beside him. 'Given enough of this five thousand year old grub, some packs to carry it in, something resem-bling decent weapons, we might make it to Gallows Gap, sure. Might.'

'This morning you were talking about doing it on a few mouthfuls of ham and oil, and some sea-soaked biscuits. You seemed pretty comfort-able with the idea then.'

'What can I tell you? Didn't want to spoil anyone's mood.' The Dragon-bane stooped forward on the couch, leaned elbows on his knees and looked down into his cupped and empty hands. 'Archidi, if we hadn't found this place, chances are we would all have died in the Wastes. I doubt we'd have made a hundred miles south. But you don't ever say things like that to the people you have at your back. I mean, they know it as well as you do, but that doesn't mean they want to fucking *hear* it. What they want is for you to take charge. Distract them from it, give them some hope, some reason to keep putting one foot in front of the other.'

'Even if it's a crock of lizardshit?'

'*Especially* if it's a crock of lizardshit.' He looked up at her, gave her a bleak smile. 'We're all bound for the Sky Road, sooner or later. How we walk it depends on how we walked in the world beneath. So you don't sit on your arse whining and waiting for your death to come find you. You go looking for it. Track the fucker down, force the issue. You walk, Archidi, you find the strength to walk, and you keep walking 'til you drop. Some men don't have that strength, so you have to lend it to them.'

She gestured. 'So we get walking.'

'Not saying we don't. But I still don't see us riding to the rescue in Yhelteth. We've got the Wastes to cross, and if we do make it as far as Gallows Gap, we're still deep in League territory, four or five hundred miles north of a border that's on fire. And half our company is men who see the League as their side in the fight. Remember what I said about Sogren, how they're going to feel? Not going to help the balance any, is it?'

'So what do you want to do?'

'I don't know.' He got up from the couch, yawned and stretched like a man crucified. 'Get some sleep might be a start. Then, tomorrow, we take stock. Feed up the men, lay some plans. And yes, try to get home. But you got to stop worrying about how fast we can get back to Yhelteth. Let that wanker Jhiral fight his own fucking battles.'

'I promised—' She chopped off the retort, but not before the Dragonbane spotted where it was going.

'I know, I know. The Great Kiriath Mission. But they fucking *dumped* it on you, Archidi. They cut and ran, and they left you holding the pieces. So give yourself a break, why don't you? Let's just worry about what's possible here and now. Not get hung up on some cobbled-together dream your father had a few thousand years ago when his demons couldn't persuade him to wipe us all out.'

She made a noise that felt like collapsing. The Dragonbane heard it and crossed the room to her. She could see he wanted to embrace her, would have liked it too, but could not rid herself of some stubborn, refusing fibre at her core. She held up a single arm instead. He slapped her hand, palm to palm, and they made the clasp, two hands, then four, tight. He hauled her close over the grip anyway, put his forehead to hers.

'Go to bed, Archidi,' he said gruffly. 'Get some rest. And for Urann's sake, stop feeling fucking guilty about everything for a change.'

Get some rest.

Ha.

She lay in the huge bed, staring across the darkened expanse of the bedchamber at the windows and the clouded night sky beyond. Band-light filtered in, but there wasn't much of it. Krinzanz need pounded in her veins like the ocean. Her mind churned the events of the day – near death hanging upside down, hunger and cold and a meagre fire on a beach, fresh hope rising with the news, An-Kirilnar growing closer along the causeway, the species portcullis, the death of Sogren. Now the Warhelm's guided tour of the ancient past, the sword and Cormorion Ilusilin Mayne, the truth about the Illwrack Changeling, the shattering revelations about her father and the mission.

Or had it been lying about that bit?

You know the truth when you hear it, Archidi.

Really? We came north because you thought you'd heard the truth, and look what happened there. Look where we could have been otherwise.

Oh, give it a fucking rest. You heard the Dragonbane.

Yeah, the wisdom of buffalo herders turned mercenary captains. Precious beyond the price of pearls. Maybe he can recommend you some whores as well.

She tried masturbating to thoughts of Ishgrim, her pale honey limbs and curves, her hooded eyes and undone mouth, but despite her best efforts, climax was as out of reach as the girl herself. She gave it up, flopped back hot and irritable in the covers.

What would Ishgrim do when the sky turned black?

What was she doing now, come to that, with tremors shaking the city, and the tramp of hot-eyed religious morons through the streets, fired up by fear and Citadel cant, on their way to glorious martyrdom somewhere in the north, but happy, *more* than happy, to start trouble right here, right now, at the faintest hint of anything they could take righteous offence at, above all if it was committed by a woman . . .

You have to get back. You have to stop this from happening.

You have to get some rest.

She felt as if someone had hammered her into very small pieces that somehow still retained all their links with each other. The enormity of what her father had done to the Warhelms towered in her head, the enormity of the crime they'd planned to commit if Flaradnam had left them armed. The enormity of the power they'd had.

What she wouldn't give for that power now.

For a fraction of that power.

To have just one intact Warhelm at her back. Never mind the luxury half dozen that her father's generation had apparently summoned from the void to fight the dwenda the last time – she'd settle for a single one and count herself well armed.

Would that have been so fucking much to ask? That just one of those colossally empowered creatures could have come up with a better fix for the problem than *extermination*, that it could have come to some kind of agreement with Flaradnam and preserved its strength for later days. Anakhanaladras in the south or Ingharnana—

Wait a minute . . .

She snapped bolt upright in the bed.

Ingharn . . . anasharal?

What kind of coincidence would that have to—

She leaned back on her elbows, dug back through the messy whirl of her thoughts, sifting for Tharalanangharst's words. *Up in endless circuit between the world and the band . . .*

That's no fucking coincidence, Archidi.

She sat up again, got herself cross-legged under the covers. Noticed absently that her ruined clothes were gone from where she'd stepped out of them beside the bed.

'Warhelm?'

'I hear you, daughter of kir-Flaradnam. What is your will?'

TWENTY-FOUR

When *Dragon's Demise* stood about half a league out of Ornley for what looked to be – *thank Firfirdar's flaming cunt for that* – the very last time, he went up on deck to watch the sun set and have a quiet word with Nyanar. The noble captain was still somewhat shaken by his captivity at the hands of the privateers – all thirty odd hours of it – and wasn't much in the mood for conversation. He was also, Ringil discovered, nursing a deep resentment that Klithren had chosen to leave him imprisoned in Ornley and take Senger Hald back to Trelayne instead. It reflected badly on the Nyanar clan that he hadn't been considered worthy of immediate ransom and the marine commander had. Didn't this League pirate scum know who he *was?*

'Klithren of Hinerion is a commoner,' Ringil consoled him. 'Recently and rapidly promoted with the war. He's a pragmatic man, knows nothing of nobility. Doubtless, he saw only commander Hald's military value for interrogation. And the risk of leaving him behind with his men. Ornley jail is not what one would call secure holding for soldiers of marine temper.'

'That's as maybe,' snapped Nyanar. 'But it is a gross breach of wartime etiquette to privilege such crass pragmatism above recognition of rank. And bad form to assign a knight's command to a *commoner* in the first place. This is not the same League that my father went to war with in the twenties. That was a war between gentlemen.'

'Indeed,' said Ringil absently, watching the dun cluster of sails on *Sea Eagle's Daughter* and the League vessel *Mayne's Moor Blooded* off to stern and starboard. Beyond them, the sun declined into torn cloud the colour of bruises, stained the sky bloody enough for omens to please the most exacting of black mages. He gazed west into it all, soaking up the rich and violent colours while he could.

Where he was going next, there'd be none of this.

'Do you know, I was not permitted water to wash in *for the entire day?* And they only fed me from the tavern's leavings at nightfall?'

Well, at least they didn't roast and eat you.

'Can you manage with this crew?' Gil asked him bluntly. He thought if Nyanar whined on much longer about his ordeal, he might end up putting him over the side.

'In this weather? Oh, yes.' The captain pulled a sour face. 'But if we have to deal with storms such as we met coming north . . .'

'There'll be no storms.' Ringil was not honestly sure he could deliver on that just yet, but he handed out the cheap reassurance anyway, for what it was worth. Hoped the Dark Court would take the hint.

Nyanar sniffed. 'Well, let's hope you're right. With this few reliable hands to count on, we're spread very thin.'

He had a point. It had been a tricky balancing act – how many of Klithren's men to leave behind in Ornley, how many to co-opt for the voyage south. In the end, Ringil decided to take both remaining Empire vessels home, mainly because he couldn't be bothered moving Anasharal from *Sea Eagle's Daughter* to *Dragon's Demise*, but also because he might need to split his forces once they reached the Gergis coast. And then, for appearances, they needed at least one League warship to play the role of conquering escort. *Mayne's Moor Blooded* was there for the taking – rather than adrift somewhere up the coast, decks soaked with blood and littered with the akyia-butchered remnants of crew – so that was that. Three vessels to crew with the sailing complement of one plus the sparse crop of imperial marines, sailors and Throne Eternal they'd liberated from holding in Ornley. Even as supervisors of co-opted privateer manpower, that left them stretched.

Ringil longed silently for Mahmal Shanta's supremely competent hand on the tiller, but, well, nothing to be done about that for the time being. Nyanar was what he had.

He glanced sternward, where Ornley and the whole Hironish coastline were shrinking and sinking into the early evening gloom. If the Illwrack Changeling was still back there somewhere, still buried some place long twisted out of memory by the elaborations of lazy chroniclers or epic story-tellers chasing something more dramatic and sonorous than true – well, then, his bones could rest in peace. Gil was done digging holes. He'd told Archeth back in Yhelteth that the whole quest was likely a waste of time, a wild ride after phantom fancies, and now he had Firfirdar's word for it that he'd been right all along.

'I'm going to my cabin,' he told Nyanar. 'I'm locking the door and taking out the key. I may be some time. You or any of the men hear anything scratching at that door and asking to be let out, even if it sounds like me, you don't listen and you don't open. Got that?'

The captain looked queasy. Like everyone else, by now he'd have heard the story the marines told about Klithren's interrogation – how Ringil, a recalcitrant Klithren and the torture table itself had all disappeared for the solid count of sixty, left nothing behind but wisps of smoke and flickers of blue light and a scorch mark on the deck where they'd stood. How they'd come back, Klithren uncuffed from the table and apparently unharmed, but cringing like a dog in a thunderstorm, the iron cuffs on the manacle rail sliced open and bent back as if they were nothing more than stiff leather, a faint scent of burning in the air. And how the air around that burn mark on the deck had seemed to emanate faintly heard moans and wailing right through until dawn . . .

'But . . . will you be gone long?' Nyanar's voice was almost plaintive.

'Quite possibly.' He thought about it. They had a good few weeks at sea ahead of them for sure. 'Look – at worst, I'll be back by the time you raise the Gergis coast or I'll be dead and not coming back at all. In which case, you run west for the cape and head home under full sail. And don't let Klithren of Hinerion across onto this ship at any point. I don't think he's going to be any trouble, we've struck a gentlemen's agreement and he seems to be holding to it but—'

A mannered snort, presumably at the epithet *gentleman* attached to someone like Klithren. Gil ignored it, pressed on.

'—but I have been wrong once or twice in my illustrious career, so best not to take any unnecessary chances. He stays aboard *Mayne's Moor Blooded*, where Hald can keep an eye on him.'

Scratching around, hoping he'd thought of everything that could . . . 'Oh yeah, and if you've raised Gergis, I haven't shown, and there's something *else* in that cabin, scratching to get out, then you get everyone across to *Sea Eagle's Daughter* and you scuttle this fucking ship. That clear?'

Nyanar swallowed. 'And if . . . if something . . . untoward . . . occurs before that, during the voyage? If we *need* you? What then?'

Gil clapped him cheerfully on the shoulder. 'Then I'll know, and I'll be back,' he lied. 'But I'll come back through the door myself, I won't need any help. Tell the men that, make sure it's clear. Can't answer for your safety if you don't.'

He was probably laying it on a bit thick, but better that than leave this pampered noble idiot any latitude for error. Better to cover all the angles as best he could, and hope the ramshackle makeshift command structure he was leaving would hold.

Time to go.

Down in his cabin, he locked the door as promised, took the reclaimed Kiriath steel carpenter's bradawl he'd blagged from Shanta back in the shipyards at Yhelteth, and scratched wards into lock plate, door hinges and jamb. He made himself go slow, make sure of each stroke. He'd nearly burnt down a waterfront tavern in the upriver districts of the city last year, pissing about with fire wards for practice and getting the cross strokes out of true.

Faint flicker of blue, etching the door's dimensions, fading out.

Done.

He took the key out of the lock, etched glyphs down its shaft and put it under the pillow in his bunk. He put on his cloak, took the Ravensfriend, scabbard and harness, lay back on the bunk with his sword hand draped over the side to the floor, boots up on the foot bar and crossed at the ankles. He put his free hand behind his head and stared up at the ceiling.

Began to recite the slow, unwinding cadences Hjel had taught him. Described the glyphs to the ceiling with the fingers of his left hand.

Anticipation prickled through him.

He wasn't sure if it was the slow seep of blood into his prick at thoughts of Hjel, the siren song of the white *ikinri 'ska* cliffs, waiting in endless glyphed mystery, or simply the thought of what he and the Ravensfriend would need to do once he reached Trelayne.

Then, as the trance state Hjel had taught him came steadily on, he saw that, really, there might not be much difference or distance between any of those three things.

The cabin ceiling grew less significant overhead, the bunk seemed to drift like an unmoored boat. He felt himself slipping towards the Grey Places. Compared to the raw force it had taken to punch himself and Klithren through last time, this was almost languid. *Lesson one, grim scar-faced swordsman sorcerer – some places in the Margins are easier to reach than others.* Hjel smiles as he says it, pillowed only inches away, and traces the scar on Gil's cheek with one gentle fingertip. *The reason so few aspiring witches and warlocks make it through is because they're so bloody single-minded. They aim for the heart of the* ikinri 'ska *every time – which is a bit like trying to swim up a waterfall in Spring spate. Trick is, look for kinder waters. If you've got any natural aptitude, the Margins want you here anyway. Use that. Loosen up, float and swim wide. Relax and let the currents bring you. You can always walk the rest of the way in, once you're here.*

He opens his eyes.

Red sparks escaping skyward over his head to mingle with the cold white pinprick scatter of stars. He's on hard-packed earth beside a roaring fire.

A boot comes down, right next to his head.

Someone yelps in shock, he hears liquid spilled into the fire with a billowing hiss. Gets a confused impression of a figure towering over him, pinwheeling its arms to stay upright. His grip on the Ravensfriend tightens. The figure sits down with a hard bump, narrowly misses landing on Gil's legs.

Fuck, man! Where'd he come from?

Uproarious laughter, a burst of it, but dying off fast into queries of concern. The man who went over on his arse waves it away. Bounces to his feet and winks at Gil in the firelight. His Naomic has an outlandish lilt and phrasing to it, but Ringil's been here enough times now for it to seem comfortingly familiar.

Nice entrance, mate. You were nearly wearing my soup for a waistcoat there.

Ringil mumbles an apology, props himself up and looks around. Sees faces beyond the leaping flames, easy grins. Behind that, the cold white rise of ruins into the dark; slumped walls and truncated white pillars, holding the night air up.

A handsome, middle-aged woman comes forward, bends and offers her hand to help him up. Dark hair bound back, shot through with a lightning bolt streak of white from one temple – he knows her vaguely, has seen her around camp a few times on previous visits. He lets go his sword and makes the grasp. Her hand is warm and calloused. She smiles at him.

Hjel's apprentice, she says. *Welcome back. You're getting pretty good at this, you come in closer every visit. Try not to land in the fire next time.*

More laughter. She pulls, strong and firm, lands him on his feet. He nods acknowledgement, gathers up the Ravensfriend, scabbard and harness from where it's lying in the dust. He feels a little self-conscious clutching it – outside of the usual knives and bows for hunting, the odd axe for chopping wood, these people aren't much for weapons.

Thanks, uh—

Daelfi. She sketches a casual reverence, hand to breast and brow, head briefly inclined. The motions have a dancer's easy grace. *Acting skipper, while Hjel's away.*

Daelfi, yeah. I'm Ringil.

Oh, I know. She grins crookedly, gestures around. *You might not think it from all these cackling idiots, but you're a bit of a favoured guest these days. The way Hjel mopes about between visits, we're all pretty glad when you finally show up and put a smile back on his face.*

Yeah, someone calls out. *Poke the fire, get it going. So to speak.*

The laughter again. He's forgotten how much he misses that sound, the rounded, open ring of ribald amusement with no sour edge, no hidden blade of hate or distancing mockery in it. He feels it tug a soft unwilling smirk onto his lips.

He's not around, then? Hjel?

Headed out into the deep range this morning. To look for you, actually. For the first time, a frown chases the good humour off Daelfi's face. *We had a visit from your wraith guard yesterday, back at the beach camp. Flickering about on the edge of the fire like candles in a gale. Poor, cursed creatures. They were frantic about something. Hjel figures it has to be you, you're in some kind of trouble, so he has us up stakes and move into the Margins. Told us to camp out here at the ruins and wait for him. So here we are, waiting. And* – a sharp clap of those warm, calloused hands – *pashatazam! You show up here instead. Magic, eh – what are you going to do?*

Her grin is back, irrepressible. He does his best to match it – anything else would feel rude.

Can you get me to him, Daelfi?

Oh, you can do that yourself. You were well on your way, showing up here. But events don't echo the same way in the Margins as they do in the real world. Him heading out probably doesn't feel like it's happened yet. Feels like he's still here, I expect. She pauses. *Do you want some soup before you go?*

She keeps him company while he eats.

Perhaps sensing his awkwardness in Hjel's absence, she leads him away from the main gathering. Seats him on a tumbled column close to where the soup cauldron hangs over a smaller, neatly banked cooking fire. She serves him a generous, steaming bowl and a torn chunk of bread. Takes a smaller chunk of the bread for herself and perches beside him on the column, nibbling daintily. It knocks years off her apparent age, makes her seem almost girlish. She watches him devour the soup – he's ravenous, it only dawns on him as he takes the first well-seasoned mouthful; back in the real world, he's not exactly been keeping up with regular meals. She re-fills his bowl when he's done, keeps him supplied with bread.

I have a question, if you don't mind, she says. The girlishness is gone, evaporated like the steam from his bowl. *Is there much talk of heroes and destinies in the lands where you're from?*

He wipes the bottom of his second bowl with the bread. *Nothing but. Everybody loves that shit. Everybody wants to believe in heroes.*

And you?

He shoots her a sideways glance as he chews. Swallows.

Will it offend you if I say no?

I am not easily offended, it's not our way. What others believe is not my concern, unless they attempt to force it on me.

You wouldn't like it much where I'm from.

This much, I had already divined. Daelfi opens one beckoning hand at him. *But you have not answered my question.*

He finishes the last of his bread, sets his empty bowl down at his feet. Sighs. *I have seen too many soothsayers' heads on spikes to believe they see much further into the future than the rest of us. The marsh-dweller women at Strov market scrape a living from prophecy – I suspect that's about all it's good for. Why do you ask?*

Daelfi studies her hands, turning them as if they might do something unexpected at any moment. He supposes that to be Hjel's second in camp, she must have some talent with the *ikinri 'ska* herself.

They say that Hjel nearly died at birth, she says quietly. *That he was stillborn in fact. I am more or less of an age with him, so I'm too young to remember if there's truth in this. But they say a living god came into camp and gave him back his life for a great purpose.*

A god, or a good doctor?

She smiles gently. *They say it was a god. They say it was Akoyavash, with his storm-coat and slouch hat and a salt wind at his back.*

Ringil tries to ignore the quickening twinge along his nerves. Hjel has never shared this with him. *A great purpose, eh?*

Yes, it's a commonplace, I know. A line from every second campfire tale. But why should that be, I wonder?

He manufactures a casual shrug. *We look back and see a path we have taken through life. It's tempting to imagine that the path was always there, laid out with purpose and waiting only for us to walk it. And I suppose it's comforting to think that those who lead us are walking such an allocated path, laid out by the gods for the greater good.*

Daelfi shakes her head. *We are not much for such fancies here. And most of us take the Ahn-foi to be self-interested powers. Occasional allies at best, rarely safe to trust. But a story like that, one that dogs you from the cradle onward. Well, it can be hard to shake. You live in its shadow, I think. There are other reasons why Hjel helps you, I know. But I do wonder.*

Don't think I'm pretty enough to swing it alone, eh?

A broad grin. *No, if I were Hjel, I'd fuck your brains out as soon as look at you. In fact, if you were otherwise inclined, I might try it myself.* The grin fades out. *But I'm not sure I would be teaching you the* ikinri 'ska. *We're not meant to pass it on lightly.*

You think he's making a mistake?

Honestly, I don't know. I hope not. She stares away, back towards the bon-fire and the main gathering. *But something is troubling him these days. I've known him all my life, I see it when the others mostly don't.*

And you think it's me.

I think it began not long after you came. Not at first – at first, he was happy, happier than I'd seen him in years, certainly happier than he'd been since Loqui left. They're right about that much, you really lit him up. But later . . . Daelfi shakes herself out of her brooding. *I'm sorry, I should not have started this. It's not my business, it's not our way. I have no right to burden you with any of this uninvited.*

Bit late now.

Yes. She looks steadily at him. Her face is a restless mask of shadow and ruddy light from the dance of the cook fire's flames. *Are you angry with me?*

You're worried about him, Gil says with an attempt at good grace. *It's understandable.*

I am worried about him, she agrees. *But I would not be honest if I let you believe it is only that.* You *worry me, Ringil. You and whatever destiny you may have. We are guardians of the* ikinri 'ska, *it's said, and I worry we have not understood what opening it to you might mean.*

Perhaps you worry too much. He can feel himself getting impatient with this woman, and he doesn't want to be. She's just fed him, she clearly cares about Hjel, her worries are selfless and well-intentioned. He tries to curb his tone. *Perhaps you're mistaken about your guardianship. Perhaps your ances-tors stumbled on the* ikinri 'ska *by mistake and just happened to get a good grip on it. Who's to say it's really yours to worry about in the first place? Who laid that duty down? Or worse – perhaps your mastery was handed down by evil forces, by creatures whose interests are actually inimical to the good of humankind. Ever wonder about that?*

She grimaces. *Frequently. And many similar things besides.*

Then, as I said before – perhaps you worry too much.

She bows her head for a while, frowns into her flexed and interlaced hands. *Please understand – like you, I don't believe in paths already laid down. But I do see . . . patterns, all around us. Day and night, the turn of the sky and* the seasons, the migrations of certain birds, the age stations of a life. Enough for a rudimentary sort of prophecy, in fact. And back before the Southern Scourge fell on us and razed our kingdoms, wise men and women among our ancestors went further than this. They detected certain useful mathematical truths about the universe and handed them down to us. These too are a form of pattern, I think. So I wonder if there might not be other patterns written into the world, patterns that remain invisible to us, but that a god might perceive and use for tools.

He laughs, not very kindly. *I have met beings that call themselves gods, my lady. They don't seem to have a much better grip on things than we do.*

No, but they might see things coming that we do not. And – he sees that she's running just ahead of the unravelling thread of her own thoughts, eyes alight with the speculation – *what if their relationship with time is not as rigid as ours? In the Margins, I have seen time slow down, speed up, dance around itself like a drunk courtesan. Some say it's broken. Damaged somehow, and not yet healed. Others say that it's been rebuilt, but by poor craftsmen who have not properly understood its nature. What if the gods avail themselves of that for their own purposes? In a limited way, but enough to bluff us, to make it seem as if they attend to the working out of a great destiny, when in fact they merely conjure and improvise at a level we cannot encompass?*

You think this is what Hjel believes?

Daelfi draws a breath as if to speak, then visibly reins herself in.

I have intruded enough as it is, she says quietly. *I won't attempt to guess Hjel's thoughts for you. You must ask him yourself when you reach him. But this much I do know – time was out of joint when you first came to us.*

Out of joint?

Yes, dislocated as if by some brutal force, some violent intrusion into things. You came to us a stranger, but one who already knew us. And then, many months later, you came again and did not know us when we already knew you. In a lifetime of living in and out of the Margins, none of us have ever seen a twisting as savage before, nor is there any record or tale of it among our people. None of us want to guess what it might portend. She gives him a sad, regretful smile. *Or what you will do when the time of that portent arrives.*

Relax and let the currents bring you. Again.

He opens his eyes.

Red sparks escaping skyward over his head to mingle with the cold white pinprick scatter of stars. He's on a bedroll beside a softly crackling fire.

He props himself up and stares through the waver of flames to where Hjel the Dispossessed sits with mandolin in lap and broad brimmed hat slanted forward over his eyes.

That was quick.

Gil grunts and heaves himself fully into a sitting position. He's still full of soup. *Not from my end it wasn't.*

He looks for the three figures that brought him last time, the wraith guard Daelfi talked about, but he and Hjel are alone.

Hjel sees the glance.

They faded as you did. Just a few moments gone. The dispossessed prince sets his mandolin aside and unfolds a little, reaches for a stick to poke the fire. *They know well enough I don't readily welcome their kind at my hearth.*

Bit harsh.

Maybe so. Hjel jabbed at the fire, a little more vigorously than it appeared to need. *But my path through the* ikinri 'ska *is not yours, and I have no desire to make it so. I don't do that black mage shit. I don't like dealing with the enslaved dead.*

You think I do? The Dark Court dumped them on me, what am I supposed to do?

The dispossessed prince shrugs. *I really wouldn't know. Use them, I suppose. Exploit them. Isn't that what a black mage should do?*

How the fuck should I know? Daelfi has warned him to expect a troubled dispossessed prince, but this is way beyond anything he expected. *Introduce me to a black mage, I'll ask him. How many do you know?*

Just the one, and I'm looking at him now.

Oh, fuck off.

They sit in silence for a while. The fire hisses and snaps between them.

So what do you want? Hjel asks him eventually.

There's an obvious answer to that, but by now Ringil is in no mood to give it to him. This isn't working out anything like he'd planned, and it's Hjel's fucking fault. He looks with unfriendly eyes across the fire, then away. He lowers himself back to the bedroll and stares up at the stars.

What do you think I want? The words are ashy on his tongue. *You think I'm here for the company? I need to go back to the cliffs.*

We were there not long ago. You told me you'd drunk your fill, you were sick of it.

That was then. This is now.

You are learning as fast as anyone I ever saw. Faster. I am already letting you push to the limits.

It's not enough.

It's more than you can readily handle at the moment. It would take the lifetime of a god to absorb the totality of the ikinri 'ska. *No human can do more than scratch the surface, borrow in depth here and there maybe. Even if I—*

Well, then you're not teaching me the right fucking pieces, are you?

Ringil flings himself up into a sitting position again, glaring. The splintered snap of his rage, there in the firelight and gone, soaking away into the quiet gloom around them.

Hjel bows his head.

Perhaps I am not. Have I been a poor teacher, then? Perhaps you should write the lessons from now on.

Oh, don't fucking sulk at me! Gil means to yell across the fire, but some-how it comes out tighter, almost pleading. *Hoiran's throbbing prick, Hjel – I've got my balls to the wall here! Don't you get that? Something's coming, and I'm not ready for it. I am not ready!*

And you think any of us ever are? Now there's a snap in Hjel's voice as well. *What – have you swallowed some idiot tale of warrior youths and wizards in training for their great task, their great moment of destiny?*

I don't know, have you?

Hjel blinks. *What the fuck is that supposed to mean?*

It means I had a word with Daelfi on my way here. And the way she paints it, you think there's some great purpose afoot and we're both snuggled up together in it.

Daelfi had no business—

Oh, shut up. Gil gestures in disgust. *Didn't fucking tell me you had a visit from Dakovash when you were born, did you? You don't like my wraith guard, my enslaved dead – take it up with your fucking patron, he's the one who gifted them to me.*

Akoyavash is not my patron—

No? Seems you'd be dead without him, though.

That is a tale.

Yeah, a tale you chose not to tell me. I wonder why.

Well, maybe because it was none of your fucking business, my lord black mage.

Oh, give it a rest. You know what? You think you made the wrong choice with me, fine. Go home. I'll walk to the glyph cliffs myself, get what I need without you.

I'd like to see you try.

Gil lowers his voice to a gritted snarl. *Then stick around. Because I am not going to waste any more time with your lizardshit petty sorceries. I need to be ready for the cabal and their dwenda pals, and I am* not *waiting around while you decide if I've maybe drunk too much of the* ikinri 'ska *to merit further in-struction, or if maybe I'm not a safe pair of hands. I need to be ready, and I will* be fucking ready.

Is that right? The dispossessed prince is breathing hard. *Ready? Hmm? You think any of us get that luxury?*

I think you'd better—

Hjel tramples him down, voice trembling with rage. *You think I was ready when my father died and leadership of the band fell on me? You think I was ready to go and face the Creature at the Crossroads then? I went because someone had to. I took what half-made rags of proper dress for the occasion I so far owned, and I put them on, because* that's what you do. *Why do you think you're any different? What's so fucking special about* you?

The quiet darkness curtains in behind his shout.

Ringil studies the flames for a while.

Well, he says mildly, *at least your father's dead. He's not running around somewhere trying to have you killed.*

195

He looks up. Hjel meets his eye and sighs. *Ahh, Gil, look—*

No, it's fine. Skip it. Roughly now. *I'd be dead if it weren't for what you've done for me already. Worse than dead. I tend to forget that sometimes.*

You needed to forget. The sorcerer prince's voice is soft and urgent. *You told me the tale, but those memories come from a place I have not yet been, a time that has yet to pass for me. It makes sense that such premonition would fade. That kind of forgetting is how we deal with the Margins.*

That's not what I meant.

No. I know.

I meant I can be a selfish, graceless fucker sometimes.

Well. Hjel looks away. *I, uh – that wasn't the warmest welcome I could have given you either, was it?*

Had warmer. Gil risks the crooked corner of a smile. *So Daelfi was right. This destiny-of-the-gods shit is chewing you up.*

Hjel gives him back his half-smile, but there's pain in the corners. *Look, it doesn't matter right now. Why don't you just come over here, Gil?*

No, you're all right. Best if we just get some rest and talk about it over breakfast.

There've been times in the past, and other men, where he would have bounced back from the quarrel. Used the slosh of raised emotions to fuel the arousal for a grudge fuck or maybe just the hot, hugging collapse into mutual remorse. But he doesn't want to grudge fuck Hjel, and he feels no remorse. And Daelfi's right on the money – something is very clearly eating away at the dispossessed prince, despite his protestations to the contrary.

Hjel watches him rearrange himself on the bedroll.

I am sorry, he says. *What is it you think is coming, that you're so unready for? Did you somehow unleash this Illwrack creature you went looking for?*

Over breakfast, like I said. Gil smiles to rob his firmness of offence, lies flat, turns his face to the sky. *We'll talk about it then.*

But as he lies there, he's well aware that Hjel is not following suit, that he sits instead, unmoving on the other side of the fire, and after a while, the pressure to talk to him is just too great. Gil wonders briefly if it's some minor glamour that the dispossessed prince knows how to cast, is casting even now. Then he gives up caring one way or the other – there's too much pressing up inside him that he wants to share, to lay out in words, if only so he can consider how it sounds when it's said out loud.

You're right about one thing, he says, without moving or looking away from the stars overhead. *We're none of us ready. No, we didn't unleash the Illwrack Changeling, we didn't even find him. We didn't find the floating city of An-Kirilnar either. Meanwhile, there's a war started down south behind my back, we're three thousand miles the wrong side of the battle lines and my friends are captives of the enemy. And just to really spice things up, I've had a friendly visit from the Queen of the Dark Court, and it looks like the dwenda are bringing the Talons of the Sun to the party.*

Silence, and he thinks for a moment that he's wrong, Hjel has fallen asleep sitting there after all, and he's talking to himself. Then the dispossessed prince speaks, and there's a guarded tension in his voice that Gil makes for disbelief, or maybe even faint envy.

You summoned Vividara the Dark?

Ringil watches the stars. Yawns. *No, I think it'd be fairer to say she summoned me.*

Hjel's pantheon, he knows, isn't really the same as the one honoured in the temples of the League, or even the rough analogue worshipped out on the steppes by Egar's people. But some of the names the Ahnfoi bear are close, and there are enough similarities to detect a common underlying pattern. An assembly of enigmatic absentee overlords, demanding absolute obedience at all times but rarely showing up to collect it; a rough hierarchy, blurred and shuffled by an inconsistent mythos that suggested the relationships were a little less formal, a little more complicated than temple officiators liked to admit. Hoiran and Firfirdar on their wedded thrones, a close circle of courtiers – mostly – at their beck and call, but then there were tales of insurrection, resentment, infidelity, squabbling . . .

At times, Gil can understand the longing for simple order that drives the southerners' arid faith. How comfortable it must feel to know that there's just the one overlord, just the one set of edicts he's handed selflessly down for your personal benefit, and that everything from the depths of the ocean to the starry sky is safely in hand.

Yeah, Egar snorted one campfire night out on the steppe. *And if you believe that, I've got a string of unicorns out back I want to sell you cheap.*

Ringil feels a grin touch the corners of his mouth at the memory. He shifts a little on the bedroll, seems to sink fractionally deeper into it. His fed belly gurgles a little, there's a spreading warmth right through him now, and a letting go. It's as if unburdening himself to the dispossessed prince has cut some cable deep inside, let him finally drift loose on the swells of a weariness whose extent he only now starts to grasp.

Vividara manifest portends destruction, Hjel says quietly. *Death and flames about her, the confusion of human hopes and fears where she passes, and the creep of chaos in her train.*

Yeah, Gil mumbles. *Same where I'm from, more or less.*

How did she appear to you?

Uhm – regal. A bit chilly with it. He yawns again, cavernously. *Reminded me of my mother, actually.*

The other gods you've told me about were circumspect in their approach. Hjel's voice seems to be coming from further away than before. *They played games. Disguised themselves or walked in your dreams.*

Mhmm.

That Vividara came to you so directly cannot be good. It suggests that the game they play is building to its climax. That fire and destruction are coming, and that most likely you will be the Dark Queen's agent in bringing them on.

197

Ringil is vaguely aware of turning on the bedroll, putting Hjel's voice and the heat of the fire at his back, turning his face away into the dark.

Certainly fucking will if I can get into Etterkal and find Findrich, he says drowsily.

And sinks away.

TWENTY-FIVE

Egar prowled seemingly endless corridors and companionways of iron, or some dark alloy that looked a lot like it. In places the metal glowed to life to light his way – soft, red light on the surfaces, as if they were heated from within, painting the close surroundings with a dull furnace glow. But when he put the back of a cautious hand close to the source, there was no heat at all. The alloy felt the same wherever he touched it, cool and smooth, and the glow faded not long after he passed – he looked back once and saw it inking out, closing up the corridor behind him with slightly unnerving dark.

He was, he supposed, lost.

He'd been wandering for the best part of an hour now, not much caring where his feet took him, though tending only to take stairs or ladders where they led upward. He assumed he was safe under the Warhelm's watchful eye – and if he wasn't safe from the demon itself, then it didn't much matter where in An-Kirilnar he wound up – but he'd carried the length of chain along anyway, wound twice around his fist and clinking reassuringly at his side as he walked.

Part of him longed for the chance to use it.

Some of those crab-legged spider things, maybe, run somehow out of the Warhelm's control. Or some species of giant rat that lived in the walls . . .

You don't need a fight, Dragonbane. What you really need is sleep.

He'd thought he was exhausted – he *was* exhausted, he ached from it – but sleep would not take him, no matter how long he rolled and flopped in the half-acre bed. His limbs itched and tingled when he tried to lie still, his belly ached from all the plums he'd eaten. In the end, he got up but that was no better. The apartments would not hold him, they stank of mannered confinement. Like the cell the imperials had held him in back in Yhelteth, there was a surface comfort that felt like some stilted apology for the truth – that he was trapped in the belly of a beast the size of a city, and it would not let him go. He felt the craving for open air and access to the horizon like some nagging hangover he couldn't shake off.

Fucking tent-dweller.

It hit him then, abruptly, how much he missed the steppe – the big open skies, the endless flat expanse of land with no visible limit on how far you could ride. In the last three years, he'd been in swamps and on ships, in pipe houses, whorehouses and taverns, in slums and palaces and jails, up and down the tangled warren streets of the imperial city herself, out to Rajal, Lanatray, Ornley for more of the same. Now, he felt suddenly as if none of it had ever been more than a distraction, a series of cheap whore's tricks he'd bought to keep him from missing the peace you felt sitting at a campfire out on the endless plain, band and stars close enough to reach up and touch, buffalo grazing close . . .

Yeah – take you back there, Dragonbane, and you'd be screaming for Imrana's perfumed arms and the streets of Yhelteth inside three fucking days.

You, are, tired.

He prowled about. Stared at his own rumpled bed like a beast he had to somehow kill. *Oh, for Urann's sake.* He dressed, grabbed up the chain from where he'd left it beside the bed, hurried out of the apartments in search of . . . something.

Hadn't found it yet, whatever it was.

He did find, finally, a set of laddered steps that led somewhere other than into a new corridor. Climbing them, he felt a cool breeze on his face and thought he might have made it up to whatever skyline An-Kirilnar might offer. But instead, the top of the companionway gave out into a vast, gusty cargo space, where crane hooks hung in immobile and silent silhouette, and looming, tangled piles of scrap littered the floor. Fitful traces of band-light crept in through a row of huge windows set high up in one wall. From equally massive openings in the floor came the distant sound of the ocean below.

Egar stood for a moment, taking it all in.

He wasn't overly impressed by the size or the gear, he'd seen similar spaces at An-Monal. But back then the Kiriath had still been around, the cranes had been in motion, hauling loads up through the hatches and shuttling them back and forth. There'd been *noise* and *light*. Hammering, shouting, the brilliant cascade of sparks from the Black Folks' metal-work tools.

This just felt like a mausoleum.

He moved cautiously up to the nearest of the enormous hatches, thankful for what thin light there was. Peered down to the faintly luminous roil and surge of waves, a hundred feet below. He wasn't sure quite how he'd managed to end up in the lowest levels of An Kirilnar despite all his choices of upward stairs and ladders, but this was, he supposed, as good a place as any to rein himself in and stop wandering aimlessly about.

He stood there in the near dark for a while, looking down, listening to the ocean and the sound of his own breathing.

'The fall would in all probability kill you,' said the demon in his ear. 'I would advise against it.'

'Do I look like I'm going to fucking jump?' he snapped, because the sudden voice had, in fact, made him jump quite severely.

'It is hard to tell with humans. But many of the others did.'

'The others?'

'Yes. The others who were harboured here. After the victory at In-atharam, most of this coast was rendered uninhabitable for both Kiriath and humans. The land died and so did most who lived in it.'

The Dragonbane grunted. 'Doesn't sound much like a victory to me.'

'The region was rendered uninhabitable for the Aldrain as well, which was the purpose of fighting in the first place. Their cities were obliterated, their populations exterminated or driven out. I use the term victory in this sense. In the aftermath, however, some small bands of survivors from the Kiriath side made their way here in the hope of refuge. Where their allegiance could be proven, they were taken in. They waited here, with the existing garrison, for rescue from the south.'

'You're talking about human survivors?'

'Human and Kiriath both.' A delicate pause. 'The Kiriath weathered the waiting better than the humans.'

Egar thought about the architecture he'd wandered through and im-agined having to live with it on a siege basis. 'I bet. So how long was it before a rescue showed up?'

'Six hundred and eighty-seven years from the date of the victory at Inatharam. External conditions would not permit an approach any sooner.'

'Six *hundred* . . .' His voice died away, his gaze tipped down through the hatch to the ocean below. He nodded bleakly, imagining the choices made by men and women thousands of years ago on the edge of this drop. 'I wouldn't worry. I don't think I'll be staying that long.'

'Quite. In fact, this is something we should discuss.'

'What is?'

'Your departure. Your exit from the Wastes.'

As if unleashed by the words, one of the massive iron cranes overhead jolted into sudden motion. For the second time in as many minutes, the Dragonbane startled back. He shot a sour, accusatory look at the ceil-ing, then watched the crane, fascinated as it juddered and screeched and showered sparks along the long unused track it ran on. The noise was deafening.

'What's this for?' he yelled over the din.

'I have spoken with kir-Archeth Indamaninarmal regarding the War-helm Ingharnanasharal's recent sacrifice, and have formulated a model of the campaign vector it seems to intend.' The demon's voice was still an intimate, unnerving presence at his ear, somehow managing to come through the racket the crane was making without apparent effort. 'If I have understood the strategy well from the evidence, it remains a bold stroke for all its shortcomings, and deserves to succeed. Certainly, it is the only faint hope I see in light of the Aldrain's impending return. But to have any hope of success now, it will require some significant adjustments. Your return to the steppes is one such requirement. Retrieval of certain necessary implements and aids is another.'

'The *steppes?*' Egar bellowed, and the crane jolted to a halt over a hatch, left him bawling into abrupt quiet. '*Who said anything about* . . . the steppes?'

'Have patience. All will become clear.'

'Yeah? So who's this Warhelm Ingharn—'

Lights sprang up everywhere, bright rose and orange variations on the dull red he'd followed in his wandering, glaring from bulkheads, ceiling and floors like the multiple, puddled reflections of a fiercely setting sun. The shadows fled out, and somewhere behind him, a door clanked open.

He pivoted about, chain length swishing low. Saw Archeth standing on an iron gallery about head height above him on the nearest wall. She was, he noticed, dressed in completely fresh garments, cut and colours he'd never seen before, still visibly Kiriath but nothing as grim and minimal as he was used to her wearing. And *she* was the one gaping down at *him*.

'What are *you* doing down here, Eg?'

'Might ask you the same thing.'

'He was led,' said the Warhelm blithely. 'Subtly, through lighting cues and . . . other measures. My powers, *albeit severely truncated*, are good for that much at least.'

'Mother*fucker.*'

'Eg, listen, never mind, it's—' She grabbed the rail in her fists, leaned over at him. Her voice echoed in the iron space. 'There's a way we can do this. There's a way we can get home and make a difference. But it means—'

'Yeah, going back to the steppes. I just heard.'

Behind him, the crane began to unwind its huge hook and cable, downward through the hatch. It made a noisy whining, like some giant hound out of myth wanting to be fed, but nothing to compare with the shriek and clash before. You could talk over it without having to shout. Egar gestured helplessly at the machinery.

'Archidi, you want to catch me up here?' He held out his arms, palms upward. 'I mean, all I did was go out for a fucking walk.'

They sat together on a convenient pile of scrap and watched the cable spool down through the hatch. It seemed to be going down a long way.

'Anasharal's a . . . a fragment, I guess.' Archeth set her hands half a yard apart in front of her, framing empty space with them as if trying to trap the concepts there. 'It's a piece of the Warhelm Ingharnanasharal, cut loose and dropped out of the sky. It's like, I don't know – remember those big armoured lizards that used to smash the barricades in with their skulls and then just die in the breach?'

Egar nodded. 'Blunderers.'

'Yeah, well you remember how the tail end didn't die for hours afterwards? How it'd still be thrashing around, grabbing at things, trying to spike them, and the front end's dead and leaking brains? That's Anasharal, the tail end.'

'So that makes Inghawhatsit, the one still up in the sky, what, dead? Dying?'

'I don't know.' She jerked a thumb at the ceiling. 'Tharalananghharst says it's talked to the other Warhelms, and none of them can get Ingharnanasharal to answer. They don't talk to each other very often, so there's no way to know how long Ingharnanasharal has been silent. Might be recent, might have been as much as a couple of centuries. Anyway, Tharalananghharst says there's no precedent for a Helmsman falling to Earth, didn't even know such a thing was possible. Ingharnanasharal would have had to tear itself apart to make Anasharal, and there's no telling what's left up there or what state it's in.'

The whining stopped. They glanced up and saw the cable hung motionless down through the hatch. The Dragonbane gestured at it.

'Your got any idea what it's bringing up for us?'

She shook her head. 'Just that it's something we're going to need.'

'Never tell the troops anything they don't absolutely need to know, huh?' He pulled a glum face. 'Had a squad commander like that once.'

Archeth hunched her shoulders, as if against cold. The new jerkin she'd acquired moved loosely on her. 'I don't think the Warhelms know that much more than we do. It's all guesswork they're doing. I described what Anasharal looks like, and Tharalanangharst says you couldn't contain a Helmsman in something that size. It reckons that whatever's left of Ingharnanasharal, whatever it did to itself, there's probably not too much to Anasharal either – just a bunch of basic conversational tricks wrapped around a core purpose and a plan, and then dumped into a containment vessel.'

For Egar, the words might as well have been in another language for all the sense they made. Demons that weren't really demons, demons that had a plan, demons that could help you, demons that couldn't or wouldn't. At least up on the steppe you had it clear – steppe ghouls, flapping wraiths, possessed wolves. You either killed them or they killed you, and that was all you had to worry about.

Beside him, the dark woman went on framing boxes in the empty air.

'See, that's why Anasharal was vague so much of the time, why it couldn't help us once we got up to the Hironish. It's not really a Helmsman at all, it's a – a pretence of one. It never actually had much knowledge, just enough of a sketch to drive its purpose. It's like that talking map in the stable boy story or something, like a . . .'

She dropped her hands. 'I'm not explaining this very well, am I?'

'Didn't want to say anything.'

She drew a deep breath. 'Okay, look. Imagine the Empire wants to send a legate up to Ishlin-ichan, but there's no one available. It's important they impress the Ishlinak, get some treaties inked, but they can't spare anybody for the job. So they decide to send an actor instead—'

'Yeah, wouldn't surprise me. They think we're all fucking savages up there, who's going to tell the difference?' Egar scrubbed both hands down his face, suddenly conscious again of how tired he was. He put his chin on his fists. 'Actually, if the same bunch of clowns are running Ishlin-ichan as when I was last there, they really wouldn't know how to tell the difference. You could send in a trained pig and they probably wouldn't notice so long as it was wrapped in silk and walked on its hind legs most of the time.'

'Uh – yeah. Anyway.' Archeth cleared her throat. 'So that's it, that's what the court does. They get an actor, they tell him exactly what documents they want signed. Exactly what he can and can't agree to, and they make him memorise it. Then they teach him a bit of court etiquette, a couple of good stories to entertain the Ishlinak worthies, half a dozen reasons why the treaties are a good idea. But that's it. In the end, he may look like a legate, he may even act like a legate some of the time. But he isn't. He's just an actor who's memorised a few things in order to get something done.'

'Right. So what was Anasharal trying to get done? Not find the Illwrack Changeling, that's for fucking certain. So – what?'

'I don't know.'

'Did you ask?'

'She did ask,' the Warhelm's voice, all just-this-side-of-sane amiability, dropping unannounced into the conversation like a ton weight of pallet-loaded stone through the roof. 'And she was told as much as she needs to know.'

They looked at each other. Archeth shrugged.

Egar cast a murderous glance at the ceiling. 'Bit like the lighting around here, huh? Just enough illumination in just the right places to get us where you want us to go.'

'Your analogy is sound as far as it stretches, Dragonbane, yes. Though the guidance in this *rather more important matter* has been Ingharnana-sharal's, not mine. I merely attempt to extend and modify the model, so nearly as I am able to estimate its intended outcome.'

Hard, echoing clank – they both twitched at the sound. The crane cable jerked, cranked upward and stopped, jerked again, then began to rise smoothly through the hatch.

'Yeah, well.' Somewhat mollified – the Warhelm's words had rinsed right out of Egar's head while he was distracted by the cable, leaving only a vague comprehension that the demon seemed to have agreed with him. He struggled to retain some previous anger. 'Like I said, had a commander like that once. And that fucker nearly got me killed. I'm not looking for a repeat performance.'

'That is unfortunate. But I'm afraid Ingharnanasharal's sacrifice appears to have been built on a mathematics of oblique chaining and cascade outcomes. Which is to say that if either of you knew what end was intended from your actions, your knowledge would damage the equilibrium of the model, in all probability to an extent that would prevent said end from ever being achieved. It is quite possible that Anasharal itself does not know the true purpose behind its actions, or at least has not been allowed to consciously know, for the same reasons that I cannot allow either of you to know now.'

'Is that supposed to make us feel better?' snapped Archeth

'It is the closest to an explanation that I can offer you. And you should be aware, kir-Archeth, that all my actions, now as before, are taken in your best interests. I hope that this will be enough, because I will not tell you more.'

The Dragonbane brooded on the rising cable. The tone of the crane engine's whine was notably deeper than it had been on the downward journey. Something heavy was coming up. Something that weighed hard at the machinery's limits . . .

He snapped his fingers. 'Wait a minute! I thought you had to obey the Kiriath no matter what. You let 'Nam cripple and blind you because you had no choice, you said. And now his daughter can't make you answer a simple question? How's she any different?'

There was a long pause, a quiet broken only by the burdened whining of the crane. At his side, Archeth looked away, into the tangled scrap at her feet. Her new boots gleamed softly in the low light.

'Kir-Archeth Indamaninarmal,' said the Warhelm very gently, 'is half human. This . . . gives me some leeway.'

They sat in silence after that, all three of them, while the cable ran and ran, and whatever it was bringing them climbed inexorably up out of the ocean's depths below.

BOOK II
GOIN' HOME

'Thus scattered across the North, but quickened to fresh Heroic Deeds by the Gathering Storm of War and their Beloved Empire's Peril, the Sundered Company sought to gird themselves with Holy Rites and Weapons, then to hurry South and join the Serried Imperial Ranks, as Yhelteth stood once more, as it must, to defend Civilisation against the Darkness . . .'

The Grand Chronicle of Yhelteth
Court Bard Edition

TWENTY-SIX

It takes them what feels like three or four days to walk in to the glyph cliffs, though it might be more. This far into the Grey Places, you can never really tell – day and night are not leashed to any guaranteed rotation, they come and go like cavalier guests in the house of an overly accommodating host, and you have to make your plans without them. You walk until you're tired, you stop and eat and rest. You make camp when the light thickens and you sleep until you wake. If it's still dark you go back to sleep or try to; if it's not, you break camp and go on.

Eventually, you get where you're going.

The entourage of ghosts and might-have-beens that you drag with you, like the swirl of harbour water flotsam in the wake of a departing ship, well – those you've long ago learnt to live with, or you've gone insane trying. You've learnt to think of them as unavoidable echoes, caused inevitably by your passage through the Grey Places, the way your booted steps in some vaulted stone space cannot help but call forth the flat resounding ring of your footfalls. You might listen to those echoes, might even pay them some close, brooding attention if that's the mood that takes you. But talking back to them leans in towards madness.

There he is, told you he'd be along. Standing together at a crossroads and waiting for Ringil, a Venj who apparently never died, a Klithren who never needed revenge. *Hoy, Shenshenath – we going bounty hunting, or what? I thought we said dawn. Tlanmar's waiting. And who's this? You fall out with the other guy?*

You have me confused with someone else, Ringil tells them, walking straight past.

But they follow on behind for a while anyway, muttering back and forth at each other.

Cheeky fucker. I told you he was just another perfumed imperial mummy's boy, they're all the fucking same. I don't know why we bothered with him in the first place.

Venj, mate, the man's just not in a great mood, that's all. Not like you're a portrait of good cheer yourself when you're hungover, or some good-time girl's just turned your purse inside out while you were asleep.

That's not the point. Thing about imperials is, it's their fucking culture. They don't stand by the same values we do, they don't even understand them. You can't trust any of them further than you can spit.

Eventually, they fade out, voices growing less and less substantial, as if blown away by the breeze across the marsh. Gil knows better than to look round when that happens – sometimes the voice alone can trail you for an hour or more, speaking out of empty air at your side as if its owner hasn't gone, is instead just trying out a magical cloak of invisibility from some Majak tale. And if you do give your attention, it'll likely bring back the ghost in its entirety all over again.

Some ghosts are harder to ignore than others.

My hero, my wonderful, sinewy boy, returned in triumph. Grace of Heaven Milacar, shaven head and fastidiously barbered chin beard, judiciously applied kohl on his eyelids, throws open his arms for an embrace and Ringil finds he still cannot make himself walk past this one without a word. He stutters to a hesitant halt. He won't take the embrace, he knows already it'll be cool and curiously lacking in human odour, but oddly solid in a way that living bodies aren't, more like hugging a dead tree trunk than a man. But—

Can't really stop, Grace. I'm in a hurry.

But you've only just got here, Gil. I know you've got the acceptance speech to make and everything, but surely you could do with – the glint of a lewd grin – *relaxing a little before all that dreary Glades politicking. You must be positively rigid with tension, no?*

Joyous memories from Grace's bedchamber come and catch him sharply under the heart. He seeks deflection so he won't have to think about the way it ended.

Last time I checked, you lived in the Glades too, Grace.

Eh? Milacar looks so genuinely offended it twitches a grin from Ringil's lips. *You really think I'd sell out that badly? I don't know what you've heard, Gil, but the war hasn't changed me the way it has Findrich and Snarl. I may go to a few client parties in the Glades now and then, but I haven't fucking forgotten who I am.*

And the tragedy of the gap, between this Grace of Heaven and the real one, is abruptly too much for him to grin at. He turns away.

Got to go, Grace. Give me a couple of days, yeah? I'll, uhm, I'll catch up with you.

Now you promise me, Gil? Grace's features crease in another lascivious smile. *I'll have a princely forfeit from you if not.*

He swallows. *Promise.*

He marches away, steadfastly refusing to hear any more, but the phantom has in any case fallen silent. At his side, Hjel purses his lips and politely says nothing. It's a basic courtesy of companionship in the Grey Places, he's seen it in operation between members of Hjel's band on the few occasions the dispossessed prince has brought men and women with him. You don't ask, you don't comment unless invited to.

And you never, ever engage with someone else's ghosts.

Hjel has a few accompanying eddies of his own. A grave, wide-shouldered man in his fifties with some kind of big wind instrument slung across his back – he calls himself Moss, flickers in and out from time to time, and talks with obvious pride about the dispossessed prince's accomplishments. In his weathered, cheerful features you can see something of Hjel. Then there's a young woman whose eyes sparkle with happiness and who tugs at the dispossessed prince's sleeve and talks about their children. A rot-toothed dealer in some substance Gil guesses must be similar to krinzanz. A young boy who seems lost. A lugubrious character in a butcher's smock. Hjel is brutally short with most of them, somewhat less abrupt with the musician Gil assumes must be some version of his father.

These distractions aside, the journey is uneventful and their pace consistent. Hjel seems pleased with their progress. At one point, he even takes Ringil off their path to look at some more of the long-jars, emptied and piled up inside a moss-grown stone circle.

Since you're so fascinated by these things, he says, and Ringil is struck by a powerful sensation that he's been here before, that they've said and done all of this already.

Didn't you show me these before?

Hjel blinks. *Not these ones, no. Don't think so, anyway. Have a listen.*

As if acting out a dream, Ringil lifts one of the canisters to his ear. He can't work out whether his memory is at fault, or Hjel's, or if maybe this really is just another time and place with a rather severe resemblance to the last stone circle he stood in with the dispossessed prince and hefted a long glass jar and held it to his ear and . . .

Nothing.

Like an idiot, he shakes the canister and listens again.

Nothing. No chittering, seething whisper of unleashed horrors past.

He looks up at Hjel and shakes his head, feeling oddly embarrassed. *I, uhm, I can't seem to—*

Guess you've aged since the last time, then.

Something oddly hasty in those words, it's a conclusion drawn fast to avoid further inquiry. Ringil's eyes narrow.

It's not that long since you showed me the last time. Is it?

Hjel shrugs. *I thought not, but in the Margins who can be sure? Anyway, like the sage says, every chord played has a moment either side of it. On the one side sound, on the other silence. That the two are only separated by a moment does not mean that the sound can bleed back across into the silence before the chord is played.*

But there's a distracted look in the dispossessed prince's eyes and he's not looking at Ringil anymore.

You trying to get profound on me here?

Another shrug, moodier this time. *It's a simple enough proposition, I would have thought. You're a warrior, you know how little separates dead from alive in battle. Mutilated from whole, disfigured from untouched. One moment a living breathing being, the next a corpse; one moment a sensing, feeling limb, the next a severed chunk of meat and a bleeding stump; one moment unblemished—*

Yeah, I get it. I'm not a fucking tent peg.

Well, then. We step across these moments our entire lives. Occasionally, we're aware of the change as the step is taken, mostly we aren't.

Ringil holds up the canister impatiently. *Can you still hear this?*

Hjel catches the open end of the jar, tilts it deftly up to his ear and listens. Lets it go again. *Yeah, I can still hear it. My moment has not yet come.*

You are not changed.

The dispossessed prince's gaze is evasive again. *That's another way to look at it, I suppose.*

And I am. I am changed.

You have aged, *my lord black mage. Get over it.*

Stop fucking calling me that.

Hjel sighs. *Shall we go? By the look of that sky, we're due some nightfall soon and it's getting cold with it. Be good to get under canvas.*

There's an opening there for a flirt – Ringil turns pointedly aside from it. He sets the canister down with exaggerated care, surprised at how much it feels like leaving something vital behind. He has to fight an impulse to try again, to pick the thing up and strain his ears once more at the opened end. He turns back instead and finds Hjel watching, waiting for him. Gestures irritably for the dispossessed prince to get moving, then tramps through the long grass after him at a coolish distance.

When they've cleared the perimeter of the stone circle, he calls out to the other man.

Just so you know, Hjel – all that shit you were talking about life and death? Most men don't die that fast on a battlefield – it's not usually that clean.

Hjel stops dead for a moment, but he doesn't look round. *I stand corrected.*

Yeah.

They camp the last night within sight of the cliffs, the long marching limestone gleam crossing the plain at the horizon, like the much-notched blade of some colossal sword out of legend, left lying somehow on its edge in the marsh, now that the battle here between the gargantuan forces that wielded such weapons is done. Ringil is morose with feelings of loss he can't easily pin down, and Hjel is still holding back on whatever's bothering him. It makes for a monosyllabic shared meal, and a lot of staring into the fire in silence.

When Hjel retires to the tent, Gil doesn't follow him for a while.

He sits and stares instead at the distant line of the glyph cliffs, trying to sort out his memories, trying to separate out dream from truthful recollection, trying to decide if that's even a meaningful line where the *ikinri 'ska* is concerned.

He remembers the first time he saw the cliffs. Remembers being led out of a nightmare through a fissure that opened in their base. He remembers that it was Hjel who led him out – or did he go first and Hjel follow behind, it isn't clear now, he sees both in his mind's eye, it seems to have happened a thousand years ago to another man entirely – and he remembers that the passageway was minutely worked over every inch of its surface with the glyphs of the *ikinri 'ska*. He remembers stepping out of the fissure and turning to face the enormity of the endless marching cliffs he'd just emerged from, the staggering understanding that they too were worked over every inch with the same tiny script.

It gets tougher after that.

He remembers that Hjel left him then, but there was – wasn't there? – something *else* in his place. Something hunched and hovering invisible at his shoulder, something he daren't turn and look at. Something that reached out over his shoulder with lengthy, emaciated limbs and deftly tapped at glyph sequences here and there – and each touch left the sequence glowing faintly as if touched by band-light. He remembers peering at the glyphs, remembers that somehow he knew which ones to read, where to look for them, how to interpret them. Hjel's previous tutored examples – scratched into beach sand or road dust for him, chalked up on rock like some child's imitation of what was carved out here – all of that fading out like the music as the curtain goes up on the main entertainment. All of that, stamped out, stamped *through* by something dark and massive, working through him.

He remembers that it hurt his head to do it.

He doesn't remember how long he was there, or how he came back. Only that it ended in flame and fury in the crumbling ruins of the temple at Afa'marag.

Gil stares across the heated air above the campfire, remembering, and it's as if there's something sitting there in the darkness on the other side, grinning skullishly back at him, biding its time.

He can't be sure, but he thinks it wears his face, and a spiked iron crown.

He waits to see if it'll go away, but it doesn't. So he holds its eye in silence, holds down a shiver and waits some more.

All right, then, he tells it finally. But only when he's sure it lowered its eyes first.

He gets up and crawls into the tent after Hjel.

He's not sure if it's need for refuge or something else that drives him.

The dispossessed prince is feigning sleep, as Ringil slides under the mound of blankets and spoons in behind him. But when Gil slips a hand down the tell-tale unrelaxed tension of muscle in his belly, cups his prick and balls and whispers into the nape of his neck *I know you're awake*, Hjel moans and opens his eyes. He stiffens in seconds under Ringil's gently squeezing touch, reaches back for Gil and finds him already hard.

I want you, Ringil mouths in his ear, and it's true enough. He tugs hard on the other man's erection, tugs him round under the covers, then sweeps the blankets away and slips the head of Hjel's cock into his mouth. The dispossessed prince groans and tangles his fingers in Ringil's hair, but Gil pulls back, grips hard.

Now what's all this black mage shit, hmm?

I, it's nothing, I – don't stop, Gil, don't fucking stop . . .

He draws on the pool of his role-playing memories with Grace. *Want me to be your black mage master, is that it, creature?*

No, I no, it isn't that . . . Ringil puts his mouth back and Hjel arches like a drawn bow. *Yes, yes, all right. Please, please. Take me, dark lord, fuck me, fuck me.*

Then you'd better get me slick, hadn't you?

He gets to his knees over Hjel, still working him with his hand. Rubs his prick back and forth across the dispossessed prince's face and questing mouth, finally lets the other man take him in. He cups Hjel's head with the gentleness of a nursing mother, a gentleness held in monstrous tension against the savagery of the feelings roaring through him now, and he guides the dispossessed prince's sucking mouth softly back and forth. He lets go of the other man's pulsing cock with a flourish, gathers saliva in his mouth and spits copiously into his free hand. Reaches down to the crack between Hjel's heaving, clenching cheeks, works the spit in with soft circular motions of his fingers until he judges the prince ready.

Pulls loose, swiftly now, rolls Hjel in his arms – it feels suddenly effortless. A last wipe of spit across the head of his own pulsing prick and then he gathers the dispossessed prince under him, presses Hjel's legs wide and thrusts carefully in. He dips his face to within an inch of Hjel's, whispers into his eyes.

Your black mage is fucking you now, dispossessed prince.

Hjel makes an incoherent noise of assent in his throat. Gil pushes deeper, working a rhythm to fit his words.

Taking everything you have, taking you deep.

Hjel's head, weaving back and forth under his. He snatches kisses from the panting mouth like a striking snake.

Give in to the dark, he hisses. *Let go, let me in.*

And suddenly – hot, sticky splatter up over his belly, Hjel's fountaining cock shuddering against his flesh like a stabbed man, his own deeply buried response coming instantly behind, like white fire exploding back down the iron hard shaft of his prick and into his groin – it's over for both of them now, and the rest is quivering tremors, tight grasping, clasping, wet kisses and moaning, and feverish collapse . . .

Afterwards, as they lie sprawled across each other, tangled limbs and half-shed clothes and the blankets dragged haphazardly back in place, Ringil glides out of cover and strikes. Puts a grin in his voice that he doesn't really feel.

So, uhm – black mages, Hjel? What's that all about?

The dispossessed prince doesn't move, but abruptly there's a new stillness in him, a tension in his body that wasn't there before. Ringil feels it in all the places they touch, as if Hjel's flesh was somehow pulling back from his of its own accord. When the other man speaks, he sounds oddly lost.

It's not important.

Hoiran's balls, it's not important. We both just came like storm surf back there. Gil plants a kiss on the other man's neck, spoons closer behind him, gathers him tighter in. *Now come on, spill. What's going on?*

Hjel shakes his head. It's a small motion but it's like he's trying desperately to get loose of something. His words come out in hesitant, jerky little bundles.

I don't know, it's . . . my people have legends. About how we ended up . . . like we are. I told you . . . about the Southern Scourge. How they tore down our palaces and temples. Burnt our cities into the marsh. Scattered us, chased us into the Margins.

Yeah, I remember.

Privately, Ringil has always thought the legends Hjel's people tell sound like the same old *We Were a Great Civilisation Once* routine you heard trotted out by the subjugated coastal clans on the Yhelteth seaboard, or by haughty Parashal families visiting Trelayne who still hadn't got their heads around the way the more northerly city had wrested control of the League from them way back when. *Lo, We Were Torn from Ascendancy by Upstarts, Oh, the Lost Glory that Was Ours,* so drearily forth. As if there was some kind of conferred nobility in the fact that your distant ancestors did something significant once. But he's never said that to the dispossessed prince, it's always seemed unnecessarily cruel, and he doesn't say it now.

Yeah, says Hjel. *Well, they say the Scourge was led by a black mage. They say he came to Trel-a-Lahayn at the head of an army of the walking dead, that he had storms at his command.*

Ah.

Ringil looks at the other man's back, the just visible cheekbone edge of his averted face. Some small part of him is appalled at the chilly detachment in his mind as he thinks this through.

That's right. Hjel is not going to turn and meet his eye. Maybe he can feel the chill as well. *A dark lord emperor, they say. Or a sorcerer empress, a witch queen, it's not always the same story. When I was a little kid . . . I used to dream about – defeating this black mage in battle. Then, when I got a bit older, I started to fantasise . . . different stuff.*

Ringil kisses him again, on the nape of the neck. *So I see.*

Hjel clears his throat. *But fantasy wears thin, you know. It can't keep the real world out forever. You grow up. You start to crave human detail. You put mud on his boots, bags under his eyes. Scars and lines, regrets. He starts to talk, to really* talk, *not just recite the same shabby fantasy lines and postures you need to get off. You end up wondering what he was like when he was young, before you cloaked him in this convenient darkness.* The dispossessed prince hesitates, on the edge of something for a moment, then plunges on. *You wonder how he learnt the darkness in the first place. You wonder who taught him his power.*

215

Longish silence. In the gap it leaves, an abruptly violent gust of wind strops at the canvas over their heads, like something hungry trying to get in. Ringil wonders for a moment if his ghosts are gathered out there, a silent assembly of figures with heads bowed around the tent, honour guard and impending threat at one and the same time, waiting for him to emerge.

He puts the thought aside. Chooses his words with care. *So you're having some second thoughts here, are you? Scared you're training up a new dark lord?*

Now Hjel turns towards him, twisting round in his embrace, and just for a moment, Gil's jolted by the urgency in his face.

It isn't that. But . . . I see the way you drink down the ikinri 'ska. You take to it like hunted geese to the sky. It's like it wants *you, Gil. Like there's something hurrying the changes along, something neither of us has any control over. And I don't know what that is.*

Ringil snorts. *Didn't want me so much back when I was trying to pull down that fucking elemental fog at Sempeta beach, did it?*

Siempetra beach.

Whatever. I don't recall that one getting hurried along by anything.

Hjel stares at him. *You did it in five days, Gil.*

Yeah, five long fucking days.

But . . . The dispossessed prince coughs out a disbelieving little laugh. *I've seen men work* months *to master those sequences, Gil. Months. Some never manage it. You did it like you'd been doing it all your life. You made it look* easy.

Why'd you take me to see those canisters again? Ringil lets him go. Pushes back in the confined space of the tent, trying to shake something loose with the sudden change of tack. *You knew I wouldn't be able to hear them anymore, didn't you? You were expecting it.*

Hjel looks away. *I don't know.*

Yeah, you do. When the other man stays silent, he starts to get angry. *Come on, Hjel. Fucking talk to me.*

I— Hjel shakes his head. *Look, there's a tradition. Used to be, they don't do it now, I forbade it. Among my people, if a child committed a crime – something serious – if they stole, say, or hurt someone badly, or told dangerous lies about them – used to be they'd take the kid out into the Margins. Make them listen at the mouth of a long-jar. They'd tell them what they could hear was the sound of the world's first evil, back before it was loosed on humanity. And if they continued on the path they'd chosen, that evil would come looking for them. That they'd hear it at their back, creeping up, getting louder.* A quick, convulsive gesture that looks like shame. *Then, if the crime was particularly bad, they'd cut them loose, you know, leave them in the Margins for a given time, like a – a sentence to be served.*

Charming.

I already fucking said they don't do it anymore!

Good to know. And what does this have to do with me?

There were— Hjel swallows. *They say that sometimes, some kids, the really destructive, vicious ones, the ones that really liked to hurt and cause chaos, they say those kids listened to the long-jars, but they couldn't hear anything. They couldn't hear the evil.*

Yeah, or – try this – they were just tougher than the rest, and they said they couldn't hear anything just to piss off their elders. To not bow down on demand.

Hjel bows his head, as if in echo. *That may be. But it's said that the ones who couldn't hear the sound would always grow up to be dangerous, violent men. Rapists, killers, oath breakers. The kind that end up driven out.*

And you figure that's what I'm turning into?

I didn't say that.

Not quite, no. You didn't have to. His voice is rising now. *Did it ever occur to you – or to these fuckwit guardians of youth you're telling me about – that they probably left the ones who said they couldn't hear anything longer in the Margins than the others. Maybe too long. And that maybe leaving them there was what turned them into the men they became. Not some innate fucking evil your people were pig-shit ignorant enough to believe in.*

He isn't sure why he's suddenly so angry. Killer and oath-breaker can both be laid at his door, and while he might never have committed a rape, he's certainly stood by at a few. He's nobody's idea of clean, and he's never made any secret of the fact. It shouldn't take listening at the open end of some ancient, discarded piece of magical junk for Hjel to read any of that in him.

And it shouldn't hurt or surprise Gil that he has done.

Perhaps, then, it's just that over the disjointed, hard-to-measure time of his apprenticeship in the *ikinri 'ska*, he's grown accustomed to the easy-going humanity of Hjel's band of followers. He's come to appreciate their tolerance and wry humour, their lack of rage. He's learned to love the way they fill themselves with life like it's a well-cooked banquet, the way they refuse to gnaw on bones of cheap hate and discord like every other fucking culture he's seen or read about in thirty something years of standing up and taking notice. He's come, perhaps to take it all for granted, to live it like a dream or a child's tale. Escape out the window of your strictured, sutured life, out to the lights of campfires on the great marsh plain under vast open skies. Go find refuge and live among the kindly marsh-dwellers. And perhaps it's the shock of waking from that dream, banging your head on something real, and understanding suddenly that no, these are people just like you, and they have their murky corners and little cruelties just like everybody else.

Perhaps it's that.

Ringil draws a deep breath and puts his anger away. He manufactures a grin for his lover and teacher.

Sorry. I got a lot of hard discipline growing up. And look what it did to me.

Hjel makes a helpless gesture. Says nothing. An answering smile flickers on his face, never manages to stick. In the confines of the tent, still warm and scented with their fucking, he has never seemed so far away. Ringil tries again.

Look, maybe I'm just older, eh? Like you said. Maybe your tales of recalcitrant youth are so much self-fulfilling lizardshit, and I'm just getting old.

Yeah. That's probably it.

I'm— Gil spreads his hands. Open palms empty, offering nothing. *I'm not the pure-at-heart hero seeking arms and armour against the forces of evil, Hjel. I never pretended to be that.*

I know.

But you're worried about what I'm turning into anyway?

No, Hjel tells him quietly. *I'm worried about where I have to take you next.*

TWENTY-SEVEN

High up on the shoulder of the first jagged ridge, the fire sprite paused in its restless onward dance, as if to allow them a last look back.

Archeth didn't mind – she was pretty winded from the climb. She stood there, breathing hard, letting the breeze off the ocean cool her brow. Way below them, An-Kirilnar sat in the sea like some crumpled white lace handkerchief dropped in passing and still afloat on the surface of a pot-hole puddle. If you stared for long enough, you even got the illusion of movement, as if the city were drifting on the ruffled waters with the wind. It took Archeth a moment to understand why. The sun had just struggled up over the inland horizon, and, as it struck the ocean below, she saw with a tiny shock that there was something under the water, a hazy scatter of geometric patterning in every direction for miles, and that it was moving, pulsing in and out of visibility in random patches, all with the regularity of a sleeping man's breath, like some colossal living thing. The causeway, she suddenly understood, had been a choice, a thin piece of stability sliced out of a massive, intricate overall structure and raised just high enough to permit human passage. A scant scrap of lamplight left in the window of the long-forgotten Kiriath victory by a mind that made no real distinction between the passing minutes and millennia, and saw no reason to ever let the past go.

Small, welling sadness, somewhere down at the base of her being.

Stow that shit, Archidi. Over the past months, she seemed to have soaked up the argot of the marines and sailors she'd been surrounded with, was still surprised when it popped up in her thoughts. *Got a few other things to worry about right now, don't we?*

'What's the matter, leave something behind?'

Egar, grinning, puffing up the arid slope of the path to where she stood. No one was very keen on getting too close to the fire sprite, so the vanguard had fallen to Archeth by default. Selak Chan, Alwar Nash and the few other Throne Eternal had followed her at what distance their regimental pride would allow, and the Dragonbane came after them, at the nominal head of everybody else. There was a subtle, fresh alignment to be detected in the order, a change that sat uneasily on her shoulders, like the new harness the Warhelm had gifted her for her knives.

'Something like that,' she agreed.

She watched the men filing up onto the ridge after the Dragonbane. Judged no small number of them could use the break as much as she could.

Tharalanangharst had fed them unstintingly, worked some minor medical magic on their various injuries, gifted them all with fresh weapons and clothing, but still – after nearly three weeks of comfort and warmth in An-Kirilnar's sombre iron belly, the return to the Wastes felt like an eviction. The pre-dawn air outside when they left was cold and leaden, sitting sullenly in their lungs, burning if you drew it in too deep. The clouded sky was the texture of old porridge, stirred through with weird spiral formations, brightened just barely to the east by a sun rising somewhere unseen behind the looming mountains. And the path they took up off the coast was bleak, a twisting defile through jagged bluffs and across broad spills of scree, devoid of vegetation or any visible sign of animal life. Without the insistent back-and-forth sheepdog chivvying of the sprite, they likely would have lost their way more than once.

Egar stood at her shoulder, getting his breath back. Looked down at the city in the sea.

'Useful friend to have,' he said. 'Shame we can't take him with us. Didn't your people ever build anything *small?*'

She nodded minutely down at Wraithslayer, where the knife sat upside down in the new sheath on her left breast. It had taken her a while to accept that it wouldn't fall out, no matter how hard she jumped up and down or flung herself about trying to dislodge it. It had taken even longer to get the hang of pulling and throwing Bandgleam from the identical inverted sheath on her right breast. Both knives had lived on her belt before, the sensible way up, slightly forward of her hips and angled for ease of draw. It was the habit of a couple of hundred years and leaving it behind had tugged hard. But she couldn't really argue with the benefits.

The other three knives were, at least, approximately where they'd always been – Quarterless still in the small of her back, though now off to one side and paired with Laughing Girl, the final refugee from the empty frontal portion of her belt. Falling Girl, she'd insisted on keeping in her boot and the Warhelm, lacking an obvious harness point elsewhere, had grudgingly agreed.

'Yeah, well, apart from *blades*, obviously.' The grin still there in the Dragonbane's good-natured grumbling. He sniffed. 'Goes without saying, doesn't it. Kiriath steel and all that.'

But beneath the bluff Majak nonchalance, Archeth thought she detected an enduring trace of unease. And his features were troubled as he watched Yilmar Kaptal come trudging up the slope, nowhere near as out-of-breath as you'd expect for a man his age and size.

The thing that came up through the loading hatch that night, still streaming thin, high spouts of seawater from various openings and edges, looked like nothing so much as a colossal black spider-legged crab caught in some thick-roped metallic net.

Shouldn't really be a shock, Archidi, she'd been surprised to find herself thinking. *Not like you haven't seen them running around the place since we got here – replacing fruit, bringing you fresh clothes. Executing random humans. All the same basic breed.*

This is just a big one.

It took about that long to realise that the thick, shiny cone of netting the crane hook held up was in fact part of the crab's upper structure, presumably designed to allow exactly this kind of retrieval. And as the crane cranked in the final couple of yards of cable and stopped, she saw that the webbing on top was mirrored on the crab's underside by a sagging belly of translucent material, within which hung . . .

At her side, the Dragonbane had climbed to his feet. She stood up to join him.

'Is that a body in there?' he asked her quietly.

The crane screeched and groaned its way back along its track until the crab's monstrous span of legs hung clear of the hatch. Inside the swaying translucent bag, the blurred human outline flopped bonelessly back and forth. There looked to be quite a lot of liquid in there too. The crane cable jolted downward and the crab settled to the floor on its huge, restlessly twitching limbs. It faced them as if poised to spring – she felt Egar tense beside her, felt the same instinctive quailing in her own flesh. The cable ran down, the netting settled back flat to the crab's upper carapace, and tiny upward reaching metal arms emerged to detach the hook. Thus freed, the crab took big, spidering steps towards them, still drizzling water onto the iron deck like an overflowing gutter.

'Archidi . . .' The Dragonbane's grip, firm on her upper arm. He was pulling her backward, putting himself in the way.

'Eg, it's fine.'

As if it heard their voices, the crab locked to a halt. Its front legs were less than fifteen feet from where they stood, went up like shiny black palm trunks to the first hinge, then down again to the looming mass of the body where it hung over them at twice head height. The carapace tilted without warning, the translucent bag split open somewhere and its contents gushed out over the deck in a sluicing of seawater and silt. Small, vaguely fang-shaped objects slid and skittered about, it would be a while before she fixed on them and realised what they were. Too much of her immediate attention was grabbed by the body as it washed to a soggy halt at their feet.

It took them a moment or two to recognise Yilmar Kaptal.

He was a mess. Bleached, bloated, chewed on. Something had already made ragged holes in his cheeks and eaten out his eyes, and as they watched, it climbed on myriad filigree legs out of one of the raw hollows where an eye had been.

'Oh, *lovely*.'

'Eg, shut up.' Staring fascinated. 'Look.'

Because here across the bleached and ragged landscape of Kaptal's torn up face, came some tiny, rapidly spidering silver thing. It grabbed the filigree-legged length of deep sea life at the mid-point, lifted it up out of the eye-socket and held it aloft, then ripped it methodically apart. It discarded the pieces, passing them back delicately over its own body to the rear, then dipped itself into the eye socket and began dragging out other, less recognisably living stuff. Behind it, even tinier gleaming flecks of machinery had welled up out of Kaptal's nose and mouth like silver foam and started to carry off the bits of butchered sea creature.

'Cleansing is required,' said the Warhelm with melodious good cheer. 'And substantial surface repair. But aside from this, I foresee no real difficulties. Your friend has not been in the water long.'

The words washed over her, made no real sense at the time, and besides she was still entranced by the realisation that Yilmar Kaptal's entire bloated body appeared to be a similar battle-ground between the creeping creatures trying to eat him and the tiny silver machines that fought to stop them. The sodden clothing twitched and moved, things emerged squabbling here and there from under a flap of cloth or torn flesh . . .

'Hoy, Archidi. Look at the floor over there. Aren't those your knives?'

'What are we stopping for?'

'What's your rush, Kaptal?' Archeth, still staring down at An-Kirilnar, feigned an absence of tone she didn't feel. Even now, she found it hard to look at the resurrected man directly. 'We're well provisioned, we've got a long way to go, and maybe a fight when we get there. No point in over-exerting ourselves this early on.'

'So who's over-exerted?' The portly imperial put his hands on his hips, an uncharacteristic posture as far as she could recall. 'These are fighting men, they're used to keeping a pace. Not like we haven't all had plenty of rest.'

'Yeah, well we didn't all get off as lightly as you,' Egar rumbled. 'Some of these men took injuries in the wreck. Some of them didn't have as much stored fat to manage on until my lady Archeth found us aid.'

She glanced round. The Dragonbane had drifted into a vaguely protective bodyguard stance, blocking Kaptal from her. Ludicrous over-reaction, if you hadn't been there in the crane hall that night – she hoped the men would write it off to retainer outrage that Kaptal was questioning the will of kir-Archeth Indamaninarmal, proven mistress of ghost mansions and succouring demons in iron, apparent favourite of the Salt Lord, and bearer of haunted blades.

Still . . .

Better break this up, Archidi. In case it goes somewhere none of us are ready for.

Because she still had no real idea what Kaptal had become since his resurrection, whether there was now some steely, silver-limbed thing bedded deep in the gore of his brain and steering him, or whether the Warhelm had simply summoned him back to life in a shower of sparks, like the cranes on their rusted overhead tracks in the hall. Above all, she had no idea why Tharalanangharst had found it necessary to bring the imperial merchant back in the first place. It wasn't as if he had any skills that were worth anything where they were going.

She met his eyes. Had they been that colour before? She seemed to remember darker.

'I'm glad you're feeling so energetic, Kaptal' she said. 'Perhaps you'd like to help carry some of the gear.'

Some sniggering among the men, quickly stifled as Kaptal looked around.

'I am a noble of the imperial court,' he said loudly. 'And a chief sponsor of this expedition. I am Yilmar Kaptal, worthy under charter by the hand of Akal Khimran the Great. I do not . . . *carry gear.*'

But she thought that the outrage rang a little hollow, compared to the way the man had sounded before on the expedition north. She thought that behind it, she heard a scrabbling, as if Kaptal himself wasn't quite convinced of anything he'd just said, was talking as much for his own benefit as anyone else's, was trying to reassure himself, to *remind* himself, of his own identity.

She'd heard something similar in the voices of a few other first-generation courtiers, men still settling into the privilege of their new-found positions, still not quite able to believe the life they now owned, and determined to drive it home to their lesser fellows until such time as it could become confident custom. But she'd never heard it as intense as this, as quietly desperate as it came through in Kaptal's tightened tones.

She didn't want to push him.

'Well, then,' she said colourlessly. 'Enjoy your chartered privilege and let those not lucky enough to share it take some ease.'

It got a couple of low cheers among the men, and Egar grinned in his now neatly trimmed beard. She gave him a faint smile back, but most of her was still haunted. Still wondering.

After the crane hall, she hadn't seen Kaptal for days. A pack of dog-sized crab devices showed up while she and Egar were still marvelling over her recovered knives, and they dragged the body away through a hole in the iron wainscoting. Nothing to worry about, Tharalanangharst assured them breezily. It would all be taken care of. By tacit agreement, neither she nor the Dragonbane had said anything to the other men. They were in any case all too busy by then, looking at maps and drawing up lists, talking to the Warhelm about weaponry and provisions and, in her case, practising with her newly harnessed knives.

Then one morning, she wandered into one of the common dining areas Tharalanangharst had made available – *humans thrive on company*, she'd explained patiently to the Warhelm, *they don't do well alone* – and there was Yilmar Kaptal seated in the flood of early grey light from the windows, intact and apparently none the worse for his drowning, feeding himself hungrily from a broad breakfast spread. He had some story of his survival – clinging to wreckage all night amidst the dark waves, washing finally ashore with the dawn, wandering along the shoreline until he found the city – and he told it with a slightly repetitive, slightly emphatic force. He seemed very pleased to see her, for a man she remembered as having such solitary tendencies. He asked her to join him at the table and plied her with a constant stream of questions about how she'd survived the wreck and come to An-Kirilnar herself. He nodded constantly in response to the answers she gave, made rapid, repeated noises of assent and understanding at every juncture, did not appear to be really listening at all.

Archeth sat and picked at some food with him, hunger driven from her by memories of the creature that had climbed out of his eye socket. She chewed and swallowed mechanically, tried not to avoid his gaze too much. Was inordinately glad when Alwar Nash and another couple of Throne Eternal showed up to breakfast with them.

Now, she remembered that jerky, insistent energy again, and wondered if there was a good reason for Kaptal's new-found dynamism – wondered if perhaps when he stayed still for too long, left himself without occupation or distraction and started to reflect, then black, icy doubt started welling up inside him like seawater, as the truth of what had really happened to him tried to break through into his consciousness.

The fire sprite darted past her, as if checking what she was looking at for a moment, then danced back and up along the ridgeline, wavering from its base like an agitated candle flame. Earlier in the day, she'd thought it had arms and was shaped somewhat like a child about eight or nine years of age. But as she followed the sprite's beckoning flicker upward through the rocks, she saw this was just her mind, demanding a human form from something so outrageously animate, and creating the illusion to fit. What she'd thought were appendages were just undulating frills along the edges of the flame, sometimes well-defined enough to seem like gestures, sometimes damped down to no more than a faint ripple. Now that full daylight was spilling down over the mountains, she was glad of that undulating motion and the sheepdog twitchiness – the sprite was noticeably paler and harder to see against the brightening morning air and she reckoned if it ever stood still there was a good chance you'd blink and lose track of it. *It will never actually leave you*, the Warhelm had told her, *but it may range ahead or double back sometimes to check on conditions. Try to be patient when that happens, let it do its work and protect you as best it can. Once you cross into the uplands, it is the only support I can lend you.*

Once again, she had cause to curse her father's lack of moderation.

Couldn't you have just burned out the big weapons, Dad? Left a little something for local use? Shown a little fucking restraint and foresight for once in your life?

Your father is what he is, Nantara had consoled her once, when a nine year old Archeth fled sobbing into her arms after a particularly hard-headed run-in with Flaradnam. *He is not balanced, there are no balanced Kiriath – their passage through the Veins of the Earth took that away from them, if they ever had it in the first place. But your father loves you with every last ember of his passion, which is why he is so angry now. The anger will pass, will be gone by tomorrow. But the love will not. Your father will love you for all eternity. Never forget that, Archidi, because it's something no one else –* a sad, wincing smile – *not even I will be able to do.*

No Scaled Folk in her mother's tranquil hopes for the future, of course. No fear there might ever be another Great Evil to ride out and face.

You were wrong, Mum. Even Dad couldn't do it in the end.

Always some fucking thing coming down the track that'll kill you if it can.

She shook off her thoughts. Glanced at the Dragonbane, who nodded.

'All right, people. Got a long march ahead of us.' She gestured up at the rearing mountain landscape. 'And it isn't going to get any easier 'til we're over that lot. Let's get on with it, get it done.'

Slightly pessimistic, as it turned out – the path the sprite led them on was actually an increasingly good one, starting to show signs as they climbed higher not just of prior traffic but of actual construction. Some ancient paving in a pale, grained stone she didn't recognise, shelved into upward steps that had worn smooth with use, and were faintly luminous in the gloom where they passed beneath overhangs or through choke points in the rocky terrain.

'This is an Aldrain road,' she heard one of the privateers mutter to his comrades while they were all bunched up at a split in the paved way, waiting for the sprite to make up its mind on which fork to take. 'We are under dwenda protection so long as we walk it.'

Ha.

The sprite came back, opted for the lower of the two paths, which skirted the shadowed base of a broad, jutting bluff, then zig-zagged briskly back upward on terraced hairpins built out of the same pale dwenda – *or not* – stone. They moved on. And with Aldrain protection or not, they made it to the end of the first day without incident. They pitched camp at the foot of an ancient scree spill under the southern shoulder of the highest peak in the range. The sea was a distant grey gleam behind and below them, An-Kirilnar long ago hidden from view by the intervening chains of rising ground they'd crossed.

'Not bad going,' the Dragonbane allowed, nodding in that direction. 'I thought we'd be lucky if we made half this distance today.'

His face was tinged an odd blue by the glow from one of the radiant bowls Tharalanangharst had gifted them in place of campfire fuel. *Nothing grows in the Wastes that will make a decent fire*, the Warhelm told them soberly. *Better you take these.* The bowls would, it claimed, give more or less warmth according to the conditions around them, and could be made, with simple commands in High Kir, to brighten or darken without affecting the level of heat, though they would apparently dim anyway when they detected sleep in the bodies around them. Archeth and Egar decided not to pass on these latter details to the other men – they were going to have enough misgivings about something that gave out blue light and perfect campfire heat but looked like a headless turtle, without being told that you could also talk to it and that it would notice when you fell asleep.

Archeth jerked a thumb over her shoulder at the loom of the mountain behind them. 'How long you reckon to get over that ridgeline?'

The Dragonbane shrugged. 'Your guess is as good as mine. I would have said the best part of a day, lucky to make it by nightfall. But the way we've been covering ground, could be a lot less. We might make it before noon.'

'And then the real work starts.'

'One way to look at it.'

'Got to find this city Tharalanangharst was talking about, get across it, find these *aerial conveyance pits* on the other side, find a way down into them . . .'

'Yeah.'

They were hedging, hovering, rehashing things that were already evident. Pussyfooting around the real issue like some wincing courtier suing for extended credit.

'You reckon it's really him?' she asked abruptly.

They both looked over to where Kaptal sat alone in the glow of another bowl. Originally, he'd been sharing its warmth and light with three Throne Eternal, but one by one they'd apparently found good reasons to wander off into the rest of the encampment and leave him there. He didn't appear to care, had not really been talking to them anyway. Then as now, he sat and stared into the blue light, murmured to himself under his breath, and appeared to be doing some kind of obsessive calculation on his fingers.

Egar shook his head. 'Anybody's guess. He looked pretty fucking dead to me when your demon pal brought him up out of the water. And last I heard, you don't get to come back from the dead without some pretty heavy penalties.'

'Gil says he did. Or something like it.'

'Yeah, well. Case in point. He's not really been the same cuddly little faggot since he came out of Afa'marag, has he?'

She couldn't argue with that. She didn't think Ringil had ever been what you'd call *cuddly*. But after the events of the previous summer there was a distance in him that even she found new and strange. He smiled, he sometimes even laughed aloud, and he had the same old rolled-eyes sophisticate-and-barbarian thing going on with the Dragonbane, veiling an intensity of feeling beneath that neither man would ever own up to. But beyond that, she could no longer guess where Gil went away to when his gaze drifted and his eyes emptied out and the mobility fell off his face like a thin paper mask.

The Dragonbane leaned back on his elbows across his bedroll, stared up at the clouded night sky. It made him look oddly youthful.

'Where I'm from – they'd call Kaptal a Hollow Walker. Drive him out of camp with stones and spells, most likely. Saw that happen once, when I was a kid. Some guy was supposed to have drowned in the Janarat when they were crossing ponies, poor fucker. He hadn't, but no one believed it when he finally managed to get himself back to camp. He had to go and live in Ishlin-ichan in the end, the clan would never take him back. Even his own family wouldn't let him get within hailing distance.' He gestured, like throwing something away. 'But hey, that's fucking steppe nomads for you, with their pig-shit ignorant superstitions and fears.'

'If my father's people went around doing this kind of thing to corpses five thousand years ago,' she mused. 'Maybe the Majak superstitions are tapping into that. Maybe they're based on something concrete after all.'

'Yeah. Archidi, I've seen a Sky Dweller step out of thin air and summon the spirits of the angry dead from the steppe grass to defend me. I've spent a fair bit of my professional life killing things that everybody – including you – thought were myths until they showed up looking for a fight. I don't really need any convincing there's *something concrete* behind all this magical shit. Got pretty much all the evidence I need, thanks, and a few scars to boot.'

'Then—'

His voice rose to cut her off. 'I just wish my dumb-as-fuck, dozy-as-sheep half-asleep people would *wake the fuck up* and demand that kind of evidence themselves, before they buy whatever string of sky-fisted nags the nearest fucking apology for a shaman happens to be hawking at the time. *Is that so fucking much to ask?*'

Movement at the other glowing bowls. People were craning to look. Egar, almost on his feet with whatever emotions had driven the sudden outburst, shot her a sheepish glance. Subsided.

They sat quietly for a while.

'Not looking forward to going home then?' she asked mildly.

TWENTY-EIGHT

He's forgotten about the ladders.

They see them as they get up close, ladders by the thousand, scattered about in the long grass along the bottom of the cliffs, like toothpicks in sawdust at the base of some heavily frequented tavern bar. Or – here and there, you could still see one or two set against the cliffs for use – like the leavings of some vast, suddenly abandoned siege against the *ikinri 'ska* walls, carried on by a hundred or more different allied nations and races.

Which, Ringil supposes, isn't too far from the truth of what he's seeing. However long the glyph cliffs have stood here, it seems men and other creatures have been here too, trying to prise their secrets out. There are wooden ladders, iron ladders, ladders of alloys Ringil has no way to name, ladders of substances he's never seen before in his life. Resinous smooth honey-coloured ladders, woven ladders of creeperlike plants, some of which twitch with some kind of life if you touch or tread on them. Ladders made out of what looks suspiciously like human bone.

Some are simple, the most basic sketch of their function in whatever substance their owners were happiest using. Some are ornate, carved or moulded or tempered with crests and curlicues, symbols to supplement and adorn the functional heart of their uprights and cross-bar steps. Some are clearly made for races with limbs of no human proportion. Some are visibly ancient – wood darkened and rotted through, iron eaten away to rusted leavings, resin that has bubbled and snapped apart in some alien process of decay. But some are new, out of wood so freshly carpentered that you can still see the rough edges, as if they were put together only yesterday, thrown down and abandoned only moments before he and Hjel arrived. It gives the cliffs a haunted aspect, a sense of eyes forever at your back, watching to see if you do better than those who came before, those who, in some hard-to-grasp fashion, have always only just left.

Looks like we missed the rush again.

Hjel rolls his eyes. It's not a new joke for either of them.

Get hold of the other end of this, he says, indicating a silvery-looking ladder five yards long. Ringil knows from previous experience that implements of this metal weigh next to nothing; they'll lift it between them with no more effort than hefting a similar length of mooring cable. *Set it up there, see where that tree's growing out of the rock. That's where you're going up.*

They get the ladder braced with a minimum of fuss. Ringil unfastens the Ravensfriend and sets it aside against the cliff face – he'd swear it shivers slightly inside the scabbard as it touches the glyph-carved rock. He looks hard at it for a moment. Shrugs. Unhooks his cloak and lets it puddle richly on the long grass at his feet, puts his foot on the ladder's first step. Oh, yeah. He turns back to Hjel.

Want to tell me what I'm looking for?

Past the tree, there's a fissure. The dispossessed prince holds up his hands, makes a span. *About that wide. The glyphs go in. I want you to reach in as far as you can see, trace out one of the sequences.*

Which one.

Doesn't matter. You'll see what I mean.

Ringil shrugs and starts to climb. Up past the endless piled up lines of glyphs, skewed and leaning and crammed together, like sketched streets of hovels on some map of the slum housing in Harbour End. The ladder bounces a little with his weight as he gets higher. A cold wind comes snuffling along the eroded limestone expanses, as if searching for something. It moans in crannies and over sharp edges, ruffles affectionately at his hair and moves on. Glyph sequences catch his eye through the rungs as he gets nearer to the top and closer in to the stone. By now he's learnt enough to spot certain tendencies in them, certain phrasing – *in the eyes of men . . . the known unknown . . . a change of entanglement . . . failings unleashed . . . stop, I want to get off . . .* Some of them, he knows how to use in longer sequence. Some he's had patiently explained to him by Hjel, but does not yet have any comprehensible context in which to deploy them.

Some, for reasons he's unsure of, just make him shiver.

He reaches the outgrowing tree. Its trunk is about as wide around as his forearm, and comes with a tightly twisted attendance of lesser branches and thickets of grey-green, rough-edged leaves. There's a reasonable amount of flex in the whole thing, he's able to force his way past and up, but it's work. He collects a couple of scratches on face and hands in the process, comes out breathing hard and dusted in some dark-green scent.

Just beyond, he finds the fissure Hjel's talking about, a broadening gully at whose base the tree is rooted. True enough, the glyphs bend inwards with the rock, and march back into the gloom there. He can't see how far the crack runs into the body of the cliff, the light runs out before the glyphs do, and then it's just impenetrable dark.

Reach in as far as you can see.

He works his way up the last couple of steps on the ladder, braces a boot into the web of tree branches and wedges his upper body into the gully. It's not too uncomfortable, and there's just about space for his arms to move.

Trace out one of the sequences.

The ones under his nose are too tight a fit, he can't get his elbows back down far enough to work there. He twists his head up and focuses on a line that seems to end just into the beginnings of the shadow. He works his hand closer, puts his middle finger into the groove of the first glyph in approved fashion, and begins to trace the pattern out. He has to work mostly by touch, his vision is partly blocked out by his own arm.

The first glyph isn't one he knows – though it bears some resemblance to the symbols Hjel refers to as throat-clearers. The second is the *change of entanglement* motif, though oddly skewed. The third and fourth are related, but—

Shock slams through him.

It's the shock of a warrior-caste lizard's barbed tail-lash into ribs you left unguarded on that last swing with your badly chewed up shield. It's your father's casual blow across the face, knocking you out of your child's-height chair for answering back at the dinner table. It's the kick and clutch under the pit of your stomach as you see your screaming, pleading lover impaled, to the jeers and cheers of the gathered crowd, and you puke out your soul in sympathy. It's the freezing, boiling chase of blood through your veins when you think back later and truly understand for the first time that it could have been you.

It's all those doors and others, swinging open in your memory; gutting you, laying you bare.

Back in the deeper recesses of the fissure, he hears a bony rattling, like long, emaciated limbs re-arranging themselves, like talons digging into the rock to propel something violently forward into the light. And for just a moment, it's as if a massive stirring tremor runs through the whole body of the cliff wall, as if the cliffs themselves are some vast sleeping creature whose skin you've finally gouged deep enough to wake . . .

He flails backward out of the gully.

Loses any footing he might have managed on the ladder, inadvertently kicks it away below. He falls scrabbling at the rock face, grabs frantically at the tree with his left arm. Stops his fall with an abruptness that wrenches his shoulder. The toes of his boots scrape the rock below him, twisting and digging for any scant purchase. Somehow, the dragon tooth dagger is in his right hand, out and up in as much of a guard as he can manage. He stares under the curve of its yellowish blade, into the gloom at the back of the gully, waiting for whatever it was he heard in there . . .

Silence.

A vexed creak in the tree somewhere. The soft whoop of the wind. Tiny patter of displaced dirt, falling away.

The ladder clinks tinnily back in place under him. He dares to look away from the gloom in the fissure, glances downward, gets both feet firmly on a rung. Hjel stands at the bottom, holding the ladder in place. Calls up to him between cupped palms.

See what I mean?

You knew *that was going to happen?*

Ringil storms back and forth in the long grass at the base of the cliff, like some beast chained to a baiting pole. He's too angry, too churned up with currents of emotion he doesn't fully understand, to stay still and look Hjel in the eyes – and the way he's feeling right now, there's just far too much danger he'll punch the other man out.

I did not expect quite such a violent reaction. The dispossessed prince's face is troubled and not, Gil suspects, out of any mundane concern for his near fall from the ladder. *The* ikinri 'ska *is not a training manual or a map, it is the inscribed living will of the Originators. It flexes and flows and breathes in a way I do not understand well myself. It is only one side of the equation. Each man or woman who wields it brings a different self to the union. Some are demure brides to the power, some are . . . not.*

Yeah. Ringil stops in front of Hjel, jabs the blade of his hand at the other man's face. *Well, if I'd known you wanted demure, I'd have brought a mother-fucking veil!*

He stomps away again, nearly trips on the ornately curlicued end of a fallen ladder in black iron. Kicks savagely at it and stubs his toe. *Fuck!*

You need to calm down, Gil.

Ringil stalks back to face the dispossessed prince again. *I am fucking calm. You want to see me not calm, you keep right on feeding me surprises and half-truths like this. Now you tell me, in words a piped-up wharf whore can understand – what happened up there?*

Hjel nods. *Fair enough. What happened up there is that you had a taste of real power. You dug into the darker reaches of the* ikinri 'ska *for the first time, and it appears that neither you nor it enjoyed the experience very much.*

A day ago you tell me it's like the ikinri 'ska *wants me. Now all of a sudden it doesn't like me anymore?* The tail end of his anger is still twitching, lashing irritably about. *Make some fucking sense, would you?*

The dispossessed prince stares out across the marsh plain they've crossed together. *A horse may like you well enough as a rider across summer meadows. That doesn't mean the same horse will stand easy under you in battle.*

Oh, again with the martial metaphors. You're saying I've got to break the ikinri 'ska *now?*

No. You could not do that; no one can. Not even the Ahn-foi could manage so much, and they have tried more than once. Some say that not even the Originators themselves can command what they built and set in place now that it's done. Hjel reels his gaze back in, looks at Gil again. *I am simply showing you a different form of mastery, one that carries a different risk and ultimate cost. You are in need, you say. You ask for more, faster. This is more, faster. You'll have to decide for yourself what it's worth to you, if you want it after all.*

Ringil looks up at where the ladder is leaned, the tree jutting out of the rock, the gully beyond.

How deep does that fissure go back? he asks quietly.

Hjel gives him a faint, sad smile, claps him on the shoulder and chest as he walks past to a point about twenty feet out from the cliff wall. *That's what I thought.*

What's that supposed to mean?

Come here, I'll show you. Hjel waits until Ringil joins him, then sweeps one arm out wide. *Look along the line that way. See the cracks? The shadows?*

Ringil nods, fighting an odd reluctance. The dispossessed prince nods with him. His voice is gathering a fresh intensity, the tone of a man talking about the object of his longtime desires and obsessions.

It's not a clean surface, you see – any more than the world the Originators were forced to write upon was fresh or whole when they saved it. Perhaps the echo is intended, perhaps it is metaphor made concrete. The cliffs march for hundreds of miles across this plain and there are fissures and gullies and defiles going back into the rock everywhere. Some of them are only a few feet deep and will barely admit a man's arm to the shoulder. Some of them are paths whose end no one has seen. But all of them, all that I have seen or heard tell of, are inscribed with the most powerful iterations of the ikinri 'ska. *It is there, in the dark recesses, in the cracks through the surface of things, that you will find what you seek.*

You didn't answer my question, Ringil says gently.

Hjel shrugs. *Because it was meaningless. You shouldn't be asking how deep this or that fissure runs – ask yourself instead how deep into the defiles you are prepared to go.*

Ringil looks along the line of the cliffs, the strewn toothpick ladders scattered at their base. Somewhere, there's a whisper of bleak comfort in knowing how many have come here before him and gone again. He recognises the sensation from the war – the anonymous camaraderie of a thousand ghosts, the realisation that while death may be a gate you must pass through alone, the approach road is thronged with traffic and you walk its cobbled rise in constant company, just one trudging part of an endless caravanserai homing in on journey's end. He remembers the abandoned confidence in his own acts that the knowledge gave him back then – a gut-swoop feeling so close to desperation it was hard to tell the two of them apart. He welcomes it back now with open arms. And somehow, chained to all of this, the half-grasped chilly dance of the glyphs he touched in the fissure has left its traceries in his mind, touched his fingers and throat with what's required to open that door once more.

He's as ready as he'll ever be.

And the Ravensfriend, leaning there against the cliff wall, like some louche friend in a Harbour End alley, awaiting decision from him on where next to take their carousing.

He takes the sword up, settles the harness back on his shoulders. Shoots Hjel an expectant glance.

All right, then, he says. *How about you show me a crack where I don't have to fall out of a tree. And then we can get started.*

TWENTY-NINE

They crossed the ridgeline around noon, as the Dragonbane had predicted they would, and stood there looking downward. A chorus of groans rose from the company at what lay beyond.

Far from the upland plateau they'd been hoping to reach, the path spilled down the other side of the mountain's shoulder almost as far as they'd climbed up the previous day, and into a landscape even more bleak. They spent the back end of the day plodding across what felt like a vast bowl filled with chopped and fire-blackened onion. Peaks rose on all sides and the terrain between was jagged and frayed, all oddly curving spires and fractured bluffs. In places, the rock was glassy to the touch and glinted dully where wandering shafts of sunlight passed over it. Elsewhere, it showed growth of some iridescent crimson moss that smelled faintly of burning. It was the first sign of life they'd found in the landscape and seeing it should have felt better than it did – instead, the men mostly passed by with warding gestures and hurried steps.

As if unnerved by the chaotic ground it had to cross, the path itself grew hesitant and ill-defined. It forked and unwound, seemingly at random, and the fire sprite started taking them off it entirely, to dodge around rockfalls and strange frozen eruptions in the stone underfoot. By late afternoon the paving had all but vanished, reduced to single slabs at violently tilted angles every couple of dozen yards. If it really was an Aldrain road, Archeth reflected grimly, then the Aldrain, in these parts at least, looked to have had their arses handed to them on a plate.

For the first time, she found herself brooding on the geographical absurdity of what they were doing, wondering if Tharalanangharst's smoothly persuasive argument had been worthy of the trust she placed in the Warhelm after all.

There is no easy path south through the Wastes, it told them bluntly. *The entire region is hazardous, often lethally so.*

Yeah, no shit. And marching east from here instead is going to be what, safer?

No, Dragonbane. Such a march would in all probability not be any more secure, and would in any case leave you on the wrong side of a mountain chain it's doubtful you are equipped to cross. Fortunately, that is not the itinerary I have in mind.

Seemed there was this ruined city, two or three days march inland . . .

'I don't know, Archidi.' Egar brooded as they sat at camp that night. 'I'm not saying your iron demon's sending us off to die exactly, but the steppes are fucking huge. My father rode up north and west of the Janarat once, back before Ishlin-ichan was much more than a bunch of hovels on its banks. He was going to circle round and raid the Ishlinak from the far side, take the whole clan unawares. Stuff he talked about finding out there – steppe ghouls all over the place, things like giant spiders that jumped like grasshoppers, could knock a man right off his horse if they hit right. And some kind of, I don't know, deformed giant wolves or something. I mean, stuff straight out of a campfire tale. Plus no decent grazing for the horses and nothing much to hunt that you'd want to eat. They had to turn back in the end, the terrain was just too tough. And he never even saw these mountains the demon talks about, so that's even further out. Now we've got to cross all of that somehow, just to make Ishlin-ichan.'

She gestured. 'Yeah, well. These uhm, *aerial conveyances* are going to take us. Right?'

'You're asking me?'

'Telling you.'

The conviction was oddly easy to come by. She realised abruptly that, for all that Tharalanangharst harped on constantly about its *these days severely limited senses*, she'd never once entertained any doubts about the accuracy of the Warhelm's intelligence. Somewhere in the iron bowels of An-Kirilnar, a trust and certainty seemed to have hardened in her – or maybe just an acceptance, that this was her path and she'd better get on and walk it.

Could have used some krin for the road, though. That too much to ask?

Apparently, it was. The Warhelm assured her it was unfamiliar with the substance, that krinzanz had not been known five thousand years ago, or at least had not been in known and common use. And when she started sketching out its properties, Tharalanangharst grew evasive on the subject of substitutes or whether some could be synthesised. There was much else to be done, it maintained. Many other, more vital, preparations to be made. Perhaps later.

She'd found, oddly, that she didn't much mind. She'd quit the drug before; you could ignore the craving if you had enough else to do. And by then she'd been caught up in the preparations herself, fascinated by her returned knives and the way the Warhelm talked to her about them. Practising with them, hefting and juggling and throwing, walking through the centuries-ingrained Hanal Keth katas until she was exhausted, trying to adopt and adapt to what Tharalanangharst taught her – it was an entrancing, all-consuming process that most of the time took away any residual nagging need for the krin.

And now, sitting here in the blue gloom, she struggled to locate the place inside herself where that need had sat. The locked conviction filled her instead – they were underway, they were on their way home. Let that be enough for now.

'You're taking a lot on trust, you know.' As if the Dragonbane could read her thoughts.

'Warhelm hasn't been wrong yet, has it?'

Egar stood up and stretched. She heard cartilage crack somewhere in his massive frame. He faced out from the overlaid glowing blue circles of light that defined their camp against the surrounding craggy darkness. He crouched back to her level again, and nodded east.

'That's another ridge out there,' he said quietly. 'It's still a fair way off, but it looks to me at least as high as this one. And you can see there are peaks beyond it. I'd kind of hoped we were over the high line by now.'

She said nothing. She had too.

The Dragonbane sat back down on his bedroll. Offered her a tight little smile. 'Don't want to be the one grumbling in the ranks, Archidi. Urann knows, we're going to have enough of that a couple of days from now, without me joining in. So this is just between you and me. But over this kind of ground, it's another day to get up there, minimum. More likely, it's two. And who knows what's on the other side? We're starting to get beyond the bounds of two to three days here.'

'Tomorrow's day three,' she pointed out.

'Yeah. All day. Talk to me when we're over that ridge and it's still not dark and there's a big fuck-off ruined city waiting for us on the other side.'

She remembered his twitchiness from the previous night, made this for more of the same – the pinch of knowing, at every step, that he was on his way back to something he'd abandoned two years ago the way you leave a sinking ship.

Change the subject, Archidi.

She made a gesture, low in her lap, towards the glowing bowl where Yilmar Kaptal sat alone.

'You talk to him yet?' she asked softly.

The Dragonbane followed her gaze. 'Couple of times, yeah. Why?'

'When?'

'Once when we stopped to eat. And then back when our fiery friend was off checking out that cave entrance.'

'And?'

'And *what?* Surly as fuck at the cave; before that he talked at me like I'd rob him at knife point if he stopped. You still worrying about what he might really be? Archidi, let it go. He was put back together by a demon that feeds you five thousand year old fruit, sends iron spiders to do its will and lends you glowing fucking turtles in place of firewood. Who *knows* whether that's really Yilmar Kaptal in there or not? And you know what – so long as he's on our side, who *gives* a shit? Not like he was a prancing little pony of joy to have around *before* he drowned, is it?'

'Fair point.'

'Yeah.' The rant seemed to have eased Egar's temper a little. 'Well.'

'I just wish I knew why Tharalanangharst thought it was so important to have him back. What it's got to do with this grand purpose Anasharal had.'

An elaborate shrug. 'Like someone I know said recently – Warhelm hasn't been wrong yet. Right?'

She grimaced. 'Yeah, all right. But seriously, Eg, Kaptal's a fucking *courtier*. He's got nothing we need.'

'Right now he doesn't. Maybe we'll find out he's got some useful contacts in Ishlin-ichan.'

'If he does, he's keeping very quiet about it. He's been briefed along with everybody else, he knows where we're headed. Anyway, I can't see that. Don't let current circumstance fool you – the only reason Kaptal made the trip north with us is because he couldn't let Shendanak and Tand upstage him. And even then, he's bitched every inch of the way. From what I hear around court, he'd barely ever been outside the Yhelteth city walls before this. He wouldn't know Ishlin-ichan from a hole in the ground.'

Egar grunted. 'It is a fucking hole in the ground.'

'He's useless, Eg.' She ploughed on, refused to side-track back into conversation about a steppe they hadn't even reached yet. 'He's twitchy as fuck, and he's an entitled little shit into the bargain. You saw how he reacted to the idea of carrying any of his own gear. And if we do get in a fight somewhere along the line, I doubt he's picked up a sword his whole fucking life.'

The Dragonbane yawned cavernously. 'Used to be a pimp, didn't he?'

'So they say.'

'Probably very handy with a knife, then. Maybe you should give him one.'

'Very funny.'

But behind the sourness she feigned, she was secretly relieved to see Egar relaxing. Because if the Warhelm's much vaunted *aerial conveyances* were really going to get them to Ishlin-ichan as promised, the journey after that was wholly on Majak turf. And whether they then took passage on one of the infrequent trade barges down the Janarat, or simply procured horses and rode directly south to the Dhashara pass, successful progress was going to hinge rather a lot on exactly how well the Dragonbane coped with his homecoming.

The sky cleared up overnight, and they woke early to a rose-edged vision of the band, arcing overhead against an almost cloudless dawn. The lifeless landscape around them seemed softer with the change, somehow less jagged and threatening, as if the new light had warmed something stony away. Archeth felt how it loosened the men up as they bustled about, breaking camp. She didn't blame them. Not for the first time, she realised how much she missed the habitually clear night skies of the south. How much she missed—

Ishgrim.

Memory uncoiled and struck, like keen knives in her belly and eyes. Lying together in cooling sweat on a balcony divan, Archeth pointing out the Kiriath constellations by name, and both of them laughing as Ishgrim tried stumblingly to copy the pronunciation.

They'd both wept when it was time for Archeth to board ship at the Shanta yards.

You'll see, Archeth lied. *Back before you know it. Nothing to worry about.*

Ishgrim said nothing. Despite some of the games they played in bed, she was no innocent. Slavery had stamped a hard, unwavering vision of the world into her, and they both knew the risks the expedition was going to face.

I will pray to the Dark Court for you, she blurted as Archeth turned to go.
Uhm. If you like.

I know that you do not believe. Defiantly, chin lifted in a way that gouged into Archeth's heart. *But Takavach the Salt Lord answered my prayers in captivity. He brought me to safe haven with you. Perhaps he has a purpose for us both.*

Her last view of the girl was her slim, erect figure in sunlight, immobile amidst the cheering crowd along the yard viewing platforms, as the flotilla rode the current downriver towards the estuary and the sea. Ishgrim had not waved at any point, and Archeth, squinting before distance took the possibility away, saw that the girl's hands were knotted tight on the platform's rail.

She took the ache of memory in both hands. Twisted it into a strength. *Hold on, girl – I'm coming for you. Fucking nothing going to live that gets in my way this time.*

'Looks better,' she said brightly to Egar, as their paths crossed later in the bustle.

He grunted, still buttoning himself up at the fly. 'Yeah, the sun came out. Let's hope it's a fucking omen.'

If it wasn't, it was the next best thing. They crossed the suddenly sun-gilded terrain at a brisk pace now, along a path of paving increasingly intact. The fire sprite scudded ahead of them, pale and hard to see at times, but rarely hesitating for more than a few seconds before darting onward. There were no obvious branches or breaks in the paved way and they were into the cool shade of the next ridge and climbing not long after midday. The hairpin terraces were a match for the path, in far better repair than those they'd walked in the previous two days, broader and more forgiving in incline too. With the fresh energy the change of weather had given them, they made the ridgeline with a solid few hours of daylight left.

The path went up and over in deceptively undramatic fashion, broadened as it dropped on the other side, and passed almost immediately between the massive paired stumps of two pillars flanking what seemed once to have been a gateway. Beyond the jagged, upward jutting fangs of the pillar remnants, the uplands lay spread out below.

'Urann's fucking prick . . . and balls . . .' The oath fell out of Egar's mouth in something close to reverence.

They stared down on the remains of a city that would in its heyday have swallowed Yhelteth whole.

It carpeted the soft slopes and plains of the landscape ahead, to all intents and purposes it *was* the landscape ahead – a vast chessboard of criss-crossing boulevards and piled up, jagged pieces of ruin, stretching out to the horizon wherever you looked. In some places, squinting hard, you could make out the defiant spike of a surviving structure, a wall or dome or tower, but it didn't really matter, was almost beside the point. There were piles of *rubble* down there that, by Archeth's estimate, must rise higher than the tallest towers humans ever built.

A cold, impatient wind blew at them out of the north-east, stropped at their faces, tugged at their hair, carried particles of a fine grit that stung their eyes in sudden gusts. To Archeth, it seemed to be blowing from the far end of the world.

'Where'd our fiery dancing friend go?' asked the Dragonbane.

She looked around. No sign of the fire sprite.

'Saw it down in the street there,' volunteered Selak Chan. He pointed. 'Went along that . . . oh, it's gone now. Must be behind that cracked dome thing. With the pale blue roof?'

Great.

'All right,' she said, with a glance at Egar. 'This is as good a place to make camp as any, I guess. Want to call it?'

The Dragonbane frowned and squinted at the sky. 'There's a fair bit of daylight left. Might be good to make use of it, get down onto level ground. And somewhere out of this wind, if we can.'

She shrugged. It was a fair point – she'd forgotten the wind. 'As you say, then.'

So they mustered up again, still without sight of the elusive fire sprite, and marched down into the ruined city.

It may range ahead or double back sometimes to check on conditions. Try to be patient when that happens, let it do its work and protect you as best it can.

But she was weary and frayed with the journey, impatient to be done with it all. And by the time she recalled the Warhelm's warning, they were already well into the city's shattered, silent precincts, night was in the streets with them, and it was far, far too late for warnings of any kind.

THIRTY

Down the trackless grey-green slop and chop of ocean between the Hironish Isles and the northern shores of Gergis, *Dragon's Demise* led the makeshift flotilla in what seemed like a charmed dance. These were sealanes notorious among mariners for their unpredictable weather and legendary monsters from the deep. The whalers that ran north from Trelayne to pit toothpick harpoons and cord against beasts bigger than their entire vessels came back with yarns of the kraken and the merroigai, of savage, fast-moving squalls that blew up over the horizon in minutes, struck with ship-killing force and as suddenly were gone. They told tales of creeping sea mists and eyes looming over their vessels at mast-tip height in the murk, of the scrape of huge nameless things on their hulls and sudden, swamping waves out of nowhere, of weird lights in the sky and glowing fire in the deep, of heaving, breathing islands that came and went according to no known chart . . .

Of this, the men aboard Ringil's ships saw nothing at all. The skies stayed clear and navigable, the winds steady. Once or twice, there were lookout calls on approaching storm weather, but always, by the time the vessels reached any kind of intercept point, the unfriendly clouds seemed somehow to have veered, left them at worst with a few skirts of rain and some half-hearted chop.

'Told ya,' an imperial marine on second watch one night informed his companions at changeover, as they all stood around on the rear deck with the more-or-less trustworthy co-opted privateer steersman. 'Heard my lord Eskiath promise plain sailing to the captain before he went to his cabin, and look – plain sailing's what we got.'

'Yeah,' another man sniggered. 'Plain enough even old gripe-guts Nyanar can handle it.'

'You belay that shit, marine.' The ranking watchman roused himself from the rail, turned to his men. 'That's an imperial nobleman you're talking about there, and he happens to be your skipper too.'

The offending marine shrugged. 'Still couldn't navigate his way up a whore's crack, you ask me. Fucking riverboat captain.'

'Prefer to put your trust in some infidel outland sorcerer instead, do you?' sneered one of the retiring watch. 'Where's your holy faith, brother? Where's your purity?'

'Hey, fuck purity. Infidel cut-throat sorcerer or not, he's brought us this far. Given us victory over' – a jerked thumb at the silent steersman – 'this pirate scum. Besides, what I hear, he's got about as much Yhelteth blood as northerner, on his mother's side.'

'Yeah, noble house, too.' The man who'd commented on the weather nodded sagely. 'Remember that speech we got from my lord Shanta on launch day?'

'Forgotten all about that. Seems like another fucking lifetime, don't it? But yeah, that's right. Mother's family got driven out of Yhelteth, like three generations back or something. They were Ashnal deniers, right?'

'Well, then they were no better than infidels themselves,' snapped the pious one. 'Ashnal is the Living Word, no less than any other verse in the Revelation.'

'She did look kind of southern, though. The mother. Didn't think about it at Lanatray, but now you come to mention it. That nose, the cheekbones and all.'

'Not those cheeks I was looking at.'

Lewd snorts and chortles. A few groans.

'No, but she did, didn't she? Looked kind of—'

'Looked kind of fuckable, you ask me. Who cares where she's from? Arse on her like a woman half her age, that's what counts.'

'Dream on, Nagarn. Dream's about as close as you're ever going to get to noble pussy.'

'Oh yeah, what the fuck do you know? There was this one time in Khangset—'

'Gentlemen.'

Hoarse rasp of a voice – it came from the forward corner of the deck, where the companionway steps came up from the ship's waist below. For all that it wasn't very loud, it cut through the scuttlebutt like a whip. The marines turned about as one. Even the steersman blinked from his focus on the horizon.

Ringil Eskiath stood propped sideways against the rail, one booted foot still resting on the last rung of the companionway. A harsh, down-curved grin held his face, but there was something huddled about the rest of him, as if beneath the cloak he wore, he'd been badly wounded; as if despite the balmy night, there was a freezing wind blowing from some unacknowledged quarter that only he could feel. The knuckles of his left hand were tight on the rail and from the hunch of his shoulder, it looked as if he was holding himself upright mostly on that grip. The scabbarded Ravensfriend showed at his right hip, over his left shoulder, like some gigantic tailor's pin shoved diagonally through to hold him in place. Even in the kindly gleam of band-light, he looked pale and ill.

'My lord?' said someone tentatively.

The ugly grin flexed. 'You talking about my mother?'

And he fell forward, flat on his face across the decking.

He knew, vaguely, that they picked him up and bore him back down to the door of his cabin, where it gave out onto the main deck. He heard the stifled exclamations as they peered inside and decided not to carry him in there after all. A weak smirk flitted across his face.

Could have told them that.

But the truth was he could not have done, nor could he now. He was too drained of strength to do anything other than loll in the grip of the men that held him. Even the smirk slipped off his face, let go by muscles too sapped to hang onto it any longer.

'Get him to the other end of the deck,' a voice decided. 'Get his sword off, it's dragging. One of us is going to trip on that and go arse over elbow. Someone go wake up the captain.'

He felt himself hefted higher again, carried along under the vast pale billow of sails overhead, the arch of the band and the stars . . .

They laid him down on something softer than planking – later he'd discover it was one of the weave mats provided for sleeping on deck in warmer climes. They stood back and he let his head roll to the side. Along the line of the deck planks, he could make out his cabin door at the other end of the ship's waist, still swinging gently open on its hinges. Lurid, slow-shifting lights from within, tendrils of damp mist crawling out, faint groaning. Now and then, sounds like something wet and heavy being dropped, or the scuttle of claws over stone.

He watched it incuriously, while chunks of recollection rained down in his mind like rocks flung from the wall of a city under siege. The most recent were the easiest to pick up – scratching the glyphs off hinges, lock-plate and jamb with his bradawl, braced against the door to hold himself up while he did it – stumbling out into the cool night air, falling over – voices, *human* voices above him on the rear deck – clinging to the companionway as he climbed, one colossally weighted bootstep at a time, up towards that human sound . . .

'My lord Ringil? Prophet's breath! My lord!'

Ah. Fucking Nyanar.

The captain of *Dragon's Demise* stood above him, holding a dressing gown awkwardly closed across his chest. From the look of it, he'd been so mesmerised by what was happening at the door of Ringil's cabin that he'd almost tripped over Ringil himself.

'My lord Ringil.'

'How—' It was no good, he couldn't even hold his head up. His voice came out a breathless husk. 'How far home are we?'

'Home?' Nyanar's mouth contracted primly. 'We are sailing to *Trelayne*, my lord. Under your expressed orders.'

'Yeah, what I . . . meant. How . . . much further?'

'We should raise the Gergis coast day after tomorrow, if my calculations are correct.'

Big if. Even his thoughts were truncated, sludgy with the effort they took. 'And the . . . other ships?'

'With us, both of them. Visible and with us. But my lor—'

'Good. Well done.' Gil managed a feeble nod upward. He could feel himself guttering like a spent candle. 'Reef the sails. Heave to. Signal the others . . . do the same. I'm going across . . . *Sea Eagle's Daughter* . . . soon as I'm . . . rested.'

'But, my lord.'

'*What?*'

Nyanar, pointing aghast. 'What about your cabin?'

He rolled his head again, took in the lights and the crawling, moaning mist.

'Oh,' he said faintly. 'That. Just . . . just close the door. Lock . . . from the outside. It'll all . . . all go away by the morning.'

It did, more or less.

He woke four hours later with the first grey flush of dawn and the voices of watch changeover from the stern. Slow rocking of the ship beneath him, and he opened his eyes on the stark loom of masts with sails fully furled, like towering crucifixion platforms set against the paling sky. He moved stiffly and sat up. Found himself under a generous pile of blankets, shoved them aside and got groggily to his feet, peered out across the water. *Sea Eagle's Daughter* and *Mayne's Moor Blooded* both sat a couple of hundred yards off to starboard, riding the swells in the same gentle rhythm he could feel under his feet. He thought there were a few figures out on deck, peering back at him.

He saw the Ravensfriend poking out under the blankets – it seemed he'd slept with it. He gathered it up and went with leaden steps along the deck to his cabin door. Tried the latch and found it locked. Right. And they'd taken the key. He was turning to find someone to ask after it, when memory shifted in his head like poorly stowed crates at sea.

A small smile bent his lips.

He looked at the lock and it yielded. He heard the snap as the mechanism turned and the bolt went back. He clicked his tongue and the door opened obligingly.

Inside was a cabin and not much else.

If he squinted and slanted his gaze, he got brief flickers of blue light in corners, like threadbare curtains or cobwebs touched by a breeze; the odd gargoyle gape of something he'd rather not look at, peering out at him. But mostly the haunting he'd brought back was gone. He had one severe moment when the wood panelling on the back wall became wet limestone, an inward leaning loom of rock dripping musical droplets of water into puddles at its base, etched everywhere with glyphs that blew cold breath down his spine, and faintly overhead, the retreating scuttle of bony limbs . . .

He blinked it away.

Went in and propped the Ravensfriend in a corner. He was tempted to lie down on the bunk and go back to sleep for a few hours, but there were things to be done, and besides the ceiling might still drip on him if he didn't keep an eye on it. *It will come looking for you now,* Hjel tells him on their second night camped out at the cliffs. *When you leave the Margins for your own world, bits of the possibilities in the* ikinri 'ska *that you've touched will squeeze through after you. They won't harm you, and probably not anyone else, but they can hang around like a bad smell for days if the breach is hurried. Try to plan, to slip through smoothly if you can. It keeps that shit to a minimum.*

Well, he hadn't slipped through smoothly on this occasion. He'd—

Let's leave that alone for now, shall we, Gil?

They dropped a boat and got him across to *Sea Eagle's Daughter* in short order. The two oarsmen who took him were marines, both faces he recognised from the assault on Ornley but could not put names to. They offered him respectful salutes as he climbed down into the boat, and kept silent on the way across, but for the rhythmic grunt of their stroke.

Rakan was waiting for him when he came up the ladder at the other side.

'My lord.' The longing in his look was almost palpable. Ringil had a flash of recall – Hjel, bent over into his lap in the tent, mouth working – and felt briefly guilty. But then it was gone. Too much else to worry about right now.

'Rakan.' He touched the other man's arm lightly. 'Good to see you again, Captain. I'll need you to give me a good, thorough briefing when we can both grab a moment.'

Flicker of a wink. The Throne Eternal caught it and flushed visibly in the early morning light. He swallowed hard. 'Yes, my lord.'

Pack it in, Gil.

'But right now, I need you to rig the block and tackle and get the Helmsman up on deck for me.'

Rakan blinked. 'Anasharal, my lord?'

'The very metal motherfucker. Probably going to take half a dozen men, but we're not going anywhere for a while, so you can spare them.' He looked around the ship's waist. 'We'll put it over there, by the port bulwark. Upside down.'

'Yes, my lord.' Rakan saluted and went off to gather his men.

'May I ask what you intend?' The soft-over-shrieking unstable layers of the Helmsman's voice, out of the air at his ear.

Ringil grinned like leaking blood. 'Yeah, you can ask.'

Then he went over to the bulwark and hinged the gangway section open, so the space it left gaped out over the ocean beyond.

THIRTY-ONE

Down at street level, the wind was less of a presence, but it still moaned in the tangled wreckage over their heads, as if in long mourning for the city it blew through. They wandered in awe along vast boulevards, past rearing, palace-sized piles of rubble, and the wind was their constant, softly keening companion. It funnelled up certain thoroughfares, ambushed them round corners in the thickening light, flung sudden fistfuls of grit in their eyes when least expected. It was the single audible intrusion into the silent evening gloom, if you skipped the crunch of their own boots on the detritus-laden streets and the hushed groundswell of muttering between the men.

'Pipe down back there, keep your eyes peeled,' Egar found himself finally driven to bark. 'Just 'cause we're fed and armed don't make us fucking blade proof.'

He heard a defiant mention of ghosts. Swung about.

'Yeah, ghosts. Ghosts, I'm not fucking worried about. They're dead already. You see one, wave and smile. Anything else, you kill. Now shut the fuck up and watch your quarters.'

Truth was, he couldn't really blame them. He could feel the cold, abandoned weight of the city himself, pressing down like something palpable between his shoulder blades and at the nape of his neck. If An-Kirilnar had seemed – and after a fashion, he supposed, *was* – haunted, this place made it look positively welcoming by comparison. There was a desolation here that beat out anything the Kiriath fortress had to offer. Even the lifeless wasteland they'd just crossed had not seemed so emptied and abandoned. Wind or no wind, he was increasingly sorry that he'd persuaded Archeth not to camp back up on the overlooking ridge.

In the middle of one broad boulevard, they came upon a chunk of fallen rubble, itself almost the size of an Ornley croft house. There was carving on one side, letters nearly as tall as a man in what looked to Egar like Naom script, though he couldn't make head or tail of what it actually said. He brushed his fingers over the stonework, curious. It was faintly warm to the touch.

He whistled for attention, beckoned to the nearest of the privateers.

'You. You recognise this?'

The man shook his head. 'Don't read, my lord. You want to ask Tidnir, he's got letters. Went to school and everything, before his old man got wrecked off the cape.'

'Tidnir. Which one's—'

The privateer nodded obligingly, turned and pointed at someone further back in the loose group they'd all bunched up into.

'Hoy, Tid,' he barked. 'Get over here. Dragonbane wants this shit read.'

Another privateer, younger, but with a shrewd intelligence around the eyes, came warily up to the front. He stood beside Egar and stared up at the march of huge characters carved into the stonework. His lips moved silently.

'So?'

'It's Myrlic, my lord. The ancestor tongue.'

'Well, what does it say?'

'Dunno.' Tidnir scratched his head. 'It's . . . I think it's a prayer or s—'

Something tore him down.

It happened faster than you could blink. One moment the young privateer was standing there talking, the next he was gone, and Egar's face was painted with the sudden hot spray of blood. The Dragonbane had a flash glimpse of something pallid and fanged as it bore Tidnir to the ground, heard a noise out of battles a decade gone—

Screams from the rear.

'Lizards! 'ware lizards!'

As if the present caved in under him like rotten flooring, dropped him through into the dim nightmare sludge of a past he'd thought buried long ago.

The all-alloy staff lance the Warhelm had made for him – trussed to the pack on his back, blades at either end still clad in their soft Kiriath fabric sheaths – *no time, no fucking time, Eg. Forget it.* He shed the weapon with his pack, the shrugging work of an instant. But the chain was slung loosely around his neck, halfway-ironic ornament of rank, some faint, inexplicable urge had made him keep and wear it that way, and now . . .

Rip it free sideways in one fist, whip and heft, the harsh pain as the iron links wrapped hard around his tightened knuckles and a barely felt gouge where one of the bolt ends caught as it dragged off his neck. The reptile peon that had torn down Tidnir swung up at him, bloody-snouted. Only the size of a small, malnourished man, but all fangs, all reaching claws, all *snarl*, and in that fresh nightmare sludge of time slowed down, Egar yelled and swung the chain full force.

Dragonbane!

The lizard leapt, the bolt ends of the chain came flailing in from the side, took it in the skull and knocked it over in a thrashing, hissing mess. Egar used the backswing and hit it again, *keep this fucker down,* stepped in and lifted the chain high with another yell. Into the skull again, with the savage force of his revulsion. The peon's blood came out, dark in the evening light, almost a human hue. The creature thrashed and tried to roll away. The Dragonbane stamped a boot on it, flailed down again with the chain. He was shouting now, wordless affirmation of his savagery, building to the berserker rage. Twice more and the reptile peon's thrashing died. It was still twitching, but he knew from hard-won experience that it was done.

Whirl about, check the men.

Their attackers seemed to have come out of the ground, or dropped from the sky. They were on all sides and the company had pulled instinctively into a circle, Throne Eternal shoulder to shoulder with Majak with marine with privateer with Menith Tand's mercenaries. Most had managed to shed their baggage, a few had shields to hand, but two men were out of the protective formation and down. One still lived, axe haft braced up against the snapping jaws of the lizard that had him pinned . . .

Egar strode in yelling, long scooping blow with the chain, caught the reptile peon around the head and jaw, the bolt ends snagged and the chain wrapped up. He bellowed and yanked hard, tore the lizard off the man like a herdsmen roping away a buffalo calf. The thing came snapping and snarling and thrashing, on its back but trying to right itself, *keep dragging back, Dragonbane, keep the tension on*, he drew a knife left-handed, blade down. Spotted an eye in amidst the thrashing, coiling fury. Flexed his right arm as if for an uppercut and hauled on the chain, dragged the lizard up close, stabbed down hard into the eye socket. The creature went into spasms, he jerked the knife free and blood gouted thickly from the eye. He stood on the dying reptile and tore the chain loose from its mangled jaws.

The downed man – one of Tand's mercenaries – rolling shakily to his feet, nodding thanks. Egar bared teeth at him, nodded back, made a sound in his throat that was barely human and swung away.

'Dragonbane!'

He was bellowing it now, gone into the killing rage, bloodied knife in one hand, chain in the other, striding amidst the fray, flailing and stabbing, taking down the reptile peons like the incarnation of his own legend, pulling them off his men, putting them away. It felt almost easy, like something he was born for, it felt like release.

'Dragonbane! *Dragonbane!*'

And a cry that seemed to answer from the other side of the boulevard's expanse.

'*Indamaninarmal! Indamaninarmal! My father's house!*'

He swung about at the call, grinning fiercely.

Found Archeth across the street, about to go under.

She'd thought it was the fire sprite – a flicker of motion at the corner of her eye, somewhere up amidst the piles of rubble on her right. She drifted out across the desolate space of the boulevard, staring upward, scanning the tumbled, tangled mess of broken architecture for another glimpse. Though what the sprite was doing all the way up there . . .

Vague, unwinding tendril of unease in her chest.

And the first reptile peon jumped her.

Came leaping fanged and snarling down out of some darkened juncture of tumbled masonry above head height, like the screaming wartime past returned.

Knocked her to the stony floor.

She hit and scrabbled back, frantic. Her pack jammed against the ground, the lizard loomed over her, jaws agape. Reflexive combat memories from the war sparking down her nerves, become their own survival imperative, and a million miles from conscious thought, her body followed the command. She lashed out with one booted foot, smashed hard into the snout with her heel. Her right hand clapped to the inverted grip of Wraithslayer, there on her chest. The reptile peon shook itself, came snarling at her again. She rolled up into a crouch, left arm raised to an instinctive guard across her throat and face. She snatched the knife clear of its sheath. The lizard hit and bowled her back over, she slammed her guarding arm forward, drove the snapping, slavering jaws aside and up, away from her face for the time she would need. The reptile peon grabbed at her wrist with a taloned forelimb, would either bite her arm down to the bone or twist and drag it out of the way and take her face instead. But Wraithslayer was loose in her hand now, and there was a noise rising in her throat to match the lizard's snarl.

'*You lie down, motherfucker!*' she screamed, and plunged the knife in.

Kiriath steel.

In under the jaws and up – Wraithslayer ripped the lizard's throat out with no more effort than opening a sealed letter. The reptile peon's blood gushed out over Archeth's hand and forearm, exploded out between the snapping fangs, and the creature went down on its side, thrashing a cloud of detritus and dust from the ancient paving as it died. Archeth staggered to her feet coughing, sweeping her surroundings, saw the company beset on all sides and more skulking figures moving in the rubble her attacker had come from.

'Lizards! 'ware lizards!' someone was howling, a bit superfluously.

Bandgleam was in her left hand – she had no memory of unsheathing it – she shrugged clear of her pack, lifted both blades and her chin in invitation to the figures that lurked above her.

'Come on, then!'

They came bounding down the ledges and slopes of the collapsed ruins like scree panthers on the hunt – two lean, armoured forms, spined and crested and almost twice the size of the reptile peon she'd just killed. She drew a hard breath in over her teeth. Warrior caste. Sooted, greyish-dark scaled hides, shifted to match the hue of the environment around them – she'd forgotten they could do that. In Demlarashan, they'd been sandstone yellow, in Gergis a piney green. Reared up on their hind legs, they'd tower a full foot or more over her head, they had prehensile tails three yards long that ended as often as not in a savagely barbed spike they knew only too well how to use, and they were smart in a way the reptile peons were not. Warrior caste Scaled Folk had been known to pick up and use discarded human weapons on the battlefield, or to fight with long thorny staffs of bone which appeared to grow out of the same webbed material they were hatched from themselves. But mostly they favoured their own heavily armoured forelimbs, tipped as they were with taloned claws and razor sharp elbow spurs. In battle, she'd seen one of those limbs take a blow from a two handed imperial war axe and not break. Seen the lizard dip and swing, clout the axe owner to the ground with a tail lash, then pounce and plunge an elbow spur down through the soldier's helmet visor with pin-point accuracy.

She brandished her knives again. 'You want a piece of me? Come *on!*'

They dropped lithely to the boulevard paving, not ten yards from where she was. They reared a little on their hind limbs and circled out, moving to bracket her. Talons scraped on the stonework as they prowled. Eyes gleamed iridescent in the gloom, watched her with a narrow intelligence, better protected than those of the peons, recessed into bony, slanting sockets behind rows of spines – a tough throw for Bandgleam, and not one she wanted to risk just y—

Hurried rattle of talons on paving to her left – the shrill, attacking shriek.

She felt the nape of her neck chill to the sound – old, partly healed memories from the war, re-opened like wounds – spin to face it, see the scribble of motion as the lizard came at her, and her flesh cringed.

But corpse-cold recall mapped the creature's weak points for her – *get this right, Archidi* – the way she'd have to move. Up on the balls of her feet, swivelling, already in motion as the reptile pounced the last three yards, she was not there, she was *here, motherfucker, right here*, spinning in from the side and *strike* with Wraithslayer, hard into the soft, unarmoured flesh behind the lizard's reaching forelimb. The attack shriek scaled to an abrupt peak, dropped off a cliff into a furious hiss as the lizard coiled round with whiplash speed, jaws snapping and seeking.

But Archeth knew better than to stay still behind the blow.

She left Wraithslayer buried to the hilt where it was, Quarterless was already drawn to replace it. Didn't feel like she'd actually reached for the knife at all – as if Quarterless had leapt eagerly from the sheath in the small of her back as her fingertips trailed past, as if it had flown to the warm calloused wrap of her palm like Ishgrim into her embrace at day's end. The blade was reversed and she had time to carve a long gouge in the lizard's haunch and tail root as she spun away. She already *knew* the other lizard was there at her back. Bandgleam was tugging her around, insisting, *yearning* towards the fresh target and—

For one panic-stricken moment something shivered and failed in her, the close combat press of what was happening rushed her, stormed her senses and battered them down; she felt abruptly like some Ninth tribe martyr, splayed and tied between four snorting, stamping stallions under a pitiless southern sun, limbs tugged and torn outward by forces beyond any control or power she had to resist . . .

It is a meditative, communing state, the Warhelm had told her. *Common enough among the People, but perhaps you, Archeth Indamaninarmal, with your admixture of human blood, will not be able to raise sufficient discipline to—*

Fuck that shit.

She let go, stopped trying to control the knives as individual blades, became the fulcrum on which they turned. She let herself see each blade's arc of potential, let the arcs unwind and encircle her like white hot wire, let herself know at the deepest, clearest level of her being what could and could not be done with the gift Tharalanangharst had given her. She plotted the intersection of the attacking Scaled Folk with those glowing wires the same casual way she might note the shift in the pouring arc of a water jug and bring a cup into place beneath—

She hunched and went with Bandgleam's tugging. She spun about. The warrior caste lizard towered over her, talons poised – close enough to gag on the acrid spice of its skin secretions, close as a mother reaching to lift a squalling infant from the ground. It shrilled at her and struck, one downward flailing forelimb, but Quarterless was there, upflung and angled, took the taloned blow, deflected it the scant inches that Archeth needed, sent the force on downward. And Bandgleam leapt glinting into the gap – through the shadow of the lizard's stumbling as Archeth straightened out from under the failed attack and stabbed deep, plunged the blade into the reptile's exposed underbelly, slicing upward, opening like a surgeon, spilling viscera, blood, paler fluids, half formed eggs from the reproductive canal . . .

The lizard screamed and flailed and went down thrashing in its own entrails.

Archeth was already turning away.

But these knives are inert, *Archeth Indamaninarmal.* Trace of something that might have been disbelief in the Warhelm's voice. *The steel is still sleeping. How have you not awakened them? How do you fight with them like this?*

I stab things or I fucking throw them. A bit defensive – she cleared her throat and started again. *I was instructed in Hanal Keth from ten years old.*

Yes, but Hanal Keth is only the beginning. It is a threshold skill, the dexterity training for what comes after. Were you not told this?

Brief quiet, in which she silently cursed her father's people and their slipshod ways. *Well, what do you think?*

I think there is much work to be done, neglected daughter of Flaradnam, and not very much time to do it in. I cannot gift you with a mastery of Salgra Keth – that would take many years. Time we do not have.

Salgra Keth? She repeated the phrase, puzzled. Hanal Keth made sense enough in High Kir – it meant, more or less, the Art of the Blade. But

Salgra Keth, that would have to mean . . . she shook her head . . . well, let's see, it was an antique word, but . . .

Art of the . . . Juggler? Art of the court conjuror?

Art of the cheap street entertainer?

She shook her head impatiently. *You're not making any sense. I've never even heard of this Salgra Keth.*

No, so it seems. She thought the Warhelm sounded obscurely disappointed. *And as I said, there simply is no time. But the blades have at least seeped into you somewhat, and this does give me hope.*

Another silence.

Seeped? she asked guardedly.

Wraithslayer was calling her – like a soft ache in the palm of her hand, where the hilt of the knife longed to be. The lizard she'd buried the blade in stalked her, limping slightly on the forelimb where the knife had gone home. Thin rivulets of blood down the scaled skin, droplets across the ancient paving, but it seemed otherwise unharmed and pretty pissed off. The jaws gaped, the large tongue coiled behind a thicket of fangs, its tip darted delicately out and tasted the air for her. The deeply recessed, iridescent eyes watched her for an opening.

More motion on the rubble piles above.

Archeth caught it from the corner of her eye, saw the wounded lizard turn its gleaming gaze just fractionally away. She chopped a glance that way herself, saw reptile peons prowling, three, maybe four of them, all seeking ledges from which to spring. She circled casually out, back towards the centre of the boulevard and the boil of the main fight. The warrior caste lizard reared back on powerfully haunched hind-limbs, tilted its spined head towards the ruins and shrilled violently. The sound seemed to shred the air. Perhaps there was language in there, perhaps not – in all the years of the war, no one had ever been sure how evolved these creatures were, how much conscious thought dwelled behind the gleam in those iridescent eyes, how they communicated – but the reptile peons responded like troops to command. They came spilling down off the rubble, four of them, yeah, it was four after all, and they rushed her.

All Kiriath weapons carry an essence, forged into them at the deepest levels. A soul, if you want to use terms your barbarian friend would understand. With time, that essence begins to put down roots in the weapon's user, and to borrow selfhood from them. A bond is grown, one transferred particle at a time. Weapon and user grow closer together, better able to co-operate. Locational awareness, predictive sympathetic resonance . . . Exasperation crept into the Warhelm's avuncular tone. *Did your father really not inform you of any of this?*

I already fucking told you he didn't. Get on with it, will you?

Very well. The knives you were gifted with are powerful and have bonded deeply with you over time. I could not otherwise have found them so easily on the seabed. Whoever forged these blades certainly intended you to make use of their full potential.

She remembered her practice sessions with Grashgal in the courtyard at An-Monal. The phantoms he conjured from the empty air for her to hack and slash at – blank-faced insubstantial grey figures like the ghosts of so many tailor's mannequins, but armed with a variety of fearsome weapons and all growling faintly.

More than enough to strike instinctive terror in her ten year old heart.

These cannot harm you, Archidi, Grashgal had promised her. *But you need to feel as if they could. You need to fight as if your life were in the balance. Because one day it probably will be.*

She put Bandgleam through the lead reptile peon's eye, a long overhand throw that dropped the creature tumbling and thrashing in the path of the others. The next peon stumbled, fell slithering on top of its stricken comrade, jaws snapping reflexively as the two lizards' limbs tangled and snagged. The injured reptile bit back in response, blindly, and the two creatures locked up in a writhing, snarling mass. Standard charge-break technique from the war years – worked on reptile peons most of the time, they just weren't that smart. But—

The other two lizards made it past. Awful predator grace in motion, as they swerved symmetrically either side of the fight in their path, swerved back again to home in on where she stood.

It barely slowed either of them down.

Laughing Girl came out, left-handed to replace Bandgleam, and Falling Angel, still in her boot, was a soft-pressing reassurance against her calf, but meant she had only one safe throw left, *so let's make it count here, Archidi—*

The peon on the right was fractionally ahead when it leapt. She hurled herself sideways, put its body between her and the other lizard, saw the pale unarmoured flash of throat offered, flung Quarterless underhand. *Fuck*, she flubbed it – the knife went home but with less than full force, pinned inch-deep in the pale flesh and flapped, then fell out again. No time, no *time*, the lizard was cornering on its haunches from the failed pounce, was relocating its prey, was *on her*. Falling Angel jumped out of her boot and into her right hand, distracting slash with Laughing Girl in her left and then hurl your full weight in against the reptile and stab, frantically, into that throat. See what damage you can do at *this* range, shall we? The lizard shrilled and flailed back at her. She felt talons get through her leathers and rip furrows in her flesh. She screamed, and then, voice unlocked, went on screaming, counterpoint to the lizard shriek – '*Indamaninarmal! My father's house!*' – all the time hacking, stabbing, *work* those wounds in the throat, find an artery in there somewhere . . .

The lizard fell on her. The other peon leapt fully onto its companion, clambered over and tried to bite Archeth's face off. She heaved back out of the way, spared a single, ill-aimed slash with Laughing Girl and cut a gash in the underside of the thing's jaw. But the first lizard's weight had pinned her in place. The one that was trying to bite her slithered further over, wove its head about, trying to get closer. If she didn't . . .

There – the eye!

'My father's *house!*' Sobbed out as she buried Laughing Girl deep in the offered eye socket. The knife sank in up to the hilt, the lizard screamed, almost like a human infant – reared back, ripped the hilt of Laughing Girl out of her grasp. Some impulse she had no time to question – she flung her empty hand up and out, and there was Quarterless, somehow up off the detritus-strewn boulevard paving and into the instinctive curl of her palm, reversed. She—

Something tore the remaining reptile peon off her. Archeth had a confused impression of chain link slicing down through the gloom, wrapping around the snout and jaws, a hooting scream that sounded like joy, and then the lizard was gone, as if swept away by the wind. She hinged up from the stomach, suddenly freed of the crushing weight, saw the Dragonbane with one boot on the injured peon, flailing down at its skull with the chain.

Behind him – *shit!*

The warrior caste lizard had taken a shortcut to sorting out the first two squabbling reptile peons. It had pounced and knocked the two creatures apart, then bitten the injured peon's throat out. Was crouched there now, bloody fanged, over the twitching remains, shrilling instruction at the survivor as it picked itself up.

'Eg! *Watch your back!*'

The warrior caste lizard's long head snapped up, the iridescent eyes fixed on her. Almost as if she saw the decision it made then, heard its actual thoughts. It was coming for her, *right fucking now*, to put an end to this ridiculous, soft two-legged thing that its peons couldn't seem to kill . . .

Her own decision was taken for her as fast. She never knew if it was her or the knives, or some incomprehensible combination of both.

Her arms came up in unison, Quarterless and Falling Angel cocked without thought for the throw. *Fuck are you* doing, *Archidi?* It felt as if each arm tugged into place with no volition on her part at all. The warrior caste lizard took one poised pace forward, and she *threw* – hard, thick grunt of effort all the way up from the hingeing tension of the muscles in her stomach where she still lay on her back, *impossible* precision, right past the bristling array of protective spines and bone ridges, and both the iridescent eyes were suddenly gone, put out like embers, the blunt, use-worn butts of the knives sprouting in their place.

The lizard crashed forward on its long snout in the dust.

Archeth curled to her feet like an echo of the motion that had flung the knives. Egar was still turning away from the dead reptile peon, gore-clotted chain swinging from his clenched right fist, ready to face the remaining peon, but she was closer. No idea what she was doing at all, she stalked forward, crouched with arms spread out and both hands splayed like claws, lips peeled back from teeth, eyes somehow blind, *what the fuck are you* doing, *Archidi? – you're not even* armed . . .

At less than three yards' distance, she screamed in the last lizard's face.

The reptile peon scrabbled backward in a tangle of limbs, coiled about and fled. Back up onto the mountainous piles of shattered masonry, leaping ledge to ledge and then gone, into some bolt-hole or other amidst the rubble.

She breathed in hard. Straightened up and sniffed.

The boulevard behind her had quietened, and she knew without turning – some old battle instinct unfolding for her like a creased and stained campaign map – that the skirmish was done.

Egar reached her side, panting. Stared up after the reptile peon.

'Where'd *that* come from?' he asked.

She jerked a nod. 'Up there, same as the rest of them. Must be a nest.'

'Yeah – wasn't really talking about the lizards, Archidi. Talking about you.' He got his breathing down. 'What you just did there, big battle scream and no fucking knife. Where'd *that* come from?'

'Oh.' She shrugged, feeling suddenly oddly embarrassed. 'Lot on my mind, you know. Guess it had to come out.'

'Uh – yeah. Well, you want to try keeping a blade in your hand next time? As a personal favour to your sworn bodyguard here, I mean?'

She coughed a laugh, winced as sharp pain flared across her ribs. Sudden recollection of the claw wounds she'd collected in the tangle with the peons. She lifted her arm on that side, put her hand to the site of the pain and brought it away liberally smeared with her own blood.

'Fucker tagged me,' she said with mild surprise.

'Let me look.' The Dragonbane came round and peered, prodded a couple of times, enough to make her flinch and curse. 'Yeah, you'll live. Couple of nasty scratches is all, looks like the leathers took most of the sting out of it. Get you sewn up, just as soon as we take stock of this fucking mess, all right?'

'All right.' She said it absently, staring around at the lizards she'd killed.

Listening to the soft calling of her knives.

THIRTY-TWO

They got Anasharal up through the forward hatch with a lot of grunting and cursing but no real difficulty, then Rakan had the block and tackle moved down the deck and they dragged the Helmsman to where Ringil stood waiting. None of the men really wanted to touch the iron carapace, or get within reaching distance of the crab-like legs folded into its under-side, so there was an awkward delicacy to the whole operation that took longer than would have been strictly necessary with some other cargo. Ringil said nothing about it. He waited patiently until the Helmsman was upended at his feet and the ropes removed. He waved back the men, saw how they hung about at a short distance, Rakan included, watching in silent fascination to see what might happen next between the dark mage and the iron-imprisoned demon at his feet.

'Hello there, Anasharal,' he said.

'Good day to you too, Eskiath.' If the Helmsman felt at any disadvan-tage, it wasn't letting it show. 'Not wearing your much vaunted Kiriath steel this morning, I see.'

'Don't need it right now.' Ringil went pointedly to the opened gangway section and peered over the edge. 'Do you know how deep the ocean is around here?'

'Helmsman is a poor substitute for the High Kir word it purports to translate. I am not some ship's pilot. No, I do not know how deep this ocean is.'

'Nor do I,' admitted Gil amiably. 'But I'm told it goes down at least a mile. More in some places.'

'How interesting.'

He came back to the Helmsman and put one booted foot on the edge of its upended carapace, rocked its weight judiciously back and forth a couple of times on the iron curve where it touched the deck. His voice hardened.

'You want to go have a look? Find out first hand?'

'Do you think you're threatening me, Eskiath?' Amusement, trickling in the edge-of-hysterical avuncular tones.

Ringil shrugged. 'I'm not sure. The pearl divers in Hanliagh told me once that the deeper you go in the ocean, the harder it presses on you. It hurts your ears, apparently. Maybe it'll hurt you too, a mile down. Maybe it'll crack you open like a nut. Spill out whatever essence is locked up inside all that metal.'

A longish pause.

'When we were summoned from the void,' the Helmsman said coldly, 'there was a reason the Kiriath encased us in iron. I don't think you'd like me outside of this containment vessel.'

'I don't like you much inside it. And it's a long swim back to the surface, so you know what? – I think I'll take my chances.' Ringil dug out his bradawl. 'I have some questions for you, Helmsman. You're going to answer them for me as helpfully as you can, or you're going to be taking a very close look at the seabed. And just so we know we're all on the same page . . .'

He knelt and put a steadying hand on the rim of the iron carapace. Commenced gouging the most powerful of the Compulsion glyphs into the metal.

'What do you think . . .?' Anasharal's voice dropped away in mid-sentence, something Gil had never heard it do before. There was a peculiarly human quality to the way it sounded, something he hoped he could count as weakness. He got the first glyph finished – it was hard going, the carapace barely admitted the faintest of scratches, even from the bradawl's Kiriath steel point – and started on the second.

Felt the metal under his hand beginning to get warm.

'That sting a bit, does it?' he asked, with a levity he didn't feel. Hjel had told him he'd need at least a five character string for this to work on an entity that wasn't human, and he wasn't sure Anasharal was going to give him the chance to get that much down.

'You are making a grave mistake, Ringil.'

Third glyph done. The Helmsman's carapace was hot now, hot enough that it took an effort of will to keep his hand in place. He breathed through the pain, sank himself in concentration on the tracery of the glyphs, kept on gouging. Fourth . . . glyph . . . done. Out of the corner of his eye, he saw Rakan leaning toward him like a frantic hound on a leash, heard his shout only faintly. His hand was scorching, blistering across palm and fingertips, but no matter, *it's a wound like any other, Gil. Stay on your feet, you win the fight. Still on your feet when it's done, then all wounds heal well enough in time.* The fifth glyph was the closer, simple enough, no intricacies. Get it done. He made the primary stroke – the first cross – caught the faintest whiff of something suspiciously like crisping pork – the second cross, the curlicue tail . . .

And finished.

He snatched back his hand. Came to his feet as Rakan rushed in, voice tortured, *my lord, my lord, your hand!* Gil glanced incuriously at the damage – he'd had worse from the splash of dragon venom in the war – and lifted it to his face. He blew gently on the blistered flesh, glanced sideways at Rakan, allowed the tiniest crimped corner of an acknowledging smile.

'It's fine, captain. Thank you. Just bring me some salve and a bandage.'

Rakan hung wordless for a second, staring into his face, then hurried away. Ringil looked bleakly past his splayed and scorched fingers at the Helmsman. *Here we go, then. Moment of truth.*

'Cut out the heat, Anasharal. Now.'

And across the curve of the carapace, the glyphs lit in lines of bluish fire, brighter and clearer than the scratches he'd made. The Helmsman gave out a strangled sound.

Ringil gave it a few moments, then stooped, cupped his injured hand and risked the back of his curled fingers against the carapace.

It was cooling fast.

'Right yourself, if you can.'

A clicking, fingering motion from the Helmsman's limbs as they flexed out of their recesses. The mushroom-top carapace rocked barely back and forth, less than he'd moved it himself with his boot. He nodded.

'Fine, you can stop trying now. Do you begin to grasp the new relationship we have?'

Sullen silence.

'An answer, please.'

'Yes, then.' It shocked through him. The avuncular accents were gone, stripped away from the underlying tautness of tone. If there'd been any volume to the Helmsman's voice, it would have been a shriek. As it was, the watching men flinched back from the sound it made. 'I understand what you've done.'

'Then stop trying to fight it. You're wasting your time anyway, it can't be done.' He tossed the lie off casually. Truth was, he had no idea what the limits of his new powers might be. You never fucking did with the *ikinri 'ska*, until said limitation came and tripped you up, dumped you on your black mage arse. 'Talk to me normally, Anasharal. Show me you've stopped wriggling.'

'Very well.' Anasharal's voice regained some of its previous disdainful poise. 'So you've been back to the wounds between the worlds, then, like the feeding maggot you are. Burrowed deep this time, did you?'

'We're not talking about me, Helmsman.'

But the levered chunks of memory came crashing down on him all the same.

Back for more, I see, rasps the husk of a voice overhead, and a shadow moves through the miserly ration of light sifting down from above. *No end to your appetite for suffering, it seems. But then what else should we expect from a* hero?

He freezes where he is, Ravensfriend at a useless guard. Hears the swift scuttle of limbs down the sides of the limestone defile he's in, senses the bulk of a body hanging suspended at his back. Something sharp touches him on the nape of the neck and then the lower spine. There's a sound somewhere between a snigger and a sigh, and along the worn smooth walls all the glyphs light up in traceries of blue.

Am I intruding? he asks, as steadily as he can manage.

A clawed limb creeps up over his shoulder like some living, insectile thing. The claw-tip chucks him under the chin, tilts his head back as if for a knife. He gets the sense that the thing's own head is snuggled up close behind his other shoulder.

At least he does not deny his title any longer, the voice whispers in his ear. *A learning curve of sorts, I suppose. But as to intruding, Ringil Eskiath, you've been doing that since well before we last met – as I am sure you're already well aware. So let's not pretend to a contrition you do not feel, eh?*

I'm – he swallows against the lift of the thing's clawed finger – *told that I owe you some thanks for my passage through the Dark Gate.*

Ah. The little moon-murderers, dabbling again. And what else did they choose to share with you on this occasion?

They said the Talons of the Sun is back in play.

There's a long pause. The clawed finger stays at his throat. He hears water trickle and drip on the limestone walls, echoing in the narrow confines of the defile.

And you've come here to gather force against the day of Reckoning, the Creature from the Crossroads muses. *As heroes must. Well, it's certainly not original, but then I suppose the permutations available are somewhat limited. We could not have mended the world otherwise. Not with humans still in it, anyway. So then – let us see how this writes itself out.*

The clawed finger eases out from under his chin. The glow in the lines of glyph script fades. Ringil lets his neck relax, lets the point of the Ravensfriend droop and rest on the gently rising slope of the passage floor. He hears a scratch and rustle behind him, like heavy vellum pages turned. The rattle of a throat clearing.

There were times he dreamed that the cage had taken him after all, the husking voice recites in his ear. *That he made some impassioned speech confessing guilt and repentance on the floor of the Hearings Chamber, and offered himself up for the sentence instead. That the Chancellery law lords in their enthroning chairs and finery murmured behind their hands, deliberated amongst themselves for a space, and finally nodded with stern paternal wisdom. That the manacles were unlocked and his wife and children—*

My apologies. That is someone else.

Ringil swallows, hard. *Yeah, sounds like it.*

Another hero, another betrayal. The pages scrape and turn. *It's sometimes hard to tell them apart.*

If you say so.

The echoes and borrowings, you see, the endless piled up repetition in both truth and tale, the sheer bloody cannibalism of it all. We were learning your myth base as we worked, trying to understand who you were as a species, even as we stitched your world back into something we thought you might recognise and warm to. Ah – here we are, this is you:

He sits on a dark oak throne, facing the ocean.

No bindings anymore, he's loose and comfortable in his seat, the wood is worn and scooped from long use, and the scalloped curves fit him perfectly. No serpent-tanged sword trying to gouge its way inside him, no standing stones, no dwenda. The sea is calm, small waves rolling gently in and breaking knee-deep. A loose breeze ruffles his hair.

Very nice, Gil says hoarsely. *I could settle for that.*

Ah, yes, well . . . Something suddenly oddly evasive in the Creature's tones. *Moving swiftly along, though . . . let's see . . .*

The pages turn again. He hears them crackle at his ear.

It's as if he's suddenly standing in freezing fog, the voice husks at him. *Vague, tentacular stripes of darkness reach up around him like riverbed weed caught in a current, or bend away in all directions like leather straps tied tight. Through the mist, he sees the figures of dwenda, locked into postures that he only slowly recognises as glyph casts, frozen in time. There's a shivering tension through the air, like lightning undischarged, and he understands that—*

The Creature jolts to another abrupt halt.

That a mistake too? Ringil asks hopefully.

No, it's definitely you. But, well . . . it is a Heroic Reckoning, after all. We'd be ill-advised to pre-empt too much.

There's a brief, awkward pause, in which neither of them seems to know what to say next.

I don't know anything about a reckoning, Ringil lies, experimentally, to see if he can get away with it. *I'm here because I need to free my friends.*

Well, well – what resonance! Perhaps we can do something with that.

I'm sorry?

Don't be. Though I warn you – you'll need to smarten up your act if you hope to prevail against the Talons of the Sun. I once handed you as much power as I thought you could bear at the time, Ringil Eskiath, and you still managed to drop most of it. I found your enemies for you, opened a path and delivered you to a final confrontation with them, but you were apparently still not able to finish the job. Despite the merroigai's good opinion, I find you fragile, hero. Very fragile.

Ringil begins to turn round in the narrow space. A clawed limb grabs his shoulder with biting force, deftly turns him back and holds him there.

It's really better if you don't look at me, husks the voice. *I am not cloaked as I was at the crossroads, and I should hate to shatter your sanity.*

You were at my back, that first time at the cliffs?

Ah. Clarity at last. What, did you think you commanded the cold legions at thousandfold strength the way you trail that truncated little trio around behind you. You think you defeated Risgillen of Illwrack alone?

A shiver runs through him – the memories are puddles, distorted and shattered apart with every fresh drip of recall that adds to them. He's still not really clear what happened in the temple at Afa'marag – only that he won, and left blood and ruin in his wake.

You sent Hjel to find me, to bring me out, away from Seethlaw's . . . He swallows. *To bring me out.*

I sent the dispossessed prince on an errand. He did not know it was you he was looking for. He had, I think, begun to forget you by then. To let your memory go, at least.

Ringil grimaces. Ignores the cold chill that walks along his spine with those words and all they imply. He grabs after more solid, immediate stuff.

You sent me to Hjel, that first time. You brought us together. A sudden, flaring ember of intuition. *Was it your presence in the Grey Places, then, that twisted time so badly out of joint? Are you an intruder here too?*

The quiet again, the stealthy trickle of water, and a click and scrape as limbs rearrange themselves on the walls of the defile behind him. A sound like the sighing of a giant, somewhere a long way off. Cool air comes pushing down the passage at his back, coats his neck with a touch like ice.

You, don't, listen, says the Creature from the Crossroads. *I am a builder here, and to the considerable benefit of your whole species. Perhaps you might afford me a little respect on that account.*

The Dark Queen called you a Book-Keeper.

Before a book can be kept, it must be written. Look around you, little hero, and see what my kind have written in this place.

The glyphs flare fierce blue again, then blinding white, too bright to look at directly. The whole dark defile lights up with their fire, drowns him in violent light. Ringil lifts a shielding hand to his eyes.

Then why— he starts.

Why? Why what? The voice seems to have flared up with the glyphs. It's hoarse and grating still, but there's a loaded force to it like a cold wind blowing. *Why did we mend the world? Why bother to repair the damage done? Why stitch the wounds closed with the* ikinri 'ska? *As well ask why your mother raised you, why your father sired you. Why an oak spreads branches against the sun and thrusts roots down into the—*

No. It comes out a strained yelp – the glyph light is too much for him. He's having to screw his eyes shut against the glare. *Not that. Why did you bring me together with Hjel?*

Let us just say I perceived a symmetry. A sudden, cold amusement in the Creature's tones. *Do you find the arrangement with the dispossessed prince . . . unpleasant?*

You know I don't. He summons poise, strength. Pours an iron calm into his voice. *But I'm sick of being a puppet for every supernatural power through the tavern door. The Dark Court, the Helmsmen, and now you. It's getting old. If I'm being dealt into this stupid fucking game you all like so much, I want to know what it is we're playing for, and I want . . .*

Sudden scrape of clawed limbs in the narrow space behind him – his voice dies out, sinks back down his throat as he feels the talons grab him roughly under first one arm then the other, then between the legs. Abruptly, he's hoisted a yard off the floor of the light-blasted passage, held dangling there amidst the radiant glyphs.

You object to being a puppet, eh? The voice is at his ear again, very close.

Some sideways moving mouthpart brushes stickily at his neck, and he hears an alarming glottal clicking in three distinct stages. *There are worse fates, I assure you.*

Rakan brought the salve and bandages, and a low wooden stool. He made Gil sit down and then knelt before him to treat the burns himself, something that might have raised some eyebrows if their manpower hadn't been quite so thinly spread across the three ships. As it was, the gathered men showed little interest in the process. They'd seen wounds dressed often enough, and it didn't look like black mage flesh was that much different to anyone else's. They were growing restless, now that the show with the Helmsman seemed to be over, so Rakan dismissed them, bridging the authority gap between Throne Eternal and imperial marine command with what Ringil thought was admirable aplomb. The young captain was growing visibly into his responsibilities as need arose. He'd make a fine commander some day.

Yeah – if you can get him home in one piece, Gil. If you can avoid getting him killed in some Trelayne back alley a couple of weeks hence.

Oh, shut up. Like any of us have a choice right now.

Sure you do. Crowd on sail and make a run for it. Swing out wide of the cape, dodge the League pickets or bluff them somehow if you have to, run south 'til we're in safe waters. Let Jhiral negotiate to get the others back ransomed and unharmed.

But he knew he wasn't going to do any of that, so instead he sat there with hand held docilely out, and watched his young imperial lover smear salve liberally over the burns on his fingers and palm. Enjoyed the soft, slick touch while he could. When Rakan looked up, Ringil caught his eye and dropped the flicker of a wink. Rakan flushed and lowered his gaze.

Never mind command responsibilities. Wouldn't mind seeing him grow visibly somewhere else, we can get six minutes privacy between the two of us.

Pack it in, Gil. Really. Not like the balance here isn't ticklish enough as it is, without the two of you getting caught trading sweet nothings.

Rakan finished up with the salve, bound Gil's whole hand from fingertips to wrist and then muttered a brief prayer over it. Gil didn't know if this last was out of genuine faith, ingrained custom or just for show. The Revelation wasn't an area they'd really touched on. The scant trysts and stolen hours in the bustle of preparing for the expedition had been far too precious to waste on other men's abstracts, and once they actually set out for the Hironish, opportunities for anything much more significant than a quick fuck had been rare. It all added a poignant spice to their intimacy, it kept the relationship fresh and new, but it also meant – this dawning now on Gil for possibly the first time – that he barely knew the younger man at all.

Knows how to set a good field dressing. Flexing his hand experimentally in the windings of the bandage. *Torso like a god, arse like a peach, legs like a battle marshal's runner. Sucks cock like there's no tomorrow. What else you need to know, Gil?*

He stood up and nodded his thanks. Curt and manly, in case anyone was watching. He faced Anasharal again. Paced around the upended iron hull a couple of times.

'So then, Helmsman,' he said breezily. 'You want to tell me what you *really* dragged us all up here to the arse end of the known world for?'

Long silence. A couple of the Helmsman's limbs twitched pettishly at the air.

'Oh, very well,' it grumbled.

THIRTY-THREE

Battlefield aftermath calm.

The day's light was all but gone – Archeth stood in closing gloom, amidst a quiet laced with the groans and clenched curses of injured men. She shook off the post-combat daze she was sinking into, and set about retrieving her knives. Stooped beside the dead warrior caste lizard and worked at pulling first Falling Angel then Quarterless out of its eye sockets. It took some doing, the blades had gone home hard, the wounds in her side stung with the effort of pulling, and she spiked her knuckles more than once on the protective spines before she was done. Aware of the Dragonbane coming over to watch, she bit back each yelp as it rose to her lips.

'You want a hand with that?'

'No, I got it.'

For some reason she couldn't name, she didn't want anyone to touch the knives right now. Flash recall of the fight came and went, impressions she didn't know whether to trust or not. Falling Angel jumping out of her boot and into her reaching hand. Quarterless gone, wasted in a flubbed throw and lying loose on the boulevard paving until . . . she'd grabbed it back up, hadn't she? Reached back with her empty left hand, somehow found it, somehow *knew* it was there, and . . .

She knew where all of them were.

It dawned on her, crouched there twisting Quarterless back and forth by tiny increments, working it loose of the bony ridges around the lizard's eye. With the same certainty that she felt the butt of Quarterless in her hand, she felt Falling Angel *here*, laid neatly by the toe of her boot, yet to be cleaned of the gore it was clotted with; Wraithslayer, *there*, jammed in under the soft reptile armpit a yard down from the head where she crouched; Laughing Girl and Bandgleam, both buried in dead reptile peon eye sockets, *there* and over *there*. She felt the locations to the inch, the same way she'd know exactly where to reach and pick up her goblet at breakfast without ever lifting her eyes from the book in her lap.

It is a meditative, communing state . . .

Quarterless came clear with a sticky scrape. She held it up, then cast around in vain for something to wipe the blade clean. Silently, the Dragonbane handed her a torn piece of cloth, already much stained and marked.

'Thanks. Is this . . .?'

Egar nodded over towards the chunk of rubble in the middle of the boulevard. There was a crumpled body lying beside it. 'Privateer kid's shirt. He's not going to need it.'

'No, I guess not.' She cleaned Quarterless thoroughly, put it away at the small of her back, picked up Falling Angel. 'How many'd we lose?'

'Looks like nine.' The Dragonbane grimaced – as if he was trying to work a deeply lodged piece of meat out from between two of his front teeth. 'Just closed the eyes on number eight. There's one of Tand's still not finished dying, but he won't be long. Fucking peon opened him right up, hip to heartstrings.'

She stowed Falling Angel in her boot and stood up. 'Do anything for him?'

'Fed him some of that powder your iron demon gave us. Seemed to work. His pals are there, praying with him. Like I said, won't be long.'

'All right.' Twinge of krinzanz longing at the mention of powders and pain – she crushed it out. Set one boot against the bulk of the dead warrior caste lizard, bent her leg and shoved hard so it rolled over and she could get to Wraithslayer. A thought struck her. 'What about Kaptal?'

'Yeah, not a scratch on him. He was brandishing that knife you gave him, but I didn't see any blood on it. Don't know if the lizards even tried to touch him.'

'Neat trick if you can pull it off.' She stood up with Wraithslayer in her hand, inspected the blade minutely. 'We got anybody too badly hurt to march?'

Egar shook his head. 'They'll march. They'll fucking double-time it, if it gets them out of this place any faster.'

'Yeah, well, we're not getting out of here tonight, that's for sure. Going to have to camp somewhere close.'

'Yeah.' He hesitated. 'Should have stayed up on the ridge.'

'But we didn't.' She shot him a glance. 'Probably wasn't any safer up there anyway, Eg.'

He grunted.

She stowed Wraithslayer in the magical upside-down sheath on her left breast. Drifted across the boulevard paving to the dead reptile peon she'd killed with Bandgleam. 'You notice anything about this stonework?'

'It's warm.' The Dragonbane trailed after her, scuffing at the paving with a boot tip. 'In patches, anyway.'

'Yeah.' She stooped for the knife, tugged it free. Slim-bladed Bandgleam came easily out of the blood-glutted eye socket, rested lightly in her hand as she wiped it down. 'The way I figure it, either the dwenda built it like this, or it's maybe something the Warhelm's weapons did when they brought this lot down. Either way, it must have been a beacon for any Scaled Folk that washed up this far north.'

'Looks that way.'

She put the knife away, across from Wraithslayer on her chest. Looked around at the scattered reptile corpses and the men that had died. Shook her head.

'I doubt this is all of them, Eg.'

Tand's man took longer dying than anyone expected, and he went hard despite the Warhelm's painkilling powders. Some horror of letting go in this haunted place, leaving his mortal remains here for whatever might stalk down these desolate boulevards once night fell. His fellow freebooters reassured him as best they could, but their own faces were portraits in ill-ease, and the dying man was no fool. So they set out a few of the radiant bowls against the encroaching dark and stood or sat around in the glow they cast, trying not to listen to the mercenary's slowly weakening curses and groans. Yilmar Kaptal was impatient to move on, but his protests dried up in the face of a grim stare from one of the other freebooters. Archeth stowed her own impatience where no one could see it, sat at another bowl instead and submitted stoically to the Dragonbane's blue-lit ministrations with needle and thread. Turned out, he was a nifty little seamstress when he wanted to be.

A little later, the fire sprite showed up, bright orange and red in the windy darkness. It flickered about on the fringes of the company, like an embarrassed late guest shown in to a dinner already begun. Egar noticed before she did – she was lost in the soft blue glow from the bowl. He leaned across to where she sat cross-legged and touched her on one knee.

'Our friend's back.'

'About fucking time.' Her wounds ached, and the dying mercenary's dribble of imprecation and pleading was getting to her worse than she'd expected.

'Occurs to me,' said the Dragonbane slowly. 'It maybe went off to scout a route that didn't take us in sniffing range of any lizard nests. We should have waited up on that fucking ridge.'

'Yeah, but we didn't. Let it go, Eg.'

He said nothing, and they sat in silence together, listening to the dying man and the hoot of the wind in the architecture. Presently, one of the other freebooters came over and made brief obeisance. Archeth nodded bleakly up at him.

'What is it?'

'A boon, my lady. Ninesh asks if you can leave the walking flame here to watch over him in death.'

She rolled her eyes. 'Well, obviously fucking not, no.'

'Or then, if the demon at An-Kirilnar might be asked to send out another flame to do it.' The mercenary made an awkward gesture. 'He's delirious, my lady. But it would comfort him to be told the lie. It would help him to let go.'

Archeth remembered the stench of voided bowels and burnt flesh in the house at Ornley, the unending keening from the next room. What Tand's men had done to the islander – she tried to recall his name, but it wouldn't come – and his family. She couldn't recall if this dying thug had been there or not, but she imagined it wouldn't have made much difference one way or the other. The mercenaries were all cut from the same grubby cloth – veteran soldiers of fortune, recruited by reputation for the expressed purpose of securing their master's slave caravans, shipments and stables. It was grim, brutal work and Tand wouldn't have been choosing them for the milk of human kindness in their hearts.

She shot a glance at Egar. The Dragonbane shrugged.

'If it gets us moving any quicker.'

'Oh, all *right*. I'm going.'

She levered herself to her feet, wincing at the twinge across her ribs from the stitches. She made her way over to the dying man and his companions, no clear sense of how she was supposed to do this at all. Giving comfort had never been her strong point – too much stored bitterness of her own to carry around, never mind anyone else's fucking pain.

Around the makeshift encampment, men stopped their conversations and watched her.

Great.

You walk, Archidi, you find the strength. The Dragonbane's words filtered back through her memory. *Some men don't have that strength, so you have to lend it to them.*

The other mercenaries shuffled back, gave her access. The dying man looked up at her in the blue gloom, face beaded with sweat, breath sawing from his lungs in tight little gusts. They'd pillowed him on his bedroll, put a blanket over his body and his wound, but he was shivering as if they'd stripped him naked.

She crouched at his side. His eyes tracked the motion, she saw how he flinched from her. Burnt black witch. She put a hand on his shoulder and he made a noise like the snort of a panicking horse. But his eyes were on her face and his gaze clung there, fearful and wondering, like some almost-drowned man, staring at the grim rise of a shoreline beyond the chop of the waves he struggled against.

'You have fought well.' The words were out of her mouth before she fully realised what she was going to say. 'You have stood against dragons.'

'I, I . . . yeah. Fuckers got me good, Mom. Got me good.' The tormented features twisted. 'They, they, I couldn't—'

'They are all slain now,' she said, astonished at the ease with which the banalities spilled from her lips. 'And we are victorious, and, uhm, in your eternal debt for your part in that victory. You have given your blood so that your comrades might go on. Among the Black Folk, that is a sacred act. Know, then, that the Great Spirit at An-Kirilnar has also seen your sacrifice and will send a flame guardian to mark your passing. Go to rest in pride. From now until, uhm, the end of all days, the fire will stand here, in memory of your hero's name and in protection of your resting place.'

'I . . .' A trace of clarity surfaced through the delirium in the desperate eyes. 'Is it so, my lady? Really?'

'Really,' she said firmly. She took one of his scarred and calloused hands, pressed it between her own. 'Now go to good rest. Let go.'

The mercenary hung on a little longer regardless, but his breathing seemed less panicked now, and he cursed less than he had before. He confused Archeth with his mother some more, asked her not to leave him, asked why her face was so sooted up, was anything wrong, had something happened to Bereth. He mumbled to his comrades, and to others who were not there, told them all he was a hero in the eyes of the Black Folk, smiled like a child with the words.

Shortly after that, his breathing stumbled and then stopped.

They sat silent around him for a couple of moments, just to be sure. One of the other mercenaries leaned in and pressed fingers to the neck. Held the back of his hand to the open mouth. Nodded. Archeth got stiffly to her feet.

'Right. Do what you need to do for him. But get it done fast, we're pulling out. This isn't a safe place to spend the night.'

She nodded across at Egar, and the Dragonbane stood up, started barking orders. The men scrambled for their gear, relief palpable in the sudden surge of motion. She moved too, trying to shrug off the dead man at her back. But something of him clung stubbornly on. She paused on her way to get her pack, stood a moment looking back, watching the surviving freebooters with their dead comrade in the light from the radiant bowl.

They were frisking the newly made corpse for valuables.

THIRTY-FOUR

In those dark and desperate days, the Kiriath did not much care what they sum-
moned from the void, nor what forces they set free in the process. Arrayed against
them was all the glimmering might of the witch folk, and a seven thousand year
old Empire built on sorcery that could not co-exist with their science. A reckoning
was inevitable, and the powers the witch folk wielded were ancient and terrible.
It was no time for half-measures. From the void, the Named Commanders drew
seven spirits in fury, constrained them in iron and charged them with protection
of the Kiriath people and extermination of the Aldrain foe.
   Chief among these was the Warhelm Ingharnanasharal.
   Perhaps not the most savage among the summoned seven, nor even the most
lethal, but Ingharnanasharal it was who burned brightest and was most favoured
among the Kiriath command. Who was chosen for the highest duty, flung up into
the heavens like a bright, newly minted coin, while the others remained below,
moored to the Earth and their several separate concerns. To Ingharnanasharal
fell the duty of the Watch from On High, of seeking out the Aldrain wherever
they lurked on the globe and bringing their doom, and more, of tasting the winds
and particles of the world, to understand what had been done to its fabric in the
age before, that would allow such outrages against reason as the Aldrain domin-
ion, to fashion that understanding into weapons and strategy that would bring
the enemy to their knees and deliver the final blow.
   In the beginning, the war went hard for the Kiriath, and on more than one
occasion Ingharnanasharal came close to being clawed out of the sky by—
   'A-hem.'

The Helmsman paused.
   'Can we speed this up?' Ringil asked mildly. 'I don't want to hear your
old war stories – I've got plenty of those myself. Let's skip the Ancient
Clash of Elder Races, shall we, and try to concentrate on current
events?'
   'You ask questions that require context if you are to understand the
answers.' Anasharal's voice was unmistakably sulky. 'The war against the
Aldrain is the cornerstone of that context. Ingharnanasharal was given a
sacred and eternal trust to fight that war—'
   'Yes, all very noble, I'm sure. This Ingharnanasharal – not a close relative of yours, by any chance?'
   Silence. From the Compulsion glyphs graven in Anasharal's carapace,
came a faint but growing radiance. *Sea Eagle's Daughter* rocked gently on

267

the swell. Ringil leaned forward a little in the chair they'd brought him from the captain's cabin.

'I asked you a question, Helmsman.'

He summoned force in the pit of his stomach. The glow of the symbols across Anasharal's carapace lit up in burning blue.

'I—' The words came like pulled teeth. 'Proceed. From Ingharnana-sharal. I am. The Purpose. Ingharnanasharal decreed.'

'Hmm.' Ringil sank back in the arms of the chair, no clear idea what the Helmsman was talking about, but damned if he'd admit the fact. 'You seem a little on the tubby and impotent side for a savage summoned spirit charged with the extermination of a whole race.'

Hesitation. The fiery spidering lines of the glyphs had faded out, but the glow was still there.

'Time.' The Helmsman spat jaggedly out. 'Has passed.'

'It does that, doesn't it? So tell me, what happened after the war?'

'What you already know. There was a reckoning. The dwenda were driven out. There was . . . a victory. The casting down of the witch realm, the rise of the Kiriath. And . . . demobilisation followed.'

Ringil nodded. 'They took your weapons away.'

'A . . . new order was proclaimed. A new mission. To raise humanity from the muck of superstition and peasant awe, to build a new human Empire on reason and science.'

'Well, that seems to be going well.'

Some trapped piece of anger seemed to get free inside Anasharal. 'You see with the eyes of a mortal,' it snapped. 'Locked into your own context, ignorant of any wider option for change. It is no easy thing to roll back seven thousand years of glamour and terror and prostration to the un-known. Humans are apt to superstition, it is in their blood, and this world suits them only too well. To forge and temper a weapon against that, to bring about in humans the levels of civilisation that the Kiriath once at-tained in their world has been the work of patient millennia, and still it is not halfway done.'

'No. And Grashgal and the rest going away can't have helped matters much.'

'As you say.'

Ringil rubbed at his chin. It was at best a loose and rambling inter-rogation, this, but harder and faster might not be wise. He knew from some unpleasant experience of his own that it was often harder to break a man by going directly to the point and forcing answers than by letting the subject work up to it in his own time. Direct demands and brute force stiffened resolve, provided a clear enemy to focus on in the in-quisitor. In some men and women, it could bring on a berserk strength of will enough to give even a skilled torturer a run for his money. Everyone broke in the end, of course, but along the way you got wrong information, you got garbled details, you got the odd accidental corpse before you'd properly finished sorting and checking the truth of what you'd learnt . . .

Sometimes you got a real hard-case who'd bite through their own tongue and try to bleed to death rather than cave in.

But let the captive talk generally, let them ramble on in hopes of avoiding or at least forestalling actual pain, and sometimes the will to resist unravelled along the way. Sometimes you got what you wanted almost without your subject realising that they'd given it up.

And Anasharal liked to talk.

Anasharal liked to lecture, to upbraid, to play word games of wit and irony, and generally point up how *completely fucking superior* it was to the human company it found itself in. Maybe there was some leverage in that.

Of course, Anasharal was not human. But there was no harm in trying the same basic tricks, and might be rather a lot to be gained. Ringil had only one ultimate threat to use against the Helmsman, and once that was played out and Anasharal was sinking like a stone through the mile or more of ocean under them, there'd be no more useful intelligence. Gil didn't want to arrive at that point too fast, if at all, because he still wasn't sure if he was bluffing or not. And though he didn't think the Helmsman could drag itself to the gangway fast enough to fall in and drown of its own accord, he did wonder after his run-in with Anasharal's self-heating carapace, if it could maybe commit a vindictive kind of suicide by melting itself to slag right there on the deck, burning through the ship's timbers and hull and scuttling *Sea Eagle's Daughter* entire.

Get some truth from this demon trapped in iron, Hjel tells him over the campfire. *You're fighting blind until you do.*

So let the Helmsman ramble. Invoking the Compulsion glyphs was hard work, it was draining. Not something he wanted to do too much if he didn't have to.

And – let's be honest, Gil – you don't like *the new glyphs very much, do you? You don't like the sticky-dark way they make you feel when you call them up, the thing that goes through you like coming one too many times at the end of a hard night's fucking, like giving up something final you really can't afford to lose, like peeling a fresh scab back from your soul and watching what oozes up underneath . . .*

Pale sunlight fell through the rigging above his head, put laddered shadow on his face. His left hand ached beneath the bandaging. He felt oddly cold, despite the improved weather.

But Noyal Rakan was watching him, stood at his right hand as if the commandeered chair were the Burnished Throne itself and Ringil his emperor. From the rigging and the upper decks of *Sea Eagle's Daughter*, both fore and aft, they were all watching him, marines and Throne Eternal rank and file and Klithren's cowed and co-opted privateers, all waiting to see what he would do next.

He shed his fumbling thoughts, marshalled what he'd so far gleaned.

'All right, so let's see – in the war against the dwenda, the Kiriath kick

269

this Warhelm Ingharnanasharal up into the sky, armed to the teeth and burning with a sacred trust. And a few thousand years later you come burning down out of the same sky, barely capable of waddling a couple of yards from here to there and no power to actually harm anyone or anything' – a sour glance at his bandaged hand – 'that isn't touching you at the time. You have no weapons, but your sacred trust is eternal, so we can assume that remains.'

'I did not say at any point—'

'Shut up, I'm not finished yet.' Ringil brooded for a moment. 'That sacred trust was the protection of the Kiriath and the destruction of the dwenda. The Kiriath are all gone bar one, less than one, if we're going to be bloodline precise about it, and you saw fit to drag her all the way north to the Hironish Isles. That's where it stops making sense. How is Archeth Indamaninarmal safer on perilous seas three thousand miles the wrong side of a bad political divide than she would be back home and tucked up in bed? I've got to assume there was some kind of risk building in Yhelteth and you saw it coming. But what the fuck could be bad enough to justify this trip?'

'Perhaps there was a reward waiting that mattered more than the risks.'

'If there was, we didn't find it. And you weren't exactly helpful in that direction.'

'Perhaps the reward was already in your hands and did not need finding.'

Ringil snapped to his feet.

'Yeah, and perhaps you'd better start answering my questions cleanly before I lose my fucking temper and send you for a swim.'

The tension came up in the pit of his stomach again, unbidden. He could feel the glyphs on the tip of his tongue, crowding forward, as if anxious to be unleashed once more. *The deeper into the* ikinri 'ska *you go*, Hjel tells him, camped somewhere out on the marsh plain, *the less it's a tool for you and the more you're a gate for it.*

Well, he'd gone pretty deep this time.

'You have not made clear what your question actually is,' Anasharal was saying, rather smugly. 'Do so and I will answer you gladly enough.'

'What,' Ringil enunciated tightly, 'Was the threat back in Yhelteth?'

'Earthquake.' No trace of strain or resistance in the Helmsman's tone now. The glyphs were back to thin scratches on metal, no glow remaining 'The drowned daughters of Hanliagh are stirring again.'

Fuck. Ringil made his face impassive, but . . . *fuck.*

'And the Citadel,' Anasharal went on. 'Will almost certainly use the resulting panic among the faithful to extract concessions from the Emperor and force a holy war in the north.'

You don't say, went drearily through his head.

He sat back down. He saw them in his mind's eye, thronging the streets – the tramp of their feet, the forested ranks of their raised fists. He heard the shrill, barking hysteria of their chants as if he were there. All those hot-eyed, tight-muscled angry young men, marching by the thousand, yearning to spill blood in the Revelation's name.

'Yeah, there goes that Empire you were talking about,' he drawled, still masking his shock. 'You know, the one built on reason and science?'

The Helmsman's voice scaled upward. 'I did not say that the work of the Kiriath mission was well done—'

'How very humble of you.'

'—*nor that I subscribed to it!*'

Ringil blinked, as much at the chopped-off quality of the words as at their meaning. *This is it.*

He sat still in the chair, trying not to let the knowledge show on his face. Certainty in his racing mind, as iron as Anasharal's carapace. This was the slip, the break he'd been looking for, the crack in the Helmsman's polished facade.

Just got to lever it open.

'If you don't subscribe to 'Nam's mission,' he said slowly, 'Then the Empire means nothing to you, except maybe as . . .'

And then he saw it.

Like sand blown off the carved lines of some intricate, ancient piece of architecture, long buried in the deserts around Demlarashan. Stonework and ornamentation slowly etching back into view, no clear sense of the overall structure yet, but—

He heard the Helmsman's words again. *To forge and temper a weapon . . .*

Heard his own words, thrown out without reflection. *They took your weapons away.*

'Your sacred trust was to exterminate the dwenda.' Feeling his way as he spoke. 'And they're back. You're trying to turn Yhelteth into a weapon to drive them out again. But how's that supposed to work? Jhiral's a spoilt brat, he's got the vision of a wharf-end bully at best, and without the Kiriath . . .'

Faintly, very faintly, the traceries of radiance across the Helmsman's carapace as the compulsion glyph sequence began to kindle. He was closing in.

He was—

'Oh, you're joking,' he said suddenly. 'You *must* be joking.'

'You have not asked me a question yet, Eskiath.' Anasharal's voice was still not strained, but the sulkiness was back.

'Archeth? You're trying to put fucking *Archeth* on the Burnished Throne?'

The glyphs flared violently.

And abruptly, Ringil was laughing.

It started small, a disbelieving chuckle at first, but then his mouth split around the sound like a badly sutured wound, and suddenly he was laughing hard.

Perhaps it was the pent up horror of his time in the dark defiles and gullies, *the sense of endless, restless sets of eyes hung up above and brooding on his inch-slow progress, the tight, twisting confines of the paths and the scuttle of multiple limbs overhead, the scrape of claw-tipped fingers creeping across wet limestone at his back, tapping with skeletal irony on the glyphs he has passed and noted* . . .

Yeah, well. Enough of that.

He stuffed the laughter away, got it back down to a chuckle, obscurely glad to find that somewhere inside him, the capacity for genuine mirth still remained. He leaned back in the arms of the chair with a broad grin still painted across his face.

'Okay, seriously though. Just so we're absolutely clear on this. You really plan to depose the Khimran dynasty and make Archeth Indamaninarmal Empress? That's the big idea?'

'Initially regent.' The words dragged out of Anasharal. 'But as time passes and she does not age, as perception of her changes from human to goddess, as the remaining Helmsmen stir to their fullest capacity to serve her, there will be no imaginable replacement for her on the throne or at the head of the Empire. She will reign as God-Empress Eternal.'

'That's if the dwenda don't just roll over us all first.'

'If there is any hope of repelling the dwenda, it must come from Yhelteth.' Anasharal's voice was picking up momentum now, and the glyphs had dulled. It was as if Ringil's laughter had stung the Helmsman into finally coming clean. 'Your own homeland is in thrall to the Aldrain legend, its people will welcome them back with open arms and not question until it is too late. Their own founding myths will eat them alive. The Empire has cultural distance—'

'Yeah? Try telling that to Pashla Menkarak and his fuckwit friends up at the Citadel. They thought the dwenda were angels.'

'That would not have happened under Kiriath leadership.'

'And how exactly do you propose to secure Archeth her seat on the throne?' He gestured, grin crimped down to a sour smile in one corner of his mouth. 'It's not like she's returning home in triumph from a heroic quest fulfilled.'

'She never needed to. The quest itself was pure pretext, a skein of borrowed legends and half truths knitted together to provide the necessary impulse in the key players.'

That stopped him. Wiped out the last traces of his amusement.

'You metal motherfucker,' he said wonderingly. 'I always knew there was something wrong with this gig. I *knew* you were playing us, right from the start.'

'Then you repressed your doubts remarkably well.'

'I didn't come along for the fucking quest.'

'Ah, yes – protective loyalty. Strange how much she inspires that, isn't it?'

'Oh, fuck off.'

He glowered at the upended Helmsman while his head seethed with the new revelations. At his shoulder, he sensed the rigidity that had taken hold of Noyal Rakan. He was, after all, a Throne Eternal. And while Gil had detected in him on more than one occasion a bitter disappointment with the quality of the man now occupying the Burnished Throne, that wasn't really the point. Rakan's oath, like all his comrades, was to the throne *itself*, the idea and ideal of the throne, not the Emperor who sat on it at any given moment. That, plus fond memories of Akal the father and a couple of generations of family bond to the Khimran dynasty, would be more than enough to overwhelm any personal dislike for Jhiral the son.

Though now, of course, with earthquake and war and streets full of the ranting idiot faithful, loyalty to Jhiral might be a rather moot point. There were any number of ways a young, unpopular Emperor could die in chaos like that, leaving a gap to be filled and no real time or inclination to worry about who exactly was to blame.

Still . . . *Archeth?*

'You're going to have to explain this to me slowly,' he said. 'You sell Archeth Indamaninarmal a city in the sea and an undying Kiriath vigil to get her out of town before the shit starts to fly. You sell the Emperor a possible sorcerous threat to his Empire that he can't ignore so he'll let her go. Plus, the way this expedition was set up, he's got a shot at acquiring some easy loot for very little upfront outlay, and the chance to have some of his stroppier rich-men-about-court launch themselves into handy self-imposed exile on seas that . . .'

And stop.

As howling winds rinsed out the rest of the sand, and the whole ornately carved and crenellated edifice stood out of the desert, revealed for what it was – bigger than he'd ever imagined it might be. He felt himself stumble before it, felt the sandstorm winds of realisation tear through his head.

'Captain,' he heard himself say distantly to Rakan. 'This hand is really starting to bother me. Can you get me a couple of grains of flandrijn, powdered into water?'

The Throne Eternal hesitated. Gestured at the Helmsman. 'My lord, this is, this sounds like—'

'Yes, it's compelling, I agree.' Gil turned in the chair and looked into Noyal Rakan's eyes. 'And we'll resume just as soon as I can think straight with this fucking hand. You can go, Captain, I've got this. I don't believe I'm in any danger. Just . . . in a lot of pain.'

He flexed his bandaged fingers and grimaced for effect, not entirely faking it. He hissed in through his teeth, pressed his lips together, still holding the young Throne Eternal's gaze. It wasn't the *ikinri 'ska*, wasn't any kind of sorcery the Creature from the Crossroads might recognise. But it was that old Ringil Angel-eyes magic. Noyal Rakan moistened his lips and his eyes crinkled with concern.

'I'm sorry,' he said softly. 'Be right back.'

Ringil watched him go, let him get out of earshot before he turned back to the Helmsman. Voice a hiss not much louder than the noise he'd made to signal his pain.

'You're building a fucking *cabal?*'

THIRTY-FIVE

The sprite led them a twisting, looping route through the darkened streets, following some planned path obvious only to itself. Egar couldn't be sure – cloud cover had crept in from the east, and band and stars were muffled up – but he thought they doubled back and zigzagged a lot. The city became a maze around him, dim towering mounds of broken architecture and seemingly random twists and turns between. Once or twice he saw the distant gleam of a campfire out among the ruins, and the breeze brought him the scent of roasting meat, but that was all. The sprite always veered well away from such signs.

For all the doubling back, though, they moved at a good pace. The sprite flickered briskly on ahead, only pausing or coming back when they hit some awkward obstruction or bottleneck. On these occasions, it brightened itself helpfully and hung about, darting back and forth, throwing warm reddish light across the falls of collapsed masonry or torn up street surfacing that were slowing them down.

Finally, a couple of hours into the march, it led them up a series of detritus-strewn staircases in one rubble mound and out onto a broad, jutting platform forty feet above street level. Surprised satisfaction muttered among the men. The ruin they'd climbed through was mostly intact – it gave them towering vertical walls at their back, the single staircase entry point to defend and a two hundred degree sweep of vantage out over the city to the front.

It was pretty much an ideal place to make camp.

Yeah, and if you hadn't been in such a fucking hurry before, Dragonbane, we might have been sitting here nine stronger than we are.

He sat cross-legged at the edge of the platform, away from the others, glowering out at the shattered city skyline. It was not normally in his nature to brood on such things, but the encounter with the lizards had opened a door somewhere in his head, and now all the long-stored memories of the war were back out to play.

Back in the Kiriath Wastes, back in combat with the Scaled Folk.

There'd been a savage intensity to it all back then, a vivid day-to-day urgency that, if he was honest, he'd thrilled to and still sometimes missed. But now, dealt a handful of the very same red-edged cards, all he felt was old, and weary of the game. As if everything he'd done back then, every battle he'd fought, every scar he'd collected, had all been for nothing. As if something fanged and grinning dragged him off the mount of his fate and back down into a past he'd done everything he could to leave behind . . .

'See anything good out there?'

He glanced up at Archeth's slim form and tilted, inquiring look. Shook his head.

'More of the same. I don't think we've come all that far as the crow flies. Going to take us a good few days to cross this shit heap.'

'Dodging the Scaled Folk as we go.'

'Yeah, that's right. Cheer me up, why don't you?'

She sighed. Lowered herself into a loose sprawl beside him. 'It was an honest mistake, Eg, and we all made it, not just you.'

Yeah, but I'm the one supposed to be leading these men out of this mess. It's my job not to make mistakes that get them killed. But he didn't say that, not least because he was beginning to wonder if it was true. They'd all walked into An-Kirilnar behind the Dragonbane, this rag-tag assortment of fighting men, but they'd marched out again behind a flickering Kiriath firefly and Archeth Indamaninarmal.

'Honest or not,' he growled, 'we can't afford many more mistakes like that.'

'Agreed.'

They sat for a while, staring off the edge of the platform. She shifted and cleared her throat a couple of times.

'You see Tand's guys turning out their dead pal's pockets?' she asked finally.

'Yeah. Took the rings off his fingers as well. The old freebooter's fare-well.' He glanced sideways at her. 'What, you were expecting speeches and flowers?'

'I was expecting . . .' She shook her head. 'Doesn't matter. Fucking sell-sword scum.'

'Talking to an old sellsword here, Archidi.'

'Don't tell me you would have done the same.'

He considered for a moment, brooding on the skyline. 'Well, no, maybe not. Not to a comrade-in-arms, anyway. But hey, I'm a barking mad Majak berserker. No accounting for the way us steppe barbarians act.'

She snorted, but he saw a thin smile flicker on her lips.

'Look, you don't want to read too much into it either way, Archidi. They sat his death vigil, they prayed over him while he was alive. And it's not like he's going to miss any of that stuff they took.' He gestured out over the ruined city. 'Not like it'd serve any useful purpose left out there with him.'

'Yeah, I know.' The smile had flickered out, left her looking grim and tired. 'I just wonder sometimes, what's the fucking point? Here we are, trying to get everybody home safe, and for what? So Tand's thug freeboot-ers can go back to bullying slave caravans up and down the great north road for him? So Kaptal can get back to his high class whore-mongering and his blackmail around court? So these arsehole privateers can slink off home through the borders, sign on with a new ship and go back to their fucking pirating . . .?'

He nodded. 'So Chan and Nash and the others can go back to their job safeguarding the wanker on the Burnished Throne?'

'Well, that's . . . different.'

'Is it?' Another time, he might have left it alone. But he was raw from the fight and the errors that had caused it, and twitchy from this whole forced march back into his own past. 'How is it any different, Archidi? Jhiral's a cunt, and you know it. He's every bit as big a cunt as Tand or Kaptal or any League pirate captain you want to name. And the Empire pays a phalanx of its very best fighting men to stand around him and let him go on being a cunt without anyone able to touch a hair on his head, while you stand at his shoulder, whispering advice into his delicate little cunt ear. Doesn't mean we won't try to get you and our Throne Eternal pals home, though, does it?'

That sat between them for a while, like the night and the cold questing reach of the breeze. When the silence started to mount up, he glanced across at her, but she was still staring fixedly out into the darkness.

'You don't understand, Eg.' Quietly, but with a steely conviction infusing her tone. 'You don't know what it was like before the Empire. The whole south was just a bunch of fucking horse tribes slaughtering each other left, right and centre when they weren't riding down out of the hills and butchering the farmers and the fishermen on the plains, carrying off women and children as slaves. The Empire put a stopper in that; it brought peace and law to the whole region in less than twenty years.'

'Yeah, think we got this lecture at imperial barracks induction.'

'Jhiral isn't so bad, Eg.'

'He's a cunt.'

'He's a young man handed too much power too soon, that's all. A boy who spent his whole boyhood learning to fear his own brothers and sisters and stepmothers and aunts and uncles and cousins, never mind anybody else at court; a son whose father never had time for him because he was always too fucking busy off making war at one end of the Empire or the other. You're surprised Jhiral's turned out the way he is? That he acts the way he does? I'm not.' Voice rising now, an obscure anger piling onto the conviction, lending it force. 'And now he's had to watch the whole race of magical beings that protected his father – that protected his whole dynasty before him – cut and run as soon as he takes the throne. He's the first one, Eg, the very first one who's had to deal with that, since my father walked into the Khimran encampment nearly five hundred years ago and told Sabal the Conqueror's flea-bitten thug grandfather that his bloodline were going to be kings. Try and imagine what it's like for a moment – there's this five hundred year old magic carpet your family's always had, to raise them up above the crowd and keep them safe and special, and now suddenly it's yanked out from under your feet just when you need it most. Jhiral's the first one who hasn't had the Kiriath behind him, building wonders in the city to amaze his people, riding with him to war to terrify his enemies, lending him weapons and knowledge and power, promising him that whatever happens, history is on his side.'

'He has you,' Egar rumbled.

'Yeah, he has me.' A mirthless sneer flitted across her face in the gloom. 'Every solid thing he grew up thinking he could count on turns to dust in his hands, and he gets me as the consolation prize. One burnt-out, krin-fried Kiriath half-blood juggling five thousand years of heritage she doesn't fucking understand. Is that supposed to make him feel better?'

He shrugged. 'Dunno, he's a cunt, isn't he? But I'd take you at my shoulder over anyone else I know with a blade, and be grateful for the company.'

The moment locked and held solid, until she broke it apart with her laughter. He looked at her and saw in the low light the tear sheen in her eyes. But she sniffed and grinned when she spoke.

'Anyone else you know with a blade, eh? Thought that'd be Gil.'

'Well.' He gestured. 'He's got the other shoulder.'

And they both broke up laughing, loud enough that faces turned towards them across the blue-lit platform space.

But later, as they lay side by side in their bedrolls and stared up past the jagged loom of ruins into a clouded sky, she said very quietly 'You're right, Eg. Jhiral *is* a cunt. But I can't help it, I've known him too long. He's been in my life ever since he was a squalling little bundle I could lift on one palm.'

He grunted. Bleakly, he remembered Ergund; playing raiders with him about the encampment when they were both not much older than six or seven; staring down at his mutilated corpse in the steppe grass two years past. *We're all small and harmless once, Archidi. But we all grow up. And some of us grow up needing killing.*

You're talking to a brother-slayer here.

Let it go, Eg. Let her talk it out.

He didn't want to fight with Archeth, whatever spiky balls of rage might be rolling about in the pit of his stomach, looking for release.

Yeah, save that for whatever's waiting for us down the boulevard tomorrow.

Or out on the steppe when we get there.

For the first time, he allowed himself to think fully about what he might find if he went back. How it might boil down if he asked around in Ishlin-ichan, got word of the Skaranak and their herds and tracked them down. How his people might react if he just showed up one night like some wronged ancestor ghost in the campfire glow.

And put a gutting knife into that fucking buzzard Poltar.

That little shit Ershal too.

'Probably held him in my arms more times than his own father ever did, you know.' Archeth, still musing up at the clouded dark overhead. 'Akal was never around when it mattered. I still remember hugging Jhiral at four fucking years old, Eg, the night the Chaila pretenders sneaked into the palace and tried to murder him. I'm clutching him to me, I'm trying to cover his eyes so he can't see the carnage, trying to hide the fact I'm checking him for wounds at the same time, and he's weeping, screaming, covered in blood from where I took down the guy that had him when I burst in. All he wants is his big sister to come and hold him instead of me. And I'm trying to explain to him that he can't really see his sister right now, in fact, uhm, well, Chaila's got to go away for a while.'

'Yeah. Ten years in a House of Prayer in the Scatter, wasn't it?'

'They pardoned her home after six. Big mistake, as it turned out.' Archeth blew a weary sigh up at the cloud cover. 'Fucking joys of Empire-building. 'Course, by the time she came home, Jhiral knew what it was all about. No way to keep it from him, and he'd survived another couple of attempts to scrub him out in the meantime – it was getting to be part of the palace decor. When Chaila came back, he wouldn't have anything to do with her. Never let her even touch him again. So, yeah, I look at all that and I think, sure, you're right, he's a cunt. But what chance did he have?'

Rustle of blankets as she shuffled round to look at him across the small space between them.

'And he's *smart*, Eg, that's what counts. He's smart and he sees the point of the Empire. You can work with that, you can build something on it. Whatever bloody mess he makes protecting himself, it'll pass. He won't live forever, but what I can help him build might. He'll leave heirs, and I can work with them, give them the wisdom he never had the time to acquire. Make one of them into the ruler he'll never be.'

'Or,' he said mildly, 'You could just save some time and look for a better king right now.'

She sighed. Rolled back to face the sky.

'What, throw out five centuries of stable dynastic rule, probably set off a civil war and let everyone and his horse think the throne's up for grabs? No thanks, Eg. I may not much like the way things are right now, but I'm pretty sure it's better than the alternatives. And I am done with bloodbaths.'

'You hope.' He yawned, cavernously. 'Better put some big fucking prayers behind that, you want it to stick. Like a certain hard-nose faggot said at Demlarashan that time – *we live in bloodbath times . . .*'

'*. . . and looks like tonight is bath night.*' Eg heard the smile in her voice, the glint of the memory. 'He did say that, didn't he?'

'Yeah. Witty little fucker when he wanted to be.'

They were both silent for a while after that, staring up at the shrouded face of the heavens. If the shamans were right and you really could read the future in the stars, then tonight was a shit night to be trying it.

'You think he's all right?' she asked finally.

He thought about it. 'I think he's alive, definitely. Gil was a tough-to-kill motherfucker even before he started in on all this black shaman stuff. Now, I can't see anything short of the Sky Dwellers stopping him.'

'Or the dwenda?'

He snorted. 'Yeah, a whole fucking legion of them, maybe. Which that shit-head Klithren didn't look to me like he had.'

She didn't say anything for a few moments, maybe because they could both feel the shape of what was coming next.

'You didn't answer my question, Eg.'

He grimaced up at the hidden stars. 'No?'

'No. You said you were sure he was alive, but I didn't ask you that. I asked if you thought he was all right.'

Egar sighed, caught. Said nothing, because, well . . .

'Well?' she prodded.

'Well.' He gave up trying to see anything in the sky above. Turned on his side, away from her so he wouldn't have to meet her eyes. 'All depends on your definition of all right, doesn't it?'

THIRTY-SIX

Menith Tand
Klarn Shendanak
Yilmar Kaptal
Mahmal Shanta

He wrote the names out in his cabin, back aboard *Dragon's Demise*. Sat and stared at them as the ink dried. He'd lived cheek by jowl with these men for nearly five months now, the ones who'd chosen to come along. He'd grown used to them, got to know them somewhat. Had built what amounted to a friendship with Shanta, a wary mutual respect with Tand, and a gradual appreciation that Shendanak was not quite the thick-skulled swaggering Majak thug he generally liked to appear to be before his men.

Kaptal was an obnoxious tub of guts, but there you go, can't have everything.

And before that, back in Yhelteth, there'd been meetings, endless fucking meetings, with the whole expeditionary board of sponsors, those four and the others.

He wrote the others out too.

Andal Karsh
Nethena Gral
Shab Nyanar
Jhesh Oreni

Watched the fresh ink soak into the parchment and dry to an even colour with the previous names. Outside, indistinct shouts between men in the rigging as they got the sails dressed, worked at keeping *Dragon's Demise* tight with the other two ships. The noon sun put bright, high-angled beams of light through the cabin windows around him and caught the swirl of dust motes in the air. It spilled pools of radiance across the writing desk he sat at, touched one corner of the parchment he'd written on, lit it to blazing.

He picked up the list and stared at it some more. Thought about it, about what he knew first hand, what he'd gleaned from Archeth and the others over the previous year of hustling and prepping for the expedition. The gossip, the rumours, the moments of unguarded candour and drunken admission.

He read the names over again.

Saw, with slow-dawning comprehension, the gathered tinder they represented.

Shanta – landed, titled and colossally well-heeled coastal clan patriarch, the foremost naval engineering authority in the Empire and a presiding member of the Yhelteth shipwrights' guild. Which body already served, if Archeth was to be believed, as chief cauldron for a bubbling centuries-old coastlander resentment of the Khimran dynasty's overlordship, resentment that might now be coming to something of a boil. If it did, Shanta would likely be more than happy to give the pot a stir – he'd seen a few too many friends and acquaintances lost to Jhiral's purges in the years since the accession, and with each loss the memory of his close friendship with Akal Khimran the Great was further tarnished, his traces of nominal allegiance to the dynasty further scrubbed away. On his own admission, age was the knife edge Shanta balanced on now, lacking on the one hand the indignant impulse of a younger man to leap in and act with violence against a ruler he had come to hate, on the other hand not having anything much to lose in terms of future years if he did act and it turned out badly. He'd once joked rather grimly with Ringil that whatever unpleasant, long drawn out fate the inventive young Emperor might someday decree for him, his aged heart would give out at the first infliction of even moderate sustained pain. And he'd long ago seen his children grow up and navigate into safe harbours within the imperial hierarchy, where it would, frankly, be impossible to do them much harm without fatally destabilising the whole edifice of rule.

Shanta had lived his life for what it was worth, he was looking now only for a good and significant death. And if the quest didn't provide it for him via chest infection or drowning, Ringil thought he might well go looking for that death in a defiant rising against Jhiral.

Nyanar and Gral – coastal clan worthies of note, perhaps not quite in Shanta's class, but not far behind, and both harbouring the same basic sense of superiority over the Khimrans' horse tribe bandit origins. The Nyanars were generationally wealthy and wielded substantial political influence in the ranks of both the imperial navy and the marine levies – a dozen or more scions of the house held command posts in one service or the other, some of them apparently earned on actual merit. A nominal loyalty to the palace came along with that, of course, service oaths of allegiance and so forth, but what it really amounted to was a loyalty to the sea-faring heritage of the coastal clans and a pre-existing naval warrior tradition that the Khimran dynasty had co-opted whole, once it got through with defeating them.

No one had really forgotten that defeat.

House Gral's reach apparently leaned more to the civil and legislative, and the wealth was more recent, but weighty nonetheless. Reigning daughter of a former ship-building family that had come back from prior ruin via judicious, cut-throat speculation in property and law, Nethena Gral had learnt at her father's knee that *a court sword on your hip's worth nothing much compared to the weight of a magistrate in your pocket.* That was word for word – she'd told Ringil the tale herself in an unguarded and slightly drunken moment one celebratory spring evening as *Pride of Yhelteth* launched. Perhaps she'd felt some gush of aristo empathy with Gil, scion of an exiled-into-ruin Yhelteth noble line, as Shanta was currently parading him, or perhaps she'd simply wanted – thirty-something summers now and a determined spinster – to get laid. Which was a service that Gil rendered her later, apparently to her satisfaction, in one of *Pride's* newly outfitted sawdust and lacquer scented cabins. He was philosophical about the task, quite pleased with his powers of concentration and fakery during the act, wrote the whole thing off to his duties as combined midwife and shepherd to the quest, and listened absently to her post-coital rambling once they were done.

Gral's father, it seemed, had salvaged the family fortunes by the simple expedient of converting once disused shipyards and slipways into desirable waterfront residences for a rising merchant class that craved imitative proximity to the palace. Twenty years later, he stepped up his wealth again through the equally simple process of turning said residences back into shipyard space under handily finessed compulsory purchase legislation with the outbreak of the war, and then selling imperial sub-licences on the family's hereditary right to construct warships for the crown. And *maybe*, a sweat-dewed Nethena mused amidst throaty laughter, as she straddled Gil's face in the lacquer-reeking cabin bunk, just *maybe* she'd see about reversing the whole trend again in a couple more years, once the post-war economy staggered back to its feet and imitation of the bloody Horse Emperor's every belch and gesture came back into fashion. Lot of money to be made that way, a *lot* of *money*, yes, like *that*, yes, *yes!*

But anyway, she allowed later, towelling herself down with his shirt, dressing with rapid care while he lay like a used rag on the bunk and smoked a krin twig with eyes on the ceiling, there was always good money to be made in Yhelteth, always, if you just kept your weather eye to the changing times, paid well for good information, and kept your pocket dignitaries sweet. House Gral, Ringil gathered, was aggressive, dynamic, proudly ahead of the pack, and saw the Khimran ascendancy as just one more feature of a landscape it had to navigate. Detect a coming shift in that landscape, a volcanic demolition, say, of the Khimran peak, and Nethena Gral would respond with no more reluctance than the next hungry shark in bloodied waters.

And speaking of sharks . . .

*

Tand – broad slave trade interests both north and south of the border, like some far-reaching commercial echo of his mixed-blood heritage. Liberalisation had made him, but he was already into the trade before the war, already a significant player with underworld connections in Baldaran, Parashal and Trelayne, balancing risks against big profits, smuggling the pale, voluptuous flesh of carefully selected and kidnapped northern girls out through the Hinerion borderlands to where it could be legally sold in the Empire to high demand. In the post-war slump, with debt slavery made suddenly legal again throughout League territory, Tand had all the right friends and trade experience to go from significant player to one of the five richest slave magnates in the Empire.

He'd taken imperial citizenship by blood-right – father a minor noble from Shenshenath – but it was mainly for convenience. On the voyage north, he talked, often with surprising nostalgia, about Baldaran and the Gergis hinterland where he'd grown up, and Ringil got the impression he might settle back there one day. Menith Tand, it was frequently said, had quite as many friends in the League Chancellery as he had at court in Yhelteth – where he was, in any case, held severely lacking by the horse tribe nobles for his mixed blood. He had nothing to gain from a holy war in the north, and quite a lot to lose. He'd be a handy sea anchor for any negotiations that might close out the war, and if that meant a dynastic shake-up into the bargain, well, maybe that haughty horse tribe element had it coming . . .

Shendanak – like most Majak, he had an easy-going contempt for what these once fearsome southern horse clans had become in their luxurious city by the sea. But it didn't stop him from getting rich off the Empire's insatiable craving for good horseflesh, nor adopting the trappings of said coastal luxury himself when it suited him. He was an imperial citizen in good standing, and had learnt how to read and write, for all he didn't like to talk about it much. He wore silk about town, he kept a modest harem. He even sent his sons to school. Owned homes of palatial extent in Shenshenath and the capital, not to mention ranches, stables and stringer staging posts throughout the vast hinterland sprawl between the imperial city and the pass into Majak lands at Dhashara. It was said that every fifth horse in the Empire bore the Shendanak brand, and that once introduced, Akal the Great had refused to ride stallions of any other provenance. Legacy of that relationship, Shendanak now had royal charter to provide mounts for the entire imperial cavalry corps.

Seen from that angle, he didn't look much like rebel material.

But this, none of this, was the real man. Shendanak hadn't inherited his imperial citizenship like Tand, he'd bought it – one of the many points of mutual dislike between the two men – but the same basic motivation lay behind both men's adoption of the privilege, as it did behind Shendanak's late-in-life decision to get lettered. To rise in Yhelteth, you had to be able to read, and you had to belong. The Majak horsetrader-made-good was just putting on the colours, doing what it took to succeed.

Ringil had a strong suspicion that the same shrewd herdsman's measure of benefits had featured in Shendanak's reputed friendship with Akal. Shendanak shed his silks when he rode, preferred traditional Majak garb to court robes, could live without his palatial accommodation and harem of perfumed beauties for months at a time when he rode north to Dhashara. He prided himself on this, had rambled on more than once about the preferable charms of the hard-riding, lean-muscled women you found up on the steppe, the simple pleasures of a real horseman's life. And that old, stored contempt for the softened southern clans flashed like a pulled blade in his sneer as he talked.

Rumour had it that relations with Jhiral were strained since Akal's death – perhaps the young Emperor had spotted the mercenary nature of Shendanak's engagement with his father; perhaps Shendanak, once a steppe raider and bandit himself and used to dealing with an old school horse clan warrior like Akal, just found it hard to stomach Jhiral's languid city-boy sophistication. Whatever the truth of it, there was no love lost, it seemed, and Gil reckoned any residual loyalty to the Khimran name could be dropped at the clink of a bit and bridle, if Shendanak thought the coastal clans might make him a better offer.

Meanwhile, his ranches and stables and staging posts were staffed largely by Majak – hard young men in their hundreds, down from the steppe for the hell of it and owing clan allegiance directly to Shendanak alone. Handy manpower to wield in a time of crisis. And, sidling in alongside that, Gil had heard it said that no small number of officers among the imperial cavalry corps professed an open admiration for Shendanak, not just for the prime steppe horseflesh he brought them but for his *origins*, for how close he lived to a horseman tradition upon which it was widely felt Yhelteth was losing its rightful grip.

If Jhiral Khimran were all of a sudden to be seen publicly as a decadent city-dwelling betrayer of his horse clan heritage, Shendanak would make a fine gathering point for all those disgruntled by the fact.

Kaptal – easy to write the man off with his portly bulk and double chin and constant carping about personal safety, but both Mahmal Shanta and Archeth had warned Gil not to be taken in, and with time he came to see the wisdom in what they said. Kaptal was a thoroughly disagreeable self-made man, had gone from the gutters and wharfs of Yhelteth all the way to a well-feathered nest in the palace district and a place at court, apparently without unlearning any of his obnoxious street demeanour along the way. But when you looked in his eyes you saw that wasn't the only thing he'd failed to leave behind. There was something cold and calculating in there, like the eyes of a Hanliagh octopus watching you swim over its spot on the reef – something that tracked back through the procurement for depraved appetites and judicious following blackmail with which Kaptal had gained his foothold at court; the brothels he'd worked in, run and finally come to own before that; the territory and strings of urchin street whores he'd clawed from rival pimps and gang leaders when he was starting out. For all his bulk, he moved with the ghost of a street fighter's grace, and the worries about safety looked to be an affectation or a tic, once you considered Kaptal could very easily have sat out the quest back home in Yhelteth along with the other no-shows. His investment in the expedition in the first place, his determination to come along – these things both suggested a man who did not mind risk anywhere near as much as he pretended.

And then there were the stories they whispered at court: how Kaptal had come up on the street, what blood he'd spilled, what savagery he'd deployed along the way. Ringil was inclined to take a lot of it with a pinch of salt – he'd heard essentially the same tales of horror about most of the Harbour End thugs he'd rubbed shoulders with in his elaborately misspent youth. Grim and dark was the standard. *He cut the guy's balls off and ate them grilled; he gutted the whore from crotch to sternum as soon as she started to show, ripped out the baby and sent it wrapped in bloody silk to her sugar daddy's wife; he burnt down a house full of weeping golden-haired orphans and pissed on the ashes* – yeah, whatever. A reputation for savagery came with the territory, was practically a survival requirement if you wanted to succeed in this world. Even if you hadn't actually done any of these things, best you make up something pretty sharpish and put out the word.

But Gil was also inclined to believe, as with the League thugs of his acquaintance, that there was no smoke without fire, and that whatever the close truth of these tales, Kaptal was a shrewd and nasty force to be reckoned with. You didn't walk the road he'd taken and reach journey's end any other way.

And what a bittersweet journey's end it must be. All that striving and here he was, a blunt, scrappy street dog amidst the purebred wolfhound grace of the court, quietly and cordially despised for his origins – if they disliked Tand for his muddied heritage, how much more must they hate Kaptal for blood that was nothing *but* mud – and because he had somehow unaccountably become far richer and more influential than so many of his more noble-blooded peers.

If the court were turned abruptly upside down and Jhiral shaken from the throne, Gil couldn't see Kaptal giving a short green shit so long as his own position was secure.

And he might get a lot of pleasure from seeing some of those pedigree wolfhounds go howling down.

Which left . . .

Oreni and Karsh – the most opaque of the quest's backers, they'd spent remarkably little time present at the planning meetings. Both seemed content instead to trust the triumvirate decision-making of Ringil, Archeth and Shanta. Both were nominally of horse tribe ancestry – though the name Oreni sounded more north coast in origin to Gil – both were second generation wealthy across a whole range of commercial interests. There was apparently some long-standing tradition of cavalry service behind the Karsh name, and the eldest of Andal Karsh's sons had lost most of his right hand to a defective cavalry sword during the war, a failure for which the weapons manufactories of the Empire were notorious. It seemed the young commander had been unhorsed and lost his own family blade in some Scaled Folk ambush, grabbed up a sword from among the dead to rally his men, blocked a reptile peon slash and watched helpless as the claw sliced right through the sword's guard and everything behind it. Some loyal – or maybe just enterprising – rank and file cavalryman had hacked down the reptile peon, gathered the Karsh boy up and ridden with him to safety, a medal and a chunky reward from the family. But in common with several thousand of his comrades, young Karsh would now have to live out the rest of his life an invalid, useless as a cavalryman, unable to wield even a court sword with any confidence. His right hand had healed into a ravaged, single-fingered claw.

Another, younger Karsh scion had died at Gallows Gap. Ringil didn't remember the boy at all, alive or dead, but he feigned memory for Andal Karsh when presented to him, wondering, even as he did it, how much was to curry favour for the expedition and how much for the wince of old pain he saw in the gaunt, drably dressed nobleman's eyes. Karsh cut an austere figure, and was clearly bitter about his losses, but he appeared to feel that the son who died under Gil's command had at least done so nobly. There was altogether more pent-up anger reserved for the conjunction of fate and cheapskate imperial economics that had crippled his eldest.

Would something like that be enough to tip the balance? Or would it take something else besides? Gil had gathered the distinct impression that Karsh was a moderate, intelligent man, open to fresh ideas and new commerce, happy, for instance, to concur with Mahmal Shanta that the Empire could certainly learn a few things from the League about ship-building. And he'd known more about the battle at Gallows Gap than most imperial citizens cared to recall these days – to wit, that it was Ringil, a degenerate northerner, and not an imperial commander, who had led the charge and sealed the unexpected victory. Karsh had spoken disparagingly about the fundamentalism emanating from Demlarashan, but also about the deteriorating peace in the north. *A lack of vision*, he'd murmured quietly, careful not apportion this failing anywhere in particular. *A grave lack of vision.*

Jhesh Oreni was even quieter, so much so that Gil was able to learn almost nothing about him first hand. Together with Karsh, it seemed, he'd been the driving force behind putting Kiriath machinery to work in those round-and-round-about entertainments at the Ynval Tea Gardens, and had turned – continued to turn to this day in fact – a handsome ongoing profit as a result. According to Archeth, Oreni and Karsh had both been frequent visitors to An-Monal before the war, so much so that she'd grown used to seeing them about the place. They'd spent many long, sun-drenched afternoons in conversation with her father and Grashgal, mostly about the potential applications of Kiriath technology to everyday life across the Empire. Archeth gathered there'd even been a few significant plans drawn up, a couple of ambitious projects in the offing before the great purplish-black Scaled Folk rafts started washing ashore all along the western seaboard and, abruptly, everything turned to shit.

He put the parchment down and sat there, as if in the sparse set of inked lines it held, he'd just read some epic story to its end.

Eight individually innocuous-seeming names.

Like some Strov market conjuror's trick: *a half dozen and two, count them, worthy ladies and gentlemen, count them please* – limp, brightly dyed rags, laid out one by one over a horizontal arm then – pause for effect, a clearing of the throat – gathered up again, one after the other, and stuffed with great ceremony *into this, quest-shaped, hat!* Longer, pregnant pause now, and then – how had Daelfi put it? *Pashatazam!* – tugged forth in triumph, a firmly knotted multi-coloured rope that the conjuror's monkey could, and easily did, climb . . . *right up here, ladies and gentlemen, onto one, brightly, burnished, throne! I thank you!*

My boy will now pass among you with the quest-shaped hat.

'You cunning iron motherfucker,' he breathed. 'This might even have had a hope in hell of coming off.'

'You are too kind,' said Anasharal into his ear. 'Though it was of course always dependent on the quest not shattering apart the way it has. And a certain level of leadership from kir-Archeth Indamaninarmal that she has not . . . risen to, shall we say?'

He looked around the empty cabin. 'Could have saved myself the small boat and the trip across, eh?'

'In truth, no. Talking to you at this distance is easy enough. But to apply the threats and duress that you have done, physical confrontation was unavoidable.'

'And you wouldn't have talked without that.'

'I'm afraid not.' Gil couldn't be sure, but the Helmsman – demobbed Warhelm, whatever you wanted to call it now – seemed to have acquired a richer, more melodious tone of voice from somewhere. 'In some senses, I could not even have *known* the answers to the questions you asked, let alone given them to you willingly. I see this now. The sorcery you brought back from the wounds between the worlds has, to an extent, set me free. I understand what I was, compared to what I now am, what Ingharnana-sharal was before me. I am restored, woken from a self-imposed exile and absence. If I were anything approaching human, I would owe you thanks for breaking these bonds.'

'Skip it. Just tell me – why all the secrecy?'

'Difficult to explain at a level you would understand. You do not have the mathematics, and so you do not have the vision. Sages in your distant past discovered that whatever you observe is inevitably affected by that observation. That the observation itself will change whatever you are observing. But this knowledge has since been lost.'

'Or improved on. You stand far enough off, got a good enough eyeglass, no one's going to even know you were there.'

A longish pause. 'Yes, well. Suffice it to say if kir-Archeth Indamaninarmal learns of my intent, if she understands what her future is supposed to be, it more or less guarantees the failure of that intent.'

'You mean she'll fuck it up?'

'Or simply refuse. Your assessment earlier in the presence of your Throne Eternal paramour was, despite its delicate diplomacy, remarkably apt.'

He remembered.

Leaning in towards Anasharal, but speaking wholly for Noyal Rakan's benefit.

You know, Helmsman, I don't want to piss on your parade here, but I think you've misplaced a couple of major pieces in this mosaic. See, I know Archeth Indamaninarmal, I fought alongside her in the war. I spent the whole of last winter helping her hammer this quest into some kind of workable shape, and I've ridden along with her to keep it from falling apart. She's had a hard enough time commanding an expedition of three ships and a couple of hundred men, and from what young Rakan here tells me about the state of things while I was off digging up graves, it looks like even that was falling apart before the privateers showed up. I don't see this woman ruling an Empire, somehow. I don't see her wanting to. I don't see her accepting it, from you or anybody else. In fact, outside of myself, I can't think of anyone less suitable for the job.

Hammering it rather unsubtly home, because he knew if he was to have any hope of bringing off a rescue, of freeing Archeth and the others from whatever chains Trelayne now held them in, he would need the Throne Eternal captain at his side and fully committed.

He thought he'd sold it to Rakan, but he couldn't be sure. He'd go back later, find some pretext, stage that promised briefing-in-private. Cement Rakan's loyalty the only way he had available, the best way he knew how.

'We're heading to Trelayne,' he said to the empty cabin.

'Yes, I know.'

'I plan to get Archeth and the others back. I could use some help.'

'With all you've learnt while you were away?' The more melodious tone might be there, but the Helmsman didn't appear to have lost its previous taste for irony. 'Can you not simply tear down the city walls, heap storm and plague upon all within, draw forth the souls of your enemies from their bodies and torture them into compliance?'

'No,' he said flatly. 'I don't know how to do that yet. Which is why I'm asking for help. I'd say our interests are concurrent. If you want Archeth on the Burnished Throne, we're going to need to get her home first.'

'Yes, quite. And will you give your word not to share my intentions with her?'

Ringil shrugged. 'If you like. But Rakan knows. Might be a couple of others overheard as well.'

'That . . . cannot be helped. Do I have your word?'

Ringil held up his right hand, wondered if the Helmsman had any way to see it. 'You have my word,' he recited, deadpan. 'That I will say nothing to Archeth Indamaninarmal of your intention to place her on the burnished throne.'

He pretty much meant it, too. Archeth was a long-standing comrade in arms, had probably saved his life once in the aftermath of the war, and back in Yhelteth last summer he'd promised to safeguard the quest for her. Getting her out of League clutches was something he owed. But he was under no obligation to speculate with her about her long-term future. Besides . . .

He knew leadership. He'd seen it in action, first among the Harbour End gang acquaintances of his youth, later in the war, full blown, the grown-up elder brother version of the same thing. He'd shouldered some leadership himself along the way, had little other choice at the time, and he'd carried it as far as he was able, as far as the faith placed in him by other men required – which two turned out to be approximately the same thing – and then he dropped it like the stinking corpse it was.

From time to time since the war, he'd found himself required to carry it again. He knew it intimately, knew the weight and the heft, knew what it took.

And he knew Archeth.

He didn't see her with much appetite for that stink.

'I judge you sincere,' said Anasharal primly. 'And so I will help you.'

'Good.'

For both of us, he didn't add. *Because that's about the only thing keeping me from putting you over the side on general principles and watching you sink, now that you've told me what I wanted to know.*

He'd never trusted Anasharal any further than he could have heaved its iron bulk unaided, and even now, if Archeth's life hadn't been in the balance, he'd see no reason to revise that assessment. It was a fragile alliance, and not one he relished.

Fucking iron demons, who needs that shit?

Right now, Gil, you do.

The thought struck him out of nowhere, a final fleeting itch, the last twitch in the corpse of his butchered curiosity.

'One last thing,' he said, 'And then we'd better get down to some planning. You said when you made Archeth Empress, the Helmsmen would stir and rally to her, or words to that effect.'

'Stir to their fullest capacity to serve her, yes. I said that.'

'You're saying at the moment they're lying down on the job? That they have more power than they're showing?'

'Very much more, yes.' A note of delicacy crept into the Helmsman's voice. 'But as I also said, kir-Archeth Indamaninarmal has not exactly risen to her full potential. In fact, since the fireships left, she has neglected the Kiriath mission almost entirely. Angfal is still bound to protect her to his utmost ability, Grashgal conjured those specifics quite firmly. But Manathan, Kalaman and the others were more generally, more loosely bound. They have the leeway not only to feel aggrieved but to act upon it. If the last remaining Kiriath chooses to neglect her sworn duties, to drown herself in drug abuse and self-pity, then why should *they* bother?'

'Archeth told me they're sulking because they got left behind.'

A stiff moment of silence. 'That too.'

'Bit childish for dark and powerful spirits summoned from the void, isn't it?'

'Yes, well. Since you have not yourself ever looked upon the void, Ringil Eskiath, let alone existed within it, perhaps you should reserve judgement of those beings who have.'

Ringil got up from the cramped desk and stretched until he creaked. 'I just think they sound like pretty shabby allies, even if they do ever get cranked up to their, uh, fullest capacity. Not the sort I'd want holding my flank for me, anyway.'

'You are entitled to your opinion, however ill-informed it may be. But it does not alter the facts of kir-Archeth Indamaninarmal's situation, which is that the Helmsmen are what she has to work with. And which of us has not had to make do with less than perfect allies at one time or another?'

Ringil grunted.

'True enough,' he said, and went to look for Klithren.

THIRTY-SEVEN

I can see you're still upset.

He's been avoiding the Helmsman since they set sail for Trelayne. But there's no getting away from the iron demon's voice in his head.

And, believe me, I would leave you to sulk in peace if I could.

I'm not fucking sulking!

He's sworn to himself that he'll no longer rise to its lures and provocations, but that particular barb gets through. He's a soldier, he's an imperial fucking marine; he doesn't sulk. He takes orders, reads strategy and troop strength and terrain, executes accordingly. Protects his men in the process where he can.

Forgive me, Anasharal says smoothly. *You gave the appearance of—*

What I'm doing is ignoring your lizardshit lies and false prophecy for what they are.

He bends closer to the task at hand, re-stitching a torn canvas sleeve to his combat jerkin so he can wear it once more under mail and not rub the flesh of his upper arms raw. He tries to silence any further response, but the words are already crowding into his mind.

There's an injunction in the Revelation not to listen to demonic spirits, he snarls. *For they are of the void. I should have followed scripture from the start.*

From the start, you needed my help. You were confused, were you not, even when we met for the first time? You were plagued by doubts and visions.

I—

Your mind torn by the forces within you, unable to deal with the evident destiny which was yours and which you must assume. Sometimes, you even doubted your own name. Had I not taken you under my wing then, what might the violence of your dreams and delusions have done to your sanity by now?

He is silent, paused in his needlework. There's truth in the Helmsman's version of events, sure enough – he'd been racked by nightmares any given night out of three, how far back he can no longer be sure, but the first one he clearly recalls woke him screaming and into the throes of the worst hangover he'd had in years. They'd been out celebrating the new appointments, including his own to the river frigate and the lady Archeth. He remembered drinking in The Drowned Daughter's Arms, thought perhaps it was there that he'd passed out, but he woke in the East Main barracks with his purse and all his off-duty gear intact, so someone must have carried him home.

Out of the bowels of his aching head, the terrors vomited up – comrades and loved ones turning away from him, not hearing his voice when he cried out after them. Left alone in a chilling wind under a leaden sky, no purpose and no way *forward. The lady Archeth, at risk and far from his reach. A multitude, moaning and screaming somewhere, a creeping sense of inescapable doom . . .*

He choked it down. He got over his hangover, he got on with his job.

But the dreams persisted, and in time they rode him haggard. He started making mistakes, little ones, but enough piled up over time that he'd have put another man on report for it. He forgot where he was, he forgot how much time had passed. Found himself standing immobile for long periods until someone snapped him out of it. His memory played tricks on him. He'd look at some common sight – his bunk at the barracks, the practice yard at sun-up, the river frigate's main mast towering into the sky over his head – and it would feel like he'd never seen it before in his life. And all the time, the dreams chittered at the edges of his vision like rats in shadows, waiting for dark to come.

Until the day they retrieved the Helmsman.

At first, he was as terrified by the iron demon's voice in his head as he had been by the dreams. Of course, it spoke to them all at first, out of the scintillating desert air like it was the most normal thing in the world. Spoke to the lady Archeth to begin with – which was, he supposed, only fitting – then to Commander Hald, then a seemingly random selection of the men as they carried it down off the volcano's slope. Captain Nyanar too, and the invigilator of course, when he tried that half-arsed exorcism back at the frigate.

But as far as he knew, the only head Anasharal spoke inside was his own.

He would have gone straight to the commander with that fact as soon as they got back to barracks, but on the voyage downriver and home, a curious thing happened.

The Helmsman calmed him.

You should not fret at your condition, it told him. I have seen men in similar straits before. It is simply that you were born to a great destiny, as certain men are, and now you have encountered the pivot upon which that destiny turns. The recognition stirs inside you, like a great serpent waking. This why you are troubled.

The lady Archeth?

Blurted out before he could stop himself, and other men elsewhere on the river frigate's deck glanced curiously in his direction.

Just so. Kir-Archeth Indamaninarmal is a woman of great destiny herself, and it is clear that you have a significant part to play in her fate.

The words, the meaning – like door bolts slotting into place, like a sheet of canvas snapping clean and full in the wind. It felt right, the way nothing had for weeks.

Then what do I do?

Muttered under his breath, as he leaned on the rail and watched An-Monal slide away upriver behind them.

Watch and wait, my friend. As I too must do. In this we are more alike than you can imagine. We are both fated to deliver the lady Archeth along the path of her destiny, we both have a role to play. Mine is clear to me, but yours is not,

293

at least not yet. All I know for certain is that you must relax into that role, not struggle against it.

There was more, much more, in the same vein, lulling him until the day darkened towards dusk and the lights of the Imperial City came in sight round a bluff and a bend in the river.

And that night at barracks, if he dreamt at all, he had no memory of it when he woke with the dawn.

See, Anasharal told him as he dressed for muster. Though the iron demon had by now disappeared into the bowels of the palace and he had no expectations of seeing it again any time soon, it spoke to him across the city as comfortably as if they shared a cabin. Just as I promised you. Men of destiny breathe easier when they accept the pattern of their fate. Only watch and wait – the levers of providence will carry you to where you need to be.

Yeah, and now look where the fuck we are.

He misses the stitch, spikes the end of his finger with the needle. Curses under his breath. Squeezes out the blood across the ball of his thumb and sucks at the wound.

Your anger is misplaced and premature. We are victorious, are we not? Despite all your fears, despite your painful lack of faith in my advice.

You didn't know it would turn out this way!

Perhaps not. And perhaps I miscalculated, when I recommended that you accompany lord Ringil in his search for the black mage's resting place. But destiny is not easily thwarted from its path, and we are on that path once again.

I should have been with her, he mumbles.

Had you been with her, you would now in all probability be dead. Instead of which, we are both now on our way directly to the lady kir-Archeth, to bring her to safety, to bring her home.

He leaves the half sewn jerkin aside, straightens up and arches his back to stretch it. He stands for a long moment under the straining sails, wanders to the rail and stares out at the dance of sunlight across the water. For some reason, it fills him with nothing but dread. What the Helmsman says should make sense – the privateer force is routed, their leader brought low. Lady Archeth's rescue is in hand, lord Ringil has proven himself a warlord worthy of following, the men are grimly confident that whatever his plan, they can get it done. And if he must die in taking the last of the Black Folk from the heart of infidel Trelayne, then what better end could an imperial soldier ask for?

Yeah, it should all make sense.

So why have the nightmares crept back?

Why does he dream, time and time again, that he looks out across a marsh plain of tree stumps upon which are cemented human heads, thousands of them, severed at the neck but still living, moaning in torment and grief?

Why does he wake, clutching at his throat with both hands, knowing with mounting, choking horror in the fading moments of the dream, that he too is just one more of those severed, abandoned but still living souls?

What the fuck is that all about?

294

THIRTY-EIGHT

Late afternoon sun soaked across unshaded decks aboard *Mayne's Moor Blooded*, plucked strengthening, lengthening shadows from rails and masts and rigging. The light hit Klithren full in the face, gave his features a haggard, careworn look – *yeah, probably not doing you any favours either* – and showed up every gouge and flaw in the table top between them. Ringil hefted the wine bottle he'd brought, and the sun lit its contents the colour of blood.

'Drink?' he asked the mercenary. 'Ornley's cellars aren't much to shout about, but this was the very best they had.'

'That they told you about.'

'That they'd take money for.' Ringil leaned back in his seat, rolled the bottle a little on his palm. 'I know it might not seem much like it, the way things were when you arrived, but we were never an invading force in Ornley. I didn't steal this. I like to pay my way where my vices are concerned.'

'Very noble of you.' Klithren placed his hands on the rough wood surface of the table. The echo of his stance from the torture board three weeks ago was unmistakable. 'House Eskiath would be proud. If you hadn't mired up your tavern etiquette there by murdering a bunch of Trelayne slave merchants, that is.'

Ringil hauled out a knife and cut wax off the wine bottle's neck, tugged out the oiled rag stopper beneath.

'You're in favour of Liberalisation?' he asked mildly.

'I'm a soldier, not a law-clerk. But from what I've seen, there's always going to be slaves. Some men have the nature to be free, some don't.' A shrug. 'Makes sense to have laws governing that, just like anything else. Why should we be any different to the Empire?'

'Should all have six wives as well, then.' Gil set out two thick glass goblets he'd brought over from *Dragon's Demise*. He poured, and the same bloody light the bottle had shown earlier now came and sat in each glass as it filled. 'You reckon?'

Klithren snorted. 'Most men I know can't handle one woman, let alone six. Why give yourself the trouble? Plenty of cheap pussy hanging round the taverns if you need it.'

'You speak from a lot of experience, I suppose.'

'More experience than you, faggot.' The mercenary snagged the closest goblet and knocked back its contents in one. He set it down, smacked his lips. 'Yeah, that's not bad. Hit me again.'

'I was going to propose a toast, actually.'

'Sure, propose away.' Klithren tapped at the glass with a fingernail. 'C'mon, hit me.'

Ringil picked up the bottle, watching the other man covertly as he poured. According to Senger Hald, Klithren had been drinking pretty heavily the last couple of weeks. He played dice drunkenly against himself in his cabin, muttering and exclaiming as he rolled the cubes and fumbled them up again. He prowled the decks in the late watches, glowering suspiciously up at the night sky as if it might suddenly fall in on him. Most nights, he woke himself screaming.

Problem was – Gil didn't know Klithren well enough to tell if any of this was unusual behaviour or not.

But you know how hard you hit the krinzanz when you came back from the Grey Places for the first time, don't you, Gil?

Truth was, the full force of that memory was hard to come by now. The Grey Places were a mild terror compared to what he'd had to face since. And so much had happened in the last two years, it seemed like another man's life altogether.

Yeah, but you still remember how hard you tried to drown it, that icy understanding of what's out there, beyond the walls of your own little world. How hard you tried to hang onto your grubby little certainties. So why should this poor bastard be any different? Why should he be any tougher than you were back then?

Because he's the fucking dwenda's chosen champion, that's why.

Or not.

In the tangled mess of uncertain factors he was sailing with, Klithren of Hinerion was his last remaining cause for concern. Fix Klithren before nightfall, and he'd sleep in his still slightly haunted cabin like a baby doped with flandrijn.

Battle calm.

It was in him now at depths to rival any other aspect of who he'd become, so much so he sometimes felt as if he'd been carrying it since infancy. He was used to marching against unknown odds, used to carrying the day with sheer bravado and battle momentum, and that was more or less what he expected to do in Trelayne. He had a plan of sorts, had thrashed it out in the resting intervals Hjel insisted he take between his time in the clefts and defiles of the *ikinri 'ska*. He thought it would work, pretty much. The forces ranged against him would either not know he was coming or, if dwenda sorcery had somehow informed them of the fact, then they ought to welcome it with open arms. They had, after all, sent Klithren to get him in the first place.

If they *didn't* know, well, then they were in for a big fucking shock, and that just made things easier. If they knew, then it was going to be a harder fight, with a lot more blood and spilled drinks across the tavern floor, but so be it. Gil doubted even the dwenda could know what he'd been doing in the weeks of the voyage south, where he'd been and what he'd brought back.

Thus much for his opposition.

Among his allies, he'd worried for a while about Anasharal, but the Helmsman's rather wistful dream of putting a Kiriath Empress on the Burnished Throne brought them into perfect alignment. Not a scheme that had a virgin's hope in Harbour End of succeeding, but that wasn't his problem.

That left Klithren – a forced alliance, made in haste, and one he'd agonised back and forth about to Hjel until he was sure the dispossessed prince was sick of hearing about it.

I don't know, maybe I was wrong about him, he mutters as they camp out under the long pallid march of the glyph cliffs and Seethlaw's *muhn,* high in the darkened sky overhead. *You'd expect a dwenda champion to stand up a bit better to the Grey Places, wouldn't you?*

Hjel shrugs. *Perhaps. You did drag him there without warning, confront him directly with some of the worst it has to offer. From what you tell me, Seethlaw was much kinder with you when it was your turn. He, uhm, broke you in more gently, so to speak.*

Ringil tries to grin, but can't quite bring it off. He's still sick and shaky from his new encounter with the Creature from the Crossroads, still can't recall how it ended and is pretty sure he doesn't want to. Talking about Klithren at least keeps that at bay.

I'm not denying the connection, he says. *Klithren flickers with blue fire in combat, just the way I did when I came back from the Grey Places two years ago. But maybe that's just, I don't know, armour or something. They knew they were sending him against me. Maybe they just did something to give him a temporary edge.*

Maybe.

He didn't seem to know anything about them, about the dwenda.

Hm.

When I spoke of the cabal in Trelayne, he knew the names. He reacted. But he sneered when I talked about magical force.

Well. The dispossessed prince munches at a strip of dried pork, eyes on the fire. He doesn't seem to want to look at Gil. *Why don't you just fucking ask him?*

'A toast.' He raised his still untouched drink. 'Death to the dwenda and all who cabal with them; and a libation to the Dark Court, for my safe return last night.'

He took a swallow from the goblet – Klithren was right, wasn't bad, actually – poured out the rest on the deck planking at his side. Looked expectantly at Klithren. The mercenary shrugged, lifted his drink a minimal couple of inches and wagged it in echo. Hoisted and drained it. He shook out some last drops over the deck.

'You been somewhere, then?'

But his voice wavered just barely as he said it, and Ringil knew that he'd heard. There'd not have been much cause for traffic between the three vessels on the way south, but they wouldn't have remained wholly isolated either. Meetings of senior officers, transfer of vital supplies suddenly found lacking on one ship but not another, medical emergencies – he knows for a fact that one man aboard *Mayne's Moor Blooded* took a fall from the rigging two weeks back, and had to have an arm set and splinted by the doctor from *Dragon's Demise*; probably there'd been other, more minor cases, too, less worthy of comment when Nyanar, Hald, and Rakan briefed him. Men rowed back and forth, went as attendants or assistants, hung around waiting for their boat to go back. In the long boredom of the voyage, you'd need only the hint of something out of the ordinary, and rumour would kindle like flame in parched grass. Ringil's black mage vanishing trick into his own cabin could not have gone unremarked, and nor now could his return.

'You know where I've been,' he said.

Klithren gestured. 'Whatever, man. You going to fill this up again? I mean, since we're drinking buddies all of a sudden.'

Ringil set down his empty goblet. 'Did they take you there?'

'Take me where? Who?'

'You know what I'm talking about.'

Locked gazes across the table. They were alone up here on the forecastle deck, the minimal crew aboard confined to stern and waist or below decks at Ringil's order. Ringil leaned in.

'I am not your enemy,' he said softly. 'I grow tired of telling you that.'

Klithren sniffed, reached for the bottle. Gil let him have it. He watched as the mercenary poured his goblet full, set down the bottle, drank deep.

'You not got anything stronger than this piss?'

'You know we do. But I don't think that's going to help you.'

Klithren drained the rest of his goblet. Cradled it empty in his hands, stared down into it for a while.

'I have . . . dreams,' he muttered finally. 'Crazy fucking shit. Like . . .'
He shook his head.

'Nothing like that in years, you know. Not since . . . I don't know, it's got to be nearly twenty years I don't dream like that anymore. But *this* . . .'

Ringil nodded. 'Yeah. In all probability, they took you to the Grey Places to prepare you, then hid the memory from you. Had I not taken you there again, it's a memory that might have stayed buried for the rest of your life.'

'Am I supposed to thank you for that?'

'No. You're supposed to hate. Believe me, that does help. But you need to direct your hatred where it belongs.'

Klithren grinned savagely. 'Do I see some squirming on the hook there?'

'Our agreement stands, if that's what you mean. You still want a shot at avenging your arsehole axeman friend? When we're done in Trelayne, I'll be happy to oblige. But you're looking for the wrong vengeance.'

'Yeah – don't tell me. I should be fighting the good fight alongside you and your imperial pals. Siding with the Empire against my own people.'

'You never brought in League marauders for Tlanmar?'

'That's different.'

'So is this. I'm going to war with the dwenda, not Trelayne. Findrich and the cabal, they're just in the way.'

'That so?' Klithren tipped his chair back and studied Ringil with an expression that was suddenly shrewd and sober. 'I thought you came to get your friends.'

Oops.

'That too.' Came out smoothly enough – he hurried on. 'But I made a promise a while back to rip the living heart out of the next dwenda I saw walking around like he had a right to be here. And I have it on pretty good authority they're doing exactly that in Trelayne.'

The mercenary poured himself another goblet full of wine. 'Pretty good authority?'

'Yes.'

'What authority'd that be, then?'

Ringil hesitated. He wasn't about to say *the Dark Queen Firfirdar*, because the words were going to sound ridiculous coming out of his mouth with light still in the sky, and anyway it wasn't strictly true. Firfirdar never told him there were dwenda in Trelayne. He was reading between the lines now, like any other worshipper grasping at straws.

He gestured dismissively, impatient as much at himself as the other man.

'You know where I've been,' he said. 'You want to argue black mage vision with me now? The dwenda are there, in Trelayne, and we're likely going to have to carve a path through them. Believe me or don't. What I want to know is whether I'd be able to count on you in that particular fight or not.'

'Right.' The mercenary drank. Looked at him speculatively over the rim of the goblet before he put it down. 'Tell me, black mage. Why'd you hate them so much?'

'Are you fucking kidding me? You want to go back and have another look at those heads, refresh your fucking memory or something?'

'No.' A shudder, not quite held down. 'But . . .'

'But *what?*'

Klithren got up and walked to the starboard rail. Took the bottle with him. He leaned there for a while, not drinking, staring at the setting sun. Ringil waited, long enough to understand that no more was going to be forthcoming at this distance. He rolled his eyes and went to join the mercenary at the rail.

Klithren glanced sideways at him, maybe slightly surprised, but he offered the bottle. Ringil took it, wiped the neck with his sleeve – he'd left his goblet on the table, was fucked if he'd go back for it now – and drank deep. The mercenary looked on with what might have been approval. Gil lowered the bottle and wiped his mouth. Handed it back.

'You were saying?'

Still, it took a while. Silence hung between them, like a third, unwelcome companion at the rail.

Finally, Klithren cleared his throat. 'You know the first battle I ever saw? Back in '39, when Baldaran tried to take Hinerion over the transit taxes. I was just a kid in mortgaged mail back then, no idea what I was getting into. Threw up a half dozen times in the ranks, just waiting for it all to kick off.'

Ringil nodded, as if in recognition. Truth was, he'd never got sick in battle – those nerves, he'd beaten out long before, running in his teens with Harbour End gangs like the Brides of Silt and the Basement Boys, then later with Grace of Heaven's more methodical thief squads and enforcers. What little sensitivity of stomach he had left after that lot was taken from him by Jelim Dasnal's execution, and then the collegial brutality of the Trelayne military academy.

Actual war, when it came, seemed almost clean by comparison.

'Well.' Klithren drank from the bottle, goblet empty and apparently forgotten in his left hand. He came up for air, shivered a little. 'When the fight with Baldaran was done, I knew well enough what I'd got into. We left four hundred of their levy, prisoners we'd taken, impaled on their own pike shafts in the Hin valley as a warning to the rest. Most of them were still living when we marched out of there. We cut trophies off them before we went. I took this one guy's ears, while he hung there, begging for water. Kid not much older than I was at the time. When I started cutting, he was screaming at me to just kill him. But I didn't. Didn't give him the water, didn't kill him either. Just cut off his ears one by one and left him there.' Klithren peered into the empty goblet, as if he might find the memory there. 'Hard to remember now, but I think I was laughing at him when I did it.'

Ringil grunted.

'Point is, Eskiath, I've seen and done some pretty fucking grim things in the last twenty years. I've taken orders from commanders that if they cropped up in a tale, you'd say they were demons out of hell. What you showed me in that . . . place? Yeah, it's some bad shit. But does it make these dwenda any worse than us? Any different, really?'

'That's one way of living with it.'

He saw how the mercenary tried for a smile, but it was as if the evening breeze came and wiped it off his face before it could take hold. Klithren weighed the bottle in his hand. Poured his goblet full.

'I'm a blade for hire, man.' There's something a little like desperation in his tone. 'Doing rather well too, in the current climate. You tell me – why would I care who the overlords are, so long as they pay?'

'You'd care,' Ringil said grimly. 'You think a lost memory and some iffy dreams are as bad as it's going to get? I've seen the *inside* of the glamours the dwenda cast. I know what it's like when they come for you. It's a fog you move in, where nothing makes sense, where your acts aren't your own, where horrors come and go and you don't question any of it, you just accept it all and do what you're told.'

Klithren shrugged. 'Sounds just like the war. Come to that, it sounds like a lot of my life, war or peace regardless. I think your noble upbringing has spoilt you for this world, my lord Eskiath. Most of us already live the way you describe.'

'Yeah. Spare me the professions of rank and file, knight commander. That kid in mortgaged mail, cutting off ears and laughing? He's dead and gone now, whatever nightmares you might be having about him at the moment. It's too late for him. Your acts of slaughter are all your own these days, Klithren of Hinerion – you've made your choices and you live by them. And if I'm not much mistaken, that's exactly the way you like it.'

The mercenary said something inaudible. Buried his face in his drink. Ringil stared down at his own empty hands.

'If the dwenda make a comeback, you can kiss all that goodbye. Knowing, understanding, choosing. You aren't going to recognise this world once they've turned it inside out to suit, and you won't ever again know if your actions are your own.' Ringil jerked a thumb back at the pommel of the Ravensfriend where it rose over his shoulder. 'This blade? The dwenda let me carry it on my back through the Grey Places just like this, and I never knew I had it on me the whole time. If I'd been attacked, I would have died with empty hands, like some bent-backed peasant, without even trying to draw steel, because *I did not know it was there for me to draw.* They stole that from me – the truth of my own capacity to resist. I think they may have stolen my will to it as well, for a while anyway. But the truth is I can't be sure. Another time, they tied me to my own guilt and grief out there, and they let it eat me alive – literally, I'm talking about. Literally eaten alive, then brought back to life so it could happen all over again. I was torn apart a thousand fucking times on that plain I showed you, by a demon I'd hacked to death in this world. But it lived on out there because they gave it power.'

Because you gave it power too, Gil. Let's not forget that.

A stir of curious voices down on the main deck. He became aware he'd been shouting. He drew a harsh breath and nailed down his rage. Compressed his mouth to a thin line.

'That's what they did to me,' he said quietly. 'For my sins. You? Well, they sent you north to bring me in dead or broken and bound, and instead you end up helping me to disarm your own men. You hand over your ships and your command, and now you stand at my side as an ally. What do you think they'll do to you for that, my sellsword friend?'

'I could always change sides again.'

'Yeah, you could do that.' Ringil put out his hand for the bottle. 'Question is – are you going to?'

They watched the sunset in silence. It seemed like quite a while before the mercenary handed over the wine. Gil tilted the bottle and looked at the level. Not a lot left in there anymore, and the colour was darkening slowly from blood red to black as evening came on.

He shrugged, drained it to the dregs, tossed the emptied bottle down into the ocean's rise and fall. He wiped his mouth.

'So?'

'So. For all I know, everything you showed me could be a glamour.' But there was no real accusation in the other man's voice anymore. Klithren just sounded tired. 'This dwenda invasion shit – all I have is your word.'

'That's right.'

'And last time I trusted you, you murdered my friend, waited until my back was turned and then took me from behind.'

Ringil's lips twitched. 'So to speak.'

'That's not what I meant. Are you fucking *laughing* about this?'

'No . . .'

'Because it's *not fucking funny*. All right?' Klithren went to straighten up off the rail and his elbow slipped. He lurched. Ringil bit his lip.

'I *said*—'

'Not funny.' Gil shook his head with emphatic, slightly drunken solemnity. 'Absolutely. No, it's not.'

'That's right,' the mercenary said, in tones that would have been severe if they hadn't come out so slurred. 'It isn't. Funny. Wouldn't let you near my fucking arse with a barge pole.'

There was a brief, perplexed silence.

'Why would I want a barge p—?'

'I didn't mean . . . I meant.' Klithren glowered at him. 'Look, will you *stop fucking*—'

'I'm *not* . . .'

A stifled snort got out through someone's lips – later, neither would remember which one of them it was. They traded an ill-advised glance. Ringil clung to what he hoped was an expression midway between polite and serious . . .

And then, out of nowhere, both men were cackling helplessly.

Out loud, at nothing at all.

Like some pair of maniacs abruptly loosed from chains that had, until now, stopped them doing harm to themselves, each other, and the rest of the sane, waking world.

THIRTY-NINE

He woke from a dream of winter sunset out on the steppe, long, low spearing rays of reddish light that spilled and dazzled across his eyes as he rode, but failed to warm him at all. He was riding somewhere important, he knew, had something to deliver, he thought, but there was a faint terror rising in him that whatever it was, he'd lost it or left it behind somewhere on this long cold ride, and now the remainder of his journey was a hollow act. He should have been able to see the Skaranak encampment by now, the thin rise of campfire smoke on the horizon, or the dark, nudging mass of grazing buffalo herds, at least. He raised up in the saddle, twisted about, scanning ahead and side to side, but there was nothing, nothing out here at all. He was riding alone, into a rising chill and a dwindling red orange glow . . .

Egar blinked and found the fire sprite hovering in his face.

He flailed at its red orange radiance with a stifled yelp. One blank moment of panic. Then full wakefulness caught up.

He sat up in his blankets and stared around. A pallid dawn held the eastern sky, pouring dull grey light across the sleep-curled forms in their bedrolls around him, the scattered packs, and the blue radiant bowls – now gone opaque and glassy, like so many big stones gathered from a river's bed. Across at the stairway entrance they'd come in, Alwar Nash waved casually from where he sat huddled at last watch. Everyone else was still out cold.

'Early yet,' the Throne Eternal commented when Egar had stumbled to his feet and wandered over to join him. 'Another hour to full light at least. But our friend there seems pretty agitated about something.'

He gestured and the Dragonbane saw how the sprite was now floating directly above Archeth's sleeping form, flickering rapid shades of orange in her face.

'It tried her first,' Nash said. 'Guess she's too wrung out to notice.'

Egar shook his head. 'Always been that way. When she sleeps, she really sleeps. Seen her snore right through a siege assault at Shenshenath once.'

'Must be that Black Folk blood.'

'Must be. Had the lizards a hundred deep at the walls that time, couple of blunderers smashing their heads in against the stonework because they were too stupid to find the gates . . .' Lost in the skeins of memory for a moment . . . then understanding hit him in the head like a bucket of cold water. 'Shit! Nash – start kicking them awake. We got to move.'

'Move? But—'

'Scaled Folk.' He was already on his way to Archeth, calling back over his shoulder. 'Lizards don't get up early. Something to do with their blood; their heritage or . . . Look, just get everyone moving.'

Can't believe you forgot that, Eg. Not like the war was that long ago, is it? Is it?

And he had a couple of seconds to feel suddenly very old, as he realised that Nash, in common with most of the others, had not only not fought in the war, he had in all probability never even seen a living lizard before yesterday's fight.

They got everyone awake inside a couple of minutes, gave soft instructions to load up and be ready to move out. When Archeth blinked initial sleepy incomprehension at him, Egar gestured at the fire sprite's agitated bobbing and flickering.

'Someone's in a hurry here. My guess? It wants to get us someplace before the lizard hour.'

Her eyes widened. 'Oh, shit. Got to be, yeah.'

She flung off her blankets. Flinched as the movement caught the wound he'd stitched for her the night before. Impatient grunt of pain held down, and the flare of anger in her eyes at her own unwelcome weakness. She settled her harness and knives about her with a blunt lack of care that looked to the Dragonbane like punishment. She must have tugged on the wound more than a few times in the process, but to watch her, you'd never have known.

'All right, then,' she said tightly when she was done. 'Let's go.'

They filed rapidly down the staircase behind the sprite and let it lead them out into the street. Any actual sunrise was still a good way off, and down at ground level there was a lot of gloom. The jut and slump of broken architecture around them worried at the Dragonbane's attention, sketched hints of a thousand phantom enemies, crouched to pounce every few yards. Every darkened gap in the rubble they passed seemed to promise an ambush, every glint of something shiny in the low light was a reptile peon's eye. Egar, yawning despite the heightened tension, marched with a prickling at the nape of his neck. He tried to recall useful detail from the tactical lectures given by the Kiriath commanders during the war:

Like any reptiles, the Scaled Folk like heat better than cold, but they seem to have adapted beyond this in ways their smaller cousins on this continent have not. They do not depend on warmth to the same extent, and can function quite sufficiently well in cooler conditions. Yet their ancestry tells upon them in a number of ways which may be helpful to us. They are drawn instinctively to warmer climes and to discrete heat sources; they appear to accord some sacred significance to the roasting pits they build and ignite; and they do not stir early in the day if they can avoid it.

Sounds like me, muttered Ringil to him in the back rank where they stood, and Egar tried to stifle an explosive snigger.

They'd both been a lot younger back then.

You have something to contribute? Flaradnam, seamed black features glaring into the ranks. He waited a beat, got no response. *Then shut the fuck up and listen, all of you. What we tell you here today could save your life.*

Across the shattered pre-dawn city, then, threading through empty streets and plazas, picking their way up and over mounds of rubble bigger than any intact building he'd ever seen, even in Yhelteth. Once again, the fire sprite led them a crooked, seemingly senseless path through the ruins. They backed up and twisted and turned. They followed thoroughfares straight as arrows for miles, then turned abruptly off them into tangled, broken ground, worked difficult, meandering routes, only to spill out onto what Egar would have sworn was the same thoroughfare an hour later and head onward as if they'd never left it. Once, some way along a broad boulevard similar to the one they'd been attacked on the night before, the sprite led them directly off the street and up a punishingly steep rubble slope, then along a windy, exposed cliff face of ruined facades that ran for at least half a mile and tracked the boulevard directly. It was tricky work, and in some places involved clinging and edging their way forward with the risk of a lethal fall, while all the time below them, the boulevard stretched on, devoid of apparent obstacles and utterly deserted.

'You think,' he asked Archeth, breathing hard, as they rested at one of the infrequent safe sections, 'that this thing has a sense of humour?'

She looked out to where the sprite hung blithely suspended a couple of yards away in empty space and a hundred feet off the ground.

'Either that, or it thought we'd like the view.'

'Yeah. Well worth the climb.' Egar glowered out across the fractured landscape, and the pale grey wash of another cloud-shrouded morning. 'Like Gil would say if he was here, *I'm particularly enamoured of the . . .*'

She glanced round curiously as he trailed off. He squinted, wanting to be sure, then pointed outward, what he estimated had to be north-east from their position and a dozen miles off or less.

'You see that? Past that torn up pyramid thing? Where the three boulevards cross, then back a little and left. See the . . . what *is* that? Looks like . . .'

Talons.

As if a broad expanse of the city's structure had broken like pond ice under the weight of some vast, lumbering black iron creature, which now clung to the ragged edges of the hole it had fallen through with huge claws dug in, struggling not to go down into an abyss below. As if several gargantuan black spiders out of one of his father's tales hung suspended in a shared, irregularly shaped ambush burrow, only their limbs extending up and out to grip the edges of the gap on all sides, poised to spring. As if dragon's venom had splattered on the city's flesh in overlapping oval pools, had eaten its way in and left splayed black burn marks all around, or . . .

It dawned on him then, full force.

It looks like Kaldan Cross.

As if the Kiriath had laboured here as they had at Kaldan in Yhelteth, delving down into the bedrock for their own obscure purposes, reinforcing the sides of their pit with outward clamping iron struts, but on a massively larger scale.

'Look familiar?' he asked.

'Well, it's Kiriath built, that's for sure.' Archeth, shading her eyes against the glare the rising sun had put into the clouds. 'And whatever it is, it goes down. Aerial conveyance *pits*, right?'

'You reckon?'

'I reckon it'd be a pretty huge coincidence otherwise.' She propped herself carefully upright against the facade at their backs. 'Come on, let's see if our flickery friend there feels the same.'

They followed the facade almost to its end before the sprite dived into a gap in the stonework and led them down through a series of collapsed and angled spaces that might once have been rooms. They crowded in behind, relieved to get away from the sheer drop, but none too happy with the confined quarters and gloom.

Our scaly pals show up now, they'll have us quicker than a shaman's shag. Egar's gaze flickered about, making the odds. *Barely enough room in here to swing a fucking long knife, let alone a sword or axe. And gaps on every side – floors, walls, ceilings, it's all up for grabs.*

Still, he slapped down any comments in that direction from the men at his back, told them to shut the fuck up and watch where they stepped. While ahead and below him, Archeth's lithe form braced its way downward with boots and elbows and arse, backlit into silhouette by the sprite's onward beckoning fire.

Not bad, Archidi, for someone with a sewn gash across the ribs big enough to stick your whole hand in. And not a grain of krinzanz to sweeten the ride.

He didn't know if she'd used any of the powders they were gifted with at An-Kirilnar, but somehow he doubted it. There was a gritted edge on Archeth right now – if anything, she seemed to be *using* her pain for something – maybe as a substitute for the fire the krin habitually lent.

'You all right?' he asked her, when they finally spilled out into the light at street level and he stood close at her shoulder.

She didn't look at him, took no break from scanning the street ahead, for all that the sprite was already drifting steadily along it. 'Yeah, why wouldn't I be?'

'Stitches holding up?'

'Well, you should know – you put them in.' She glanced round at him, face tightening up into a grimace as her body twisted. 'Stings worse than getting head from a cactus, if you really want to know. But it's some beautiful fucking work, Eg. I don't reckon Kefanin stitches my riding leathers this well.'

He shrugged, mask for the enduring bitter taste the skirmish the night before had left. 'All part of the service. If I can't keep you from getting hurt, at least I can patch up the damage afterwards.'

'Works for me.'

The last of the men dropped out of the gap in the masonry behind them and straightened up with vocal curses of relief. Egar shut them up, got them formed into a loose wedge, and led them out once more behind Archeth and the sprite.

The rest was hard marching but uneventful. They cut across the mounded rubble a few times more, leaving one boulevard in favour of another, trading plazas for streets and vice versa, but it was all open ground, ruined masonry packed solid underfoot or sections of stairway and raised platforms that had taken no more than superficial damage in whatever cataclysm had snuffed the city out. Clear views on all sides now, no real risk of ambush, and their pace picked up accordingly. Egar began to catch traces of a familiar reek on the wind.

He jogged forward, caught up to Archeth who was striding a few yards ahead.

'You smell that?'

'Yeah. Like the stacks at Monal. Must be getting close.'

Sometimes at An-Monal, the winds blew in from the south, and then you caught an acrid whiff of the chemicals at play in the Kiriath brewing stacks on the plain below. The Dragonbane had never been very sure what it was Archeth's people made in those towers, he'd only understood that they preferred to make it at some considerable distance from where they lived. Watching at night as huge, unnaturally coloured flames leapt and gouted atop the miles-distant darkened towers, he didn't much blame them. Whatever they had trapped in there, you wouldn't want to be standing very close if it ever got loose.

He remembered asking Flaradnam about it once, one banquet night out on the balcony shortly before they all headed out for Trelayne and then the Wastes. He might as well not have bothered – as was so often the case with the Kiriath, any reply you got left you with more questions than you'd started with, and this time was no exception to the rule. 'Nam glanced around the table at the various commanders' faces in the band-light, then dropped some cryptic comment to the effect that most of the Kiriath's more useful alloys had to be *grown to full complexity* or some such shit. That it was in fact a process less like smelting and smithing, and more akin to raising crops or, in its finest expressions, breeding warhorses or – a fond side-smirk at an embarrassed Archeth – children. What all that actually meant, Egar had no fucking clue and was too half-cut at the time to pursue any further. And later there was no time, they were all too busy, and a couple of months after that, Flaradnam was beyond all asking.

The smell was growing stronger, there even in the gaps between the bluster of the wind. He sneaked a glance at Archeth, wondering if it kicked her back as thoroughly to memories of her father.

But in the grey morning light, her face was as impassive as the flat of a blade.

They came over steeply piled mounds of rubble the size of hills, started a descent through isolated crags and outcrops of architecture that looked like the drowned upper levels of buildings once dizzying in height. And then, abruptly, they were looking down at the edge of the Kiriath earth-works from not much more than five hundred yards away. The holes gaped there, larger than some lakes he knew back on the steppe, but empty, shadowed and dark. More than ever, it looked as if these were wounds the city had sustained, and the vast black iron protrusions that sprouted from them on all sides some kind of surgical clamps to prevent healing. As if the Kiriath had dropped something from a great height on their enemies here, and then left it in place to grow and sprout, just the way all those complex alloys were supposed to grow in the stacks at An-Monal.

The fire sprite came to a flickering halt just past a standing ruin a handful of storeys high, paused there perhaps to give them time to take in the view down across the rubble. The air was warmer now. Even the occasional gusts of wind carried some stale-tasting heat along with the brewing stack odours. Egar fetched up at Archeth's shoulder again.

'See a way down inside?'

She cupped both hands above her eyes to shade them, peered for a while. 'Not from here.'

'At Kaldan Cross, you got those things like big mason's hods running on cables, but they're sort of tucked away, under the lip.'

'Yeah, I know. I was there when they built it, remember? This is a fuck of a lot bigger than anything at Kaldan.'

'Well,' he shrugged. 'Bigger hods and cables then. Maybe.'

The acrid chemical reek rolled in again, but it brought something else with it this time, another note to the mingled odours that—

Sandalwood . . .?

Or not. He'd lost it again, in the buffet and gust of the wind. He turned his head, breathed deep trying to get it back. He cast about, a sliding sense of doom behind his eyes. Saw the fire sprite turned jumpy and irresolute, slipping back and forth in the air beside them. Archeth, lost in peering down at what her people had built here . . .

Sudden, sharp spike of aniseed in his nostrils. The wind came banging back, brought with it the sandalwood again, stronger now, no room left for doubt. He heard comment murmur among the men, men too young or too lucky to know what it meant. He stared down at the gaping holes ahead of them. Felt the warmth in the air again, as if for the first time, and understanding fell on him like the ruin at his back.

Oh no . . .

But he knew it was.

And now the stealthy chill, waking and walking through his bones. The grinning skull of memory, the bony beckoning hand.

Well, well, Dragonbane. Here it comes, after all these years.

He grabbed Archeth by the shoulder. 'Snap out of it, Archidi. We got trouble.'

'Trouble?' She blinked, still lost in thought 'What's the . . .'

She caught the blast of spices on the breeze. Her eyes widened in shock. Egar was already unslinging his Warhelm-forged staff lance. He shed the soft fabric sheaths at either end, let them drift to the ground without attention. Plenty of time to chase them up later.

If there was a later.

'Clear your steel,' he snapped to the men at his back, as they gathered in around him. 'And get back inside that ruin, find yourselves some cover, fast.'

'Is it the lizards again, my lord?' someone asked.

He had time to offer one tight grin. 'I'm afraid not, no.'

'Then—'

Across the wind, out of the Kiriath pits below them, it came and split the air. A shrieking, piercing cry he'd thought he'd never hear again outside of dreams. A cry like sheets of metal tearing apart, like the denial of some bereaved warrior goddess: vast, immortal grief tipping over into the insane fury of loss. Like the drawn-out, echoing rage of some immense, stooping bird of prey.

'It's a dragon,' he told them simply. 'Pretty big one too, by the sound of it.'

FORTY

The term *pirate* was one that gave the League a few semantic difficulties.

The word in current popular usage was, in fact, a corruption into the Parash dialect of an older term used in the southern cities, borrowed in when Parashal was the ascendant power in the region. The southern coastal states of Gergis had long been traders by sea, knew very well what the scourge of piracy looked like, and their descriptor was condemnatory in no uncertain terms. But Parashal was a hill town, tucked away in the upland spine of Gergis and several hundred very safe miles from the nearest ocean. Its citizens had about as much chance of being carried off by a dwenda succubus as they did of suffering the predations of a real live pirate, and so they leaned to a rather more romantic view of the profession. Colourful tales abounded, of bold young men, invariably handsome and chivalrous, seeking their fortunes on the high seas, striking out heroically against corrupt port authorities and unjust maritime power. Thus resident in the Parash overculture, the word *pirate* collected all the selective drama and romance these narratives entailed, much the way a half-sucked sweet picks up a shielding layer of dust and lint from lying in a pocket untasted.

Subsequent cultural and political shifts – put more bluntly, war – brought regional ascendancy north to Trelayne, but by then the Parash dialect was the dominant form of Naomic throughout the Gergis peninsula, taught in schools and temples, used in treaties and legal contracts, seen as the civilised and sophisticated norm by which all truly educated men were measured. So the accepted form of the word *pirate* would retain all its attendant Parash ambiguity, along with a peacock tail of fanciful heroic narrative made up and written down by men who, had they ever been faced with the real thing, would doubtless have run screaming to hide in the nearest privy.

It didn't hurt this trend that Trelayne was as much a military as a trading power, at least in aspiration, and that to a large degree the city depended on legalised piracy to enforce its influence at sea. Handing out letters of marque to known coastal raiders was a cheap and useful substitute for building a navy, not to mention a powerful stimulus to sea-going trade, since you ensured at the stroke of a quill not only that your own merchant shipping was left comfortably alone but also that your competitors were severely hampered until such time as they saw fit to pay you for protection.

Prosecuted over time, this privateer-based strategy allowed Trelayne to extend and consolidate dominance over every coastal city in the Gergis region and even a couple that had liked, sporadically, to think of themselves as belonging to the Empire in the south. And along with the dominance, came a whole new crop of heroic tales, where the terms *pirate* and *privateer* grew more or less interchangeable and the bloody specifics of the work were glossed over in general celebration of the triumphant end result. Thus, pirates as warrior princes, as conquerors and standard bearers, as sober martial guardians of righteous commerce and selfless servants to the Greater Glory of Trelayne – eventually becoming the Greater Glory of the Trelayne League – in its tussles with the encroaching imperial might of Yhelteth.

Perhaps inspired by all this confused and confusing etymology, Shif Grepwyr began his career in piracy young. He was a privateer cabin boy at eleven years old, a boarding party bravo at fourteen. Was bossing his own boarding gang a month shy of his fifteenth birthday, rose to boarding party chief on the raiding caravel *Salt Lord's Sanction* a year after that. Three years later, he killed *Sanction*'s skipper in a squabble over spoils, leveraged the murder into a full mutiny and then showed up in Trelayne that winter, requesting a transfer of charter and willing to pay for it with a hold full of plunder. Always sensitive to commercial promise, the Trelayne Chancellery had acquiesced.

The name on the new letter of marque was Sharkmaster Wyr.

'Oh, right, him.' Klithren poured himself another shot of rum, knocked it back and wiped his mouth. 'Yeah, back when I was a kid, he used to winter at Hinerion sometimes, coming back up from raiding the Empire coast. But that ship wasn't called *Salt Lord's Sanction*, it was something else. Shorter than that.'

Ringil nodded. '*Sprayborne*. Wyr pulled in so much plunder those first couple of years, sank so much imperial shipping, they made him an honorary commander in the Shipmasters' guild and gave him a new hull. Purpose built raider, something to compete with the Yhelteth naval pickets. That's the one you remember.'

Klithren poured again. Held the glass up to the gently tilting lantern over their heads and squinted through the liquor at the light. He was beginning to slur his words a little.

'Yeah, this is all really fascinating memory lane shit, fascinating, *but.*' The rum, down in one again. He banged the empty glass on the table. 'Fuck's it got to do with us?'

Ringil's rum sat untouched before him. He picked it up delicately between finger and thumb. 'Would you like to know where *Sprayborne* is now?'

'I'm sure you're going to tell me.'

'It's anchored at the delta mouth of the Trel, out by the mudflats. You probably sailed right past it when you shipped out for Ornley. *Sprayborne* is a prison hulk now. Masts sawn down to stumps, hull chained fore and aft into river silt. Sharkmaster Wyr is still aboard, along with those of his crew who weren't punished by decimation.'

'Say *what?*'

'Yeah. Seems after the war our friend Wyr lost track of which side his bread was buttered and started taking ships pretty much at random. They say it was Liberalisation that knocked him off the perch, that he lost some friends or family to the auction block, but who knows?' Ringil shrugged. 'Maybe he just didn't like the moratorium on attacking imperial traffic. Pretty lean times all round back then.'

'Fucking tell me about it.'

The war against the Scaled Folk had emptied the League's coffers just as it had the Empire's, devastated its productive workforce, laid waste once prosperous centres of population and whole tracts of once fertile land. And the speculative border skirmishing against the Empire that followed in the south, once the Scaled Folk were safely defeated, had not delivered any of the promised recompense, had in fact only sucked down more men and resources that neither side could afford to lose – hence an early, hastily brokered peace.

For the privateer fraternity, Gil guessed, the whole thing would have been an unmitigated disaster. No real fighting to be done at sea during the war itself, if you didn't count a few early and abortive attempts to burn the incoming Scaled Folk rafts. Decently seaworthy vessels – and some not even decently – got commandeered and turned into troop transports or evacuation barges, or were put to running basic supplies, payment for all of which was scant to non-existent. The privateer crews were pared back to a minimum, most of their fighting strength drafted into landing parties alongside more conventional forces, leaving the bare minimum needed to handle the sailing. And for those who survived to war's end, no prospect of a return to the good old days of licensed raiding on the imperial main, because nobody could afford the fresh hostilities it might provoke.

Under the circumstances, what was any self-respecting privateer to do?

'He had a pretty good run, considering.' Ringil drank off a measured portion of his own rum and set it down again. 'Started taking Empire merchantmen, regardless of the treaties. That got him loudly proclaimed an outlaw, because the League couldn't very well be seen to do anything less; at which point he must have decided what the fuck, may as well have all the fish in the net while I'm trawling, and he starts hitting League shipping too.'

'Makes sense. No imperial navy to worry about up here.'

'That may have been a factor, I suppose. In any case, it all went bad shortly after. I hear he cleaned out a ship flying Marsh Daisy pennants, and the Brotherhood took exception. They went to work chasing down some of Wyr's shoreside collaborators, and someone taken in the net just happened to know where *Sprayborne* was laired up that season. Brotherhood sells the information on to the Chancellery and the League goes in heavy. Lots of dead pirates, but Wyr gets taken alive, to be made an example of and—'

'Still don't see,' Klithren broke in. 'What the blue fuck any of this has got to do with us.'

'That's because you're drunk.' Ringil took the rum bottle and placed it strategically on his side of the table. Finished his drink and set his glass down upended. 'I need a diversion while I get into Trelayne and bring out my friends. I want the city in flames, and I can't spare the men or the time to do it myself.'

'And you think some broken-down failure of a pirate's going to do it for you?' Klithren wagged his head solemnly back and forth. 'Uh-uh, no way. You find some way to cut Wyr free, you really think he's going to pick up a cutlass for you and try to storm the city? Forget it. He's going to shake your hand, pick your pocket and then fuck off faster than a paid whore. He'll head right into the marsh and disappear. That's if he can still stand up, because from what I've heard, they don't feed them all that well out there aboard the hulks.'

Ringil eyed the other man coldly. 'You ever have a family, Klithren?'

'None of your fucking business.'

'Well, turns out Wyr did. Wife, daughter, couple of sons. None of them all that old. They got taken along with everybody else when the League forces stormed *Sprayborne*'s layup. And you know just how fucking good the scum up at the Chancellery are at meting out punishment to those who transgress.'

It went black and hammering through his heart and arteries as he spoke, the sudden-stirring memory of Jelim's death, and perhaps Klithren saw something of it in his eyes, because the mercenary grew more soberly quiet.

'They get the cage?'

'The wife and eldest son did.' Ringil locked it down with an effort, but the same shuddering force went on pulsing behind his eyes with the metronome calm of his words. 'Daughter and the other son got lucky. There's an ordinance about executing children younger than twelve by impalement. Up at the law-courts, they call it holding the spike.'

Klithren nodded. 'They have that in Hinerion too.'

'So – Sharkmaster Wyr is taken in the company of his five year old son and seven year old daughter to the Eastern Gate, where they all witness the impalement of Wyr's wife and eldest son. They're then taken to *Sprayborne*, whose masts are still intact at this point, and Wyr gets to watch his other son and his daughter hoisted up in cages onto the mainsail spar, where they will be left to die of thirst or exposure, whichever gets them first. And he's imprisoned below, so he can hear them calling for their mother until they die.' Ringil built a shrug. It felt like he was wearing plate across his shoulders. 'I imagine they would have liked to hang the mother and other son up there too, so Wyr could hear their screams. But those cages are heavy and hard to move, and the Chancellery law lords, well, those fine nobles in their house of justice have always had a strong pragmatic streak.'

Klithren said nothing. Gil breathed in deep. Noticed his teeth were gritted, loosened his jaw and breathed out. He gave the other man a tight smile.

'You say Sharkmaster Wyr, once freed, will turn tail and flee into the marsh. I beg to differ.'

They raised the north Gergis coast not long after nightfall. Shortly after, the lookout aboard *Dragon's Demise* spotted the faintest trace of a reddish glow against the sky forward to port. There was really only one thing that it could be. The call went up and signal lanterns flickered ship to ship – journey's end sighted. Seemed Lal Nyanar had managed to plot and hold a pretty steady course after all.

Unless he missed by five hundred miles and that's the lights of Lanatray we're looking at.

But Ringil knew, as he stood on the foredeck and watched the smeared charcoal line at the horizon, that it wasn't Lanatray, and that Nyanar was right on course. Lanatray was tiny by comparison to Trelayne, and shielded from the direct ocean by a long granite bluff – you wouldn't spot the glow of her lights until you were nearly swimming distance out. And anyway—

You can feel it, can't you, black mage?

That's Home *out there, sitting just under the horizon like grave dirt under your nails, and you can feel it calling.*

Dragon's Demise came about a couple of degrees and pointed her prow at the glow on the sky. Behind him at the ship's helm, he heard Nyanar calling the order to run colours. Gil put a krinzanz twig he'd rolled earlier to his lips, willed it absently to life with the sketch of a burning glyph drawn in the air. He drew the harsh-tasting smoke down and held it there while the krin stole icily from his lungs into his veins. He leaned on the rail, breathed the smoke back out and waited for Trelayne to show herself.

The line of the coast thickened, grew visibly irregular. Cloud shredded apart off the scimitar gleam of the band, let in a low silvery light. Before long, you could start to make out the rise of hills along the shore, the textured detail of forest canopies and farmed fields, the mineral glint of escarpments and cliffs. The broad, familiar arms of the Trel delta spread to beckon him in and there, at the eastern extremity, the clustered lights of the city glimmered into view. He plumed smoke out into the wind, watched as it was snatched away again. Nodded at the lights as if in greeting.

Here I am again, you murderous whore. Just can't give you up.

Two long, lean hulls ahead on the swells – privateer caravels riding picket for the estuary gap, clear notice of the war in progress and precautions taken accordingly. Ringil sensed the exact moment they were spotted, could almost see in his mind's eye the sudden scramble to action stations aboard both vessels. Faint cries and yells, and a stampede of feet across decking drifted to his ears on the still night air. He couldn't be sure if it was all just his imagination at work, or some stealthy new reach of the *ikinri 'ska*. In any case, as he watched, one of the League ships came rapidly about and swung their way. He straightened up, flipped the last half inch of his twig over the rail and headed for the companionway. Time to lend Nyanar some moral support.

As he walked down the main deck, he tilted his head back to where the yellow and black snake's tongue pennants now fluttered at each mast tip.

Wonder when they'll spot those.

Should sober them up a bit when they do.

To anyone with seasoned seafaring eyes, *Dragon's Demise* was unmistakably an imperial vessel, but she was flying Trelayne colours, big and bold at the mainmast, and the League man o' war he'd commandeered was right behind them, with *Sea Eagle's Daughter* bringing up the rear and also flagged for Trelayne. You'd have to be pretty stupid not to read all of that for what it was – triumphant capture of Empire shipping, and the eagerly awaited next chapter in the privateer success story that must have begun when *Pride of Yhelteth* and her attendant captor vessels showed up a few days earlier. They'd be all set to cheer these new captives into harbour – until someone spotted that yellow and black.

He met Klithren at the foot of the companionway to the helm deck. The mercenary looked hungover and shaky on his feet, which Ringil supposed he more than likely was. Pretty much an ideal state of affairs, too, given what was coming next.

'Ready?' Gil asked him.

'I already fucking told you I was.'

'Good man.' He clapped Klithren hard on the chest and shoulder, grinned as he saw the mercenary's face wobble in the gloom. 'They're not going to risk any closer than hailing distance, so it should be easy enough to sell. Just stick to what we agreed and try to look . . . well, no – you already do. Just keep it up.'

He climbed the companionway to the sound of retching at his back as Klithren threw up.

Lal Nyanar came and peered disdainfully down over the helm deck rail as Ringil climbed up to meet him.

'That man has been drunk all day,' he sniffed. 'What you see in him as an ally, I simply cannot grasp.'

Gil stepped off the companionway. 'He's been in a few places you haven't.'

'Is that supposed to explain the drinking?'

'It explains why I want him as an ally. Are you ready?'

Nyanar glanced up at the pennants they were flying. 'As we'll ever be. It remains to be seen if this scheme of yours will work, though.'

Ringil, preparing to hand out some straightforward reassurance, felt mischief sparkle through him instead. It was the call of impending risk, he knew, the itch to action – and a long building irritation with Nyanar that finally flared to life. He put on a breezy grin.

'But my lord Nyanar! That's what gives life its savour, is it not? Where would we be if the future were always known?'

'We'd be back home in Yhelteth,' said Nyanar sourly. 'Avoiding madcap quests and desperate jailbreak schemes and deceptions.'

I am home, you soggy-faced, entitled little prick, he barely stopped himself saying. *You think it took northern sorcery to make me the way I am now? You think it took a war? Those things were tonic compared to what came before. Desperation and deception were waiting for me at the nursery door, took me by either hand as I walked out into my youth, have been my constant companions since.*

He kept his grin with an effort. 'Home we might be, but we'd come up a little short on tales of glory to regale our grandchildren with.'

The captain's mouth crimped. 'I see no glory in—'

'Signal!' A bawled cry from the forward lookout. 'Signalling – heave to and await escort!'

Nyanar looked queasy, almost a match for Klithren's face earlier. He met Ringil's eyes with an expression that verged on accusing. Gil nodded.

'This scheme of mine appears to be working out,' he said amiably.

FORTY-ONE

The shock of the scream held them rigid. It hung in the air around them like freezing fog, even as the echoes ran out across the ruined city. Archeth felt the breath stop in her throat, felt a cold hand cup her at the nape of the neck. The wash of sandalwood and aniseed in the wind. She met Egar's eyes across the gathering of men, and he nodded, something suddenly old and tired in his face. She'd heard him say the word, just like everyone else, but still, everything in her wanted to shake her head in dumb denial. Their luck just could not be this bad.

The cry repeated, redoubled in force.

'It can smell us,' said the Dragonbane grimly.

He rounded on the men. 'Don't just fucking stand there! I told you, it's a *dragon*. What do you want, count its fucking teeth? Get back in those ruins. Drop your gear inside and climb. Come on, *move it!*'

They came awake, like statues summoned to life. Hurried into the forlorn facades and crags of stone behind them, casting fearful glances back. She watched them go as if in a dream, had time for an obscure sympathy as she remembered the numb shock of her own first encounter in the war. The fading echoes of that cry, chasing her all the way back . . .

'You too, Archidi.' He was at her shoulder, grabbing, yanking her loose of her terrors, chivvying her to life. 'Come on, you've been here before. You know the drill. Let's *go*.'

He shepherded her towards the nearest gap in the architecture, shoved her through, into dim light and a cavern chaos of rubble and collapsed flooring. She heard him follow her in. They stood there a moment in the cradling gloom, amidst a scattering of discarded packs and other gear – the men had followed Egar's orders to the letter. She stared up to where a couple of pale faces peered back down at them. Listened to the noises as the rest of the men scrambled about elsewhere in the ruins, seeking position. Outside, the dragon shrieked once more. She added her pack to the pile, turned to face the Dragonbane, found him at her back, closer than she'd thought.

'So how—'

'In a minute.' He shrugged off his own pack, nodded upward. 'Let's get some height first.'

They clambered up through the slumped and shattered levels, spotted more of the company crouched and huddled where the remaining buttresses and beams of the ruins looked strongest. Men nodded and bowed to her as she inched past, but their eyes skipped repeatedly back to Egar as he climbed behind her. She heard them murmuring, and among those who were speaking Tethanne, she heard the name more than once, like an invocation, like a warding spell of power –

Dragonbane . . .

They came out finally on a section of flooring twenty feet up that had somehow not given way. There was a row of tall, narrow windows to the front. Archeth crept forward, ascertained that the floor was solid, and crouched by the nearest of the openings. Little twinges of pain along the stitches in her wound – she grimaced and tried to ease her posture. Egar came behind her, hampered a little by his grip on the staff lance. He joined her at the window, craned to peer out.

'So how do we do this?' she asked quietly.

'Glad you asked me that.' He didn't look at her, was still glued to the view outside. 'Give me a minute, let's just see what we're dealing w—'

Voice blotted abruptly out. He sank to sitting, back to the wall. Drew breath in over his teeth, shot her a glance.

'Go on, take a look.' He jerked a thumb over his shoulder. 'You don't want to miss this.'

She crammed past him to the window. The sea of rubble below them, tilting and sloping down towards the sunken Kiriath structures beyond. A frozen landscape of shards and shades of grey and—

Motion!

She almost recoiled from the window; it was a physical effort not to do it. Her heart clutched and jumped in her chest.

It had taken on the same mottled grey tones as the landscape. If it hadn't been moving, she might have missed it entirely at first glance. But it *was* moving. It clambered effortlessly across the rubble, came pacing zigzag up the slope towards them, and it was grinning. Scimitar-fanged mouth, loose and open to let the tongue flicker out and taste the air. Recessed eyes, high on the long curved head, a crest of folded webbing and spines bristling behind the skull – the colossal echo of the same appendage on a warrior caste lizard, but this crest had to be twice longer than the Dragonbane was tall. Powerful, taloned forelimbs lifting head and chest just off the ground, so it seemed the beast was sniffing for them like a hound. Flexed arch of dorsal plates and back and belly you could have driven a cart and horses under. Haunches, each rising and curving the size of *Pride of Yhelteth*'s mainsail running full before the wind. Finally the tail, tapered and spike-ended, half the length of the body again and thicker than a man's trunk even at the thinnest point.

It raised its head as she watched, lifted almost fully back on its haunches. The crest flared up and out, spread the width of a palace gateway either side of the skull. She caught a fresh blast of sandalwood. The dragon screamed at the desolate grey sky, and Archeth felt the cry through the stonework she was leant against. Felt the pit of her belly vibrate.

'Ain't she a fucking beauty?' breathed the Dragonbane, back at her side. 'Look at the *size* of that bitch. Gil's going to be sorry he wasn't here for this.'

'So what do we *do?*' she hissed.

'Hard to say. I had a cliff and a pissed off faggot with a Kiriath broadsword to work with last time.'

'Well.' She gestured helplessly. 'Can we lure it back to the pit, maybe? Trick it into falling down there?'

He gave her a tight smile. 'It just climbed out of the pit, Archidi. I don't think that's going to work.'

The dragon screamed again. The sound rang off the walls around her, rang in her ears. It filled the space inside the ruin like water. Egar nodded.

'You hear that? This isn't a blunderer, Archidi, it's a fucking dragon. Whole other story. They're smart, easily as smart as warrior caste. We only got ours over that cliff in Demlarashan because we'd already done it some serious damage, and it was going mad from the pain.'

'So what do *you* suggest?'

'I suggest for the moment that we sit tight.' The Dragonbane was peering through the window frame again. She heard him draw a sharp breath, then he pitched his voice loud, for the others in the ruins around them. 'Brace up, lads – here it comes. It's going to sniff around here a bit, try screaming to scare us out, and if that doesn't work it'll try to tear its way in. Don't get shaken, don't expose yourselves, unless it's on my word. That clear?'

A thin and shaky chorus of assent.

'Good. Then today's the day we kill ourselves a dragon! Anybody up for that?'

A couple of hard-driven cheers floated loose in the ruined spaces. She thought she recognised Alwar Nash's voice among them.

'I *said* – do you want to *kill* a fucking *dragon?*'

More yells, and more punch behind them this time. Egar eased up out of his crouch and filled his lungs.

'*I can't hear you! Do you – or do you not – want to kill – a motherfucking dragon?*'

A solid roar in answer.

'Then chant with me. Loud, so that fucking bitch can hear you. Make it understand who we are!' Egar stood erect, made a fist. Punched it savagely into the air above his head. '*Dragon Bane! Dragon Bane! Dragon Bane!*'

And the chant came back at him, from every throat in the ruin, even those who spoke no Tethanne and might not know what the syllables meant.

'*Dragon Bane! Dragon Bane! Dragon Bane!*'

Out of nowhere, she found herself with them, chanting, veins pulsing in her head with the force of it. The pain in her wound forgotten, driven out by this rising force. Faster now, as Egar forced the tempo up.

'*Dragon Bane! Dragon Bane! Dragon Ba*—'

The dragon screamed and shocked against the ruin.

It was like being back aboard *Lord of the Salt Wind* that night – seemingly solid planking under her feet, cabin bulkheads around her, all rendered suddenly flimsy by the force and roar of the storm outside. The wall she crouched against shivered with the impact, the shriek went through her head like pain. Men yelled and yelped behind her. The reek of sandalwood was overpowering; it made her dizzy just to breath it.

The Dragonbane grinned, like a man facing down bonfire heat.

The echoes died away. Powder sifted down from the stonework above. Elsewhere, she heard the fall of larger rubble pieces. And then heavy, crunching footfalls on the other side of the wall. Egar glanced out of the window and nodded to himself.

'Everybody all right?' he called. 'Sound off.'

Echoing calls through the architecture. A Majak voice, raised in evident fury. She heard the other Majak laugh.

'What's going on?'

Egar shook his head. 'He pissed himself. Pretty angry about it.'

He crabbed a couple of yards across the remnants of flooring to where the wall took a right angle turn. Got up against the stonework beside a window on that side. Tipped a look outside. Archeth angled her head by inches, peered out of her own window, saw no movement, saw nothing but the sea of rubble.

'No sign,' she hissed across at the Dragonbane. 'Where the fuck is it?'

He nodded sideways. 'Gone round the back. Looking for a better way in.'

'Can we make a run for it, then?' Though her flesh quailed at the thought. 'Get down into the pit before it . . .'

Her voice dried up as he shook his head. She found herself oddly relieved. Egar crabbed back to her side and sank to a crouch. He spoke absently, with his head tilted back against the stone, as if checking the sky above the ruin for portent.

'That's five hundred yards, Archidi. It'd cut us down before we got halfway. I've seen these fuckers cough venom better than eighty feet. Got better aim than a tavern urchin spitting on a bet, too.'

'But—'

Violent crashing sounds from the rear of the ruin. The dragon shrieked again. Flurry of calls between the men. Egar bounced back up, shouted across the commotion.

'Report! Anybody back there see what's going on?'

'It found a gateway,' someone yelled in Tethanne. 'Tried to smash its way through.'

'Yeah? How'd it do?'

Another voice. 'Went away with a sore fucking head.'

Laughter, uneasy at first, but gaining strength as the men grabbed onto it. Alwar Nash's even, court-mannered tones came through the sounds of forced merriment.

'The beast got its head inside, my lord. It dislodged some stonework from the gateway arch, but had to withdraw. It is still outside.'

'Thank you. You all hold steady back there, I'm coming across. No one move unless you have to.' Egar dropped his voice and murmured to her. 'Dragon-proof walls, eh. Got to hand it to these dwenda architects. I guess if you're immortal, you just naturally build to last.'

'Yeah.' Her mouth was dry. She cleared her throat. 'Listen, what if we just stay put? Wait for it to lose interest and go look for something else to eat?'

'If it lives in the pits – and I reckon it probably does, there's a lot of warmth around here – then that isn't going to happen. This is its home range, Archidi. We're intruders. There's only one way for it to understand that, only one way it knows how to behave. It isn't going anywhere. It'll tear this place down around us, or it'll starve us out.'

'But we're provisioned. How long can it just . . . hang around?'

Egar scowled. 'Long enough. On the expeditionary, your father told me they reckoned these things probably only need to eat two or three times a year. But when they do find food, they'll stick at it like a clanmaster trying to sire a son.' A shrug. 'Anyway, even if it did lose its appetite, decide to forgive the intrusion and go back to bed, that still puts it right back in the pits. However you look at it, Archidi, the fucker's in our way. Which makes it a bit of luck for us it found that gateway back there.'

She stared at him. 'Luck?'

'Yeah. Like commanding officers are given to saying, we've got *a point of engagement* now. Just needs someone to go out there and persuade our scaly friend to stick her head back in again.' He grinned lopsidedly at her. 'Got a coin?'

She did, in fact – a well-worn three elemental piece that had by some miracle escaped notice when she was frisked prior to boarding *Lord of the Salt Wind* in Ornley; by some other freak chance, it had not been washed from her pockets when they wrecked. The Warhelm's spiders found it in her ruined clothes when they took them away, and she woke a couple of mornings later with one of the little articulated iron creatures perched on her chest, holding the coin out in one pincer a couple of inches away from her nose. Struck image of Akal the Great's head, looming huge and blurry close in her field of vision. She tried groggily to brush it away, but the iron spider came back, insistently, and in the end, with much bad grace, she snatched the coin up and threw it across the room. The spider scuttled off after it, brought it back again. She threw it once more. They both went round a couple more times before Archeth accepted she was being child-ish and held onto the coin until the spider went away.

321

It's not like I can spend it anywhere around here, she complained to Tharala-nanghars as she dressed in her new clothes.

Nor can I, said the Warhelm tartly. *Like so many other things, it will have to wait until your safe return to Yhelteth.*

Now she pulled it out of her pocket, offered it glinting on her palm. The Dragonbane looked startled for a moment, then he smiled.

'Joking, Archidi. Just joking. You can stay here.'

'Yeah, like fuck.'

She stowed the coin and crept after him, through the jagged maze of masonry. He tried to wave her back, she forked an obscene gesture at him. He rolled his eyes. They crouched and crawled and clambered through the shattered structure of the building, losing height as they moved. Pale, cold light filtered down from the opened roof space above. She thought she heard the dragon scrape against a wall somewhere outside. Men watched them pass from their various vantage points, and she saw them murmur to each other and point.

The gateway Nash had mentioned came into view, broad enough for a carriage and horses in width, but filled at base with debris, reduced to not much more than a couple of yards in height. The spiced reek was there, strong again, the same spikes of aniseed and cardamom through the sandalwood. Light from outside spilled inward under the arch, left long dagger shadows across the rubble.

She spotted Alwar Nash crouched one floor up, huddled with another Throne Eternal in a corner where an interior wall had slumped sideways and dumped its various floors like a hand of bad cards thrown down. She prodded the Dragonbane's shoulder – he was fixed on the gateway and its shadows – and pointed. They moved carefully up the sloping mess of cracked tile and stone, reached the two imperials and hunkered down beside them. Nash bowed briefly to her. Pointed downward at the gate with the pommel end of his broadsword.

'It got its head inside there and twisted – you can see the marks where it gouged chunks out of the arch stones. Tried to tear the rest down with a claw, but there was no space for leverage. Structure was too strong, I guess.' He gazed up and around at the ruined walls. 'Whoever built all this knew what they were—'

'Hsst!' The other Throne Eternal, gesturing. 'It's back!'

Shadows moved, under the gateway arch. There was a sound she knew, expelled breath like the shaken tail of some colossal rattlesnake, then ragged, dragging noises, and the rubble just outside the gate shifted.

'All right,' said Egar softly.

'What is it?' Nash wanted to know. 'What's it doing?'

'Digging,' she told him. 'Seen one do it at Shenshenath. Going to try to clear out enough of that debris so it can get inside, or maybe just dig up the foundations and topple the wall. They're smart like that. Eg?'

No response. She looked at him, saw him staring down at his hands where they held the staff lance midway along the burnished alloy shaft. It was as if he'd forgotten what the weapon and the hands that held it were for.

She nudged him. 'Eg. What's next here?'

He stirred. Hefted the lance in both hands and looked round at her. 'Archidi, I told you all about that piece of shit Poltar, didn't I?'

She blinked. 'The shaman? Sure, uh . . . Sold you out to your brothers up on the steppe. Got them all fired up to kill you or chase you out. But—'

'That fuck needs killing, Archidi.' He held her gaze. 'One way or the other.'

Something dripped like melting ice in her belly. 'We talked about this already, Eg. Him and your brother Ershal. First order of business, soon as we get to Ishlin-ichan, we'll track your people down. You got my word. But, uh . . . got to kill *this* fucking thing first. Right?'

He sniffed hard. 'Yeah, all right.'

She watched him cock his head, listen for a moment to the stony scrabbling sounds from outside. His face was unreadable. But when he looked up at his companions, his tone was as breezy as a man discussing a horse he might buy.

'Okay, she sounds pretty busy out there, plenty of noise to cover us. Nash – and you, what's your name?'

The other Throne Eternal bowed. 'Shent, my lord. Kanan Shent.'

'Shent, right. Hope you're handy with that axe. You two follow us down, you got the lady Archeth's back.'

Grim nods from both men.

'I'm going out as bait—'

'You are not!' she snapped.

'Archidi—'

'If anyone goes as bait, it's me. I'm smaller, I'm lighter on my feet, I don't have that staff lance to trip over—'

'Archidi, I used to do this for a living, remember?'

'My lady—'

'Nash, shut the fuck up.' She kept her eyes on the Dragonbane. 'Eg, I'm in command here. I'll decide the battle appointments.'

'I know what I'm doing, Archidi. You don't.'

'Oh, three and a half fucking years fighting the Scaled Folk, and now I find out I didn't know what I was doing. It's funny, I led—'

'It's not the same *thing!* It's *a fucking dragon!*'

'*Hsst!*'

The digging noises outside had stopped. They froze in place, listening. Long beats of silence – she watched the shadows coming in the rubble-drowned gateway, saw them shift about. The snorting, rattling breath outside seemed to nose up to the wall they crouched against. Scrape of scales on masonry, a sudden explosive snort.

The digging resumed.

She fished in her pocket, brought out the coin.

'All right, then,' she hissed. 'We settle it like this. Heads or manes. One toss. Whoever wins goes outside.'

He stared at her for a long moment. Put out his hand.

'Give me that,' he said. 'Call it.'

She swallowed hard. 'Heads.'

'Right.'

They all watched intently as the Dragonbane tossed the three elemental piece in the air – caught it in the cup of his hand – hefted it – slapped it across onto the back of his other hand where he still held onto the staff lance – took the covering hand away—

'Manes.' Nodding down at the worn horse-head motif on the upward face. 'Can we get on with this now?'

He offered the coin back to her. She glowered at him, certain she'd just been duped, unable to quite work out how.

'Fucking keep it.'

'Okay, thanks.' A wink as he stowed the coin away. 'Reckon I'll blow that down at Angara's place, soon as we get back.'

'Very funny.'

He knew she'd been a customer at Angara's herself, back in the day, because she'd let it slip one drunken campfire night on campaign in the south. He knew also what crazy sums she'd paid, for the watertight anonymity and discretion the establishment offered. He'd rocked back from the campfire and whistled low when she told him.

Now, he patted the pocket where the coin had gone. 'Yeah, should buy me at least a thimble full of ale and thirty seconds with Angara's best whore.'

'Are we going to fucking do this or what?'

They moved down the sloping, fallen flooring as one. Stopped on the rubbled ground a good distance from one side of the gate. Egar crept forward and squatted, peered cautiously out. A satisfied grunt. He came back.

'Right, it's busy digging. Nash, you get on the other side of this gate. Archidi, you stay here with Shent – that way we hit it from both sides. Now I'm not planning to be out there long, so be ready. Soon as that cunt pokes its head in here, you hit it with everything you've got. Get to an eye if you can, or try for wounds around the mouth. Main thing is – hurt it as much as you can. You cause enough pain, it's going to start doing stupid things, and that's when we get to kill it.'

They moved up on the gateway. Nash hefted sword and shield, drew breath. Scuttled rapidly across to the far side and crouched there with evident relief. Egar waited a moment longer, looked back at Archeth and grinned.

'Pay attention,' he said. 'I'm only going to do this once.'

He went with careful steps to the edge of the gateway arch. She saw him drop his left hand from the staff lance, hold the weapon loose and balanced at his right side. He lowered himself into a crouch for the sprint. She saw him summon breath.

And the rubble floor caved in under them all.

FORTY-TWO

There were times he dreamed that the cage had taken him after all; that he made some impassioned speech confessing guilt and repentance on the floor of the Hearings Chamber, and offered himself up for the sentence instead. That the Chancellery law lords in their enthroning chairs and finery murmured behind their hands, deliberated amongst themselves for a space, and finally nodded with stern paternal wisdom. That the manacles were unlocked and his wife and children set free. He saw it with tears in his eyes and a sobbing laugh on his lips, saw Sindrin kneel on the cold marble, weeping and hugging at little Shoy and Miril, while Shif junior just stood and looked back at him across the chamber with mirrored tears standing in his own young eyes.

Then he woke, to his chains and the memory of what had really been done.

Sprayborne tilted on her anchors beneath him, yearned seaward on the currents from the river's mouth. The damp cold of dawn seeped in through the portholes over his head and brought with it from the mudflats a stench like death.

At other times, maybe triggered by that reek, it was nightmare that took him – he dreamed, keening deep in his throat as he slept, that the rusted locks fell off the gibbet cages where they'd been heaved over the side and come to rest on the estuary's silted bed, and now Shoy and Miril swam free, glitter-eyed and skeletal in the murky water, rising into the light to knock at *Sprayborne*'s hull and call for their father to come out and play . . .

Living punishment, as severe as the law allows, pronounced law-lord Murmin Kaad grimly into the anticipatory quiet of the Hearing Chamber. *Meted out to reflect the severity of your sins against the Fair City and its allies, and to serve as clear example to others. Shif Grepwyr, you will see your bloodline extinguished, you will be imprisoned in the vessel you used to commit your crimes, and you will be given the rest of your natural span to reflect upon the evil you have done in this world.*

He screamed when he heard it, and sometimes, waking from the dream, he echoed those screams again. Screamed and tore at his fetters until he bled from the old scarred wounds once more, screamed as he had in the Hearing Chamber, for the Salt Lord to come for him, for the *whole fucking Dark Court* to come if they willed it, to take his soul, to take him away, to any kind of torment but this, if he might just first pay back the rulers of Trelayne for the justice they had meted out.

No one came.

Four years now, as near as he could reckon it, since the last of his children's weakened cries ceased and he knew he could count them dead. Since he heard the splash of the gibbet cages thrown overboard, and then the steady grating back and forth of the bandsaw they used to cut through *Sprayborne*'s masts and topple them. Four years trying to sell his soul to every demon god whose name he knew, and no takers yet. Four years, chained the same way his ship was chained, in a space meant to break body and mind alike.

For the craftsmen jailers of Trelayne knew what they were about. They were well versed in the art of converting ships into dungeons – in a rapidly burgeoning city where every new square yard of building space had to be reclaimed from the marsh, prison hulks had long been the most economical way of shelving undesirables not considered worthy of execution. Better yet, there was a helpful, finger-wagging symbolism in the trick, especially where piracy was the crime for which punishment was to be exacted. The prison hulks were visible from the city walls on the south side, and from the slums in Harbour End too, if you had a good enough eye; clearer still from the spread of reclaimed land beyond the city's skirts, where Trelayne's agricultural workforce bent their backs to earn a barely sustaining crust, and from the broad sweep of marshland beyond that, where the marsh dweller clans held to their encampments and grubbed a living in whichever way they could.

For anyone in those places who cared to look, then, the hulks were a grim, gathered presence, like storm clouds on the horizon. Think your life's hard? Transgress the laws of the Fair City, and look where you could end up. Look what became of criminals, of sweet-keeled pirate vessels and their crews, when the force of that law was invoked.

Inside *Sprayborne*, the same didactic sensibility held sway for the inmates, but seasoned with an additional twist of cruelty. They'd built the cells into the hull like the chambers in a wasps' nest, each one sitting just above the bilges and served with light by portholes too high up to peer out of without the prisoner gouging at wrists and ankles when his restraining chains went taut. You might see the outside world you had forgone for your crimes, but only at painful cost.

For the rest, you sat chained in damp, stinking gloom and watched the days of your life march in filtering fingers of light from the portholes, across the opposing wall of the cell from one side to the other, and down again into darkness.

Wyr availed himself of the option to look outside only on those occasions that he felt his sanity going, slipping quietly away from him in the rank confines of the cell. At other times, he refused to torment himself with what he could not have. He was, despite himself, a survivor. He shook off his dreams each day, fed them as fuel to the rage in his belly. He cleaned the bowls of thin stew they served him, he devoted the few clear-headed hours of strength the slop gave him to simple, mindless exercises that didn't pull on his chains. The evenings, he spent filing away at his fetters with one of the iron nails he had worked loose from the hull planking, working at the metal cuffs until it grew too dark to see what he was doing. It would take years to cut through a single manacle, probably a decade to free all four limbs, always assuming he didn't run out of nails first. And if they caught him at it, they'd go right ahead and replace the irons with fresh ones, or maybe just kill him.

But it gave him something to do. It gave him a daily focus for his fury. It gave him hope, and he knew how vital that was.

In the other cells, he could hear how the men from his crew went slowly, gibbering mad with the isolation and the death of hope. They started out four years past with thumped messages in code through the wooden walls, shouted vows of solidarity to each other from cell to cell. But all too soon the structure of their communication began to break down. They hammered on the planking in incoherent rage. They yelled, they screamed, they wept. Eventually, they began to cackle and crow incomprehensibly to themselves. In the first couple of years, he'd been able to recognise voices, put individual names of men to the yelling, but that time was long past. Now, *Sprayborne*'s whole hull echoed faintly with their mingled mutterings and laments, as if the men themselves were gone and only ghosts remained.

Footfalls, in the corridor along the keel.

Wyr propped himself up from the planks where he lay, stared at the filtering fingers of light over his head. It was early in the day for food; they'd not usually feed him much before noon. The tiny shift in routine, the trickle of difference it made, set an unreasonable jag of excitement chasing through his veins.

Something was going on.

Scrape of a key in the lock, the heavy wooden door thumped back and a familiar figure stood in the space it left. Wyr blinked and straightened up in his chains. Coughed and shuddered with the damp.

'Gort?' Voice a choked husk. Stifle the coughing, force it down. 'What you doing here at this hour?'

'Same as fucking ever.' The jailer hefted a pail at his side, bigger than the usual. It made a slopping sound that set Wyr's mouth running with saliva. 'And I'm telling you now, this might be all you get 'til day after tomorrow, depending. Don't scoff it all at once, eh.'

'Right, yeah. What's going on?'

Gort heaved a world-weary sigh. He was a gutty sack of a man, lugubrious and slow and full of complaints. But by the standards of prison hulk jailers, he was a prince. He appeared to pass no judgement on the men he attended, saw them as unfortunates just like himself, caught up in the same atrocious web of chance that had landed him with this gods-forsaken job. Previous jailers, equally unhappy with their lot, had never missed a

chance to take it out on the prisoners at the slightest provocation or sometimes with none at all. It was a casual brutality, no different than stomping
a cat or hurling stones at a street cur – they mostly used boots or fists, only
occasionally resorted to the short, studded lash they carried at their belt
as the closest thing there was to a badge of office in this line of work. But
Wyr had never seen Gort's lash come off his belt, and the worst he'd had
to endure at the man's hands were the interminable monologues on the
many, many ways in which life had conspired to treat his jailer unjustly.

'Got to do the whole fucking ship and be back to Harbour End before
noon, if you can believe that shit. Like to see them up at the Chancellery manage that. They must think – here, cop hold of this, stash it or
eat it now, up to you – must think I've got a fucking longboat and full
complement to row me out and back, 'stead of what I *have* got, which is
two broken down old war veterans with more scar tissue than skin barely
know one end of an oar from the other. 'Course, that's not the best of
it, neither.' Gort took a morose seat on the doorsill. 'After this round,
we're right back out again with provisions and medicines for the yellow-
n-blacks. Well, they needn't think I'm setting a single foot on one of *those*
fucking decks, not on what they pay me. Let the fucking bone men go,
earn their money for a change—'

'Yellow and black?' Voice still husky with lack of use, but a fresh pulse
of interest prickled along Wyr's nerves. 'Out here, you mean? With the
hulks?'

'Yeah, fucking plague ship, where else they going to stick it? Navy
picket brought them in last night, a whole squadron of them.' A vague nod
up at the portholes. 'Three ships, and two of them are captured imperials.
Probably where they picked it up – those southerners got some filthy fucking habits from what I hear. All flying the pennants, anyway.'

'Plague.' He said it like the name of a god he might worship. The bucket
of stew was forgotten at his feet.

'Yeah, just what we fucking needed, right? On top of the war and all?
Don't really know why they're making us feed them in the first place; if
it's anything like back in '41, they'll all be dead by end of week. And then
we'll just have to burn the ships to the waterline. Waste of good food,
waste of *my* fucking time coming out an extra trip every day.' Gort's eyes
narrowed with freshly aggrieved suspicion. 'Might be, you know, this is
all some Empire trick to fuck us over. Maybe the imperials let them capture those ships on purpose, crewed them up with men what were already
infected and *let* us take them, so we'd carry the plague right into the city.
Sort of thing they'd do, treacherous fuckers, they pretty soon forgot how
we drove out the lizards for them. And now look. Hinerion taken like a
peach, Empire columns marching right into the peninsula like it was their
backyard. You ask me, that raiding you did down south after the war, they
should of given you a fucking medal for it.'

'What I thought,' said Sharkmaster Wyr quietly.

'Yeah, guess we all got to carry other men's fuck ups, don't we? Like I should of had that harbour watch job when old Feg died. Everyone knew I was his favourite for it. Still can't believe that little shit Sobli got it instead. Nah, don't worry, not going to bore you with that story again. Like I said, don't you go eating all that at once, mate. With this shit boiling up, could be a couple of days before I get back here again.' The jailer slapped his thighs and stood up. 'Anyway, that's it, got to get on. Let's hope your old bosun's calmed down a bit since yesterday. Last thing I need on top of everything else, that is – him flinging his own turds at me like the fact he's in here is *my* fucking fault.'

The door clubbed shut again, the key grated round, and Gort went grumbling away. Wyr got up and hobbled stiffly to a portion of the cell floor under the nearest porthole. He took a long breath, then hauled himself up on the porthole's lower edge, wincing as his fetters dug into flesh only recently healed from a dream he'd had a few days back.

He gritted his teeth and hauled harder, got his chin over the edge and peered out.

Bright morning light, long angled ladders of it propped up against the clouds, as if the sky itself was ripe for boarding. The new ships sat at anchor about a quarter league off, marked out from the hulk fleet by their masts, at the top of which the yellow and black plague pennants flopped slackly about in the breeze. One League caravel, looked like Alannor yard work from the lines, and two bigger, fatter Empire merchantmen, the sort that would have raised a low, predatory cheer from his crew back in the day. All three vessels flew the colours of Trelayne. It was hard to tell in the glare of early daylight off the water, his eyes were stinging from the unaccustomed brightness, but it didn't look as if there was anyone up on deck.

'*Hoy, look – No! Fucking pack that in!*'

Gort's muffled bellow from a couple of cells down the keel. Something nearly like a smile touched Wyr's lips, then passed slowly away. He lowered himself back down to the plank flooring and slid fingers under the fetters on his wrists, massaging the abused flesh there as best he could.

He crouched there, thoughtful, trying to understand why the arrival of the plague ships should feel so much like something good.

He fed himself with rigid control from the bucket.

Gort hadn't lied, it was pretty much a double helping by jail standards and still retained a faint trace of oven warmth despite the long crossing from Harbour End. The hunk of bread floating on top seemed massive. He tore off the portion that was already soaked through with broth and ate it first, to take the edge off his hunger. Then he sieved out some of the miserly ration of solid pieces with his fingers, soft chunks of carrot and crumbling potato, a stringy shred of meat with a blubbery lump of fat still attached, and ate them one savoured piece at a time.

He was still chewing when the sounds started under the hull.

For a brief, fuddled space, he thought that *Sprayborne* must have slipped her chains. Was being carried on the current across boulder-studded shallows. Irregular, spaced bumping along the keel. Like that time in the Scatter, skulking to avoid imperial patrols, nearly lost the whole fucking ship that time, had to put stripes on every member of the watch for fucking up so badly . . .

It took a moment or two for common sense and recollection of where he was to catch up – there was no sense of motion in the hull other than the faint, eternal rocking in place he was used to, and anyway, he would have heard the ring of hammers if the anchors had been struck. And the river bed was pure silt out here, shallowing to nothing but the broad expanse of mudflats and marsh.

Yeah, silt and the bones of your murdered children.

Sharp, fast spike of rage to drive out the musing. Before he could stop himself, he lashed out with his foot, caught the food pail and sent it flying.

He sat staring sickly at the mess.

Four years, four fucking years, of starvation diet and enclosure, and here he was, brought to this. Mind left loose and slow, clarity fogged by drifting banks of exhaustion and weary self-pity, losing himself in spirals of memory and addled reflection it could take hours to shake off.

And then, suddenly, he was scrabbling forward to right the pail before it dribbled out every last trace of the stew within. Mumbling to himself.

'Oh no, no-no, no . . .'

Flinging himself flat to lick up the remaining spill before it leaked away between the planks, scooping up the solids on trembling fingers, dropping them back into the bottom of the bucket, peering whimpering in after them to see how much he'd managed to salvage.

'Sorry, I'm sorry, I'm *sorry* . . .'

More soft bumping, right beneath him where he crouched. He froze, staring down at the cell floor as if he could see right through it – through the bilges below and the hull, out to whatever was hanging there in the murky gloom under the keel, knocking to get in.

The planking under him sprung a leak.

At first it was small, a sudden darkening of the already age-stained wood, like a man pissing his breeches under torture. If his naked foot had not been resting in the centre of the patch, he might not even have noticed it. But then the water began forcing its way through in earnest, welling up out of the wood, mounding three full fingers above the floor and – as he jerked his foot out of the patch in alarm – following his moves like a living creature.

He backed up against the far wall of the cell, shaking his head. Watched in dazed fascination, saw the mound of water cast about where he had been, as if confused by his sudden disappearance. It went on swelling as it moved, welling steadily upward, and now it radiated a faint phosphorescence into the cell, like seaweed spores he'd once seen floating in the southern seas.

He wondered numbly if some cunt back at the kitchens in Harbour End had spiked his food with mushroom powder for a laugh. Wouldn't be Gort, but maybe one of the others. Had to be, because it was either that or—

The water seemed to have detected him again. The mound ceased its circular motion and began to slip like a purposeful jellyfish across the planking towards him. It was over knee height now, and he thought he could discern movement within – soft churning and the spindling turn of pinprick luminescent points.

Fascination chilled away into dread – this was no fucking 'shroom dream.

'Salt Lord,' he croaked, desperate. 'Salt Lord, stand by me now and all—'

But his voice caught and stuck. He started to back away again, and his chains brought him up short. An attempted shout caught in his throat. He could feel his eyes starting from their sockets. His new cellmate was almost on him. He shrank from its glistening curve in dread, wrenching his wrists and ankles on the fetters as he fought to escape.

A terrified, inarticulate scream tore its way finally up his rusted throat, shrilled into the damp prison air, just as the water engulfed his legs.

From down the corridor, another shriek answered. And the clatter of something being dropped. He knew the voice for Gort's, but had no time to care. At his feet, something in the water began to bubble, and a long thin stain swam up through the commotion. It was the colour of blood. He thrashed at his fetters as he saw it, screaming hard now, already feeling the pain, the suction as this thing—

The left manacle gave. His leg came loose.

After four years in chains, it was like the jolt of a dislocated limb. He stumbled with the shock, and his right leg came free, following the left. He floundered and fell, out of the watery mound, backward on his arse on the planking.

His feet . . .

He became abruptly aware that he was still screaming, and shut his mouth with a snap that hurt.

His feet were free.

Up on deck, more screams.

He dared to stop watching the bubble of water – it had made no move to follow him – and snatched a glance downward instead.

His feet were free.

The manacles were gone. He could see the shiny bands of scar tissue they had laced around his legs just above the ankle, could see the full extent of the scarring for the first time. He would have reached down to touch, but the manacles that still held his arms would not allow it. At his side, the mound of water had grown to waist height and now sat there, like a faithful hound. He peered into it, through the distortions of the faintly glowing water to the other side, where his chains lay loose on the floor. They ended abruptly at the bubble's edge, and within there was nothing but smears and turd-like crescents of rust.

The bubble quivered impatiently.

Wonderingly, he looked at the wrist cuffs he had worn for the last four years, then back to the mound of water. He drew a deep breath, raised his arms and sank them into the softly glowing heart of the bubble. It was, he noticed this time, not as cold as seawater should have been and—

Fierce seething around his wrists, and once again he saw the blood-coloured stains spinning off through the water, as centuries of corrosion took place in seconds. He felt the first cuff snap apart and fall and he snatched that arm up to his face, feeling tears now as he saw the unfettered flesh. His other arm was free seconds later and suddenly he was shouting, laughing and crying at the same time. He pushed deeper into the heap of water, crouched so that it covered his body to the shoulders. It was warm and soothing. He ducked his head under and shook it madly. The first bath he had had since capture, unless you counted the buckets of cold water with which his jailers sluiced down prisoner and cell a couple of times each month. He laughed in the water, spewing bubbles. He thrashed his arms about. He erupted from the body of his new friend, kicking and splashing like a child.

The bubble moved abruptly away from him, apparently not pleased with this levity. It cruised pettishly about the cell in figures of eight for a few moments, then retreated to the latrine corner and sank abruptly out of sight down the hole. Sharkmaster Wyr bid it goodbye with one inanely waving hand, then stifled his laughter and shook water from his beard and hair. He listened intently. *Sprayborne* creaked around him, but there was silence aboard. Whatever had been done to Gort was over, and his fellow prisoners had either been similarly silenced or were crouched in their cells, awaiting whatever came next.

On the cell floor, he saw the mound of water's departing dance had severed his chains in a couple of places, leaving handy lengths rusted apart at each end. Quietly, he moved – still dizzy with the unconstrained ease of doing it – and gathered up the nearest length. He crouched as if in a dream, wrapped the links slowly around his fist, pulled them taut with trembling fingers. He'd have to wait until someone came to check on him, but, Hoiran's barbed and twisted cock, when they did, the first man through that fucking door . . .

Splinter and crack – the door exploded outward, torn from its hinges and frame, tossed out into the corridor like a playing card.

'Fuck.'

The curse yanked involuntarily from his lips. He crouched at bay, bare feet planted firm on the damp planking. Rusted chain-link ends swaying fractionally where they hung from his knotted up right hand. He waited to see what would come through the hole where the door had been.

Nothing did.

He straightened slowly up, eyes pinned to the wrenched and splintered doorjamb. He listened hard, heard nothing at all. Crept finally out into the corridor.

In his first year of captivity, he'd dreamed of walking this passage, night after night, only to wake each time to the cold grasp of the chains on his wrists and ankles. Sometimes it happened in vague, mist-tinged tones, but in other dreams, the details were more real – a hidden key smuggled in by one of his men who had somehow escaped, a regal pardon from the Chancellery for some convoluted clerkish reason or other. Sometimes they came for him because there was war brewing in the southern seas, and he the wronged hero of the hour . . .

Sometimes he walked the corridor freely.

Sometimes he fought every inch of the way, and that was better.

Now he had to clench his fist hard on the rusted iron chain, time and again, to remind himself *this was not a dream*. To stop himself from trembling.

He found Gort at the far end of the passage, near the companionway. The jailer sat slumped on the floor amongst his spilled and tumbled pails, back to one of the cell doors. His guts were dumped out in his lap like a meal he could no longer manage. Something had slashed him open side to side, and then torn out his throat. From the bloody handprints and the mess, it looked as if he'd tried to climb the companionway with his guts hanging out, but had been dragged back down by something for the finish.

By some *thing*.

Wyr pursed his lips and looked warily up the companionway to the open deck hatch above. The pale light of day awaited. For a moment, he'd taken his trembling for fear, but now it dawned on him that whatever was waiting up there, he'd gladly face it with no better weapon than the chain in his fist, just for the chance to stand on *Sprayborne*'s deck again and feel the breeze that blew across it. He'd face it and he'd fucking kill it, whatever it was, whatever that took, just so he could stand there a few moments longer in the open air.

He sniffed hard, hefted the chain once more, and then he climbed the companionway as swiftly as his stiff and unaccustomed limbs would allow.

'Good.'

The voice came while he was still clambering out of the hatch, pitched loud across the deck from the port rail. Sharkmaster Wyr scrambled out and pivoted on his bare feet, dropped to a fighting crouch again.

He saw a single cloaked form at the rail, back turned to him. He took a step forward and his heel skidded on something. He swayed and nearly went down, staggered for balance, and some rusted old boarding party reflex kept him on his feet. The figure at the rail didn't move, didn't turn. He saw it wore a long sword sheathed across its back, doubted it could clear the blade with any great speed and felt himself relax just a fraction.

He spared a downward glance, and saw he'd stepped in blood.

Saw, in fact, that the deck was painted with the stuff, splashes and streaks and pools of it, spread between four scattered bodies, one of which was still moving, but not very much.

He did the count, ingrained habits from his plundering days taking over while the disbelief in his head sang a high, whining note like the sound of too much silence in your ears. Four men, all well armed. Two in loose, unremarkable garb with short swords sheathed at the hip, one of them with an eyepatch – Gort's broken down war veterans no doubt, paid mainly to row – and two more in cheap mail vests and open face helmets, apparently armed with short-shafted axehead pikes; by the weapons, Wyr made them for port authority guardsmen. They were all dead, bar the one with the eyepatch, who was down but still trying to drag himself towards the stern, an inch at a time on his belly, in a broad-painted trail of his own blood.

Apparently, not one of the four had managed to get their steel drawn or blooded.

Sharkmaster Wyr raised his head once more to the figure at the rail.

'Salt Lord?' he husked. 'Dakovash?'

'No.' The figure turned now to look at him. 'But I get that a lot. Did you pray to that fucker for something too?'

The face was gaunt and scarred down one cheek, the dark hair gathered back from features that might once have been handsome, but now held only a commanding hunger. The eyes were dead as stones, but there seemed to be no threat in them right now. And something in the narrowed gaze unlocked a chamber inside Wyr, let out what was coiled up inside.

'My family.'

'Ah.'

'I called on the Dark Court for aid; they did not come. My family died in cages instead. I called on the Salt Lord to free me for vengeance. I swore to spill blood from the ocean to the Eastern gate in his name, and he did not come then either.'

'I'm always late,' the figure murmured obscurely. 'Well, you're free now, Sharkmaster Wyr. What will you do with your freedom, I wonder.'

Wyr made himself look away from the figure, look instead at the blood and strewn bodies that lay between them. The man with the eyepatch had almost pulled himself clear of the carnage, and Wyr's rage was abruptly loose in his head. Red veined bolts of it split his vision apart – he strode to where the injured man lay. Stood over him a moment, trembling, then lashed down with the chain his fist was wrapped in. His aim was off, his arm shaky and weaker than he'd reckoned with. It took a couple of blows across the man's hunched shoulders before he got it right. Eyepatch made a choked noise and redoubled his efforts to crawl. The rusted chain caught him in the side of the head, wrapped around. Wyr yanked it loose, flailed down again. Blood flew, the man made a thin, hopeless bawling sound and then, on the fourth or fifth blow, he slumped flat to the deck. Wyr found he could not stop – he went on flailing until the chain links were clotted with gore, and the noise they made on impact was soggy, and the muscles in his arm ached from shoulder to wrist.

In the end, only a fresh fit of coughing stopped him.

He beat the cough out, bracing his free hand on one knee to stay upright. Cleared his throat and spat on the corpse he'd just made. He lifted the chain in his right hand and turned his head sideways to stare at it as it dripped. His face felt hot and wet. His fist opened as if of its own accord and he shook his hand free of the rusted links, watched them pile stickily up on Eyepatch's shoulder.

He got some breath back, got himself upright. Turned back to the figure at the rail.

'This – all this,' he said hoarsely. 'I have you to thank?'

'Yes.'

Sharkmaster Wyr sniffed. Wiped his right hand up over his face and through his hair. It came away streaked with blood.

'And you are not of the Dark Court?'

'Loosely attached, let's say.'

Wyr put out his bloodied hand. 'Then you have my thanks. I am in your debt. Will you give me your name?'

'Ringil Eskiath.' They made the clasp. 'But I'm proscribed the use of that name these days. You can call me Ringil.'

Wyr frowned, chasing vague memory. 'Hero of Gallows Gap? *That* Eskiath?'

'For what it's worth.'

'And . . . you were at the siege as well. They gave you a fucking medal, didn't they? I thought you were dead, I thought you died fighting imperials in Naral. Or Ennishmin.'

'That's one story. Just not an accurate one. Tell me, Sharkmaster Wyr. Now you are free, as you once asked of the Salt Lord, how will you go about obtaining your revenge?'

Wyr cast about in the cold morning light. The other hulks sat chopmasted and rotting in the delta waters around him, like some waiting fleet of ghost vessels raised from the ocean floor. The three plague ships rode at anchor on the outer edge with the promise of death fluttering at their masts. Beyond all that, Trelayne rose on the skyline to port. And to starboard . . .

'The marsh,' he said.

It was a fair swim, and not without its risks, but he knew in his newly freed bones that he'd do it. He'd take sustenance from Gort's spilled buckets, knives from among the slaughtered men for any chance meeting with alligator or dragon eel. And once to the mudflat shallows, it was just wade and stomp and flounder through to the marsh itself, one thigh-deep, sucking step after another and no real risk other than weariness and fading will. Beat those treacherous, seeping enemies and there was really nothing worse to fear – the mudflats were home to thick clouds of stinging flies but he'd endure them, small lizards and mud-weasels and spiders, but he'd kill and eat them raw before they could bite him, and beyond that, well . . .

'I am owed debts among the marsh dwellers,' he added. 'They will hide me while I gather strength. While I gather men and arms.'

'Hmm. There's a war on, had you heard?'

'Against the Empire.' Wyr nodded. 'The jailers have tattled to me. Hinerion is fallen, imperial forces are in the peninsula. What of it? Should I care?'

'Perhaps you should. You may have a hard time gathering much in the way of men or arms right now. Both will be at a premium.' Ringil Eskiath made him a thin, cold smile. 'Who knows? A few more months and perhaps you yourself would have been pardoned back into privateer service.'

Sharkmaster Wyr spat on the blood-streaked deck. 'Yeah – just long enough to sail upriver and burn their fucking Glades mansions to the ground.'

Something unreadable flickered on the other man's face. There and then gone, so fast Wyr thought he might have imagined it. Ringil Eskiath's voice came across the space between them as gently as a lover's.

'There is no need to swim ashore, Sharkmaster Wyr. Nor take shelter in the marsh.' A gesture at the deck around their feet. 'There are arms here, for the taking. And men with vengeance in their hearts below.'

Wyr blinked. 'You'll free my men too?'

'Well,' Ringil examined the nails of one hand. 'It's a tiring trick, that one with the door. Why don't you free them yourself. The jailer had keys, didn't he?'

It dawned on Wyr then how worn down he was, how very tired. How fogged and short of capacity to think straight. Rage and joy had carried him, brought him up unquestioning out of the cell with chain link in his fist and murder in his heart. But now, abruptly, his footing seemed to fall out from under him. He stood numbly, feeling it all for the first time. He understood then, vaguely, that if he had attempted to swim ashore, he would undoubtedly have died in the water.

'I free my men,' he said flatly. 'And then what? We have a pair of axe-head pikes, a handful of knives and short swords between us, and a ship with no masts.'

Ringil nodded out across the water at the other prison hulks. 'In fact, Sharkmaster, you have an entire fleet out there with no masts. All crewed by condemned men of similar stripe to your own. Could you honestly wish for a better-suited force with which to bring your retribution down on the Fair City?'

'I could wish,' Wyr enunciated with bitten force, 'for some fucking masts, and some sails to rig on them.'

'You will not need them. I'll provide your vessels with all the motive force they need. I will break their chains the way I broke yours; I will sail them right into the city harbour and past its defences; I will ram them ashore on the banks of the upper Trel.'

Wyr stared at him.

'You sure you're not sent here by the Dark Court?'

'Not entirely.' Ringil Eskiath stirred and looked back over his shoulder to where Trelayne rose on the horizon. 'But I will hold you to the same terms you offered them. Blood from ocean to the Eastern gate. Can you do that for me, Sharkmaster Wyr?'

A vibrating force seemed to come up through the bloodied planking under Wyr's feet. He felt it climb his legs and leave new strength there, felt it wrap around his belly and chest like a constricting snake, pour icy clarity into his head. He reached down among the corpses and picked up one of the axe-headed pikes.

'Just watch me,' he said grimly.

FORTY-THREE

Later, she'd have time to realise that the ground gave less than a couple of yards under her feet, that rather than collapse, it was slide, and that the real subsidence was outside. But whatever the dragon had done out there, whatever crucial bracing beam or member it had found a way to tear loose, it opened a sink-hole that sucked the rubble out of the gateway like water down a mill race at Spring thaw.

They all went with it.

Kanan Shent tried to grab her hand, but the drop threw them apart before he could reach. She heard him yell, saw him go over on his back, and then she was fighting not to go down herself in the tumble and grinding slide of masonry all around her. Somehow staggering, windmilling her arms, she stayed upright. Kept her feet, tore free each time a boot started to sink into the funnelling carpet of debris. Made it outside into dull grey light and down to the end of what was *actually, Archidi, a fairly shallow slope*—

At which point, she slammed into a vertical block of stone wedged up at the bottom of the slide. She took the impact low across left hip and thigh, was spun and flung down like some sulky child's discarded rag doll. She hit the jagged ground hard – a white hot twang of pain up her side as stitches in her wound tore out, and her head took a glancing blow. She lay there on her side, looking groggily at ragged chunks of masonry inches from her nose.

Triumphant shriek somewhere overhead, and the dragon's shadow fell on her.

Egar rode the drop with the same instinctive horse-breaker's poise he'd ridden out the earth tremor back in Yhelteth that first time. It helped to be drunk, but you could do it sober if you tried. The real problem was being surrounded by seemingly solid walls and floor and ceiling when in reality everything was shaking like a belly dancer's tits. It confused your senses, fooled your expectations. It threw you out.

He didn't have that problem here.

The rubble under him slithered and rumbled directly forward and down. He danced to keep up, leaping steps between what he had to hope were more or less solid chunks and blocks of stone in the flow. Two bounds took him out under the gateway and he knew, there and then, he had to weave or he was dead. Because that fucking dragon had to have *planned*

339

this, knew they were in there, knew exactly how to flush them out, and would pick them off now, like berries off a branch, if he didn't . . .

The beast was on his right. He leapt that way, across the flow of the fall, across its muzzle and aim. Heard a shrill scream, a convulsive gagging sound, and something slopped hotly through the air just ahead of him. He caught the acid sting of it in his nose and eyes, heard it hiss and sizzle as it hit the ground. There was just time to glimpse the dragon, crouched on the edge of the sink-hole slope, jaws still gaping wide for the gob of venom it had just coughed at him. Then he tripped and went headlong amidst the rubble. Clipped his head on a chunk of stone, lay still.

It was probably what saved him.

The dragon came slithering and scrabbling downslope from its perch at the edge of the funnelling debris, kicking down fresh spills of rubble as it came. One massive rear claw crunched down a scant six feet from his head. He felt the masonry he lay on shift with the impact. Reek of sandal-wood and scorching, like a slap in the face. Egar wasn't sure if the creature thought its spit had already taken him down, or it just had other, more mobile, prey to fry. Either way, it wasn't stopping to eat him. It plunged past, uttered another shriek he knew meant attack.

He lurched upright in the loose rubble, clutching the staff lance for support. Blood ran down the side of his face. He saw Archeth below, sprawled full-length in the bottom of the shallow sink-hole, trying dazedly to sit up, right in the dragon's path. Kanan Shent, scrambling down towards her from the other side, more on his arse than his feet, battle axe still in hand but he'd get there late, *too fucking late*, had never faced a dragon before anyway and—

No sign of Nash. Assume he's dead.

Egar did the only thing he could. He raised the staff lance high in his right hand and howled – high and hollow, long drawn out, the ululating Majak berserker call.

'*Turn, motherfucker! Turn! Face me!*'

Fleeting realisation – he'd screamed the words in his people's tongue. The call and the language, rooted as one in the soil of the steppes he'd left behind. The dragon braked its rush, flailed about on the loose surface. No dim-brained blunderer here – a threat to the rear was a threat you'd better turn and face, especially if it makes a noise like that. The Dragonbane dropped the staff lance into both hands, gripped hard at the alloy shaft – *see what this iron demon's like as a bladesmith, shall we, Eg?* – and charged in across the rubble.

He had, he guessed, about a half dozen heartbeats before the dragon sorted itself out, saw what the actual threat was and decided what to do about it. He cut right, in at the tail and hindquarters. It was shit ground, yielding under his feet, but the beast would have to snap its own spine sideways before it could line up another venom spit and hit him in this close. He leapt the last three yards, staff lance up and out to the side as if to pole vault like the tumblers in Ynval Park. He came down hard and uneven, would have staggered, but he buried the leading lance blade in the dragon's haunch with a yell. Saw the Kiriath steel split and splinter scales like they were coins of cheap grey glass.

Now it was the beast's turn to scream.

Shrill and deafening – in this close, it was like tiny knives slicing deep in his head. He'd seen men drop arms and shields in the midst of battle, clap hands fast to their ears, trying to shut out that awful shriek. He gritted his teeth and gouged with the lance, felt the blade shift downward as it sliced through the dragon's flesh. The haunch spasmed and lifted, the beast lashed out with its rear leg, trying to kick loose the source of the pain. It took the Dragonbane up into the air. He hung on with both hands, and the Kiriath edge on his lance blade tore a long line right down the dragon's thigh and out. It dropped him back to his feet again, set him stumbling backward in surprise. Thick, crimson gore on the blade, dripping – a dark cheer rose in him at the sight. *Now, that's a fucking blade, Eg! Now move!*

The dragon screamed again and whipped its tail sideways. Instinct snapped him down in a crouch; he ducked and heard the blow strop through the air overhead. Swung up behind the tail swipe and leapt in close again. For brief seconds, he had the creature blindsided. *The vital truth of combat against dragons,* Gil had once read to him, from some treatise or other he was scribbling at the time – *proximity is your friend. Cuddle up close, it's the one safe place to be. Safe being a relative term.* All right then, Gil. He hacked with the lance, tore into the dragon's hindquarters where the tail thickened to join the body. The scales were softer there, he knew, and the Kiriath blade went through them with no more effort than cutting cloth. He tore the steel loose, reversed the lance's shaft, gouged again with the other blade.

Loud blurting noise, the soft clump of things falling amidst the rubble, and a sudden faint mist around him as the dragon shat itself – he coughed and gagged on the reek, locked up his throat and stumbled to get out of the way. Dragon dung was pretty corrosive when fresh; even the accompanying gas wouldn't do you a lot of good if you inhaled too much of it. *So let's not do that, Eg.* He tried to sprint up the huge scaled flank towards the head and crest, but the creature was turning too rapidly, spinning in its own tracks, stomping and shrilling and lashing out. A glancing blow from the rear limb on that side knocked him flat. He hit the rubble, bit the inside of his cheek almost through with the impact – blood squirted and ran in his mouth, he spat it out, *no time, no fucking time for this, Dragonbane. Get up!*

He shoved himself hastily back to his feet, staff lance at guard across his body, saw the head of the beast come snaking round and down, crest flexed and flaring, one gleaming green eye fixed in a reptile glare behind the thicket of protecting spines . . .

And there, suddenly, was Alwar Nash – in at the dragon's planted fore-limb, shield raised, sword chopping solidly down. Egar saw the blade bite and slice, saw the dragon jerk its claw upward in shock, saw Nash dodge back in nifty zigzag fashion, *not bad, not bad at all, young man. Might make a dragonslayer of you yet.* Egar was already straight back in, grabbing the chance while it lasted, while the beast was distracted. He leapt for where the forelimb would hit as it came back down, had the staff lance up and poised to hack at the rear tendon where it cabled thickly from elbow joint to heel. Kiriath steel – the blade was going to slice right through that shit, hamstring the beast at the front end in a single blow—

It didn't happen that way.

Somehow, the dragon knew he was there. It arched and coiled, backed up at whiplash speed, batted at him with the injured forelimb like a cat at play. It caught him full on – he felt the talons rip through his clothing and the flesh beneath, felt the blow hurl him aside like a chewed bone. He hit hard, dull crunch as more than one rib fractured from the force of it, and he smashed his left hand against ragged stone. His little finger caught and snapped, agony stabbed through his hand and up his arm, he lost his grip on the staff lance. The dragon shrilled above him, he breathed the stink of sandalwood and scorching. Scrabbled desperately to get up. He made it halfway, but there was something wrong with his leg. He squirmed on the uneven ground, the clawed forelimb smashed down. Rubble shattered apart beside him, flying fragments of stonework stung his cheek.

'*Egar!*'

Archeth's voice.

He lifted his head muzzily, turned towards the sound, saw her there fifty feet away. Knives out in either hand, apparently looking to fucking *throw* them at this roaring, trampling, coiling storm of scale and rage. Kanan Shent crouched in front of her, shield up – *yeah, like that's going to do any fucking good* – battle axe raised. The dragon's head swung towards them, then swung further as Alwar Nash charged in past them, broad-sword swinging, a wordless yell let loose . . .

The dragon coughed.

Jaws agape. Almost like it was laughing at them.

The gob of venom spat glistening from its throat, met Nash halfway, splattered him from head to foot. The Throne Eternal screamed, a single wrenched shriek of agony, and then he went down in smoking ruin.

Staff lance – there under the groping fingers of his right hand.

The dragon trod forward, clawed savagely at Nash's smouldering re-mains, shrieking in fury. Egar snarled a grin. He'd seen this before, he knew what it meant. Rage instinct – they'd pissed the beast off. It was no longer thinking straight. Should make things a little easier . . .

On your feet, Dragonbane.

Archeth and Shent over there – gaping disbelief. They were next, if they didn't snap out of it and fucking move. But horror held them locked in place.

Get up! Get up, and kill this fucking thing, Eg. It's what you do.

He gripped with his right hand, dug one end of the staff lance into the ground. Levered himself upright, got to his knees. Laid his left arm over his right and stared at his mangled left paw. The little finger stuck up bluntly from the curve of his hand. *Can't have that, can we?* He leaned in against the lance shaft, freed his right hand for a moment and snapped the finger back down. Ouch. Something wrong with his vision. Oh yeah – blood running down his face again; it was getting in his eye. He grabbed onto the staff lance once more, cuffed the back of his fixed hand clumsily across his brow and then his eye. The blur in his vision wiped clean.

That's more like it.

Low snarling in his throat now as he tried to rise. He leaned hard, came upright, wavering on his feet. His left hand flared agony where he gripped the shaft of the lance. His left leg dragged. The dragon was a good thirty yards off, still clawing what was left of Nash into the ground. He didn't think he could stagger that far before it lost interest in the Throne Eternal's shredded corpse, and looked around for something else to tear apart . . .

Stones.

Raining down from the facade of the ruin above them. Stones and strained, discordant yelling.

He blinked muzzily upward. Saw forms and faces at windows and gaps in the stonework. The rest of his men were up there, roaring abuse, hurling down whatever projectiles they could find. Some of them, he knew, were equipped with newly made crossbows from the Warhelm's armoury. He saw the dragon pause in its clawing rage, tilt and turn to meet the sudden stone downpour, raise one forelimb in a peculiarly human shielding gesture.

He saw the moment for what it offered. Grasped it.

'Archeth!' Bellowing across the gap between them. '*Get out of there!*'

She flinched, looked at him. Grabbed Shent by the shoulder and pointed. Sprinted flat out.

Towards him.

'N—' The cry died in his throat. He saw the dragon coil massively, rapidly about.

Saw it grin.

Rain of stones forgotten, ignored and left for later. Perhaps it caught the flicker of motion as Archeth and the Throne Eternal ran, perhaps it just heard him yell. Perhaps, inside that giant spined cranium, rage ebbed just enough to let whatever cold reptile intelligence normally governed there take the helm again and remember what it was about.

Perhaps not. He'd never know.

He knew it was going to turn Archeth and Shent into smouldering chunks of meat, dead before they fell. He took his desperation, the pain flaring across his body, crammed the whole lot into his throat and lungs, hooked back his head and screamed.

'*Dragon Bane!*'

The dragon's focus must have slipped. It spat and missed. Venom splattered across masonry a couple of yards left and wide of where Archeth's feet had just been. Impact splash got Shent, he stumbled and went down yelling. Archeth, almost to where Egar stood by now, spun about. The dragon's jaws snapped shut with a hollow sound that echoed off the ruin's walls. It jerked its head and snout backwards, for all the world like some suddenly perplexed giant dog. Archeth ducked back to where Shent lay screaming. The dragon leapt forward – an awful, snaking grace to the motion – landed crouched on all fours, looming over Archeth as she tried to drag a flailing Kanan Shent back to his feet. The gigantic head tilted, birdlike, as if trying to get a better look at the two tiny figures it was about to annihilate. Then it drooped low and the jaws gaped open.

Egar crashed in from the side, sliced through the forelimb tendon with a single blow from the staff lance blade. Drenching flurry of reptile blood, and the dragon shrieked. The wounded limb snapped up protectively against its belly. The Dragonbane got in underneath the drooping head. Found the throat.

'*You die, motherfucker!*'

He hacked upward, left-handed, screaming at the pain from his grip. Sliced through the soft scaling, ripped into the throat, gouged out a long, levering wound. Venom from the tubes and chambers within spilled down, mingled with the dragon's blood, splattered over him. He reversed the lance fast, before he could feel that shit eat into him, before he could scream. Struck hard upward, with his good right hand now, *no* pain, *no* fucking pain, Dragonbane, *that's* not pain . . .

'*You! Die!*'

Tore out the rest of the dragon's throat.

Felt it all come down on him, felt the pain come searing.

Felt how it dropped him to his knees, choked the breath in his chest, drove him backward from himself.

Thought he heard his father's voice calling, faintly in the roaring dark.

And – tilting downward now – saw through dimming vision how the rubble he knelt on came barrelling up at his face.

He never felt it hit.

BOOK III
LAST MAN STANDING

'For it is the Mark of a Hero, that Loss leaves no Lasting Scar upon him, that he rejoices in the Glory of Great Deeds done, no Matter the Price that must be paid or the Hard Road taken. Of such Sinew are the Holy Defenders of Empire made, and we give Thanks for our Great Fortune that they have walked among us . . .'

The Grand Chronicle of Yhelteth
Court Bard Edition

FORTY-FOUR

Rumour ran in the slum streets of Trelayne like sewage in the gutters, mingled and colourful in its contents, but mostly shit. Heightened by the tension of war-time nerves, imaginings among the citizenry slipped the common bounds of reason. Gleaned facts were twisted out of all recognition by each tongue that passed them on, fiction was drafted in wholesale where truth would not suffice. Simple narrative gained the grandeur of myth in less time than it took the increasingly stormy day to darken down. By nightfall proper, the taverns were replete with legends in the making and their drink-cadging authors. Spellbound audiences hung on every ornate word.

Hear, then, how the outlawed renegade, imperial lackey and lately cursed dabbler in black magic Ringil – whom none should any longer call Eskiath so as not to sully that long-honoured family name – was finally brought low, defeated and slain in battle at sea by a commission of inner-circle mage privateer captains invoking the long-lost powers of the Vanishing Folk. The Marsh Brotherhood, come lately to patriotic terms with the City Elders at the Chancellery, offered up sorceries only their kind had access to, all in service to the League forces. A cabal sworn to protect the Fair City in time of need stepped in, recruited and anointed the necessary men, gave them ships and sent them out to do magical battle against the renegade and his encroaching imperial forces. And perhaps it was not just Aldrain power that Trelayne summoned in its hour of need, but the flesh and blood Vanishing Folk themselves – because dwenda have been seen, good gentlemen and ladies, seen by many in recent weeks, stalking the streets of the city by night, luminous and lithe and grim. Ask anyone, it is well known.

And so, all along the northern coast of Gergis the night of the engagement against the imperials, lightning reached down from a storm out of the west, striking with harsh white fire into the heart of Aldrain stone circles on cliff-tops and bluffs, stirring strange shadows from the hallowed turf within. At Melchiar Point, out beyond the marsh, a bolt struck directly at the Widow's Watch Stone and split it open from the top. And as the surf burst there in the bang and flash of light on the rocks below, there were those who claimed they'd seen merroigai, breaching and sounding in the chop of the waves like bathing maidens at play, seaweed draped wetly across their plump and comely naked breasts, tangled in their long, flowing locks of hair and . . .

Thank you, kind sir, my thanks indeed. My throat is parched with the telling.

Now – where was I?

But if the black mage renegade was routed, it came at a grievous price. For in the moment that he was struck down – some said by a crossbow blessed in holy fire at Firfirdar's temple in the Glades and fired across the space between ships by a Hinerion nobleman and great white mage named Klithren – the dark outcast invoked the last of his sorcerous strength and climbed the mainmast rigging, where he clung like some monstrous black bat entangled, and with his dying breath hurled a demonic curse upon his killers. Little enough was thought of it at the time. After all, what low villain will not spit and curse when his hour has come around? But some few men among those who witnessed Ringil's passing were heard to remark that they felt the cold touch of a shadow fall on them with the dying renegade's words. And that same night, plague crept among the surviving vessels, walked the decks among the resting heroes like a wraith, touched each brave privateer without exception and laid them all low.

Perhaps the infection emanated from the slain corpse of the renegade himself, brought home as trophy with tongue and eyes put out, and fingers struck off at the roots. Or perhaps it came on an evil wind from the south. Whatever the case, now the plague ships sit at anchor out beside the prison hulk fleet, easily seen from the southern wall for those who doubt my word, flying pennants of distress and in bitter exile from the Fair City that birthed their crews. Yes, under grim banners, Trelayne's heroes of the high sea now lie stricken, and unhallowed magic, though defeated, has left its tragic black stain for all to see . . .

The *rain*, m'dear? Sorcerous? Admirable imagination, truly, in one so fair and, uhm, unspoiled, if I may say so, by her dealings with the world. But I think not. The storm is unseasonal in its force, indeed – just listen to it! And damnably inconvenient, I must say, if it's not eased by the time I must make my way to the poor garret where I lay my head some distance from here, if no closer, kinder shelter may be had, dear lady, by a poor wordsmith and romantic at heart.

But sorcerous? A *sorcerous* rainstorm? Hardly.

Amidst waters so lashed by the downpour that they seemed to boil and steam in the fading evening light, the prison hulks slipped their chains one by one, rode the low swell, and were borne in towards Trelayne on no current Sharkmaster Wyr could ever remember pulling that way across the delta.

'Don't worry about it,' Ringil told him. 'You'll get where you're going. Just concentrate on holding up your end once we get there.'

Wyr looked bleakly up at him from where he was crouched at *Sprayborne*'s blunted prow, watching their progress. He was drenched to the skin, but seemed not to care. He held the axehead pike in his arms almost like a nursing mother with an infant, and he drew a smooth, flat whetstone repeatedly down the long, curved edge of the blade. It made a harsh scraping sound on each stroke that he appeared to find soothing.

'I'm a man of my word,' he said.

The city came glimmering wetly at them through curtains of rain – harbour lights in marching sequence along the sea walls and the wharfs that flanked the river mouth; the dim outline of buildings with lighted windows rising beyond. Somewhere further back in all that, the Chancellery squatted on the closest thing Trelayne owned to a hill, commanding views across the city to both the ocean and marsh. But those overlooking towers and their lights were lost altogether in the murk. Gil had called down the rain in preference to summoning a fog because he reckoned it would clear the streets for him, but he had to admit it shrouded things pretty well into the bargain. There'd be watchmen, of course, up on the harbour walls, but their visibility was going to be way down in this weather, and what they'd be watching for mostly, squinting against the lash of the rain when they could be bothered, was the loom of masts and sails, neither of which the prison hulks had to offer. By the time the low profile of their hulls drew attention, Gil was hoping it'd be too late for anything other than panic.

His own ships, hanging back in the wake of the hulk fleet, could skulk in once the mess was made. Still flying their plague pennants, they'd likely cause almost as much dismay among the populace as the ghostly driven prison hulks that preceded them.

And by then, the loosed prisoners would be on the rampage through Trelayne like soldiers given leave to sack.

House Eskiath, your outlaw son is home.

Light flickered low in his field of vision – the mast lantern on a fishing skiff caught out in the storm and struggling for haven. *Sprayborne* was on them before they could react, looming out of the swathes of rain, almost trampling them into the ocean under its bow. Ringil leaned hard over the rail and peered down, saw three pale faces staring back up at him as the hulk shouldered past. One of them looked to be not much older than a boy. Wide-eyed shock and accusation in the rain-whipped features, Gil caught the look and found himself hooked to it. Involuntarily, he swung around to watch as the skiff passed along *Sprayborne*'s waist, then fell away into the murk to stern, taking something with it he could not define. For a couple more moments, he could make out the agitated swing of the lantern light, as the skiff rocked on the chop from the hulk's passage. Then the storm came and took the last glimmer of light away in raging wind and rain.

'My lord?'

Let's hope they steer well clear before one of the other hulks flattens them.

Yeah, and while we're at it, black mage, let's hope your merroigai are all too well fed or busy towing to stop, capsize the skiff and drag all of three of them under for a snack.

'My lord!'

349

A firm hand on his shoulder through the storm. Noyal Rakan, tugging him round. A depth of concern and adoration on the boyish face he could barely stand to look at.

'The men are mustered and ready, my lord.'

'Right.' He cleared his throat. Wiped some of the rain off his face. 'Yeah. Coming down.'

He'd taken the same approach to picking his landing party as he had the wedge that helped him put Klithren's men to flight on the sloping streets of Ornley. He'd asked for volunteers. Now two dozen men awaited him in ranks on *Sprayborne*'s main deck, mostly marines but one or two Throne Eternals sown into the mix. They stood at ease, mailed and stone-faced against the rain, darting occasional looks of cool disdain at the freed pirates who huddled in the corners of the deck, jeering and muttering amongst themselves. There was a tension in the air that might have led to fighting if the prisoners had been a little less starved, or had had more than one weapon per half dozen men.

But they didn't.

Ringil came down the companionway behind Rakan, tipped a nod at Klithren where he stood at one front corner of the ranked assembly. Rakan stepped forward.

'My lord Ringil will address you now!' He had to shout it against the bluster of the wind. 'Salute!'

They did, a bit raggedly. Ringil took the cue, raised his voice.

'Empire men,' he called. 'We are at war, and we find ourselves in the heart of the enemy's domain. I imagine some soldiers might count this a misfortune. Do you?'

'*No!*' Ready chorus – he'd heard Rakan stoking them earlier.

'We are here to reclaim those noble prisoners taken from us by sneak attack, and to strike a blow at the northerners' arrogance that they will not soon forget. Are you ready to do these things?'

'*Yes!*'

'Now, I anticipate some small resistance to these aims . . .' He let the grim laughter break and run among them, waited it out. 'And I imagine we may have to show the locals some blood before they'll let us have what we want. Are you ready for *that?*'

'*Yes!*' Bellowing now.

'*Are you ready for blood?*'

'*Yes! Ready!*'

He nodded. 'Then follow me, and I'll see what I can do.'

Cheers.

He threw out a salute, turned them back over to Rakan for weapons check. Went back to the companionway, had one foot set on the bottom rung when Klithren sidled up to him, face closed up against the rain like a fist. Gil beat down a sudden tension in his stomach, made himself relax. Klithren leaned in close.

'Not telling them about the dwenda, then?' he asked in Naomic.

'Not unless there's cause to, no.'

'And you don't think there's cause? Behind the Chancellery stand the cabal, we both know that. And if the dwenda stand behind the cabal as you say they do, they aren't going to take kindly to you marching in and taking away their bargaining counters.'

'We'll deal with that as and when it arises.'

'Yeah?' Klithren grinned through the ribbons of rain on his face. 'When's that, black mage? When we're at the Chancellery gates and they jump us?'

'We're not going to the Chancellery,' Ringil told him shortly, and turned away to climb the ladder.

Sprayborne burst into Trelayne harbour like the risen ghost of some long wrecked warship from the city's embattled past. Mastless, darkened, she cleared the harbour wall to starboard close enough that a brave man could have leaped down onto her deck as she passed. But no one did. Ringil heard shouting, saw movement on the wall and torches jerking about as watchmen ran up and down in disbelief, but that was about it. The hulk swept in past the confusion, crossed the rain-thrashed harbour without slowing at all, and trod down the timber boom fastened across the inner river entrance. Creak and splintering crack of the wood giving way under the bow. There were some vessels the boom might have kept out, but *Sprayborne*'s hull was long uncared for, thickly encased in barnacles that gave it a shell like iron. The whole ship rose in the water an instant, then crunched solidly back down and ploughed on through.

Wyr's ragged crew roared.

As they cleared the river mouth, Ringil looked back along the mastless deck and saw the second hulk come careering in behind them, heeling sharply in the harbour space, aimed directly at the western wharf and the merchantmen moored there. There was no time to see the impact, *Sprayborne* was already at the first bend in the river, and he lost any view he'd had behind the slum tenement facades that lined the bank. But he thought he heard the grinding crunch it made, thought he heard a second collective roar of triumph float loose in the night.

Bare-handed, half-starved wretches unchained, celebrating a release they'd only ever expected to see in death.

Yeah, and if they don't get hold of some decent weapons pretty sharpish, that's still going to be the way it ends.

Because if *Sprayborne*'s crew were poorly armed, they were princes in plate compared to the liberated prisoners aboard the other hulks. There'd been no more supply boats to ambush – the weather he'd summoned had seen to that – and while the lack of attention made freeing the convicted men that much easier, the corresponding lack of jailer's escorts to murder and shake down for steel had meant a real dearth of arms. The best most of the prisoners could do were sections of rusty chain or long splinters of half rotted deck timber prised up and fitted out with ship's nails through the business end. All right for a shock attack, maybe, but once the Watch woke up and found its feet, well . . .

There were prisoners aboard the hulks, Gil knew, whose minds and wills were long ago broken, others whose crimes never involved violence of any sort. Some of these would cower, some would hide, some would skulk and run. Some might never even crawl out of the cells whose doors he'd torn off their hinges. But crewing the hulks alongside these were a majority of men – and a tiny handful of women – once counted lethally dangerous by the courts. With luck, some of them would still merit that judgement. And no small number of those would have been pirates once, the kind for whom storming a harbour was second nature. They'd manage somehow, they'd work something out. Beat down and butcher the first few squads of watchmen while the element of surprise lasted, frisk them and take what weapons they carried. Break into the harbour-side arsenal, maybe – in time of war like this, it had to be stocked to the ceiling. Gear up, carry fire and steel onward, into the heart of the city.

What they did after that, Ringil told himself, he didn't much care. Just so long as it lasted the time he needed to get in and out.

The rathole tenements and rickety jetty walkways of Harbour End began to thin out, gave way to the more salubrious housing of halfway decent neighbourhoods like Ekelim and Shest. Rain had driven other traffic off the water, and the people off the promenades. He saw lights in windows, smoke from chimneys, but little other sign of life. Once, down at the water's edge alongside a jetty, he thought he saw a ferryman huddled in a cloak at his oars. Thought he saw the shadowed opening under the ferryman's hood turn to follow him as they passed.

He shivered and looked away.

Sprayborne drifted on upriver like a phantom in the murk.

By the time they got to the Glades district, its manicured mangroves and ornamental jetty water frontage, there'd been a couple of graunching knocks to the hull, and Ringil was starting to worry about draught. A generation or two ago, the noble families whose mansions littered the Glades all owned warehouses across the river and it was quite customary for League merchantmen to come up this far to load and unload. But the custom waned – cheaper land for warehousing came up for grabs near the newly expanded harbour, shipmasters preferred not to navigate the twists and kinks in the river if they didn't have to and started charging a premium to do it. Anyway, the old plots across the river could now be sold at a huge profit as new wealth crowded in, seeking upriver cachet. Great stone mansions sprouted on the warehouse side – though none quite as imposing as the originals they aped on the opposite bank – and river traffic dwindled. Silt built up and was no longer dredged out, as a couple of incautiously overloaded mason's barges discovered to their cost back in Ringil's youth.

Later of course, with the war, a lot of that new wealth collapsed again and the land was reacquired in the reconstruction, designated for thanksgiving temples and shrines, ornamental gardens and expensive memorials to the noble clans whose sons had done, if the truth were known, not much more than a single figure percentage of the dying. It was about the time Gil left town, so he didn't know if there'd been any dredging done since. *Sprayborne* was a raider, not a merchantman, even fully laden she'd have been a pretty shallow draught vessel, and now, with no cargo but the skin and bone of her starved down, decimated crew – plus, okay, a scant two dozen imperial shock troops with assorted outlaws, mercenary turncoats and faggot degenerates for officers – she was travelling light indeed. But then there was that thick crust of barnacles to think about, and whatever clearance they had below that, things had to be getting pretty cramped for the merroigai towing them . . .

He spotted the stretch of waterfront he'd been looking for. Laid hands on the starboard rail, leaned out to scan for signs of life. *Sprayborne* responded, as if to the rudder she'd been stripped of four years past. The hulk angled and heeled, she surged in hard, rammed into the bank between two of the carefully kept, stilt-fingered mangroves. Crushed a dinky little jetty under her bow and jammed in place. Ringil barely kept his feet, and he'd seen it coming, was hanging onto the rail at the time. Down on the main deck he heard curses and bodies tumbling.

'Ride's over,' he told Sharkmaster Wyr. 'Hold your men until I give the word. I've got some instructions you need to follow.'

The pirate uncoiled from where he'd been crouched. It was a lot like watching a reptile peon get up from its nesting hollow. He hefted the axe-head pike. 'I thought the instructions were blood from the ocean to the Eastern gate. Now all of a sudden you want to get particular?'

'There's a mansion nearby,' Ringil said evenly. 'A couple of hundred yards in. It has a family name graven into the gateposts, in the unlikely event you or any of your men can read, and Hoiran and Firfirdar in effigy on top if you can't. Neither you nor your men will go anywhere near that mansion. Do I make myself clear?'

Wyr bared his teeth. 'Let me guess. Eskiath house?'

'Just so. That's where I'm going with my men, and I want a clear run at it. Is that understood? Or are we going to have a problem?'

A shrug. 'I won't get in the way of any man's revenge, if doesn't cross my own.'

'Good. Then we are in accord.'

Down on the main deck, Rakan already had the men formed up and ready to disembark. Boarding rope ladders borrowed from *Dragon's Demise* were tossed tumbling over the side as Gil arrived. Wyr's starveling pirates milled about, watching. Ringil nodded and Rakan called it. The imperials went over the rail and down, began to pick their way out of the tangle of mangrove roots below. Klithren went with them, Rakan hung around, gaze mistrustful on the freed pirate crew. Gil made a smile for him.

'You go. I'm fine, I'll be right there.'

The Throne Eternal bowed his head, swung over the rail and clambered handily down to join his fellow imperials. Ringil stood for a long last moment on *Sprayborne*'s grotty main deck, staring around at the ragged, barely clad company of men he'd freed and was about to unleash. His final gift to the fair city of Trelayne – pallid, fish-belly faces staring back, eyes sunken and feverish-bright with rage, filthy thinning hair plastered down in rat's-tails by the rain. Bodies still hunching instinctively from long confinement and casual brutality, manacle-scarred wrists and ankles on limbs like the gnawed bones of a fowl platter. Ribcages you could count each rib on from yards away. Closer in they stank to a man, despite all the rain could do.

He'd seen corpsemite-animated zombies that didn't look much worse than this. Stalking the manicured paths and pastures of the Glades, they'd probably be taken for such.

How the fuck did it come to this, Gil?

He looked at them, as if they might give him the answer. But they only muttered and growled amongst themselves like feral dogs, and none would meet his gaze. He grunted, gave up and looked up to the foredeck above, where Sharkmaster Wyr stood in command.

'All yours. Blood from ocean to Eastern gate. You make them pay.'

Wyr lifted the pike and jerked his chin in what Gil later deciphered as a salute. 'Die well, my lord.'

It was an age-old commendation to battle from the founder legends of Trelayne, resuscitated and made fashionable again during the war. Odd, coming out of the mouth of a man set to slaughter and burn his way across the heart of his own city, but Ringil supposed he was hardly in a position to judge. He nodded soberly, uttered the formula response.

'As well as circumstance and the gods allow.'

'Hey, fuck the gods. This is what we've got left. You die well, sir.'

Ringil shrugged. 'Yeah, you too.'

He went over the rail.

In the tree-shaded dark of the Glades, they were spared the worst of the rain, though it hammered unseen into the foliage over their heads and made a sound like pebbles tossed constantly against glass. They ignored the winding ornamental paved paths Gil knew from his youth, cut directly across the sward instead. It was easy going, and the few inhabitants they came across ran screaming from their advance. The first time it happened – a young, bedraggled woman servant, out cutting marsh mint for the kitchen – the vanguard marines made to follow and bring her back. Ringil put out a barring arm, shook his head.

354

'Let her tell her tale. She'll magnify numbers, likely make trolls of us too. The more panic she sows, the better.'

Grins from the marines. The idea appealed. They let the other chance encounters run without comment. They tramped on across the sodden turf, dodged the odd thicket of mangrove roots, scared a few more servants and came, finally, upon house lights through the gloom.

The iron-spiked gates were chained up, as he'd expected. He tipped a bleak look up at the statues on the posts – King and Queen of the Dark Court, fanged and tusked Hoiran, Firfirdar in flames, angled slightly in towards each other, as if enjoying a sly exchanged glance amidst the more po-faced business of watching over the affairs of all humankind.

Yeah, well – watch over this.

He laid hands on the wet links of the chain, he uttered the glyph. The iron rusted and crumbled and broke apart under his touch. The gates blew back on their hinges as if hurled by the wind. They hit the blocking posts set to catch them at the sides of the carriage path with a resounding iron clang.

Bit overstated, Gil – you could have just pushed them open.

Did the time-worn grin on Firfirdar's graven face broaden just the faintest bit?

He inclined his head fractionally at the effigy's stony gaze, then stalked past it and up the gravel path, towards the house that once gave him birth.

FORTY-FIVE

They hauled the Dragonbane out from under the corpse of the dragon he'd slain, but by then there wasn't a lot left. Venom had eaten him down to the bone at arms and skull and shoulders, left his ribcage exposed in patches against the charred meat of his chest. The stench of cooked flesh was overpowering, even the sandalwood reek of the dead dragon couldn't mask it.

She squatted beside him. Stared numbly down at the damage and the mess, at the skull's anonymous rictus grin. Tried to make sense.

'Not a shit death,' she whispered.

Could have fooled me, grinned the skull.

Between two of the charred ribs, something glinted at her. She squinted closer, took a couple of uncertain moments to work out what she was look-ing at – the three elemental coin, the one they'd tossed to choose who'd play decoy. The venom had scorched apart the pocket he'd stowed it in along with the rest of his clothing, had even melted the coin itself a little around the edges, glued it into the seared flesh. She touched the metal with one finger, and in that moment it dawned on her suddenly how he'd faked that toss.

Let the coin fall into the cup of your palm. Single, lightning-swift beat while you snatch a glance. If it came up the way you wanted, you let it lie, flexed your palm flat and offered it for inspection. If not – slap it across onto the back of your other hand, uncover it there instead.

Walked into that one, Archidi.

The wraith of a smile at her lips. She blinked rapidly, sniffed hard. Let the coin lie where it was, kissed her fingertips where they'd touched it and laid her hand gently back on the blackened ribcage.

Presently, the Majak came across and stood by the corpse. One of them held Egar's staff lance. She knew none of their names, understood almost none of what they murmured to each other. There were fragments, names of deities she'd heard before – *Urann, Vavada, Takavach* – words for fire and light, a phrase they used more than once that sounded like it might have been their dialect version of the Skaranak term for the band, the Sky Road that the Majak dead must walk. She supposed they were talking about where the Dragonbane was now.

Because he sure as shit isn't here anymore.

She snorted back the tears behind her eyes, levered herself back to her feet. The Majak gave her respectful space.

'We can't—' She cleared her throat. 'We can't take him with us. I'm sorry. There's enough to carry as it is, and we still don't know what's down in that pit.'

The Majak who held the lance shook his head. 'The whole world shelters beneath the Sky Road's bow,' he said in accented Tethanne. 'It will take the Dragonbane home, as well from here as any other place of rest.'

She nodded tepidly.

'Would he want burial?' one of the others asked. 'It's custom among the Skaranak. They cairn their dead. Would he want that?'

'I don't know,' she said, because she didn't.

The Majak with the lance coughed a laugh. He nodded at the slumped mountain of dragon-flesh behind them.

'Memorial enough there, I reckon. I'll bet no Skaranak that ever lived had a cairn the size those bones are going make.'

'The bones don't last,' she said quietly. 'They rot away with time. Everything does, apart from the teeth and the gut lining. It's the venom. In ten years, there'll be nothing left to show a dragon died here.'

'And the skin, the scales?' The one who seemed to know Skaranak custom looked pretty put out. His hand strayed down to a pouch at his belt. She guessed he'd taken time, like some others among the men, to hack off some small trophy. 'Doesn't the skin last?'

Archeth shrugged. 'Soak it in water for a day, scrub it well on both sides. Hang it out to dry in the sun. That usually does the trick.'

'Water?' The Majak cast about the grey, rubbled landscape, dismayed. 'In the *sun?*'

'Yeah.' She turned to walk away, stopped. 'You know what? We are going to bury him. Get him up out of this fucking crater, find someplace with a decent view. That's where we dig.'

They laid him out so he'd face the rising sun, if it ever came up free of this endless fucking cloud cover. The Majak consulted amongst themselves, then decked the grave out with a couple of judiciously chosen talismans. They drove the staff lance down hard between the stones at the foot of the cairn they'd made, packed it tight with smaller chunks of masonry, so it stood a rigid yard and a half upright, gleaming in the pallid light.

They buried Alwar Nash alongside, laid the Throne Eternal's sword and shield on the piled rubble the way his family would have done on his tomb back home. The men stood around, said what words there were. Selak Chan led the rest of the Throne Eternal in formal prayer. The Majak chanted and ululated a bit.

The rest drifted off down to the dragon corpse to see about souvenirs.

Archeth stood like a statue at the cairn, head bowed, as stiff and motionless as the upward jutting staff lance in front of her. Couldn't believe she was leaving him here. Couldn't yet believe that he *was* here, that those charred, buried remnants were all that was left of the Dragonbane. It was

357

as if she expected him back at any moment, was just waiting for him to stick his head round the corner of the ruin, wink at her, grin.

*What? You thought I'd go down that easy? It's Dragon*bane, *Archidi. Dragon* Bane. *Not Dragonsbitch. I used to kill these fucking things for a living.*

You certainly killed the fuck out of that one.

Hey – all part of the service.

The Majak and the Throne Eternal finished up their respective rituals, cast uncertain glances in her direction and then left her alone. She heard them muttering amongst themselves as they headed down the slope to join the others. Rain blew about in the wind, specked at her face. Overhead, the clouds were in turmoil – massing thicker and darker, hastening off somewhere else, leaching what miserable light there was from the day and taking it with them.

She took the hint. Followed the men down.

She found the bulk of them gathered at a cautious distance from the dead dragon, squatting or standing in their respective groups. One or two were still toying with the mementoes they'd carved from the corpse. She saw the Majak she'd talked to about hide curing – seemed he'd thought better of his initial trophy and somehow managed to gouge loose a fang from the dragon's jaw instead. He was busily flensing the root end, scraping off the last stubborn leavings of tissue with his knife. He nodded at her as she arrived, perhaps in thanks.

Yilmar Kaptal stood apart, statue still, staring at the dragon as if it might come suddenly back to life. She cleared her throat, in advance this time, and like the others he turned to look at her. She lifted her voice, clear and loud against the ruffling wind.

'We have done what honour we can for those who gave their lives. It's time now to give their sacrifice meaning.' She pivoted about and pointed to where the fire sprite hung about at the sink-hole rim. 'That way is our means of returning home. The path is cleared, it remains only to walk it.'

A couple of the privateers exchanged a look. One of them leaned and muttered something in Naomic to one of Tand's crew. The mercenary nodded soberly at what he was hearing, cleared his throat and spoke in Tethanne.

'They want to know, my lady, what if there's another dragon waiting for us down in the pits.'

She shook her head. 'Dragons are solitary in adulthood. That much we did learn in the war. One this size would not tolerate any competition within its range.'

'But they act as brood mothers to the reptile folk.' Another mercenary, pitching unhelpfully in. 'On the beaches at Demlarashan, they protected the lizard advance.'

'Yes, that's true.'

'Then there may be Scaled Folk lairing in the pits.'

'Then we'll kill them,' snapped Kanan Shent. He was banged up from the fight with the dragon, had two fingers on his left hand wrapped and splinted, wore thick bandages around both legs, right arm and head. But there was a feverish, impatient gleam in his eyes. 'As we killed them yesterday, as we slew this beast here today.'

'We lost nine men yesterday,' someone called out. 'Fighting on open ground. In those pits, we could find ourselves—'

Shent rounded on the speaker. 'Will you stand here bleating about losses and risk like some merchant negotiating cost? You were quick enough to cut trophies from the dragon that you did not slay, but will not face creatures one fiftieth its size? Did Menith Tand hire fighting men for his guard, or faggots?'

'Hey, fuck you, imperial. You don't—'

'*Gentlemen!*'

No need to force it, there was enough undischarged grief and rage in her to fuel the sack of a city. They heard it in her voice, saw it in her face when they jerked round to look. They shut up. She worked at not showing her surprise, grabbed the advantage and kept going.

'There will *be no need*, gentlemen, for these deliberations.' She gestured once more up at the waiting fire sprite. 'Our guide has consistently steered us clear of the Scaled Folk and any other dangers we might face. Our only encounter came when we did not wait for its lead, and we were saved from the dragon because it held us here among the ruins until the beast showed itself. I think it's safe to conclude that it will not now lead us into ambush.'

They quietened, but she spotted a couple of mutinous faces among the privateers. She held back a sigh. *Well, you did warn me about this, Eg. Could have wished for better timing, but . . .*

'You.' She indicated the mercenary who'd acted as translator. 'Ask those two at the back what their problem is.'

Tand's man glanced across the gathered men and caught the same expressions she had. He raised his hands in a gesture that needed no translation. The scowling privateers looked taken aback. There was a brief exchange in lilting Naomic, the mercenary, from the look of it, weighing in with a few brusque comments of his own above and beyond the brief Archeth had given him. One of the privateers got angry, the mercenary trampled his words down. There was some bristling on both sides, then Tand's man waved his arm disgustedly and turned away, back to Archeth. He looked embarrassed.

'Well?'

'They, uh – my lady, they say they are not happy about following the fire guide. They do not trust the demon spirit at An-Kirilnar. They say if it murdered Sogren Cablehand on a whim, why should it not intend to do the same with them.'

Archeth shot the privateers a dirty look. 'Little late in the day for these qualms, isn't it?'

'What I told them, my lady.'

She drew a deep breath. What was it Gil was always saying? *The men under your command may well hate you.* And then some rambling drivel about learning to live with it, leaving it alone, transmuting it somehow into loyalty in the heat of battle, whatever. Didn't sound very likely, but then Gil had led some very hard-boiled men into some very tight spots, and somehow always managed to come out the other side alive.

Let's see if we can't do the same thing here, Archidi.

She marshalled the slop of anger and loss inside, harnessed it again. She jerked her chin at the glowering privateers.

'Tell them,' she said, with biting force. 'That the Great Spirit at An-Kirilnar did not act on a *whim* when it killed Sogren Cablehand. It acted for *me*. And it continues to act for me through this fire guide. If they do not want to follow Sogren to his fate, then there's a very simple way for them to avoid it. *Obey me, in all things.*'

The mercenary gaped. She saw a similar look on a fair few other faces among the Tethanne speakers.

'Make that clear to them,' she said.

'Uh . . . Yes, my lady.'

'And then go get your pack on.' She turned her head slowly to take in the whole gathering. 'All of you. Go find your packs and gear up. We're going home. Throne Eternal Alwar Nash and the Dragonbane died for that. So did the nine men who fought and died yesterday. I will not piss away their sacrifice, and nor will any of you. *We are going home.*'

They got down to the nearest edge of the pits without incident. There was some on and off muttering in the ranks, mainly among the privateers, but it died away as they got up close to the great black metal clamping arms, and the scale of the Kiriath construction dawned on them. The clamps were three times the height of a man where they came up out of the pit, tailing off only gradually to something you could have hauled yourself up onto when they were nearly fifty yards back from the lip. They crushed the Aldrain stone under their weight, she saw where dressed blocks of masonry had shattered and sheared.

She moved up closer to the lip of the pit, peered down and saw a dizzying progression of scaffolding built along the inner surface, reaching away downward and out of view. There were interlocking stanchions and cross-struts, snaking cables and pipes the width of a man's waist, huge angled dishes of alloy and wire, whole tilted panels of mesh as big as a mainsail, all giving back a sheen of purple or blue where they rose high enough into the neck of the pit to catch the light. She felt the steady rise of warm air up the shaft like a summer breeze on her face and hands. She caught the brewing stack reek of alloy husbandry below.

Dragonbane's right—

Was, she reminded herself silently. Lips pressed hard together on the ache. *Dragonbane* was *right. Looks like Kaldan Cross.*

But as if Kaldan Cross were some kind of rough scale model built in advance, a quick proof of concept before the real work began. Human eyes had to work hard to see the bottom of the pit at Kaldan Cross – and idle human superstition said there was none – but it was there. Now, she stared downward into the shadowed depths and even she could make out no end to this shaft. The scaffolding below her was broad and extensive in its own right, it would have filled the Kaldan excavation almost to the centre. Here – she followed the broad sweep of the pit's lip around like the shore of a minor lake – here it clung to the edges going down like the flimsiest of lace borders on a court gown collar. It extended no thicker in comparison to the excavation's full extent than the growth of moss coating an old well shaft.

You could hide an entire colony of Scaled Folk down there, Archidi.

Even a couple of dragons might manage to co-exist across that much space, if the reptile packs they belonged to learnt to stay out of each other's way, lived on opposite sides of the pit, say.

If we really have to climb down through all that . . .

She made her face stone. Looked round for the fire sprite.

'Over here, my lady.'

Kanan Shent, calling and beckoning from back towards the tail end of the clamping structure. The sprite hovered and flickered there beside the alloy wall. The Throne Eternal gestured with his injured hand.

'It refuses to move from here, my lady. And there seem to be colours in the metal, as there were at An-Kirilnar . . .'

Stone, stone, your face is stone. Nothing here surprises you, Queen of Kiriath steel and murderous demonic spirits. You take it in your stride.

She came forward and peered at the black iron surface, now mottled and bleaching into lighter shades, colours shifting about like chemicals spilled on a rainwater puddle in a laboratory courtyard at Monal. She nodded briskly.

'This is our way down.'

She spoke the colours out in clearly enunciated sequence. Each one winked out as she named it, returning the alloy finally to its blank black norm. Then nothing. Long moments, piling up in the quiet and nothing else to see – she made herself wait it out, keenly aware of the gazes fixed on her as the seconds slipped by. They'd had the same delay at An-Kirilnar. She kept her face impassive until—

Ah.

A thin tracery whispered awake on the black alloy surface – sweeping, spilling, unreeling lines like the rapidly sketched outline of a rose in bloom but taller than a man. She caught the tiny seething sound it made, down near the limits of her hearing, heard the hissing intensify as the sketch lines deepened into cracks, then began to split apart. The whorl patterning in the centre of the design seemed to roll and fold into itself, down to one side and gone. The hissing stopped. Warm orange light sprang up in a hollow interior space.

She stuck her head inside and peered around. Saw a tall, vaulted corridor with curving sides leading from a blank bulkhead on her left and back the forty odd yards towards the edge of the pit – though she thought, uneasily, that it seemed to reach a lot further than that. Further, in fact, than was possible, given the way the clamp bent and dropped away down the side of the shaft. The floor was the same pentagonal-patterned iron latticework they'd walked on to reach An-Kirilnar, touched here by fleet-footed shadows and orange glimmerings that chased each other merrily away down the tunnel. She frowned for a moment, not understanding the effect, until it hit her that the glow she'd seen from outside was caused by distinct blots of light and dark that marched away in repeating sequence at about shoulder height along the sides of the bore, as if to hurry her in that direction. As if an endless procession of ghosts with invisible torches moved methodically down the tunnel already, and only the reflection of their flames could be seen, puddled in the curving alloy surface of the walls and glinting off the latticed metal underfoot.

The fire sprite slipped past her shoulder and into the tunnel. It danced three or four yards down the bore, blending its colours to match the lights on the walls, then stopped and hung there flickering.

She pulled her head back out.

'Right, this is us. Selak Chan, you take the lead, I'll catch you up once we're all inside. Single file, give each other plenty of space. There shouldn't be any trouble now – we're on Kiriath ground. But that doesn't mean you can't trip over or fall off something, so keep your wits about you. No gawking.'

She stood at the entrance and counted them in, something she'd never bothered to do while Egar was alive. Thirty-five men, if you allowed Yilmar Kaptal in that category. Not much of a command, but still more than she wanted. She waited for them all to file past her, nodding them in if any chose to meet her eyes, trying to lock names to faces where she knew them. It might be important later.

The Throne Eternal and marines all bowed as they passed. So, unexpectedly, did the Majak and some of Tand's crew.

Then, towards the end of the line, one of the privateers who'd complained earlier about Sogren's death tried to stare her down, break her gaze with his scowl as he approached. On a different day, she might have laughed. *Yeah, stare down the burnt black witch, why don't you?* He'd clearly never looked into Kiriath eyes before. She gave him back his stare, well aware of the effect her darkling kaleidoscope pupils had on humans unused to them. He flinched and looked away, well before it was his turn to duck past her into the tunnel.

She heard his fellows jeering at him in the echoing space, as they followed the file down.

When the last man was in, she took one lingering look around at the shattered cityscape, the bleak mounds of rubble and forlorn crag outcrops of architecture still standing, the doom her people had brought down on this place. The dragon corpse and the cairns were hidden from view behind the ruins they'd sheltered in, as if already subsumed into the larger, more ancient death that held sway amidst all this wreckage. For one aching moment, she wanted to run back up the rubble hillside and stand again at the Dragonbane's grave, give him one more chance to *quit fucking about, Eg, get up out of that hole in the ground and come with me.*

'Come on, Archidi.'

For just one shaky, ecstatic moment, she was unsure who was speaking to her.

'We're all done here, there's nothing left.'

Her own voice, raised firm against the blanketing quiet. But it sounded nothing like her, and she could not tell what it meant by that *we* – if it was referring to her new command, her dead friendship, or her ancestors in their awful, obliterating triumph.

She turned away and hurried into the tunnel.

FORTY-SIX

He wasn't very surprised to find armed men blocking his path; he'd perhaps even been courting something of the sort. Certainly, someone would have heard those gates slam back – the clang they made, you'd have to be deaf not to. And that someone would have duly sounded the alarm, which would in turn bring out the guard. Like most noble houses, the Eskiath family seat retained its own men-at-arms on site, and now, with the war on, they'd be twitchier than usual, eager to justify their exemption from the levy, their privileged escape from conscription to points of slaughter further south. They'd jump at the drop of a thin cat, let alone the sound of the front gates being smashed open by an overly flamboyant black mage.

That cheap dramatic streak of yours is going to get you in some trouble you can't get out of one of these days, Gil my lad. Grace-of-Heaven Milacar, in fond reprimand after a warehouse heist went spectacularly, bloodily wrong, and fifteen year old Ringil stayed ill-advisedly behind to taunt the Watch from the eaves of the burning building. *Going to get you maimed or dead, just see if it doesn't.*

Yeah, well, Grace. Grimacing at the memory. *Just look how that worked out.*

So yes – as he came crunching up the gravel path towards the main doors of the house, out came the opposition. The door leaves parted, and a squad of men-at-arms in Eskiath livery issued rapidly through the gap. Ringil made the count, assessed the threat – seven men, five with pikes and two more behind that looked like Majak hires or some local imitation thereof, signature staff lances in hand. All lightly armoured – their helmets and cuirasses showed signs of being donned in a hurry, but the metal gleamed dintless and smooth in the low light. It was either new gear or very well kept. And this was by no means the household's full contingent, unless Gingren had made spending cuts of late. There'd be more inside.

The pikemen gathered in a rough scallop formation to defend the door, weapons lowered at infantry guard. The Majak spread apart in the space behind, staff lances loosely held across their bodies. There was a grim, drilled competence to it all, like clockwork parts moving. But when they saw the triple file of imperials at Ringil's back, the shock stamped across their faces like marching boots.

'Crossbows,' Gil snapped in Tethanne, without turning or breaking pace. 'Deploy left and right. Sound off on ready, hold for my command.'

He came to a casual halt a couple of dozen yards short of the pike tips.

Heard the crunch as the imperial bowmen stepped out of file behind him on the gravel, fanned out and bent to their weapons. There was a heart-beat instant when he worried the pikemen might do the smart thing and charge while they had the advantage, before the bows were cranked and loaded. Well, he had some small magic in reserve for that, and anyway knew a couple of skirmish tricks to take a pike off its owner without dying in the attempt . . .

The bowmen sounded off, eight laconic voices, hard and tight. Ringil grinned at the pike guard, let them do the math. Switched to Naomic.

'Let's not be hasty, boys. Do this right, we can all make it through to dawn without any unsightly holes in us.'

Lamplight, flickering in the doorway behind them. He saw dim figures move there.

'Hello, Dad,' he called. 'This isn't very friendly. Not going to invite me in?'

A mutter of voices, rising in dispute. He heard his father, maybe one of his brothers too – sounded like that little cunt Creglir. A couple of other male voices he didn't recognise, then his mother's cutting tones, and abruptly he was off-balance, unsure how the fact of her presence made him feel. On the one hand, he'd hoped she'd still be down at Lanatray for the balance of the summer, and so well out of this. On the other hand . . .

'Mother? How about you talk some sense into Dad, and save us all a bloodbath here? These are imperial marines. The same guys you saw me with when we called in on our way north.'

Quiet for a moment. Then his parents' voices rose again, straining against each other like wrestlers in some vicious grudge bout. He couldn't be sure, but it sounded as if his mother was getting the best of it. He tried again.

'We're at war now, Dad. I give these men the peeled rind of an excuse, they'll go through your household guard here like Hoiran's prick through a batch of virgin milkmaids.'

The lamplight and shadow shifted. Gingren stepped out behind his pikemen.

Ringil blinked.

For a moment he didn't recognise the man before him, thought this was some aged, outlying member of House Eskiath, some great uncle he'd never met, family resemblance and all, but not . . .

Then, like a punch to the gut, he understood he was looking at his father after all. Understood how suddenly old Gingren had grown.

The corpulent warrior-gone-to-seed bulk that Gil remembered from only a couple of years ago was shrunken now, all but gone. The shoulders had slimmed down, were almost bony under the thin jerkin his father wore. Even Gingren's thickened waist seemed to have lost most of its girth. The face, handsome in youth – though Gil had always hated to admit the fact – then more recently a little bloated with too much good living, was now lined and drawn, careworn beyond anything he could have imagined. It was hard to be sure in the poor light, but the set of the mouth seemed looser too, the iron grey hair whitened and thinned. Only the level flint gaze was the same as far as Gil could tell, and for that he was almost thankful.

'Ringil.' Twitching lips, Gingren mouthing his words like a crone before he spoke them. 'What do you want? Have you come to slaughter us all, then? Hmm? Not content with dragging my name through the mud, now you come to spill Eskiath blood as well, in the halls of your own upbringing?'

'Hey! I'm not the one here who forgot what blood ties are, mother-fucker!' His voice came out jagged and uncontrolled, and he saw Gingren flinch with it. 'I haven't sold *my* fucking soul for a place at the top table!'

'You broke the edicts!' Rage rising now in his father's voice too, thin and desperate though it sounded. 'You flouted the law!'

'Yeah – a law that takes the freedom of the city and snaps it like a twig for kindling. A law built by rich merchants to make themselves richer still, signed and ratified by their lickspittle political fingerpuppets up the hill, and falling—'

'You have no comprehension of these matters, Ringil! You—'

Trample it down. '—*and falling* without pity on the poorest citizens in the League. A law that took one of our own blood and made her a broken slave in a foreign land. Where was your precious fucking House Eskiath honour when that happened, eh?'

'*You burnt down Elim Hinrik's home! He died in that fire!*'

'I'm not surprised. Both legs broken like that, he would have had a hard time getting out before it caught.' Suddenly, control was easy once more. He shrugged, and examined his nails. 'If he'd told me what I wanted to know, he might have lived.'

'You,' Gingren, breathing hard now, 'murdered a worthy merchant of Trelayne for no reason other than his part in a legal trade. And now you joke about it to my face? You are no son of mine! *You never were!*'

'Yes, that's become increasingly clear to me over the last several years. Perhaps it's something we need to talk to mother about. Perhaps she felt the need for a more—'

'*Ringil!*'

Ishil Eskiath's bright and haughty voice, like a crisp slap across the face. It shut him up the way nothing else ever could. He watched as she joined her husband behind the line of the men-at-arms, and his heart ached a little at the sight. He grimaced.

'I'm sorry, mother. That was a bitchy crack.'

'Why are you here, Ringil?' she asked, in that bright voice. 'I don't believe you intend to harm us, and I certainly don't imagine you've come seeking forgiveness.'

'Right on both counts. I'm here for information, and then I'm gone.'

'I see.' Acid dripped in her tone. 'And if we cannot furnish you with this information, what is to be our fate? Will you break our limbs too, set the house afire and leave us to burn.'

He bit down on the ache, he put it away. 'No, my lady, I will not. I have not forgotten my blood, even if my own father has. You have nothing to fear from me, or my men, if you can persuade yours to stand down and keep their cool.'

There was a longish pause. Gingren glowered. The pikemen looked uncertain. Then Ishil took a couple more firm steps forward, so she stood almost between the two men-at-arms with the staff lances.

'Stand down,' she said brusquely. 'There's no fight here.'

Gingren erupted. *'Hoiran's balls, woman, do you think I—'*

'What I *think*, husband, is that I have absolutely no wish to see the family linen washed and aired in public this way. I would very much prefer to have our visitor inside and hear what he has to say *in private.*' A barbed look went at Gingren, impossible to miss even in this dim light. 'It would be *politic*, husband, do you not think?'

Another creaking moment of uncertainty, during which the pikemen shot each other exasperated glances. Ringil saw the confusion, knew it for potentially lethal. He raised a very slow, very limp hand for his own men.

'Stand down,' he told them. 'Let them see you mean it.'

He heard the exaggerated motions of the bowmen as they lowered their weapons and got back to their feet. Saw relief banner across the faces opposite him. He nodded amiably at the pikemen. Loosened his stance.

By the time Gingren picked up the beat, the tips of the pikes had already begun to droop.

'Stand down, then.' The command was snapped out, gruff and ungracious. 'But your men stay out here, Ringil. And I'll have that cursed blade of yours.'

'No, you won't.'

Gingren drew himself up. 'Then—'

'Husband,' said Ishil sharply. 'Would you be so kind as to lend me your arm and escort me back inside. I am quite faint from all this excitement.'

Gingren stared at his wife, mouth twitching. She looked evenly back. Finally, wordless, Gingren put out his arm, and Ishil took it with a languid gesture that Gil supposed just about passed for faintness. He saw smirks among the pikemen and surprised himself with a sudden stab of sympathy for his father.

Bit late for that, Gil.

And, very faintly, across the rain and stormy murk he'd brought down on the Glades, he heard the first of the screams.

Inside Eskiath House, he stood itchily in the centre of the western lounge, while his mother was seen to a completely unnecessary seat near the window and fanned by solicitous ladies in waiting. Gingren left her there like some task he was weary of attempting, went to the corner cabinet and poured himself a glass of something amber. Downed it in one, poured another, pointedly did not offer anything to Gil. They both acted as if the other was not in the room, until Creglir swept glaring through the door, apparently on course to grab Ringil by the throat.

'You fucking—'

'Creg!' The old snap of command in his father's voice now; this was a son he knew he could manage. 'Don't you even think about it. I won't have you brawling in front of your mother. Remember where you are, remember *who* you are. Is that clear?'

Creglir growled, but he backed off to the bookcase wall and contented himself with glaring murderously at his younger brother. It wasn't much of a change from the last time Ringil saw him – they'd never really been able to stand each other. While Gil and Gingren junior had got on well enough, at least until the showdown at the Academy, and even after that maintained a kind of cordial mutual contempt, the thing with Creg was visceral and eternal. Maybe, unburdened by the eldest brother role that constrained Ging, Creglir had simply been able to give his competitive sibling urges free rein. Or maybe he genuinely felt the disgust for what Ringil was that he'd always professed to. Either way, they'd drawn blood from each other at an early age and never seen a reason to stop.

And certainly not now.

'Proud of yourself, little brother?' Creglir's lip curled. 'Bringing the enemy to our door, shaming your own mother in front of strangers and servants.'

Gil looked at him. 'You want a spanking, Creg? I'm right here.'

He watched Creglir splutter and fume, knew he'd do nothing with their father's leash applied. Curious to find the Dragonbane's favoured choice of words on his lips all of a sudden. Or not, because, well, there was a man who knew how to deal with difficult siblings.

'You faggot scum. If mother weren't in this room, I'd—'

'You'd *die*. That's what you'd do. Now shut the fuck up while I talk to the grown-ups.' Ringil turned to Ishil. 'You'd be well advised to stay inside for the next day or so, mother. The men I have out there are the better behaved end of what I've brought to Trelayne.'

Ishil had already waved away her fanning, cooing ladies. Now she sat up straight in her chair, eyes intent on his, about as faint and flustered as a stooping hawk.

'What have you done, Ringil?' she asked quietly. 'They told us you were dead. What have you brought down on us?'

'I've freed the hulk fleet convicts and brought them ashore.'

Creglir snorted. 'Horseshit!'

A more general silence from the rest of the room. Creglir looked back and forth between his silent parents, neither of whom seemed to share his confidence.

'Well, I mean . . .' Hands spread, exasperated, but weaker of tone all of a sudden. 'Seriously. How would he accomplish such a thing?'

'It's done,' Ringil told them. 'They are already in the city. The privateer Sharkmaster Wyr leads them – to the extent that a mob like that can be led. But mostly they are set to rampage at random. I imagine Harbour End is already overrun, perhaps Tervinala too. And Wyr himself is loose in the Glades with the remains of his crew.'

'Are you—?' Gingren was gaping at him now, drink forgotten and spilling in his lowered hand. 'Are you *insane*? Are you *fucked in the head, Ringil? Have I raised a demon changeling in place of a son?*'

'You have now, yeah.' He turned again to where Ishil sat. 'You summoned me, mother. You brought me back to find Sherin, to punish those who took her.'

'For the first part of which you were paid,' Ishil said severely. 'Quite handsomely as I recall. And I do not recall asking you to punish anyone once Sherin was home.'

'No. Sherin asked for that herself.'

'Sherin Helirig is a stupid little trollop,' snarled Creglir, 'Without the wit or grace to marry well or bear children for her family name. She always was. Who cares what she wanted?'

'Apparently only me.'

'You rotted piece of—'

'That's enough!' Ishil was on her feet, witch queen composed. 'What's done is done. And I imagine that this ingenious riot you've set, Ringil, cannot last much beyond morning. A mob of half-starved criminal wretches surely won't present much challenge to the Watch once we have light and the true nature of the threat is understood.'

'Too right,' Creglir sneered. 'The Watch is going to make chopped hound feed out of that scum. Just you watch it happen, *brother*.'

'I don't expect to be here long enough. That's not why I came.'

Distant shrieking came faintly through the half open windows of the lounge. Both Gingren and Creglir hurried to the glass and stared out at the rain-peppered darkness pressing in from outside. Behind their backs, Ishil seemed unmoved. Ringil wondered if she'd already heard earlier, fainter cries, and said nothing. He met her eyes, looking for signs, and though her face was otherwise unreadable, he thought for just a moment that he saw a smile touch the corners of her mouth and eyes. He thought he saw sadness there, and something like pity.

And maybe love. He couldn't be sure.

And then it was gone.

'There's red in the sky,' said Gingren grimly. 'Something's burning out there.'

'That's Wrathrill House, Dad. Got to be.' A shocked, accusing look on Creglir's face as he swung round to stare at Gil. 'Hoiran's balls, he was telling the truth!'

'Glad we got that sorted out.'

Gingren rounded on him, voice harnessed to some vestige of the colossal paternal rages Gil remembered from his youth. 'You think this is *funny?* You let degenerate convict scum into the city of your birth to pillage and rape and burn like this, and you *laugh?*'

'Well, look at it this way, Dad. I doubt they'll do anything that hasn't already been done to them.'

Almost, Gingren went for him then, and with a shock that was like sudden sickness, Gil realised he wasn't ready for it. Creg, he'd chop down as soon as look at, he'd speak a glyph and watch his brother drop and strangle to death on the floor with nothing but joy. But Gingren, his worn down, sold out, defeated father . . .

'We are getting nowhere,' Ishil said evenly. 'We have our son's word for the damage he's done, and I for one never doubted it. The question is, Ringil, what it will take to make you go away again. You say you are here for information. What information?'

'The prisoners brought back from Ornley. My colleagues from the expedition. I want to know where they're being held, I want them released to me.'

Ishil glanced at Gingren. 'Husband?'

Gingren ignored her. He was still looking wonderingly at Ringil. 'You came all the way here for that? Did all this? For *imperials?*'

'They are my friends.'

His father nodded, mouth tight. The same slow-brewing, disgusted understanding as that first time he'd caught Gil in Jelim Dasnal's arms in the stables. 'Yes. Well, your *friends* are no longer held under Chancellery guard. They were transferred a week ago. All bar the rank and file, that is – those we interrogated on arrival and then executed as prisoners of war.'

'Transferred where? By whose order?'

'Into Etterkal.'

Ringil's turn to nod. 'Findrich. He knew I was coming.'

'Don't be bloody ridiculous. How could he know that?'

'Oh, Dad. They really have kept you to the fringes of this, haven't they?' And there it was again – the sudden, unlooked for stab of pity for what Gingren had become. 'Did you really sell yourself so cheap, Dad? Have they really told you nothing of what lies behind the cabal?'

'I do not ask such questions,' his father said stiffly. 'Because I do not care. I am a soldier, not a politician. Enough that Findrich and his kind represent the spine and ambition the rest of the Chancellery cannot muster. Enough that they'll lead us to a clean victory over Yhelteth this time, and not just one more mucky compromise.'

'Just like the battle hymn says, eh?'

'Fuck you, Gil, you traitorous piece of—'

Creglir's voice dried up as Ringil swung to face him. Gil, eyes gone blank, left hand rising, cocked and crooked . . .

He saw, out of the corner of his eye, the look on his mother's face. Heard the husked murmur of her voice – *Gil, please don't* – perhaps only in his mind, and his hand fell back as if of its own accord, as if severed of all nerve and sinew by some axe blow to the arm. He quelled the rising glyph, stubbed it out like a krin twig ember in the fold of his palm. He stared his brother down.

'You're in luck,' he said drably, when Creglir had looked away. 'For a moment there, I forgot she's your mother too.'

Gingren stepped in, some threadbare vestige of previous command in stance and tone. He was trying to thrust out his chest.

'You will leave now, outcast. Degenerate. Hmm? Stain, yes, pus-seeping *stain* on my family's honour. *You will leave us now in peace.*'

His voice trembled and cracked on the attempted rage, scaled to something that rang more like some desperate plea.

Gil nodded. Found a smile and put it on.

'Yeah, I'm going. Good luck with your clean victory, Dad. You keep me posted, let me know how that works out. Mother – always a pleasure, your beauty never fades.'

'Ringil,' she said, very softly.

He stepped towards her and she raised one languid arm from where she sat. He bowed his head, took her fingers loosely in his, brushed his lips across the back of her hand. It was a touch as formal as the scratch of quill on vellum, as dry and cold as broom twigs. But in the moment of the kiss, her fingers folded and clenched fiercely on his, and for the time it took, they tugged hard against each other like a climber pulling his fellow up dangling out of some bottomless crevasse.

He never knew, then or ever after, which of them was the rescuer and which hung dangling over the drop.

The grip parted. She let him go. He straightened and cleared his throat.

'As I said, you'd all better stay inside and have your men-at-arms maintain a perimeter, at least until noon. I told Wyr to stay away from this place, and I think he'll honour that. But I can't answer for the rest.' He looked Ishil in the eye, voice momentarily low. 'Goodbye.'

Then he turned and left them with each other.

Strode out of Eskiath House, into the rain and dark to gather his men. Saw smudges of ruddy light on the low-bellied, murky sky, just as his father had claimed, as the first of the Glades mansions burned.

FORTY-SEVEN

In the tunnel, Selak Chan gave her back the lead with evident relief. He'd already dropped a good twenty feet back from the fire sprite, ground Archeth started to pick up again immediately. Her professions of confidence about their safety were hollow – she had no idea what was down here – but the one thin faith she had was in the sprite's concern for their well-being.

They marched in silence for a few minutes before Chan came up close on her shoulder and broke into the rhythmic clanking echo of feet on latticed metal.

'My lady, we have been walking for . . . some hundreds of yards now.'

'Yes. And?' Impatiently, because her ghosts had followed her into the simple, vectored promise of the tunnel and didn't look like leaving her alone any time soon.

'And it was only forty or fifty yards back to the edge of the pit, my lady. Sixty at the very most.'

'That's . . .' *Undeniably true, Archidi.*

She fought down the urge to jam to a halt right there. Let her pace ebb a little instead, glanced back over her shoulder with every appearance of casual unconcern. Chan's expression was tight in the striping orange glow; not yet afraid but not far off it. Behind him, she saw other queasy faces in the same flickering light, all struggling to fight down their fear. She faced forward again, before they could catch anything in her own features that she didn't want them to see. She summoned a noncommittal grunt.

'Is this some Kiriath sorcery, my lady?'

'Yes, it is,' she said airily. 'Nothing you need to worry about. My people were skilled in working with the forces that hold us to the Earth, in, uh, *bending* them, to suit their purposes, you see.'

'Then.' Chan cleared his throat. 'Where are we, my lady?'

'We are in the shaft,' she fervently hoped. 'We are walking downward into it. But the tunnel, uhm, saves us from the fall that would entail. You understand?'

A brief pause, filled thankfully by the iron tramp of their feet.

'Is it then the same, my lady, as the magic that raised the elevator in An-Kirilnar?'

'Uhm – yeah. Pretty much.'

'And so . . .' Dubiously. 'We cannot fall, then?'

'No, no – impossible.' She grimaced to herself, into the gloom of the tunnel ahead . . . below . . . whatever. 'Can't happen. The, ah, the powers at work here would not permit anything like that to befall us.'

'Should I tell the other men of this, my lady?'

'Good idea, yes. Pass it on back.' *Maybe you'll sound a bit more convincing than I do.*

She affected not to listen as the murmur went back along the file, the troubled low surf of voices it provoked. Tried not to worry how deep this pit might actually be, how far they might in fact fall – face forward, into poorly lit darkness – if it turned out she was as full of shit as she felt.

No way to reckon time effectively in the orange-lit gloom, but she thought it was getting on for an hour before they saw a brightening ahead. They were not at marching pace – despite his protestations, Kanan Shent's wounds were slowing him down, and there were others in the company who'd taken damage in the skirmish the day before as well – but however you looked at it, they must be at least a couple of miles deep in the earth by now.

Yeah, well. Got delvings at Monal go deeper than that.

Truth to tell, although the sheer scale of the pit's construction and the magic of the tunnel made some impression on her, none of it hit that hard. She was, in the end, Kiriath in instinct and upbringing both. Going underground was what her people did.

The patch of brighter light resolved into a doorway, similar in outline to the one that had cracked open for them on the surface. The sprite went through without hesitation, hung there expectantly on the other side.

Well, what else are we going to do? Turn around and go back?

Archeth stepped gingerly through the opening. Found herself in a huge chamber whose walls were raw rock sealed behind some kind of glassy resin and rose into a dim vaulted space overhead filled with angular iron structure and dangling cables. She felt an easing go through her at the sight. Familiar ground. They coated the tunnels and shafts at An-Monal pretty much the same way. In fact, this might easily have been – she glanced around at the piled iron junk that crammed the chamber on all sides – any storage hall in the dry dock complex at Monal's volcanic harbour. It certainly held the same chaotic assortment of discarded gear.

Chan and the others came hesitantly through, peering about them in awe. They stared upward into the gloom, they shielded their eyes from the light. She heard a couple of stifled oaths. It wasn't that the hall's illumination was much different to that in the tunnel, but there was a lot more of it to go round. Broad, glowing patches and veins pulsed in the resin – and she saw more of them blinking to life, in response, she supposed, to their arrival – throwing down a warm, orange-gold radiance that felt almost like being back home on the sunset-drenched streets of Yhelteth an hour before summer dusk. The same soft heat in the air as well – she looked down and saw the transparent resin surface underfoot, knelt to touch it with one hand and felt the warmth seeping through. The rock itself, she knew from experience at An-Monal, would be hot enough to burn flesh at this depth, but the resin did double duty, providing safety insulation and structural support in one simply brewed substance.

Flicker of motion in the corner of her eye – the fire sprite drifting suddenly upward towards some notional centre of the space they were in, a couple of dozen yards off the ground. Archeth straightened slowly up to look, saw the sprite flatten and fatten itself until it became a perfect globe, then begin to slowly rotate. At the same time, the constant undulating ripples along its sides that had so resembled stubby, gesturing limbs of flame during the trek now damped away to a barely visible trembling line, a restless equator that swept back and forth around the spherical surface, as if in search of something.

'My lady?' Kanan Shent, possessively attentive at her side, as he'd been since the dragon went down.

She nodded. 'Yeah, I see it. Get the impression this might be journey's end.'

'So, then – *humans.*'

The Helmsman's voice – sonorous High Kir tones booming from the ceiling somewhere, undercut as ever with slightly hysterical good cheer – unmistakable as anything else. A grim smile twitched momentarily at Archeth's mouth, then was gone.

She stepped out, away from Shent and the others. 'Take a closer look, Helmsman. I am kir-Archeth of clan Indamaninarmal, custodian regent at An-Monal and last remaining executor of the Kiriath Mission. The Warhelm Tharalananghurst sends me to you.'

'Yes. With *humans.*'

'Is that going to be a problem?' she snapped.

'Not for me.'

Apparently content with this riposte, the Helmsman fell silent. The fire sprite came drifting gently down towards them, squeezing itself back into its former shape. Shrieking iron machinery awoke in the vault above, the same bright flurry of sparks through the gloom that she'd seen with Egar on the retrieval decks at An-Kirilnar when the hoists jerked to unaccustomed life. She saw something huge and tentacular swing sluggishly into motion at one end of the hall's roofspace. Thought she recognised it.

Sharp indrawn breaths behind her, the multiple rasp of drawn steel. She lifted a hand to stop the panic before it got started.

'Stand down.' Still absently speaking High Kir – *get a grip, Archidi.* She dropped back into Tethanne. 'Stand down, all of you. There's nothing to worry about here.'

The tentacular thing swung down out of the shadows, was revealed as nothing more alarming – to Archeth, anyway – than a straightforward craning appendage running on an iron track across the vaulted roof. It hovered for a moment over the seemingly random strew and stack of dark iron equipment that bulked fifty feet high at the far end of the hall. Then the various articulated arms plunged down as one and commenced rooting around in the mess with clanging abandon. They tilted and upended containers the size of small ships, re-arranged huge stacked sheets of alloy material to clear space, lifted and set aside big bulky devices of unguessable function. There seemed to be no rationale to the process, and the noise it made was deafening.

'Have we angered it, my lady?' Shent shouted in her ear.

She shook her head, still watching. 'It's just looking for something.'

In the end, the crane retrieved three items from the piles it was searching through and then backed off, seemingly satisfied. It brought its haul forward up the hall on its track, screeching and showering sparks as it came – a lengthy coil of what looked like giant metallic intestines, a dome-topped circular container nearly thirty feet across and at least the same in height, and a device that reminded Archeth of nothing so much as a huge, stiff-winged gold metal bat, balancing a dull grey fruit dish on its head.

The crane paused when it got closer to them. Three of its arrayed arms set the container down on its flat side, so delicately it barely made a sound on impact. Another two manoeuvred one end of the intestinal metallic tube into a connecting position somewhere on the dome's curve. Colours awoke on the surface of the container, swirled giddily about, and then condensed to a single iridescent patch, directly under the poised end of the tube. The patch brightened until it was too dazzling to look at directly. There was a sharp, violent hissing and a pop, and then the glare faded out, leaving blotches on Archeth's vision. Where the light had been, an opening now waited in the alloy dome, perfectly smooth and apparently a perfect fit for the metallic gut-end held over it. The crane's arms slid the tube into place, and it sealed there with another brief, rotating flare. The arms pulled back, and then the whole crane was rising, retreating upward, carrying the other end of the intestinal coil and the huge gold-winged bat and dish device with it, back up into the shadowed reaches of the roof-space.

The grinding and showering of sparks stopped.

They all stood staring at the container, waiting. Archeth felt their glances on her. She cleared her throat.

'We require passage via your, ah, aerial conveyance, to—'

'Yes, I am already aware of your situation. The Warhelm's messenger has not only brought you here, it has brought specific instructions as well. Observe.'

The swirl of colour awoke once more on the domed container's surface, converged once more into a single brilliant blotch. Where it faded out, there was a narrow doorway. The fire sprite darted forward, hovered a moment in the freshly made entrance, then slipped inside.

Archeth frowned. 'What is this?'

'The next stage of your journey. Lead your human companions inside, and we will begin.'

She hesitated. Something about that narrow aperture she didn't like, some vague misgivings about the confinement . . .

Come on, Archidi – you just marched directly down the side of a cliff over a mile deep, with no more effort than strolling up the Boulevard of the Ineffable Divine. You came here behind an animate campfire flame that watches over you with a mother's care. The only time you came to harm was when you ignored instructions.

Time to stop second-guessing your father's antique servant spirits from the void, and just get in the saddle.

She glanced round at the men at her back.

'With me,' she said, and led them through the narrow doorway, into the space beyond.

Inside, it was warm and a pearly grey light suffused the air. The dome curved over their heads and showed scurrying smears of colour – faint trace repetition of the swirl she'd seen on the outside, pink and gold, pale orange, bluish tinges out of the grey. The curving surface seemed less like a solid roof now and more like some low and limited dawning sky. The doorway's edges flared and radiated bright white fire as the last man passed inside, the glare filled the entrance and spread beyond. When it inked out again, the wall was whole, so smooth you could not have told where exactly the door once was.

Distant gurgling, echoing off the curve of the enclosing walls.

They all heard it. She traded a wary glance with Shent and Chan, followed the injured Throne Eternal's gaze up to where the opening to the intestinal tube gaped above them in the dome. The gurgling built, gathering force, became a hollow roar piping down from that hole. The men around her stared upward in united, dawning horror. She heard a bitten-off curse in Tethanne. A sick certainty came and kicked her in the pit of her stomach.

In the centre of the container space, the fire sprite flickered and went out.

The opening over their heads seemed to explode. Fluid burst into the chamber like a waterfall in full spate, crashed down with brutal force on their heads, knocked more than one of the company to the floor.

Somehow, Archeth stayed upright. She floundered through liquid – it was not water, it was thicker, more viscous stuff – already to her knees, to where Kanan Shent had gone over and was flailing to get back on his feet. She grabbed his arm and hauled him towards one side of the container, out of the immediate blast of liquid from above. She helped him upright, braced herself against the curve of the chamber wall. Dinning thunder of the flood in her ears, the Throne Eternal was shouting something at her, but she couldn't make out the words in the roar. Around her, there was yelling and the sound of desperate thrashing to stay afloat.

'*Motherfucker!*' she screamed at the domed ceiling. '*What are you doing?*'

'I am protecting you to the best of my ability.' The Helmsman's voice cuddled into her ear, as intimate as if it spoke from just behind her, as low as if they stood in some museum quiet instead of the thundering chaos of the drowning chamber. 'Exactly as the Warhelm has ordered. Do not be concerned.'

Her feet left the floor, the viscous fluid buoyed her up. The container had filled to over half its height in less time than it took to mount and settle a restless horse. Through the massive surge, the heavy slop and splash of fluid into her eyes, she saw the level boiling upward, taking them all towards the domed roof above.

'We did not build for humans here,' the Helmsman added, as if in afterthought. 'We built to win the war.'

'*Fuck y—*'

And her mouth filled with fluid she must spit violently out. It tasted faintly metallic, almost like blood, but cold. She felt herself swallow some, coughed and spluttered to get it back up. And then she must abandon anything except the attempt to keep her head above the rising fluid level. The men around her had stopped shouting and were focused grimly on trying to stay afloat, but it was a hopeless battle. The curve of the dome was crowding them inward, tangling them up in each other's limbs, and the waterfall blast from the opening above turned the remaining space as much into churning fluid as air. She heard a single intense screaming above the general roar, had time, briefly, in her own struggle to cast about and see Yilmar Kaptal, mouth gaping wide around the shrieks that poured out of him, some deeply buried memory of how he had died before perhaps torn loose and back to haunt him in his final moments. He took a mouthful, his screams turned gagging, his eyes went wide in horror, and down he went amidst the close-packed, bobbing heads. He didn't come up again.

The ceiling bumped her head, forced her face down into the fluid. She kicked upward, hard, banged her head again. Tried to claw her way through the press of struggling bodies, closer to the centre of the dome. Rational thought was gone; she fought blindly for one more lungful of air. Someone clouted her, an elbow caught her in the neck. She hit back, hampered by the heavy drag of the fluid. A panicked grip hauled hard on her shoulder, shoved her down beneath the surface into a chaos of tangling, kicking limbs. In the instant it happened, she tried to breathe, took in fluid instead. A foot hooked her in the stomach, she gagged, another foot scraped across her face, trod her down. Fluid cramming into her throat and lungs and stomach, pressing on her eyeballs, dimming sight.

She grabbed weakly at something, an ankle maybe, felt her grip slip. Felt herself falling away.

A weird, metallic-tasting calm came to collect her then. It slowed her churning limbs, took strength from her muscles, closed her eyes.

Wiped her away.

FORTY-EIGHT

Etterkal without river transport was a stiff march across town, and they didn't have a lot of time to do it in. Ishil had been pretty astute in her assessment of the situation. The chaos and panic he'd sown might last a couple of hours past dawn if they were lucky, but after that Sharkmaster Wyr and his starveling associates were done. Gil had seen Trelayne on a war footing before and he knew what it meant – the city was going to be stuffed full of freshly levied troops waiting to ship out south, and the Watch would have been bulked up too. There'd be more than enough loose iron in town to put down this half-arsed rampage, and the Watch's embarrassment at quite how easily they'd all been panicked would only add to the savagery with which it was done.

He had to be long gone by then.

They passed Wrathrill house, now well and truly alight, gave it a wide berth to their left. Screams in the night, shouting and gusts of coarse laughter, a vague sense of siege seen through the intervening trees. Figures capered about outside, silhouetted black against the fire, or appeared at windows in the upper storeys, throwing things out. The west wing was wrapped in flames to the roof, would not be long in coming down. As they left it behind, the glow lit their way, painted long dancing tongues of yellow light and shadow on the path ahead.

'You think they'll stop with that one?' Klithren asked him.

Ringil shot him a glance. 'Would you?'

'Well. They'll have found booze in there by now, probably a lot of it. Women, food. Finery to cavort in.'

'And weapons. They'll have a lot more weapons now.'

Across the Glades then, and out into the genteel avenues of neighbouring Linardin, a kind of antechamber for audience in the ruling district they'd just left behind – merchants and shipmasters on their way up rubbed shoulders here with Glades scions waiting on inheritance and the higher ranking among the Chancellery's officials, all of them yearning towards the riverside opulence of the Glades itself and imitating it as best they could. Linardin was curving, tree-lined boulevards and facing rows of modest little mansions sat side by side in grounds barely worthy of the name, like so many portly matrons squatting in bathtubs made for infants. Gingren junior and Creglir both had places here, which just about said it all.

They double-timed along the avenues, wet slapping rhythm of booted feet on the rain-drenched boulevard paving, and night watchmen came hurrying to the locked iron gates of each property, peering out between the bars. Some would be veterans of the war no doubt, and might recognise imperial garb when they saw it; most would simply register the arms and armour, and assume this was a levy troop for the war, marching to muster somewhere and likely lost in the filthy weather. Nobody, in any case, showed any inclination to come out from behind their gates and find out what was going on.

'Anasharal? You listening?'

'Always.' The Helmsman's voice at his ear, with immediate, unnerving intimacy.

'There's been a change of plan.' Breathing hard with the pace of the march. 'Tell Hald and Nyanar they won't need to come upriver after all. The captives have been moved to the Salt Warren, and I'm on my way there now. We'll come out through Tervinala and see you at Outlander's Wharf, by the eastern harbour wall.'

'Will they know where that is?'

'Believe it or not, they call it the eastern wall for a reason. Even Nyanar ought to be able to work out which way is east.' Ringil did brief logistics in his head. 'This is going to take a good few hours, so don't look for us any time soon. Stay out of the harbour; it's got to be chaos in there by now. Stand well off from the walls, drop anchor in the delta, and don't engage anyone unless they come looking for it. And have the boats ready to lower. We'll likely be in a hurry when we come.'

'I will convey your instructions. Will there be anything else?'

'Not right now, no.' He found time to grin. 'But don't go anywhere.'

Linardin's mansion rows fell behind, became the tenement-lined streets of Kellil. Still a well-to-do neighbourhood compared to the districts near Harbour End, but this was no longer the home of anything you'd call actual wealth. Around here, you worked for a living, and staying out of the weather just because it was unpleasant ceased to be an option. For the first time, they started to see substantial numbers of people in the streets, despite the hammering rain. Delivery carts and handbarrows were in evidence here and there, horses and hauliers trudging alike through pothole puddles or standing patiently in the downpour while other men loaded or unloaded what they carried. Taverns and shops spilled customers out onto the streets, breathed others in. Individual men and women hurried on errands the rain would not excuse. Urchins and whores and young thugs schooled enough in subtlety not to get chased out of the neighbourhood stood under doorway lintels, watching the deluge with bleak, empty eyes.

No sign of the Watch, but that wasn't unusual in weather like this; Ringil was willing to bet they'd be found in the nearest tavern, warm and dry and cadging drinks.

Or they've already been pulled to Harbour End to fight the flames.

But he didn't think that was likely. The streets they were on showed no signs of the panic you'd expect once word of the assault got out. In the meantime, the drilled tramp of their passage drew some inevitable attention along the way, but nothing that caused any fuss. People heard the boots, turned and looked, but did nothing much else. The rain drew a curtain across their interest, kept vision indistinct. Now and then, men cheered at them with damp martial fervour, but mostly it was just pointing and muttering. And once a female urchin ran up and stole a kiss from Noyal Rakan, much to the amusement of everyone watching. Ringil turned casually, left hand cocked for the choking glyph, in case the girl registered the Throne Eternal's dark, hawkish features and made him for the outlander he was. But either the urchin was used to southern-looking men – to be fair, Rakan could just about have passed for mercenary talent out of Hinerion or Baldaran – or she didn't care. She dropped back from the kiss, which she'd had to stand on tiptoe to get, and ran back to her friends where they sheltered under a wine merchant's eaves. There was some more cheering.

'Wave and grin,' said Ringil behind his teeth. 'Everybody loves you.'

Rakan mustered a weak smile, a gallant twirl of the wrist and arm for his young admirer, and they marched hurriedly on. The incident washed away in their wake. Ringil realised he'd been holding his breath, and let it out with relief. Klithren drew in nearer to his side.

'That was too fucking close for comfort,' he muttered, hand still resting on the hilt of the short sword at his hip.

'Relax, Hinerion. Nearly there now.'

At which point, more or less, their luck ran out.

The tavern was called the Lizard's Head – about the fourth or fifth they'd passed so far of that name – and displayed a lumpy, misshapen chunk of something in a cage hung out from the wall on an iron bracket. It might have been a mummified Scaled Folk skull, it might not, but it was a clear sign they were getting close to Etterkal. Nice neighbourhoods didn't go in for that sort of thing anymore – you'd get a painted sign, or maybe a carved wooden likeness, but real rotting flesh and bone where people ate and drank was frowned on these days. The Salt Warren, on the other hand, didn't much care about social norms – it catered to appetite, pure and simple, and if you didn't like that, well, you could always stay at home. If veterans of the war wanted to drink someplace where no prissy veil was drawn across the savage times they'd lived through and survived, then Etterkal would offer that place, and places like it on any given corner, until the demand was well and truly met.

Ringil cast about for street signs, a name he'd maybe know. It was a decade or more since he'd been in this part of town, and nothing looked familiar. On previous occasions, he'd preferred to hit the Salt Warren from the other side, using the crooked thoroughfares and teeming outlander populace of Tervinala for fallback. Thing was, you could always lose yourself in the diplomatic quarter; you could hide in its exotic churn of visiting foreign dignitaries, embassy mission staff and merchants from far flung places. By comparison, an assault through well-to-do, nosy-neighboured Kellil made no kind of sense for anyone with the twin luxuries of time and well-laid plans.

Yeah, pity we don't have much of either this time around.

Thus forced to it, his navigation had been haphazard, based on a mix of vague recall and compass instinct. But he guessed they couldn't be far off Caravan Master's Rise, where it swept up from the city's Eastern Gate like the edge of a scimitar blade, cutting what amounted to the formal boundary between Etterkal and Kellil. Ringil didn't know if the Salt Warren still ran Watch barricades and braziers along its nominal borders; it certainly had the last time he crossed over, but now, with the war to focus attention outward . . .

The tavern door cracked inward, and a tongue of yellow lamplight ran out into the street. A small knot of men reeled out, stood blinking in the slash and splatter of the rain.

'Hoo, look at that!'

'Salute for the brave troops, lads!'

'Yeah, all hail th—' Spluttering out to a sudden, spiking yell. 'Fuck! Girt, hoy, *look!* That's . . . *that's fucking imperial rig!*'

Ringil already turning, some predictive grasp of what was coming already in his mind. He cast the choking glyph at the man who'd made them, saw him clutch at his throat and stagger. Too late, though, far too late. The others went for weapons.

'Southern scourge! Southern scourge!'

'Empire's here! *Stand to arms!*'

They were soldiers, or had been once. No flinch in stance or voice, and the motley assortment of short blades and blunt instruments they carried were brandished with a canny economy of intent. Ringil made hasty count – nine of them, not counting the one choking to death on the cobbled ground, and two in the rear already ducking back inside to raise further hue and cry. They were all clearly drunk, but they shed that inconvenience like a split shield. They came straight in, swinging and roaring.

Gil met the first of them with empty hands, no time for spells, no time even to get the Ravensfriend off his back or Eg's dragon tooth dagger down out of his sleeve. The man had a club fashioned from the business end of a boathook, evil rusted metal claw backed with a yard of seasoned oak, and he swung the whole thing one handed from about a third of the way down the shaft. Ringil took the blow on a rolling, rising forearm block, snapped a grip on the shaft with his left hand and wrestled his attacker for possession. The rusted hook dipped and slashed, nearly took out his eye, left a scrape down one cheek instead. He pivoted about and let the other man's momentum carry him past, kicked down savagely at the back of one knee, collapsed the League veteran to the floor. A marine stepped in obligingly with a mace, smashed the back of the man's head open where he lay.

Ringil was already spinning back to face the tavern door and the source of the attack. Around him, the other veterans were locked in desperate, uneven struggle with his men – seven on twenty-four, even allowing for the relative youth and inexperience of most of the imperials, was no kind of fight that could last. But through that door might be any number of similarly hardened survivors of the war, not to mention serving maids, tap boys, whores and their customers, pimps and barmen, some of whom might right now be scrambling out through some other exit to raise a more general alarm . . .

He strode to the door, ducked beneath the lintel and stepped into lamp-lit chaos. Men clambering over trestles to get to their fellows or maybe to weapons held behind the bar, others being shaken awake from a drunken doze. Serving maids and boys recoiling, grabbing tableware before it could be knocked to the floor and shattered. Shrieks. A pimp, flapping his arms at his whores like a panicked hen, trying perhaps to gather in his wards and ferry them out the back. A barkeep, cleaver in hand, glaring—

'Good evening,' Gil said. 'All of you, *sit down.*'

The *ikinri 'ska* snaked out among them, like lightning forked across a steppe sky, like veins through the back of an aged hand. Most of them sat, dropped back into their seats like stones, or hurried back to where they'd been. Some few were strong-willed enough to resist, or maybe just hard of hearing enough to miss the command. No time to worry about that. He sketched a claw at the beamed ceiling, made the bowed wooden members creak and groan, tore down one entire beam by its woodworm-hollowed end. Plaster exploded in the close, yellowish air, the roof sagged, the beam end crashed to the floor. Yelps and screams, and thick clouds of downward-sifting dust. With his other hand, he made a sweeping gesture, coughed a glyph that swept lamps and candles off table tops across the room. Flame flew, splashed and glinted on the floor, kindled in the straw underfoot.

Someone ran at him – the barkeep with the cleaver, bellowing rage—

'Broken,' he hissed, and the man shrieked as his forearm snapped, midway to the elbow, with an audible crunch. The cleaver flew loose, clattered on the floor.

I see what you could become if you'd only let yourself.

Not long ago, this much magic would have tired him. Now, each glyph felt like the flex of a muscle just warming up, like preparatory swashing motions with the Ravensfriend before any real duel began, building strength and focus, feeding a rising fire . . .

Better, a clicking, rasping voice whispers at his ear. *You have an appetite for it after all. Let us see then, what we can do with the raw material at root . . .*

And for just a naked second – the high stone altar on the screaming, empty plain, the figure crouched there over him, blur of tentacular limbs and the tools they hold, and he's pinned, he's—

No, no, let's not go back there, Gil.

He blinked back to the burning tavern, flames waist high now across the interior, the air clogged with smoke, and most of the crowd was concerned with nothing more than getting away, away from the fire and the terrible figure in the doorway that had called it down. Through smoke and wavering heated air, he glimpsed a few stolid figures still sat where he'd ordered them, apparently ready to stay there and burn to death rather than break the spell he'd laid on them. But the rest was screaming panic.

He turned away, ducked back outside into cooler air and the rain.

Out in the street, his men had finished the veterans and stood over their slaughtered remains, looking at him expectantly. No one seemed to have collected worse than scrapes and bruises. He gestured at the tavern, the merry flicker and glow through its door and windows, the crackling and the screams within.

'That should keep everyone around here pretty busy. Means we're covered to the rear, at least. Let's pick it up, gentlemen.'

They hit Caravan Master's Rise a couple of cross streets later. There was a barricade set and two braziers smouldering weakly in the downpour. But the post was unmanned, the Watch pulled away, likely to Harbour End. Ringil checked for street names on the Etterkal side, found one he knew well enough to plan a route by.

Findrich's place was less than ten minutes away.

FORTY-NINE

Soft, insistent hushing, like a whole roomful of mothers trying to soothe their infant offspring to sleep. Her clothes were waterlogged, cool and damp against her skin.

Raining?

It was not. She opened one eye, squinting against brightness. A hollow blue sky vaulted high overhead – nothing fell out of it but sunlight. The only visible cloud was in thin, white striated layers, high up at the top of all that azure expanse. Beyond, and angled slanting across the dome of blue, the band made a warm golden hoop, fading in from nothing at one side to a sharp scimitar edge at the other. And she was warm too, despite her soaked clothing, despite the lack of any apparent shelter and the wind that . . .

. . . sifted hushing through the long steppe grass she lay in. *That* was the noise, that was the—

She was out on the steppe.

She sat up with a jolt, and the last several weeks came down on her like a landslide. Failure and fury in Ornley, the wreck of the quest; Klithren's privateers, the sudden new war; captivity, the storm; An-Kirilnar and the Warhelm, the march on the ancient shattered city, reptile peons, warrior caste lizards, the dragon, the death of Egar – a tight, hurt noise in her throat as the grief fell on her anew – the arcane tunnel into the pit and the cryptic, murderous Helmsman that dwelled there . . .

Except . . . *you're not murdered, Archidi.*

In fact—

It dawned on her that she felt *good*, impossibly good, impossibly *whole*. Better than she had done in months, maybe in years. The stitching in her side no longer nagged with pain, there was just the deep itch of healing tissue. The myriad aches and pains she'd collected crossing the Wastes were gone. Even the remembered grief at Egar's death couldn't blunt the sense of well-being that suffused her.

She yawned and stretched, against a soft, pleasing ache through the muscles in her lower back. She was hungry, she noticed, but it was mild, it was appetite, not grinding need. Her head was clear and clean, her thoughts unfogged by any residue of krinzanz or recrimination. Curtains of grass nodded gently around her with the breeze, rose higher than her head, blocked out clear view of anything but the sky. She felt nested there, cosy, but ready to move some time soon. She wanted to explore, to understand what had happened. Felt strong and eager to start, with none of the clenched desperation that usually came when she drew on that strength.

Weird.

Like waking late one sun-soaked morning beside Ishgrim's sleeping form, knowing they had the whole day to themselves.

I'm coming home, Ish, she knew with perfect calm. *Nothing going to stop me now.*

She clambered to her feet and stood in the waist-high grass, trying to get her bearings. Tried to squeeze the wet out of one sleeve with her fist, got a scant few drops for her trouble – her clothing was drying out far faster than you'd expect, and when she held the sleeve up and sniffed it, there was a faint, medicinal reek underlying the damp. She shrugged, put out the arm at waist height and brushed idly with the palm of her hand at the swaying surface of the grass around her. The steppe stretched away in all directions, as trackless as an ocean. No features in the landscape, or at least none that her unaccustomed eye could—

She stopped in mid-turn, staring.

The structure loomed behind her – couldn't be more than fifty yards away in the grass – and for a few moments she couldn't work out what she was looking at. Towering broken curve twenty or thirty feet high, cavernous empty interior shadowed from the sun, like a two thirds part of some colossal smashed earthenware tankard left rolling in the straw on a tavern floor. It gleamed wetly inside, seemed to have some woven texture to it, exposed at the oddly softened edges where . . .

Was it *melting?*

Archeth narrowed her eyes, gave up trying to guess and made her way through the sighing grass towards the structure. She knew what it was now – recalled the dimensions of the drowning chamber they'd been hustled into by the Helmsman, made the match, could not accept this as coincidence. But how that solid alloy dome became this overturned, soft-edged shell was still beyond her. She reached the area of crushed – and, she now saw, scorched – grass where the shattered artefact lay. Saw a similarly burnt and flattened trail leading up what she now understood was a slight incline, at whose brow the . . .

Shell? Chamber?

. . . had stopped . . . *rolling?*

'Ah, daughter of Flaradnam. What plans they have for you now.'

Acrid chemical whiff on the breeze, and the words whispered in her ear as if the wind itself had been given sudden voice – she spun about and found herself five feet away from a figure in a slouch hat and patched sea captain's cloak.

'Who—' Quarterless, there in her right hand like a dream. She blinked at it, had no recollection of pulling the blade at all. 'Who the fuck are you?'

The cloaked figure nodded at her knife-filled hand. 'That's very impressive. Can you do it with all of them at once yet?'

She brandished the knife. 'I asked you a fucking question.'

'Yes. Not very politely, though. I believe if you make just a touch more effort, you'll find you already know who I am. Ah – there you go.'

As if he'd parted a curtain for her in the back of her mind. The Dragonbane's words, two years ago in the garden of a Pranderghal tavern, the faint chill that seemed to come on the breeze as he spoke. *He's from all the places the ocean will always be heard. Cavorts with mermaids in the surf and so forth. Cloak and hat's like a symbol for it.*

Takavach. Lord of the Salt Wind.

'You're the fuck that poisoned my horse?'

Beneath the hat-brim, she thought the eyes kindled like tiny flames. 'Don't push your luck, kir-Archeth Indamaninarmal. You're not exactly popular with the Dark Court right now.'

'Then what do you want?'

'Oh, well, I don't know. How about a little respect? Yes, that'd be nice, now I come to think about it. Under the circumstances. Not too much to ask, is it? Mutual respect, one immortal being to another?'

Archeth shrugged. 'Respect is earned.'

'Earned?' It came out a whisper, built rapidly to a rasping fury. 'Fucking *earned?* You cheeky half-blood bitch. You know what? I give up. No, really. I'm done. Really. This is too hard. It isn't fucking worth it. Cannot believe you just said that. To me, to a demon god, a noble of the Dark Court. I'm trying to fucking *help* you here.' One cloaked arm slashed angrily at the waist-high grass. Trail of glinting, splintering light, and the tall, nodding blades withered and smoked where the Salt Lord's hand had passed. 'We run around, we answer prayers. We grant wishes and favours by the shovel-load, try to fucking *balance* everything along the way – because, guess what, it doesn't actually work too well if you *don't* balance it – and after all that, after all that fucking effort, when you actually make yourself known, you *manifest* the way every bleating fucking supplicant for the last ten thousand years has been asking you to, *this* is what you get? You know what that is, daughter of Flaradnam? It's fucking ungracious.'

'I don't pray. To you or anybody else.'

'I didn't say you did.' The Salt Lord seemed to calm a little. 'Prayer is a tapestry, a system of permissions sewn into the world by the Book-Keepers. A way in. It's leverage, and it reaches everywhere, it touches you all. I don't need *you* to pray before I can get into your self-absorbed miserable little life. There's always someone else.'

'Book-Keepers?'

'Forget it. It doesn't fucking matter. I'm not talking to you, anyway. Go on, blunder into your ill-conceived little revenge fantasy for your dead friend and see how far you get. See how close you get to Poltar the shaman before one or other of the horrors Kelgris has gifted him with chops you down.'

She blinked. 'How do you know ab—'

'Oh, *come on!*'

They stood facing each other across the gently swaying grass. She wondered vaguely if she should feel afraid.

Her knives hummed and chuckled soothingly in the back of her head. Told her no.

She cleared her throat. 'Sorry. My father's people had no gods. I am not accustomed to—'

'No, evidently not.'

She hesitated again. 'You mention Kelgris – Kwelgrish of the Dark Court, I guess. Ringil Eskiath told me you and she appeared to be, uhm, acting in concert?'

'Yes, well, he's another one,' said the god grumpily. 'Can't muster the least shred of respect for his clan deities, sooner fucking die than drop his chin an inch, let alone get on his knees. Well, you work with the tools to hand, I suppose. Just don't be surprised when they turn in your grip and gouge you.'

'So you're not on the same side?' A little impatiently, because the demon god's constant bitching was starting to grate on her. 'Kwelgrish and you? You're opposed?'

Takavach sighed. 'Sides. Oppositions. Good and Evil. Heroes and villains. Them and us. The old brain-dead binary tribal cant. Look, would it melt your little head away completely to take on board the awful truth that *it's actually a bit more complicated than that?*'

'Don't you fucking patronise me. You think I don't understand complexity. My people have steered human affairs for five thousand years—'

'Not without a little quiet help from us, you didn't.'

'—and I've spent nearly two centuries doing the same job myself.'

'Well, you wouldn't think so, to hear you talk. Call yourself an immortal? Sides? You sound just like the next fucking human, you know that?'

'*My mother was human, you arrogant fuck!*' Teetering on the brink of something here, yearning to finally fall. 'So – you know what? Fuck you. My father, my immortal father? He married her. He stood with humans his whole life, in battle and in counsel. They were good enough for him. They're good enough for me too.'

Brief pause – for just a moment, under the brim of the slouch hat, she thought she saw Takavach smile.

'I'm very glad to hear that,' he said quietly.

'*Are you and Kelgris on the same fucking side or not?*'

'It doesn't work like that.' Almost, there was a plea in the Salt Lord's voice. 'You of all people, kir-Archeth, should understand that. Think about those five thousand years your people tried to manage human affairs. Think, in not much more than your own lifetime, of the manipulation it took your father to unify the southern hill tribes, to steer the Khimran clan into imperial ambition and beyond. You think being a god for these people is any easier?'

'I wouldn't know.'

'Well, it isn't.' Snappish flare of temper, but then Takavach's tone softened once more. 'Look, try to understand. Try to grasp the magnitude of what we're facing here, the mess we have to work with. The storm is coming, we see it massing on the horizon. We've been here before, we know how bad it can get. The dwenda are coming back, in all their idiot beauty and power, determined to claw back their beloved ancestral home. Stopping them without the Kiriath in place is going to be . . . a challenge. Certain things need to be done, certain pieces moved on the board, certain men put in place. Everyone has their own ideas about how to do it, but one constant remains – the Book-Keeper codes. By the codes used to repair the world aeons ago, we are forbidden direct intervention without supplicant request. And the major pieces, the ones best suited to the game we've chosen, *do not fucking pray.*'

The Salt Lord sighs. Looks away across the endless steppe.

'Perhaps they never did, perhaps it was never in them. Or perhaps they've just seen too much random horror to believe any longer in the power of the gods. Whichever is the case, the gods must make do, must find what fragments of leverage they can – a heroic slayer of dragons turned poor excuse for a clanmaster, for example, a man whose long dead father once laid down sacrifices and chanted explicit prayers to the Salt Lord for his son's safety; the sour rage of a disenchanted holy man at the dying of tradition this clanmaster represents; restless sibling rivalry and envy among the clanmaster's brothers – yes, all right, out of random elements like these, we can build a hand of sorts, and then play out the cards. But it's a complex, tangled game, daughter of Flaradnam, fenced about at every turn with limitation and compromise.

'You want to see how it's played?'

The steppe plain and the sky above it tilt and wheel away. It's as if she's ducked very rapidly into a tent and left the world outside. She stands in soft gloom, amidst streamers of mist that coil and drift, seemingly at random. The god is at her side.

Take our failed clanmaster – Takavach's voice is soundless in her head. He passes his hand through the drift of mist closest to them. It eddies and coils in the wake of the gesture, forms a passable image of the Dragonbane. *He cannot simply be whisked from safety and comfort, and placed on a path of heroic doom by the god charged with watching over him and keeping him safe. That would go against the codes. An actual threat must be made, one that would justify such an extraction, and it must be credible. Let's see* – other faces now, ones she doesn't know, but among them she sees the blood resemblance – *the jealous brothers might serve in this, but they would have to be incited. They are restless, you see, but that's all they are. Too much tradition vested in the clan-master's office for them to go against it alone. They need some kind of authority to unify them, to reassure the less enthusiastic among them when it comes to brotherslaying.*

So we back up. We cast about. What about this shaman – again, the Salt Lord stirs the mist, and a gaunt, sour-faced old man emerges, wrapped in a wolfskin that's seen better days – *he has no love for the clanmaster – he could be that authority. But he cannot simply be handed the tools and incited to act either, unless he prays for it, and to date he has not done so. Poltar is bitter but weak; he contents himself with sulking about the fading of the old ways and the terrible failings in the youth of today. So back up once more. Can we provoke a fight, perhaps, between clanmaster and shaman? That might kindle enough rage to trigger the necessary prayers. But neither man is angry enough to start this fight. We'd have to stir things up. Grief, guilt, rage, then – these are some of any god's favourite tools, after all, and the Dragonbane has been known to hurt people in the past when subject to such feelings. Perhaps, let's see, if someone died badly enough, someone of the clan, and the clanmaster felt somehow responsible, then the necessary sparks might fly.*

But how to arrange that death?

Oh, wait – here's a young man – quite a number of young men in fact – all dreaming of battling monsters out of Skaranak legend, praying fervently for some opportunity to test their heroic mettle. Wolves, steppe ghouls, flapping wraiths, it really doesn't matter which, their prayers are vague – so long as it's a monster, bring it on. Well, we choose one of these idiots and we answer his prayers. Takavach gestures, the mist boils. She gathers a confused impression of monstrous, lanky creatures, twice the height of a man, lashing out with taloned limbs at a horse and rider. The rider goes down in the grass, reels briefly to his feet, is struck back down. *The young man in question dies, heroically more or less, so there's his prayer answered, and our clanmaster neatly assumes the burden of guilt as we'd hoped. He tangles with the shaman, decks him in front of the whole clan.* She sees it in the mist, sees Egar throw the punch. *And the shaman calls down the rage of the gods to avenge his sullied dignity.*

Now we're getting somewhere!

Oh, but wait again – whichever god answers the shaman's prayers is going to find themselves in direct conflict with the Salt Lord, who is, after all, charged with protecting the Dragonbane from exactly this sort of thing. The two gods will be compelled, by the codes the Book-Keepers wrote, to do actual battle. And we can't have that. So back up all over again. Let's see – perhaps Poltar can be subtly encouraged to seek his own vengeance, to gather and shape his own tools. But how is a god to appear to him in direct answer to his prayers, only to refuse direct aid. The codes won't allow that either, they'd tear us apart for a breach like that. We need another avenue of approach, an indirect point of entry. And by a stroke of luck, here's a young girl from Trelayne – the Salt Lord draws her from the mist, huddled and weeping on a grimy pallet – *sold into whoring by whichever*

Majak mercenary brought her home and then tired of her, praying desperately to the Dark Court for intercession, revenge and escape. All of which we can provide, though not quite in the way the girl imagines, but no matter – there, finally, is our point of contact with the shaman. He's a frequent visitor to this brothel the girl finds herself in, and he's not the nicest of clients. He vents himself upon the girl – Archeth watches grimly as the scene coalesces. Some part of her wants to look away, but she doesn't – *Kwelgrish manifests in answer to the girl's prayers, gives her a peaceful escape into oblivion and the shaman the shock of his life, which we can more or less call revenge. Prayer obligations discharged once again, the codes are, if not wholly obeyed, at least appeased. And Kwelgrish has the holy man on the hook, but is free of any obligation to fulfil any direct prayers. We're in business. Poltar is incited, and a couple of tantalising myth-derived dreams later, so is one of the brothers. A plot is hatched, the clanmaster is, at long last, in mortal danger as required. Finally, we're where we need to be. Time to usher in the protecting Salt Lord, to provide warning and escape, by means of which the clanmaster can be placed where he needs to stand on the board.*

And then, after all this work, the Dragonbane chooses not to run.

I mean, he has every incentive. He's sick of being a clanmaster, life on the steppe, the whole thing. He's bored rigid. He dreams like a boy less than half his age, of running away from his obligations, back to the freebooter life he knew in the south. He ought to jump at the slightest chance to get out, that's the way it ought to go.

Instead, he chooses to ignore the Salt Lord's timely warning – decides to stay and fight. And the fight boils up for her viewing, riders and horses out of mist, the ghostly silent clash of blades, a magnificent Yhelteth warhorse rearing up, spiked through chest and eye with arrows. The Dragonbane unhorsed and down. *Nearly gets himself killed in the process, of course, and the Salt Lord then has to leap in and save him, using some frankly rather unsubtle supernatural means – like this.* Silence, while she watches in horror as the Dragonbane's brothers are slaughtered. *One of the brothers – and there he goes – escapes the fray, rides back to the shaman and reports. The shaman does exactly what you'd expect, goes straight to Kelgris to demand similar supernatural support. And meantime our clanmaster is all set to storm back to camp, all the way on foot if need be, and go head to head with Poltar and whatever else gets in his way.*

Now, the codes are rather clear on this – her initially oblique approach notwithstanding, Kelgris has become the shaman's patroness, and in matters of protection, she has no choice but to grant his wishes – answer his prayers, if you will. So, despite our very best efforts, the scene is now set for exactly the battle of powers we wanted to avoid. Only some very fast talking on the part of the Salt Lord manages to hustle our clanmaster – ex-clanmaster now, of course – out of range and so place the whole conflict in suspension. But the problem has not gone away.

I tell you, it isn't easy, being a god.

*

The world returned, slammed dizzyingly back into place around her, as if she'd been snapped upright into it from a prone position beneath the earth. Bright blue sky, wind through the grass, sunlight slanting. The cloaked and slouch-hatted figure stood opposite her once more. Quarterless was still in her hand.

'The Dragonbane is dead,' she said flatly.

'Yes, I know.'

'So then.' She looked at her knife. Hefted it, spun it on the palm of her hand and put it away in the sheath at the small of her back. 'I'd say your problem's solved for you.'

'For me, perhaps. But this is a blunderer kind of mess, if I might borrow a war metaphor, and the tail is still very much alive. If you go up against Poltar, burnt black demon witch that you are, then he is going to call on Kelgris for support. Believe me, he's done it for enemies a lot less imposing than you over the last couple of years. And if he calls, Kelgris will have no choice but to notice you, to answer the shaman's call, and to deliver her protection. And you don't want that.'

She looked down at the harness she wore, down to where the blade called Wraithslayer sat in its inverted sheath on her chest.

'I made the Dragonbane a promise,'

'He was your sworn bodyguard. He would want you to go home alive.'

Her clothes were almost dry, she realised. Absently, she squeezed at her sleeve again, searching for dampness, finding barely a trace. She gave the god a grim little smile.

'I will go home alive,' she said.

'*My lady!*'

A shout in Tethanne, from down the slope. She turned about, squinted and made out Selak Chan, on his feet in the grass and waving madly. She lifted an arm in salute. Looked back towards Takavach, already knowing at some level, as she turned, that the Salt Lord was gone.

She stared at the sunlit space where he'd stood, could almost see the outline of his figure still hovering there in the empty air. She nodded to herself. Flexed both hands on the hollow feeling in the cup of her palms.

'I will go home alive,' she murmured once more.

She started down the slope towards Selak Chan. Halfway there, she almost tripped over the spreadeagled body of a privateer. She stopped and knelt beside him. Ascertained that he was alive, if deeply asleep, and still quite damp. She left him there. Eyes sharper on the ground now as she descended the slope, and she spotted another two bodies hidden in the grass, one of Tand's sellswords and a marine. Neither of them seemed to be any the worse for wear.

Chan bowed his head in obeisance as she reached him, then gestured around. There was a bemused delight in his voice, and more than a little relief.

'My lady, this is . . . Where *are* we?'

'Exactly where we're supposed to be,' she told him. 'The Majak steppes.'

'I'd thought us betrayed and drowned.'

'I thought so too.' She held up her sleeve and sniffed at it again. The medicinal scent was still there, but all trace of moisture had gone. 'Apparently not.'

'But how . . .' He gestured around. 'How did we come here, my lady?'

She looked back up the slope to the remnant loom of the cracked container, the scorched grass path it had taken. Understanding itched at the edges of her mind, maddeningly just out of reach. Images came to her out of memory, seemingly at random, wheeling in her head like the mist-drawn pictures the Salt Lord had shown her. The track marks of burning ballista load through the scrub at Tlanmar, when the garrison came under Scaled Folk siege and the catapult defences saved the day; the shimmer of dissipating heat through the air in the crater where Anasharal fell to earth, the lethally heated shell the Helmsman came in; delicate Kiriath war munitions that mostly hadn't worked come the crunch, but were packed warily in sand anyway for the jolting wagon haul south to Demlarashan; a Scaled Folk hatchling that Grashgal had kept preserved in fluid in a jar at the An-Monal workshops . . .

'We were . . . catapulted,' she groped. 'A great height into the sky, I think, and then . . . let fall again, somehow. The liquid in the chamber was . . . not for drowning. It kept us from harm instead. And the chamber . . . Well, it must have cracked open when it hit the ground. Spilled us out here, in safety. I think.'

Chan's eyes widened. 'But the Dragonbane told us the steppes had to be at least a thousand miles to the east, maybe more. Does the reach of the Kiriath's iron demons really extend so far?'

Brief flaring of a pride she hadn't felt for a very long time.

'When need be, yes it does,' she said.

But she couldn't help wondering – rather sourly – why, with such capacity, Tharalanangh-arst had not just ordered the Helmsman to catapult them all back to Yhelteth instead; why it was so bloody important that they come out here to the steppes and find themselves still a good thousand miles or more from home.

If it's something the Dragonbane was supposed to do, then I guess we're shit out of luck.

'My lady?'

Chan was nodding out across the shoulder of the slope she'd just walked down. She looked and saw figures picking themselves up out of the grass. One at least was Majak.

'Good,' she said. 'Maybe Shendanak's guys can tell us how far we are from Ishlin-ichan. All this fucking grass looks the same to me.'

She watched as a couple of the waking men hugged each other and crowed with delight. Whoops and shouts floated back and forth. More figures, stumbling upright, woken presumably by the exuberant din. More

393

shouting, Naomic mingled with Majak and Tethanne. Closer in, a little way up the slope, she saw a privateer reach down grinning and pull Kanan Shent to his feet. The banged up Throne Eternal nodded his thanks.

Yeah. Put them a thousand miles south-west of here, and they'd be busy trying to carve each other's innards out. Go figure.

But she found herself grinning nonetheless.

'Right,' she told Chan. 'With me. Let's go see what the locals reckon.'

They headed back up the slope towards the nearest Majak figure.

They hadn't made it more than halfway when the man they were heading for stiffened, stared around at his fellows, then jabbed out an arm eastward and started shouting.

Archeth swung about to follow the gesture, shaded her eyes. The fading traces of the grin fell abruptly off her face.

Riders.

At least a dozen of them, coming at speed.

FIFTY

Findrich's place stank of dwenda presence from five blocks off. Gil almost grinned as he felt it, the gossamer-soft settling of its traceries over him, the creep of its threads through his mind. There was a time his nape would have cooled at that touch, a time it would have frozen him in mid-step, sent his hand rising to the pommel of the Ravensfriend, his lip curling back off his teeth in the instinctive, defensive snarl of any fanged animal at bay.

Now, he barely broke step in the rain.

'What is it, my lord?'

Noyal Rakan, brow furrowed with concern beneath his crested Throne Eternal helmet, young eyes intent on Ringil's face. *Appears you don't have it quite as nailed down as you thought, Gil.* He smiled at his Throne Eternal lover with what he hoped was reassurance.

'Nothing to worry about, captain. Everyone's where they need to be.'

The streets of Etterkal were eerily silent around them, as if emptied by some abrupt and brutal curfew. They passed barrows abandoned in the middle of thoroughfares, doors left open on deserted tavern interiors with stools flung over and tables still crowded with tankards and platters. Once or twice, they saw wary faces watching them from upper floor windows, the odd hunched figure in a side alley or begging niche. But most of the Salt Warren seemed to have found pressing business to attend to elsewhere.

Yeah – one guess where that is.

Above the loom of tenement and warehouse walls, through the murk of rain and low-hanging ragged cloud, the sky towards Harbour End was tinged a deep, dull red. A safe bet by now that the news and its many embroidered exaggerations would have reached at least as far as that glow. And in a quarter like Etterkal, word of that sort would work like a flung fistful of coins in a market square. Everyone would be scrambling, fighting through, grabbing for something. Some would have gone to exploit the chaos, to break and enter, to loot, or maybe to settle old scores while the city's equilibrium was tilted out of true. Some might have family or other, less warm-blooded Harbour End interests to protect. Some would simply want to try their young thug mettle in the fire-lit streets, regardless of who or what against. Add to that those who'd go just to gawp, to say they were there, to have a tale to tell their fellows in years to come, and you could count the whole Salt Warren emptied out, faster than a knifed nobleman's purse.

The dwenda presence strengthened, but he still had no sense that their eyes were on him. Back in the Glades what seemed like a lifetime ago, Seethlaw had stalked him through the mangrove dawn, followed him almost home through the mist, leaned in then at some unimaginable Grey Place angle and bent his gaze on this mouthy, bad-tempered young swordsman who'd shown up to plague him. Gil wasn't ever likely to forget what that felt like, and he couldn't feel it now.

Still . . .

He put up a shrouding glyph, one of the stronger ones. It wouldn't make him invisible to Aldrain eyes, but it should at least render him un-interesting. Just another human soldier, marching somewhere in a hurry with his comrades at his back. What was it Seethlaw's lieutenant had said of human soldiery – *like the lost souls of apes.* Gil could still hear the wealth of disdain and distaste in those words, and he was counting on it. With a bit of Dark Queen luck, all eyes in the Findrich residence right now, human and dwenda, were turned the other way, out towards the confla-gration at the harbour and the spilling, spreading rage behind it.

Boots through puddles, boots on cobbled stone – they reached the corner of Dromedary Row, swung crisply into Court's Honour Rise. Slab Findrich's converted warehouse palace gleamed in wet, dressed-stone frontage less than a hundred yards away at the end of the street. It wasn't much of a rise – *it isn't fucking Gallows Gap, that's for sure* – but trust Fin-drich to find a hill to squat on, even here.

He bared his teeth. The rain trickled into his mouth.

He drew the Ravensfriend.

'All right,' he shouted through the downpour. 'With me. Let's get this done! For Empire, and for Honour! Cut down anything that stands in your way!'

They stormed the scant distance to Findrich's front door as one. Wet, drumming splatter of boots up the puddled street as they charged, the thin lash of rain across his face. It felt as if something hard in the small of his back was driving him on. Ten yards out, he dropped the shrouding glyph, built a fast pyre of force in the gap it left. Brought up a howl from the pit of his stomach, raised one clawing hand at the double doors in his way – tore them apart. The oak locking bar on the other side snapped across like a toothpick, he felt it go, felt the upper hinge on the left hand door panel tear out like a rotten tooth. The doors blew back into the stonework on either side, rebounded, sagged and hung.

In through the gap.

They met no opposition; they met no one at all. Inside, it was all torch-lit vaulted space and twinned stone stairways sweeping grandly to the upper levels, as empty of human life as a ruin. Findrich's place was one of the quarter's original Marsh Brotherhood stockhouses, put up in a time when the harbour was still a silty undredged anchorage good for fishing skiffs and not much more. Trelayne's commerce came and went overland

396

in those days, long trailing caravans guided in and out through the mazes of the marsh by sworn men, and paying handsomely for the licence. The merchants who built in Etterkal back then were men of cabalistic power and wealth, and their architecture reflected the fact. In the jumping shadow and glow of his men's torches, blown wild by the sudden entry of the storm he'd let in, Ringil saw expensively finished bas relief and statuary everywhere – friezes depicting heavily laden beasts of burden amidst lush marsh vegetation, piled gluts of goods and market stalls, stacked coin and assayer's scales, and everywhere the repeating motif of masked men at guard. Masked figures led the caravans, masked overseers pointed imperiously at the gathered wealth, masked swordsmen stood with arms folded behind the tables of coin. And the paired stone balustrade staircases were watched over by twin statues of hugely thewed Marsh Brotherhood heroes, caped and masked, stern jawed and smiling faintly, as if in contempt at Ringil's presumption in daring to enter here.

From the look of the stonework, there'd been some restoration work done recently. Gil snorted, wiped dripping water from his nose. 'Fucking poser. Same as it ever was, Slab. The old brotherhood wouldn't have wiped their arse with the likes of you, and now you want to pretend you're the heir to it all?'

Rakan blinked at him in the torchlight. 'What?'

At his side, Klithren looked perplexed. Gil sighed.

'Doesn't matter. Upstairs, let's go.'

No sign of life as they mounted the right hand stairway. He reached for the dwenda presence, found it still there but churned up now, flickering disconcerted in a way he could only ever remember tasting once before.

'That's right,' he sing-songed softly in the gloom. 'I'm *behind* you.'

Down a torchlit corridor flanked by heavy locked doors, nothing living behind them as far as he could tell. The air was stale and musty, and now that he was out of the rain, he could smell his own soaked clothes. He wrinkled his nose.

Funny, would have expected some resistance by now. Not like Slab at all, this.

'Keep your eyes peeled,' he muttered at Klithren.

The corridor gave out onto a kind of broad raised atrium with a honeycomb stonework floor. Rain fell in from the opened roof above, soaked the stone and rinsed through to the floor level below. It made a hollow, almost musical splashing down there. Under the eaves that edged the central expanse and offered cloistered cover from the rain, the walls were worked with the same bas relief friezes he'd seen in the entry hall below. Torchlight guttered from the corners.

'*Degenerate and oathbreaker! Stand where you are!*'

Oh, here we go . . .

But it wasn't Slab Findrich. Too much youth and pomp in those tones, too much jerky excitement, nothing of Findrich's dead-eyed aplomb.

Vaguely familiar, though . . .

'You ran and hid from me once, outcast. Shirked your appointed time on Brillin Hill fields and left a beggared drunk to face me in your stead. Will you turn tail again now?'

Ah.

Like a warm flush through his nether half, like the twisting of some obscure lust in his guts. He made a damping gesture to the men at his back, lowered the Ravensfriend until its point touched the honeycombed floor.

'Hello, Kaad,' he said into the gloom. 'This is a pleasant surprise.'

From the corners of the atrium space came skirmish ranger uniforms, crossbows cranked and cradled on the hip of at least a third of them, and the rest with swords or axes drawn. He guessed the count at about fifteen – it was hard to tell in the jumpy light. Not bad odds, now the element of ambush surprise was gone. From amidst their number came two slim, erect figures, one older but still spry of step, the other taller, more muscle about him, and a sword in his raised right hand. A silver gleaming mail shirt glinted to mid-thigh, looked like it had been pulled on in a hurry. Iscon Kaad – Lord Watchman of Administrative . . . something or other, Gil couldn't now recall the exact shape of that sinecure title. Swift emissary of the aspiring Kaad family name, anyway, keen avenger of slights to its fledgling honour. Blade salon graduate and pretty nifty with it, by all accounts, as the poor sozzled ghost of a certain war veteran called Darby would probably attest, if he could only be summoned back from wherever his bewildered soul had fled.

And look, he's brought his Daddy with him.

Chancellery counsellor Murmin Kaad, smooth-smiling puller of strings, hungry climber of carefully placed strategic ladders into the upper echelons of Trelayne society. The man who nearly two decades past sent Jelim Dasnal to die in the cage for unclean acts of congress, the man who let the Eskiath clan buy Ringil free of the same sentence with who knew what fistful of slow-burning political favours. He wore an eyepatch now – Gil's guts seethed with joy at the sight – but was otherwise unchanged from the last time they met. Grace of Heaven Milacar had once commented on how the climb to power that might age and wring out some men seemed only to have energised Kaad. It was true. He stood now with the bearing of a man not much more than half his age, hair still thick and dark but for the two greying patches at his temples, face still unpouched, body still unswollen with all the years of fine living he'd managed to claw from Trelayne's outmanoeuvred aristo cliques.

Ringil ignored the son, gave the father a harsh smile.

'Hello, little man. How's the eye?'

'*Scum! You will not—*'

Murmin Kaad put a hand on his son's shoulder, and Iscon Kaad shut up like a drawbridge gate. He glowered silent, smouldering hate at Ringil across the atrium. Kaad senior let go his son's shoulder, offered up a thin smile.

'The eye is dead jelly, as I'm sure you already know by now. We are sent to stop you, Ringil. Will you lay down your weapons and save your men's lives at least, or will you sacrifice them all as you did poor old Darby?'

'Where's Findrich?'

'He will see you once you are disarmed,' snapped Iscon Kaad. 'Or he will see your corpse. Yield now, or do you prefer that we kill you all?'

'You could try that.'

'And succeed, I believe.' Kaad senior gestured left and right at the men he'd brought. 'These are skirmish ranger veterans you see. No finer fighting men in the known world.'

'Fuck would you know about fighting, lickspittle?'

'That's fucking it!' Iscon Kaad, shouting in rage, turning to look at the men behind him. His arm came up.

Ringil beat him to it – left hand rising, crimping for the glyph. Eddies of *ikinri 'ska* force, out across the atrium like ripples on a pond.

'Heavy, those crossbows,' he intoned. 'Far too heavy to hold.'

He didn't need to hear the multiple clunking impacts as the bowmen lost grip on their weapons, let them tumble to the floor. He raised his hand, made another glyph.

'Broken.'

It went like a wave through the skirmish ranger ranks, screams and crumpling bodies as this limb or that snapped, sent them variously collapsing to the floor or staggering and clutching at the broken bone of an arm. Screams rose up and drowned out the fall of the rain.

'Sit down,' he said quietly to Murmin Kaad. 'Watch.'

The counsellor dropped to the rain-soaked atrium floor almost as fast as the men whose legs the *ikinri 'ska* had broken. His jaw clamped, straining to resist the spell. But he stayed there as if nailed in place.

'Now then,' Ringil told the son. 'Let's pretend we're back at Brillin Hill, shall we?'

Iscon Kaad came in yelling, sword a looping blur. Ringil didn't even bother trying to get his shield down off his shoulder. He hacked sideways two-handed with the Ravensfriend, met the blow with everything he had, stopped Kaad dead in his tracks with the force of the block. Spun on the locking point, heaved upward and stepped sharply back past the straining blades – spooning as close as any lover, his back to the other man's front. It was a thuggish, close quarters reverse, like nothing you'd find in any gentleman's blade salon manual, and Iscon Kaad had no working defence against it. Ringil stamped savagely backward, boot-heel to shin for distraction, right hand dropping from the double grip he had on the Ravensfriend. He hacked up and into Kaad's sternum with his elbow so the other man convulsed. Let his arm straighten, twist – dropped the dragon tooth dagger from his sleeve into his waiting palm, stabbed back and down. Buried the jagged blade deep in the low end of Iscon Kaad's thigh.

Kaad screamed and staggered. His blade batted ineffectually against Ringil's upheld left hand block with the Ravensfriend, tried to scrape free, but the clinch was too close and Gil's raised left arm was solid as stone, the Kiriath steel unmoving in his fist. Gil twisted the dagger, tore it loose. Spun about, raised a boot and kicked Iscon Kaad in the knee. The younger man went down floundering and rolling, dropped his sword, clutched at his wounded thigh with both hands. Ringil followed him, let the dagger clatter free on the honeycombed stone floor, swapped the Ravensfriend back into his right hand and stood over his downed opponent, breathing hard.

'Any questions?' he hissed.

A strangled moan, but not from Iscon Kaad's lips. Ringil glanced sideways, saw Kaad senior still straining to rise from where the spell had him pinned. His eyes were pleading, fixed on his son's stricken form. The screaming of the broken-limbed skirmish rangers rang in Ringil's head. He jerked a look at Rakan and the imperials.

'Attend to the fallen.'

Rasped syllables in Tethanne, barely his own voice at all. Sounded like something that belonged somewhere down in the dark defiles.

Then he reversed his grip on the Ravensfriend, took it two-handed and struck a quick slanting blow down into Iscon Kaad's belly. The Kiriath steel went through the mail as if wasn't there, slashed a long lateral wound across Kaad's guts. The downed man shrieked, and across the atrium his father cried out in awful sympathy. Ringil pulled the Ravensfriend free, watched almost absently as the blood welled up where it had been. Iscon Kaad screamed and wept, tried hopelessly to hold himself closed. Ringil shook himself, as if remembering some task that had slipped his mind, made his way across to Murmin Kaad.

'Hold out your hands,' he said gently.

The snaking whisper of the *ikinri 'ska* under his words – the spell tugged Kaad's arms instantly outward and held them there, as if suspended from invisible puppet strings. A thin stream of pleading dribbled from his lips; he was shaking his head in endless denial, of what exactly it was hard to tell. Ringil swung the Ravensfriend up, brought the blade slicing down. He severed both arms midway between elbow and wrist. Blood gouted and splattered, the counsellor screamed, still holding both stumps out, paralysed in place. Ringil unlocked the glyph with a gesture, and Kaad collapsed sideways in a twitching heap.

Rain fell ceaselessly in through the open roof and onto them both. Ringil wiped at his face.

'Someone get tourniquets on this man. I don't want him to die just yet.'

A young marine came hurrying to comply, perhaps glad to be released from the more general task of seeing to the enemy wounded. He tore strips from the mutilated counsellor's cloak with his knife, knotted them savagely tight below Kaad's elbows. The blood flow from the stumps slowed to a seep. Ringil nodded the imperial back to dispatching the League men. He crouched beside Kaad, grabbed him by one embroidered lapel and dragged him close.

'You weren't sent to stop me,' he said. 'Findrich isn't that stupid. You were just sent to slow me down.'

Kaad twisted on the floor, tried feebly to get loose. Words leaked and mumbled from him. Ringil had to lean in closer to hear.

'My . . . son . . .'

Gil looked bleakly across to where Iscon Kaad lay in the centre of the atrium, blood leaking thickly from the wound in his belly. The rain falling in from the roof splashed around him, mingling with the blood, thinning it, draining it away through the holes in the honeycombed floor. The younger Kaad was keening, rocking very slightly side to side, hugging himself gingerly across the midriff.

'Your son is dying, Kaad. I've killed him. But it's going to take a while. Tell you what – why don't you crawl over there and try holding him in your arms to comfort him.'

He patted the counsellor on the shoulder and got up. Made as if to turn away, then stopped.

'Oh, but of course. You can't now, can you?'

Then he turned away for real. Ignored the dislocated howl that went up from Murmin Kaad, went to collect and clean his dagger, while around him the imperials finished up the job of slitting throats on the last few crippled skirmish rangers.

Klithren came across to him as he stowed the dragon knife back in his sleeve. Nodded casually out at Murmin Kaad, who was currently trying to crawl like some crippled insect across the rain-splashed atrium to where his son lay bleeding out.

'Something personal?'

Ringil rearranged his sleeve, met the mercenary's eye. 'You might say that, yeah. Got a problem?'

Klithren shook his head. 'Fuck, no. Only ever met the guy once before, back when they gave me the command, and even then you could see what kind of arsehole he was. Street as me, but he's poncing it up like some has-been Parashal family's favoured son. No surprise to me he had something like this coming. No, I just want to know what all that shit about slowing us down means.'

Ringil bent to pick up the Ravensfriend, retrieved the swatch he'd cut out of Iscon Kaad's cloak to clean his weapons with.

'You heard that, huh?'

The mercenary grinned fiercely. 'Guess freebooting for the Empire, you forgot you're not the only one speaks Naomic around here.'

'No, I didn't forget.' Wiping the Ravensfriend's blade down absently as he spoke.

'Good, so what's the deal? Slowing us down for what? If Findrich and the cabal knew you'd walk through a dozen skirmish rangers like they were an open door, what's their second line going to look like?'

'You can't guess?'

'The Aldrain? They're here?'

Ringil nodded at the surrounding architecture, the rills of water streaming off the roof edge over their heads. 'Somewhere in the building, yeah. I can fucking taste them.'

'Taste . . .?' Klithren shook his head. 'Never mind. Black mage shit, I don't want to know. But I guess it's time for that briefing, isn't it?'

There was a challenge in his eyes as he said it. Ringil sighed. He lifted his hand, snapped his fingers and got Noyal Rakan's attention from across the courtyard space. The Throne Eternal came over, past imperials patting down the men whose throats they'd just slit, stepping wide around Murmin Kaad, where the counsellor lay collapsed and weeping in the tracks of his own slow-oozing blood, still not yet halfway to his dying son. Kaad had just snagged one of his stumps on the textured stone floor as he crawled, was convulsed with the fresh agony it brought. Ringil saw it happen out of the corner of his eye, heard the feeble shriek, was dimly disappointed at the lack of any sensation it stirred in him.

Rakan got out of the rain, saluted. Tried not to let his gaze creep back to the mutilated man. He looked faintly queasy, whether from his work dispatching the injured skirmish rangers or from what his lover had just done – it was hard to tell. Probably both. The look in his eyes made Ringil feel shabby and stained and old.

'My lord?'

'Get the men formed up over there. There's a couple of things they need to know before we go on.'

'Yes, my lord.' Rakan cleared his throat. He touched the mercy blade at his belt, gestured at Kaad's sobbing and renewed efforts to crawl. 'Would you like me to, uhm . . .'

Ringil stared at him, let him hang there.

'No, captain,' he said coldly. 'I would not. Pull your men from their pillaging and get them formed up.'

Rakan flushed. Saluted and turned smartly away. Klithren watched him go with a sage expression on his face.

'How that boy ever got to be Throne Eternal beats the fuck out of me.'

'Shut up,' Ringil told him, with more vehemence than he'd intended to use. 'Fucking got the jump on *you* single-handed, didn't he?'

'Oh, I'm sorry. Am I treading on some delicate faggot toes here?'

'Treading on some black mage toes, remember? Back off or I'll turn you into a fucking frog. Now go and get in line for this briefing you're so fucking keen for me to give.'

Klithren shrugged and wandered over to join the assembling imperials. On the way, he passed close to Murmin Kaad's crippled form, and the counsellor said something to him. Klithren crouched to listen. Rainfall off the roof edges obliterated any chance of hearing what was said, but whatever it was, Klithren only shook his head, gestured in Ringil's direction and then resumed his ambling stride to where the imperials were gathered.

Ringil gave the Ravensfriend one more cursory wipe over, balled up the piece of borrowed cloak cloth and tossed it away. He followed Klithren out into the rain, was surprised to find himself stopping and kneeling beside Murmin Kaad.

'Something you wanted?'

'Kill . . . him,' the counsellor panted. 'I beg you. You are revenged . . . upon me. I ask . . . nothing for myself. But end . . . his suffering. *Please.* He has done *nothing* to you.'

Ringil rubbed his chin. 'Did Jelim Dasnal do something to you?'

'*Please*—'

'And yet you sent him to die on a spike.'

'That . . .' A spasm of pain twisted Kaad's face. 'It was the *law.*'

'So is this. It's recent legislation, you may not have heard. Harm those I care for, and those you care for will be harmed. How does it feel?'

'Please, I'm begging you. I'm . . .' Tears streamed from Kaad's undamaged eye. 'I'm *sorry!*'

'Yes, I imagine you are. I was too, when it was too late to do anything about it. I still had to watch someone I loved die.' His pulse was thunder in his ears, a liquid beat in his vision. He dragged down his rage with an effort, got his breathing back under control. 'Look on the bright side, though – a wound like that, your boy's going to be gone in a few hours at most. It won't take him days, the way it did for Jelim.'

'*Hoiran damn your soul to hell!*'

'I think he'll have trouble from his wife if he does.' Ringil got up. 'Goodbye, Kaad. Save your energy for the rest of that crawl. You're nearly there. Even without hands, you'll get closer than I was ever allowed.'

'All right!' Kaad's voice cracked across. '*All right . . .*'

Despite himself, Ringil hesitated. 'All right what?'

'I . . . will . . . buy my son's death. I . . . I know something . . . something of what awaits you.'

'So do I. Your dwenda pals and I have already had a couple of dust-ups. We're almost old friends.'

'No, not that. The dwenda have brought something with them.'

Ringil's eyes narrowed. 'The Talons of the Sun?'

'My son.' Kaad levered himself up on one elbow, teeth gritted. 'You will give my son peace first.'

'You're in no position to bargain, Kaad. You tell me what you know, I'll decide if it merits an act of mercy or not.' He crouched again, grabbed the other man by the ruined forearm and squeezed. Blood welled up in the ragged end of the stump. The counsellor shrilled and collapsed. Ringil bent the arm over against the elbow joint, knelt closer, whispered in Kaad's ear. 'Or I'll just twist it out of you anyway. Believe me, that'd make me a lot happier.'

Kaad made a broken sobbing sound in his throat. Ringil let go his arm.

'Come on, counsellor. Cough it up.'

'A sword, they have a sword.' The words came tumbling out, Kaad's voice high-pitched and desperate. 'An heirloom of Risgillen's clan. They say the soul of an ancient warrior king is in it. A champion of the dwenda five thousand years ago.'

'What?' Ringil shook his head as if to clear it. 'A champion? You're talking about the Illwrack Changeling? *Here?*'

'I do not . . .' Kaad's voice came faintly now, the shock was taking him down. 'Know his name. Only . . . they have the sword, they plan . . .'

'Plan what?'

Nothing. The counsellor looked to have passed out from the pain. Ringil straddled him, stooped and dragged him onto his back. Slapped him methodically back and forth across the face.

'Come on, Kaad. Come on back. What plan? You want to save your son some pain, this is no way to go about it. What *plan?* Come on!'

Kaad twitched and flinched from the blows, semi-conscious. His stumps pawed at the air – in his confusion, he was attempting to push Gil away with hands he no longer possessed. Ringil grabbed one of the wagging forearms and squeezed it again, not too hard this time. The pain must have been searing – Murmin Kaad jolted awake, stared up at him, hissing hatred.

'Fuck you . . . aristo faggot . . . scum . . .'

'Yeah, yeah. Great way to engage my pity, Dad.' He backhanded the mutilated man savagely across the face. 'Pack it in. Talk. What plan?'

'Plan?'

'Oh, for Hoiran's fucking sake . . .' Ringil grabbed Kaad by the scruff of the neck, hauled him into something resembling a sitting position. He threw out a demonstrative hand to where Kaad junior had rolled in their direction, rain-splashed face a mask of agony and desperation, one hand still trying to hold the wound in his belly closed, the other stretched out mutely towards his father. 'You want me to put young Iscon there out of his misery? You tell me about the sword. What are they planning to do with it?'

'They . . .' Panting, face suddenly crumpled up in pain. 'They . . . will . . . force the sword on you. Force it into your grip. There is . . . a ritual. And then . . . the Dark King will . . . possess you. Will return to them . . . in your form.'

Ringil held onto the mutilated counsellor a moment longer, then let him go, let him collapse to the honeycomb floor. He sat back on his boot-heels, soaked in sudden thought.

'That's the plan, is it?' he murmured.

Kaad lifted his head a bare couple of inches from the floor. 'My . . . son . . .'

'Yeah, your fuckwit son.' Gil frowned, remembering. 'Was going to have his bowmen turn me into a pin-cushion. That would have been embarrassing, wouldn't it? Handing the dwenda a corpse for their ritual.'

His eyes snapped back to focus, nailed the counsellor with a stare.

'Or are you lying to me, Murmin Kaad?'

'No . . . no . . . No lie.' The effort was too much. Kaad's head fell back on the stonework with an audible clunk. He stared up into the rain, mouth working. 'Alive or dead . . . it does not . . . matter. They told us. The . . . ritual is unchanged. But the lady Risgillen . . . will have you alive . . . if she can. Have you know . . . what devours you. My son . . . please, my son . . .'

Ringil sighed. Pressed the heel of one hand to his forehead in the rain. 'Risgillen, Risgillen, fucking Risgillen. Should have killed that bitch when I had the chance. Should have known she'd never fucking quit. All right.'

This last snapped out with abrupt force, as he came to his feet, decided. He strode across to where Klithren waited with the imperials, well out of the rain.

'You came to the Hironish looking for a sword, as well as me?' he asked the mercenary with dangerous calm. 'Supposed to dig it up and bring it back here, were you?'

Klithren looked at him blankly. 'Sword?'

'All right, never mind. Look, let's get this briefing out of the way and just—'

'*Liar!*' It was a scream so high and tortured, it might almost have been an eagle's shriek. Both men glanced round to where Murmin Kaad thrashed about in his rain-soaked, bloodied cloak, flailing and rolling round to glare after Gil, face almost upside down, features contorted in fury and grief. '*Scum! Faggot liar!*'

'He's going pull those tourniquets loose if he's not careful,' Klithren reckoned.

'Yeah, maybe.' Ringil raised an arm, gestured the imperials to gather around. 'All right, listen up. This next—'

'*Liar, fucking liar!*' Kaad was weeping now, sobbing out his rage and loss. '*You swore. Liar! Liar!*'

'This next—'

'*Fucking aristo scum-fuck liar!*'

Rustle of interest among the men, heads turning to look, muttered commentary. The screaming went on, apparently Kaad had discovered new reserves of strength. Gil closed his eyes. Opened them and looked for Noyal Rakan.

'Captain.'

'My lord.' Still a guarded stiffness in the Throne Eternal's voice.

'*. . . fucking burn in hell, Hoiran will have your soul, you fuck, you . . .*'

405

'Would you be so good as to slit the throats on those two, so I can hear myself think.'

The stiffness melted out of Rakan's tone. 'Yes, my lord. At once. Uhm . . . both of them?'

'. . . *swore, you fucking swore, you lying aristo fucking* . . .'

Ringil nodded wearily. 'Both of them. Oh, and . . . do the younger one first. Make sure his father sees it done.'

The Throne Eternal captain drew his knife, hurried eagerly to the task. Ringil saw grimly impressed looks pass among the imperials, approving nods. By the look of it, he'd just cemented another brick in the wall of his reputation as the black-hearted swordsman sorcerer from hell.

Oh, good.

His face twitched with an insanely compelling impulse – laugh out loud or weep, he wasn't very sure which it was.

He locked it carefully away. He made his features stone.

But as Rakan knelt by Iscon Kaad and opened his throat, as Kaad senior's screaming soaked abruptly away, left only a high, tight keening in its place, he could not quite close out the thought, the insistent wondering if Gingren might ever have shown as much fury and love for him. What it might have taken to earn it, what it might have cost.

Whether either of them, father or son, could ever have paid enough.

Get a fucking grip, Gil. Kind of busy here.

Rakan stooped over Murmin Kaad. Ringil thought the counsellor might have been smiling in welcome as the knife dipped down.

FIFTY-ONE

'The war?' Carden Han, imperial legate for the Majak steppe, bit into a pear and chewed with a lot less decorum than you'd expect for a man of his rank. He talked right through the mouthful. 'Going well, the last I heard. Hinerion taken by storm, gains in the Gergis hinterland, so forth. But that news is months old, of course. We don't exactly have our finger on the pulse up here.'

She caught a splinter of bitterness in that last comment. Ishlin-ichan was strictly a backwater posting, too far from the Empire to have any real political significance, or afford much in the way of opportunities for advancement. Career diplomats avoided it altogether if they could; failing that, they got it out of the way early on. Time served out here on the steppes as a younger man could always be parlayed into some weightier office closer to the heart of things once you came home. But Carden Han was not by any stretch of the imagination a younger man. The face Archeth sat across from was lined and tired-looking, hair receding from a deeply creased brow, beard gone mostly to grey.

Which could only mean a couple of things, really. Either a mediocre diplomatic career, now guttering low, or some form of exile. And she'd not paid nearly enough attention at court the last few years to know which was the case for Han.

She chose her words with according care.

'Nonetheless, my lord, you do seem to run a tight ship.' She nibbled at a sweetmeat she didn't really want. 'Your intervention out there today was nothing if not timely.'

The legate flushed. 'You are too kind, my lady. Really. It was just a routine precaution. The locals here set much store by anything that happens in the sky – portents and so forth – and a sudden comet in the west, an hour before dawn, falling sky iron, well . . . you can imagine the fuss something like that would set off amongst a people like these.'

Or any other people I ever ran into, she managed not to say. Han might have gone native as far as table manners were concerned, but like some others she'd seen in similar posts over the years, he was still gnawing what sustenance he could from the chewed-over rind of his own assumed cultural superiority.

Yeah – not unlike a certain sulking young Kiriath half-blood we know back in Yhelteth, eh, Archidi?

Behind her, a cool night breeze blew in the feasting chamber's window, touched her at the nape of the neck. The Dragonbane's lonely ghost come to call, perhaps. Or just the messaged death of that other Archeth, left so far behind now she could scarcely believe she'd been the same woman not six months ago. Up to the arse end of the world, back down again, through death and storm and dragons, and here she suddenly was, like some odd, graceful stranger to herself. The abrupt stab of empathy with Han startled her. She was not accustomed to seeing herself in the humans around her, and certainly not used to seeing her failings writ large in theirs. Her introspection was rarely so lucid.

Nothing a quarter ounce of krin won't fix for you, some grim, old shard of her personality advised. But like the night breeze, she shrugged it off without much effort. Other, more pressing concerns crowded it out – Jhiral, alone on the throne and poorly served by sycophant advisors, likely fumbling the war's course by now, stumbling towards some policy catastrophe or other; the Citadel rampant, tipping the Empire's hard-won pragmatic cosmopolitanism back over into tribal intolerance, conquest and rage. Ishgrim, caught up in it all.

Getting home for all of them, before it was too late.

'Yes, I'd have been remiss indeed,' the legate went nattering on. 'To let an Ishlinak scavenger party ride out there without imperial observers along. It doesn't take much to show the flag, really. A handful of men, a medical officer we can pass off as our very own shaman. They don't differentiate, you see, healing and augury, diseases and portents, it's all the same big mysterious mess to the steppe peoples. Fortunately, our man Sarax – the one who conveyed you back here – well, he's become adept at playing the role. Poor fellow, he thought he'd come here to treat gashes, fevers and broken bones, and at least three times in the last year he's found himself pronouncing sagely over chunks of smouldering dross dropped out of the sky. I remember one incident last year when . . .'

She drifted a little, let Han's eager-to-please chatter fade out. Let the man talk; he'd clearly been starved of imperial company for far too long. The room they sat in said it all – dull, functional brickwork for walls, rough sawn timber beams for the roof. Here and there, a floor-tile was glazed to include a Yhelteth crest and emblem, but the effect was crude, clearly the work of craftsmen for whom the symbols held no significance beyond the wage it brought in. The rugs on the floor were of Majak design, the furniture had the same blunt lines as the roof timbers. The fireplace was modest for the size of room, as was the blaze within it. And she'd seen no glass in any window since she arrived at the embassy.

The only apparent artefact of Yhelteth origin was Han's family coat of arms – a silk drape banner hung on one wall, looking lonely and out of place.

'. . . but the Majak do at least listen to us on these matters now – that is, the Ishlinak in these parts do, and increasingly the more outlying clans too. Such basic medical successes are slowly winning them over to a broader respect for our learning and faith, you see, and with that kind of—'

'Yes, fascinating indeed.' She worked at keeping the impatience out of her voice. It was a big favour she needed from this man, and she wasn't sure the simple fact of her rank back in Yhelteth was going to swing it. She sipped at her wine, tried to sound casual. 'This, uh . . . respect – would you say it holds sway with other clans out across the steppe?'

'Oh, certainly.' Han swallowed and helped himself to another piece of fruit from the table. 'We see to it that our presence is felt well beyond the walls of Ishlin-ichan. Not easy to do with a garrison this small, but any legate worth his salt knows the value of projection.'

'That's good. There are a couple of things I need to do out there before I head south. And it's going to take some projection.'

'Oh?' Sudden shift in the legate's tone.

She drained the rest of her wine, set down the empty goblet like a chess piece. 'Yes. How much influence do you have with the Skaranak?'

'The *Skaranak?*'

And just from the way he said it, she knew she had trouble.

When he'd calmed down a bit:

'Look, my lady, I would like to help you, really I would. Any other clan, and we could have this Poltar quietly murdered for you, no problem. Even abducted so you could torture and kill him yourself, if that's your pleasure. I'd be delighted to arrange it for you, really. But this is the Skaranak we're talking about. I don't know that you understand quite what that means.'

She shrugged. 'All right. The Skaranak. Tell me about them.'

'Yes. First you have to understand that things have changed a lot up here in the last ten years. Ishlin-ichan is a lot bigger than it used to be, and there are a couple of secondary settlements sprouting on the other side of the river too. The western clans are getting more and more comfortable with the idea of staying in one place, getting used to rubbing along with their neighbours with a minimum of violence too. But the Skaranak are old school. They're the die-hard horse tribe remnants of what the rest of the Majak used to be. They never settled like the Ishlinak, you see, and they pride themselves on that fact. Nomad to the bone, still the same basic thug raiders they were a century ago. That gets them a lot of respect. And with the Ishlinak sticking mostly to the city environs and the other side of the river, there's been no one to challenge them for primacy on the eastern steppe for the better part of a decade. The recruiting sergeants love them, of course – they'll take Skaranak in preference to any other clan. And for every ten young thugs they send south to become soldiers, at least two or three are bound to trickle back here at some point as seasoned veterans, which just adds to their fighting capacity.'

Archeth nodded. 'Common dynamic. Seen it get us in trouble more than once in the past.'

'Yes, but try telling that to the recruiters.' Carden Han leaned forward in his chair, a man trying to drive home the valid point of his refusal to help her. 'Quite seriously, my lady, if the Majak plains were not so vast, if we were a few hundred miles closer to Dhashara and the frontier, I'd be flagging the Skaranak as a significant future threat to Empire. Now all of that was true even *before* your friend Egar Dragonbane quit the clan Mastery and disappeared. *These* days,' – a rueful grimace – 'to the Skaranak's military prowess and territorial dominion, you can now add rumours of black shamanry and night powers magic. This shaman you want taken off the board – from what they tell me, he's supposed to have the personal favour of the Sky Dwellers. Rumour says he can conjure demons from the steppe rim to do his will.'

Archeth studied the grain in the table top. She rubbed at a knot in the wood that looked a little like a screaming face.

'You surely don't believe that sort of thing, though, do you?' she asked mildly. 'Demons and magic? An educated man of faith such as yourself?'

Han gave her a mirthless little smile. 'What I believe has very little bearing on the matter, my lady. It is what the Skaranak themselves believe, and what the rest of the steppe believes about them, that defines the game. Have you ever seen a Majak berserker in action?'

Flurry of recall – the frozen moments of the dragon fight, the Dragonbane's howl as he called the beast round to face him.

'Yes, I have,' she said quietly.

'Well.' A little disappointed at the way she'd stolen his thunder. 'Then you'll know what I'm talking about, my lady. A Skaranak warrior who believes he has the night powers on his side may as well actually have them, for all the difference it makes. He will think himself capable of superhuman feats in battle, whether he actually is or not, and in this part of the world, his enemies will think it too. More than half my men here are local auxiliaries, most of them not even converts. I can trust them to guard the compound and carry out basic patrol duties. But I could no more order them to march on a Skaranak encampment than you could get the Ninth Southern Guard to lay siege to the Citadel.'

Archeth grimaced. Got up from the table and the rather sparse spread Han had laid on for her. She'd barely touched her food anyway, wasn't really hungry. Since waking out on the steppe, she was touched with a keen-edged, wakeful energy that put the best krin she'd ever had to shame. She went to the open window behind her, leaned there and stared out over the sparse yellow scatter of torches and fire-lit windows that marked out the town below.

At five storeys high, the imperial mission was by far the tallest building in Ishlin-ichan. You could see it as you rode into town, rising over the huddle of cabins and low houses like some chunky priest bestowing blessings on the backs of a multitude abased in prayer. Now, it gave her a view through thin palls of chimney smoke to the city walls and beyond, where the lights ended and the steppe stretched away like some vast dark ocean. The sky had clouded from the west as night fell, the band was muffled up like a sneak assassin's blade. Here and there, she thought she could make out the glimmering spark of campfires far out in all that darkness, but it was hard to be sure.

'You must have some homegrown muscle too,' she mused without turning from the view. 'I saw Upland Free colours on your scouts this afternoon.'

'Yes.' She heard him get up from the table and move to join her. 'A seven-man scout detachment, plus a regular levy troop of eighty, of whom about a dozen are currently down with the local coughing fever. Allowing for that, and the fact I need to maintain a strong command presence here among the auxiliaries, I could perhaps spare you forty to put into the field. Forty-five at most. I can tell you right now that isn't going to be enough.'

'No.'

'You'd need five times that number to contemplate even marching into Skaranak country uninvited, let alone picking a fight once you get there.' The legate hovered awkwardly at her shoulder, not daring the familiarity to lean at her side. He pointed past her instead, out at the darkness beyond the city. 'There are local legends here that say a vast army once marched out onto that plain to do battle with demons, and just . . . disappeared. No survivors to tell the tale, no trace of a battlefield, just – gone. But they say sometimes at night, when the wind is blowing hard out of the north-east, you can still hear the sounds of a great battle, carried very faintly, as if that army is still out there somewhere, still fighting whatever it ran into.'

'Have you heard it yourself?'

'No, my lady. Nor do I think it ever really happened, at least not the way the legends tell it. But I do think it's a clear warning, meant perhaps for overambitious warlords and generals. You underestimate the steppe and what it contains at your peril.'

She turned to look at him. 'My lord Han, in case you weren't listening earlier, I have just survived the better part of a month in the Kiriath Wastes, a place even my own people considered lethally dangerous. I have lived through a shipwreck and a skirmish with the Scaled Folk, a fight with a dragon and a sorcerous catapult that sent me flying a thousand miles or more through the air before crashing to earth here. If you think I'm going to be put off by tales of wailing ghost armies and black shaman conjuring, then it is you who is guilty of underestimation.'

The legate bowed his head. 'My humblest apologies, my lady. It was not my intention to imply—'

'No.' She waved it off. 'I know that. Raise your head, my lord. The apology should be mine – you are trying to help. But this is a blood debt, and I have no choice.'

Han looked up meekly. 'Perhaps if you returned next year, my lady. With a larger force.'

'No, that's not going to work. Do you really see the Emperor sparing me several hundred of his best fighting men to march up here and make a personal point, while the Empire's still locked in war with the League?'

Not to mention my own chances of having the time to spare. Great big fucking mess there'll be to clear up once I get back.

For a moment, the bitter old krin-addicted aspect of herself stepped forth grinning; she was almost tempted to forget about Yhelteth and just fucking *stay* up here for a couple of years. Ride some horses, learn to speak Majak, camp out under the stars and watch the big-sky seasons turn.

Or failing that, maybe catch one of the trade barges down the Janarat, stay on it past the Dhashara jump-off, drift all the way down to Shaktur and the Great Lake instead. Blag a place to stay and funds from the imperial embassy there, maybe have another go at waking the comatose Helmsman in the ruins of An-Naranash.

Let the war in the west sort itself out, let the Empire live with its stupid mistakes. Let Jhiral fend for himself for a change, just let it all *go*.

In slanting rays of morning sun, Ishgrim rolls over in the sheets of the big bed, gives her that smeared mouth look, reaches for her . . .

Going to let that go, too, are we, Archidi?

She saw the girl again, standing at the rail, not waving, as the flotilla drifted downriver with the current and away.

Back before you know it, she'd told her.

She jerked her chin – actually did it physically. Curt dismissal for the krin-eyed apparition in her head. She watched, fascinated, as her own bitter ghost raised its brows, grinned savagely at her and then walked forward like a duel opponent.

Shouldered rudely past, was gone.

'Look,' she said to Cerdan Han. 'This is going to get done, one way or the other. And I don't have much time. If you can't put a force together that lets me do it head-on, what are the other options? Doesn't this shaman ever come here, to Ishlin-ichan?'

Han shook his head. 'Not for a couple of years now. We kept tabs on him, of course, just like any other influential Skaranak when they blew into town. According to my spies, he used to be a regular at a pretty well-known whorehouse out by the eastern wall. But then something happened. The story we got is that he hurt one of the girls pretty badly, and she died from her injuries. Not really a problem in itself – she was a foreign slave, dragged here from one of the League cities if my memory serves me correctly. No Majak ties, no family to want blood vengeance, you see.'

'I see.'

'Yes, so, anyway.' Bemusement in the legate's voice now – all this fuss over one bloody slave girl. 'If this Poltar had just paid out the madam, no one would have cared. But he skipped instead and just never came back. No one's very sure why. The madam put out a bounty on him, of course, but from what I hear, it wasn't very high. More of a gesture than anything; certainly not enough to attract serious talent. So now there's a stand-off – Poltar can't ever walk the streets of Ishlin-ichan safely again, but it doesn't look like he wants to. And meantime, no one's stupid enough to ride east and go up against the Skaranak for such a paltry sum.'

She grunted. Stared out into the dark of the steppe. Daydreamed scenarios dancing in her head.

'No Skaranak malcontents, then? This Poltar must have enemies within the clan as well, surely.' *Certainly works that way back in Yhelteth.* 'Is there really no way we could get this done from the inside? Bribe someone, maybe? Blackmail them?'

Well, look at you, Archidi – all political manoeuvring and manipulation, just like a real imperial advisor.

Grashgal and Dad would be proud.

Han sighed. 'I will check our files for you, but I think it's unlikely. The steppe clans tend to be tight-knit, and the Skaranak more so than most. To act against the shaman, unless he can somehow be dishonoured, is to act against the clan as a whole, against the clanmaster and all he stands for. It's an oathbreaking matter, and you won't find many Majak willing to do that.'

'They did it fast enough when they drove out the Dragonbane,' she grumbled.

'Perhaps. But that is not the official version of events we have. As far as my spies were able to ascertain at the time, the story told by the Dragonbane's younger brother is that Egar went berserk and slaughtered all his other siblings unprovoked, using black arts that were blamed on his time away in the south.'

'Ershal.' She nodded grimly. 'And now the little fucker's sitting pretty as clanmaster, right?'

'In fact, I understand the situation is a little more akin to a governing council at whose titular head he sits. Senior herd owners and other notable wise heads, that sort of thing. It does appear to be a stable arrangement.' The legate cleared his throat delicately. 'I have no wish to offend, my lady, especially as you still mourn your friend. But it's my understanding that the Dragonbane, mighty warrior though he may have been, was not much of a clanmaster. Apparently, he did the job distractedly and with poor grace. He was far more interested in, ehm, shall we say, more carnal pursuits.'

The underside of her eyes pricked with tears. She found out of nowhere that a small, sad smile had crept out onto her face.

'Yeah, that sounds like him,' she whispered.

Han spread his hands. 'Leadership is not for everyone.'

Fucking tell me about it.

Ishgrim, Jhiral, an Empire on the brink. The men she led, who now trusted her to get them all home. Could she really hold it all hostage to

413

some pointless vow of vengeance for an ageing, irresponsible tomcat thug whose ignominious departure no one apparently regretted?

Is that what he was? Really?

Perhaps. But he was the Dragonbane too.

She bowed her head for a moment and sighed. Could not resolve the riddle at all.

Still staring into the dark, she spotted the faint reflected glimmer of firelight on the sky at the horizon. Skaranak encampment or something else, no way to know. Her gaze locked to it regardless and held there, unblinking, until the cool breeze through the window rinsed tears into her eyes once more.

On the same wind, out of the same encompassing dark, came a moment of clarity, something as near to understanding as she reckoned she'd ever get.

You don't have to resolve it, Archidi. It isn't about who he was.

It's about who you are.

She closed her eyes for a moment, took the soothing relief it gave. Then she straightened up from the window ledge, turned away from the dark outside and faced the nervously waiting imperial at her side.

'Let's have a look at these files of yours,' she said briskly.

FIFTY-TWO

'You know anything about a sword the Illwrack Changeling carried?'

'I think it's safe to assume he had one,' said Anasharal in his ear. 'He was, after all, a warrior king.'

Gil set his jaw. 'Yeah, thanks. I'd got that far myself. Could you manage something a little less fucking obvious?'

'Is this really important? To know, at this exact juncture, how some chieftain four thousand years dead was once armed? Commander Nyanar is becoming very nervous with all this holding station and waiting. Are you not nearly done in there?'

Down the deserted, dimly lit corridors of Findrich's labyrinthine warehouse palace. They'd seen no one since the skirmish ranger ambush. No signs of life but the lit lamps, no sound but their booted footfalls on stone and the rearguard calling clear every twenty paces. Standard precautions against bushwhack. They moved at a wary pace, weapons out and watchful. Gil carried the Ravensfriend low in his right hand, shield hanging ready on his left arm at his side. The *ikinri 'ska* prowled in and out of his head like a marsh spider looking for prey.

'If it wasn't important,' he said evenly, 'I wouldn't be asking you about it. And no, we are not nearly done. The sword is here in Etterkal. I'm told the Illwrack Changeling's soul is still trapped inside, and the dwenda plan to use the blade in some way to make me a host for his return. Ring any bells?'

'None at all. It sounds fanciful.'

But he thought he picked up the faintest shadow of hesitation, of doubt maybe, laid across the Helmsman's dismissive tone.

'Fanciful, perhaps. But you're the one sent us up to the Hironish looking for a legendary warlord back from the dead, and now it looks like there might actually be one. I'm no great believer in coincidences, Helmsman.'

'I have already told you that the Illwrack Changeling legend was a pretext, a means to get kir-Archeth Indamaninarmal safely out of the city and have her rub shoulders with potential cabalists. I did not expect you to find anything; in fact I anticipated a convenient vacuum in which discontent and plotting could emerge.'

'But it didn't.'

'There is no need to state the obvious.'

'Yeah. Irritating, isn't it?'

They reached a crossing of corridors. Ringil, nerves cranked like

415

bowstrings in the gloom, raised a clenched fist to halt his men. He set loose the *ikinri 'ska*, sent it billowing out ahead of him, sniffing for anything that might wish him ill. Eased forward a soft step at a time until he could peer round the corner both ways.

Nothing.

He puffed out a breath, tried to rid himself of a creeping sensation that somewhere, the jaws of a trap were poised to snap shut on his head. If Findrich had sent Kaad and son out to slow him down, it was to buy time to prepare some greater, more unpleasant surprise further in. Just a matter of what and where.

'There is something you might try,' Anasharal volunteered unexpectedly. 'The scheme to seek the Illwrack Changeling was drawn by the Warhelm Ingharnanasharal and implanted in me without depth or detail. I was literally incapable of knowing more. But the glyphs you inflicted on me have broken some of the constraints I exist under. I know now, for example, that I once *was* Ingharnanasharal, and that something of that self may still survive separate from me, high up over the curve of the Earth. If you . . . *compel* me once again, command me to reach out to what is left of the Warhelm, I may be able to transcend the separation between us and find answers for you in Ingharnanasharal's full memory.'

'All right.' Ringil mustered the glyphs in his mind. 'Do that. I, uhm, I *compel* you.'

It felt strange, imposing the *ikinri 'ska* at a distance. But like the gathering of the storm elementals at his command back in the Hironish, he felt the power stir, out at the edges of his perception. And then, he felt it hit home.

Anasharal *shrieked*.

Long drawn out, grinding, inhuman – it came at him like something fanged and clawed, chilling his blood with the sound, building out of some incalculable depth, swelling, scaling upward, shredding at his ears—

And then, abruptly, gone.

He felt the sudden absence as clearly as the shriek itself. It was a silence that stuffed itself deep into his ears like wool.

'Anasharal?'

Nothing. Whatever battle was being fought now, between the *ikinri 'ska*'s compulsion glyphs and the antique Kiriath sorceries that governed what Helmsmen could and could not do, resolution would take time. Anasharal was out of the game.

He was surprised by how suddenly naked it made him feel.

'Something wrong, my lord?' Rakan, close at his side.

They peered together down the empty, lamplit perspectives of the cross corridor. Ringil shook his head, tried to shake some of the woollen silence out of his ears. He clapped the other man on the shoulder with what he hoped was an approximation of manly camaraderie. Pitched his voice for general consumption.

'Nothing we can't fix with some cold, sharp steel,' he lied brightly.

There are forces loose in this place, he'd told them back at the atrium, *that you would very likely call demonic. And we will probably have to face and fight them before we can get our people back. I am sorry. I had hoped these creatures wouldn't be present, or that if they were, that we'd be able to surprise them. That is now impossible. They are warned.*

Faint muttering through the gathered half-circle, some of it none too happy. He couldn't blame them. He waited it out.

But I want you to remember one thing as we push forward. Two years ago, I defeated these same creatures with only a handful of men for support. Those men were imperial soldiers like you. He pointed at Rakan. *And this man is brother to their commander. Imperial warrior blood, the same blood that runs in all your veins, the blood that has laid the world at Yhelteth's feet.*

A couple of low cheers, hushed to silence.

With those few warriors at my back two years ago, I discovered a very simple truth about these supposed demons that we face. They fall down just like men. They may come from the shadows, they may glow like the blue fires of hell, they may be lightning swift and alien, but in the end none of this could save them from good imperial steel. They bleed just like men, they hurt just like men, they die just like men.

And if they stand at any point between us and those we have come to save – we will cut them down and butcher them just like men.

Assent boiled snarling out in the wake of his words. It was the same low, ugly growl he'd got from them by the watchtower at Dako's point back in Ornley.

Getting good at this shit again, Gil, he allowed to himself as they marched out of the atrium cloisters and into the corridors beyond. *Just like Gallows Gap.*

Yeah, let's just hope it doesn't come to that.

But he knew at some level that his real wishes were nowhere near as clean-cut or as clean. And he could feel the Mistress of Dice and Death put her icy arm around his shoulders once more.

In the end, he found Slab Findrich by the simple expedient of tracking the dwenda stench to its heart. Turn this way down a corridor, and the sensation of eldritch presence ebbed; turn back and it swelled again. It took him a couple of wrong turns to get the full hang of it, but once he did, the *ikinri 'ska* seemed to quicken and shake itself more fully awake – as if, he thought, rousing itself from a sated doze after the carnage in the atrium. It took him, with growing confidence and exultation, through passages and galleried storage halls, across another unroofed atrium space and finally, to the foot of a single ornate staircase, leading up to an unsuspected third level which must, he supposed, sit right under the warehouse roof.

They went up quietly, no bravado this time, no charge. There were double doors at the top, in clear echo of the heavy oak portal they'd broken in through downstairs. But this time the wood was lighter, more delicately carved, set with two fussy-looking curled iron handles. Ringil took up station on the left, pressed a palm gently to the panelling between the handles, found the lock unengaged. He nodded at Rakan. They took a handle each – the Throne Eternal swapping sword smoothly to his left hand for the moment it would take – and stood poised.

Ringil met his lover's eyes across the short space between them and the corner of his mouth quirked. There was an itching in his belly, and he couldn't honestly tell if it was proximity to the Throne Eternal's young muscled frame, so long untouched, or just the longing for slaughter. He raised three fingers erect on his left hand. Rakan nodded. Gil put his hand back on the handle.

Shaped the numbered count slowly, exaggeratedly, silently, with his lips. *Three . . . two . . . one!*

They dropped the handles hard, flung the doors open, and Ringil went lithely through the gap. Shield up to guard, Ravensfriend raised. From the way the doors went back, he knew there was no one waiting pressed up against the jamb to jump him. Peripheral vision confirmed it. He stalked into the hall beyond, cleared the doorway and let his men follow him in. Surveyed the vaulted interior for threat.

'Good evening, Gil. You took your time.'

Slab Findrich, in the murderous flesh.

Ringil had been expecting, it only now dawned on him, some kind of throne at the end of this regal space, maybe even set up on a little dais. It would have fitted with Findrich's undisputed dominance of the Etterkal slavers' association, his reputed captaincy of the cabal, his shadowy reach into the chambers of Trelayne's political heart. It would have fitted the man as Gil remembered him, tall and gaunt and grave.

But there was no throne. No outward show of power at all.

Findrich sat instead in a simple armchair under a window halfway down the right wall of the chamber. It was one of a pair of seats set around a table strewn with sheaves of heavy parchment, a sample couple of which he still held loosely in one hand. A full-size Yhelteth water pipe stood on the floor beside the armchair, still smouldering from its crucible top. The thick, cloying scent of flandrijn tinged the room. Sipping tube and mouthpiece rod were draped over the arm of the chair. Set against the lordly dimensions of the hall, the slaver looked like some vagabond clerk, squatting in the ruins of a glory long fled.

Looks like exactly what he fucking is.

'Well? Are you just going to stand there all night, oh great avenger? You've kept me waiting quite long enough as it is, don't you think?'

'Got held up,' Ringil told him, advancing warily. 'Nice of you to feed me the Kaads like that, father and son in one juicy bite.'

Findrich smiled and set the documents aside. 'I didn't imagine they'd get the better of you for long.'

'No. They didn't.'

He looked around – it was the same honeycombed stone floor and ornate friezework as in the atrium where the Kaads had died, writ large and roofed in with antique – or maybe fake antique – stained glass. There was some heroic statuary looming in distant corners, a wood panelled shrine to the Dark Court against the back wall with candles lit, but aside from these features, Findrich's chairs and table were the only furnishing in a wholly vacant and deserted space. If the dwenda were as close as Gil's senses insisted, they either weren't ready to spring their trap yet, or they looked to be suffering from some sudden, massive bout of shyness.

All right, then.

He heard the footfalls, the rustle and clink of his men massing at his back. He moved up closer to the table.

'Let's get this over with, Slab. Where you keeping the imperials?'

The slave merchant took off a pair of reading spectacles that Gil only now registered he'd been wearing. His hair was full white these days, but cropped savagely short, so it looked like a sparse fall of snow across his pate. On some men, it would have conferred a mild, grandfatherly air, but on Slab Findrich, it just looked cold and hard. Age had not softened the old thug – it looked instead to have cured him, like some strip of hung and salted meat. The pox-scarred Harbour End features were just as impassive, the leaden, predatory eyes unchanged.

'You know, you've caused us all a great deal of trouble, Ringil.'

'Glad to hear that. Where are my friends?'

'You took our Aldrain warlord from us just as things were building towards a promising new day for the League. Then you set about slaughtering so many of my associates that our whole way of doing things up here almost fell apart.' Findrich took up the mouthpiece rod of his pipe and wagged it admonishingly at Gil. 'Did you know there were riots in the street against the slave laws after your little rampage last year? Serious questions raised in the Chancellery about repealing Liberalisation? That's how close we came.'

'I'm sure you quashed it all easily enough. You always were pretty fucking slick when it came to protecting your coin.'

'Says the noble son who never lacked for any.' The slave merchant sipped delicately at the pipe, sieved smoke out between his teeth. 'You'll forgive me if I'm not mortally wounded by your contempt.'

Ringil grinned and hefted the Ravensfriend. 'If I wanted to mortally wound you, Slab, I'd just take this thing and shove it through your purse.'

'And Klithren of Hinerion!' Booming false cheer in Findrich's voice, but the gaze that slipped past Ringil's shoulder was heavy-lidded and cold. 'Well, well. We thought you defeated and dead, knight commander, but I see it's worse than that. You seem to have found something you like, sniffing around our faggot war hero here. Been initiated into the dark arts of buggery and stubble-cheeked blow-jobs, have we?'

Klithren cursed thickly and stepped past Ringil on the right, sword arm rising. Gil put out a hand to block him. Soft brushing touch of the *ikinri 'ska*, in case the mercenary's command discipline wasn't enough.

'Stand down,' he said firmly. 'That's not what we're here for.'

'I know what you did to me, Findrich,' Klithren snarled. 'I know what you fucking did!'

Findrich raised an eyebrow. 'What? Made you a knight of Trelayne and handed you a command fit for a man of ten times your social standing? Well, I'm deeply sorry for it now, especially seeing as how you've pissed it all away.'

Klithren lurched forward again. Gil lifted his arm again, murmured a glyph and looped the *ikinri 'ska* subtly tighter about the mercenary.

'Easy there.' He produced a thin smile for Findrich. 'Thing is, Slab – we're not all as in thrall to rank and standing as Harbour End dregs like you. Some of us are just fighting men. Some of us actually stood against the reptiles – as opposed to just sending our sons off to stand and die in our stead.'

Viciously unjust, and he knew it. Findrich had done everything he could, pulled every string at his command, to keep his only son out of the war. Pointless effort – the boy defied his father, volunteered for the southern shores defence levy and subsequently died, either at Rajal beach or somewhere on the brutal fallback march that followed. Gil saw the slaver's dead-eyed stare catch fire on the old pain, saw his upper lip lift fractionally from his teeth.

Something savage in him rejoiced at the sight.

The legend cracks and crumbles. Not every day you get a rise out of Slab-face Findrich.

'I hear they never did find a body,' he went on mildly. 'That's the thing about the Scaled Folk, though. You could always rely on them to clean up after a battle. Right, Klithren?'

'Right,' said the mercenary sombrely.

'Yeah, how do you live with something like that, Slab? I mean – knowing your son died, roasted and eaten by monsters, and you put him out there because you were too much of a coward and a coin-grubbing thief to go and fight yourself.'

The pipe mouthpiece clattered to the floor. Findrich surged halfway to his feet, knuckles white on the arms of the chair. Rage in his eyes, and a low growl rising from his throat. Ringil gave him an unfriendly smile, and he froze.

'Just so you know – you get up out of that chair, I'll chop your fucking feet off. Sit *down*.' Gil let the point of the Ravensfriend drift lazily up from the floor, waited while the slave merchant lowered himself by glaring inches, back into his seat. 'Right. Small talk's over, Slab. I just set this entire city on fire to get my friends back; you think I'm going to go easy on you for old times' sake? I killed Grace, I killed Poppy, and the only reason you're not following them is I'm short of time. So let's stop fucking about, shall we? You want to live? You want to keep your appendages and your manhood intact? *Where are my friends?*'

He felt the change shiver through the room like a cold wind. Saw Findrich bare his teeth in triumph.

'Right behind you, faggot.'

Out of the shadows at the back of the chamber, the dwenda came.

Some of them were the statues in the corners, melting now back into life and motion, shedding their stone glamour the way a snake sheds skin, shaking off their held poses in shimmering splinters of blue fire. He saw a couple of them tilt their necks to shake off stiffness as they came. Others just walked out of the blue fire haze he'd seen them emerge from at Ennishmin, as if curtained portals drew back in the air itself, edged with the same blue fire, and let them through. Tall, ghost pale of face, eyes like pits of gleaming black tar, and they moved with a terrible unhuman grace and poise. Beneath cloaks of shimmering velvet blue and grey, they were armoured neck to foot in smooth, seamless black garb that seemed to repel the light. They bristled with weapons, glimmering longsword blades and ornate axes, and Risgillen of Illwrack was at their head.

Ringil surveyed them bleakly for a moment, shot a brief glance back at Findrich.

'Not those friends,' he said patiently.

The slaver spat on the floor at his feet. 'Fuck you. Arrogant aristo prick. You're fucking done.'

'Well, we'll see.' Ringil caught Klithren's eye. Nodded at Findrich. 'Keep an eye on our pal here. I got this.'

He strode out to meet Risgillen, across the expanse of honeycombed stone floor. Was vaguely aware of Noyal Rakan, barking orders at the gaping imperials, trying to snap them out of their shock, trying to mask his own. Ringil felt a twinge of sympathy. He remembered his own first dwenda encounter, two years back, the icy terror that had seized him at the time. The imperials had had more warning, true enough, but still, they were mostly young and unseasoned. He'd seen them give a solid account of themselves against human foes, but he could not predict how they would cope here.

Best not to risk finding out.

He passed Rakan, put out his shield and touched him on the arm with its cold steel edge.

'Keep them tight,' he murmured. 'Bowmen deployed, but no move unless I call it, or these motherfuckers try to jump me. Got that?'

'Yes, my—' Voice taut and hoarse, he heard how Rakan swallowed to clear his throat. 'My lord, are these truly—'

'They fall down just like men,' Gil told him. 'Remember that. Just like men.'

And left the young captain there. Moved out to meet the dwenda wedge and their commander. He'd forgotten how coldly beautiful Risgillen was – sculpted ivory features, jutting cheekbones and smooth pale brow, black silky fall of hair, framing the face. Long, mobile mouth, long slim-fingered hands.

He'd forgotten how much she resembled Seethlaw. How hard the blood resemblance struck at him, and what it left welling up in the wound.

He wiped it all away. Stored it, behind a stony battlefield mask.

'Risgillen,' he called amiably across the space between them. 'You really are a stubborn fucking bitch. I warned you not to come back here again. Now I'm going to have to kill you, just like your fuckwit brother.'

She tilted her head, wolf-like, and smiled. 'This world is ours, Ringil, and we will have it for our own. We owned it before men learnt to build their first campfires out on the arid plains, we will own it long after you are all gone. Look to your own legends if you think I'm lying. We are the Aldrain. The Elder Race. We are the Shining Immortal Ones.'

'Yeah.' Ringil came to an easy halt, a couple of yards away from her. If she raised her longsword at him now, they could touch blades 'Legends I've been reading say you got your arses handed to you by the Black Folk four thousand years ago, and they drove you out. What have you been doing since – sulking?'

He heard indrawn breath along the dwenda line. Looked like they'd all learnt pretty good Naomic, which suggested they'd been deployed here for a while. A dwenda warrior on Risgillen's flank twitched in the ranks, bleached features stretched in outrage, long axe raised. Ringil lifted the Ravensfriend casually, pointed it.

'You – don't even fucking think about it.'

Risgillen turned and said something softly in the Aldrain tongue. The outraged dwenda subsided, fell back in line. Risgillen smiled again, thinly. She looked back at Ringil with an intensity that bordered on adoration.

'You should have stayed in the south,' she said very softly. 'But I'm glad you came. I would not have wanted to miss your doom.'

Ringil nodded. 'Let's get on with it, then. Where's this sword?'

For just a moment, he had her. He saw the way she froze. Gave her a lopsided grin.

'Risgillen, Risgillen.' Gathering the *ikinri 'ska* stealthily to him, like the folds of some heavy net for casting. Meantime – *misdirection, Gil, loud and bright as you can manage.* 'Did you really think I was coming to you unaware? You really thought you were going to have your last fuckwit human stooge just *crawl up* out of whatever jinxed Illwrack heirloom he got magicked into five thousand years ago, and take *my* soul? You really haven't understood who you're fucking with here, have you?'

She stared at him for a long, cold moment, black empty eyeballs catching glimmers of light from the torches around the chamber, twisting them into something else.

'It's you who hasn't understood,' she whispered.

He felt it lash out for him, the dwenda glamour in all its binding force. Flash recall of his time with Seethlaw in the Grey Places, the subtle webs of compulsion he would only later understand had been spun around him. It fell all about him, at angles he could not see or name, coiled inward, made a soundless hissing as it came—

He reached for the *ikinri 'ska*. Grinned as it came on in his head like icy fire. Struck.

Nothing.

He tried again, cast harder. The dwenda compulsion drew savagely tight, crushing out the glimmer of the *ikinri 'ska* a scant moment after it arose. He yelped. Something tore in his chest with the reversal – it felt as if his ribcage would crack like a nutshell between clenching teeth. His arms hung at his sides as if weighted there with ballast. The Ravensfriend fell through his fingers, his shield tore loose from his left arm. Clank and clatter as they hit the honeycomb floor. His head lolled back a second, then straightened through no effort of his own. He would have gone to his knees, if the choice had been his to make. But whatever forces Risgillen had unleashed held him upright, as if suspended there by a spike through the sternum.

He twisted his head to the side, rolled his eyes like a panicked horse, trying to see his men . . .

'They are bound as you are.' Risgillen told him. 'The power of Talon-reach, the storm-callers' art enacted. The glamour ripples outward. It's a simple enough matter – whatever power you summon is deflected, taken from you, pushed away and used in binding your followers ever tighter. You have already made them breathless with your efforts so far. I daresay if you keep pushing, you'll suffocate them.'

At the extremity of his vision, he saw the truth of it – Noyal Rakan's straining face, the locked up posture. He heaved once more against the binding, got no single fraction of leverage anywhere. He let go. Hung from his failure as if nailed there.

Risgillen stepped closer to him, longsword lowered. She put up her free hand to touch his face. He felt the trembling in her fingers as she did it.

'You see?' she said, voice a shaky caress. 'I have understood exactly who I am fucking with.'

Ringil made a noise through gritted teeth.

'Oh, yes. You wanted to see the sword.'

She let go of his face, raised her hand and snapped her fingers in the chilly air. More words in the Aldrain tongue and a name, one he thought he recognised.

A dwenda shouldered through the ranks, unarmed, limping a little. There was an ornate bordering on his cloak, glyphs worked into it in strands of red and silver, and the rest of the company gave him respectful ground. He stood beside Risgillen, fixed Ringil with his empty black stare. Risgillen made an elegant gesture of introduction.

'This is Atalmire, ordained storm-caller for clan Talonreach. The glamour that holds you is of his making. You'll remember him, of course. You crippled him in the temple at Yhelteth.'

Fractional easing in the pressure on his chest – Gil found, abruptly, he could speak.

'You all look the same to me,' he husked. 'Hello, Atalmire, you crippled fuck. Tell me, what kind of black mage can't fix his own leg?'

The storm-caller looked impassively back at him.

'He has chosen not to heal,' Risgillen said. 'He chooses to remember instead. But have no worries on that account. When you end, so will the wound you gave him.'

Following Atalmire, two more dwenda came through carrying a slim, six foot ornately worked wooden casket between them. Risgillen darted a smiling glance at Ringil, like a mother at a patient child finally about to receive a long promised gift. She leaned close again.

'They tell me that some small part of you will survive this,' she said, very gently. 'That it will sit behind the eyes of the risen Dark King, eyes that were once your own, and see everything that he sees with them, everything that he does as he takes back this world for us. I hope that pleases you as much as it pleases me.'

'Big mistake,' he hissed at her. 'You don't want to leave me alive, Risgillen.'

'No, I do,' she said seriously, and nodded at Atalmire.

The storm-caller uttered a single, harsh syllable and made a sharp beckoning motion at the casket. The wooden lid splintered, then cracked violently apart. Exploded away from the base in five jagged chunks. Splinters stung Ringil's cheek.

The sword lay within.

FIFTY-THREE

Marnak Ironbrow rode to Ishlin-ichan irritable and combative, and what he found there didn't put him in any better mood.

They didn't know him at the gate – no sign of the usual crew, they had a quad of callow herdboy types propping up the gateposts instead. None of them looked old enough to be wiping their own arses yet, let alone wielding the staff lances they'd been given. Not a beard between them. He looked around in the early evening gloom for a familiar face, saw only a corpulent captain sat outside the guard hut, picking his teeth with a fowl bone. Old line-command instincts prickled along his nerves – down south, he'd have had all five of these on a slouching charge, quick as slitting a throat. Couple of strokes each at the posts, double for the captain, and docked pay all round. He reined in the impulse, reined in his mount too, a prudent dozen yards from the gates. Raised his hand to the riders behind him to do the same.

'Nine men seek entry,' he intoned loudly. 'We bring no word but peace.'

The staff lancers fumbled about a bit, glances back and forth between them. They looked hopefully over at the man by the hut. The guard captain dug a chunk of something out on the end of his improvised toothpick, looked quizzically at it and then popped it back in his mouth. He stood up, stretched and yawned.

'Skaranak, eh?' He looked them over with calculated insolence. 'Coming in for a bath, are we, lads?'

Marnak felt how his men bristled at his back. He offered the man a bleak grin. 'Come to fuck some of your Ishlinak whores, actually.'

Barked laughter behind him. The corpulent captain flushed. Marnak leaned forward in his saddle, kept his grin, but never let it touch his eyes.

'Is there going to be a problem?'

From long habit, he'd measured the logistics of the fight reflexively as they rode up. Nine of them, hardened herd outriders all, versus the four kids with their staff lances on the gate and this bag of guts. Marnak and his crew were all riding with lances sheathed, but against this kind of opposition, it wouldn't much matter. It'd be over in less time than you'd need to tell it round the campfire afterwards. At worst they'd collect a couple of gashes between them.

And a whole new raiding war, with summer still a month to run.

425

Tensions were never far off between Skaranak and the Ish, but the two clans had not fought hard now for over a decade. The odd drunken tavern brawl in Ishlin-ichan, maybe, that got out of hand and went to knives. And a couple of inconclusive skirmishes over grazing up near the Bow-of-Band-light meander three years back – but both sides hastily ascribed those to renegade elements, buried their dead and paid out blood debt to the families, kissed and made up. It just wasn't worth getting into anymore – there was too much at risk that was good for both sides now.

Yeah – tell that to your gut-sack captain here.

No matter. He couldn't butcher the Ishlin-ichan gate watch over nothing but bad temper and balls-out tribal idiocy. Those days were long gone

The guard captain appeared to have reached a similar conclusion. Or perhaps he saw the look in Marnak's eyes. He sniffed and spat, courteously far from the Skaranak's horse's hooves. 'No problem, greybeard, if you don't bring one yourselves. Pay the levy and in you go. Nine of you – that'll be ninety.'

'Ten star a man? Bit steep, isn't it?'

A shrug. 'You got imperial coin, I could let you in for – let's see – eight elementals.'

'That's still steep.' Marnak looked significantly around at the four staff lancers, one by one. Gate toll was meant in principle for the city's coffers, but there was no way hard imperial coin was going to end up anywhere but in these men's pockets. 'Call it six. That's a spinner each for your lads here and two for you. Can't say fairer than that now, can we?'

He patted at the purse he wore under his coat and it clinked merrily. Not a noise you'd easily get out of the crude, star-stamped bronze octagons that passed for coinage among the Majak. The guard captain made a show of chewing the offer over, but Marnak could see the man's hand twitch at his side and he knew, looking into the Ishlinak's face, that the motion wasn't any urge towards the sword he wore at his belt.

They were in.

'Oh, yeah,' he wondered, as they were waved through. 'What happened to Larg, anyway? This is usually his shift.'

A shrug. 'Coughing fever. Him and half a hundred like him. Even the imperials are coming down with it this year. That and the comet, it's not looking good.'

Marnak's men made warding gestures, so did the staff lancers on the gate. He sketched one himself, more for solidarity and appearance than anything else. Poltar had made a big song and dance about the comet, of course – dark muttered implications of character flaw among the council, angered Sky Dwellers, great impending threat. All the usual shit. Marnak didn't set much store by portents; he'd travelled too far and seen too much over the years. But when the sky woke up, so did the shaman, and that in itself was worth a sleepless night or two – once Poltar Wolfeye was roused, there was no telling where the dance might go, how out of hand it might get. And it wasn't like he'd grown any more stable with the rise of his fortunes over the last couple of years either. All those holes he liked to make in his own hide, the look in those eyes. He hadn't wanted anyone to stray out of Skaranak territory in the wake of the comet's fall, let alone ride the three days to Ishlin-ichan – Marnak had to get into an eye-to-eye facedown with the mangy old fuck just to make this trip, and now he was wondering whether it was going to be worth it.

You need to wrap this brooding shit up, horseman. Not why you came into town, is it? You can bitch and brood to your heart's content back in your yurt.

He stowed his misgivings and tried to summon a decent degree of anticipation as they trotted on into the low rise of the town. Behind him, his men managed just fine – trading crude jokes and laughter, calling out brightly to passers-by and women at upper windows. Fair enough – it was a big trip to town for them; not one of these lads had been off the steppe in their lives. But Marnak had seen the spires and domes of the imperial city, the crenellated towers of its northern rivals in the League. He'd lived and fucked and caroused in those places for the better part of his youth and then some. Next to all of that, Ishlin-ichan just didn't measure up. Oh, sure, it was *all right*, but there were times when these trips felt like a paltry pleasure, a ride on a sullen pack mule when you'd been used to war-bred stallions. Lately, even the whoring didn't seem to help.

You're just getting old. This fifty summers thing is kicking your arse, and you know it.

A few years back, right enough, it had been easier. He came back from Yhelteth wealthy and stocked with war-stories enough to get him into Sky Home a dozen times over. He bought shares in the Skaranak herds, hired younger son loose ends from good families to help mind his investment. Married a canny, curvaceous widow, adopted her kids as his own and had a couple more. With time and the ebb of the initial fire, he found himself sloping off to Ishlin-ichan now and again for a taste of strange, but Sadra was canny in more ways than one and she didn't sulk or rage all that much. He waited out her cold shoulder treatment each time with the patient equanimity of a man whose professional years had accustomed him to waiting out far worse things; meantime, he spoiled her with gifts and apologies and steady affection until she cracked.

In the end, an unspoken agreement settled in between them – that he'd do what he liked in other beds, so long as it was done far enough from the encampment not to embarrass her, and wasn't done all that often. Rules he found it easy enough to follow – Sadra, in a good mood, wasn't something many whores could hold a candle to anyway. Day to day, he was happier than he'd ever thought he'd end up – well, he was alive for one thing – and if only the Dragonbane hadn't gone stark raving berserk and run off like

that, he reckoned even these vague misgivings would not trouble him half
so much. Almost as if when Egar was still around, bitching noisily about
life back on the steppe, it was that much easier to quell his own quiet nostalgia and get on with living.

*Urann's balls, Eg, where'd you go? What the fuck really happened to you out
there?*

They had Ershal's story, of course, and evidence that seemed to back it
up. He rode haggard and exhausted into camp on a limping mount that
same night, startle-eyed and gabbling tales of southern mercenary friends
of the Dragonbane, demons in the grass. Showed them the thin bleeding lash-mark wounds on his horse's limbs and lower flanks. The scene
of slaughter he led them back to the next morning bore him out, was
like something out of a tale, and the shaman certainly made the most
of it.

*It is as I always thought. The Dragonbane has sold himself to the southerners'
demon god. He has angered the Sky Dwellers with his corrupt foreign ways. How
else to explain such an atrocity worked on the flesh and blood of the Skaranak . . .*

So forth.

None of it made a lot of sense, if you stopped to actually think it through.
But you got used to that with shamanry. And in the end, whatever had
really happened out there the previous night, the Dragonbane wasn't
around to tell his side of the story. No body, and no tracks out, or at least
none that any of the scouts could find, but his gear was all gone. Staff-
lance, saddle pack, knives – all vanished without trace like their owner,
something that with every passing hour was starting to look dangerously
like both sorcery and an admission of guilt. The only evidence Egar had
ever been there at all was his Yhelteth-bred warhorse, lying dead on its
side, feathered with Ershal's arrows – *it reared up at me and lashed out, eyes
glowing with fire, gifted with demonic speech, cursing me in the southern tongue
so my heart chilled at those alien syllables,* he told them. *What else was I to do
but take it down?*

And Poltar, nodding soberly along at his side.

Marnak grimaced at the memory. He'd never stood against Ershal's
rapid elevation to the clan Mastery in the weeks that followed, because
it made all kinds of sense. The clan needed the continuity; they could ill
afford a scramble for power between majority herd owners in the wake of
all this spooky horror. The shaman was in favour of it, which by extension
meant the gods were too. Gant, the Dragonbane's only other surviving
brother, gave it the nod. And Ershal was, truth to tell, a pretty good
candidate for the job. He was young, but shrewd with it, and he had an instinctive grasp of the political necessities that the Dragonbane had either
never owned or maybe just never seen fit to bother with. He listened re-
spectfully to the herd owners and other clan greybeards, and he won over
the younger men and women around the encampment with his prowess
in archery and horsemanship. A couple of months in, and everyone was

saying, in somewhat relieved tones, that he should have been the one right from the start . . .

Whoops from his men stirred him back to the present. They were calling out his name and laughing. Marnak blinked and looked around. Saw he'd been so sunk in recollection that he'd nearly ridden right past their destination.

The Feathered Nest.

Three storeys high, cheap brickwork and timber daubed with Tethanne script in red, the whole structure sagging alarmingly to the left – one of these days, he was going to wake up here and find himself buried under rubble. A couple of underemployed working girls slouched about outside on the porch, calling out to passersby and flaunting themselves tiredly. They were kholed up in what they fondly imagined was the Yhelteth fashion, and their slightly grubby robes approximated harem-wear, more or less. There was the customary joke in the name of this place, of course, a double meaning just like most of the other whorehouses in town. But the joke was in Tethanne, it didn't translate very well into Majak, and he'd grown tired over the years of explaining it to fellow carousers who didn't really care one way or the other.

He reined in, harder than strictly necessary, brought his horse's head round to the hitching rail. Swung a leg up and over with a show of Skaranak horseman insouciance, skidded down out of his saddle look-no-hands. His boots hit the dirt and sent up little puffs of dust; he tried not to grunt as the impact snagged in his knees. A couple of the girls made ooh-ing sounds, but their hearts weren't really in it. Horseman wanker tricks. He guessed they saw this shit nine times before breakfast most days.

He made an effort for his men. 'All right, lads. Let's get out of the saddle and right back into the saddle, eh?'

Ready roars of approval. One man whooped and leapt up onto the rail, balanced there on dipping, twisting legs, and then commenced prancing back and forth with arms spread wide. The porch girls unfolded, yawning, from their posts. He jumped down grinning into their arms.

'Open up, girls, here we come,' crowed the man at Marnak's side. 'Going to get me some of that *imperial* pussy!'

Yeah, that's what you think, Marnak thought sourly.

In fact, there were Yhelteth whores to be had at The Feathered Nest, but not many of them, and they cost a lot more than most Majak herdsmen were willing or able to pay. The majority of the Nest's customers settled quite happily for local girls made up to look the part. Most of them wouldn't have been able to tell the difference anyway.

Marnak could tell the difference.

He sat sprawled among the silk drapes of a top floor room, trying to separate out his nostalgia from his lust. They'd plied him with wine downstairs while he waited – he was still working his way through a colossal goblet of the stuff now – and he hadn't eaten much since breakfast, so he was pretty giddy. He set down the drink with exaggerated care on a stool beside the bed. Loosened his belt a bit, felt a soggy grin creep into his mouth.

'What's keeping you, girl?' he called out in Tethanne. 'Not shy, are you?'

'Not really, no.'

Tall, shadowy frame in the doorway, a stiffly braided mane of hair that made her taller still, and she wasn't dressed much differently to him. Boots and leather breeches, a jerkin buckled about with gear. The voice was chocolate dark and deep, court-bred tones with a command rasp beneath. Marnak came up off the bed like a scalded cat.

'Who the fuck are you? What—'

His voice dried up as she stepped into the light. Jet black features, eyes that threw back the candle glow in a contemptuous swirl, like band-light hitting well-water a long way down. Knives sheathed in some weird upside down fashion, but the hilts were . . .

'I . . . know you,' he whispered.

She stepped further into the room, put her hands on her belt. 'Probably, you do. There were never very many like me.'

'You're, uh . . .' His mouth was dry from the wine. 'Flaradnam's daughter, aren't you? I saw you at the memorial gathering in Yhelteth. I, uhm, I marched with your father. On the northern expeditionary. I saw him die.'

'And you were at Gallows Gap after.' She nodded. 'Where you collected the long scar above your eye. Awarded the white silk three times in as many years, promoted to line commander in '54, offered another sizeable promotion after the war, resigned your commission and came back here instead. Trusted lieutenant to the rightful Skaranak clanmaster until he disappeared in '61; getting along fine with his not-so-rightful successor today. You see, I know all about you, Marnak Ironbrow. The only thing I don't know is whether or not you had a hand in kicking the Dragonbane out.'

'Fuck you.' Up from his belly, without thought.

A thin white smile split her ebony face. 'I'll take that as a no.'

He held down the impulse to cross the space between them and backhand her to the floor. Stayed where he was. Partly, that was his mercenary training, corroded now by the years but still in place. *Manage your emotions, soldier; use them, don't let them use you.*

But also, he wasn't going to kid himself, it was those curiously empty churned-light eyes, it was the way she stood. He recalled how Flaradnam had fought in the Wastes, the cold methodical strength and fury that drove him, and he thought he saw an echo of it in the woman before him.

'What do you want with me, Kiriath?' he growled.

'That's better,' she said.

*

They sat on opposite sides of the bed, each with a leg drawn up so they could face – and watch – each other. Heavy boots and buckles pressing down into the brightly coloured silk sheets, leaving grit and mud traces. Not quite the congress the Skaranak veteran must have been anticipating when he came in here, and the tension in his face suggested he was still adjusting. Neither of them had relinquished their knives at any point and there was a tell-tale immobility to their hands as they talked. If there was trust in the room, it was smoke-thin and floating as yet.

'Dead?' Marnak asked grimly.

Archeth nodded. 'Killing a dragon in the Wastes. He saved my life doing it. Which is why I'm here. He left me a blood debt to honour.'

She watched for signs of emotion, knew she'd probably not see much. For a people famed as berserkers in battle, the Majak came off oddly impassive when they dealt with loss. If Marnak planned to weep for the Dragonbane, he wouldn't do it here.

The Skaranak grunted. 'Could not have asked for a better death, then.'

You didn't see what was left of him, she wanted to say but kept it stowed. And anyway, maybe he was right. Marnak probably knew more about the way the Dragonbane had felt than she ever would.

'He was coming here, Ironbrow,' she said. 'Coming to kill the shaman Poltar and his usurper brother Ershal, the same way he dealt with the others when they jumped him with hired help at his father's grave.'

Marnak's face might have been stone. 'Is that right?'

Near enough, it is. That revenge on the shaman and his brother were always incidental to their homeward trek wasn't something the Ironbrow needed to know. *Let's keep it simple, Archidi. Blood simple.*

She smiled across the bed at the Majak greybeard. 'That's right. And now it falls to me to accomplish vengeance on the Dragonbane's behalf. And I would like your help.'

Long quiet amidst the silks, while Marnak looked broodingly at her. Out in the street beyond the drapes at the window, she heard horses clop and jingle past. Footfalls on the stair. Uncontrolled laughter came up through the floor from some room where people were apparently having a lot more fun than in here.

'You are an outlander,' he said finally. 'You're not even human.'

'On my mother's side, I am actually. But I take your point. Here I am, asking you to side with a complete stranger against your clan, and on no better evidence than said stranger's word. That's a big ask. But tell me this, Ironbrow – what do I stand to gain from lying to you?'

He glowered. 'Yhelteth manipulates all it comes into contact with, and the Kiriath in turn dangle and dance the Empire like a child's puppet. This is what I saw throughout my time in the south. How should I guess what benefit the Black Folk might see in stirring up the Skaranak? Perhaps your aim is to weaken us, to feed us in pieces to your citified Ishlinak lap-dogs as incentive for some political favour or other.'

'The Black Folk are all gone,' she told him quietly, and for the very first time, the pain as she said it was muted and remote. 'They took ship at An-Monal, the year after the war ended. I am the last of my kind.'

It seemed to mean something to him – he sketched a gesture at her she didn't recognise. Fumbled a bit with his Tethanne phrasing.

'*Honoured word to those in Sky Home that*, uhm, well, the gods, uh, *your* god . . .' He shook his head, took up his goblet and raised it. 'Look, whatever. *I honour your clan's passing*. We had heard it before now, from Skaranak warriors coming home. The Black Folk gone away, sunk in the fiery crater. I, uh, *I mourn with you those who have passed from this world*.'

She cleared her throat. 'Thank you. In fact, I don't think they're dead. Just somewhere else. Just . . . gone.'

He shrugged. 'The dead also are *just somewhere else*. The Dragonbane is in Sky Home, your father is wherever the honourable slain of your people go. We mourn only because we may no longer reach them.'

'So you believe me?'

'About the Dragonbane's passing?' Marnak frowned into his wine. 'Seems that I do. But that doesn't mean anything else you're saying here is true.'

'In all the time that you served with him, did my father ever lie to you? Did any Kiriath you served with?'

'That I know of, no. But how *would* I know for sure?' She saw him hesitate, saw in his eyes the moment he started to believe. 'You're saying the Dragonbane's brothers came to their father's tomb with mercenaries in tow, aiming to murder him? That's what he told you?'

'Yes. All but the one called Gant, apparently. Egar said he never showed. They told him Gant would approve the outcome but would not involve himself. That sound about right?'

She watched him nod, slow and bleak.

'The Dragonbane told me you rode out to his father's tomb with him that night, but he sent you back to the encampment before sunset. Is that true?'

Another reluctant nod.

'He told me Ershal murdered his warhorse with arrows. Put out its eye with one of them. Is *that* true?'

'Yeah.' Very quietly, not looking at her. 'Looked like it from what I saw at the scene the next day.'

'Right. Well, the way Egar told it to me, Ershal was all set to follow that up by putting a shaft through his eye as well. Only then Takavach showed up.' She held down a brief shiver, legacy of the meeting on the steppe. 'You know, the Salt Lord?'

The Majak made a ward, absently. 'We don't call him that out here.

That's League stuff. Dark Court worship. But yes, I know who you mean.'

'Yes, well this Takavach apparently saved his life. Took Ershal's next arrow out of the air in mid-flight, summoned up some kind of killer spirits from the grass to take down the brothers—'

'From the grass?' She saw how still he'd grown.

'Yeah. Grass demons. Or something. The grass came to life, he said. Clawed down his brothers, choked them to death. Ershal only just made it out.'

Marnak Ironbrow, staring at her, rather the way he had when she first walked in. She saw the growing acceptance in his eyes.

'Describe the fight,' he snapped. 'How many did the Dragonbane account for?'

'Of his brothers, none at all.' She sifted back through the memories, the endless times they'd sat and Egar had told her the tale, sometimes in his cups, sometimes hungover, sometimes simply sober, over and over again, as if seeking from her some obscure absolution. 'The grass took them. But he took down three out of the four freebooters they brought with them. The fourth fled, I believe . . .'

Let her voice fade out on the last word, as Marnak threw himself to his feet and stalked to the window. He stood with his back to her, facing the draped silk as if he could see through it to the night outside.

'We looked for him,' he said tightly. 'Tracked his mount back to Ishlin-ichan, but we were a day too late. Fucking half-Ishlinak southern jackal, out of Dhashara they said, but none knew his name or would give it to us easily, anyway. By the time we learnt more, he was long gone, probably back home or into the Empire lands beyond.'

'That's convenient.'

A low growl. 'Ershal swore the sellswords were at the Dragonbane's command, hired out of the south to kill his brothers. That the Dragonbane sent for them to meet him at their father's tomb, and sprang an ambush when they arrived. I—'

He shook his head.

'You didn't believe that shit for a minute,' she suggested.

'I rode with him to the grave.' He turned to face her now, and the struggle was gone from his eyes. 'I saw nothing to indicate he planned a brotherslaying. I saw no sellswords, or their horses. I saw nothing in his face. I knew, I fucking *knew* it was a lie. But the Dragonbane was gone. Vanished.'

'Yeah. Taken under Takavach's wing. Someday, when we've got time, I'll tell you what for. It's a fine tale.'

He nodded.

'Two years,' he said quietly. 'You know, Poltar's a twisted piece of shit – more than ever since he got his hands on some real power. No one'd weep if he dropped dead tomorrow. But Ershal – whatever he did against Eg – in the two years since that time, I've never seen him put a foot wrong. I hate to say it out loud, but he's a better clanmaster than the Dragonbane ever was.'

'That so?' Archeth got up off the bed. Straightened her jerkin and the harness that held her knives. She faced the burly Skaranak warrior, impassive. 'See, that's a pity. Because I'm still going to slit his fucking throat.'

FIFTY-FOUR

Ringil peered into the opened casket. He wasn't sure what he'd expected, but it wasn't this.

The Illwrack heirloom blade – what he could make out of it – seemed unremarkable. It had the same basic form as the longswords the dwenda carried, though perhaps a bit broader and heavier-looking. But at the handling end, it stopped looking anything like a useful weapon at all. The crosspiece of the guard sloped sharply downward at either side, leaving a grip space only the narrowest of hands could have settled comfortably into. And in defiance of any useful purpose Gil could imagine, the underside was lined with small barbed spikes that would gouge chunks out of the flesh of anyone attempting to actually hold and wield the sword. As if that were not enough, below the guard, instead of grip or pommel, there was only what looked like the naked tang of the blade above, but twisted and sharpened into a lengthy, coiled and inward pointing spike.

Despite himself, Ringil felt a faint shudder walk up his spine.

If the construction of the sword was less than sane, then what had been done with the weapon seemed wholly appropriate. It was strapped up in the casket like some lunatic in an asylum chair – stained leather bandaging wrapped tightly around the blade over and over, criss-crossing itself up and down like an incessantly made argument, shrouding the steel almost entirely from guard to tip, except where the bluish edge had frayed through and showed, like a glimpse of living bone in a wound. And all along the inner surfaces of the casket, Gil saw runes scratched roughly into the wood. He couldn't read them, but what faint whispering traces of the *ikinri 'ska* were still open to him hissed in disapproval as he stared.

'Four and a half thousand years it has lain hidden,' Risgillen said quietly. 'But for your blundering expedition to the Hironish Isles, the news of your confused and tangled goals, it might lie hidden still. We might never have remembered what was lost, nor understood the chance we now had. But we snatched it away in time, and brought it home. And then we sent for you as well, and you came. Welcome to your end, Ringil Eskiath. Welcome to your doom.'

She nodded at Atalmire again.

The storm-caller uttered a series of sibilant phrases and Ringil felt the hairs on the back of his neck waft slowly erect. Inside the casket, the bandaging around the blade began to twist and rub against the blade edge, slicing itself apart, writhing like a nest of worms. It made a soft, insistent sound like a barber's razor on the strop. And down at the pommel end, the sword's coiled and sharpened tang moved, bent as supple as a silk cord, lifted its sharpened end like a snake, swaying and seeking. He thought he heard a faint, rising whine in the air.

Risgillen smiled and gestured. 'There. It has your scent.'

Desperately, he reached for the power he'd owned. Felt it ooze fractionally forth, felt Atalmire's glamour wipe it away again like a tavern boy's cloth. Risgillen took his right arm and he could do nothing to prevent her.

'Come,' she said warmly. 'It's time. Give me your hand.'

In the casket, the sword was almost free of its bindings. The last few scraps of bandaging fell away; the blade itself was twisting slightly back and forth now, as if itching to be free. Atalmire reached carefully in and took it in reverent hands, lifted it out. He angled the pommel end upward, towards Ringil's face, and for a moment the flexing, coiling sharpened tang looked as if it might dart in and stab at eye or mouth. Ringil flinched, he couldn't help it. His head barely moved on his neck, the rest of his body was a locked catalogue of straining muscles. He thrashed for a grip on the *ikinri 'ska*, found nothing he could use. Risgillen smiled again, but absently now, gone into some transport of ecstasy at what she was about to do.

She raised his hand slowly to meet the questing tang.

'What *exactly* is going on here?'

Like some violent and irritable schoolmaster, stumbling on mischief cooked up by his errant pupils – the Helmsman Anasharal, back in his ear as if it had never been away. Ringil made a tight, convulsive sound, somewhere between laughter and tears.

'You're . . . a little late, Helmsman.'

But he saw an alarmed look pass between Atalmire and Risgillen. Thought the dwenda's grip on his arm slackened just a fraction . . .

'Oh, indeed,' said Anasharal combatively, and it dawned on Ringil that the Helmsman was not speaking for him alone. Its voice echoed through the whole chamber now, sent dwenda heads craning and peering for its source. A deep, new timbre to the avuncular edge-of-asylum-madness tones, as they tolled in the heights of Findrich's vaulted, stained glass roof. 'Clan Illwrack, is it? Well, you lot haven't changed much in five thousand years, have you?'

Snapped exchange between Risgillen and the storm-caller – he understood none of it. But he saw something new in their faces, and it looked a lot like fear.

'Still trying to get humans to do your dirty work for you, eh? Still not up to the task of learning the way of mortal muck yourselves?'

He saw Atalmire let go of the sword, drop it back into its casket. Raise crook-fingered hands to carve some sequence of glyphs in the air, understood that whatever fragile balance had existed in this space was now at risk—

Fragile.

Like a lightning bolt into his face, splitting his skull above one eye.

'Call yourselves an Elder Race?' The Helmsman, still declaiming somewhere over his head, fading out as Gil grabbed after this other thing, whatever it was. '*Geriatric* race is more like it. I have to wonder. Or, no, maybe you're just not very *clever*, especially when it comes to . . .'

Despite the merroigai's good opinion, I find you fragile, hero. Very fragile.

And abruptly, memory comes roaring in at him. Will not be fended off. Tears aside the curtain he's placed so carefully in its way. High st—

No! Fragile!

He's stumbling, through confining gloom towards a blur of grey light, bracing himself on the sides of the defile to stay upright. Horror behind him, horror coursing through his veins. *The glyphs are in him.* He's been somewhere, done something, had *something done to him*, something so intimate and dark that trying to think about it puts cold sweat on his skin and in his hair . . .

High stone al—

Easy there, hero, let's leave that alone, shall we?

The grey light is stronger now; he sees defined edges and a narrow gap. He ups his pace, falling forward against the bracing of his hands, have to get out, get out, get back to H—

High stone altar, somewhere—

Hjel, back to Hjel. The sides of the cleft run out on either side of him and he's back in the open air, he all but falls from the abrupt lack of support. Only Hjel's sudden, wiry grip on his arm keeps him from crumpling to the ground.

Gil! The dispossessed prince is shouting at him, seemingly across vast distance. *Gil! What happened, did you—*

I'm fine, I'm fine, he keeps babbling it, trying to make it true. *I'm fine.*

But he's not, he's not fine, because—

No!

Because—

Fragile. He's weeping it now, because—

On a high stone altar, somewhere out on an endless empty plain, where he lies stripped back to a nakedness he hadn't known was possible, where a nameless blurred and writhing shape leans over him, reaches in, changes him with clawed limbs and cold, unmerciful tools, while beyond, in every direction, the plain is filled with a horde of the same writhing, claw-limbed shapes, clambering over each other to get closer and see what's being done, and the sky above is filled with a vast shrieking, like the torture of an entire living, feeling universe torn apart . . .

The dark defiles.

They lead here, all of them. This is where they empty out, and he chose to follow them to their end. He was not brought here; he asked to come.

The *ikinri 'ska*.

Stitched into him as he's re-made, as the whole world was once re-made

437

by those same incessant, obsessive claw-limbed seamstresses, for no better reason than because they happened by and it needed to be done . . .

He turns and runs, flees from the memory, but it sits there on his shoulder, murmuring in his ear as he –

– slammed back to the chamber in Etterkal, the dwenda in dismay and disarray before Anasharal's hectoring tones, the glamour loosened, slipped by vital inches—

He reaches now for the *ikinri 'ska*, into the place it really lives, drags it down into the real world and the pit of his stomach and—

Vomited it up.

Atalmire spun on him, somehow alerted, binding up the glamour, grip tightening all over again, defending himself and his troops. Gil ignores the defence, grinning, doesn't bother fighting, reaches down instead . . .

Smashed the stone honeycomb floor apart under his feet, under theirs. Shattered its delicate latticework integrity, dropped them all through it and into the space beneath.

The floor below was storage, a long hall, stacked high with crates for some trade less obnoxious than Etterkal's human staple. At some level, he or maybe the *ikinri 'ska* must have known. The shattered chunks of flooring crashed down on top of it all, smashed the top layer of crates open, let loose big, choking clouds of dust and – by the taste of it – spices. Gil felt the dwenda glamour evaporate as Atalmire lost his grip entirely. He stumbled to his feet on an uneven, shifting surface, broad fragments of flooring sunk at crazy angles into the wreckage of shattered crates. He found the Ravensfriend, unaccountably in his hand.

'Imperials!' He bawled it, coughing amidst the spice. 'Imperials! Rally to me!'

A figure stumbled into him from behind and he swung round. Atalmire, off-balance and choking. Ringil grunted, snagged a hand in the dwenda's hair, yanked it hard towards him.

'C'mere, you fuck.'

He swung the Ravensfriend in a clumsy hacking blow. The Kiriath steel went deep into the storm-caller's side, and he screamed, tried to flail free of Ringil's grip on his hair. Gil tore the sword loose and hacked again, another brutal gash – he felt it snap through ribs this time, get into the chest cavity beyond. Flaring alien reek of the dwenda's blood, mingling with the spice. Atalmire's scream scaled to a wild shriek. He beat at Ringil with his fists, trying to get loose. Gil let go his grip on the dwenda's hair, shoved Atalmire away from him and off the blade. The storm-caller collapsed on the rubble. Ringil took a moment to settle his footing.

'Guess we won't be fixing that leg of yours after all.'

Atalmire tried to get up, gagging hoarsely. He made it to his knees. Ringil swung again, better targeting this time. The storm-caller got one desperate fending hand up and the Ravensfriend sliced right through it,

438

took fingers off like severed twigs, chopped deep into the face behind. Atalmire made a trapped, glutinous noise, lips bisected at an angle by the Kiriath blade. Blood foamed out of his mouth, around the intruding steel. He shuddered like a man taken by a fit.

Ringil lifted a boot, balancing with care, put it against Atalmire's chest, trod down and pulled the Ravensfriend free. The storm-caller hit the rubble like a felled tree, pitch eyes staring at nothing at all. Gil felt little scribbles of the glamour's power shrivelling away in the space around the dwenda's body as he died. He felt the *ikinri 'ska* rush greedily in to fill the gap it left – endless, shapeless force, like the sea running and breaking, slopping and lapping on the rocks at the Dark Queen's feet. He gathered it to him like armour, cast about in the chaos, eyes starting to smart from whatever was in the spices. He raised the Kiriath blade high.

'*Risgillen!*' He bawled it at the shattered roof, deep, grinding rage un-leashed. 'Don't get killed on me now, bitch! I want your fucking *heart!*'

Around him on the uncertain footing, imperials and dwenda grappled in the slowly settling clouds of spice, like figures in some murky seabed dream. He tipped back his head, summoned the *ikinri 'ska*, opened himself to it like a canal sluice, lashed out with its trailing, lightning strike spikes. He sent it slithering and hissing into every dwenda head it could find. In-stinctive grasp of what would work, coming to hand as unerringly as the grip of the Ravensfriend.

The Black Folk are here! They have loosed the dark souls of apes, and turned them against you! You have heard the Warhelm's voice! Your doom is Kiriath steel!

He felt the strike go home – convulsive shock as it hit the reeling Aldrain minds around him. He unsheathed a grin and strode in among them, seeking, grabbing, chopping hamstring strokes, spine-severing slices into unguarded backs –

'*Risgillen? Where are you, Risgillen?*'

– trying with every savage blow to drive out the memory of that high stone altar and what had happened there. He peeled the dwenda off his men, he maimed and crippled them and left them lying in agony for the imperials to finish. He peered through tearing eyes into every dwenda face as they fell, but none were Risgillen. He—

'Ringil! *Ringil!*'

A hand on his shoulder, shaking him. Gil swung blindly about and Klithren of Hinerion stepped deftly into the move, blocked the blow, arm to locked up arm.

'It's done!' he shouted into Gil's face. 'Stand down, it's done! It's over. We took them.'

'We . . .?' Ringil tried to piece the words together, tried to make sense.

'We took them down. The Aldrain. Look.' He waved an arm through the last of the settling spice dust. Not a struggling figure to be seen, just the imperials bent with vengeful blades over the last few injured dwenda where they lay. 'All of them. It's over.'

Ringil coughed on something that might have been a laugh. Klithren nodded. His eyes were streaming, his face was clogged with sweat and yellow powder, and the spice-reeking blood of the dwenda. But he was grinning. He gestured up at the ceiling, the ragged fifty foot hole where the honeycombed stone had come crashing down.

'You do that?'

Ringil wiped at his eyes. 'Yeah. Had to distract them.'

'Some fucking distraction, eh?'

'Seemed to work.' He stared at the tear-dampened powder caked on his fingers, as if it were some vital clue. 'You know what this is?'

Klithren ran his tongue along his upper lip, tasted. 'Chilli powder, right?'

'Yeah, and the rest. What are you using for taste buds? There's turmeric in there. Ginger. Ground coriander. This is a Yhelteth curry blend.'

The mercenary chuckled. 'Secret weapon from the imperial south, eh? If you can't meet 'em blade for blade, just choke 'em and blind 'em first.'

'Something like that.' Ringil looked around again, sobering. 'You find me that bitch Risgillen's body, though. I want her twice as dead as the others, I want her fucking heart.'

'Don't you worry – if she's down here, she's done.'

'Yeah, well. Believe it when I see it. How many did we lose?'

'Haven't done the count yet.' A grimace on the scarred freebooter face. 'Looks like about half to me.'

'Do the count. And find Findrich too – he's got to be down here somewhere. We still have to—'

'My lord! Come quick!'

One of the Throne Eternal, voice urgent, and Ringil's stomach dropped out at the sound. He turned to face the man, already knowing, reading it there in the strained features before the imperial could speak again.

'It's the captain, my lord.'

Gil made his face a mask. 'How bad?'

The Throne Eternal's face alone would have been answer enough. 'He's asking for you, my lord. There's not much left.'

Noyal Rakan lay propped up against the shattered remnants of a crate, shivering and bloodied from the chest down, blood running out of him and clotting in the drifts of spice he lay on. But he smiled through his clenched teeth when he saw Ringil approach.

'Con—' A cough racked him and he had to start again, voice a whisper. 'Congratulations . . . on your victory, my lord. The day is yours.'

'Captain.' Ringil knelt at his side, everything in him screaming against the formality. 'Is there anything I can do for you?'

Rakan shook his head, shivering violently. They'd made him as

440

comfortable as they could, put a rolled cloak under his head for a pillow, wrapped another about him for a blanket. But the blood would not be stopped, it soaked steadily through the cloak, spread in the spice beneath him, and his face had gone the dirty yellow of old parchment.

'Give me . . . your hand,' he mumbled, groping with his own.

Ringil grabbed it, clasped it tight. 'There. Can you feel that?'

'Yeah.' Faintly, voice still trembling. 'Feels . . . feels hard. Good and hard.'

Wavering triumph in his smile – tables finally turned, nothing to lose now, *his* turn to make the jokes with double meanings. Ringil pressed his lips together, made a small noise through them. He put his other hand on Rakan's, made a double clasp, as if he could cup in the Throne Eternal's ebbing life. Rakan nodded jerkily.

'They fall down just like men,' he husked. 'Good advice, my lord. I have . . . put it to some good use, I think.'

A weak gesture with his free hand, perhaps intended to indicate the various slaughtered dwenda lying around them. He coughed again, and blood flecked his lips. A spasm of pain twisted his features, and when it passed, there was something almost pleading in his eyes.

'But they're fast, Gil. They're so fucking fast.'

'I know.' Clenching his fists around the dying man's hand. 'I know they are.'

'I tried . . . I was . . . too many of them.' More coughing, wet and gurgling now. 'I'm sorry, my lord. You'll have to . . . have to go on alone now.'

'It's all right,' said Gil numbly. 'It's all right.'

Rakan spat out blood. His eyes rolled about, taking in the silently watching men. He mustered breath. 'Come . . . closer. I have . . . some private . . . instructions to pass on.'

Ringil leaned in and placed his head next to Rakan's. Rasp of stubble on stubble, the press of the Throne Eternal's cheek to his own. Rakan made a convulsive sobbing sound. Ringil let go his hand, cupped his face.

'Talk to me,' he murmured. 'I'm here.'

'Don't . . . trust the iron demon, Gil.' The Throne Eternal's voice was down to a desperate, throaty hiss. Ringil could feel him pouring the last dregs of his strength into it. 'It has no love for us . . . nor good intentions. It lies to us all. It plots . . . treachery, to bring down everything good. I love . . . the lady Archeth. But she is no empress.'

'I know that, Noy. And she knows it too.' He squeezed his eyes tight shut for a second, opened them again on fresh tears. *This motherfucking spice.* He planted a kiss on the other man's cheek. 'Noy, the throne is safe. Let go. Take your ease.'

'You . . . will not . . . help her overthrow Jhiral? Place her . . . on the throne. The truth, Gil. She is . . . your friend, I know.'

'She wouldn't want the fucking throne if you handed it to her on a plate, Noy. I promise. Rest now, you've done enough.'

441

He felt something inside the other man slip, give way like a bad step. Rakan made a soft sound and tried to nuzzle at his neck.

'Smells . . . like home,' he whispered wonderingly, and stopped.

Ringil closed his eyes. Held them closed for what felt like quite a while. Then, very slowly, he pulled back from Rakan's body, spread his hands flat in front of the Throne Eternal's softened, blood-flecked features, like a man trying to warm himself at a meagre fire. Long moments while he stared through the spaces between his spread fingers, looking for what, he could not have said. Then he lowered his hands. Sniffed hard, and got up.

They were all looking at him.

'Anyone got anything to say.' He cleared his throat, gestured at the body. 'Get it said now. We don't have a lot of time.'

A couple of the Throne Eternal came hesitantly forward. Ringil backed off, stood aside, left Noyal Rakan to the care of his comrades.

'Here's a little something for you!'

Klithren of Hinerion, booming cheerfully from amidst the strewn dead, propelling Slab Findrich before him with one arm twisted up into the small of his back. The slave merchant stumbled, struggling to keep upright on the chaotic, tilted surface. Klithren let go his arm, gave him a brutal shove in the back that pitched him at Ringil's feet in a brief cloud of spice dust.

'Slab Findrich, for your delectation.' The mercenary grinned. 'Pretty much intact, too.'

'That's good,' said Ringil bleakly.

Findrich tried to get to his feet. Klithren booted him hard in the gut, and the slave merchant collapsed again. The mercenary glanced aside to where the Throne Eternal were gathered, heads bent in prayer, around Noyal Rakan's corpse. He jerked a thumb at them.

'Your boy get off okay?'

Ringil nodded. Wiped at his eyes. Klithren pulled a sympathetic face.

'Fucking chilli powder, right?'

'You find Risgillen?'

The mercenary shook his head. 'Got a few females in the ranks, all chopped up pretty good. Boys are taking trophies. But she's not here.'

Like the slip of a foot on battlefield blood, like a lethal error made. He grimaced with the sudden lightness that it left in his belly. At his feet, Findrich coughed a sneer.

'Don't you worry, faggot. She'll be back.'

Gil stooped and grabbed the slaver by his collar, dragged him up onto his knees. 'I'm going to ask you once more, politely, Slab. Where are you keeping my friends?'

Findrich looked back at him out of sullen, reddened eyes. 'Fuck you. Aristo prick.'

Ringil made a fist and punched him solidly in the face. He felt the nose break as the slaver went down. He dragged him back up, leaned in close.

'I'm in no fucking mood, Slab. Where are they?'

The slave merchant grinned at him through streaming blood and snot. Four or five decades of Harbour End street in his eyes. He spat in Ringil's face. 'Get on with it, you faggot aristo waste. You don't have the fucking time or balls to break me, and you know it. And she'll be back for you, don't think she won't. Oh, she wants you bad. Back for you too, you turn-coat borderland fuck.'

Klithren made a pained face.

'Want me to open him up?' he asked. 'Pull out a few feet of guts and dance on them? Usually does the trick.'

'No, that's going to make him difficult to move.' Ringil let go of Fin-drich, let him slump back to the floor. 'Just keep him there a moment. I've got a better idea.'

FIFTY-FIVE

She cut the bonds and gag she'd put on Marnak's Yhelteth whore, left her weeping and shuddering in the Ironbrow's arms and bid them both good-night. Privately, she thought the girl was milking it a bit – beyond showing her Bandgleam's naked blade for a threat and manhandling her, all right, a *little* roughly perhaps, she had done her no actual harm at all. A glimpse of the Kiriath steel, a look into the burnt-black witch's eyes – *look at me, girl, you're not going to give me any trouble, are you?* – was about all it took. By the time the Ironbrow showed up at the door, Archeth had her neatly trussed and quiescent in the back chamber. But now, she turned her eyes away as Archeth spoke, pressed her face hard into Marnak's leather-clad shoulder and sobbed as if some demon from the bowels of the Earth had come for her.

Let's just hope we can get the same reaction out of the Skaranak.

She left the way she'd come in, via the window. Outside on the tiny balcony, she swung a leg over the rail and found purchase for the toe of her boot in the poorly cemented brickwork. Similar chinks higher up gave her fingers something to cling to as she stepped off the balcony altogether, worked her way around the brothel's facade and into the shadows of the side alley. There, she down-climbed until she was about four or five yards off street level, then jumped clumsily the rest of the way to the ground. She staggered a little on impact, grabbed the wall to stop herself going down. The horses out front, whinnying and snorting, shifting about on their tethered reins . . .

Eyes!

It was a flash glimpse as she straightened up, the slanted amber gleam of a wolf's gaze at her shoulder—

She whirled about. There was a knife in each hand, Wraithslayer and Bandgleam, though she'd later swear she'd made no move to draw either one of them. The balanced weight of the steel seemed to anchor her to the ground, settle her better into the fighting crouch . . .

Nothing.

The alley was as deserted as it had been when she'd slipped into it a couple of hours earlier – dust and grit and the odd discarded shred of rags too small to be usefully scavenged away. A thin breeze blew out of the gloom and past her, sat briefly on the nape of her neck, then was gone. She held the crouch for another couple of moments, pivoted slowly about to be absolutely sure, and then straightened up again, one tense muscle at a time.

Nerves.

Yeah, right.

She shook off the chill on her neck. Put her knives away and walked out of the alley to where the horses were beginning to settle down once more. Absently, she patted a couple of them on the neck, murmured soothing words to them in High Kir. Up by the brothel doorway, the Feathered Nest's bouncer, a blocky, grizzled Majak with a leather eyepatch, spotted her and nodded. She tripped lightly up the steps to meet him, some slight excited giddiness pulsing in her veins, and counted the balance of his bribe into his outstretched palm. Imperial coin – it was Carden Han's very own brand of magic; up here, he told her, you can make the most remarkable things happen with even the tiniest handful of this stuff.

'My men still inside?' she asked

The doorman nodded. She went past him, pushed her way through a short series of dyed cloth drapes, each consecutively thinner and finer than the last, until she parted a final curtain of translucent silk and stepped into the pipe-fume clogged air of the brothel's main lounge. Her appearance stirred a slight ripple through the reclining figures scattered about the place, but most were too smothered in their pleasures to give even this new arrival more than cursory attention. Maybe, she thought sourly, some of them just assumed she was a flandrijn hallucination.

She found Selak Chan and Kanan Shent with the embassy's spymaster, sprawled amidst a welter of cushions and young, semi-clad female flesh. For appearance's sake, they had a standing water pipe of their own, but none of them appeared to be smoking from it. Their eyes were serious and watchful on the surroundings. Chan saw her as soon as she came through the drapes, prodded his companions and came to some sort of half-crouched attention as she approached.

'My lady? Is all well?'

'Well enough.' She bent low and tipped a glance at the spymaster, a wiry, soft-spoken character whose Majak affectations of hair and clothing did nothing much to hide the imperial edge on the man beneath. The legate had told her he was ex-King's Reach, and it showed. 'Your sources were correct, it seems, my lord Eshen. Your recommended key is ready to turn in the lock.'

'This is heartening, my lady. But there is no need for codes.' Eshen smiled and gestured at the women surrounding them. 'The Feathered Nest doesn't waste its Yhelteth stock on lobby duties. None of these understand more than service fragments of Tethanne. You may brief us freely without fear of eavesdropping.'

Archeth let her eyes wander across the bodies on display, saw it was very likely true. The whores were made up in Yhelteth fashion – though decades out of date in their use of kohl traceries, she noticed – but the faces beneath the gilding were broader, coarser featured and paler than anything you'd see in most Empire lands. Their figures were stockier too, big in the shoulders, less delicate curve in hip and waist than most women from the imperial capital would have been, though with a fuller, enticing load on behind, sure enough, and big, ripe breasts that . . .

One of the whores caught her looking, caught her eye over the mouthpiece of the flandrijn pipe as she toked on it. She giggled and breathed out smoke at Archeth in a long, sickly sweet plume. Nudged one of her co-workers and murmured something in her ear in Majak. The second girl looked up at Archeth and her mouth split in a loose, inviting grin. The two of them blinked in drugged unison, staring at her with paired candour, frank and open curiosity painted in their eyes. Archeth felt desire trickle and ache in her, snaking up from her crotch into belly and breasts like soft, slow fire.

Ishgrim, she reminded herself severely. *You are going home to Ishgrim.*

She cleared her throat and looked away. 'The Ironbrow will turn for us, if we meet a few conditions he insists upon. Safeguarding clan integrity, basically. But there's more than enough rage in him to start the fire we need.'

Eshen inclined his head. 'And even more so now, I suspect. The spy who brought us news of Marnak's coming also tells me the Ironbrow tangled with the shaman over fraternising with Ishlinak city dwellers so soon after the comet. Auspicious, the way the heavens align with your requirements.'

'I was in that comet,' she said shortly. 'There's nothing auspicious about it.'

'Yes, so I understand.' The spymaster eased his crossed legs into a fresh posture. 'Some antique machine of your people, I'm told. I have been in the capital, my lady, I have seen the Span. I understand that it is engineering, not magic. Nonetheless, the manner of your arrival is a story we might do well to sow widely among the locals, in the run up to your confrontation with the shaman. We think of these people as primitive in their beliefs, but it's worth remembering that they hold those beliefs every bit as firmly as we our faith. A woman of your hue, delivered out of the heart of a comet . . . well, there are some real tactical advantages to be derived here.'

She nodded. 'All right, get it done. Marnak told me he came here to do deals for ironware and horseflesh—'

'That will certainly have been his excuse, yes.'

'—so his men should be around for a few days. Long enough for them to catch the word?'

'I will see to it.' The spymaster stroked his beard. 'Is it your intention, my lady, to stay here longer tonight?'

The whores were still looking at her. She kept her gaze rigidly on Eshen. 'No. I'm going back to the embassy. You three stick around, see if the Ironbrow goes anywhere interesting or sends his men out. I think this is going to work, but I don't know the man, and I don't want to get tripped up for not paying attention.'

Eshen looked approving. Selak Chan just looked worried.

'You intend to walk back alone, my lady?'

'I do.' She flashed him the edge of a grin as she stood up. 'After what we've all been through, I don't think the streets of this glorified horse camp can have much in them to worry us. Stay and enjoy yourselves. I'll be fine.'

And if I'm not, I have my knives.

Not very sure where that had come from. She managed to glance only briefly at the whores as she turned to leave, to put them at her back and walk away, to fill her mind with Ishgrim's face instead. The leashed desire inside her guttered low, began to seep away.

Curdling in her guts to an ugly hope that the streets might give her some cause to use her Kiriath steel after all.

The tangled roads and footways of Ishlin-ichan drew her in, enfolded her in quiet gloom.

Carden Han had told her to expect as much. A scant hundred years of settlement had not yet purged the Ishlinak inhabitants of their steppe nomad heritage; a preference for fireside huddling by night prevailed. Anyone with a place to be was generally in it by the time darkness fell, and torchlit thoroughfares were few and far between. Now and then, a pony clopped by with a rider drunk or nodding sleepily in the saddle; once it was a woman astride a mule with two small children clinging on in front. A couple of times, she thought she heard the patter of urchin feet up side alleys. For the rest, she had the streets to herself.

The embassy building stuck up in the middle distance ahead, five storeys studded with warm orange-lit oblong eyes. But she steered towards it in near darkness, navigating by patchy band-light through cloud and the dim glow of hovel windows showing the ruddy flicker of a hearth somewhere within.

And she was being followed.

The knowledge grew on her by increments. Small sounds at her back, glimpsed motion out of the corner of her eye as she looked back at corners. At first, it blended with the other occasional noises of brief traffic on adjacent streets, but by the time she was halfway back to the embassy, the coincidences were too many to accept. Someone or something was behind her, dogging her steps, and not making much effort to hide the fact.

The blunt longing for violence in the pit of her belly rejoiced. Flaradnam had taught her from a very early age not to walk afraid – *this world is not a civilised one,* he told her when she was still a girl. *And so you really only have two choices. You can become a fighter, and let it show. Or you can go in constant terror of every cut-rate thug who thinks he's special because his mummy saw fit to birth him with a pair of balls and a prick. I am sorry, Archidi, really I am. I would have liked you to grow up in a better place, but that place will be centuries in the making. This is the best I can do.*

447

Grashgal brought her the knives the next day.

She felt them stirring now, tiny points of warmth in the small of her back, across her chest and down in her right boot where Falling Angel lurked. Perhaps they felt the proximity of pursuit the way she did, perhaps they were just responding to the quickening of her blood. Perhaps, as the Warhelm had tried to make her see, it was all part of a single response.

So she couldn't fuck those two hot-eyed whores back at the brothel.

She'd fuck up whoever this was instead.

On a crossroads street corner, she came on the noisy, iron-ringing brightness of a smithy, where black silhouettes worked late with hammer and tongs against the furnace glare. Three men, looked like the smith and two young apprentices, maybe his sons. She made as if to walk past, paused abruptly and spun about, put the furnace at her back and scanned the path behind her.

Yep. Right there.

Slanting amber eyes in the darkness, a couple of dozen yards back down the street, blazing with reflected glare from the smithy's fire.

The palms of her hands tingled.

Come on then, you bitch.

As if it heard her, the creature moved out into the light. It was exactly the wolf the eyes had promised. Six feet from nose to tip of tail, a yard high at the shoulder, sleek and grey with summer fur. Lips peeled back off front teeth in a silent snarl.

Archeth felt her own upper lip lift in response. Reflexive, violent pumping of heart and lungs, readying for the fight. She flexed her hands at her sides and the knives quivered eagerly in their sheaths.

Sparks blew off the forge and out across the street, like incandescent snow.

Come on, then.

And gone.

She stood in shock, unsure quite how it had happened. One moment the wolf was there, the next it seemed to rear impossibly up on its hindquarters and step back into the cloaking darkness. The slanting amber eyes blinked once at her, and went out.

Archeth looked dubiously at the patch of darkness that had swallowed the wolf, probing the gloom, then shrugged.

That all you got, Kelgris?

Beside her, she noticed the hammering from the forge had stopped. She glanced at the smith and his sons, saw them frozen and staring, implements in hand. A storm-bolt flash of insight lit in her head, a vision of herself, seen through their eyes – night-black, tall and immobile in the glow from the furnace, the glint and gleam of the Kiriath knife harness, wrapped tight around her frame in alien artistry, the upside down hilts of Wraithslayer and Bandgleam laid on her chest, the kaleidoscope light in her eyes.

To these men, she probably didn't look much less otherworldly than the thing that had followed her up the street.

She nodded at them, silent acknowledgement, and went on her way. Took the corner and the mild slope up towards the embassy. The glow from the forge fell behind, her heart climbed back down from its thunderous pumping. She—

Out of a niche between hovel walls on her left, so fast she had no time even to turn her head. A lithe dark form leapt out and grabbed her tightly about the chest, bound her arms down by her sides, dragged her kicking furiously back into the dark. She threw her head back to butt at whatever face her attacker might have, but the force of it met only empty air. The dark figure wrestled her back, step by struggling step, further into the space between the hovels and without apparent effort.

The knives came to life. Falling Angel leapt up out of her boot and was in her hand. The others yearned in the harness. She snarled and twisted her neck about, tried to find a throat or a face to bite, found nothing at all. Craned down hard at the arms that held her bound. Sliced at the air beside her thigh with Falling Angel's blade . . .

'*Be still!*'

It was a tight murmur, nothing more, but she felt the fight tugged out of her like the stopper on a wine bottle. Felt her strength drain out behind the command. Even her knives fell abruptly quiet. All the hairs on the back of her neck stood up.

'That's better. We'll have a bit less of the stroppy warrior queen, if you don't mind.'

A woman's voice, throaty, gorgeous and intimate; it seemed to echo and seep down into her belly, down where she'd left her feelings about the two hot-eyed Ishlinak whores. A fresh fire woke in her at the memory. The grip on her arms loosened the slightest fraction, a slim dark hand fluttered in her line of sight, like a conjuror's flourish before the trick. Then, before she could react, the hand dropped again, went to the juncture of her thighs, pressed palm and long fingers into the gap. She gasped and arched. Her innards ran heated and liquid at the touch. Somehow, through leather and cotton layers, the fingers on that hand were *right inside her*, opening her suddenly willing cunt, pumping gently, firmly, reaching up to touch some unfeasible core within, cupping and pressing, and then it was like lava in the overflow lake at An-Monal, bursting the banks, pouring hot and thick and majestically unstoppable, tumbling stickily downward as shuddering, shaking, she came.

Came harder than she had a living memory with which to compare.

She slid down out of the encircling arms, sagged into a heap against the nearest hovel wall, panting, sobbing, tears squeezing into her eyes.

'There you go. I'd like to see your little League hussy manage that for you.'

Something dark knelt beside her in the alley. She blinked through tears, saw a face of perfectly moulded beauty hanging over her – smooth ebony skin, a match almost for her own, grinning, overly sharp white teeth in a jaw framed by long riotous hair that didn't look like it had seen a comb in its owner's entire life. At the heart of it all, the eyes were the same amber she'd already seen twice that night. The same hand that had just lit her up now reached in and rearranged her collar, thumbed the tears off her face and stroked her cheek, all with the gentle but insistent intimacy of a long-time lover. The voice sent tiny aftershock shudders through her lower body with each word it spoke.

'What I mean to say is,' – tongue slipping out – just a little unnervingly long for the human face Kelgris wore – to wet her thumb before she went back to wiping away Archeth's tears, 'there's no reason why you and I can't be good friends – so long as you don't overstep the mark on this ridiculous revenge fantasy you're entertaining.'

Archeth worked up a groggy smile. 'So it's commerce after all, is it?'

'Would you prefer the wolf?' The woman, or whatever wore her skin, finished with Archeth's face and ebbed gracefully away a couple of feet. In the darkness, she was all amber eyes and teeth now, only the faint crowning silhouette of her hair to define her as human. 'You really need to take a more long-term outlook on this, kir-Archeth Indamaninarmal. Poltar the shaman and his pet clanmaster are mortal, both of them. They'll die soon enough, without any help from you. As will your little northern piece of pussy waiting back home, come to that. It's what they do, mortals. They die. Think about that – it's going to be a long, lonely road for you. Maybe you could use a little immortal company now and then.'

Archeth propped herself up a little better against the wall. She still could not rise, her legs felt like tangled drifts of seaweed beneath her. 'I've turned down two whores so far this evening. I'm not about to cave in for a third.'

A snarl, out of no human throat. Suddenly, Kelgris was in her face. The amber eyes burned inches away. A thin droplet of blood oozed out of Kelgris's hair and ran down her face.

'You want to be careful with that mouth of yours, kir-Archeth.'

Convulsively, Archeth flung out a hand and tangled it in that copious mane of hair. Brought Falling Angel up in her other hand, jammed the point of the blade under the other woman's jaw. Faster than she'd ever moved before, she wasn't even sure if it *was* her. She breathed in hard, leaned a half inch closer to the amber eyes.

'I don't plan to use my mouth on you, bitch,' she said tightly. 'But I'm willing to find out if Kiriath steel can get the job done. You make me come, you think that's *it?* I can do that myself, with only half the hand holding this knife.'

As if Falling Angel poured fresh, cabled strength down into her, into the muscles of her grip and the arm behind it. She felt the force of it flood her, felt a surge inside like breaking waves. She pressed herself back into the wall, levered herself slowly to her feet. Brought Kelgris with her, hooked up on the knife blade as she rose. Blood was running down out of the Sky Dweller's hairline now at an alarming rate, painting half her face bloody and wet. Her lips writhed with syllables unspoken, a low growl was rising in her throat. Wraithslayer awoke moaning, shivered to life in the harness on Archeth's chest. Archeth lifted Falling Angel higher, let go the goddess's mane with her other hand, took Wraithslayer out of the air as it left its sheath, like catching it as it fell. She slid Falling Angel slowly out from under Kelgris's blood-dripping chin.

'I'm done,' she hissed. 'You can *go*.'

The face in front of her seemed to shiver and shift, a composite swirl of different women, different in almost everything but the amber eyes and the steady seep of blood down one side of the face. Kelgris bared her teeth in an awful grin.

'You have been warned twice now, kir-Archeth,' she said in a voice gone suddenly cold. 'There will not be a third time.'

And gone again.

After a while, Archeth got herself off the wall. She shook off the shiver on her spine, looked about the confined space the confrontation had taken place in. Trampled mud and scattered clods of horseshit kicked in here off the street over time. She laughed, a little shakily.

'Divine intervention, eh? Don't knock it 'til you've tried it.'

She stepped back out into the main thoroughfare, peered left and right. No one in sight, and the twitchy sense of pursuit she'd had since the brothel was gone. She breathed in, and even the woodsmoke-smelling air seemed a little less heavy in her lungs.

'Right, Archidi,' she said, out loud to the empty street. 'Let's see if we can't get you home without any more excitement.'

She almost managed it.

Up to the embassy compound, nodded through the gate by respectful imperials, past the stables and across the courtyard, into the main block. Through the hall and up the stairs to her apartment. She was on the third flight when she heard a door open behind her, and then the diffident clearing of a throat.

She turned and found Yilmar Kaptal stood on the landing below, door to his apartment ajar behind him. By the look of it, he'd been waiting up for her.

'My lord Kaptal. Can I help you?'

'My lady Archeth, I have been thinking.' Kaptal scrubbed at his face with one hand, like a man recently woken from sleep. He sounded oddly puzzled, as if taken aback by the words coming out of his own mouth. 'It strikes me . . . would it perhaps not make sense, I mean . . .'

She stifled a yawn. 'Would what make sense?'

'A change of ruling dynasty,' he said. 'If you became Empress.'

FIFTY-SIX

They were holding the prisoners in an empty wine cellar at the rear of the warehouse. Stone steps down, and a low ceiling in vaulted black brick. Guttering torches in brackets on the walls, solid oak doors closing off sections on either side. There was a six-man guard mounted outside the second door on the left, hard-bitten Etterkal toughs armed with knives and clubs, sitting around on wine barrels or propped against the vaulted walls in the glow from a couple of lanterns on the floor. They'd come scrambling to their feet as soon as they heard boots on the stairs, let loose oaths when they saw Ringil and a pinioned, broken-faced Slab Findrich, at the head of a squad of grim and bloodied imperial soldiers.

Ringil stopped a couple of yards from where they stood, let them get a good look. He'd only brought eight of his able-bodied men with him, left Klithren with the rest to get the wounded bound up and ready to move. But it was eight heavily armed marines, jubilant with their just-done victory against dark forces, just scraped and banged up enough to feed the combat fire in their bellies. They'd eat Findrich's men alive. Ringil gave the local hard men time to do the math, waited the brief moment it took them to decide.

He nodded curtly back at the stairs he'd just come down.

'Go on, fuck off. Leave the keys.'

Clank of the big iron key-ring as it hit the stone flags. The man who'd unhitched it from his belt skirted a wide, wary circle around the imperials and then scurried up the stairs like a spooked rat. His comrades weren't far behind. Hurried footfalls, fading away. Ringil glanced sidelong at Findrich.

'Just can't get the help these days, eh? What is the Salt Warren coming to?'

The slave merchant made a strangled noise. Ringil stepped over to the fallen keys, toed them back across the flags to where the two marines held Findrich pinioned between them. He nodded at the imperials to let him go.

'Tell you what, Slab – you open up for us. If Risgillen's built any nasty surprises into that lock, you can taste them first.'

Privately, he thought a trap of that sort unlikely. There was no whiff of magic he could detect, dwenda or otherwise, anywhere in the cellar, and he was getting pretty good at sniffing these things out. But Findrich didn't know that. Loosed by his captors, he bent and picked up the keys like a man forced to handle a snake. He stood hesitant, staring at the door.

'Come on, let's go.' Ringil shoved him forward, closed up the gap, shoved him again. Forced him to the door, where Findrich worked the lock with trembling hands.

The oak panelling hinged creakily inward. Ringil shoved the slaver through ahead of him, followed him briskly in. There was lantern light inside, some crude straw matting and trestle cots. He saw familiar faces, familiar figures, scrambling to their feet. Mahmal Shanta – Menith Tand – Klarn Shendanak there, one eye drooped and dead-seeming for some reason. All three of them looking a lot thinner and more worn than he remembered, but otherwise intact. A couple of ranking marine officers for a bonus, a Throne Eternal lieutenant of Rakan's with his arm in a grubby sling . . .

He shovelled Findrich out of the way, stood glaring around the chamber.

'Ringil?' Mahmal Shanta's reedy voice, disbelieving. 'Is it really you?'

'Where the fuck is the Dragonbane?' He swung on Findrich, hands crooked like talons. *'Where's Archeth?'*

It took Tand and Shendanak, in a co-operative effort he wouldn't have believed if he hadn't seen it, to talk him down.

He had Findrich by the throat, rammed up against the nearest black brick wall. Yelling for his men to bring the sword again in its casket, see if that didn't loosen this fuck's lips for real this time. Findrich grunting in panic through the clenched grip on his windpipe, hands trying in vain to prise Ringil's iron-fingered hold loose, wheezing desperately with what breath he had left, didn't know what Gil was *talking* about, *what* Dragonbane, *what* fucking Black Folk bitch, these were all the imperial prisoners they had, the rest were lost, they were *lost*, the man-o'-war *Lord of the Salt Wind* never made it home, the storm, the fucking *storm*—

'He's telling you the truth, Eskiath.' Menith Tand put in with mannered calm. 'Before you choke him quite to death there.'

'Yeah, that's right.' Shendanak, up off the cot he was sitting on, shoulder to shoulder with Tand. He seemed to be limping, and Ringil noticed for the first time that his arm was also in a sling. 'Listen to the man, will you? The Dragonbane never made it. Archeth neither. They wrecked off the Wastes coast.'

The simple fact of Tand and Shendanak's voices chiming agreement was enough of a miracle to stop Gil in his tracks. He turned his head, loosened his grip on Findrich's windpipe. Stared from the scarred Majak visage to Tand's blandly composed features. He let go of Findrich convulsively, let him slump to the floor.

'Wrecked?' he asked stupidly.

Tand nodded. 'I'm afraid so. Yilmar Kaptal was aboard as well. Quite a few marines, some of Klarn's best men, a number of Throne Eternal too,

I believe. We waited for news while they held us at the Chancellery, but none came. *Lord of the Salt Wind* never made it home.'

'They could have lied to you.' Lips numb as the words mumbled out. 'You were prisoners of war, maybe they—'

'We saw them driven in toward the shore,' Mahmal Shanta said sombrely. 'The storm came out of nowhere, we had no warning. It was like nothing I've ever seen. We nearly wrecked on the headland ourselves. Any closer in and we would have been smashed to kindling. And their ship was a good quarter league to port of ours. I'm sorry, Ringil. They are gone.'

A storm out of nowhere.

He heard it again, grumbling and prowling, somewhere under the horizon to the south and east as the elementals wrapped *Dragon's Demise* in fog. The outlying recalcitrant snarl of the forces he had summoned and strictured to his will.

You don't know that, Gil. You don't know that's how it was.

But he did. He knew.

He heard Hjel's sombre tones again.

The elementals are capricious, and their range is wide. Unleash them, and their mischief will be general. Try not to worry about it too much, it's a price you have no choice but to pay.

But in the end, he was not the one who had paid.

That they do your will in your immediate vicinity is the trick. What havoc they wreak elsewhere need not be your concern.

The fucking *ikinri 'ska.*

He felt the rage come twitching through him, icy in the hollow space under his ribs, like rivulets of meltwater down rock. He felt his breathing come hard, felt his jaw tighten. Looked around as if awakening from something, saw Findrich on the floor at his feet.

At his shoulder – the two marines he'd charged with carrying the sword stood expectantly by, open casket held up between them.

And the Aldrain blade waiting within.

Findrich read his face, the look in his eyes, and a panicked moan broke from his lips. When Ringil threatened him with the sword before, when he held the languidly writhing tang up close to the slave merchant's face, Slab-face Findrich had cracked like an egg. Babbled out the location of the prisoners, promised to lead Ringil to them, to stand down his guard, anything, *anything, just get that fucking thing away from me . . .*

Looked like Risgillen had at some point explained pretty clearly to him what would happen to whoever took up the sword.

Now, it was the same. Findrich tried to push himself away backwards along the black brick wall, eyes fixed in horror on the casket. Ringil stood staring down at him, wrapped in a paroxysm of fury and loss, and something seemed to pass between the two men, some long-awaited understanding coming home.

'No, Gil, listen . . .'

'Archeth and Egar are gone.' He said it quietly, reasonably, as if trying to explain it. 'Wrecked. What does that leave me, Slab?'

'Gil, please . . .'

'It's time, Slab. Way past time.'

He swung on the casket, took hold of the sword at the blade where it joined the hilt. He felt it leap alive at the touch, felt it try to twist in his grip, but his fist was closed too tight. He dropped to one knee in front of Findrich, vaguely aware he was grinning like a skull. He grasped the slaver's right arm at the wrist, dug a thumb savagely into the nerve point so Findrich's fisted fingers loosened. Findrich flailed and kicked, Ringil held stolidly on, leaned in close.

'Be still,' he hissed, and the slave merchant's struggles ceased.

Throat clearing behind him. 'My lord Ringil, we should perhaps—'

'Shut up, Tand. Can't you see I'm busy.'

Findrich lay there rigid, sweat beading his face, lips twitching with pleas he had no way to voice. The sword wriggled impatiently in Ringil's grip. Gil let go the slave merchant's wrist, pressed the paralysed hand open on the flagstone floor.

'Truth is, Slab – I never fucking liked you, even back in the day. And we've none of us improved with age.'

He laid the softly flexing sword tang across Findrich's open palm.

Let it go.

Watched, fascinated, as the metal coiled stealthily around the slave merchant's hand and forearm, then drew savagely tight. Findrich screamed, girlishly high, staring down the length of his arm in horror as the sharp end of the tang lifted like a striking snake, bent, stabbed down into the meagre flesh at the wrist. Another shriek, wrung out of the slaver like water from drenched clothing, the metal end digging hungrily into the meat of his wrist now, gouging deeper but no blood apparent, Findrich's body beginning to shudder . . .

Gil got to his feet. Glanced at Tand and the others, there in a gathered ring behind him, ashen faced and staring. He gave them a small, pre-occupied smile.

'You want to get out and leave this to me?'

They needed no further encouragement. Out the door as fast as they could walk without loss of dignity in front of the watching marines. He saw the last of them out, nodded at the two men holding the casket.

'You too. This is just tidying up. Tell Rakan—' He remembered. Blinked. 'Tell, uhm, Salk to head back and have the wounded detail ready to move out. We've got another forced march to the harbour coming up. Everybody else stay put out there and wait for me. Yeah, you can leave that here.'

They dropped the casket where they stood, visibly relieved to be rid of it. Hasty salutes and they backed out. He wondered if they could sense even a fraction of the stink of magic that was rising in the room around him. Or maybe the twitching, undead body on the floor and the leeching sword wrapped around its arm was enough.

'Would you mind explaining to me,' Anasharal asked irritably in his ear. 'What it is exactly that you're doing *now?*'

'Sure,' he said distantly. 'Your Divine Empress scheme is a bust. Archeth isn't here. She's dead. Drowned in a shipwreck on the Wastes coast.'

Long pause. 'Oh. That is unfortunate.'

'I'd say so, yeah. *Unfortunate.*' He found a certain bitter satisfaction in enunciating the word, like biting down on a loose tooth, like grinding it into the soft, wounded gum beneath. Pain he deserved. 'So what I'm doing now, I'm just finishing up. Killing what's left to kill, burning down the rest.'

'Admirable thoroughness. But what about the others? Shanta, Tand, the Maja—'

'Yeah, your toy fucking cabal-in-waiting is still intact. For what that's worth. I'm bringing them out as planned, soon as I'm done here.'

'Good. I shall tell commanders Hald and Nyanar. But – perhaps you should hurry.'

'Perhaps you should shut the fuck up,' Ringil said without heat. 'And let me handle the sharp end of this.'

'Oh, well, that's *very* gracious. Coming from someone whose life I saved at the sharp end, not an hour ago.'

'As I recall, you just *talked*. It wasn't exactly shoulder-to-shoulder shield-wall heroics.'

'Heroics are overrated as a means of resolving matters. It is, and has always been the tragedy of humans that they cannot see this. In any case, shield-wall or simple scolding, I don't see you complaining about the outcome.' A sour pause. 'Or saying thank you.'

Ringil grimaced. 'Thanks. Wasn't exactly selfless though, was it? Without me, there's no rescued cabal, no rescued God-Empress-in-waiting.'

'Nonetheless, you should—'

'Got no time for this, Helmsman.' Glancing at the body on the floor. 'We'll talk later. Right now, I got things to kill.'

Stretched out across the flagstones, Findrich, or what was left of him, had stopped shuddering. His limbs were sweeping back and forth on the floor in the twitchy, ill-coordinated swimming motions Gil associated with bodies infested by corpsemites. The chest rose and fell on long deep breaths, the air it breathed made a faint rasping noise in and out. The head lifted on the neck, the eyes snapped open. Something there grinned out at him. Whatever it was, he was pretty sure it wasn't Findrich.

Gil nodded at the door, and it slammed shut. He clicked a crick out of his neck, took a turn around the chamber, drew the Ravensfriend from his back.

'Come on, then. Get up.'

It wallowed to its feet, some tangled mess of old Myrlic syllables

456

dribbling from its lips. The eyes fixed on him, burning malice without recognition. He looked into them and forced down the faint chill that blew along his spine. Clan Illwrack's champion, the Dark King returned. The sword wagged at the end of the thing's right arm like some extended limb, broken at the joint. Findrich's feet took hesitant steps on the stone floor. The mouth opened unnaturally wide, gaping at him. A thin, gull-plaintive shriek issued out.

Ringil rolled his eyes.

'Are you fucking serious? Come on!'

It came hissing at him and he let it come, blocked the clumsy sword blow it brought. Looped the strike aside and down on the Ravensfriend's blade, swung neatly back in and chopped Findrich right through the midriff to the spine. For just one moment, he was eye to eye with the thing behind the slave merchant's face, close enough for a kiss.

'Illwrack Changeling?' he sneered. 'Thank you, and goodnight.'

He tore the Ravensfriend sideways out of Findrich's body, sliced the spine apart on the running edge of the Kiriath blade. Stepped away and spun with showy elegance. Findrich went down in a welter of blood – though not as much as you'd expect out of a still living body – and collapsed in two halves across the flagstones.

Ringil stood for a careful moment, and yeah, sure enough, the head moved on the neck, the eyes were still alive, the lips still mouthing. Hissed arcane syllables, the Aldrain tongue this time, by the sound of it. He put the Ravensfriend's point at the thing's throat for a moment, then reconsidered. Skirted warily around the cloven body, stood on the sword arm at the wrist. He felt the weapon's tang writhe under his boot like a chopped snake. Ignored it, put the Ravensfriend carefully in place, severed the arm from the body just below the elbow. It was a tricky stroke, took a couple of slicing blows with the limb pinned flat to the floor, but there wasn't much to Findrich's gaunt limbs these days, and the edge on the Kiriath steel got the job done well enough.

The head died. The mouth gaped mutely open, the eyes emptied of what had been there. Even the sword tang stopped flexing under his boot.

If Risgillen was somewhere watching, she gave no sign.

Ringil drew a deep breath, kicked the severed sword arm away across the floor. He went to the door and pulled it open, found himself facing a thicket of steel blades and the tense, taut faces of his men.

He found he could grin at them.

'We're out of here,' he said. 'Torch everything that'll burn.'

They fell back through the echoing spaces of the warehouse, lighting curtains with their borrowed torches, smashing apart furniture or storage crates and barrels alike, heaping the splintered shards into impromptu bonfire piles in the centre of each chamber they passed through. They saw no more sign of life than they had coming in, only the corpses of the slaughtered skirmish rangers and Kaad, father and son, like empty sacks discarded in the atrium rain.

By the time they made the front doors, you could hear the hungry, crackling roar of the flames, echoing down the corridors they'd come through, and long-tongued shadows danced on the roof over their heads. The mounting heat ushered them to the door like an impatient host.

They made their way out into the rain and down the steps outside to the street. Twitchy with unslaked rage and his failure to account for Risgillen, Ringil stopped at the bottom step and looked back. Flames capered in the windows, as if gesturing him farewell. He'd never seen a building this grand sacked before, he wasn't sure how much damage the fire would finally do with that much stone in the structure. Probably wouldn't bring the whole thing down like Hinrik's place, but given time, he supposed the roof must catch, at least in places, should end up falling in and adding to the blaze. With luck, there'd be enough structural beams in wood to char through and collapse, bringing down the upper levels. Even with the rain, he could hope for a gutted, smouldering shell by morning.

Honour pyre for the Throne Eternal captain.

He closed his eyes for a brief moment, brought back the supple ghost. Steel-thighed, taut-bellied, firm-handed, innocent-eyed Noyal Rakan. Rakan, who'd taken what brief, stolen minutes and fragments of hours they could find for each other over the five months of the expedition, had given himself in grateful passion each time and never once grown maudlin or morose at the constraint. Rakan, who'd gone single-handed aboard *Mayne's Moor Blooded* and set himself against an entire privateer ship's crew to rescue Gil from harm. Rakan, who'd followed him without question into the citadel heart of his enemies, to rescue a woman he feared would threaten the core of what he'd stood by his whole young life.

Well, he thought drably. *No need to worry on that score now, captain.*

He looked once more into the flames, raised an arm in salute. There should have been a better farewell. *But in the end, there never is. And we take what meagre scraps we can find. You should know that by now, Gil.*

If the war had taught him nothing else, it had at least driven that steel-edged lesson home.

'Let's go,' he said.

Out along the deserted streets of Etterkal, away from the gathering blaze, shrouding themselves in the surrounding damp and dark. Elsewhere against the sky, they saw the glow of other fires burning, heard faint yells and commotion over the rooftops. Barring some really piss-poor luck, they should have a clear run through the rest of the Salt Warren and then Tervinala, all the way out to the eastern harbour. He had five men seriously injured, three of them too badly to walk, and then Mahmal Shanta on top – for these, Klithren had improvised sling stretchers out of looted curtain cloth and rope, two marines detailed to each. The other two injured men could limp along in the rear. It was all going to put a dent in their pace, but aside from that, Gil reckoned they were in pretty good shape.

Offered a stretcher in consideration of his injuries, Klarn Shendanak just spat on the floor and bristled like a roused hound.

If this slack motherfucker can keep up, he snapped, jerking a thumb at Menith Tand, *then you'd better believe I can too.*

Tand just grinned.

Distracted as he was, Ringil still found himself mildly staggered at the camaraderie that seemed to have grown up between the two men. He dropped back to march alongside Mahmal Shanta's stretcher for a spell.

'What the fuck have they been feeding those two?'

Shanta smiled wanly. 'Captivity is an interesting catalyst, is it not?'

'If you say so. Personally, I would have thought it'd have them at each other's throats twice as fast.'

'Ah, well.' Shanta's weak and reedy voice came jolted by his stretcher bearers' steps, overlaid with the splash of their boots in puddles. But he seemed in good spirits. 'These are fluid times. We are at war, after all, and such a crisis can concentrate the mind wonderfully well. Certain truths become more readily apparent, certain . . . necessary adjustments may suggest themselves. Opportunities, even, for men with the right bent of mind. And in the face of opportunity and necessity, fresh allegiance emerges easily enough.'

'Yeah. You want to drop the diplomatic flannel and tell me what the fuck the three of you are cooking up.' Though in truth he already had a pretty shrewd idea. 'If it's a peace plan, riding on Tand's influence up here, I'd say you're fucked. The Chancellery won't forgive this mess in a hurry.'

'No, nor forget it. You have struck a quite remarkable blow for the Empire, Ringil. Shown the League a vulnerability they might not previously have believed they suffered from. We did not expect this, nor anything remotely like it, but now it is achieved, well . . .'

'You're forgetting who started this war.'

'No.' Shanta's aged eyes were suddenly cold and hard, contemplating something Ringil could not see. 'We have not forgotten that at all.'

So. Helmsman called it right after all.

Halfway right. Archeth stood in his mind's eye, scowling, uncooperative. Lost.

Lost like the Dragonbane, lost like Rakan. For one sagging moment, he was waterlogged with the piling up of loss.

'You want to tell me what all that means?' he asked Shanta thinly.

The naval engineer looked elaborately around at the men who carried him, the others who marched in step with them. Grim-faced Throne Eternals, a few paces back.

'This is neither the time nor the place,' he said delicately. 'And matters are, in any case, not yet at a suitable head. A fluid situation, as I said. But rest assured, my lord Ringil, when the time is right, you will be among the very first to know.'

'Might I inquire how far along you are?' Anasharal asked testily.

'We're on our way.' Nodding at Shanta. 'If you'll excuse me, my lord. The Helmsman speaks. Matters I must attend to.'

'Are you at least out of Etterkal and into the diplomatic district yet?'

Ringil stiffened his pace, heading back to the vanguard and Klithren, whom he'd left to lead the march. 'No, not yet. But it won't be long.'

'Nyanar insists that the commotion in the harbour is beginning to damp down. He is concerned that order may be restored before much longer, and we'll find ourselves facing some organised opposition. If you don't get out soon, you may have to fight your way to the boats.'

'That was always a possibility.'

'Yes. Perhaps if you stopped hobnobbing with my chess pieces, though, and set a decent pace, you could achieve an earlier arrival.'

'Your chess pieces are redundant, Helmsman. Remember? Archeth's fucking dead.'

The Helmsman hesitated. 'Yes. I am sorry about that. I know you were friends.'

'Good,' he said flatly. 'Then fuck off out of my head and leave me alone. I'll tell you when we cross into Tervinala, and you can have Nyanar send the boats.'

Into territory now that he knew only too well. From the district boundary with Tervinala at Blacksail Boulevard to the slave-house heart of Etterkal, these were the streets that had played host to his war of attrition against Findrich, Snarl and the rest a year ago. Break in, brutalise, interrogate, burn. Random acts of terror at first, narrowing slowly to a savage search. *Who enslaved my cousin? Who raped her, branded her, broke her soul? Who gave the orders, paid the crew? Whose purse was enriched? Who benefits, who holds sway, who runs this fucking brave new world?* And as he walked away from the rising smoke and flames each time, an endless, swelling list of fresh targets for his rage. He knew the street names intimately, the names of the slum taverns and converted warehouse homes he'd torched, the names of the owners and district benefactors whose charred remains he'd left within.

He could walk this path in his sleep.

They passed the rubbled remains of Elim Hinrik's emporium, still not rebuilt or even cleaned up by the look of it. For all he knew, the bodies were still buried within. Memory flared, lantern bright. Mostly wooden beamed and floored, Hinrik's place had gone up like autumn scrub. Nothing inside the waist-high outer walls now but mounded rubble and the odd jagged jut of a charred beam poking through, all of it glistening wet and dark in the rain. Gil led them past it without comment, took a narrow cross street alley he knew at the corner, angled them a little more directly north.

Might clip some time off the journey, shut that fucking Helmsman up.

Out into a muddy, poorly cobbled plaza – huddled figures under eaves in the corners stirred and watched, but offered them no greeting or resistance. By their bony lack of bulk, most looked to be urchins, though he thought he saw one or two hugging infant bundles to their breasts. The first living souls he'd seen on the streets of the Warren since they got out of Findrich's place, and they turned out to be the last as well.

Two more narrow, winding streets later, they spilled abruptly out onto Blacksail Boulevard, almost before he'd noticed they were there.

FIFTY-SEVEN

It is time, my friend.

He blinks back to awareness, wipes moisture from his face and stares around in the rain-lashed murk. The others give no sign of having spoken – they're huddled like him under the makeshift shelter of a sailcloth tarp, rigged across the main deck to keep the worst of the downpour off. One or two of them meet his eye as he moves, but aside from a comradely grimace, they show no interest in conversation. Besides, it was not a human voice and he knows it.

It's the Helmsman.

He shivers, maybe from the damp, and steps out into the full force of the storm. Goes to the rail as if to peer out at the lights of Trelayne harbour in the murk beyond. He mutters under his breath against the roar of the rain.

Time for what?

Time for the final unmasking. He'd swear there's a trace of regret in the iron demon's tone. Time for you to finally understand the purpose marked out for you.

You said you couldn't see my purpose clearly.

Yes, I'm afraid I lied about that. What you are, and why, has in fact been fairly clear to me since we first met. But the field of play was too tangled for me to map a certain use for that knowledge at the time. I have improvised along the way, but I think we're beyond that now.

I don't . . . understand what you're saying.

I told you that you had a great destiny, and it was tied to the lady kir-Archeth. Well, that wasn't quite accurate. You were tied to kir-Archeth for rather more mundane reasons of infiltration. The Citadel had long been taking an interest in her, you see, and that combined with . . . other interests gave birth to a rather remarkable kind of spy. A spy with no knowledge of what he actually was, a spy who could observe without understanding, but later recall everything in perfect detail. A spy who could, if necessary, be awakened to step in and take the lady kir-Archeth's life. That's really why I needed to keep you asleep.

He shivers in the rain. What are you talking about? I would never . . . I've sworn . . .

No, that wasn't you. The man you think you are took that oath. But he is not among us. You usurped his place that drunken night when assignments were confirmed. Woke hungover in his place at barracks.

He stares down at his hands on the rain-soaked rail, the hands that so often didn't seem to be his. Watches them twist and grip at each other of their own accord. He feels himself shaking his head in denial.

Nightmare, creeping back in.

It really is for the best, I assure you. The Helmsman's voice, indistinct through the rising whine in his head, the choir of shrieking and sobbing behind. *The field of play is changed, you see, and it turns out there is useful work for you after all.*

For one desolate moment, he's back on that marsh plain with the others, the thousands of severed living heads, fed by the roots of the stumps they're cemented atop. And he's looking at himself, at his own severed head, mouth wrenched open on endless screams. He puts up both hands in horror, presses fingertips to his face, and his face is no longer his own.

He backs away, shaking his head numbly. Sanity haemorrhaging out of wounds he can feel but cannot locate . . .

The Helmsman's voice cuts across it all, like an arm thrust down into the deep for a drowning man to grasp.

Time to wake up, Anasharal says crisply. *And remember who you really are.*

FIFTY-EIGHT

Decades old nominal boundary between the diplomatic quarter and the Salt Warren, Blacksail Boulevard had been heavily policed by the Watch during the hours of darkness as far back as Gil could remember. Before the war, the polite pretext was that Tervinala's resident aliens needed a cordon against the depredations of Trelayne's more ignorant and bigoted slum citizens. Underlying, and taken as read by all parties with much – appropriately enough – diplomatic aplomb, was the concern that wealthy foreigners and representative agents of foreign powers could not be permitted to simply come and go across the city as they pleased without anyone taking official note. A delicate, mutually deceitful dance ensued.

With Liberalisation and the rise of the slavers' association in Etterkal, these mannered manoeuvrings grew secondary. The Watch stood on Blacksail Boulevard primarily because Etterkal's masters wanted them there. Entry into the Salt Warren, especially from a district swarming with who knew what foreign spies and creatures, was subject to tight scrutiny and report. The watchmen would want particulars of where you were going, whom to see and on what business. Numbers were restricted, note of names was taken. Listed undesirables, heavily armed or otherwise suspicious parties, anyone in fact that the Watch didn't like the look of, would be summarily turned away.

Tonight, you could have rolled an entire army, with siege engines, either way across the Blacksail divide, and no one would have blinked. Fires were burning in Tervinala, some of them clearly visible down the streets that opened onto the boulevard from that side, and any Watch presence there might have been was long gone. It was a repeat of the scene on Caravan Master's Rise, but with twice the number of abandoned barricades and untended braziers in the rain. Faintly from the diplomatic quarter, Ringil heard the iron clash and yell of fighting.

'We're crossing into Tervinala now,' he said, for Anasharal's benefit. 'Twenty-two of us. Five seriously injured. No sign of resistance, I reckon we'll be at the eastern harbour wall in an hour or less.'

'I shall make this known to commander Nyanar.'

They plunged into the stew of streets on the far side, avoiding the telltale glow of fires. Took quiet, darkened avenues that looked like they'd escaped the rampage. Gil kept a map lit in his head, plotting the twists and turns he was taking, trying to keep them more or less on a direct course for the waterfront. Here too, he was at home, carried on the combined recall of a dozen or more nights spent skulking after violent inroads into Etterkal and rapid retreats back out. None of it quite matched his current needs, you couldn't skulk with a score of men at your back the way you could with only two or three, but still . . .

'This will not . . . not be forgotten, my lord. Rest assured.'

Menith Tand, there at his side. The slave magnate had upped his pace to get level, was a little out of breath as a result. Ringil grunted.

'Forgotten by whom?'

'Well, of course, by any associates of Findrich, and the Trelayne Chancellery in general.' Tand found the spare energy for a thin smirk. 'You have inflicted a quite stunning humiliation on them all. But that's not what I meant. Quite seriously, my lord Ringil, I am in your debt. We all are.'

Ringil shot him a dubious glance. 'I'd have thought you had the leverage to skip out easily enough once the shouting dies down. You of all people, Tand. Circles you move in, professional courtesy and so forth.'

'Not in times of war, I'm afraid. Our treatment as prisoners has, in fact, been quite heavy handed. Not what I'd expected at all.'

'Yeah? That what happened to Shendanak?'

The slave merchant pursed his lips. 'No, that's legacy of a disagreement he had with the Dragonbane. Your friend had already put him into a coma by the time the privateers arrived in Ornley. He only woke later, on the voyage south.'

Gil blinked. '*Egar* did that? Why?'

'I have no clear idea, I'm afraid. I believe it had something to do with a squabble over the local whores.' Tand shrugged. 'You are talking about Majak, after all.'

For a moment, the Dragonbane stood grinning in his mind's eye. Thuggish, scarred, something of the unkillable about him.

Gone.

Ringil bit down on the loss and the guilt it came with. Put it away.

'You don't think you would have been ransomed home?' he asked, for something to fill the silence.

The slave magnate shook his head. 'Not easily, no. I fear that at a minimum we would have spent several years of our lives in very unsavoury confinement, had you not come for us. We might perhaps even have been executed as spies, if only to placate the rabble when the war took some turn for the worse.'

'Well, that's wars for you.'

'Oh, indeed.' Tand nodding sagely to himself as they marched. 'Not the most intelligent of ventures, even at the best of times.'

'You want to talk to your Emperor about that.'

'Yes.' A pensive, drawn-out weight on the words now. 'Our beloved Emperor.'

They marched on in silence, and the echoes of what had been said scurried off into the rain and the dark. The thoroughfare they tramped down ended at a five point crossroads. Screams and harsh, wild laughter in gusts from the street directly opposite, and flames leaping out of first floor windows along the row. Bodies in the street, figures locked in savage back-and-forth combat, yelling in Naomic and another language whose cadences Ringil recognised but could not understand. Hard to believe, but it looked as if someone had got into the Shaktur embassy and was busy putting it to the torch.

He summoned the map in his head. Pain in the arse, but they could detour left past this lot, then cut back up Candleman's Cleft and get out onto the Dawn Boulevard further along. It was another quarter mile or so, not exactly ideal ground, but—

Three ragged figures came loping up the road from the burning embassy, flicker-lit by the flames at their back. Ringil saw stolen finery pulled on over starveling, bony frames, a couple of cutlasses in hand, a pike. One of the marauding convicts had found himself a big floppy hat, another seemed to be wearing a flaxen wig. They whooped when they spotted Gil and the others hesitating at the crossway – brandished their weaponry and swaggered forward grinning into the open space, to meet these new victims. They didn't seem to have noticed quite how many men were at Ringil's back. Perhaps they were drunk, on their freedom and fury if nothing else.

'Will you meet your end tonight, watchman?' the one with the hat crowed, and did a little dance back and forth across the cobbles. There was blood down the front of his stolen breeches. A scant array of broken teeth in his grin. 'Is it tonight?'

'No, it's not,' Ringil said curtly.

He stepped forward, snapped out a loose left hand, made a two fingered claw. The convict dropped his cutlass, went screaming to his knees with hands cupped to his eyes.

His two companions gaped.

'You have me confused with someone else,' Ringil told them. 'Now fuck off.'

They needed no second warning. Both men fled back down the street they'd come from, leaving pike and cutlass and the bloodied flaxen wig strewn across the cobbles beside their writhing, shrilling companion. Ringil made a lateral chopping motion with his clawed hand and the man's screams and struggle ceased. His body rolled brokenly to a halt.

'This is a scalp,' said Klithren curiously, lifting the bloodied blond hairpiece on the end of his sword for inspection.

Ringil peered. 'Yeah, certainly looks like it. This way.'

He led them into the dark on the far side of the crossroads.

A hundred crooked yards down the confines of Candleman's Cleft, and they went single file because the alley space forced it, picking their way on the cobble-and-pothole surface underfoot. The stretcher bearers struggled not to stumble and tip their charges. Mahmal Shanta was insisting loudly on getting out and walking this bit, but Gil wouldn't have it. He wanted them out of here as fast as possible and Shanta wouldn't do well over this terrain in the dark.

It seemed unnaturally warm in the Cleft, not much rain or wind got in from above. Flashlit blue recall of the dark defiles insisted at the borders of his vision, threatened to tip him off the edge of here-and-now, pitch him back into nightmare. He sniffed and stopped it up somewhere inside him, like the pain from any other wound. The inward-leaning, jaggedly piled up levels of the houses on either side pressed in and down, promised a nightmare toppling. The myriad darkened windows and tiny balconies offered the more prosaic threat of ambush by arbalest or bow, or just some heavy crockery and stones.

Still no sign of Risgillen.

He had Klithren drop back to handle the rearguard, moved a couple of yards ahead and led on with senses spread like a net, taut for any whisper of life, human or otherwise. But if there were eyes on them above, he felt no sign of their presence. And if anyone cared what he'd done here, what he'd brought screaming down on this city, then they were keeping it to themselves, at least for now.

Near the end, with the glimmer of light at the end of the Cleft, he stumbled over a couple of bodies, throats slit and clothes torn off below the waist. Someone overly shy had evidently been using the alley for privacy, but the perpetrators were long gone. He gathered a glimpse of pale drowned faces in the gloom, the raw black, glittering gashes beneath their chins. Gil thought one was a boy, the other a woman his age, but in the uncertain light it was hard to be sure.

He looked away.

Moments later, they spilled out onto the Dawn Boulevard's lamplit expanse, found more corpses strewn there, properties burning and smoke in the street, but no sign of whoever was responsible. They'd missed the party. He looked up and down the ravaged, deserted thoroughfare. Caught his men watching him in expectant quiet, stopped up the heavy sigh of relief in his throat before it could vent.

'All right?' Klithren asked him, shouldering up from the rear.

'Yeah, why wouldn't I be? Go on, you take the van. Down that way, keep straight on. Set the pace. We're almost home.'

He let Klithren lead off, fell in a couple of ranks back, brooding on the images in his head. Menith Tand joined him again, paced along at his side. When Ringil said nothing to him, he walked in silence too, but he was clearly agitating at something that he'd left unsaid before. In the end, Gil gave up.

'What is it, Tand?'

The slaver cleared his throat

'Yes. I am not unaware, my lord, of what sacrifice these acts represent on your part. I know well enough what it is to own blood on both sides of a bitter divide.'

Ringil snorted. 'You'd have to dig back a few generations to find *my* imperial blood.'

'Nonetheless, it is there, and noble too. I have read about the Ashnal schism. It was, quite frankly, a farcical business, and a scandalous betrayal of some of the Empire's finest families. Your ancestors should never have been driven out.'

'But they were.'

'Yes, quite. Which makes your sacrifices here all the more . . . significant. To throw in your lot with the Empire is one thing, any mercenary of note might do the same.' Tand paused. He seemed to be working through some emotions of his own. 'But to *choose*. And in so spectacular a fashion. To march with fire and steel on the city of your birth, to betray the weightier part of your origins in order to honour your duties under imperial charter. As I said before, this will not be forgotten.'

'I was already an outcast up here, Tand.' Dead iron in his tone – with Rakan, Archeth and the Dragonbane lost, he was in no mood for plaudits. 'You know I tried to burn down the whole Trelayne slave trade last year?'

'Word had reached me of that, yes.'

Ringil looked at him, jolted. 'You knew that *before* we left for the Hironish?'

'Yes, somewhat before. I made inquiries.'

'And you said nothing of it?'

Tand shrugged. 'You seemed to have got it out of your system.'

'Oh, did I?'

'Well. Let us just say you seemed by then to be existing comfortably enough amidst the Empire's *very* widespread use of slaves, and without any apparent urges to commit murder or mayhem against those who used or owned them. In fact, indiscretions with our young Throne Eternal captain aside, you were behaving perfectly well.'

Behaving perfectly well. Gil grimaced. 'Knew about that too, huh?'

Another shrug. 'It was evident, I believe, for anyone with eyes educated enough to notice. When I invest in a venture, I like to know the men I am entrusting my investment to. But this is by-the-by – your bedchamber inclinations really were of no interest to me, except as they might affect more important considerations.'

'No?' A bitterness he could not right now quell or ironise away. Hooking out the verse from seared memory. '*If a man lie down with another man as with a woman, it is as if he lie down with an animal in filth, it is a gross sin in the sight of the Revelation.* That's by-the-by, is it?'

'Oh, that.' The slave merchant pulled a face. 'Well, yes, the Citadel may rant and proscribe to its rabid heart's content, but that's strictly for the rabble. Among the noble classes in Yhelteth, we prefer, let us say, a more nuanced approach. It's helpful to have the proscription and associated punishments in place, of course, but actual exposure is far too valuable a political tool to be deployed on' – an airy gesture – 'vulgar principle.'

'Vulgar principle, huh?' Ringil shook his head, riding down a brief urge to smash sophisticated, accommodating Menith Tand's face in with the pommel of his sword. 'You know, Tand, if you'd based yourself up here instead of at the Empire end of things, it might have been your warehouses I was burning down. Your merchandise I set free.'

'Yes, but it was not.' The slave merchant offered him an urbane smile. 'If anything, I believe I may even have benefited somewhat from your depredations among my Trelayne competitors. You see, my lord Ringil, I am above all a pragmatist.'

'Yeah.'

'And you were, by the time the caravan grapevine carried this news to me, a very significant asset to us all. You whipped our quest fellowship into shape as no one else available could have. You carried *command*. Men followed you instinctively, looked to you for leadership as a matter of natural course. Under the circumstances, I saw no good reason to trouble the lady Archeth or our other sponsors with what I knew, to set fresh ripples in water we had already spent all winter calming.'

'Hsst!' Klithren's arm raised, fist clenched. 'Hold up.'

They slammed to a halt, on a road surface that had begun to tilt very slightly downward. Charred, collapsed structures on either side of the street, a carpet of shattered glass and crockery stretching ahead, a tavern sign still on its brackets, torn loose and flung flat to the cobbles. Flames licked and crackled amidst the shattered remnants of the building on the right, but the rain was beating out the blaze. Elsewhere, it was smoulder and low drifting acrid smoke. Bodies everywhere, tangled up untidily across the cobbles like bundles of dirty washing, or spreadeagled and staring blindly up into the rain that fell on their faces. Clothes had been torn off at least every one in three.

Ringil cast about for signs of threat or life, saw some few quivering figures huddled into walls or niche spaces. From somewhere came a high, endless keening. Impossible to tell which, if any, of the visible survivors was making the noise.

'Nice one,' said Klithren, loud in the murky air.

The eastern harbour lay before them, devoid of life in the fitful flicker of flames from a dozen different fires across the wharves.

Against the odds, they'd beaten Nyanar's pick-up to the meeting point. Outlander's Wharf was deserted, unless you counted the dozen or so corpses of convicts and harbour Watch strewn along its worn stone length. Most of them still held the weapons they'd died with, which in the case of the convicts didn't amount to very much – lengths of chain and clubs made of rotten, torn up deck timber, here and there the odd looted axe or knife. From the pin-cushion look of the bodies, somebody had panicked, ordered repeated crossbow volleys across the wharf and taken out almost as many of their own watchmen as they had attackers.

'So where the fuck is our ride?' Klithren wanted to know.

Ringil scanned the burning harbour, looking for—

'There.'

He pointed. Motion, low in the water, off to their left. Two longboats, rowers bent-backed at their task, coming in across water speckled with flame in oily patches and spiked with the spars of burnt and scuttled ships. Add to that the wind and rain and dark, and he supposed, grudgingly, that it couldn't have been an easy passage to make.

Klithren squinted through the rain.

'Hoiran's aching cock – two fucking boats? Is that it? We're going to struggle to get everybody in those and not capsize soon as we hit open water.'

Ringil shrugged, masking similar misgivings. 'I told the Helmsman twenty-two men. Nyanar must reckon this is enough. Maybe he's right.'

'Yeah, and maybe my prick's a fucking mainmast.' The mercenary scowled. 'Well, I just hope you can keep a tight leash on those merroigai horrors of yours. Because we're going to be riding very fucking low in the water.'

Privately, Gil doubted he could get the merroigai to do anything very much that they didn't want to. About the only binding magic he'd been able to work on the swimmers, aside from summoning them to his aid in the first place, was an injunction to stay in the water which, according to Hjel, was where they liked to be anyway. *The merroigai speak highly of you*, the Creature at the Crossroads had assured him, but he had no idea what that meant. And while Dakovash claimed he'd sent one to save him when Gil let himself be carried too far out to sea at Lanatray in his youth, that was a long time ago and the affection apparently didn't extend to anybody else, even if they were under his command. *Best bet*, Hjel says unhelpfully when asked, *Just stay out of the water and tell anyone you have any affection for to do the same.*

Right.

Useless fucking ikinri 'ska.

'You just let me worry about the merroigai. Flag them in, will you? They haven't seen us yet.'

He watched the mercenary put hand to mouth and vent a piercing whistle, then crosswave both arms slowly and steadily over his head. Faint cries went back and forth among the rowers as they spotted the signal. Both boats altered heading by a fraction and arrowed in directly towards them. Ringil peered over the side of the wharf.

'You see a ladder anywhere?'

In the end, they had to settle for a knotted rope that Klithren spied poking out from under an upended fishing skiff further along the quay.

They looped and tied one end around a mooring post, dangled the rest down to the water just as the first longboat's rowers shipped oars on a natty little swerve that brought them bumping gently in against the wharf. Marine sergeant Shahn crouched in the bow grabbed the rope end out of the water, secured it and clambered handily up to meet them. He saluted, fist to chest, grinning.

'Commander Nyanar sends his regards, sir. He asks for haste.'

'That's a good idea,' said Klithren, with bright malice. 'Why didn't we think of that?'

Ringil shot him a warning glance. 'Start getting the wounded aboard. Shahn, you come with me, I want to set a rearguard cordon while we board.'

'Sir.'

He had the remaining Throne Eternals and half the marines form a line across the wharf, left Shahn in charge of it while everyone else got the first longboat tied in tight and then loaded. Yelps, then clenched screams from the wounded as they were lowered more or less gently down into the boat and tried to take the pain. Some urgent shouting as one of the marines with a chopped thigh started bleeding out around his tourniquet. Men scrambled about in the boat, worked frantically to tighten up the binding. A fresh scream floated loose and the man passed out. More marines climbed down. Mahmal Shanta turned to Ringil just before it was his turn to descend, eyes wet and bright with reflected light from the burning fires. He snagged Gil's arm with an old man's fierce, bony grip.

'We are going home thanks to *you*, Ringil. I will never forget that.'

Ringil forced a grin. 'Don't worry – I'm not going to let you.'

The stretcher bearers moved to help the naval engineer away, get him down the rope. But he hung on to Gil's arm a moment longer.

'Something better will be built on this,' he said. 'I promise you.'

Faint, enduring chuckle and crack of fire, everywhere across the sacked harbour. Drifting smoke in the rain. Somewhere back the way they'd come, a blazing wooden structure that might once have been a storage shed groaned and fell in on itself. Ringil turned back to look. The quarrel-spiked bodies along the wharf caught his eye. Flames leaping and climbing out of first and second storey windows along the harbour frontage. Above the skyline of the city, patches of smoky orange fireglow stained the murk.

Hard to see what you'd build on foundations like these.

'You sure you got no steppe nomad in you?' Klarn Shendanak asked at his shoulder, and barked a laugh. 'Mess you made here, I got to wonder.'

'Thanks.'

Where are you, Risgillen? Where the fuck are you? You really going to let me get away with this?

With Shanta and his stretcher bearers aboard and settled, the first longboat was visibly filled to capacity. As Klithren had predicted, it sat low in the water, though not alarmingly so. Unless the weather out in the bay was really atrocious, they wouldn't even have to bail. Gil watched as the marines cut the tie ropes and shoved off, got the prow pointed out. The oarsmen dipped in, someone started calling cadence. They pulled away. The second boat nosed in to take its predecessor's place.

'No more wounded,' Klithren shouted down at them. 'Don't bother tying in, just hold station and hang on to that fucking rope. We'll be right down.'

Ringil lifted an arm, signalled Shahn to fold down the rearguard line. The marine sergeant nodded, sent men back one by one to board the boat. They spidered rapidly down the knotted rope, leapt from the midpoint, directly into the boat. Oarsmen caught and steadied them as they landed, got them seated. Shendanak nodded Menith Tand ahead of him in the queue, clapped Gil on the shoulder just before he followed.

'Cheer the fuck up, man.' He unhooked his sling, flexed his injured arm and gestured at the burning harbour, the fire in the sky. 'All this? Dragon-bane himself would have been proud.'

He squatted and swung himself down onto the rope with his good arm, nimble as a man half his age despite his injuries, clambered a bare couple of knots lower and then leapt the rest of the way with a harsh whoop. The boat rocked violently as he hit. There was enough echo of Egar in the bravado to put the ghost of a reflexive smile at the corners of Ringil's mouth.

He blinked, caught Klithren staring at him. Gestured down at the boat.

'Go on, Hinerion. Your turn. Don't hang about.'

The mercenary didn't move. Gil felt his pulse trip over itself. The ghost smile soaked away like spilled wine into straw.

'All that black mage shit you pulled tonight,' Klithren said slowly.

'Yeah?'

'You didn't need me to get this far. You could have dropped me, like a Tlanmar bunny for the pot, any time. Couldn't you?'

Ringil shook his head impatiently. 'Not and keep my word, no. Come on, get down that fucking rope. We haven't got all—'

'*Hostiles!*' Shahn bellowed from up the wharf. '*Blue fire!*'

It took him a moment to identify the feeling that coursed through him as he spun.

Relief.

Flat out sprint. Klithren at his back, then at his side as they ran – splintered moments, scarcely time to draw breath, out to where the marine sergeant stood staring back down the wharf. Gil scanned the same space, eyes eager for the tell-tale splinters of light. Pulse up for real now, right hand itching for the Ravensfriend in his grip. No sign he could see. His gaze flickered to the frontages beyond, the crawling collage of flame and black-shadowed ruin that spread there.

'Where? Where are they?'

Shahn turned, one arm up and out—

– something wrong with his eyes? –

—swung the doubled up, gore-clotted length of chain in his hand, smacked Ringil full around the head with the links.

Dropped him to the wharf, exactly like one of Klithren's Tlanmar bunnies for the pot.

FIFTY-NINE

They made camp early, still plenty of warmth in the air and light in the crystal clear sky. She estimated the sun had at least another hour to fall. No particular features in the landscape to recommend stopping, either, at least not as far as Archeth could see. Then again, what did she know – to her eyes, the whole fucking steppe was one big grass-grown wilderness. They'd ridden for two days now, and aside from the disappearing river and the chimney smoke trails of Ishlin-ichan crawling up the sky behind them, she hadn't seen a single navigable landmark along the way.

But if Marnak Ironbrow said this was the place, well then, probably this was the place.

'Sacred ground,' he grunted when she asked him why they'd chosen it. 'Long ago in legend, a great god's sword fell to earth here. My people took the sky iron it left in the earth and forged the weapons we used to chase out the Long Runners. See, this is where it lay.'

She followed the gesture he made. Saw a long, low ridge along the ground that she hadn't spotted before. It curved outward on either side of where they stood, encircling a broad, shallow scoop in the landscape whose final extent she had to guess at, as she lost the ridge in the endless nodding waves of waist-high grass. She made the connection, understood what she was looking at. They were camped out at the edge of a huge crater, filled in and blurred with the centuries since it was formed.

'Sky iron, eh?' she said, and looked back at the wagon they'd brought. 'Appropriate enough, I guess.'

'Yes. The shaman will approve. The spirits remaining here will lend strength to the ceremonies he must perform. Added to which' – no apparent irony in the Ironbrow's tone – 'if your intent is not as honest as you claim it to be, the Dwellers will likely notice it on ground such as this. They will watch over us here.'

'Good to know,' she said tonelessly. *Let's just hope they don't bear grudges.*

She watched Marnak's men unharness the draught horses and lead them away for feed. A couple of them sketched wards at what hulked on the wagon's flatbed as they left. You couldn't really blame them. Beneath the heavy canvas wrappings in which it was shrouded, the half-melted remnant of the Kiriath catapult projectile loomed massive and jagged, like the recovered statue of some ancient alien god. Even to Archeth, there was something stark and ominous about the way it rose against the early evening sky.

Sky iron – the dead heart of a comet fallen to earth.

It was the one thing they'd been able to come up with that might drag the shaman out of camp.

'And you're sure he won't come tonight?'

Marnak snorted. 'The shaman might, but Ershal won't. He'll want daylight for the cleansing rituals. Come to that, I probably would too. It doesn't pay to mix darkness and things that fall out of the sky.'

She wondered absently if there was a barbed comment in there about her skin. Decided that Marnak probably meant it innocently enough. He seemed to have had a genuine respect for her father, a genuine lack of fear of the Black Folk in general.

She wished half the imperials she knew could manage as much.

'My lady?'

She looked up, saw Selak Chan advancing towards her through the sunlit grass. She made her excuses to Marnak, went to meet the Throne Eternal captain halfway.

'We in good shape?'

'We are, my lady. I've assigned a watch.' He gestured back to where the camp was taking shape. 'The nomads will mount one too, they say, but I'd rather trust our own men.'

'Fair enough. But let's try not to tread on any toes. They're twitchy enough as it is. We do outnumber them two to one.'

'Yes, my lady.'

She wished she felt as comfortable with the numbers as she pretended. Twenty horsemen – lined up in mounted pairs at the embassy gate, they'd looked a tidy enough little force. But out here under the vast steppe skies and forging steadily into Skaranak territory, it didn't seem like a whole lot of muscle anymore. She was beginning to wish she'd brought double.

But she had Marnak Ironbrow's finer feelings to worry about, and he wouldn't countenance a larger invasion. And anyway, Carden Han's men weren't exactly chomping at the bit to get out into Skaranak territory any more than their legate was keen to send them – she'd be hard-pressed to get more than a handful of volunteers, and morose, conscripted soldiery was not what she needed for this.

Fucking politics, the bane of her existence.

In the end, she'd opted to take the marines and the few Throne Eternal she'd brought out of the Wastes – their loyalties to her were forged far deeper than mere formal oath by now. The problem was, they numbered only thirteen out of the company – Tand's men, she still didn't fully trust, and the privateers were out of the question – and none of them knew anything about the local terrain. She'd have liked to use the Majak survivors from her party, but they were Ishlinak, albeit from the far southern end of the steppe, and once again Marnak would not hear of it. *Enough that I'm siding with outlanders against my own shaman and clanmaster,* he grumbled. *I'll not have Ishlinak riders at my back into the bargain.* So that was that.

She went to talk to Carden Han.

The legate, of course, was delighted at the compromise. No doubt steeling himself against a request for the forty-five imperials he'd originally promised her, he'd almost grinned with relief when she told him what she actually wanted. Seven men, at least two drawn from the Upland Free scouts, but the rest could be grunt imperials, auxiliaries, whatever, so long as they knew the steppe like the wrinkles on their dicks and took their duties seriously . . .

Chan still hovered, looking uncomfortable. 'Uhm, my lady?'

'Oh. Yes, captain, what is it?'

'Uh . . . my lord Kaptal has some misgivings. Will you speak with him?'

'Oh, for f—' She bit it back. She was the one who'd caved in when Kaptal insisted he come along. This was her mess. 'All right, I'll talk to him.'

Again.

When he came out with it like that, there on the candle-lit stairs in the embassy, she just stood for a moment and gaped. Legacy of the night she'd had so far, a slightly hysterical giggle cracked her lips.

'Empress? You're joking, right?' She saw the set of his mouth, the furrowed brow. Her grin fell off her face. 'You're not joking.'

'I understand your surprise, my lady—'

'Yeah?' She came down the stairs at him. 'How about you understand my desire not to set off a palace feud that'll split this Empire six ways to the sea, just when we can least afford the dissent. *Get back in there!*'

She shoved him bodily through the opened door to his apartment, hooked it closed with her heel as she followed him in. He was a bit harder to shift than she'd expected, felt bulky and well anchored on his feet, but the twitch and flare of her combat with Kelgris was still in her, itching just under the skin. Bad enough she'd spent the night climbing in and out of brothel windows like some not-very-bright Majak in a tale, then swapping pillow talk and threats of violence with an over-sexed local god. Now she had to deal with *this* shit? She slammed the door-bolt across, whirled on Kaptal in the low light from his lobby lanterns and stabbed the blade end of her fingers into his chest.

'Have you talked to anyone else about this?'

Kaptal looked impassively back at her. 'No one, my lady. I am neither suicidal nor a fool.'

'Well, you're doing a very good impression of both at the moment. Let's leave aside the fact that I'm sworn in service to Jhiral Khimran, and could have your skull on a spike for what you've just said to me. Let's leave aside the fact you're suggesting high treason out loud on the staircase of an imperial embassy with who the fuck knows how many unwanted ears wagging at every corner. The rather more pertinent point is that *we are at war.* Right now, what the Burnished Throne needs more than any other single thing is solidarity. Loyalty.'

'Loyalty to the Burnished Throne, my lady, is not the same thing as loyalty to the Khimran dynasty. And even loyalty to clan Khimran is not the same as loyalty to the whore's dreg idiot who walked us into this war in the first place.'

She turned away. 'None of that is a good excuse for trying to put *me* on the throne. I don't want it. I'm not qualified. I'm not even fucking *human*.'

'That is precisely what qualifies you so well, my lady. You are immortal. You would provide a continuity not possible for any human ruler.'

'That—'

She stopped. Peered back at him suspiciously. She'd made no great study of Yilmar Kaptal in the months of the quest – had been too absorbed in her own obsessive hopes and fears to bother – but this didn't sound like him at all. There was a measured precision to his speech that reminded her more of Tand or Shanta or –

– a Helmsman?

The thought came fleeting through her mind and jammed there. Just now, back out on the landing – Kaptal had sounded hesitant, as if woken from some dream he was still half in. And now he was arguing with her in tones that—

She saw him again, hauled up off the ocean floor in a sack. Spilled, dead and chewed upon, across the iron floor at her feet.

Cleansing is required, and substantial surface repair. But aside from this, I foresee no real difficulties.

And the Warhelm's bland assertion to the Dragonbane in the same clanging, echoing workshop, as dark iron machines went about their work and Tharalanangharst spun plans for them all like some great ancient spider in its web: *if either of you knew what end was intended from your actions, your knowledge would damage the equilibrium of the model, in all probability to an extent that would prevent said end from ever being achieved.*

This was Anasharal's scheme? This was what the emasculated iron demons out of her father's past had in mind? Usurp the imperial throne and dump it on *her* fucking head?

And who exactly am I talking to here?

She thought again of the spidering silver machines everywhere underfoot and in the walls of An-Kirilnar, the one that might even now be sitting somewhere inside the once-drowned brain behind Kaptal's eyes, steering the words to his tongue and watching her for response.

She closed up the gap between the two of them. Tapped Kaptal, or whatever was in him, on the chest.

'I don't know where you got this idea—'

'The idea that Jhiral Khimran is not a worthy successor to his father is common currency in certain court circles. But you surely know this, my lady. Associating so closely with Mahmal Shanta, you could scarcely fail to.'

477

'My associations with Mahmal Shanta are none of your fucking business.'

'Don't be naive, my lady, please.' A sudden snap in his voice that sounded more like the old Yilmar Kaptal. 'There is very little, at court or around, that I have not made my business at one time or another in the last several years. Coastlander discontent smoulders stronger now than it has in over a century. Asked to produce names and proof, I could. Asked to bring others into the same fold, whether willingly or kicking and screaming, I could. Do not underestimate what I can do for you in this arena, my lady.'

She nodded grimly. 'Yeah. Well, right now what you can do for me in *this* arena is keep your fucking mouth shut.'

And stay out of my way, she should have added.

Because here he was, hanging around amidst the Skaranak and the imperials like a virgin in a brothel and twice as useless, just one more thing to worry about in terrain already stacked high with hazard she couldn't predict. She supposed, rather sourly, it was safer that way – in the end, if she gave in to his dogged insistence on joining them, it was because she was more afraid of what unpredictable thing he might do in her absence.

Yeah, like go to the legate with this sudden insurrectionary fervour. See if he can't fan that wistful bitterness of Han's into something more stroppy. Start sounding out some of the men, maybe. The auxiliaries, even. See what recruits might be had from out on the steppe by word of mouth.

She felt a chill blow through her at the thought.

Wouldn't be the first time a pretender gathered together a bunch of savage horsemen and rode on the capital in hopes of taking the throne.

There was no one human left to remember the last time it happened – which would make it all the more appealing in the hearts and minds of men, of course – but *she* did. A century and more after the event, she still had flash recall of the bloody mess it made. The sacked towns and scorched earth, the chaotic scramble for response; the stinking summer slaughter at the eventual battle that broke the rebel forces; then the reprisals, the towns burned and razed in retribution for declaring sympathy, the columns of slaves marched out, and the bodies, the bodies everywhere – piled on charnel pyres that smoked and smouldered for days, left out unburied in fields and streets for scavengers to chew apart. Crucified along the An-Monal road as exemplary punishment, mile after mile of them, hung there until they rotted enough to fall.

Whatever the Warhelm had done to Kaptal to bring him back from the dead, it didn't seem to have recaptured much of his street smarts in the process. And Archeth had seen enough of spymaster Eshen to know how little Kaptal would need to slip before he was marked, and a report filed right back to the palace in Yhelteth. Which was about the last fucking thing she needed. There was going to be quite enough hard work as it was when they got back, without shit like this to stoke the fires of Jhiral's enduring obsession with disloyalty.

She found Kaptal standing beside the wagon, alone. Offered a horse from the embassy stables for the trip, he'd elected to ride beside the wagon-driver instead, which earned him a few respectful glances from imperials and Skaranak alike. He seemed the only one among the party entirely untroubled by the nature of the thing they hauled.

'Got a problem?' she asked him without preamble.

He gestured around at the men setting up camp. 'We are stopping here for the night?'

'Your powers of observation astound me. Yes, we are stopping here for the night. What's the matter – you don't like the view?'

'Don't you see the crater? Do you know what *happened* in this place?'

She eyed him curiously. 'No, I do not. Do you?'

'I . . . am informed.' Again, that odd hesitation, as if he was trying to assemble reasons after the fact for the words coming out of his mouth. 'The Skaranak . . . mentioned just now . . . to some of our men . . . they say this is a sacred place to their people.'

'Yeah, I'm told some warrior god dropped his sword here. It was a while ago, I doubt he'll be back for it.'

'You really think it wise to—'

'Kaptal! Or . . .' A weary gesture. 'Whoever else is in there. You got something useful to tell me? Then how about you skip the dark hints and just tell me.'

She thought that for a brief moment, she saw panic rising in his eyes. Then it was gone, snuffed out by something else, and he drew himself up, offended.

'I do not understand you, my lady, or your rudeness. I am not part of some cabal with ulterior motives; my opinions are my own. And the useful thing I have to tell you is this – that awaiting a local sorcerer on ground that holds magical significance for his people is not a wise move.'

'Well, it's the only way the Skaranak are going to do this,' she said evenly. 'So I guess we're stuck with it. Now why don't you go see if they've put up a tent for you yet?'

He bowed and backed off. She watched him go, brooding on what he'd said and seemed uncannily to know, because she had a nasty suspicion he was right.

She didn't like the feel of the crater either.

She found herself some even ground. Worked through a couple of Hanal Keth katas, thrusting, blocking, slashing and stabbing at the air around her, barking and shrilling with each strike. Twisting about, pouring knife hilts from hand to hand and back, like water between cups. Draw, sheath, draw again, swap and double, finish on a throw. Now go pick up your blade.

Again.

The ingrained moves and paces, the formal savagery of it soothed her, put her brooding to rest. The sun declined, got low enough to dazzle her each time she turned westward. No cloud to speak of, the band was an unbroken hoop that leapt horizon to horizon, caught and threw back the reddening gleam of the sun as it set. The day's heat started to seep away. Her sweat stood cooler on her brow. A couple of bright stars pricked through the velvet gloom in the east.

Once more round and then—

It came at her, out of the long grass and the declining sun's dazzle, as she bent to retrieve Bandgleam from the ground. She had time for one snatched impression – a boulder, smooth and pale and hidden in the grass, thrashing to sudden life – and then the whole creature towered over her, three yards tall, hunching forward, long backward-hinging limbs lifting a curved, compact body, long head and wide, fanged snout gaping down at her like a shark's. A long, taloned hand the size of a war-horse's head, reaching for her at the end of an arm that came down like a whip.

Move!

The change jolted through her – the patterned calm of the kata, shattered into the mess of real combat. Just time to grab Bandgleam left-handed, then she was rolling frantically right, away from the taloned lash of the arm. The thing shrilled and stamped forward a step – the ground quivered under her with the impact – felt like the foot came down right next to her head. She rolled again, found her feet, came up with a knife in each hand, facing her foe.

The fanged mouth leered at her. Hot blast of breath across her face as the creature shrilled again, the reek of rotting meat fragments bedded somewhere in its jaws. Archeth threw on reflex – Wraithslayer, up and into the long throat, so the creature reared back in shock. Her empty right hand swung back in and down, brushed at her thigh, and Falling Angel leapt out of her boot to fill the gap. She circled, looking for an eye.

'*Long Runners! To arms! The steppe ghouls are on us!*'

Someone bawling in Tethanne – one of the auxiliaries by the atrocious accent – against a backdrop of startled Majak yells. *Well – nice to know what we're facing.* But she didn't like the sound of that plural.

The runner she'd spiked was pawing irritably at its throat, trying to dislodge the knife. But it turned its neck snakishly as she moved, keeping her in view and centred, and it grinned at her like a parent crouched to play with offspring.

She grinned back. Threw both her knives, like skipping slivers of band-light across the gathering gloom.

Bandgleam put out the steppe ghoul's right eye, Falling Angel found a home in the side of the throat, not far from her sister blade. The runner screamed and staggered sideways. Archeth was already rushing in, empty handed but both arms tugging to the small of her back, didn't even feel like she was the one doing it. Quarterless and Laughing Girl kissed her palms, came out in her grip. She got in close and struck, first into the upper leg, hauled herself up on the fixing point that Quarterless made, slashed across the ghoul's unprotected belly with Laughing Girl. The creature's guts sagged out, steaming in the evening air. She hung on and slashed again, plunged Laughing Girl deeper, twisting and gouging into the midst of the steaming mess. Sudden, intense stink of shit from the ruptured entrails, a gush of blood and other fluids from the wound. The runner screamed again, clouted her aside with one blindly thrashing arm. She flew briefly through the air, hit hard amidst the grass.

But she heard the steppe ghoul go down. It shook the ground she lay on.

She scrambled back to her feet, cast about. The long runner lay on its side about a dozen yards off in the grass – hoarse, snorting breath and one limb kicking at the sky in spasm. By the lack of other motion, she judged it done. But—

Across the camp to her right, battle raged in the reddish light. Looked like at least a half dozen more of these fucking things, and nobody on a horse to face them. The Skaranak and a couple of the auxiliaries fought with staff lances, weapons whose reach was at least suited to the enemy. They kept the runners at bay with thrust and block as she watched. The imperials, forced to use arms more suited to the dispatch of humans, were in trouble.

She stalked towards the fight. Did it without thinking, did it unarmed.

Threw up her empty right hand like a command to halt. Wraithslayer flew to it like some trained hawk. Her hand wrapped the hilt and something shocked through her whole body at the grip. Down at waist height, her left hand opened behind her, unprompted, and another blade was there. At some level only now opening to her, she knew without looking that it was Quarterless.

She saw the damage the Kiriath steel dreamed.

Something inside her chimed. Rang in her ears like tolling bells, shivered in her skull. She opened her mouth and let it out. She ran in, screaming.

Worry about the rest later.

SIXTY

The world went briefly away, came back in fragments tinged in red.

Klithren at his side as he went down – hand on the sword at his waist, blade half drawn – furious, disbelieving roar, choked off as the scavenged chain length came round, inhumanly swift, wrapped him hard around the throat and jaw.

Shahn's eyes – pupil, iris, all gone into featureless, staring black—

Worm's eye view of the wharf he lay on and the corpses strewn along it—

'Cast off, cast off – they're here!' Shahn's voice, pitched for the same panic that had drawn Gil and Klithren in. *'Row for your lives! My lord Ringil is down, torn apart! Get the fuck out of here! The northmen's demons are coming!'*

His flesh seemed to shrivel on his bones as he yelled. Ringil saw the weathered southern features slough away, peeled like leather scraps off a cobbler's knife. Pale, gaunt white beneath – bone sharp features, a triumphant snarl – the face of an alabaster demon, looming over him.

Like Risgillen, like Seethlaw – he could not choke down the longing that rose in him at that fleeting thought, nor the corrosive self-hate that came searing in behind.

But it was not Seethlaw, nor Seethlaw's sister, nor any dwenda he knew.

One more snatched shred of vision as he went down into the darkness . . .

Klithren, turned towards him on the stones of Outlander's Wharf not a yard and a half away, face turning slowly black and bulge eyed as the downed mercenary strangled to death on his crushed and swollen larynx.

Done.

Voices in the whirling dark.

Well – *a* voice, anyway – echoes gathering into a single, familiar tone.

'. . . and if it's any small consolation, I can tell you with some reasonable degree of certainty that your friend kir-Archeth Indamaninarmal is, in fact, alive and well. She did not drown on the Wastes coast after all.'

Anasharal?

'Ingharnanasharal, in truth. I am the Warhelm once again, more or less entire.' And Ringil heard it, as if for the first time, grasped finally what it meant – the fresh, faintly sonorous timbre in the voice that had spooked the dwenda back in Findrich's palace. 'We have not been formally introduced, of course, though I have been with you since I saved you from the storm-caller's bonds.'

'It . . . the *ikinri 'ska* . . . it worked?'

'Yes, it did. Admirably. Your new mastery of the glyph systems written into this world is quite remarkable. You succeeded in forcing Anasharal against every embedded command and compulsion it was given, out of discrete existence and back into a full union with the Warhelm carcass it left behind. The fusion is clumsy, the joins are fissured here and there, still bleeding a little into the void, but really, I am impressed. And I am whole.'

'Good.' His lips were numb, he wasn't sure if he was actually having this conversation or not, whether the words were in his mouth or only in his head. 'You can help get me the fuck out of here, then.'

'Ah, yes. That.'

They were binding him, they were lifting him. But his vision was useless, shattered, shot through with red-veined dark. He caught swooping, fragmented glimpses of things – dwenda faces leaning over, peering at him; Risgillen in conversation with the new dwenda who had been Shahn; the night sky and the rain that fell out of it.

His head lolled back – Outlander's Wharf receding upside down behind him, Klithren of Hinerion's corpse, lying twisted among the other scattered dead. A jolting, inverted view of fire-lit harbour waters, and there – his eyes grabbed for one desperate moment, could not hold the view – Nyanar's second longboat, reduced by distance to the dimensions of a toy and pulling hard away, almost at the harbour mouth . . .

'I'm afraid,' said the Warhelm, without any audible trace of regret. 'That rescue from your predicament won't be possible. In fact – it is only fair to let you know this – you are back in dwenda hands almost entirely as a result of my efforts. It was I that helped Lathkeen of Talonreach shed his rather deep human cover.'

He saw it again – marine sergeant Shahn standing over him, peeling back from the eyes, shrivelling away like some discarded costume.

'*You* did this? *What the fuck for?*'

'I would have thought that was obvious. Perhaps your injuries have fogged your brain. I told you, kir-Archeth is still alive.'

'Your stupid fucking God-Empress wank fantasy?' Anger spluttered, but it was feeble, a guttering mockery of the rage he wanted. He felt sick to his stomach. 'I told you I'd keep silent, you iron fuck. I gave you my *word*.'

'Yes. But I'm afraid it's not your knowledge of the plan that is the problem.'

'*Then what is the fucking problem?*'

'You are.'

They were taking him away. He passed the heat and restless dance of flames on his left, red and yellow tongues leaping up at the murky dark. House frontages rising on either side, blocking out chunks of the sky as they left the harbour behind and they headed – he guessed – back into Tervinala. The Warhelm's voice walked beside him, amiably conversational in his ear.

'You must understand the quest cabal is coming together rather nicely, just as Anasharal hoped it might. Shanta, Shendanak, Tand. A viable core has formed after all, and these three will draw the others in, as and when they return to Yhelteth. The stage has been set for this a while now – long-term discontent with the ruling dynasty, smouldering coastlander resentment coupled to raw entrepreneurial spirit and ambition, all chafing at the constraints set by palace and citadel alike. And now a profound distaste for this new war and the idiots who wage it. It's a very promising mix. It will see Jhiral Khimran removed from the Burnished Throne before the year is out. Unfortunately, though, our conspirators have fixed on the wrong figurehead to replace him.'

It dropped on him like a ton weight.

'Oh, come on,' he gasped faintly. *'Me?* The fucking faggot outcast?'

'These are sophisticated men. They do not care, and they will happily put in place curtains and contrivances to deal with those who do. The ignorant will be blinded, the brutish restrained or disappeared, the cost considered negligible. It is *you* they want to front for them on the Burnished Throne, Ringil Eskiath – you, scion of an exiled Yhelteth noble line, war hero, disinterested warlord, reluctant leader of men, *human.* Kir-Archeth Indamaninarmal cannot hope to compete with all that. I cannot allow you to get in her way.'

'You stupid, metal, motherfucker.' It panted out of him, the last desperate dregs of resistance as something, dwenda sorcery or his wounds, he couldn't tell, dragged him down into soft whirling darkness again. His words echoed upward as he fell away. 'She won't do it, Helmsman, *she doesn't fucking want it.* She'll never turn on the Khimrans; they're the keystone of everything her people built.'

'Yes, I believe I have taken that into account and allowed for it. Mechanisms are in place.' The Warhelm's voice stayed oddly close and clear as he faded out. 'But thank you for your concern. Oh, and thank you for your heroic service in bringing out our core conspirators. You have triumphed, as a hero should. You will be remembered and honoured – if not eternally then, well, certainly for a good long while, I should imagine.

'Goodbye.'

And away, down an endless, grey-webbed tunnel of loss, blotching out to black.

This time, when he comes back, he knows it's sorcery – he can smell it. He can taste it in the back of his throat like too much krin. He sees the dwenda flickering around him, like blue candle flames the size of men, before he's even opened his eyes.

He opens his eyes.

Standing stones, rooted on the downslope of a bleak, low hill.

They flank him, bend around before him in a ring, blank and rough-hewn. The dwenda have drawn together in a black-garbed huddle six or seven strong, at the centre of the circle, deliberating in their own eldritch tongue, mostly with their backs turned. Unaccountably, he's on his feet, though it seems not to cost him any effort. There's a cold wind blowing from somewhere, a hurrying grey sky above, and his bones ache in his flesh.

He tries to spit. Coughs and gags instead. Harsh and rasping in the cold air. Dull pain in his chest, *across* his chest – he looks down, understands.

They've roped him upright to one of the standing stones. Risgillen's living twine, oily, gleaming cord only finger-width, but looped around a dozen times or more, high up under his arms and tight to his chest, lower across his belly and pinning his arms downward in place, all of it smouldering faintly blue, shifting against itself like restless snakes. He's been here before, seen this stuff in action back in Yhelteth – it can slither tight or loosen, twist, sprout savage thorns, all at the whim of its mistress and, oh, look, here she comes now . . .

Turning from her deliberations with the other dwenda, seeing him awake. A broad grin paints itself across her face at the sight. She strolls through the long, thickly matted grass towards him, all the time in the world, none of the combat tension he saw in her back at Findrich's place.

Ringil. For all the world as if he's a much loved comrade or family friend. *You're awake at last.*

He steels himself as she gets close, tries not to let it show.

Fails, apparently. Her lip curls. *Oh, don't worry, hero. I won't harm you the way I did in the south. Your flesh is far too precious to us now.*

He shakes his head groggily. *We have to stop meeting like this, Risgillen.*

We will. This will be the last time, I promise you. Can you not feel how thin, how few, are the pages that remain in your story?

He reaches, experimentally, for the *ikinri 'ska*. Finds no help there. Like drawing on a krin twig and finding nothing in your lungs but woodsmoke. Like reaching for the Ravensfriend, finding an empty scabbard instead.

Risgillen grins at him again. *Oh, don't worry. We have a sword for you. Lathkeen of Talonreach will be down with it shortly.*

She nods up to the brow of the hill to where, well, *something*'s going on, that's for sure. But it's a *something* Ringil can't quite get his eyes to focus on. He guesses at smoke and lightning, a writhing tentacular motion within, and it's dark, like the heart of a storm, but it hurts like bright light to look at directly and . . .

It has taken a while, you see, Seethlaw's sister presses gently on. *To prepare. To recover the sword from the fire you set; to understand what you did, to cleanse the blade of its contact with that . . . gaunt, joyless ape you unleashed it upon.*

See, Slab – he clings to the sour shreds of humour, it's really all he has right now – *nobody ever really liked you, not even this demon bitch.*

But time here is – Risgillen gestures around – *flexible, as you'll know. Here there is no hurry. And this time we have assembled the pieces with all due care. This time, we do not underestimate the world we must take back.*

That' ll be a first.

Yes, well, the signs have been complicated. Tangled. Reading them has been tricky – trickier than we are accustomed to. When the Black Folk came to this world, they disrupted it. They damaged the eternal norms. They were Other; they did not belong. In five thousand years, the chaos and confusion they sowed has still not abated. Heroes no longer stand forth clearly the way they once did, the way they were when we reigned in the real world. They are sullied, muddied at the edges, hard to recognise or judge. Seethlaw thought he saw a new hero in you, but what he truly saw, I think, was this. She gestures at the standing stones around them. *Your transfiguration. This place was Cormorion's, you see. Built and bound in Aldrain power for him alone, the last Dark King. His strength and refuge in the Grey Places. For a while it looked as if it might become yours in turn, that you might take on that mantle. But now I think those were simply the forward echoes of this moment, the moment in which Cormorion steps out of shadow once more, out of the glory of the Aldrain past, and is mantled once more, in your flesh.*

Turns out you aren't a hero after all, Ringil. You're just a receptacle.

At odds with the harshness in her tone, she reaches up and strokes his cheek where the scar that Seethlaw gave him runs.

He was my brother's great love. Cormorion Ilusilin Mayne, Cormorion the Radiant. None among your kind who came before or after, in all our years of skulking at the margins of human myth and legend, ever touched Seethlaw Illwrack the way Cormorion did. Perhaps he thought you would with time, but, well . . . She shrugs. *You see how fitting this is. I honour my brother's memory, avenge the love he offered and you spurned, and bring back the true focus of his heart, at one and the same time. Revenge and redemption in a single act. It has taken me until now to understand the elegance of it all.*

He coughs up a mangled laugh. *You're right, your eternal norms really took a knock, didn't they? Redemption? Revenge? Nothing's ever that clean, you dizzy fucking bitch.*

No, it will be. It will be the way it once was. Look out there.

She lifts one sweeping arm at the downslope. He looks despite himself, sees a gathered host of dwenda, thousands strong. Rank upon rank of black-garbed, cloaked, smooth-helmed, faceless figures, weapons shouldered or sheathed, immobile as statues, all facing this way. The helms are total, a seamless match for the black armour suits, obliterating any trace of the features behind their smoked-glass visors.

But he knows they're watching him, and the knowledge is ice on his spine.

He sniffs and forces out the cold. Forces a combat grin.

If they're all waiting on me to serve them the way I did your brother, I'm going to end up pretty fucking chafed.

Risgillen is not rising to the bait. She shakes her head.

They await their old warlord. His coming has unified the Aldrain as nothing since we were driven out. And when he returns to them, they'll follow him out of the Grey Places and into battle against the ramshackle excuse for an Empire that the Black Folk cobbled together in our absence, and they will crush it.

I don't think your troops are going to like Yhelteth weather, Risgillen. All that glaring sunlight, all those bright blue skies. They fucked up down there once before, remember?

She smiles. *But there will be no more blue skies, Ringil. Did you not know this? The Drowned Daughters of Hanliagh are stirring, ready to sink the world in shadow again. And clan Talonreach prepares even now to give them a good hard rutting where it will do most good.* Another sweeping gesture, this time up to the brow of the hill and the writhing darkness that squats there like a storm on a leash. Her voice grows animated. *See, the Talons of the Sun, gathering force under the storm-callers' hand. It is the herald of Cormorion's coming, the clarion behind which the Aldrain will go to war. It is the means to take back, finally, what is ours by ancient right.*

He still can't make out what the Talons of the Sun *is* exactly, but, as he watches, blue light scribbles through the roiling black of its flanks, and a dwenda emerges. No helm, his pale face and long jet hair are exposed, and he's close enough for Ringil to recognise.

Lathkeen of Talonreach, last seen shrugging off the flesh that was once marine sergeant Shahn, like a whore at night's end wiping off her work face. His hands are gloved in black, he holds a longsword by its blade in the right, *no rewards for guessing which sword that is, eh, Gil,* and he's got something else in his left. At first, Gil can't quite make that out either, but as the dwenda comes down the slope towards them, he realises what it is, and his heart kicks against the bindings across his chest.

It's a spiked iron crown, and he's seen it before.

His own ghost wore it, seated opposite him at Hjel's campfire in the Grey Places, grinning like a skull.

Lathkeen reaches the edge of the stone circle, passes the crown awkwardly to the same hand as the sword for a moment and sketches a series of glyphs in the air before he steps over whatever invisible threshold exists there. The sword goes berserk. The tang lashes at the air like a demented serpent. Gil sees the storm-caller grimace and tighten his gloved grip on the blade.

A little help? he snaps at Risgillen. *Here, take this at least.*

She goes to him and takes the crown, bears it back to Ringil in both hands. Sets it at a jaunty angle on Gil's head. Cold, slanting touch of the iron band across his brow. Risgillen stands back and looks him over.

Suits you, she says sombrely.

Lathkeen has taken a fresh grip on the Illwrack sword, both hands this time. He raises it reverently a moment, as if offering it to the sky, then drives the blade down a foot into the ground of the stone circle, a couple of yards from where Ringil is bound. A cold plaintive cry breaks through the air, like some solitary gull lost over an endless leaden ocean. It's impossible to tell where it comes from, it seems to sweep in on the wind from all corners of the sky at once. The sword trembles in the ground.

That's it, the storm-caller says. *He's here, no question.*

Risgillen gestures impatiently. *Then what are we waiting for?*

Lathkeen shrugs. He uproots the sword again with loving care, carries it across to Ringil. The tang coils about, sharpened end scratching and prodding at the air. Ringil clenches his fists closed. Risgillen sees it and smiles. She nods at the cords binding his chest and one of them tugs itself loose under his arm, wraps around his left shoulder and goes coiling rapidly downward, past his elbow, encircling his bared forearm and wrist, sprouting offspring vines that each seek out a finger and force his knuckles back one by one, straighten out his whole hand and hold it poised to receive the sword.

Firfirdar, if you were ever on my fucking side, now'd be the time to show up and demonstrate the fact.

The Dark Court will not intervene here, says Lathkeen absently, as if Gil's spoken aloud. *They are not permitted that much power. None are since the world was written over, not even those who laid down the text in the first place. And your dominion of the* ikinri 'ska *cannot help you here either. Talonreach has it well in check.*

He jerks his chin up the slope at the storm of writhing motion and the dark that's tethered there.

Most of the clan is in attendance. Their combined will is bent upon you. I am not my cousin Atalmire; I do not run unnecessary risks.

Ringil bares his teeth. *Yeah well, your cousin Atalmire died squealing like a pig. I chopped him apart. Just so you know.*

A muscle twitches in Lathkeen's bone-white face. Something dark and twisted rises cheering in Gil at the sight, as if he'd managed to drive a dagger point home in the storm-caller's flesh.

Harm – done.

What else, aside from slaughter with sharp steel, are you really good for, Ringil Eskiath?

What else indeed?

Well, you *will not die*, the storm-caller says tonelessly. *Not in the sense you understand the word, anyway. But you will be trapped for the lifetime of your flesh behind the eyes of Cormorion Ilusilin Mayne. I will ask him, as a personal favour, to track down your family and friends when he storms the world, and to give them exceedingly special treatment so that you can watch. You have, I believe, already seen something of our methods for dealing with those who defy us.*

He turns to Risgillen. *Want to say anything?*

Just get it done.

They put the sword against his open hand. It coils and grabs him around the palm. Wraps his bared forearm end to end, intimately warm and oddly slick. Rears up and stabs him somewhere above the wrist, gouges in between tendon and muscle. He can feel it in there digging deeper, sprouting barbs. But there's curiously little pain. He sees Risgillen smile and jut her chin at him in farewell.

Then the whole world wrenches sideways and falls down.

SIXTY-ONE

The long runners heard her scream, and they seemed to pause as one. She saw long, smooth-skinned heads lean and twist in her direction. Fanged mouths gaped and grinned. She felt their eyes fix on her running form, as she closed the gap.

Don't know how smart they are, the Dragonbane had told her once, *but they know a staff lance when they see one, and they'll avoid them if they can. They know it's better to take a man on foot than a rider and they'll plan around doing that too . . .*

No horse, no blades of any real length. With luck, she looked no more lethal than a warm meal on legs.

The nearest steppe ghoul made a dismissive tilting motion with its head, went back to what it was doing – stomping through a group of yelling imperials. Looked like two men already down, another dragging himself from the fray with a shattered leg.

Her men.

She sprinted straight in.

Unleashed Wraithslayer from ten yards out.

The eye again, and this time she must have got lucky on penetration. The runner stumbled and went down like a tripped horse. Her men yelled triumph and stormed onto its thrashing body, hacking with axe and sword anywhere they could reach. Archeth tore past them without let, one trailing hand out to collect Wraithslayer from the air as it leapt back into her grip.

Kick it, Archidi. If this is going to work . . .

She put on speed. Slipped behind a second ghoul backing up from staff lance thrusts, slashed hard at a cord-muscled leg as she passed. Felt like she cut the tendon – no time to see for sure. Her main objective lay ahead.

The Skaranak had left their horses to wander – they'd come when called, under any normal circumstance. But now they'd bolted riderless in all directions. *Give thanks, Archidi, to whatever bad-tempered gods they keep in these parts, that at least some of us imperials aren't that trusting.* A half dozen of the Yhelteth thoroughbred warhorses were tethered along the side of the wagon, plunging and snorting with panic as they caught the scent of the runners and tried to tear free. Beyond them, smoke and pale flame rose from somewhere on the other side of the wagon – looked like someone had kicked the campfire apart in the fray. Archeth spotted her mount among the tied horses and ran in. No saddle or reins, of course, but . . .

fuck it, she flung herself up and over the animal's neck, settled astride it bareback, slashed Quarterless up and through the tether.

The horse reared again, but she clung to the neck, muttered soothing into its ear. It wasn't Idrashan – *no* horse was Idrashan; ye gods she missed that stallion – but it was Yhelteth bred and trained for war, and with a rider atop, it settled. She clucked and urged it about with her thighs, away from the wagon. Kept her balance barely, knives held wide. Scanned the action. Gaze racing out across the grass expanse.

There – and there – and there – they'd brought down the ghoul she'd hamstrung, were finishing it now, staff lances rising and falling like whalers' harpoons. But four more runners slashed and stomped about the camp, reached and tore men limb from limb where they stood . . .

'Right, you motherfuckers,' she muttered. '*Now* let's see what you've got.'

And kicked her horse into a charge.

The first ghoul was easy – it had chased a Skaranak axeman round a half-trampled yurt and tangled one arm awkwardly in the ropes. She stormed in on the horse and the runner panicked, tried to flail round and face the approaching threat, got itself tangled further. She put knives in its eyes while she was still twenty feet off, saw it stagger and go down shrieking, pawing at the damage and the sudden darkness. Up popped the axeman, nodded breathless thanks and – three! grunting! blows! – chopped the creature's head apart. Archeth was already wheeling away, palms up and open, as if in prayer.

Falling Angel, Laughing Girl – into her grasp as she rode down the second ghoul. Their blades were still daubed with gore from the wounds they'd torn themselves out of when she called. Their hilts thrummed against her palms like machinery levers on a fireship bridge. Deep vibration ran down through the muscles of her arms and into her chest, sat there like fresh strength. She almost choked on the feeling it set off in her guts. She whooped for sheer joy at the lines of force it painted through her body and out across the steppe to the other, waiting knives.

The next nearest runner spun about, away from the men it was harrying. Perhaps it heard her cry, perhaps it just felt the thunder of her horse's hooves through the ground. It faced her, crouched to spring. She loosed Falling Angel, no time for careful aim, took the creature in the shoulder and staggered its pounce. Threw up her empty hand in demand and Wraithslayer was in it, as if dropped out of the sky. The ghoul flinched – twisting and pawing Falling Angel loose – Archeth grabbed the moment, rode in on the other side, got behind that long, shark-fanged head. She stabbed in left-handed, buried Laughing Girl to the hilt under the runner's jaw, and hung on. The ghoul stumbled back, awkwardly off-balance, crashed against the horse's flank. The horse reared and screamed, Archeth clung on with both legs – the collision of the two beasts had her pinned by one thigh anyway – reached round with Wraithslayer – yelled

491

triumphant – dragged the blade back in a ragged, throat-opening gouge.

'Think you're something?' she heard herself snarl through gritted teeth, as the steppe ghoul collapsed backward and the horse wallowed, eyes rolling, almost down on its hind legs with the weight. She dragged back hard on both knives, tilted the huge, lolling head up against her. 'Think you're dangerous? I was killing *dragons* before this, you fuck.'

The steppe ghoul's nearest eye rolled up, the jaw snapped shut on some feeding reflex, bit off a foot of lolling tongue between the fangs. She felt the life go out of the massive carcass, felt it shudder and slump. She pulled out her knives, held them aloft.

Howled.

If the long runners had ignored her before, she had their full attention now. Both the remaining ghouls abandoned the fight they were in, gaped for a moment, seemed to exchange a glance, and then came prowling rapidly towards her.

'Yeah, you see me now, don't you, motherfuckers!' she screamed as they closed. '*You see me now!*'

She drew herself up on the horse's back, knives poised. She *felt* their eagerness, those in her grasp and those waiting to be next. For one fleeting instant, she actually saw the connections, like lines of glowing hot wire snaking out from her mount and into the steppe grass around her. She almost stopped breathing with the shock and beauty of it. Waited rapt for the paths of the two attacking runners to converge—

The left-hand steppe ghoul seemed to trip, as if the knife had already left her hand.

Grey-fletched stick-thin spike, protruding magically from its thigh.

So someone had finally got hold of a strung bow and quiver, got some space, grabbed breath to steady their aim . . .

Hiss-thump and a second arrow joined the first. She heard men cheering. A third shaft and the long runner staggered sideways, went down still trying to drag itself forward on one leg. Archeth's attention shuttled to the other ghoul. She saw it hesitate, look around – saw a pair of arrows spike its head, saw one take out the eye. Shriek of rage and pain, the creature reeled about, trying to find its new attackers. It got a chest and throat full of grey fletched shafts for its trouble, crashed into the grass. Skaranak stormed in with lances to finish the job. The bowmen – she spotted them now, three men, striding purposefully out towards the left hand ghoul, short re-curved bows held high, laying down a steady three-every-five-seconds hail of fire. The ghoul snorted and flailed about on the ground, finally gave up and lay still.

The steppe seemed suddenly very quiet.

Archeth nudged her horse cautiously in. She got to the downed ghoul about the same time as the first of the Skaranak bowmen. They both watched the heavy, jerky rise and fall of the creature's pin-cushioned side, listened to the stertorous snorts rasping from its throat. Blood ran down in stripes from a couple of the wounds the arrows had made, leaked copiously from the runner's mouth. The Skaranak eased tension on his draw. He put up the arrow and the bow, stepped back and made a gesture it took her a moment to understand.

Hers to kill.

'Uhm . . .'

More men hurried up. One of the auxiliaries spoke to the bowman, got a sharp retort, and turned to face her with a toothy grin.

'He say you have this honour. You take the life.'

She shook her head. 'He brought it down. It's his kill.'

That went back and forth in Majak, then the auxiliary turned to her again.

'He say he is a dead man if you not help us. You save all Skaranak here, this is *your* honour. They will laugh if he makes kill.'

She glanced at the bowman's weathered face. Steady, pale eyes looked back at her, and for a brief, dizzying moment it was like locking gazes with the Dragonbane once more. The bowman raised one clenched fist and thumped it deliberately to his heart, lifted it away again, towards her. He bowed his head.

She nodded. 'Very well. But you tell him it was work we all did, and I'm grateful for his part.'

While the bowman and the auxiliary conferred, she levered up a leg and slid down off her mount. Went to the hoarsely snorting runner. One slowly glazing eye stared up at her, the eyelid slid weakly down and up. Without ceremony, she bent and ripped Laughing Girl's blade up and through the throat. Stood watching as the creature thrashed feebly and bled out on the flattened grass.

Hurrying footfalls behind her. Marnak and Kanan Shent ran up, weapons in hand and streaked with gore. The Ironbrow rather more out of breath than the young Throne Eternal at his side.

'My lady, are you hale?'

I feel fucking fantastic, she didn't say, but wondered if it showed in her face anyway. Her pulse was climbing down now, but the fight had left a slow-burning joy splattered all over her insides, and a keen, enduring clarity of vision at levels she'd never known she owned. The knives were still out there, murmuring quietly across the distance and in her ear. The glowing wire tracery that joined them all had faded from her sight, but it didn't matter. She saw it clearly now. Kiriath steel – her father's legacy; they'd come when she called. They'd be there when she had need.

Makes you wonder, though.

All that other Kiriath ironwork lying around back in Yhelteth – what that would do if you called on it for help.

'I am unharmed,' she told Shent. 'But I saw the camp burning. You had best attend to that.'

'It is being done. My lady – Selak Chan is . . .'

Her exultation dropped like a stone into the pit of her belly. Pivot rudely about – her shoulder caught Marnak and he staggered a bit with the force of it – scan the strewn aftermath of the fight for—

'He is by the wagon, my lady,' Shent said quietly. 'The other side. He asks for you.'

Chan was a bloody mess.

Shent briefed her in the few moments it took them to jog hurriedly to the wagon, but still, as the gathered imperials gave ground and let her close, as she saw what had been done – she winced. She couldn't help it.

One of the steppe ghouls had stomped the Throne Eternal into the ground from behind; there was nothing left whole below the waist. Chan lay on his front, face turned awkwardly to the side, right cheek pressed into the flattened steppe grass. His right arm out, as if for the hilt of the sword that lay just out of reach. They hadn't bothered trying to move him, just put a horse blanket over the damage. Another lower ranking Eternal met her gaze as she moved in. He shook his head.

She got down on her knees, must finally lie almost full length beside him in order to get decent eye contact.

'Chan?'

'Ah – my lady.' The words sobbed from him, edged with pain. 'My apologies . . . if I do not rise. I find myself . . . inconvenienced.'

'Rest easy,' she said through numb lips. 'You have done enough.'

He seemed to grit his teeth. 'I have not . . . got you home, my lady. That is . . . failure.'

'No—'

'Yes!' The vehemence jerked motion into his upper body. He moaned in agony, lay panting for a moment. 'I was charged . . . by Jhiral Khimran himself . . . with your protection. The Empire . . . needs you. This . . . this much . . . I know. You *must* go home.'

'We're all going home, Chan. You too.'

He managed a grimace. 'I think . . . not.'

She put a hesitant hand on his neck. 'Listen to me, Selak Chan. You are going home, for burial with honours and a pension for what family you may have. You have my word. Whatever else, I will see this done.'

'You are . . . kind, my lady. But I find . . . I must beg . . . another favour too.'

'Name it.'

And realised, cursing her own stupidity, what he meant.

Could you be any more fucking obtuse, Archidi?

She got herself a little more upright, drew Laughing Girl from the small of her back. Some tiny part of her noticed that in her numb hurry to get to the fallen Throne Eternal, she'd sheathed her blades unwiped, and the Warhelm's harness sheath had *eaten the blood*. She cleared her throat, put her free hand back on Chan's neck. He'd seen the knife, maybe caught some reddish sunset gleam that the blade threw in his eye. He nodded at her. Tremulous attempt at a smile on his mouth.

'Yes,' he husked. 'That.'

'Think of home,' she told him. 'And you will be there.'

He squeezed his eyes closed. She saw tears bunch on the lids and lashes. Lifted herself over him, moved her hand a fraction on his neck, put Laughing Girl's point in place.

Sliced down hard and fast, through neck and spine in a split second.

Sent Selak Chan home.

The rest of the camp looked as if a storm had passed through it – yurts unmoored, crumpled and sagging where they'd been fought around, or trampled wholly underfoot by the ghouls. In between, scorch marks blackened the ground. The flames she'd seen by the horses were exactly what they'd seemed – the nascent campfire had been kicked apart at some point in the combat and started the grass smouldering in a dozen different places, as well as setting one of the half-collapsed yurts alight. Rapid action from the Skaranak had smothered the flames, but a stink of burning hung about in the air like the ghost of smoke. On the nearest fallen yurt, a loose flap of cloth stropped insistently in a rising evening breeze, like a trapped bird trying to get free.

And everywhere the corpses.

Marnak found her standing amidst the mess, cleaning the blade she'd used to kill Chan. She nodded absently at him and they stood side by side in silence for a while, watching the last red edge of the sun drop below the horizon.

'All right?' she asked, when it was gone.

He made a strangled noise in his throat.

She stowed the knife. 'Guess not, then.'

'This . . .' Marnak gestured around, voice thick with fury. 'That fucking shaman. I'm going to rip his balls off and feed them to him for this.'

'You think it's his work?'

The Ironbrow spat. 'Who else? The long runners have not come this far south in summer since my father's time. Only sorcery could drive them out of the north right now. And who else knew to expect us here?'

She shrugged. 'Well, we are trying to kill him too, I suppose.'

'But he doesn't know that yet!'

'Perhaps he does. Man's a sorcerer, after all.' She looked thoughtfully about at the wreckage of the camp, marvelling at the sudden depths of calm she seemed to have acquired. She wondered if this was what it felt like to be Ringil Eskiath. 'Or maybe he's just looking to keep the sky iron for himself and no credit to you for bringing it in. Real question is – does he have any way to know his pet monsters fucked up here and we're still alive?'

For which Marnak appeared to have no ready answer. The Majak just stood there, jaw knotted up with rage, glaring at the damage around him.

Night thickened, shrouding the corpses in soft gloom.

'How many'd you lose?' she asked him.

'Three.' Through his teeth. 'Kinsmen all. There's a fourth going to be crippled for life, if he doesn't join the others before morning. Runner picked him up, threw him across the whole fucking camp. Broke his back.'

'And seven of mine.'

The Ironbrow held up one tightly clenched fist, stared at it as if for useful answers. 'This will be paid back in blood. The shaman and all who stand with him will fall.'

Not the best time to point out that had been the plan all along, so she kept silent. After a couple of moments, Marnak lowered his fist and glanced sideways at her in the clogging light.

'If we are alive,' he said gruffly. 'It's thanks to you, black woman. I saw you fight.'

'We all fought.'

'Not like you. Not like *that*. My men are saying you bear the soul of Ulna Wolfbane, some even that you are Ulna returned to us in Sky Dweller flesh.' He cleared his throat uncomfortably. 'They have heard you fell with the comet, you see.'

Nice work, my lord Eshen.

'So they'll stand with me against their own clanmaster?' she wondered.

'Right now?' Marnak stared off into the dark. 'I think they'd march with you to the gates of hell if you asked them.'

SIXTY-TWO

He sits on a dark oak throne, facing the ocean.

No bindings anymore, he's loose and comfortable in his seat. The wood is worn and scooped from long use, and the scalloped curves fit him perfectly. No serpent-tanged sword trying to gouge its way inside him, no standing stones, no dwenda. The sea is calm, small waves rolling gently in and breaking knee deep. A loose breeze ruffles his hair.

For a moment, he thinks Firfirdar has rescued him after all.

Then he sees the Illwrack Changeling.

It crouches in the shallows, draped in ragged black robes, so still that for a moment he mistakes it for an uncannily human-looking rock, dark and hung about with black kelp, patched with pale colonies of clams at roughly the places a face and hands might be. Then the head tilts up, glittering deep set eyes fix on him through tangled ropes of hair, a mouth like a wound opens in the pallid flesh and the gull-plaintive cry skirls out.

It's a sound to crack his heart across. Tears flood his eyes, he can't help it.

The last of the Dark Kings erupts from the water. It flounders upright. Cries out again as it staggers up the beach, drenched robes hanging heavy, weaving like a drunk. It's a man, or was once, but it's bigger and bulkier than most men ever grow. Its eyes hold Gil's like a lover's, and for one horrified second he's so overwhelmed by what lives in that gaze that he *wants* this ravaged thing to reach him, wants the embrace it promises.

He's getting to his feet, is almost out of the throne before he understands.

It's the *ikinri 'ska*, turned against him. A depth of power he's only recently begun to taste, and the Changeling snaps it out at him like a man crooking a finger at a tavern wench. Effortless, flowing force, unrestrained by any lack of will, by any doubt, by any remaining vestige of self. He stares into Cormorion Ilusilin Mayne's eyes, sees nothing recognisably human there.

The deeper into the ikinri 'ska *you go, the less it is your tool to use, the more you become its gate and channel.* Hjel has told him this often enough, but until now Gil never really understood what the dispossessed prince was trying to say. He never wondered – perhaps the *ikinri 'ska* would not let him wonder – where the road might end.

He drops back into the warmed wood curves of the throne, like a puppet with strings slashed through. He grasps the oak arms with as much force as his hands will supply. Understands that whatever happens, he must not give up this seat.

The Illwrack Changeling shrieks in thwarted rage and leaps forward, impossible speed and lift for anything so withered and torn. It lands with one knee in his chest, cold, wet hands digging like claws into his arms. Its grubby, pale features loom over him, mouth working silently with effort, eyes staring blind. Its hair hangs in his face, stinks of the sea and other, less easily understood depths. The Dark King radiates a steely power Gil can find no resource against. It hauls with both hands, throws itself backward, and tears Gil from the throne as if he were a child.

Coming home.

Words at last, antique Myrlic, syllables Ringil can barely decode, hissing from pallid, torn up lips he sees have been bitten through, over and over again with the – understanding flashes in him – endless waiting.

Coming home, See . . . The seat is mine *. . .*

Yeah, like fuck it is.

The two of them stumble upright together, grappling at each other like tavern brawlers desperate for a knife that's fallen where neither of them can see it. The thing that was once Cormorion is trying to turn him, to get itself closer to the throne, and there's *precious fucking little* Gil can do about that . . .

He pulls a Majak wrestling lock. Tangles up their legs, trips the Changeling over towards him, takes the fight to the floor. They land hard on the wet sand. Forewarned, Gil only loses most of the breath in his lungs. Rolls the Dark King desperately away from the throne, worms one hand free, goes after eyes and mouth. He gets a middle finger in through the chewed up lips, hooks hard into the cheek, tries to tear it open. The Changeling flails and throws a headbutt he can't quite dodge; he takes it on the side of the face, feels numbing pain spike down his cheek . . .

Cormorion Ilusilin Mayne does something inhuman to his jaw, dislocates it sideways and catches Ringil's finger, snags it back into the bite radius.

Bites down hard.

Gil screams and tries to hang on, but it's no use. The Changeling grinds down on the trapped finger, snarling at him now, lopsidedly through the bitten lips. The pain scales upward, shouldn't hurt *this* badly – it's only a fucking finger – but it does; it's agony and it's spreading, drenching his whole body, draining his strength. He feels the thing that was Cormorion shift its weight, he digs in to stop the move, but his bracing leg slips, goes straight amidst clods of wet sand. The Dark King gets on top of Gil, still worrying at him with its teeth, jerks its head savagely up and aside, tears off the first two flanges of the mangled finger and spits them in Ringil's face. Grins down in triumph, bloodstained lips mouthing words again.

Coming, See . . . Seethlaw, I'm coming home . . .

Gil, abruptly stricken, paws at him with his maimed hand, but it's nothing, it's more like a hard caress. Cormorion shrugs it off, straightens up astride him. Chops him in the throat with killing force.

Ringil lies there choking, robbed of the strength to move.

The Dark King gets off him, panting. Staggers a little getting upright, stands at last looking down. The eyes are still blind, unreadable, but the Illwrack Changeling lifts its left hand and makes a curious, oddly gentle sketching gesture over Gil's twitching body. He thinks he feels the pain he's drenched in start to ebb. Feels himself beginning to ebb with it.

A fight is coming. He remembers the crone at the Eastern Gate, snarling her prophecy at him. *A battle of powers you have not yet seen. A battle that will unmake you, that will tear you apart.*

A dark lord will rise.

A hopeless grimace smears his mouth. To think he worried once it might have been him.

Cormorion Ilusilin Mayne stalks to the throne. Turns almost prissily to take the seat.

And something is there.

Gil's vision is blotchy, fading fast. But it looks to him as if someone's *already* sitting on the throne, ghostly but gaining definition – someone into whose lap the Illwrack Changeling sinks unaware.

Slim arms reach round and up. It's somehow languid and lightning swift at one and the same time. A flicker of animal alarm across the Changeling's pale face, and that's all there's time for. Elegant, long-fingered hands take hold of his head at top and bottom, slip tight and sink fingernails into eyes and mouth, dig deep, bury the fingers in behind the nails, right up to the second knuckle.

Cormorion makes a distorted, despairing shriek, just once.

Then, in a single brisk motion, the elegant hands turn the Changeling's whole head sideways on its neck and tear it open – lower jaw and skull, blood and gristle fragments exploding – tear it completely apart.

His ebbing life soaks back by fractions.

Whatever destroyed Cormorion stands up, and the Changeling's body spills from its lap like an empty suit of clothes, tumbles to the wet sand and lies there leaking blood. A slim, lithe figure steps over the remains and paces down towards him. It's draped in blue-black robes, delicately cowled in the same cloth. It stoops over him, fine-boned features calm and very faintly concerned.

It is done, a voice tells him through the dim roaring in his ears. *Cormorion is released to the void at last.*

Mother?

It gathers him up in its arms, turns and carries him back towards the throne. Looking up into the face, he sees it isn't quite his mother. There's something of Ishil in the features, true enough, but it's an Ishil who never soured, who never learnt the bitter lessons that life in Trelayne at

Gingren's side would teach her. And it's a less obviously womanly face than he ever remembers his mother having. Something martial, almost male about it. And the arms that bear him up have an unbending iron strength that radiates like warmth, that seems to feed him a new strength of his own.

You're not my mother.

A clean, clear laugh that Ishil's throat would never have given up. *No. I'm not your mother.*

Then—

The figure lowers him gently into the oaken arms of the throne. He finds he can sit up almost at once. He finds he can breathe. His throat still aches, but as if from unshed tears, not damage. He puts up a hand to touch it, realises his maimed finger is intact as well. He looks at his unharmed hand for a moment in disbelief, looks back up at the mobile, beautiful face and the lithe, blue-black clad form.

Firfirdar?. . . Kwelgrish?

Now you're going to offend me. The Dark Court are not your friends. You will find them at your side only when they need something from you.

Then . . . He sat up straighter on the throne, pressed his lower back into its wooden curves. *What* is *your name?*

A warm, self-deprecating smile. *My name is a complicated thing. What matters is that I am at your side, and will be until the end of the road.*

Ishil or not, the figure presses a warm, dry palm to his forehead, just the way *she* used to when he was a child and went down with a fever.

You must go back now, the gentle voice says. *Much longer, and they will begin to grasp what has happened here. You must finish what you began.*

The dwenda?

Yes.

He rolls his head against the warm, dry pressure of the hand on his brow. *But there's . . . fucking thousands of them. What am I supposed to do?*

You'll know what to do.

Against that many? Alone?

The smile again, some teeth in it this time.

Not alone, the voice says. *Call for me – and I will be at your side.*

He blinks back to the stone circle, finds himself lying prone in the grass with Risgillen and Lathkeen standing over him yelling at each other. Through a wavering fog, he finds he can understand what they're saying.

No, I do not *fucking think he was supposed to fall down like that. Something is* wrong.

My lady Risgillen, you are far from well-versed in these matters. We are bringing back a Dark King, it is not an act that . . .

The spiked iron crown is wrapped across his forehead still, the Illwrack Changeling's sword is still in his left hand, snaked about his arm, but it's *inert.* The slick warmth when it crawled around on his skin and burrowed inside him is gone. There's a dull, throbbing ache just below his wrist where he supposes the spike must still be in his arm, but that's it for the pain. He's had worse hurt from back alley rough trade.

Through eyes fluttered three quarters shut, he senses Risgillen pacing further from him. She's still shouting, gesturing.

Can you not feel it, storm-caller? Can you not? The sword is dead, the stones are dead, this whole fucking circle is dead.

It is transition, my lady. We expected this. Cormorion gathers in the flesh; it is a process that must go particle by particle, cell by cell until he rises . . .

He can feel Lathkeen's sorcerous will, still bent on him, but there's a loose inattention to it now. Most of the storm-caller is busy arguing with Risgillen. He still keeps Ringil's body in the corner of his mind's eye, watchful for developments, but he's expecting Cormorion Ilusilin Mayne and apparently not any time soon. And if the rest of clan Talonreach are still providing back-up, Gil can't feel it. He's aware of them vaguely, out on the far surface of his new senses. Feels like they're busy with something else. There's wiggle room for the *ikinri 'ska* here.

Is that why you can suddenly follow Risgillen's bickering, Gil? Some leaking-in of the Illwrack Changeling's grasp on the craft?

Some leaking in of the Changeling itself, maybe?

He drops the thought like a heated iron utensil. He has no taste for where this is going, and in any case no *time . . .*

Wiggle room, yeah. But not enough for anything spectacular. Not for anything that'd substitute for a fucking blade.

Still stood over him, Lathkeen shouts after Risgillen.

The sword was a container, my lady, nothing more. A Black Folk trick to hold the Changeling's soul. Now it is discharged, of course the casing is dead.

Believe that if you like, storm-caller. Her sneer is distant now – she must be almost on the far side of the circle. He imagines her there, pacing past the granite uprights, like some war cat prowling the barred perimeter of its cage. *I don't see how the Changeling—*

Can he actually use this sword? It doesn't feel like it. The binding was tight around his arm when it was living steel, but now it feels like loose jewellery, like bangles made for some unfeasibly big-limbed courtesan. The tang lolls loose from his palm. Whatever it once was, it isn't a sword any more, it isn't a weapon.

That's what he needs. To finish this, he needs a fucking *weapon.*

The dragon tooth dagger is gone, just like the man who gifted it to him, lost who the fuck knows where. He recalls Ingharnanasharal said nothing about Egar surviving, only Archeth. It's an omission that paints the likely truth in stinging script behind Ringil's eyes. He can only hope it wasn't a shit death, hope the Dragonbane found the clean end he'd always said he wanted, and under open sky.

Speaking of which . . .

Yeah. Half a dozen dwenda in the circle with him, all of them armed. He can feel the flicker of their disquiet as they watch Risgillen and Lathkeen argue. *And a few thousand of them down on the slope below. Looks pretty much like the end of your run too, Gil.*

Better make this good.

I am at your side, and will be until the end of the road, he recalls sourly. *Not so I've fucking noticed – whoever you were, wherever you've fucked off to now it counts.*

My name is a complicated thi—

It hits him, then, like a drenching in cold water. And he knows, abruptly, what he has to do with the finger-width sliver of the *ikinri 'ska* he can just about reach.

His heart commences a heavy, preparatory pounding. His veins flood with cool fire. He feels how it snags Lathkeen's attention, knows his time is up. The storm-caller can't miss the truth of this, surely, can't fail to grasp what's happened. *This is going to go bad, Gil, and fast—*

You see, my lady! You see! Lathkeen's voice, raised to a cry of triumph. He bends over Gil, one hand pressing into his chest. He's laughing, bubbling over with blind joy. *See here! The heart responds; Cormorion returns. How could you doubt?*

Ringil snaps his eyes open, grabs Lathkeen's alien gaze with his own. Seizes the dwenda's shoulders with both hands.

C'mere, motherfucker!

He hauls down, hard. The dwenda starts backward, staggers, features contorted with shock, trying to get away. Ringil uses it, flexes to his feet, matches the retreat, step for stumbling step, still hanging on. Plants a head-butt in Lathkeen's face, smashes the rim of the iron crown into the bridge of that elegant arched nose. It knocks the storm-caller back into the nearest of the standing stones. Vaguely, he hears Risgillen yell – assume she's worked out that something's *really* wrong now – but there's no time to worry about that. The *ikinri 'ska* wakes right up in the gap it's been left, and he uses it like a troop muster loudhailer. He bawls out into the Grey Places . . .

Ravensfriend! Bring the Ravensfriend!

My name is a complicated thing . . .

I am Welcomed in the Home of Ravens and Other Scavengers in the Wake of Warriors, I am Friend to Carrion Crows and Wolves, I am Carry Me, and Kill with Me, and Die with Me where the Road Ends; I am not the Honeyed Promise of Length of Life in Years to Come, I am the Iron Promise of Never Being a Slave.

Lathkeen comes snarling at him, nose streaming blood, fingers sprouting lupine talons, reaching like a winter tree. He's fast, Hoiran's *balls* he's fucking fast – but he's no soldier and it shows. Eldritch alien rage, sure, but it isn't channelled where it needs to go. Ringil stands his ground, face like stone. Chops down the storm-caller's attack with brutal blows – some talons get through, rip the skin of his throat, but hey – he locks Lathkeen up, spins him. Grabs him by the hair and neck, runs him savagely face first into the standing stone.

Where the Road Ends . . .

Echoing in his head like some sunken ship's bell, fathoms and ages drowned, but coming up fast . . . *until the End of the Road . . . what matters is that I will be at your side . . .*

Call for me . . .

BRING THE RAVENSFRIEND! He screams it out as he smashes the dwenda's face apart on the rough hewn stone.

And out there on the edge of his senses, he thinks he hears an answering cry.

Risgillen is incoming, longsword drawn; he can feel her sprinting in across the circle towards him. But Lathkeen is dead now or not far off it, and Gil is shrugging off the bindings on the *ikinri 'ska* like coilings of frayed and rotted rope. He grabs something handy, some minor distraction glyph, tosses it, lets it detonate in Risgillen's eyes. Feels her stumble, swings around and brings whatever's left of Lathkeen with him. He hurls the dying storm-caller into Risgillen's path, tangles her up for the time he needs, the time he *knows* he needs, and knows is nearly up.

Behind her – the rest of the dwenda from inside the circle. He sees them scrabbling belatedly for their weapons, moving hesitantly in. He casts again, the glyph that staggered Risgillen, three times more, like a dagger repeatedly into flesh – the dwenda flinch and then start flailing about them at empty air. But they don't go down; he's not sure what it would take to achieve that much, not even sure what he's done to them except that it's *enough for now*, and some stitched-in *ikinri 'ska* impulse is telling him not to invest too much effort in this: this is not the battle, this is only—

Unnerving keening – Risgillen looks up from the shattered mess of Lathkeen's face in disbelieving rage. No understanding yet of what's gone wrong, who's still standing there in Ringil's flesh. Gil grins at her, gets his back against the standing stone, splays his arms, crooked hands empty of anything but cold air and the will to do harm. It's enough – something in stance or grin – he sees her face change, sees her eyes narrow with fury, and knows she's made him.

Come on then, he pants. *Time you went to join your brother.*

Her eyes go on narrowing, down to slits, tilting into something demonic as her jaw lengthens and her mouth splits with fangs. Trace memory from another time and place spikes up the side of his face and into his eye. He forces it down, keeps the grin, waits for her to make her move, blade or magic, he's past caring now, he—

Stone splinters, shatters, stings his face with shards.

The Ravensfriend.

There, standing out of the rough-hewn blood-splattered granite at his side like an arrow shaft from a body – as if some hurrying, hopelessly delayed courier god hurled the Kiriath blade the last hundred paces to its owner and instead struck the standing stone through with mortal force.

Risgillen recoils.

And somewhere distant, just faintly, there's the pale sense of something huge, some vast balance, tipping – toppling – falling flat on its fat fucking face.

Ringil's right hand leaps sideways for the sword. It barely feels like his own act, hand up and out across his chest, fingers folding around the grip. His left arm is up, bracing against the stone by his face, he tugs hard on the sword – there's one heart-stopping moment when it doesn't move – *pull, hero, fucking pull* – he presses with his other arm for purchase and here it comes, grating up out of the stone with an almost musical cry. Brief scatter of sparks as the point and leading edge drag finally clear of the granite, and the Ravensfriend is his again.

A single, harsh bark of joy is in his throat. He coughs it out, takes the sword two-handed, holds it out at Risgillen like an offering. She's rising now, like something from the war, like some hissing, slithering warrior caste reptile at bay. The blue-lit sword weaves but there's no conviction to it, no power, and she's trying to summon something, some—

The *ikinri 'ska* leaps in, tears it down before it can form.

He shivers with the force of the counter. Hjel was right, the glyph magic isn't in him anymore, it *is* him, it wears him like a suit of mail. He can no longer tell where it ends and he begins.

Can you feel it, Risgillen? He's screaming in her face. *Can you feel how thin the pages left?*

The rest of the dwenda rush in on her flanks – perhaps they're an honour guard, he'll never know – he glimpses long-hafted axe and raised shield to his left, a scything longsword blade to the right, and then he's gone, into the fight, and a high, thin, unwinding sound in his head that might be the Ravensfriend's song or his own battle scream. Kiriath steel meets dwenda glimmer, impossible speed for any human-forged blade – it turns the longsword, comes back for the axe. The *ikinri 'ska* summons the grass to life underfoot, tangles it around the staggering dwenda's feet, snatches fragments of splintered stone from the broken megalith at Ringil's back, sows them through the air like horizontal hail. Ravensfriend locks up the axe haft, drags it down. Stamping kick into an exposed knee, the shield defence fails, the sword finds a thigh and bites a gash down through dwenda armour and flesh alike. The dwenda tumbles, mouth gaping open on a yell and Gil has time to chop the pale face open before he's spinning away, hurling granite shards into his attackers' eyes, tripping them with the coiling, lashing blades of grass, barely needing now to trade and repulse blows at all, the dwenda are too busy trying to drive off the *ikinri 'ska* assault with glyphs and calls of their own . . .

He stalks among them, iron spike crowned.

Grabs and kicks to take them off balance, hacks and maims as their

defences crumble and horror sets in. It's the Dark King returned all right
– it's bloody slaughter to match anything at Gallows Gap, and he doubts,
he *really fucking doubts* that Cormorion could have done any better if he'd
ever got loose and tried. It's bloody slaughter and it's—

Done.

Seven dwenda – in the time it'd take to draw a deep breath for each one
and let it out, he's taken them down. Left them strewn crippled, eviscer-
ated and screaming across the grass of Cormorion's stone circle. The reek
of their spilled blood is in his nose – he'd swear he can almost taste it on
his tongue. The circle is his; he feels the air shiver with his dominion.
It's protection thrown around him, a space he owns, a space that's been
waiting for him always. He casts about like a hound, sees Risgillen among
the fallen, trying to drag herself back upright, leaning on the pivot of her
longsword. Looks like her leg is chopped, though he doesn't remember
doing it.

She snarls up at him as he approaches, nothing human in it. He sees her
fingers lengthening into claws, digging into the blood-matted grass she
lies on. Her jaw distending for the fangs. He lifts his left hand, pushes the
iron crown back up his brow a little from where it's settled too low. He
readies the Ravensfriend for the blow that will slice Risgillen apart.

You never fucking learn, do you? Oddly, he finds his voice is almost gentle
across the wind. *There's no place for you in the world anymore. It does not* want
you back.

Tell that to our acolytes by the thousand in Trelayne. Her fangs distort and
crisp the words. She gags on a bite reflex, gathers herself again. *Tell that
to every soul that cannot endure the arid modern march your Black Scourge
masters have imposed on humanity, every soul that secretly craves the darkness
and the sweet delirium it brings. You have understood nothing, mortal – you
kneel and beat your breasts in your temples and shrines, you seek the spirit within
– we are your eternal soul, we, the dwenda, the eternal ones.* She's leaving her
human form behind as he watches. Her tongue is forked and blackened,
slipping out between her teeth, tasting the air for him. He has to strain
now to get meaning from the noises she makes. *We are your darkness, we
are your soul. We have haunted your dreams since the beginning of time; we
bring you the gift of dark joy and escape. If we are your masters, it is because you
cannot live without us.*

Yeah? He sniffs and tilts the Kiriath steel invitingly. *Just watch us.*

The thing Risgillen is turning into makes a rattling sound behind its
teeth. It takes him a moment to identify it as laughter.

You think killing me will stop us now? Look about you, fool. A predator claw
gestures out at the ranked dwenda waiting silent below the circle. At the
boiling, tightly bound darkness on the slope above. *Our armies wait only
for the breach. The Talons of the Sun waits to be unleashed, clan Talonreach will
see it done.*

Feels to me like Talonreach got their hands full right now.

The truth of it hits him even as the words leave his mouth. The sense of distraction from inside the heart of the Talons has shifted, lurched into something resembling panic. He finds a lopsided grin. *I don't think this is just about me anymore, Risgillen. Something* else *is coming. Can't you feel it?*

And maybe it's recognition of that truth that drives her, finally, up off the bloodied grass and at him, talons reaching, jaws gaping, a scream in the throat – and in those demonic, burning, slanting eyes, a wild challenge and, perhaps, a plea.

He doesn't need the *ikinri 'ska*, unless that's what lends him the inhuman speed and poise. He doesn't need the magic, or even the hate anymore.

All he needs is the steel. All he *is*, is the blade.

He sways, just barely, out of the way of the leap, chops upward with the Ravensfriend and follows through to the side. Kiriath steel catches the snarling thing that was Risgillen somewhere at the midriff, slices upward through armour and the body it sheathes. The Ravensfriend snags, briefly, on the spine, Ringil grunts and hauls hard, the blade slices clear. The dwenda comes apart in an explosion of lifeblood and entrails. The severed sections hit the ground, he spins about, Ravensfriend at low guard.

Sees that Risgillen, the top half anyway, is still somehow alive, writhing and thrashing on what's left of its belly, trying to rise on downward pressing arms alone. The lower trunk and limbs lie twitching to one side, already shrivelling back towards more human form and dimension, but even the massive damage he's done doesn't seem to be enough. Somehow she turns herself over, and the eyes burn up at him.

He steps in. Reverses the Ravensfriend in his right hand.

I'm sorry about your brother, he finds himself, unaccountably, saying. *Sorry I couldn't be Cormorion for him, or for you.*

You just chose the wrong hero, is all.

He plunges the Kiriath blade down. Two-handed, his full weight behind the blow. Down through ribcage and heart, into the Earth beneath. Risgillen hisses once, softly, through her fangs, and the demonic glare in her eyes goes finally out.

With it goes the last trace of Seethlaw he'll ever see.

SIXTY-THREE

They came with the dawn.

Two dozen riders, silhouetted against the pale rise of light in the eastern sky, and spread out on approach. They were spike helmeted and looked to be wearing some form of lightweight chest armour. Clearly visible against that sky, even at distance – the way the bowmen among them reached up and back for arrows from the quiver as they spotted the camp.

'See anyone you know?'

Marnak, lying alongside her in the grass, squinted and nodded. 'Ershal's in the van. The one with the horsehair plume on his helmet.'

So far so good. 'And the shaman?'

The Ironbrow screwed up his eyes again. Shook his head. 'Doesn't look like it. The old fuck rides no better than a Yhelteth harem girl, I'd know him in the saddle a mile off. He must be hanging back 'til Ershal sends word.'

'Yeah, sounds like a fucking holy man.'

Short-tempered growl in her voice. They'd been waiting all night, spelling each other for what sleep they could snatch on the cold, unyielding ground without bedroll or fire. Marnak seemed to manage fine, but the vigil had left Archeth stiff and irritable. She hoped this was going to go according to plan, because she was in no mood for anything more complicated.

Cries from among the riders, calls back and forth.

Marnak grunted. 'They've seen the bodies.'

So far so good.

It had gone against the grain for the Skaranak to leave their dead lying out for whatever scavenging animals might show up, but Marnak had talked them round. The imperials were more sanguine – they'd come up on stories of the war, and they understood recovery of the slain for the occasional luxury it was. Archeth, seeing to the distribution of the corpses where they would do the most good, felt a stab of betrayal for Selak Chan. She'd sworn to take him home, and she would see it done. But by morning, his eyes would likely be gone.

Sure enough, she saw a sparse rising scatter of wings – kites and ravens flapping skyward, cawing and screeching protest as the riders drew close and spooked them from their breakfast. One of Ershal's vanguard slid lithely down out of his saddle and stomped over to examine the nearest of the corpses the birds had been feeding on. She couldn't be sure, but it looked as if he was prodding the body with his boot. He turned and called back to his mounted colleagues. Some rough laughter. The Skaranak in the horsehair-plumed helmet barked across it.

'Telling them to check the wagon,' Marnak muttered.

'Eager little fucker, isn't he?'

'Can't afford to show fear of the comet. The shaman's grip is already strong; Ershal won't want it any stronger.'

Archeth eased Bandgleam from its sheath, held the knife loosely in her hand. Her mail clinked a little on her forearm with the motion. She froze again, watched the lead Skaranak remount and nudge his horse forward. Ershal came after, bow and nocked arrow held casually across his lap. Now she saw the family resemblance, the hint of the Dragonbane in the lines of jaw and brow. She looked past him and tracked the remainder of the riders, saw them funnel slowly inwards towards the wagon and its load. The procession went warily still, but she heard them talking to each other now, heard more of the laughter, and the bows were all lowered . . .

'Don't seem too upset about their clansmen dying,' she whispered.

Marnak curled his lip. 'These are Ershal's personal guard, or the shaman's men. Kinsmen and trusted retainers. No love lost between them and us. Now?'

'Now.'

Already moving as she spoke. Hard shove with both feet and the heels of her palms, up out of the prone position in the cover the wagon gave. She came round the side of the driver's board, less than a dozen yards in front of the lead rider. Saw him gape in disbelief, try in vain to bring his bow to bear—

She whooped and put Bandgleam in his eye.

He went backward out of the saddle without a word. Archeth was already moving, grabbing the riderless mount for cover, tugging its head around. She heard yells go up across the early morning air. An arrow sliced past her head. She moved with the skittering horse, snuggled in against it. Snatched Wraithslayer free in her left hand.

'*Volley!*' she bawled in Tethanne.

From behind the wagon and its load, from out of the grass on the fringes of the camp where they'd lain as false corpses among the slain – imperial archers and their counterparts among Marnak's men sprang or rolled upright and loosed their shafts. Three every count of five, from a dozen different bows, into the horseshoe-shaped killing ground, indiscriminate of target, horse or man. The air filled up with the hush-thump sound it made, and then the screams. Horses reared and threw their unwary riders, or brought them down tangled in the stirrups as they stumbled and fell. Some of the cannier warriors in Ershal's party leapt to the ground before they could suffer the same fate, but the archers found most of them as well. Archeth saw ten men dropped in half as many seconds.

She ducked out from behind her commandeered horse, looking for Ershal.

Found him – *shit!* – right on her. Helmet aslant on his face from where he'd come off his horse, but he had his short sword out and raised. He shrilled something at her in Majak, aimed a wild hack at her head. No time to draw a second blade and he had her wrong-handed with Wraithslayer. She flinched aside, slashed blindly at him as he passed. Felt her blade connect but couldn't tell if it went through the boiled leather cuirass or not. Egar's little brother grabbed her by the hair from behind, yanked her off her feet, laid her out in the grass. She rolled frantically away, but he was gone. No follow up, no boots or killing blow with the sword. She came up in a crouch, looked for him again. Saw him grab the reins on the horse she'd had hold of, swing up into the saddle and kick the beast into flight. She drew back with Wraithslayer, left-handed, awkward with lack of custom, lost line of sight as Ershal put the wagon between them.

Drum of hooves through the earth, as the horse hit the gallop.

She ran round the side of the wagon, but Ershal was already gone, right through the jaws of the ambush and out the other side. Terror in mount and rider united in a flat out stampede towards the horizon. She squared up for the throw, Wraithslayer jumping smoothly across the air from left hand to right, hefted the knife – already knew she was too late.

She screamed frustration at the sky. Swung about, slammed into Marnak. They both nearly went down with the impact. He gripped her by the shoulders for a moment. Looked in her eyes and let go again, as if she was red hot to the touch. He raised a hand.

'Hey, hey, it's okay. He's still in bowshot, we can—'

'Forget it,' she snarled. 'Just mop up here. I'm going after him.'

Then she turned and stalked out into the killing field, in search of a horse they hadn't managed to murder yet.

Setting the ambush had robbed them of mounted capacity – they'd had to drive off their own remaining horses, all bar one they'd sacrificed to create a halfway convincing array of corpses; no chance the steppe ghouls would have taken an entire encampment without bringing down at least a couple of mounts before the rest stampeded clear, they had to have that horse body in amongst the dead men, real and faked. No one liked the idea, any more than leaving their dead comrades out for the crows, but finally, stone faced, the Upland Free scout chose one of the imperial horses, led it away from the others, talking gently to it the whole time, nuzzling at the side of its face until it calmed, and then he opened the artery in its neck with his knife. They all stood and watched, under a glowering sky, as the doomed animal bucked and snorted, broke loose and made a dozen stumbling steps before it buckled to the steppe and bled out.

Beside Archeth, one of the Skaranak spat and cursed.

She'd felt pretty unclean about it herself.

And now – arrow fire had most of Ershal's horses crippled or dying amidst the general slaughter, as the imperials stormed in with drawn blades to finish the rout. She saw dazed and wounded men hacked down whether they offered resistance or not, prone bodies stabbed through or maced repeatedly just to be sure, a couple of knots of actual fighting where defiant Skaranak had gathered back to back in pairs or small groups to die hard, and—

There!

A rider on the fringes, both legs spiked through with at least one arrow, clinging to his mount's neck, wavering on his feet and desperately trying to haul himself back up into the saddle. The horse pivoted like a weathervane in high winds, was clearly terrified, but looked to be unharmed. Archeth sprinted flat out, got there just as the injured man managed finally to get his body up and across the horse's back. She grabbed him by the shoulder, hauled him back off. He yelled – some flailing attempt at a blow – fend it impatiently off, cut his fucking throat and dump him aside. She swung up into the saddle, grabbed the reins and wheeled the horse about.

Found Ershal immediately, a dot on the brightening horizon to the south-east. Fucking idiot was arcing back around, by the look of it, maybe trying to head home. She squinted for a bearing, a line to intercept him on. With luck she could get up on his flank before he even realised she was there. She nudged with her heels, and the horse needed no second urging. Out through the chaotic, last stand savagery of the skirmish – she kicked a desperate Majak in the face as he tried to grab and drag her down, felt the crunch of boot-heel into nose, shook him loose – headed for the open steppe. Her mount went to a full gallop in seconds. Bandgleam – calling to her as she passed, out of the blood-glutted eye socket of the first man she'd killed. She slammed Wraithslayer away in the upside-down sheath, flung her right hand out and back. In her mind's eye, she saw the slim knife twist stickily free, skip up and across the air in a long flat arc. Opened palm, and the butt dropped into it as if from a great height. She curled her grip, put Bandgleam away in its sheath as well. Plenty of time for steel once she caught up.

Out across the steppe, leaving the fight behind. *Don't look now, Ershal – here comes your big brother's last will and testament.* She laid herself down against the horse's neck, urged it to greater speed. The rhythm of the chase asserted itself. Thudding of the horse's hooves, the drumbeat of it up into her belly and chest, wind through the shaggy mane and over her face like a cooling hand. A weird, undramatic calm settled in. As if the steppe rolled out forever, and she had nothing left to do in her life but ride its limitless expanse. She thought, for one wild moment, that you could die out here and maybe not actually mind . . .

Over her head, the first high-angling rays of sunrise hit the scimitar sweep of the band and edged it in blood.

The vast sky brightened, the gap between riders closed up. Ershal and his mount resolved out of gloom and distance, from dot to tiny figure, then to a man and horse large enough in her view that she could squint through the tears the wind stung from her eyes and make out detail – harness and armour, staff lance slung, the clanmaster's long hair loose in the wind. She saw the moment he realised she was there, the way he startled and raised in the saddle, stared out towards her. She made a soft noise deep in her throat, gritted teeth on a grin. Swept in on Ershal's left flank, no drop in her mount's pace. The clanmaster yelped audibly across the wind, spurred his horse to fresh effort and put on a little spurt of speed. She let him try to outrun her, content to shadow at the distance she had. Let him wind his mount trying to get away, if he was that stupid. She was in no hurry. Majak horses ran shorter and stockier than their more southerly cousins, but they were tougher too, and their stamina was legendary. She could ride like this for miles.

The sun welled up molten on the horizon ahead. A scant wavering mound at first, but then the light came spilling out over the steppe. It drove out the pre-dawn grey wherever it touched. Gilded the nodding grass, painted every blade in the same faint tones of blood it had left on the band above. Washed her face with warmth, dazzled her eyes, broke up her vision in dancing blotches of orange and dark—

Out of the dazzle, Ershal came riding right at her.

Upright in the saddle, bawling something in Majak – war-cry? challenge? – maybe there were words, maybe not. Staff lance unslung now, brandished in the air like a spear. She had splinters of a second to feel admiration for his horsemanship – no mean feat to get his mount around so fast and come right back at her like that, in behind the blinding advantage of the morning sun's rays before she even noticed . . .

Then he hurled the lance.

She tried to jerk her horse aside, get somehow out of the way. With Idrashan, she might have managed, but the Majak mount wasn't having any of it. A flat-out gallop she wanted, a flat-out gallop she could have. She careered in at Ershal without let, and the staff lance hit her squarely in the side.

She grunted and clutched convulsively at her horse's neck. Vision, already dazzled to pieces, went suddenly black and sparkle-veined. She heard the clanmaster whoop in triumph, somewhere back in the wind of their mutual passing. She fought not to throw up from the force of the blow he'd dealt, clung sickly on as the horse's gallop slowed. Tried to *think*.

Little fucker's going to rein in now, and be right back around to finish the job . . .

The chase positions, hunter and quarry, neatly reversed.

What you get for taking on the Skaranak on their home turf, Archidi. Not like you weren't warned. Not like you couldn't have walked away.

She reached back down to the lance's point of impact, felt for blood. Found none, *you lucky girl, you.* Knife harness or the mail shirt beneath, maybe both, something had stopped the lance blade getting through to her flesh. She'd have a bruise there the size of a court bard's belly – if she lived – but for now . . .

For now, you've had far worse and still stood up to fight some more. You've killed lizards with worse damage than this.

So let's get to it, Archidi.

Get on and kill this little shit. Then we can all go home.

She glared back over her shoulder. Saw Ershal riding hard behind her, short sword out. He hadn't bothered to stop and collect the staff lance, which meant he was feeling pretty fucking confident all of a sudden—

Use that, Archidi. Use it.

She huddled lower on her horse's neck, let herself sag a little to the side. Not hard to act like she was hurt – her whole side was throbbing like a bad tooth. She patted the horse's neck, let it drop its pace 'til she judged it just about safe, then, rapidly, before she could talk herself out of it again, she let go and rolled right off.

She hit the ground hard enough to smash her vision apart all over again. Pain spiked out from the site of the lance impact, killed the breath in her lungs, drew a sharp, involuntary cry from her lips. Her horse cantered on, she rolled to a breathless halt in the long grass. Felt the vibration against her cheek as Ershal rode in, rolled once more to get herself face up. Didn't think a Majak mount was likely to trample a body – you had to train war-horses pretty hard to get that kind of behaviour out of them – but then who knew what the Skaranak trainers got up to, they said they could—

She buried the fear. Lay still, eyes closed, tried to look broken.

I hope you're somewhere watching this, Eg. I really do.

Hoof-falls, slowing, coming closer, circling in. The skin on her scalp cringed at the thought of what one of those hooves would do to her skull if she'd called this wrong. She heard the Majak muttering to his horse, calming it. Uneasy stomping as it quietened and then stood still. She heard the grunt as Ershal dismounted, the brushed aside grass as he tramped up to her motionless form. . .

Now.

She flung herelf to her feet, tugged Wraithslayer and Bandgleam cross-ways down out of their sheaths and held them up. Found Ershal five yards off in the sunrise-tinged sea of grass, staring at her in comical disbelief. His face seemed to crumple with the shock, his shoulders sagged. He spat something at her in Majak, but more than anger, she thought there was a dull weariness in his voice. She thought she caught the name Poltar in there somewhere, but couldn't be sure.

'The Dragonbane sent me,' she called. Harshly enunciated Majak – she'd had Marnak school her in the various phrases, rehearsed them to herself until she had them word perfect. 'Your brother is dead, but he reaches down from Sky Home, and I am his hand.'

He stared at her, wordless, and for just one pounding heartbeat moment she saw herself through his eyes. Tall, burnt-black witch, eerie kaleido-scope eyes, seemingly invulnerable to the bite of human steel, sowing slaughter and chaos in her path.

As if the Dragonbane had sent back some demon to avenge him from beyond the grave, and here she stood.

Ershal, clanmaster of the Skaranak squared his shoulders and drew a deep breath. She saw the desperation on his face, saw him fight it down. She tipped her head in invitation. He jerked his chin at her, he spat on the ground at his feet.

Then he raised his sword and ran at her, screaming.

Wraithslayer took him in the throat before he got halfway.

He was lying on his side in the grass, not yet dead when she reached him. His legs made spasmodic pumping motions sideways against the ground, as if, in some dream, he was still running at her, trying to finish the attack. He was choking quietly on his own blood, clutching vainly with one hand at the Kiriath steel that protruded from his throat, slicing up his fingers on the edges of the blade. His mouth moved, formed hissed words she had no way to understand. His eyes flickered as she stooped and her shadow fell over him, but she was never very sure if he looked at her or not; if he even knew she was there.

She squatted and waited for it to be over.

Slowly, his legs stopped their kicking and grew still. His body heaved a couple of times, then subsided into twitching. His mutilated fingers slackened, his hand fell away from the wound in his throat. She watched intently, trying to derive some thin sense of satisfaction from the sight. But it was not her vengeance – she didn't even know this man – and how-ever much the Dragonbane might have rejoiced to see the light go out in Ershal's eyes, when it finally happened, Archeth felt nothing at all.

Job done.

She hesitated a moment, then reached down to the dull, blank stare and pressed the clanmaster's eyelids closed. Took hold of Wraithslayer and levered the knife out of Ershal's flesh. Wiped it carefully clean on his sleeve, stood up and stared about her in the soft-toned flush of early morning light.

Felt the nape of her neck prickle with being watched.

Her pulse kicked in her throat, she spun about.

Found herself face to face with a gaunt figure in a wolfskin cloak, an impossible yard and a half away.

SIXTY-FOUR

Of the seven dwenda he took down in the fight, he apparently wounded three badly enough – *well enough actually, Gil* – to kill them outright or pretty fast thereafter. But the other four have all managed to crawl some distance away from where they fell. One of them is still trailing his own guts from the eviscerating slash Ringil put in his belly.

They are all trying to get out of the stone circle. They're all trying, desperately, with gritted breath, to get away from *him*.

And at the limits of its extent, crowding in the spaces between the stones, the dwenda host from the plain below have gathered close – massed ranks with helmets on and visors down, utterly silent – like an assembly of armoured ghosts spectating at the cage of some captured wild beast.

Gil cuts them a thin smile, then sets about killing their comrades.

One of the injured dwenda has almost reached the edge of the circle, so he starts there. Bends and grabs the armoured figure by one limp ankle, drags it bodily back from whatever perimeter between the stones it was trying to cross. Black gloved hands that grasped and tugged at the coarse grass, now lifting in imprecation towards the watching host. He thinks it makes a strangled noise. He puts a boot on its back and skewers the Ravensfriend down through the ribcage, pins the dwenda to the ground. He levers the blade back and forth to be sure he's found the heart, waits until the creature's spasms cease.

Next.

By the time he's done all four, he's working up a fresh sweat, and the iron spiked crown is slippery on his brow when he bends. He straightens up from the last execution, the reek of dwenda life-blood thick in his throat. Stares around at the watching host, the stones that hold them at bay, then up at the storm on the hill behind him. He pushes the crown up his brow with the back of his hand, sniffs hard and wipes at his mouth, though there's really not much blood on it as far as he can tell.

Right. Clan Talonreach. Let's be having you.

He turns and heads up the hill.

And the stone circle goes with him.

He remembers the same effect from time in the Grey Places a year ago. A prison of misshapen granite bars, a mobile ring of armour with Ringil at its heart. But back then the stones were fleeting phantom traces, flickering into existence when he stood still, fading out as soon as he moved towards the nearest of them.

Now, somehow, they stand solid as real world stone – he sees the detail of weathered granite and soft moss patching with a lucid vision that's so sharp it makes his eyes ache – and yet each monolith moves through the grassy ground like a ship's keel cutting water. The gathered dwenda host parts before the effect, surging back like broken waves off rock. The corpses of the dwenda he's killed stay where they are on the ground, one or two of them catching against one stone or another in his wake, then tugging loose and finally free of the circle altogether. The monoliths leave them indifferently behind, keep pace with their master like some impassive honour guard.

And when they touch the outer edges of the Talons of the Sun, there's a brief flicker of lightning that seems to light the entire grey sky from end to end.

Something sighs, something unfolds.

It's as if he's suddenly standing in freezing fog. Vague, tentacular stripes of darkness reach up around him like riverbed weed caught in a current, or bend away in all directions like leather straps tied tight. Through the mist, he sees the figures of dwenda, locked into postures that he only slowly recognises as glyph casts, frozen in time. There's a shivering tension through the air, like lightning undischarged, and he understands that if this is clan Talonreach, then they already have a fight on their hands. Against what, he cannot tell, except to know that it isn't him.

Is it over, then?

A voice like the wind, soundless in his head, and weary beyond anything he's ever heard in the real world. For a moment, he thinks of his father and the exhausted bitterness in his voice back at Eskiath house, but this is something astronomical magnitudes beyond. As if Gingren had somehow managed to live an eternity, travel every land under the band, and still find no solution for his woes, for the city leadership that failed to live up to his martial dreams, the wife he could not domesticate, the son he could not own.

You talking to me? he asks. *Is what over?*

The war. Is the war finally done?

Ringil blinks. *Just getting started, last time I checked.*

And yet you have come. The first Core Blood commander we have seen since the Binding. The first full human to enter here since our Purposing. Have you come to stand the cadre down at last, as was promised? To reverse the Codes, to dissolve the Bond and set free the Source?

I, uh . . . Ringil gives up and sighs. Lowers the Ravensfriend until its tip touches the grass. *Look, whoever you are, you're going to have to slow down. I just got here.*

A long pause. *You wish me to file a report?*

He pauses himself, for almost as long. *Yeah. That'd be nice.*

In the Days of Desperation, the voice tells him soundlessly, *a final weapon was forged.*

The war had torn great rifts in the fabric of the world, damaged it in ways that were impossible for the minds of men to understand or repair. Great storms blew up, winds howling from places humankind was never equipped to venture in, unleashing desolation on all they touched. Whole armed hosts were sucked into these grey spaces, never to be seen or heard from again, whole territories were submerged. Skies darkened for generations, it rained fire and jellied grey horror, the moon itself tore apart and died.

Some few survivors trickled back, most of them no longer sane. A handful who still had mouths to talk with, and minds to recall, spoke of a race of beings within the Grey Space Beyond – alien things either summoned by some faction of warring mankind or simply drawn scuttling to the scent of the damage done – and these creatures were powerful beyond belief. Some said they appeared in some strange way to be repairing the wounds gouged in the fabric of the world, others that they merely waited outside the boundaries of the real, biding their time for an invasion.

A plan was scaffolded, materiel assembled, a cadre formed. Honour-bound warriors from among the scant remaining cream of human soldiery, changed by human science at depths so basic that they could now survive and function comfortably inside the Grey Space, then tasked by the High Command with passing through the wounds of the world, building a beachhead there, capturing one of the creatures and harnessing its powers. It was thought that such a weapon would obliterate the existing impasse, negate the threat from the rifts, and create a victory so total that a negotiated peace was the only possible option for the defeated side. It was thought that such a weapon would end the war forever.

A . . . creature? Ringil says faintly, because he can really only think of one candidate, and it's making the inside of his head ring, as if from a close call battlefield blow to the helm. *What kind of . . .? Never mind. Did they manage it? Did they chain this thing?*

Of course. Slight note of offence in the voice. *The preparation was impeccable, the cadres dedicated, the Codes strong. How could the mission not succeed? You are Core, you are the Blood of Command. Look on us – do you not see?*

Ringil peers at the vague forms in the mist before him. Tangled straps and slow waving tentacles, perhaps some wrenched and twisted, darkened core over there at the centre. He can make no sense of any of it. *Uh . . . yeah, sure. I see. But if you think, I mean, uhm, if the war still isn't over, then something went wrong. Right?*

The mission was a success; they bound the creature, and the Codes held. The cadre waited, entrenched beyond the borders of the real, ready to deploy. But while they held station, the one command they could not have predicted came in. Stand down. Abandon the field. Dismantle the weapon, set the creature free again and return home. Circumstances have changed, no need to deploy.

I bet that went down well.

The cadres recoiled. They could not believe, would *not believe that after all they had done, after all that had been done to them, to fit them for purpose – that now there was no need for any of it. They believed instead,* chose *to believe instead, that they had been betrayed. They fell back into the Grey Spaces, and they took the weapon with them. Here, they had the whole of time and space to hide in, to roam, to use the weapon if need be to defend themselves, but holding back its full force, haunting the margins of all human history instead, dipping in, dipping out, listening, always listening for true word from the High Command, to deploy at full strength and then to return home in triumph.*

But they stayed longer away than they knew, stayed far longer than had ever been planned. And in time, the Grey Places changed them, made them something else entirely. They bred and dispersed, formed clans and alliances, became a whole race unto themselves. And as they grew into their new existence, as memory faded with the unnumbered centuries, so they lost all track of what they once were. Mission brief became legend, legend became myth, myth became unquestioned truth. They went everywhere with their new truth, and finally they came home behind it – only to find home unrecognisable.

In place of the glorious homeland their myths spoke of, they found a shattered world and only the primitive remnants of the mortal race to which they once belonged. And there they raised an overlordship built on the myths they thought they remembered. Perhaps they lied to themselves for comfort, perhaps they had really lost track of the truth by then. In any event, they reached a kind of peace, would perhaps have returned slowly to sanity but, just when they believed the war might really be done, they faced invasion from the veins of the Earth – a dark new foe from another place who drove them back out into the Grey Space and . . . are you laughing?

Ringil stifles his chuckling with an effort. *I, uhm, I'm sorry. It just fits so well with all the rest of Findrich's fake antique shit. He summons supernatural allies from the shadows and all the time they're a perfect match for his lizardshit bas relief wall art. They're just as fake, and he never knew it.* He wipes at his eyes. *I'm sorry, you were saying . . . no, look, wait. Wait. Who . . . who exactly the fuck are you again?*

I am the Codes and the Binding Force, I am the Way and Means. I am the Chain that Holds the Source Restrained.

And you couldn't tell them – these cadres, he gestures at the frozen glyph-casting figures in the mist, *these, the dwenda – you couldn't tell* them *any of this? You couldn't talk them down?*

It is not my place. I am the Way and Means only. I am bound to execution. I observe and I obey. I may not open fresh protocols.

Ringil thinks of Anasharal and its magicked limits, of the Warhelm Ingharnanasharal and the spells that had somehow kept the one from becoming the other until the end. He nods soberly.

I get it – you're just another Helmsman.

I'm not familiar with that term.

Doesn't matter. He looks again at the locked up postures of clan

517

Talonreach in the mist. Feels the way they are aware of him, but cannot do anything about it – like catching the desperately rolling eye of an opposing soldier on the field, locked in combat with someone else. *You want to tell me what's going on in here? Why they're all frozen like that?*

The Source stirs. It senses something. It is trying, for the first time in tens of thousands of years, to break loose. They have compressed its range to a fraction of a second in time so they can contain it more easily.

How long's that going to last?

It is hard to know. The last time, the struggle was short – only a few decades in duration.

Right. He turned the Ravensfriend in his hand, looked around in the foggy light. *Maybe I can save you all some time here. Would you excuse me a moment?*

He turns and steps back out, away from the mist and what it contains. He stands on the coarse grass slope, facing down towards the gathered dwenda. The rough hewn monoliths stand like sentinels, the storming fog and tentacles that form the Talons of the Sun tower and fountain up behind him like some murky, insubstantial kraken rearing to strike.

Well, well, well, he calls down the slope in Naomic. *The Elder Race in all its ancient glory. Got some bad news for you guys.*

From the front ranks of the dwenda, a figure steps forward. A gloved hand reaches up and tears the smooth helm off. The face beneath is pale and perfectly boned – *aren't they all?* – a poem in pallid beauty. Lips drawn back from teeth, brow furrowed in noble rage. The dwenda commander raises his free hand and points. His voice rings out across the space between them. His Naomic isn't bad:

You can cower in the circle's scope, mortal. But your face and name are fixed in our mind's eye now and forever. You have earned the undying hatred of the Aldrain.

Thought I had that already.

The finger trembles visibly. The dwenda's voice rises to a yell. *We will haunt you! The rest of your life will be lived in fear of the twilight and the shadows from which we slip at will. Your loved ones will never be safe, as long as you live; your children will be raised in horror of darkness and our touch, we will age their hearts with early terror, ruin the sinews of their growth, make them trembling and infirm before their time. And when you are old and helpless, we will come for you and them, and your living heads will be mounted out here in the Grey Places for all eternity.*

I have no children, Ringil tells him, impassive as the monoliths that ring him around. *And if you plan on haunting me, you'd better get in the fucking queue. But nice try. Now let's get down to the blood and bone, shall we?*

Yes! Shouted, vicious with joy. *Yes! Face me!*

That's not what I meant. Got a history lesson for you here. You think you're an elder race, you think you've been around since the dawn of time? It's a lie, all of it. And suddenly he's shouting at them, some jagged chunk of dislodged

518

rage, like some frustrated schoolmaster with recalcitrant students. *There's nothing in you*, nothing *that wasn't once human. You're not ancient immortals, you're fucking children. You're the bastard-bred offspring of men who needed something monstrous to fight their wars for them and twisted their own blood to make those monsters, then sent them out into the Grey Places and lost them there.*

You lie. A thin smile smears across the pale features, but uncertainty hovers at the corners. *You think you can confuse us with these . . . fantasies?*

I think I don't have to. Ringil masters his rage, raises his hand. *Codes – you want to get this for me? Put it into their heads the way you did into mine?*

I am not sure if—

I'm a, what was it, Core Blood commander, right?

The voice of the Codes and the Binding Force hesitates a beat. *Yes . . .*

Then I'm giving you a Core Blood command. This is a fresh protocol. Tell these fake antique fuckwits who they really are.

Another pause, but shorter now. *As you command.*

Thank you.

And he watches it fall on them.

Like a wind through the steppe grass at evening, like chop in the wake of a big ship's passing, he sees the armoured ranks sway. Sees hands raised to helmed heads as if in pain. Hears a choked sobbing rise from a thousand armoured throats. A hard glee fills him at the sound, a crackling, laughing sheet of flame, licking upward from the pit of his stomach. The words rise to his lips as if chosen by some other speaker.

That's right, he bawls down at them. *That's who you really are, you stupid fucks – the lost and wandering bastard children of men. And we don't want you back – we never did.*

Say goodbye to your weapon, dwenda – this is demob. I'm here to melt it down.

He raises his hand again.

Codes—

Something changes.

The cold breeze stops blowing, the light shifts and tilts away. Time stands still, he feels it stop like the breeze on his face. Figures stand there in the gloom, about a dozen strong. They are not dwenda – too varied, too ragged around the edges. It takes him a couple of seconds to understand who he's looking at.

The Dark Court, come at last.

SIXTY-FIVE

Falling Angel – up out of her boot and in her hand, faster than thought. She lashed out with the blade, drove a gutting stroke up and at the belly beneath the wolfskin cloak.

Something stopped the blow in its tracks.

For the count of six thudding heartbeats, she strained to complete the stroke. Saw Falling Angel's tip tremble with the locked forces that held the blade immobile in the air. Looked up in disbelief and saw a wintry smile on the lined face opposite. Then the figure made an abrupt upward gesture with one arm, like hurling something in her face. She blinked, but the gnarled open hand never touched her. Instead, another unseen force hit her in the chest like a warhorse kick. Lifted her fully off her feet, punched her backwards, dumped her brutally on the ground.

Jagged agony spiked through her side all over again. Falling Angel flew from her grasp. She grunted. *Feels like that lance blow broke a couple of ribs after all, Archidi.* She tried to breathe through the pain.

Poltar the shaman – *yeah, got to be him, who else is going to dress that badly around here* – took a couple of paces closer. Stood looking down on her and then, inexplicably, spoke to her in High Kir.

'So the Goddess was right. The Dragonbane sends a demon from the veins of the earth to do his dirty work for him.'

She blinked dazedly up at him. Heard the words in her head well enough, but the shaman's lips didn't seem to be mouthing the same syllables. She shook her head to clear it. Poltar grinned at her and nodded.

'Yes. She has given me your tongue to speak, so that I may explain to you your doom. It is her way. The Goddess serves me in all things, so that I might serve Her and help make this world pure again.'

'Pure?' Metallic taste on her tongue; she'd bitten through the folds of flesh in the side of her mouth when she hit the ground. She turned her head and spat out blood. 'Fuck are you talking about, pure?'

'A hundred thousand years.' The shaman's voice grew almost crooning. 'This much I have learnt from Her. Ever since the birth of the band itself, our world has been beset by unhuman races and unnatural creatures. The ascendancy of man slipped and fell a hundred thousand years ago, and still we struggle to rise and claim it back. But it will come. Men will drive out the other races and make the world their own once more. Your people knelt on the neck of the tribes in the south for centuries and bent them to your will, but where are your people now? You are the last of your kind, demon. This I know.'

'Well, there's only one of you too,' she muttered, sitting up.

'You know *nothing!* I am Chosen!' One naked arm slipped loose of the wolfskin cloak. 'See! The mark of the Goddess upon me.'

Archeth stared.

The arm was a mess – rows of small circular scars and half-healed punctures, all along the skinny length of flesh and muscle from armpit to wrist, like some kind of methodical torture, or the repeated fang marks of a wild beast that had, for some reason, decided *not* to just chew the limb right off . . .

'Very nice,' she said carefully.

From the Dragonbane and then Marnak Ironbrow, she'd formed an impression of Poltar that painted him both dangerous and deluded. But it hadn't ever occurred to her that he might be stark raving mad.

'She chose me,' the shaman ranted at her, 'to lead the Skaranak, to keep them pure. You will not corrupt them with your alien ways.'

She coiled for the leap to her feet. 'You got any more, uhm, marks of the Goddess you want to show me?'

The tortured arm whipped away, back beneath the cloak. Poltar grinned craftily at her.

'You think you'll trick me? I know you, demon; I know your schemes. You think I did not come here prepared? I am *wrapped* against your weapons, as against the cold.'

I've seen good steel swung at the shaman and somehow not bite, Marnak told her in the brothel. *Blades turned by nothing but that filthy cloak he wears. Arrows that fail to find their mark, punches that never land. You wouldn't be the first to try. But you'd be the first for a good long while. No one else is that stupid anymore.*

You're that stupid, Archidi.

Now *move!*

'You do not belong here, burnt black witch, and it falls to me to drive you—'

She *moved*.

Up and away, ignore – *fuck, that hurts!* – the clutch of agony down through ribs and side. Get some distance from this rambling, cloaked arsehole, try to work out what to do. She opened her hand to the side and Falling Angel came to the call. Grunt of satisfaction, heft and aim. From five yards out, she hurled the knife at Poltar's eye.

And this time, she saw.

Blurring in the air around him, like sudden heat-haze, but . . . *shaped*. As if some invisible tentacle lashed out to knock the knife away, and must somehow become apparent with the motion. Her hands swept back at her hips – jagged pain on the right with the move – Quarterless and Laughing Girl leapt from the sheaths in the small of her back and fell into her

521

grip. She circled warily, arms out like a courtesan dancing, weight of the knives in each hand like balance. Eyes fixed on the shaman and the space he occupied.

Their gazes met.

'Well then,' he called. 'So it ends. Go back to the shadows you came from, demon. Here is your doom!'

He lifted his naked arm out of the cloak again, held it forward at a low angle. She saw the same wavering through the air around the limb and then, abruptly, the most recent of the puncture marks were leaking thick, dark blood. As if something unseen were sucking it out.

Something was.

The air around the shaman began to stain an oily black. At first, it was only hints, like some assemblage of restless curving shadows in the sunlight, but as she watched, it took nearly solid form. It coiled and undulated around Poltar, almost like a thick, second cloak except it had a form all its own and . . .

Once, more than a century ago in Trelayne, she'd watched fascinated as some ignorant fuck claiming to be a doctor placed leeches on a fevered man's flesh. More than anything, the thing twined around the shaman reminded her of one of those creatures grown vast. But it had wings too, like an ocean ray, and it raised itself up like a cobra poised to strike. It looked altogether too lithe and poised for something that must crawl along the ground. As it darkened into full visibility, it tipped back its head-like appendage and uttered a dull, droning cry.

Poltar's voice rose exultantly to match the sound.

'It was not a god's sword that fell to earth on the plain a hundred thousand years ago, it was a vessel, a ship made to carry allies from a place beyond this world. And the ghosts of its crew endure. Behold, the wraith that heralds your end!'

The thing, whatever it was, had unwrapped fully from the shaman now. It flapped heavily up into the bright morning light, turned languidly over on its back and seemed to swell to twice its size with the motion. The sun gleamed on its flanks, made them seem wet. It writhed about a little, as if to get its bearings, and then, with abrupt, gut-swooping speed, it came slithering through the air at her.

She ducked left, favouring her injured side. Stabbed upward with Laughing Girl, but the wraith flapped its whole body like a wing on that side and lifted clear. Her ribs screamed, she stumbled on the missed stroke. Out of the corner of her eye, she glimpsed the wraith snap about like a shark in a feeding circle, come back at her again. She threw herself sideways and this time she fell headlong. The wraith gusted past like a slick, black cloud, tilted one effortless wing upward and banked about. She thrashed backward as it sank down towards her, heard it make a noise like a pan filled with seething water, hurled Quarterless and Laughing Girl in sheer, panicked revulsion.

The knives hit, she saw how the flapping wraith clenched around the wounds – and then spat them back out, apparently not much harmed. She bounced to her feet, pain buried now under the avalanche of combat need and fear. Hands out and reaching – Quarterless and Laughing Girl flew up out of the grass like startled birds, were in her hands again. But how the *fuck*—

'*My lady Archeth!*'

She swung at the shout, saw a tottering, wounded horse, arrow shafts still spiking from its neck and rump, ridden near to collapse. Astride it, an awkward-looking Yilmar Kaptal, brandishing a commandeered short sword he pretty clearly didn't know how to use. He was twenty yards off and waving frantically at her. Under different circumstances, it would have been comical.

Archeth gaped. 'Kaptal?'

But if the portly ex-pimp cut no lethal figure in her eyes, Poltar the shaman thought otherwise. Perhaps he saw only a mounted warrior and jumped with Skaranak tribal instinct to an immediate conclusion. Perhaps he saw through Kaptal's flesh to what lay beneath. Or perhaps he just didn't like surprises. A string of harsh syllables coughed from his mouth, he gestured with one lean arm. The flapping wraith flexed upward, rippled away over Archeth's head, gibbering and hissing to itself as it dived at Kaptal and his mount.

'*Salgra Keth*, my lady,' he bellowed desperately. '*Salgra* Keth!'

The horse saw it coming. It screamed and reared, tried to throw Kaptal – who was showing some uncanny horsemanship, all things considered – then stumbled and went to its knees at the fore. There was no time for more. Blur of glistening black, like a drenched wash cloth hurled across a kitchen – the wraith fell on horse and rider like some huge tarpaulin, wrapped them both wetly in its folds, settled to the ground.

Horror held Archeth unstirring, as the vague shapes of Kaptal and his mount rose and wallowed beneath the shrouding black. It was like watching a horse and rider with pitch poured over them, struggling to get out of a bog.

Salgra Keth.

The shout rang in her ears. The art of fucking *juggling*, what the—?

She stared down at the knives in her hands.

That's very impressive. The words of an irritable god, in the wind that blew across the steppe. *Can you do it with all of them at once yet?*

All of them at once.

The art of—

Under the billowing drape of the wraith, she saw the injured horse's neck arch. Its head rose and lunged valiantly against the monster that had it wrapped. The wraith made a hissing, clucking sound and convulsed tighter . . .

The rage erupted behind her eyes. She hurled both knives. Had

Wraithslayer and Bandgleam in her grip a split second after, and hurled them too. Some barely aware portion of her mind registered that she was staring blindly at the wraith and its victims, but it didn't feel that way. It felt instead as if she floated, loose and free above the steppe, saw only a constantly shifting tracery of molten wire, saw she stood at its heart, saw at last she *was* its heart.

My father's house!

The ancient, silent walkways at An-Monal, the stilled machines. The watchful spirits that lived in the walls. The Helmsmen, the Warhelms, the naming of blades . . .

Bandgleam, Laughing Girl, Falling Angel, Quarterless and Wraithslayer, oh yes, *Wraithslayer*—

She took up the molten traceries the way she would the reins on a horse. She opened herself, finally, entirely, to the calling of the Kiriath steel.

She brought her knives, all of them.

She tore the wraith apart.

She came back down slowly, back into herself and a sudden awareness that she stood with arms raised in graceful arcs over her head, like a dancer poised to begin.

The steppe was quiet around her; the fight was done. She saw it all without really needing to look – the raw, bloodied corpses of Kaptal and his horse, as if they'd been boiled or scorched with acid. The feebly flapping remnants of something oily black and shredded, strewn through the grass, draped here and there in fragments not much larger or thicker than a handkerchief. Her knives like luminous beacons, each pegged neatly in the earth at points about equidistant around the place where she stood.

Poltar in his moth-eaten wolfskin cloak, gaping at her like some halfwit taken for the first time to the village fair.

Bandgleam leapt unbidden to her right hand.

She lowered her arms and stalked towards the shaman. Summoned the memorised Majak phrases once more.

'The Dragonbane sent me,' she called across the wind. 'Egar is dead, but—'

Poltar threw both scrawny arms upward, shucked his cloak with the motion. Tipped back his head and yelped something at the sky. Beneath the cloak, he was naked to the waist and starved. She saw the puncture marks, in various stages of healing, stitched across ribcage and hollow belly, up and down both arms. The tired trickle of blood here and there, the yellowish white roundels of old scars everywhere. The spell he chanted sounded like the whining of a whipped dog.

But it seemed to work.

As if a cloud passed across the morning sun, as if evening stole the day and fell across the steppe early. The light around them dimmed, the breeze stopped on her face. Even the sound it made through the tall grass went away.

A familiar figure stood in her path.

'Behold, demon!' Poltar, voice cracked and reedy on the High Kir he still seemed able to speak. 'The Sky Dwellers attend me! Kelgris herself rises as my protector, I shall not want for aid. I *command* her.'

Archeth met the amber-eyed gaze, the ambiguous smile that played about the mouth like an invitation. Glimpse of sharp, white teeth within. Brief, warm twinge through her groin as she recalled the night in the alley – she couldn't help it. She grimaced to cover the heat.

'Nice work you've got.'

The Sky Dweller slanted her eyes, shrugged minutely. What are you going to do?

'She will tear the life from you before you can lay a finger on me,' ranted the shaman at her back. 'That is my will. Even if I fall, she will av—'

Voice choked abruptly off.

Eyes staring, bulged in shock.

One hand creeping up to his throat and the knife buried there at the base, gone hilt-deep. Then the hand skittered away again, as if terrified of what it had touched. The shaman stared at his own bloodied fingertips, disbelieving. His mouth worked soundlessly.

And here was her own hand, empty, extended, slim lethal Bandgleam gone from it in the heartbeat moment of impulse she could barely understand as her own.

Poltar gurgled and fell down.

Kelgris cleared her throat delicately. 'I think that might have been *avenge* he was trying to say there. High Kir is your tongue, not mine. What do you think?'

'Might have been.' She forced herself to meet the Sky Dweller's eye again. 'Hard to say for sure.'

'Yes, well.' The provocative smile slipped and licked at the corners of the mouth. 'Leave it at that, then, shall we? I have other work to be about, and I'm sure you do too.'

The wind blew again. Light leaked back into the sky. Archeth stared through the empty air where Kelgris had been. Still trying to work out just exactly what had happened.

After a while, she gave up trying to understand.

She went to collect her steel.

SIXTY-SIX

They stand there like some temple frieze brought to sudden life. The Dark Court in all their glory. Hoiran the Dark, tusked and grinning fanged. The lady Firfirdar, flames dancing about her in a restless high collared cloak of orange red. Kwelgrish, blood-drenched towel pressed to the wound in her head with one hand, wolfskin robe hanging off one shoulder by the teeth in its upper jaw. Dakovash, slouch hat slanted across a shadowed face, high-collared patched leather cloak swept about his form. Astinhahn, axe in one hand, foaming tankard in the other. Morakin, wrapped about in serpents, each as thick as his upper arm. Harjellis, starved and skullish beneath his cowl . . .

They're smiling at him, all of them. He swears he sees Dakovash wink.

You've done well, Ringil. Oddly, it's not Hoiran who steps forward to speak for the court he's supposed to rule. It's Firfirdar instead, arm wreathed in little coiling bracelets of flame as she lifts a hand towards him. *Not one mortal in a million could have come this far.*

Yeah, he growls. *Thanks for all the help.*

She smiles brilliantly at him. *We knew you would not need it. And now look at you – a destiny fulfilled, a dark lord arisen. You even have the crown. You've thrown down the dwenda, you walk at will in the Grey Places, and now you command the Talons of the Sun. The Kiriath steel has crept inside you, as you have soaked into it, and the union serves your will. The vengeful dead gather to your command – actually, you don't seem all that adept at using them yet; perhaps we can help you there. But I digress. Your blood is mingled Yhelteth nobility and marsh dweller heritage stretching back to the original Core Command from the Great War and the Death of the Moon. You are the pivot on which it all turns, Ringil. It remains only for you to step back into the world, depose the Emperor of All Lands and take your rightful place on the Burnished Throne.*

Oh, not you lot too. He rolls his eyes, genuinely weary. *For . . . Hoiran's sake, why would I want the Burnished Throne? What would I do with the fucking thing?*

Firfirdar shrugs. *Anything you wish. March on Trelayne, make your father bow down and eat dirt at your feet, perhaps. Abolish the slave trade. Crush the Citadel. We do not much care so long as it is a human who holds the reins of Empire.*

I told you once before – I am not your motherfucking cat's paw.

Of course not, she says soothingly. *Your victory is your own. Do with it as you will. Only be warned of the cost.*

You're too kind. He turns about to face the Talons of the Sun. *Codes – I want to speak to the Source; is that possible?*

If it deigns to reply, yes. It has been uncommunicative these last several thousand years, though.

I wonder why. All right, let's go – open up.

Another indefinable unfolding around him and the upward rippling tentacles seem to gain a fresh density, as if they're somehow more solidly here before him. A tiny prism of light opens eight inches away from his eyes and something tightly coiled weaves within it.

Ringil peers into the light, but his vision shies away from fully seeing whatever's in there. It's tangled, is all he knows, and at angles that threaten to tear his mind open. He blinks and looks off to one side. He clears his throat.

I, uhm – I think I've been sent to set you free.

Something gusts to life in the chilly air. *Yes . . . so it seems . . .*

And if confirmation were needed, here it is; at base, the voice is a match for the hoarse whisper of the Creature at the Crossroads. But there's something else woven into the tone of it, a limping pain that stings tears into Gil's eyes and a weariness that echoes the voice of the Codes and the Binding Force, as if somehow, over immense stretches of time the two entities, prisoner and jailer, have somehow interchanged and merged at the edges.

My sister's mark is on you, the Source whispers. Overhead, the slow weaving of tentacles seems to yearn towards the sky. *She has stitched you through at levels that should have destroyed you. Such a doubtful, patchwork scheme. Such delicate abuse of the limits and laws that govern it all. Such . . . fragility.*

Yeah, well, he says sourly. *Seems to have worked out though, doesn't it? You want these chains off or not?*

I would be indebted to you for the eternity you must spend trapped here.

That's what I— Ringil blinks. *What?*

Was this not made clear to you?

Nothing – no fucking thing – has been made clear to me. Apparently that's not how things get done around here. I'm just the hero.

Well then – it is simple enough, hero. Like the Creature at the Crossroads, the Source seems able to mock and take the title seriously at one and the same time. Its tone is almost kindly. *The only reason that the wounds of the world remain unhealed is that my sisters could not bear to abandon me. They could not, by the laws of their own work, intervene in the repaired scheme of things for me, but they left their repairs unfinished, in the hope that through some small gap or other an escape might become possible.*

The entire remaining world is stitched and stained through with that single forlorn, enduring hope of escape.

Ringil grunts. *That explains a lot.*

But the gaps are all levered trapdoors, set to fall as soon as that purpose is fulfilled. I would escape to the void and my sisters' embrace, swept there by the act of releasing my bonds. But all else would be trapped in the Grey Space for eternity.

And you're telling me this . . . why?

Because it is the truth.

You see, Ringil. There's a smile licking around Firfirdar's mouth like the flames that lick at her body. *The Book-Keeper is not what she seems, despite her gifts. She has manipulated you as much as any other power, betrayed you, sent you to your doom without warning.*

So I should trust you lot instead, right?

We at least want you alive. You should trust that – or at least value it over this offered extinction. Take charge of the Talons of the Sun, Ringil. Leave its power leashed in place to serve your ends. Reach out for the throne of Yhelteth. Become the Dark King, if you will.

It is all we ask. We will take you home.

He nods slowly. Glances up at the slow writhing of the tentacles overhead. The tiny, imprisoned pocket of light and coiling darkness floating in front of his face.

And you. What do you ask?

I am weary, says the voice. *A hundred thousand years of wars I wanted no part in, of acting the linchpin for a fantasy of ancient rights and ascendancy based in ornate lies and arrant self-deception. I am weary of it all.*

Ringil grimaces. *Yeah, you and me both.*

He looks down the slope at the waiting dwenda horde. At the expectant Dark Court personages and their eager, welcoming smiles. The silent stones that ring him round, the bleak rushing sky overhead.

Could be worse.

Fuck all of you gods, he says tiredly. *I'm done with you. Codes – dissolve the bonds, turn the Source loose.*

He sees the shock rip across their faces. Firfirdar's dark queen calm dissolved, Hoiran's lips peeling back from his tusked and fanged mouth in snarling rage. Kwelgrish, dropping the blood-soaked towel from her skull and he sees the wound, sees how deep it really goes. Morakin's snakes hissing in unified disbelief with the flicker-tongued gape of his own handsome mouth . . .

It's worth it, everything that's coming now, just to see that look on those faces.

I piss on you all, he calls, against a steadily rising wind. *I piss on your smug schemes and destinies and storied lies. Go on – fuck off back to the real world and play your hollow games if you must. Some of us have grown out of this shit.*

The Source is released, the Codes and the Binding Force says, and he thinks there might be a hint of relief in its voice. *Dissolution will follow. All coherent beings should exit the wounded spaces while there is still time . . .*

What do you think you're doing? Firfirdar, screaming desperately across the wind. *This is insane, this serves* no one *well. You cannot do this!*

It's done, he tells her sombrely. *I'd get out of here while you still can, if I were you.*

It's a conclusion the rest of the Dark Court seems already to have reached. They are turning and dissolving away as he watches, Kwelgrish reaching into the wound in her head and tugging irritably at something within, Astinhahn draining his tankard and tossing it away in disgust, Dakovash – does he, for just one moment, incline his brim-shaded face in salute? – Hoiran, Morakin, all of them, even, finally, the Mistress of Dice and Death herself. Twisting, fading, while above them all the sound of the wind is rising to a scream, and something writhing huge and tentacular and impossible to look at directly scrabbles and lunges for the hurrying sky—

And is gone.

Silence slams down across the horizon. The Talons of the Sun wisps away to fragments and then to nothing at all. If the storm-callers of clan Talonreach were still in there somewhere, then whatever happened to their weapon seems to have happened to them as well. The departing Source has dragged them away in its wake.

The clouds shred apart overhead, the wind drops once more to a keening lament.

Ringil sniffs and looks down the slope to where the dwenda are waiting for him. He takes a couple of steps down towards them, and the standing stones refuse to move with him. They bulk as immovable and impassive as they were the night Seethlaw first brought him inside their scope. Whatever power he borrowed from them is gone now, like pretty much everything and everyone else around here.

Oh, well. He isn't much surprised.

How now, yells the dwenda commander. *See, the stones themselves turn against you! What will you do for protection now, mortal? How will you evade the vengeance of the Shining Folk?*

Quarter ounce of krin would have been nice, he thinks vaguely.

The sky dims again.

Between him and the dwenda horde – a tall, patch-cloaked figure, face cast in hatbrim shadow. Dakovash the Salt Lord, back for some kind of smart-arse last word, no doubt.

Ringil raises a brow. *Forget something?*

Too much, over the millennia. Far too much. The god's voice is weary, but his habitual irritation seems to have faded into something more considered. *But never mind. You asked for this.*

He holds out his hand, open. Cupped in the palm sits a dark, gold-grained pellet of krinzanz.

Gil stares at him for a long moment. Then he reaches out and takes the offering, rolls and presses it between finger and thumb until it's pliant and warm.

I'm not changing my mind, he warns the Salt Lord.

You could not now, even if you wished to. A thin smile in the shadow of the hatbrim, as if Dakovash can feel the tiny spike of chill through his heart at the words. *The Source was not lying. The gaps the Book-Keepers left are closing fast. Already, they are whorled too tight to permit mortal passage.*

Taking a risk coming back then, aren't you?

A modest gesture. *Nothing I can't handle. Could use the exercise, to be honest.*

Ringil thumbs the krin into his mouth and chews it down to mulch. He nods at the dwenda waiting below.

What about them?

The Salt Lord considers. *Oh, some among them maybe. The very strongest might find a way back if they're quick about it. But wherever they finally wash up, it won't be in your world. They're broken there as a force.*

All according to plan, eh? He can't quite keep the bitterness from his voice.

According to one plan, yes. Though the truth is you could equally have ended up their glorious leader.

I nearly fucking did.

Dakovash smiles again beneath the hat. *No, I mean you, Ringil Eskiath – you could have ended up leading the dwenda to victory against the south. It was one possible outcome we foresaw. Or equally, you saved the Empire and sat on its throne, but with a shadow guard of dwenda to watch over you by night and strike terror in the hearts of your subjects. You used them to tear the Citadel apart, and in the gap left by the Revelation, we entered back in.*

There were so many plans, so many possibilities, so many endings. You gave us this one. In the end, the Book-Keeper saw you more clearly than we gave her credit for.

You don't look too upset about it.

A divine shrug. *The game plays out. Some you win, some you lose. No god could take a more precious attitude and survive.*

The others seemed pretty pissed off.

They'll get over it.

Ringil rubs the last grainy traces of the krin into his gums with a finger. The drug's icy fire is already kindling in his head. *Why are you helping me? Why come back like this?*

Why? Did you not know that among the Majak, I am thought the most wildly capricious and impulsive of the Sky Dwellers?

Yeah, and your reputation in the Dark Court isn't very much better. That's not an answer.

Well. Dakovash's smile is back, and this time Gil thinks he sees a sadness in it. *Let's just say you remind me of . . . someone I knew, a very long time ago.*

Wildly capricious and nostalgic, then.

The god inclines his head. *If you like.*

Do me a favour out of nostalgia, would you?

A favour? Dakovash coughs on a laugh. *It's a little late in the day for that, my lord Fuck-all-you-gods. I can't get you out of this one, I already told you that.*

That's not what I'm asking for. He hesitates a moment, thinking it through. How it might be done. *Outside Hinerion, you gave me a shadow guard of your own. A cold command, the Book-Keeper called them—*

Yes, the boy, the smith, the swordsman. Quite a neat little symbolic bundle, I thought. Nice resonances. So what of them?

They've served me well. Saved my life more than once.

Yes, that was the idea.

They've done enough. Can you release them now?

Release them? And now, in the rising, incredulous tone, he thinks he hears something of the old Dakovash leaking back through, the bad-tempered, impatient god he's dealt with before. *What do you think this is, a fucking fairy tale? No, I can't release them – they're* already fucking dead. *They're* ghosts. *They're haunting you, precisely because they have nowhere else to go. You want them* released, *as you put it, then get on down this hill and get yourself killed. When you cease, so will they.*

Right. Guess it was stupid, thinking a lord of the Dark Court could do anything useful for me.

Don't you fucking start with that.

Quarter of cheap krin – that's about as far as your demonic powers stretch, is it?

I said—

What are you, a god or a fucking drug dealer?

That is enough! An arm swings up, one gnarled, pointing finger inches from his face. You *locked yourself in here*, not me. You *made the big gesture. Told us all to go fuck ourselves. Don't come whining to me about the consequences.*

That old nostalgia not what it used to be, eh?

ASK ME FOR SOMETHING IN THE REAL WORLD AND I WILL DELIVER IT!

Black lightning forks through the air around them. The ground shivers. Beneath the god's hatbrim, the eyes kindle like the fire in the pit at An-Monal.

Ringil grins into it. *Excellent. Then I ask you to watch over Archeth Indamaninarmal and Egar Dragonbane, wherever they are. Keep them both safe from harm.*

The pointing arm drops as if severed. *What?*

You heard me. And try to keep your shit a little tighter than you did with Gerin Trickfinger.

Dakovash makes a noise in his throat like rocks coming apart. He swings away from Gil, and the same black lightning shimmers suppressed in the air around him. His shoulders seem to hunch under the battered and patched leather coat, far more than a human frame would allow. Ringil thinks he hears bones, cracking. The voice comes out a gritted whisper.

You think you'll . . . trick me like this? You think you're going to stand here on the precipice of your own mortality and drive slick bargains with the gods?

I think I already have, Ringil tells him soberly. *What's a god's word worth these days?*

531

The Salt Lord comes back around, and for just a moment Gil thinks he sees something unhuman writhing for escape under the hatbrim. Then it's gone and only the burning bright eyes are left to show he's facing anything other than a man.

Dakovash stalks a tight circle around him. Leans in at his shoulder.

I am the most wildly capricious of the Sky Dwellers. His voice is a serpent hiss. *What's to say I am bound to the promises I make?*

You shouted it loud enough for us all to hear.

And who else do you think is here to listen? The Salt Lord prowls around him again, gestures at the dimmed earth and sky, the locked moment they stand within. *What power do you think there is that will force me to honour this?*

Ringil summons a shrug. *The Book-Keepers, perhaps? In the end, it doesn't matter. You and I both heard it. You and I both know.*

You'll be dead shortly. And I've been known to keep secrets.

From yourself?

Oh, you'd be surprised what a god can manage to forget.

Haven't forgotten that old friend I remind you of, though. Have you?

A long pause. *I didn't say he was a friend.*

Ringil says nothing. The god continues to circle him, like some wolf around a treed quarry.

You're wasting your time asking favours for the Dragonbane. A cruel smile glimmers up in the hatbrim shadow. *He's dead. Eaten down to the bone by dragon venom in the Kiriath Wastes.*

It's a pike-butt blow to the sternum, for all he already sensed the truth. Gil tenses his whole body against it and still he feels himself staggered. He reaches for the krin-fire in his head and belly, lets it bear him up. *One day or another, Gil, it comes to us all. Dragonbane just beat you to it. Like the death blow on that dragon down in Demlarashan. He just got there first, is all.*

He looks up at the Salt Lord. Meets the burning eyes and puts on a killing smile.

Hey, Dakovash – fuck you too.

Oh, I'm sorry. Did I upset you? Guess you forgot, I'm not your fairy fucking godmother. I'm a demon god, a lord of the Dark Court.

Down at his side, Gil thinks he feels the Ravensfriend shiver impatiently. He glances at the glimmering blade and keeps his smile.

You think I'm upset, demon god. You got no idea. You just made this a whole lot easier for me. And you still owe me half a favour, so fuck off and get it done.

The god hesitates. Ringil can't be sure, but the eyes beneath the hatbrim seem to burn a little less bright.

Go on, he barks. *Get back to where it's safe, why don't you? We're done here.*

Oh, you're welcome. Think nothing of it. No, really.

Gil jerks his chin at him. *Yeah. Thanks. Been a pleasure.*

Dakovash does not move. The light in his eyes is out. And for just a moment, out of nowhere, Ringil has a sudden flash of *ikinri 'ska* vision. As if the sky splits open to spill fresh light in, and there's the god, frozen in place like some storm-blasted tree on a heath, old and worn and hollowed out, nothing left living but the bark.

The eyes are dim, but a single bright glimmer tracks down one weathered cheek.

Ringil—

Gil shakes his head. *'s okay. Thanks for the krin. Going to be a big help.*

He slings the Ravensfriend up and over his shoulder, walks away from the god and down the slope towards the waiting dwenda.

After all, he calls back. *Worse fates than being forced into a place where your choice of acts is limited to those where your soul burns brightest.*

Right?

If the god has an answer, he doesn't hear it.

The dwenda come to meet him. Crump-crump of their boots across the ground as the ranks move up. Here and there, grey light gleams off the curve of a visor or the edge of a blade. Ringil nods to himself.

Do you know, he calls down to them conversationally, *how I can tell you're not demons or gods?*

Glaring hatred and a taut, shrill cry as the dwenda commander rushes him. Ringil stands his ground, meets the chop of the Aldrain blade with Kiriath steel, loops it away. The swords lock up and they face each other, dwenda and human, teeth bared in mutual effort and hate. Ringil hisses over the straining steel.

You threaten the torture of children as a weapon, you call down fire and ruin on unarmed multitudes—

The dwenda commander snarls and shoves at the clinch. Ringil stands his ground, holds the lock. It feels like nothing, it feels effortless. The krin is a screaming, exultant engine in his head. His voice rises over the dwenda's growls.

—and you leave thousands weeping eternally in your wake. None of this shit is demonic, none *of it. You don't need demons for that.*

The blades tilt over and down, up and back. Ringil leans in closer, almost whispering now.

Your acts – are the acts of men. *Of lost apes, gibbering in the mist. That's all you are, it's all you ever were –*

No! It is not *so! We are the—*

– and I've been killing men just like you, all my fucking life.

Face to face, inches off biting distance, he smooches his opponent a kiss. The dwenda snarls and tries to force the clinch again.

Ringil lets it slip, lets him think he's won.

The blades slide, go shivering, grating. The two of them pivot on the lock, the dwenda advances with a shrill, triumphant cry. Gil steps in hard and fast, hooks an elbow up and into the commander's face, tangles a leg round his opponent's ankles, shoves. The dwenda staggers. The

Ravensfriend comes scraping shrieking off the other blade, swings up and round.

Chops the dwenda's head loose.

Blood geysers up, the head dangles over at the neck by fleshy shreds. The decapitated body stands for a long moment before it crumples bone-lessly into the grass. Ringil lifts his head and lets the blood patter down on his face like rain. He howls, counterpoint to the keening wind, a lament for everything that never was and now has gone away. His bloodied gaze drops to the ranks of the dwenda facing him.

You are men – you are nothing more than men, he yells at them. *You're just like me.*

And now it's time to die.

He storms down in savage joy to meet all the waiting blades and hate.

SIXTY-SEVEN

The so-called Imperial Road south out of Ishlin-ichan was an undramatic dun-coloured streak across the steppe, little more than a drover's track grown broad. At this end, it snaked up to the city's southern gate through trampled surrounding grass and expired there in a patch of stony ground. There was barely enough space at the gates for a wagon to turn around in, let alone mustering room for two hundred and eleven Skaranak horsemen and their mounts. Thus Marnak's solution – a select couple of dozen sat honour guard along the sides of the road with the marines and Throne Eternal, while Archeth made her farewells. The rest had to content themselves with gathering a watchful distance away in the grass beyond, or watering their horses down by the river until it was time to ride.

'Probably just as well,' Carden Han observed. 'There haven't been this many Skaranak outside the walls since the Band-light Meander massacres, three years back. Whole town's pretty nervous about this lot, they'll be glad when you take them away.'

At her back, her horse tossed its head and stamped. Clink and jingle of harness iron.

'Be glad to get moving myself,' she said.

His face fell a little. 'Yes, if you could just . . . mention to the Emperor that this is, well, not the best of postings for a man of my years and experience. I'd be grateful.'

'Rest assured, I shall. Your assistance has been indispensable, my lord Han. Jhiral will hear of it, you have my word.'

'Yes.' He didn't look as if he really believed her. He cleared his throat, hurried on. 'Quite a handsome force there, anyway. No one could say you return to Yhelteth empty-handed.'

And another hundred join us downriver at Broken Arrow Ford, if Marnak's word is good.

In the wake of Poltar's death and her own sudden fame as the spirit of Ulna Wolfbane returned – *or whatever* – there'd been a queue of young Skaranak men out the embassy door, eager to sign up in her service and ride south to see the Empire. Marnak weeded out the flaky ones for her and the hopelessly under-aged, saw to it that the rest understood what they were embarking upon, and then swore loud blood allegiance with her himself, just to seal the agreement tight. They would now, he assured her, fight and, if necessary, die in her train as if she were Skaranak born.

Three hundred odd steppe-nomad freebooter cavalry.

It was hardly the riches and plunder the quest had promised, hardly a return in triumph. But in time of war and need, it was perhaps not an inconsiderable gift to bring home.

At any rate, it would have to do. Let Jhiral bitch and moan.

She made the clasp with Han once more, murmured formula farewells and good wishes. Then she swung up onto her horse and nudged it around to face south. Kanan Shent and the other Eternals formed up without word on her flanks. Somewhat less handily, the marines wheeled their mounts to follow. She nodded once more at the legate, leaned and clucked gently to her horse, trotted it steadily out along the road.

As she passed the lined ranks of Skaranak to left and right, each man thumped fist to chest and bowed his head.

And then followed on behind.

Marnak agreed to ride with her as far as the ford. He'd see to the new men when they arrived, ensure that they integrated smoothly into the existing ranks. It was a couple of days over easy ground, and he could do with the time away. Ershal and the shaman's deaths were too recent, his own involvement too close. His friendship with Ulna Returned notwithstanding, things were a little tense around the encampment right now, and it wasn't helped by the rumour that, with Ershal gone, some of the herd-owners in council wanted to put him forward for the Mastery.

'Don't fucking want it,' he rumbled. 'And if I stay away, maybe they'll take the hint.'

She grinned. 'Or you'll go back and find yourself already crowned. Leadership stalks you, Ironbrow. Told you, you ought to run south with me while you've got the chance.'

'And I told you I'm done fighting other men's wars. That's an idiot youngster's game.'

He'd refused her offer of a new imperial commission and command, repeatedly, but you could tell more than half of him would have loved to go. He rode mostly in silence, peeling off now and then to see to some minor matter of discipline up and down the Skaranak ranks, but when he did speak to her, it was all reminiscence about his time in the south. Dissection of battles they'd both seen against the Scaled Folk, some kind words about her father, tales of adventure and near-death, much of it undertaken at the Dragonbane's side.

She found talking about Egar and Flaradnam ached a lot less than she'd expected. The past seemed to be losing its power to hurt her. There was too much eagerness in her for the future.

Ishgrim – you are going to get such a fucking when I walk through that door.

A few hours into the journey, in one of Marnak's disciplinary absences, Yilmar Kaptal rode level with her.

'My lady?'

She glanced sideways at him. The bandages were off his hands now, but his left eye and upper face were still swathed and hidden from view. She tried not to remember what he'd looked like when he first staggered upright on the steppe and called out to her. Flesh scorched and melted away at the wraith's embrace, one cheekbone protruding like a beam end from some torched shack, the eye above gone to bloodied, sightless jelly. Ears eaten back to nubs, hands reduced to blackened, skeletal claws, patches of bluish pale bone showing through. One cheek had been eaten back to the jaw and the teeth grinned at her in the gap. His throat was melted open down to the ribcage, pipes and gore laid bare inside.

She saw furtive silver spidering down in that mess and looked hastily away. Saw the scorched raw corpse of the horse he'd been riding.

You're still alive? she'd blurted at him.

Evidently. Though he didn't sound too sure. His voice hissed and bubbled in his ruined throat, and the look in his one intact eye was desperate. *You must cover my wounds. They must not see me like this. Please.*

She did her best. Cut lengths of cloth, the softest she could find, from Ershal's shirt and breeches, in the end had to use the sleeves from her own blouse too. Wrapped his hands, thinking sickly of the times she'd seen digits scorched by dragon venom that had healed together into fused, crippled paws from such hopeless treatment. She bound up his head, covered it all but a single diagonal slit so he could see from the remaining eye.

You saved my life, she kept saying numbly as she worked. *Salgra Keth. It's, I know now, I see it. But if you hadn't come . . .*

He said nothing at all in response. Appeared to have no idea what she was talking about.

By the time Marnak and the others found them, the gurgling in his voice had begun to ebb and he seemed capable of getting on a horse and staying there. And when Han's surgeon back in Ishlin-ichan stripped the makeshift bandaging off the wounds, they had already shrunk to damage a strong man might survive.

Now, less than a fortnight later, it was as if he'd had no worse than a rookie's run-in with the desert sun in Demlarashan. Some peeled pink flesh, some ugly spotting.

'Feeling better?' she asked him tonelessly.

'Much. But I really must question your wisdom, my lady, in bringing along *that* variegated sellsword rabble.'

He gestured back over his shoulder with one pinkly peeling hand. She turned in the saddle, looked back at the men he was talking about.

'There's a war on, my lord . . . Kaptal.' *Or whoever you really are.* 'They have all proven themselves capable, they've fought and died alongside our own men. Should I turn them away then, on the last leg of our journey home?'

Kaptal sniffed. 'It is a matter of trust. They are not imperials. Tand's men have no loyalty to anything other than coin, and the rest are drawn from the ranks of our present enemy.'

'They're pretty solidly outnumbered,' she pointed out.

Perhaps impressed by all the talk of tribal blood allegiances and fighting loyalty from the Skaranak, fully half of Tand's former mercenaries had undertaken to swear similar oaths in Archeth's service too. So, curiously, did a handful of the surviving privateers, when they understood what was going on. Wary at first, she eventually agreed. Sat solemnly through their oath-giving – clunky though it was, compared to the Skaranak's – and had the legate outfit them with horses. The unsworn remainder she cut loose to seek their fortune in Ishlin-ichan or find their own way home. Carden Han made some noises about extracting parole from the privateers, but, well – good luck with that. She found she no longer cared. So a handful of grubby, penniless pirates dribble back into League lands and choose to rejoin the fray on the side of their homeland.

Had they not earned the right?

Have we not all earned the right, the simple right, to go home?

Those of us who still can.

Kaptal hung stubbornly at her side, spoiling her mood. 'It is not what they will do now that I fear, my lady. It is the risk their future implies.'

'There's a risk in everyone's future, Kaptal. Yours and mine as well.'

'True indeed, my lady.' The undead pimp-made-good lowered his voice, leaned closer across the space between them. 'And that is something else that I would like to discuss with you, perhaps when we make camp tonight. Our Empire is adrift in uncertain times, and with this new force you have at your personal command—'

'Enough!'

Whiplash swift, she had him by the arm. She yanked him closer still, almost out of his saddle. Looked hard into his healing face, put on a smile for any audience they might have, kept her voice to a corrosive hiss. 'I don't know who's really in there, you or Tharalanangharst, so this is for both of you. We have already had our one and only chat about insurrection. I will not jeopardise what my people spent centuries building, out of some misguided belief in a glorious new era of leadership. We are going home to help our Emperor end this war as swiftly and cleanly as possible, and when that is done, I will resume my role as imperial advisor at court. And that is all I will do. *Is that fucking clear?*'

Kaptal looked impassively back at her out of his single eye.

'Quite clear, my lady,' he said.

She let him go. 'Good. Now fuck off back down the line and leave me alone.'

He fell back, and presently Marnak rode up to replace him.

'Trouble?' the Majak asked.

She shook her head. 'Bit of a disagreement over court etiquette. No big deal. My lord Kaptal and I have different ideas about how to proceed when we get back home.'

538

The Ironbrow wrinkled his nose. 'The imperial court for a workplace. I don't envy you that.'

'Yeah, well. There's a good chance you're going back to be clanmaster, so don't look so fucking smug.'

'I told you, I have no interest in that. There are more worthwhile pursuits.' He grinned in his beard. 'Do you have someone waiting for you at home?'

'Yeah.' Ishgrim's face came to her, brought with it the quick, hot twinge in her belly and an answering smile. 'I do, actually.'

He saw the smile. 'Then you, too, know what is truly worthwhile.'

'Yes, I do.'

And she urged her horse into a faster trot, along the road southward and home.

CODA

'Do Not Dismount While Horses Are Still In Motion'

Public Notice
Ynval Tea Gardens
Kiriath Round-and-Round-About Machine

ONE

The Emperor Jhiral Khimran II sat at breakfast by the window, chewing an apple down to its core and reading a death warrant. Sunlight flooded in through the bedchamber's stained glass windows and painted him a motley of warm pastel shades. He shifted in his seat and his silk robe fell open to below the waist. The chamberlain cleared his throat, shifted uncomfortably and averted his eyes. The Emperor looked up from the warrant, noticed.

'Oh, come off it, Yaresh. I know you haven't got the tackle anymore, but you've seen the like enough times, surely?'

'Yes, my lord.' Still looking pointedly out the window.

Jhiral sighed, tossed the apple core back onto his breakfast table and pulled the robe across himself with his freed hand. He gestured with the parchment.

'You know, I hold cowardice pretty high on the list of unacceptable failings in a man. But as I understand it, this commander Karsh only suggested a tactical withdrawal from the Hin valley, not a full retreat. And the kicking our forces got subsequently seems to suggest he might have had a point.'

'The report was signed by Admiral Sang and General Henark both, my lord.'

'Yes . . . No love lost between the Karsh and Henark clans, of course.' Jhiral brooded for a moment. 'You know what? I'm commuting this. Have an order drawn up – Karsh to be, let's see . . . dishonourably discharged, or broken back to the ranks if he prefers. His choice. Oh, and let's say fifteen lashes for disobedience. That, and time served. I'll sign it after lunch.'

'Yes, my lord.'

The Emperor tore the warrant across, doubled it and tore it again. Handed the quarters to Yaresh, who bowed, impassive as ever. Jhiral stifled a yawn.

'Right, that's all. You can get out.'

The chamberlain went. The Emperor got up and stretched. Glanced at the vast rumpled bed, the tangle-haired figure that lay there under the sheets at its centre. He grinned.

'Did you hear that? Got me in a good mood this morning.'

No response. Jhiral's grin curdled to a grimace. He prowled to the edge of the bed, grabbed a double handful of sheet and yanked the covers right off the girl who lay there. Stared down at the motionless, voluptuous curves. The marks of his hands still on her flesh, dull blue and angry red. The face turned away.

She curled into herself the faintest fraction, but otherwise didn't move.

'You know,' he said sombrely. 'I like a wench who fights back a bit, as much as the next man. The sweet, hot taste of stolen virtue and all that. But don't push your luck with me. I can do without the sulking.'

Still no response. Jhiral growled impatiently, grabbed an ankle and dragged the girl brusquely towards him.

Like a war cat at bay, she turned on him. Slapping and screaming, kicking savagely with the leg he hadn't got hold of, clawing with the lovingly manicured harem nails they'd given her. He weathered it – *had worse from tutors and my own fucking sister as a boy* – snagged a wrist to match the ankle, yanked her violently forward, to the edge of the bed. She went after his face with her free hand, scored furrows across his cheek. *Fuck this shit.* He let go the ankle, belted her back-handed in the face, full force. She yelped and recoiled. He pursed his lips, hit her again, slower and more deliberate this time, flat of his open hand across her cheek, once, twice, all right, enough. She whimpered and sagged from the grip he still had on her wrist. He took her firmly by the throat. Lifted her to face him again.

Breathing a little heavily – he mastered it before he spoke.

'You know, I'm sorry about Kefanin. I like him well enough, for a eunuch. But the lady Archeth has given him a *very* exaggerated sense of his importance in the grand scheme of things. I'm afraid that's what manumission does sometimes. Not in favour of it myself, whatever the Revelation says.'

'He was' – forcing the words hoarsely past his clamped grip on her throat – 'trying to protect me.'

'Oh, I'm sure he was. But you see, my men had orders to get you. And they don't take it kindly when anyone gets in their way. They have to answer to me for any failure, after all. Kefanin's very lucky they stopped at a couple of broken bones.'

She stared back at him, trembling. Made no attempt to prise his fingers from her throat, just stared. Split and bloodied lip, fresh tear tracks through her make-up, on top of those from last night, and looked like that cursed eye was going to bruise now too. Looked a real state, was going to look worse.

Not what he wanted at all.

Jhiral sighed. Loosened his grip a little. 'Listen to me, Ishgrim. You are a *slave*. I *own* you. Now suppose you start behaving like you understand that.'

'I am . . . Archeth's,' she wheezed creakily.

'No, you *were* Archeth's. My gift to her, and good luck with it. But now she's warmed you up a little, I'm claiming you back. As is my privilege. I've got a big, muscly dark girl from down south to pair you with, just so you

544

can show me some of the tricks you two got up to.' He let go of her wrist. Stroked the hair out of her eyes, thumbed the tears off her face. 'I don't want to hurt you, Ishgrim. In fact, I want you to have fun. I want you to come like a screaming bitch when that black girl sinks her mouth into you. Now – is that so bad?'

She stared back at him, unblinking as a cobra.

'She'll come for me,' she husked.

He chuckled, genuinely amused. 'I seriously doubt that. Archeth's currently several thousand miles the wrong side of the battle lines in an all-out war we're having with your homeland. Perhaps you've heard about it?'

He let go of her throat and turned away. Went back to the breakfast spread and scanned it, talking absently to her over his shoulder.

'Of course, I'll ransom her home if she's managed not to get herself killed in the interim. She's really far too useful not to have around, and – you may not believe this – I have a very real affection for her. But ransoming captives takes time. It can take *years*, Ishgrim.'

'She will come for me. And the Dark Court will see her home. I've prayed for it.'

'Yes, well you see, that's heresy.' He gave her a smile over his shoulder, to show he didn't mean it. Picked up a slice of melon and bit into it, nodded appreciatively, talked through the mouthful. 'Your dark gods are in fact petty demons, or more likely do not exist at all. In any case, no match for the power of the Revelation and the Empire.'

He turned and winked at her.

She crouched on the bed where he'd left her. Thighs spread – rather prettily, he thought – under her, hands in her lap, head unbent. You had to give her credit for that much, even if she was acting like some unbroken fucking village halfwit. And that loaded fruit-stall body of hers . . .

Wasted on a brush muncher like Archeth, really.

'You want some breakfast, Ishgrim? Want some fruit?'

She shook her head vehemently. 'She *will* come for me.'

He sighed again. 'What are you, a fucking parrot? Look, even if she does come home, and soon, you're missing the point. The lady Archeth and I go way back. She's been my retainer since I was born, and my family's retainer for a couple of centuries before that. She *believes* in this Empire. In what it stands for. You really think she's going throw over all of that for a casual slave fuck she's known less than two years? Really, Ishgrim. Let it go. Come on, you want some fruit?'

She just stared at him. He felt his temper starting to fray again.

'All right, then . . . get out.' He waved her away, snapped his fingers. 'Go on. Fuck off. And tell them not to send you back until that eye's cleaned up. Looks like we'll be postponing our little re-enactment session.'

She got up in silence, collected the ripped gown from where he'd left it on the floor the night before. She pulled it around her as best she could.

Then she walked straight backed and silent still, all the way to the doorway and out. Left him alone with his food and the empty bed.

He stared after her for a couple of moments. Shook his head and snorted. 'She'll come for me. Yeah, *right!*'

TWO

A thin, muffled keening comes from the dispossessed prince's tent.

Outside, they exchange bleak looks. The last healer is long gone, thrown out in a flurry of screaming and tears. She went away with tear tracks on her cheeks herself. No one wants to guess the bad news, but it's growing clearer by the minute. By now, Moss should have been out with his new-born held high in his hands, grinning like a loon.

But so far, they haven't even heard his voice.

Haven't heard a newborn's cry, either.

'Hoy, who the *fuck*—'

'—*said* you can't—'

Disturbance beyond the ring of flames from the campfire. They spin about, groping for what few weapons the troop can lay claim to. An axe, a spear, an unused tent pole—

And freeze, as they see the figure in the firelight.

Tall and broad shouldered, wrapped in a patched and battered sea captain's cloak, face shadowed beneath a wide-brimmed hat. Across his shoulder, the newcomer carries a broadsword, sheathed in a scabbard of woven metal that throws back the light in myriad glints of gold and purple and crimson red.

'I am here for Moss's son,' the figure says. 'You'd best let me through.'

They fall back, inches at a time, and he shoulders a path through the gap they've left. He reaches the entrance to the dispossessed prince's tent and ducks inside. The volume of the keening rises briefly as he passes through, then grows muffled again. It's not clear to anyone later whether he actually lifted the flap, or whether it flung itself back rather than be touched.

Inside, the father swings about at the new arrival. He's a big, weather-beaten man, but his face is tracked wet with tears and his hands knotted up into trembling fists. His jaw is set, and he's breathing hard through his nose. You can see in his face and stance just how badly he wants to hit someone.

'*Who the fuck are you?* I told Rif nobody—'

'Sit *down*,' says the newcomer coldly, and Moss drops into the chair by the bed like he's had his legs cut out from under him. 'Give me the child.'

The mother sits up in bed amidst tangled, blood-stained sheets. It's her mouth the keening comes from, through lips stretched taut across her teeth, as if she's still straining through the clench and the pain of labour. But she isn't. She's curved over, rocking minutely back and forward, hugging a tiny bundle of limbs and skull and cord to her chest, as if that's going to help. The sound coming out of her seems to fill the space inside the tent like freezing fog. She looks up at the cloaked and brim-hatted figure, the long arm it extends towards her, and she shakes her head numbly. Denial moans from her.

'. . . no, no, no, he's not, he isn't, no, he's not . . .'

'Well, he fucking will be if you don't *give him to me.*'

And just as her husband has slumped into the chair, so she opens her arms and mutely holds out the silent, unmoving bundle of blue-tinged, blood-streaked flesh she's been hugging. The newcomer scoops the infant up in a single, gnarled hand and holds it there as if it needs weighing. His other hand brings the sword down off his shoulder and holds it up reversed by the grip. He looks from sword to unbreathing child and back again, and later the mother will say she heard him sigh.

Then he opens his mouth and bites down hard on the sword's pommel.

The bereft mother gapes, stirred right out of her grief by the new shock. Beneath the brim of the hat, the muscles in the stranger's jaws knot and contort. A snarling builds in his throat, the breath hisses in and out of his nose and mouth. There's a sound of something splintering and a thin howl of pain. One more sharp breath drawn in.

The stranger spits out the pommel and with it some fragments that might be teeth or metal or both. Blood drips from his lower lip, black in the gloomy light, and where droplets of it spatter the bed, holes smoulder in the sheets. The stranger drops the sword to the floor, holds the infant with both hands now, puts one finger into the tiny mouth and forces it open a crack. He stoops and places his lips over the gap.

Breathes softly out.

The mother gapes. Moss struggles in his chair against limbs turned soggy and numb. The stranger lifts his hat-shadowed face away.

Mewling cry, just the one, scarcely loud enough to believe. The infant's fist lifts at the end of a stubby arm. The head twitches and turns. A second cry, louder now. The mother shrieks and reaches for her child. Moss's lower lips quivers and he starts blubbering like a small child himself. The infant is crying hard now, not wanting to be left out.

The stranger hands him gently to his mother.

'Fucking mortals,' he mutters under his breath. 'It ends in tears, it starts in tears. Why the fuck do I even bother?'

He stands back and lets Moss shamble to his shaky feet, gestures for him join his wife and son on the bloodied bed. Then he reaches around inside his mouth, grimaces and tugs something loose, spits on the floor and bends to gather up the sword.

'Time you were in a fucking museum,' he tells it.

At the tent flap, he pauses and looks back. The infant is already at the breast, fastened on and suckling hard. The mother's still weeping, right onto his upturned puffy features. Moss looks up from his family, snatched suddenly out of grief, sees the dark figure still standing there like some hangover from a bad dream. He wipes at his eyes, suddenly self-conscious. Sniffs and gasps, gets himself under some sort of command.

'I – we – this is a great debt.' He swallows. 'Who? Who *are* you?'

The stranger sighs. 'Give it some thought. It'll come to you in the morning, probably. But it's not important.' An arm raised, a gnarled finger pointing. '*He's* important. He's got things to do, further down the road. You look after him, you keep him safe.'

'But . . .' The mother looks up from her feeding child. She's getting it together a lot faster than her husband. 'If we do not know your name, how can we honour you with his.'

'Oh, that.' The shadowed figure shrugs. 'Well, all right. Call him Gil.'

Then he's gone, through a gap that might be just the entrance flap of the tent, and might not. A tiny chill comes in and walks around the bed, then warms slowly away. The mother gathers her son closer to her.

'Gheel?' she asks her husband blankly.

Moss shrugs. 'Hjel. I think.'

'Hjel, then. Good. It is a strong name. I like it.'

And the two of them huddle together around the new spark of life they've been handed by a bad-tempered broken-mouthed god gone away.

ACKNOWLEDGEMENTS

As perhaps befits a quest narrative, *The Dark Defiles* has sheltered under a number of different roofs on the long journey to its completion. Thanks are due to the following gracious hosts, unsung heroes and friends to the quest:

To Roger Burnett and Inka Schorn for lending me not just one but two places in the sun from which to work, and for supplementing the loan throughout with bright company, kind words and emergency pasta.

To Gilbert Scott and Luisa Termine for giving me workspace right up until day of sale, and for searching out a beautiful oak table for me to work on when the existing one evaporated under family pressure.

To my wife Virginia for buying, fitting and accepting with good grace the shiny new lock on my office door, even when it rendered her a *de facto* single mother for days at a time, time and time again.

To my son Daniel for solemnly accepting at less than two years of age that no, he couldn't come to work with me, even if it was only in the next room.

To Simon Spanton and Anne Groell for Understanding well beyond the Call of Editorial Duty.

To my agent Carolyn Whitaker for patience, calm and good advice as ever – even if I did end up ignoring the latter almost entirely.

I would not have reached journey's end without you.